Isaac Asimov Presents

THE GOLDEN YEARS OF SCIENCE FICTION

Isaac Asimov Presents

THE GOLDEN YEARS OF SCIENCE FICTION

SIXTH SERIES

33 Stories and Novellas

Edited by
Isaac Asimov and
Martin H. Greenberg

BONANZA BOOKS
New York

This 1988 edition is published by Bonanza Books, distributed by Crown Publishers, Inc., 225 Park Avenue South, New York, New York 10003, by arrangement with Daw Books, Inc.

This book was previously published as two separate works entitled:
Isaac Asimov Presents the Great SF Stories 11 (1949) and
Isaac Asimov Presents the Great SF Stories 12 (1950)

Printed and Bound in the United States of America

Library of Congress Cataloging-in-Publication Data

Isaac Asimov presents the golden age of science fiction : sixth series / edited by Isaac Asimov and Martin H. Greenberg.
p. cm.
ISBN 0-517-65754-6
1. Science fiction, American. 2. Science fiction, English.
I. Asimov, Isaac, 1920- II. Greenberg, Martin Harry.
PS648.S31797 1988
813'.0876'08—dc19 87-33847
CIP

ISBN 0-517-65754-6
h g f e d c b a

CONTENTS

FOREWORD

The years 1949 and 1950 saw into print some of the best science fiction ever written. The technology and the fears brought about by the atomic age pressed new horizons and the concept of absolute mortality upon the world, and it was through this most disturbing vision that the science fiction giants finally found their wings. In this, the sixth volume in the highly acclaimed series of anthologies edited by Isaac Asimov and Martin H. Greenberg, the reader will find a thoroughly satisfying collection of stories guaranteed to beguile the mind and shake the soul. Selections by legendary writers such as Arthur C. Clark, Damon Knight, C. M. Kornbluth, Clifford D. Simak, and A. E. van Vogt make this volume a must-have for the science fiction addict or historian, readers just beginning to explore the field, and that eternal (and non gender-specific) audience, the Common Man, for whom many of these cautionary tales have been written.

C.L.S.

ACKNOWLEDGMENTS

Asimov—Copyright © 1949 by Street & Smith Publications, Inc.; copyright renewed © 1976 by Isaac Asimov. Reprinted by permission of the author.

MacDonald—Copyright © 1976 by John D. MacDonald Publishing, Inc. Reprinted by permission of the author.

Padgett—Copyright © 1949, Renewed by Catherine Moore Kuttner. Reprinted by permission of Don Congdon Associates, Inc.

Phillips—Copyright © 1949 by Street & Smith Publications, Inc. Reprinted by permission of the author and his agents, the Scott Meredith Literary Agency, Inc., 845 Third Ave., New York, NY 10022.

Padgett (Prisoner in the Skull)—Copyright © 1949, Renewed 1977 by Catherine Moore Kuttner. Reprinted by permission of Don Congdon Associates, Inc.

Hamilton—Copyright © 1949 by Standard Magazines. Reprinted by permission of the agents for the author's estate, the Scott Meredith Literary Agency, Inc., 845 Third Ave., New York, NY 10022.

Clarke—Copyright © 1949 by Standard Magazines; copyright renewed. Reprinted by permission of the author and his agents, the Scott Meredith Literary Agency, Inc., 845 Third Ave., New York, NY 10022.

Simak—Copyright © 1949 by Street & Smith Publications, Inc.; copyright renewed by the author. Reprinted by permission of Kirby McCauley, Ltd.

Kornbluth—Copyright © 1949 by Standard Magazines. Reprinted by permission of Robert P. Mills, Ltd.

MacDonald, Philip—Copyright © 1949, Mercury Press, Inc.

Sturgeon—Copyright © 1949 by Mercury Press, Inc.; copyright renewed. Reprinted by permission of the author and Kirby McCauley, Ltd.

Bradbury—Copyright © 1949, Renewed 1977 by Ray Bradbury. Reprinted by permission of Don Congdon Associates, Inc.

MacLean—Copyright © 1949 by Street & Smith Publications, Inc., 1962 by Katherine MacLean; reprinted by permission of the author and the author's agent, Virginia Kidd.

Kuttner—Copyright © 1949, Renewed 1977 by Catherine Moore Kuttner. Reprinted by permission of Don Congdon Associates, Inc.

Schmitz—Copyright © 1949 by Street & Smith Publications, Inc. Reprinted by permission of the agents for the author's estate, the Scott Meredith Literary Agency, Inc., 845 Third Ave., New York, NY 10022.

Knight—Copyright © 1950 by Galaxy Publishing Corporation; copyright renewed. Reprinted by permission of the author.

MacDonald—Copyright © 1950 by Standard Magazines; copyright renewed © 1978 by John D. MacDonald.

INTRODUCTION

In the world outside reality it was a most important year, one that saw the Soviet Union detonate a nuclear weapon and the victory of the Communists in China. On January 20 President Truman urged in "Point Four" of his inaugural address that the United States share its technological and scientific knowledge with "underprivileged areas." NATO (the North Atlantic Treaty Organization) came into being formally on April 4 and would soon be a major factor in American foreign policy. The Republic of Eire officially came into existence on April 18. In a relatively rare state name-change, Siam became Thailand on May 11, one day before the Berlin blockade was ended by the Soviets. West (the German Federal Republic) and East (the German Democratic Republic) Germany were established on May 23 and October 7.

The defeated Chinese Nationalists under Chiang Kai-shek began to evacuate their remaining forces to Formosa on July 16; the People's Republic of China, ruled by Mao Tse-tung and Chou En-lai, was proclaimed on October 1.

President Truman announces on September 23 that the Soviets have successfully tested a nuclear weapon.

The American domestic economy undergoes a series of major strikes, including a bitter dispute in the coal fields. Congress raises the minimum wage from 40 cents to 75 cents an hour.

During 1949 Simone de Beauvoir published *The Second Sex*, a work that greatly influenced the postwar feminist movement. The great Selman Waksman isolated neomycin, giving yet another important antibiotic to the world. Jackie Robinson was the Most Valuable Player in the National League, batting an impressive .342, while Ralph Kiner led the majors in home runs with 54. Hit songs included "Dear Hearts and Gentle People," "I

Don't Care if the Sun Don't Shine," " Scarlet Ribbons," and "Rudolph the Red-Nosed Reindeer."

The Volkswagen automobile was introduced in the American market but it got off to a very slow start—only two were sold in 1949. A gallon of gas cost 25 cents. Marc Chagall painted "Red Sun," while *The Goldbergs*, sometimes called American TV's first situation comedy, became a hit. Joe Louis retired as heavyweight boxing champion and Ezzard Charles became the new champ by defeating Jersey Joe Walcott. Nelson Algren published his powerful *The Man with the Golden Arm*, while important and popular films included *Adam's Rib*, the tremendous *White Heat, All the King's Men, Sands of Iwo Jima, Twelve O'Clock High* (war pictures were particularly popular), and *She Wore a Yellow Ribbon*.

Pancho Gonzales was U.S. Tennis Champion. Anaïs Nin published *The House of Incest*. Top Broadway musicals included *South Pacific* starring Ezio Pinza and Mary Martin, and *Gentlemen Prefer Blondes*, with the wonderful Carol Channing. Ponder won the Kentucky Derby. Jacob Epstein produced his sculpture of "Lazarus." Silly Putty was introduced and became a big success. The New York Yankees won the World Series by beating the Brooklyn Dodgers (sorry again, Isaac) four games to one. A pack of cigarettes cost 21 cents. The legitimate stage was graced by *Death of a Salesman* by Arthur Miller and *Detective Story* by Sidney Kingsley. Graham Greene published *The Third Man*. *Amos 'n Andy* came to television.

A loaf of bread cost 15 cents. The National Football League and the All-America Conference merged, bringing the Cleveland Browns into the NFL, which they were to dominate for the next decade. Alger Hiss was convicted of spying against the United States for the Soviet Union.

The record for the mile run was still the 4:01.4 set by Gunder Haegg of Sweden in 1945.

Mel Brooks was (probably) still Melvin Kaminsky.

In the real world it was another outstanding year as a large number of excellent (along with a few not so excellent) science fiction and fantasy novels and collections were published (again, many of these had been serialized years earlier in the magazines), including the titanic *1984* by George Orwell, *Lords of Creation* by Eando Binder, *A Martian Odyssey* by Stanley G. Weinbaum, *Exiles of Time* by Nelson Bond, *Skylark of Valeron* by E. E. (Doc) Smith, *What Mad Universe* by Fredric Brown, *The Fox Woman* by A. Merritt, *The Incredible Planet* by John W.

Campbell, Jr., *Sixth Column* by Robert A. Heinlein, *The Sunken World* by Stanton A. Coblentz, and *The Star Kings* by Edmond Hamilton. Two important anthologies were *The Best Science Fiction Stories, 1949*, the first annual "Best of" anthology, edited by E. F. Bleiler and T. E. Dikty, and *The Girl with the Hungry Eyes and Other Stories*, one of the first "original anthologies," edited by our own Donald A. Wollheim.

Important novels that appeared in magazines in 1949 included *Seetee Shock* by Jack Williamson, *Flight into Yesterday* by Charles L. Harness, and *Needle* by Hal Clement.

Super Science Fiction reappeared on the newsstands, this time edited by Eijer Jacobsson. Other sf magazines that began publication in 1949 were *Other Worlds Science Stories*, edited by Raymond A. Palmer, and *A. Merritt's Fantasy Magazine*. However, all these paled beside the launching in October of *The Magazine of Fantasy*, published by Mercury Press and edited by Anthony Boucher and J. Francis McComas—with its name changed to *The Magazine of Fantasy and Science Fiction*, it would soon become a major rival to *Astounding* and certainly one of the most important sf magazines of all time.

More wondrous things were happening in the real world as five writers made their maiden voyages into reality: in February, John Christopher (Christopher Youd) with "Christmas Tree"; in July, Kris Neville with "The Hand From the Stars"; in the Fall issue of *Planet Stories*, Roger Dee with "The Wheel is Death"; in October, Katherine MacLean with "Defense Mechanism"; and in the Winter issue of *Planet Stories*, Jerome Bixby, with "Tubemonkey."

Gnome Press, under the leadership of David Kyle and Martin Greenberg (the *other* Marty Greenberg) began publication during 1949. The *Captain Video* TV series took to the airways.

The real people gathered together for the seventh time as the World Science Fiction Convention (Cinvention) was held in Cincinnati. Notable sf films of the year were *Mighty Joe Young* and *The Perfect Woman*, the latter based on a play by Wallace Geoffrey and Basil Mitchell.

Death took Arthur Leo Zagat at the age of 54.

But distant wings were beating as Malcolm Edwards was born.

Let us travel back to that honored year of 1949 and enjoy the best stories that the real world bequeathed to us.

And now, on to 1950...

In the world outside reality it was a very violent year. On June 25 North Korean troops crossed the 38th parallel and invaded South Korea. The United States, under the banner of the United Nations (the Soviets were out of the building protesting something else, and couldn't use their veto), went to the assistance of South Korea with air strikes and an expeditionary force. The North Koreans advanced steadily, forcing the U.S. and Republic of Korea troops back to a small area on the southern coast of the peninsula. Defeat was narrowly averted when General Douglas MacArthur engineered a remarkable landing far behind enemy lines at Inchon. Allied forces then pushed the North Koreans back across the border, pursuing them all the way to within a few miles of the border with the People's Republic of China at the Yalu River. However, on December 28 hundreds of thousands of Chinese troops crossed the Yalu and began to force the Allies back as the year ended.

Earlier, on January 25, Alger Hiss was convicted of perjury in testimony regarding his membership in the American Communist Party. Anti-communism reached fever pitch with the emergence of Senator Joseph McCarthy of Wisconsin, who charged in a speech that he had a list of "known communists" working for the State Department, and the passage on September 20 of the McCarran Act, which forced even suspected communists and former Party members out of government service. Especially vicious was the publication *Red Channels,* a book that accused American citizens, particularly figures in the entertainment industry, of communist connections. Careers and lives were ruined on hearsay and through guilt by association.

Other highlights of the year included American recognition of Vietnam, the seizure of Tibet by Chinese Communist forces, and the formal decision by the Truman administration to develop the hydrogen bomb. The biggest heist in American history occurred when seven men took $2,700,000 in cash and money orders from the Brink's Express Company in Boston. French Foreign Minister Robert Schuman advocated a plan for the sharing of Europe's coal and iron ore deposits—this proposal would eventually lead to the formation of the European Economic Community or "Common Market."

On August 25 President Truman ordered Federal troops to seize the railroads in order to prevent a threatened strike. The President was the object of an assassination attempt on November 1, when Puerto Rican nationalists attempted to break into Blair House, where the Trumans were staying—one guard and one attacker were killed.

During 1950 the mambo became a dance craze in the United States. Uruguay defeated Brazil 5-4 to win soccer's World Cup. The Federal Bureau of Investigation issued its first "Most Wanted" list, while *What's My Line* and *Your Show of Shows*, the latter starring Sid Caeser, were hits on television. Minute Rice and Sugar Pops appeared on grocery shelves. Pablo Picasso sculpted "The Goat" as Charles M. Schulz's *Peanuts* debuted in the newspapers. Outstanding novels included *The Wall* by John Hersey, *A Town Like Alice* by Nevil Shute, *The Short Life* by Juan Carlos Onetti, and *Across The River and Through The Woods* by Ernest Hemingway. There were 8,000,000 television sets in the United States, serviced by over 100 TV stations. Orlon was introduced by DuPont.

Joe Louis attempted to regain his heavyweight boxing championship, but lost a decision to Ezzard Charles. Americans were the mostly proud owners of over 40,000,000 cars. Top films of the year included *The Asphalt Jungle, All About Eve, Sunset Boulevard* starring Gloria Swanson, Jean Cocteau's *Orpheus, Kind Hearts and Coronets,* and the wonderful *The Lavender Hill Mob*. The last two featured Alec Guinness. The Cleveland Browns won the National Football League Championship, while the New York Yankees defeated the surprising Philadelphia Phillies four games to none to take baseball's World Series. Cyclamates and Sucaryl were introduced, and the Wallace and Wyeth laboratories developed tranquilizers. Two of the most influential books were *The Human Uses of Human Beings* by Norbert Wiener and *The Lonely Crowd* by David Riesman, Reuel Denney and Nathan Glazer.

The Haloid Company of Rochester, New York, produced the first Xerox copying machine. Middleground won the Kentucky Derby, while Al Rosen and Ralph Kiner led the American and National Leagues in home runs. Marc Chagall painted "King David." It was a wonderful year for the theater as *The Country Girl* by Clifford Odets, *Come Back Little Sheba* by William Inge, and *Member of the Wedding* by Carson McCullers all opened on Broadway. The Diners Club was founded as book publishers rejoiced. Popular musicals included Irving Berlin's *Call Me Madam,* and Frank Loesser's *Guys and Dolls*. America was singing "Cherry Pink and Apple Blossom White," "It's So Nice to Have a Man Around the House," and "If I Knew You Were Comin I'd Have Baked a Cake."

Florence Chadwick broke the record for swimming the English Channel. Smokey the Bear became the symbol for fighting forest fires. There were about 2,520,000,000 people in the world. Death took George Bernard Shaw and painter Max Beckmann.

Mel Brooks may have still been Melvin Kaminsky.

In the real world it was a simply terrific year.

In the real world the eighth World Science Fiction Convention (the Norwescon) was held in far away Portland, Oregon. Also in the real world *Galaxy Science Fiction* was born and under the editorship of H. L. Gold quickly established itself as one of the premier magazines in the field. If this was not enough, *The Magazine of Fantasy*, launched the year before, changed its name to *The Magazine of Fantasy and Science Fiction*, and also rapidly achieved excellence, transforming *Astounding Science Fiction* from the "Big One," to one of the "Big Three." The tide continued to rise with the appearance of Damon Knight's excellent *Worlds Beyond*, Raymond Palmer's/Beatrice Mahaffey's *Imagination*, Malcolm Reiss' *Two Complete Science Adventure Books*, and a refurbished *Future Combined With Science Fiction Stories*. In England, Walter H. Gillings started *Science-Fantasy*, an uneven magazine but one that would enjoy a long life. These events overshadowed the folding of *A. Merritt's Fantasy Magazine* in October.

In the real world, more important people made their maiden voyages into reality: in January—Cordwainer Smith with "Scanners Live in Vain", in February—Paul Fairman with "No Teeth for the Tiger"; in March—Gordon R. Dickson (co-authored with Poul Anderson) with "Trespass!"; in April—Mack Reynolds with "Isolationist"; in the summer—Richard Matheson with "Born of Man and Woman"; in November—Chad Oliver with "The Land of Lost Content"; and in December—J. T. McIntosh with "The Curfew Tolls."

More wondrous things happened in the real world as outstanding novels, stories and collections were published in magazines and in book form: James Blish began his "Oakie" series of novelettes, while L. Sprague de Camp and Fletcher Pratt published their first "Gavagan's Bar" story. *The Dreaming Jewels* by Theodore Sturgeon appeared in *Fantastic Adventures*, Judith Merril's first anthology, *Shot in the Dark*, appeared in paperback, and sf fans had the pleasure of reading *Pebble in the Sky* by Isaac Asimov and *The Martian Chronicles* by Ray Bradbury as part of Doubleday's new science fiction line. A. E. van Vogt brought together earlier stories in an attractive package and produced *The Voyage of the Space Beagle*. On a more serious note, veteran science fiction writer L. Ron Hubbard published an article entitled "Dianetics, the Evolution of a Science" in *Astounding*, which eventually led to controversy, to the distraction and temporary loss to sf of several important writers, and, incidentally to the establishment of something that considered itself a new religion.

The non-print media began to embrace science fiction with the release of *Destination Moon,* (based very loosely on Robert A. Heinlein's juvenile novel *Rocketship Galileo), The Flying Saucer, The Perfect Woman,* the unforgettable *Prehistoric Women,* and the moody *Rocketship* XM. *Tom Corbett: Space Cadet* debuted on television.

Let us travel back to that honored year of 1950 and enjoy the best stories that the real world bequeathed to us.

Isaac Asimov Presents

THE GOLDEN YEARS OF SCIENCE FICTION

THE RED QUEEN'S RACE

By Isaac Asimov (1920–   )

***Astounding Science Fiction*, January**

Marty Greenberg does have a tendency to pick my stories for this series. Not all of them, of course, but more than I think he ought to. Unfortunately, he insists on having the sole vote in this matter. He says I am too prejudiced to vote, which is ridiculous on the face of it. However, I don't dare do anything to offend him, for he does all the skutwork in this series (Xeroxing stories, getting permissions, paying out checks, etc.) and does it most efficiently. If he quit on me, there would be no chance whatever of an adequate replacement.

And then having picked a story, he refuses to write a headnote for it. He insists that I do the job alone.

Well, what can I say about "The Red Queen's Race"?

1. I wrote it after nearly a year's layoff from writing because I was working very hard to get my Ph.D. Once I got it, I went back to writing at once (with RQR as a result) and since then I have never had a sizable writing hiatus (or even a minor one) in my life.

2. Someone once said to me, "I didn't know you ever wrote a tough-guy detective story." I said, "I never have." He said, "How about 'The Red Queen's Race'?"—so I read it and it certainly sounds *tough-guy detective. I've never been able to explain that.*

3. If you were planning to write anyway (I wouldn't ask you if you weren't) do write to Marty to the effect that you loved this story. I want him to think highly of himself and of his expertise, and not even dream of quitting the team.—I.A.

Here's a puzzle for you, if you like. Is it a crime to translate a chemistry textbook into Greek?

Or let's put it another way. If one of the country's largest atomic power plants is completely ruined in an unauthorized experiment, is an admitted accessory to that act a criminal?

These problems only developed with time, of course. We started with the atomic power plant—drained. I really mean *drained*. I don't know exactly how large the fissionable power source was—but in two flashing microseconds, it had all fissioned.

No explosion. No undue gamma ray density. It was merely that every moving part in the entire structure was fused. The entire main building was mildly hot. The atmosphere for two miles in every direction was gently warm. Just a dead, useless building which later on took a hundred million dollars to replace.

It happened about three in the morning, and they found Elmer Tywood alone in the central source chamber. The findings of twenty-four close-packed hours can be summarized quickly.

1. Elmer Tywood—Ph.D., Sc.D., Fellow of This and Honorary That, one-time youthful participant of the original Manhattan Project, and now full Professor of Nuclear Physics—was no interloper. He had a Class-A Pass—Unlimited. But no record could be found as to his purpose in being there just then. A table on casters contained equipment which had not been made on any recorded requisition. It, too, was a single fused mass—not quite too hot to touch.

2. Elmer Tywood was dead. He lay next to the table; his face congested, nearly black. No radiation effect. No external force of any sort. The doctor said apoplexy.

3. In Elmer Tywood's office safe were found two puzzling items: *i.e.* twenty foolscap sheets of apparent mathematics, and a bound folio in a foreign language which turned out to be Greek, the subject matter, on translation, turning out to be chemistry.

The secrecy which poured over the whole mess was something so terrific as to make everything that touched it, *dead*. It's the only word that can describe it. Twenty-seven men and women, all told, including the Secretary of Defense, the Secretary of Science, and two or three others so top-notch that they were completely unknown to the public entered the power plant during the period of investigation. Any man who had been in the plant that night, the physicist who had identified Tywood, the doctor who had examined him, were retired into virtual home arrest.

No newspaper ever got the story. No inside dopester got it. A few members of Congress got part of it.

And naturally so! Anyone or any group or any country that could suck all the available energy out of the equivalent of perhaps fifty to a hundred pounds of plutonium without exploding it, had America's industry and America's defense so snugly in the palm of the hand that the light and life of one hundred sixty million people could be turned off between yawns.

Was it Tywood? Or Tywood and others? Or just others, through Tywood?

And my job? I was a decoy; or front man, if you like. Someone has to hang around the university and ask questions about Tywood. After all, he was missing. It could be amnesia, a hold-up, a kidnapping, a killing, a runaway, insanity, accident—I could busy myself with that for five years and collect black looks, and maybe divert attention. To be sure, it didn't work out that way.

But don't think I was in on the whole case at the start. I wasn't one of the twenty-seven men I mentioned a while back, though my boss was. But I knew a little—enough to get started.

Professor John Keyser was also in Physics. I didn't get to him right away. There was a good deal of routine to cover first in as conscientious a way as I could. Quite meaningless. Quite necessary. But I was in Keyser's office now.

Professors' offices are distinctive. Nobody dusts them except some tired cleaning woman who hobbles in and out at eight in the morning, and the professor never notices the dust anyway. Lots of books without much arrangement. The ones close to the desk are used a lot—lectures are copied out of them. The ones out of reach are wherever a student put them back after borrowing them. Then there are professional journals that look cheap and are darned expensive, which are waiting about and which may some day be read. And plenty of paper on the desk; some of it scribbled on.

Keyser was an elderly man—one of Tywood's generation. His nose was big and rather red, and he smoked a pipe. He had that easy-going and nonpredatory look in his eyes that goes with an academic job—either because that kind of job attracts that kind of man or because that kind of job makes that kind of man.

I said: "What kind of work is Professor Tywood doing?"

"Research physics."

Answers like that bounce off me. Some years ago they used to get me mad. Now, I just said: "We know that, professor. It's the details I'm after."

And he twinkled at me tolerantly: "Surely the details can't help much unless you're a research physicist yourself. Does it matter—under the circumstances?"

"Maybe not. But he's gone. If anything's happened to him in the way of"—I gestured, and deliberately clinched—"foul play, his work may have something to do with it—unless he's rich and the motive is money."

Keyser chuckled dryly: "College professors are never rich. The commodity we peddle is but lightly considered, seeing how large the supply is."

I ignored that, too, because I know my looks are against me. Actually, I finished college with a "very good" translated into Latin so that the college president could understand it, and never played in a football game in my life. But I look rather the reverse.

I said: "Then we're left with his work to consider."

"You mean spies? International intrigue?"

"Why not? It's happened before! After all, he's a nuclear physicist, isn't he?"

"He is. But so are others. So am I."

"Ah, but perhaps he knows something you don't."

There was a stiffening to the jaw. When caught off-guard, professors can act just like people. He said, stiffly: "As I recall off-hand, Tywood has published papers on the effect of liquid viscosity on the wings of the Rayleigh line, on higher-orbit field equation, and on spin-orbit coupling of two nucleons, but his main work is on quadrupole moments. I am quite competent in these matters."

"Is he working on quadrupole moments now?" I tried not to bat an eye, and I think I succeeded.

"Yes—in a way." He almost sneered, "He may be getting to the experimental stage finally. He's spent most of his life, it seems, working out the mathematical consequences of a special theory of his own."

"Like this," and I tossed a sheet of foolscap at him.

That sheet was one of those in the safe in Tywood's office. The chances, of course, were that the bundle meant nothing, if only because it was a professor's safe. That is, things are sometimes put in at the spur of the moment because the logical drawer was filled with unmarked exam papers. And, of course, nothing is ever taken out. We had found in that safe dusty little vials of yellowish crystals with scarcely legible labels, some mimeographed booklets dating back to World War II and marked "Restricted," a copy of an old college yearbook, and some correspondence concerning a possible position as Director of Research for American Electric, dated ten years back, and, of course, chemistry in Greek.

The foolscap was there, too. It was rolled up like a college diploma with a rubber band about it and had no label or descriptive title. Some twenty sheets were covered with ink marks, meticulous and small—

I had one sheet of that foolscap. I don't think any one man in the world had more than one sheet. And I'm sure that no man in the world but one knew that the loss of his particular sheet and of his particular life would be as nearly simultaneous as the government could make it.

So I tossed the sheet at Keyser, as if it were something I'd found blowing about the campus.

He stared at it and then looked at the back side, which was blank. His eyes moved down from the top to the bottom, then jumped back to the top.

"I don't know what this is about," he said, and the words seemed sour to his own taste.

I didn't say anything. Just folded the paper and shoved it back into the inside jacket pocket.

Keyser added petulantly: "It's a fallacy you laymen have that scientists can look at an equation and say, 'Ah, yes—' and go on to write a book about it. Mathematics has no existence of its own. It is merely an arbitrary code devised to describe physical observations or philosophical concepts. Every man can adapt it to his own particular needs. For instance no one can look at a symbol and be sure of what it means. So far, science has used every letter in the alphabet, large, small and italic, each symbolizing many different things. They have used bold-faced letters, Gothic-type letters, Greek letters, both capital and small, subscripts, superscripts, asterisks, even Hebrew letters. Different scientists use different symbols for the same concept and the same symbol for different concepts. So if you show a disconnected page like this to any man, without information as to the subject being investigated or the particular symbology used, he could absolutely not make sense out of it."

I interrupted: "But you said he was working on quadrupole moments. Does that make this sensible?" and I tapped the spot on my chest where the foolscap had been slowly scorching a hole in my jacket for two days.

"I can't tell. I saw none of the standard relationships that I'd expect to be involved. At least I recognized none. But I obviously can't commit myself."

There was a short silence, then he said: "I'll tell you. Why don't you check with his students?"

I lifted my eyebrows: "You mean in his classes?"

He seemed annoyed: "No, for Heaven's sake. His research students! His doctoral candidates! They've been working with him. They'll know the details of that work better than I, or anyone in the faculty, could possibly know it."

"It's an idea," I said, casually. It was, too. I don't know why, but I wouldn't have thought of it myself. I guess it's because it's only natural to think that any professor knows more than any student.

Keyser latched on to a lapel as I rose to leave. "And, besides," he said, "I think you're on the wrong track. This is in confidence, you understand, and I wouldn't say it except for the unusual circumstances, but Tywood is not thought of too highly in the profession. Oh, he's an adequate teacher, I'll admit, but his research papers have never commanded respect. There has always been a tendency towards vague theorizing, unsupported by experimental evidence. That paper of yours is probably more of it. No one could possibly want to . . . er, kidnap him because of it."

"Is that so? I see. Any ideas, yourself, as to why he's gone, or where he's gone?"

"Nothing concrete," he said pursing his lips, "but everyone knows he is a sick man. He had a stroke two years ago that kept him out of classes for a semester. He never did get well. His left side was paralyzed for a while and he still limps. Another stroke would kill him. It could come any time."

"You think he's dead, then?"

"It's not impossible."

"But where's the body, then?"

"Well, really— That is *your* job, I think."

It was, and I left.

I interviewed each one of Tywood's four research students in a volume of chaos called a research laboratory. These student research laboratories usually have two hopefuls working therein, said two constituting a floating population, since every year or so they are alternately replaced.

Consequently, the laboratory has its equipment stack in tiers. On the laboratory benches is the equipment immediately being used, and in three or four of the handiest drawers are replacements or supplements which are likely to be used. In the farther drawers, in the shelves reaching up to the ceiling, in odd corners, are fading remnants of the past student generations—oddments never used and never discarded. It is claimed, in fact, that no research student ever knew all the contents of his laboratory.

All four of Tywood's students were worried. But three were worried mainly by their own status. That is, by the possible effect the absence of Tywood might have on the status of their "problem." I dismissed those three—who all have their degrees now, I hope—and called back the fourth.

He had the most haggard look of all, and had been least communicative—which I considered a hopeful sign.

He now sat stiffly in the straight-backed chair at the right of the desk, while I leaned back in a creaky old swivel-chair and pushed my hat off my forehead. His name was Edwin Howe and *he* did get his degree later on. I know that for sure, because he's a big wheel in the Department of Science now.

I said: "You do the same work the other boys do, I suppose?"

"It's all nuclear work in a way."

"But it's not all exactly the same?"

He shook his head slowly. "We take different angles. You have to have something clear-cut, you know, or you won't be able to publish. We've got to get our degrees."

He said it exactly the way you or I might say, "We've got to make a living." At that, maybe it's the same thing for them.

I said: "All right. What's *your* angle?"

He said: "I do the math. I mean, with Professor Tywood."

"What kind of math?"

And he smiled a little, getting the same sort of atmosphere about him that I had noticed in Professor Keyser's case that morning. A sort of, "Do-you-really-think-I-can-explain-all-my-profound-thoughts-to-stupid-little-you?" sort of atmosphere.

All he said aloud, however, was: "That would be rather complicated to explain."

"I'll help you," I said. "Is that anything like it?" And I tossed the foolscap sheet at him.

He didn't give it any once over. He just snatched it up and let out a thin wail: "Where'd you get this?"

"From Tywood's safe."

"Do you have the rest of it, too?"

"It's safe," I hedged.

He relaxed a little—just a little: "You didn't show it to anybody, did you?"

"I showed it to Professor Keyser."

Howe made an impolite sound with his lower lip and front teeth, "*That* jackass. What did he say?"

I turned the palms of my hands upward and Howe laughed. Then he said, in an offhand manner: "Well, that's the sort of stuff I do."

"And what's it all about? Put it so I can understand it."

There was distinct hesitation. He said: "Now look. This is

confidential stuff. Even Pop's other students don't know anything about it. I don't even think *I* know *all* about it. This isn't just a degree I'm after, you know. It's Pop Tywood's Nobel Prize, and it's going to be an Assistant Professorship for me at Cal Tech. This has got to be published before it's talked about."

And I shook my head slowly and made my words very soft: "No, son. You have it twisted. You'll have to talk about it before it's published, because Tywood's gone and maybe he's dead and maybe he isn't. And if he's dead, maybe he's murdered. And when the department has a suspicion of murder, everybody talks. Now it will look bad for you, kid, if you try to keep some secrets."

It worked. I knew it would, because everyone reads murder mysteries and knows all the clichés. He jumped out of his chair and rattled the words off as if he had a script in front of him.

"Surely," he said, "you can't suspect *me* of . . . of anything like that. Why . . . why, my career—"

I shoved him back into his chair with the beginnings of a sweat on his forehead. I went into the next line: "I don't suspect anybody of anything *yet*. And you won't be in any trouble, if you talk, chum."

He was ready to talk. "Now this is all in strict confidence."

Poor guy. He didn't know the meaning of the word "strict." He was never out of eyeshot of an operator from that moment till the government decided to bury the whole case with the one final comment of "?." Quote, Unquote. (I'm not kidding. To this day, the case is neither opened nor closed. It's just "?.")

He said, dubiously; "You know what time travel is, I suppose?"

Sure I knew what time travel was. My oldest kid is twelve and he listens to the afternoon video programs till he swells up visibly with the junk he absorbs at the ears and eyes.

"What about time travel?" I said.

"In a sense, we can do it. Actually, it's only what you might call micro-temporal-translation—"

I almost lost my temper. In fact, I think I did. It seemed obvious that the squirt was trying to diddle me; and without subtlety. I'm used to having people think I look dumb; but not *that* dumb.

I said through the back of my throat: "Are you going to tell me that Tywood is out somewhere in time—like Ace Rogers, the Lone Time Ranger?" (That was junior's favorite program—Ace Rogers was stopping Genghis Khan single-handed that week.)

But he looked as disgusted as I must have. "No," he yelled. "I don't know where Pop is. If you'd *listen* to me—I said micro-temporal-translation. Now this isn't a video show and it isn't magic; this happens to be science. For instance, you know about matter-energy equivalence, I suppose.''

I nodded sourly. Everyone knows about that since Hiroshima in the last war but one.

''All right, then,'' he went on, ''that's good for a start. Now if you take a known mass of matter and apply temporal translation to it—you know, send it back in time—you are, in effect, creating matter at the point in time to which you are sending it. To do that, you must use an amount of energy equivalent to the amount of matter you have created. In other words, to send a gram—or, say, an ounce—of anything back in time, you have to disintegrate an ounce of matter completely, to furnish the energy required.''

''Hm-m-m,'' I said, ''that's to create the ounce of matter in the past. But aren't you destroying an ounce of matter by removing it from the present? Doesn't that *create* the equivalent amount of energy?''

And he looked just about as annoyed as a fellow sitting on a bumblebee that wasn't quite dead. Apparently laymen are never supposed to question scientists.

He said: ''I was trying to simplify it so you would understand it. Actually, it's more complicated. It would be very nice if we could use the energy of disappearance to cause it to disappear but that would be working in a circle, believe me. The requirements of entropy would forbid it. To put it more rigorously, the energy is required to overcome temporal inertia and it just works out so that the energy in ergs required to send back a mass, in grams, is equal to that mass times the square of the speed of light in centimeters per second. Which just happens to be the Einstein Mass-Energy Equivalence Equation. I can give you the mathematics, you know.''

''I know,'' I waxed some of that misplaced eagerness back. ''But was all this worked out experimentally. Or is it just on paper?''

Obviously, the thing was to keep him talking.

He had that queer light in his eye that every research student gets, I am told, when he is asked to discuss his problem. He'll discuss it with anyone, even with a ''dumb flatfoot''—which was convenient at the moment.

''You see,'' he said like a man slipping you the inside dope on a shady business deal, ''what started the whole thing was this neutrino business. They've been trying to find that neutrino since the late thirties and they haven't succeeded. It's a subatomic particle which has no charge and has a mass much less than even an electron. Naturally, it's next to impossible to spot, and hasn't been spotted yet. But they keep looking because without assuming that a neutrino exists, the energetics of some nuclear reactions can't be balanced. So Pop Tywood got the idea about twenty years ago that some energy was disappearing, in the form of matter, back into time. We got working on that—or he did—and I'm the first student he's ever had tackle it along with him.

"Obviously, we had to work with tiny amounts of material and . . . well, it was just a stroke of genius on Pop's part to think of using traces of artificial radioactive isotopes. You could work with just a few micrograms of it, you know, by following its activity with counters. The variation of activity with time should follow a very definite and simple law which has never been altered by any laboratory condition known.

"Well, we'd send a speck back fifteen minutes, say, and fifteen minutes before we did that—everything was arranged automatically, you see—the count jumped to nearly double what it should be, fell off normally, and then dropped sharply at the moment it was sent back below where it would have been normally. The material overlapped itself in time, you see, and for fifteen minutes we counted the doubled material—"

I interrupted: "You mean you had the same atoms existing in two places at the same time."

"Yes," he said, with mild surprise, "why not. That's why we use so much energy—the equivalent of creating those atoms." And then he rushed on, "Now I'll tell you what my particular job is. If you send back the material fifteen minutes, it is apparently sent back to the same spot relative to the Earth despite the fact that in fifteen minutes, the Earth moved sixteen thouand miles around the Sun, and the Sun itself moves more thousand miles and so on. But there are certain tiny discrepancies which I've analyzed and which turn out to be due, possibly to two causes.

"First, there is a frictional effect—if you can use such a term—so that matter does drift a little with respect to the Earth, depending on how far back in time it is sent, and on the nature of material. Then, too, some of the discrepancy can only be explained by the assumption that passage through time itself takes time."

"How's that?" I said.

"What I mean is that some of the radioactivity is evenly spread throughout the time of translation as if the material tested had been reacting during backward passage through time by a constant amount. My figures show that—well, if you were to be moved backward in time, you would age one day for every hundred years. Or, to put it another way, if you could watch a time dial which recorded the time outside a 'time-machine', your watch would move forward twenty-four hours while the time dial moved back a hundred years. That's a universal constant, I think, because the speed of light is a universal constant. Anyway, that's my work."

After a few minutes, in which I chewed all this, I asked: "Where did you get the energy needed for your experiments?"

"They ran out a special line from the power plant. Pop's a big shot there, and swung the deal."

"Hm-m-m. What was the heaviest amount of material you sent into the past?"

"Oh"—he sent his eyes upwards—"I think we shot back one hundredth of a milligram once. That's ten micrograms."

"Ever try sending anything into the future?"

"That won't work," he put in quickly. "Impossible. You can't change signs like that because the energy required becomes more than infinite. It's a one-way proposition."

I looked hard at my fingernails: "How much material could you send back in time if you fissioned about . . . oh, say, one hundred pounds of plutonium." Things I thought, were becoming, if anything too obvious.

The answer came quickly: "In plutonium fission," he said, "not more than one or two percent of the mass is converted into energy. Therefore, one hundred pounds of plutonium when completely used up would send a pound or two back into time."

"Is that all? But could you handle all that energy? I mean a hundred pounds of plutonium can make quite an explosion."

"All relative," he said, a bit pompously. "If you took all that energy and let it loose a little at a time, you could handle it. If you released it all at once, but used it just as fast as you released it, you could still handle it. In sending back material through time, energy can be used much faster than it can possibly be released even through fission. Theoretically, anyway."

"But how do you get rid of it?"

"It's spread through time, naturally. Of course, the minimum time through which material could be transferred would, therefore, depend on the mass of the material. Otherwise, you're liable to have the energy density with time too high."

"All right, kid," I said. "I'm calling up headquarters, and they'll send a man here to take you home. You'll stay there awhile."

"But— What for?"

"It won't be for long."

It wasn't—and it was made up to him afterwards.

I spent the evening at Headquarters. We had a library there—a very special kind of library. The very morning after the explosion two or three operators had drifted quietly into the chemistry and physics libraries of the University. Experts in their way. They located every article Tywood had ever published in any scientific journal and had snapped each page. Nothing was disturbed otherwise.

Other men went through magazine files and through book lists. It ended with a room at Headquarters that represented a complete Tywoodania. Nor was there a definite purpose in doing this. It merely represented part of the thoroughness with which a problem of this sort is met.

I went through that library. Not the scientific papers. I knew there'd be nothing there that I wanted. But he had written a series of articles for a magazine twenty years back, and I read those. And I grabbed at every piece of private correspondence they had available.

After that I just sat and thought—and got scared.

I got to bed about four in the morning and had nightmares.

But I was in the Boss' private office at nine in the morning just the same.

He's a big man, the Boss, with iron-gray hair slicked down tight. He doesn't smoke, but he keeps a box of cigars on his desk and when he doesn't want to say anything for a few seconds, he picks one up, rolls it about a little, smells it, then sticks it right into the middle of his mouth and lights it in a very careful way. By that time, he either has something to say or doesn't have to say anything at all. Then he puts the cigar down and lets it burn to death.

He used up a box in about three weeks, and every Christmas, half his gift-wraps held boxes of cigars.

He wasn't reaching for any cigars now, though. He just folded his big fists together on the desk and looked up at me from under a creased forehead. "What's boiling?"

I told him. Slowly, because micro-temporal-translation doesn't sit well with anybody, especially when you call it time travel, which I did. It's a sign of how serious things were that he only asked me once if I were crazy.

Then I was finished and we stared at each other.

He said, "And you think he tried to send something back in

time—something weighing a pound or two and blew an entire plant doing it?''

''It fits in,'' I said.

I let him go for a while. He was thinking and I wanted him to keep on thinking. I wanted him, if possible, to think of the same thing I was thinking, so that I wouldn't have to tell him—

Because I hated to *have* to tell him—

Because it was nuts, for one thing. And too horrible, for another.

So I kept quiet and he kept on thinking and every once in a while some of his thoughts came to the surface.

After a while, he said: ''Assuming the student, Howe, to have told the truth—and you'd better check his notebooks, by the way, which I hope you've impounded—''

''The entire wing of that floor is out of bounds, sir. Edwards has the notebooks.''

He went on: ''All right. Assuming he told us all the truth he knows, why did Tywood jump from less than a miligram to a pound?''

His eyes came down and they were hard: ''Now you're concentrating on the time-travel angle. To you, I gather, that is the crucial point, with the energy involved as incidental—purely incidental.''

''Yes, sir,'' I said grimly. ''I think exactly that.''

''Have you considered that you might be wrong? That you might have matters inverted?''

''I don't quite get that.''

''Well, look. You say you've read up on Tywood. All right. He was one of that bunch of scientists after World War II that fought the atom bomb; wanted a world state—You know about that, don't you?''

I nodded.

''He had a guilt complex,'' the Boss said with energy. ''He'd helped work out the bomb, and he couldn't sleep nights thinking of what he'd done. He lived with that fear for years. And even though the bomb wasn't used in World War III, can you imagine what every day of uncertainty must have meant to him? Can you imagine the shriveling horror in his soul as he waited for others to make the decision at every crucial moment till the final Compromise of Sixty-Five?

''We have a complete psychiatric analysis of Tywood and several others just like him, taken during the last war. Did you know that?''

''No, sir.''

"It's true. We let up after Sixty-Five, of course, because with the establishment of world control of atomic power, the scrapping of the atomic bomb stockpile in all countries, and the establishment of research liaison among the various spheres of influence on the planet, most of the ethical conflict in the scientific mind was removed.

"But the findings at the time were serious. In 1964, Tywood had a morbid subconscious hatred for the very concept of atomic power. He began to make mistakes, serious ones. Eventually, we were forced to take him off research of any kind. And several others as well, even though things were pretty bad at the time. We had just lost India, if you remember."

Considering that I was in India at the time, I remembered. But I still wasn't seeing his point.

"Now what," he continued, "if dregs of that attitude remained buried in Tywood to the very end. Don't you see that this time-travel is a double-edged sword? Why throw a pound of anything into the past, anyway? For the sake of proving a point? He had proved his case just as much when he sent back a fraction of a milligram. That was good enough for the Nobel Prize, I suppose.

"But there was *one* thing he could do with a pound of matter that he couldn't do with a milligram, and that was *to drain a power plant*. So that was what he must have been after. He had discovered a way of consuming inconceivable quantities of energy. By sending back eighty pounds of dirt, he could remove all the existing plutonium in the world. End atomic power for an indefinite period."

I was completely unimpressed, but I tried not to make that too plain. I just said: "Do you think he could possibly have thought he could get away with it more than once?"

"This is all based on the fact that he wasn't a normal man. How do I know what he could imagine he could do? Besides, there may be men behind him—with less science and more brains—who are quite ready to continue onwards from this point."

"Have any of these men been found yet? Any evidence of such men?"

A little wait, and his hand reached for the cigar box. He stared at the cigar and turned it end for end. Just a little wait more. I was patient.

Then he put it down decisively without lighting it.

"No," he said.

He looked at me, and clear though me, and said: "Then you still don't go for that?"

I shrugged, "Well—It doesn't sound right."

"Do you have a notion of your own?"

"Yes. But I can't bring myself to talk about it. If I'm wrong, I'm the wrongest man that ever was; but if I'm right, I'm the rightest."

"I'll listen," he said, and he put his hand under the desk.

That was the pay-off. The room was armored, soundproof, and radiation-proof to anything short of a nuclear explosion. And with that little signal showing on his secretary's desk, the President of the United States couldn't have interrupted us.

I leaned back and said: "Chief, do you happen to remember how you met your wife? Was it a little thing?"

He must have thought it a *non sequitur*. What else could he have thought? But he was giving me my head now; having his own reasons, I suppose.

He just smiled and said: "I sneezed and she turned around. It was at a street corner."

"What made you be on that street corner just then? What made her be? Do you remember just why you sneezed? Where you caught the cold? Or where the speck of dust came from? Imagine how many factors had to intersect in just the right place at just the right time for you to meet your wife."

"I suppose we would have met some other time, if not then?"

"But you can't *know* that. How do you know whom you *didn't* meet, because once when you might have turned around, you didn't; because once when you might have been late, you weren't. Your life forks at every instant, and you go down one of the forks, almost at random and so does everyone else. Start twenty years ago, and the forks diverge further and further with time.

"You sneezed, and met a girl, and not another. As a consequence, you made certain decisions, and so did the girl, and so did the girl you didn't meet, and the man who did meet her, and the people you all met thereafter. And your family, her family, their family—and your children.

"Because you sneezed twenty years ago, five people, or fifty, or five hundred, might be dead now who would have been alive or might be alive, who would have been dead. Move it two hundred years ago: two thousand years ago, and a sneeze—even by someone no history ever heard of—might have meant that no one now alive would have been alive."

The Boss rubbed the back of his head: "Widening ripples. I read a story once—"

"So did I. It's not a new idea—but I want you to think about it for a while, because I want to read to you from an article by Professor Elmer Tywood in a magazine twenty years ago. It was just before the last war."

I had copies of the film in my pocket and the white wall made a beautiful screen which was what it was meant to do. The Boss made a motion to turn about, but I waved him back.

"No, sir," I said. "I want to read this to you. And I want you to listen to it."

He leaned back.

"The article," I went on, "is entitled: 'Man's First Great Failure!' Remember, this was just before the war, when the bitter disappointment at the final failure of the United Nations was at its height. What I will read are some excerpts from the first part of the article. It goes like this:

" '. . . That Man, with his technical perfection has failed to solve the great sociological problems of today is only the second immense tragedy that has come to the race. The first, and perhaps the greater, was that once these same great sociological problems *were* solved; and yet these solutions were not permanent because the technical perfection we have today did not then exist.

" 'It was a case of having bread without butter, or butter without bread. Never both together . . .

" 'Consider the Hellenic world from which our philosophy, our mathematics, our ethics, our art, our literature—our entire culture, in fact—stem . . . In the days of Pericles, Greece, like our own world, in microcosm, was a surprisingly modern potpourri of conflicting ideologies and ways of life. But then Rome came, adopting the culture, but bestowing, and enforcing, peace. To be sure, the *Pax Romana* lasted only two hundred years, but no like period has existed since . . .

" 'War was abolished. Nationalism did not exist. The Roman citizen was Empire-wide. Saul of Tarsus and Flavius Josephus were Roman citizens. Spaniards, North Africans, Illyrians assumed the purple. Slavery existed, but it was an indiscriminate slavery, imposed as a punishment, incurred as the price of economic failure, brought on by the fortunes of war. No man was a *natural* slave, because of the color of his skin, or the place of his birth.

" 'Religious toleration was complete. If an exception was made early in the case of the Christians, it was because they refused to accept the principle of toleration; because they insisted that only they themselves knew truth—a principle abhorrent to the civilized Roman . . .

" 'With all of Western culture under a single *polis*, with the cancer of religious and national particularism and exclusivism absent; with a high civilization in existence—why could not Man hold his gains?

" 'It was because technologically, ancient Hellenism remained backward. It was because without a machine civilization, the price of leisure—and hence civilization and culture—for the few, was slavery for the many. Because the civilization could not find the means to bring comfort and ease to *all* the population.

" 'Therefore, the depressed classes turned to the other world, and to religions which spurned the material benefits of this world—so that science was made impossible in any true sense for over a millennium. And further, as the initial impetus of Hellenism waned, the Empire lacked the technological powers to beat back the barbarians. In fact, it was not till after 1500 A.D. that war became sufficiently a function of the industrial resources of a nation to enable the settled people to defeat invading tribesmen and nomads with ease . . .

" 'Imagine then, if somehow the ancient Greeks had learned just a hint of modern chemistry and physics. Imagine if the growth of the Empire had been accompanied by the growth of science, technology and industry. Imagine an Empire, in which machinery replaced slaves; in which all men had a decent share of the world's goods; in which the legion became the armored column, against which no barbarians could stand. Imagine an Empire which would therefore spread all over the world, *without* religious or national prejudices.

" 'An Empire of all men—all brothers—eventually all free . . .

" 'If history could be changed. If that first great failure could have been prevented—' "

And I stopped at that point.

"Well?" said the Boss

"Well," I said, "I think it isn't difficult to connect all that with the fact that Tywood blew an entire power plant in his anxiety to send something back to the past, while in his office safe we found sections of a chemistry textbook translated into Greek."

His face changed, while he considered.

Then, he said heavily: "But nothing's happened."

"I know. But then I've been told by Tywood's student that it takes a day to move back a century in time. Assuming that ancient Greece was the target area, we have twenty centuries, hence twenty days."

"But can it be stopped?"

"*I* wouldn't know. Tywood might, but he's dead."

The enormity of it all hit me at once, deeper than it had the night before—

All humanity was virtually under sentence of death. And while that was merely horrible abstraction, the fact that reduced it to a thoroughly unbearably reality, was that I was, too. And my wife, and my kid.

Further, it was a death without precedence. A ceasing to exist, and no more. The passing of a breath. The vanishing of a dream. The drift into eternal non-space and non-time of a shadow. I would not be dead at all, in fact. I would merely never have been born.

Or would I? Would I exist—my individuality—my ego—my soul, if you like? Another life? Other circumstances?

I thought none of that in words, then. But if a cold knot in the stomach could ever speak under the circumstances it would sound like that, I think.

The Boss moved in on my thoughts—hard.

"Then we have about two and a half weeks. No time to lose. Come on."

I grinned with one side of my mouth: "What do we do? Chase the book?"

"No," he replied coldly, "but there are two courses of action we must follow. First, you may be wrong—altogether. All of this circumstantial reasoning may still represent a false lead, perhaps deliberately thrown before us, to cover up the real truth. That must be checked.

"Secondly, you may be right—but there may be some way of stopping the book: other than chasing it in a time machine, I mean. If so, we must find out how."

"I would just like to say, sir, if this is a false lead, only a madman would consider it a believable one. So suppose I'm right, and suppose there's no way of stopping it?"

"Then, young fellow, I'm going to keep pretty busy for two and a half weeks, and I'd advise you to do the same. The time will pass more quickly that way."

Of course he was right.

"Where do we start?" I asked.

"The first thing we need is a list of all men and women on the government payroll under Tywood."

"Why?"

"Reasoning. Your specialty, you know. Tywood doesn't know Greek, I think we can assume with fair safety, so someone else must have done the translating. It isn't likely that anyone would do a job like that for nothing, and it isn't likely that Tywood would pay out of his personal funds—not on a professor's salary."

"He might," I pointed out, "have been interested in more secrecy than a government payroll affords."

"Why? Where was the danger? Is it a crime to translate a chemistry textbook into Greek? Who would ever deduce from that a plot such as you've described."

It took us half an hour to turn up the name of Mycroft James Boulder, listed as "Consultant" and to find out that he was mentioned in the University Catalogue as Assistant Professor of Philosophy and to check by telephone that among his many accomplishments was a thorough knowledge of Attic Greek.

Which was a coincidence—because with the Boss reaching for his hat, the interoffice teletype clicked away and it turned out that Mycroft James Boulder was in the anteroom, at the end of a two-hour continuing insistence that he see the Boss.

The Boss put his hat back and opened his office door.

Professor Mycroft James Boulder was a gray man. His hair was gray and his eyes were gray. His suit was gray, too.

But most of all, his expression was gray; gray with a tension that seemed to twist at the lines in his thin face.

Boulder said, softly: "I've been trying for three days to get a hearing, sir, with a responsible man. I can get no higher than yourself."

"I may be high enough," said the Boss. "What's on your mind?"

"It is quite important that I be granted an interview with Professor Tywood."

"Do you know where he is?"

"I am quite certain that he is in government custody."

"Why?"

"Because I know that he was planning an experiment which would entail the breaking of security regulations. Events since, as nearly as I can make them out, flow naturally from the supposition that security regulations have indeed been broken. I can presume then that the experiment has at least been attempted. I must discover whether it has been successfully concluded."

"Professor Boulder," said the Boss, "I believe you can read Greek."

"Yes, I can,"—coolly.

"And have translated chemical texts for Professor Tywood on government money."

"Yes—as a legally employed consultant."

"Yet such translation, under the circumstances, constitutes a crime, since it makes you an accessory to Tywood's crime."

"You can establish a connection?"

"Can't you? Or haven't you heard of Tywood's notions on time travel, or . . . what do you call it . . . micro-temporal-translation?"

"Ah?" and Boulder smiled a little. "He's told you, then."

"No he hasn't," said the Boss, harshly. "Professor Tywood is dead."

"What?" Then—"I don't believe you."

"He died of apoplexy. Look at this."

He had one of the photographs taken that first night in his wall safe. Tywood's face was distorted but recognizable—sprawled and dead.

Boulder's breath went in and out as if the gears were clogged. He stared at the picture for three full minutes by the electric clock on the wall. "Where is this place?" he asked.

"The Atomic Power Plant."

"Had he finished his experiment?"

The Boss shrugged: "There's no way of telling. He was dead when we found him."

Boulder's lips were pinched and colorless. "That must be determined somehow. A commission of scientists must be established, and, if necessary, the experiment must be repeated—"

But the Boss just looked at him, and reached for a cigar. I've never seen him take longer—and when he put it down, curled in its unused smoke, he said: "Tywood wrote an article for a magazine, twenty years ago—"

"Oh," and the professor's lips twisted, "is *that* what gave you your clue. You may ignore that. The man is only a physical scientist and knows nothing of either history or sociology. A schoolboy's dreams and nothing more."

"Then you don't think sending your translation back will inaugurate a Golden Age, do you?"

"Of course not. Do you think you can graft the developments of two thousand years of slow labor on to a child society not ready for it? Do you think a great invention or a great scientific principle is born full-grown in the mind of a genius divorced from his cultural milieu? Newton's enunciation of the Law of Gravity was delayed for twenty years because the then-current figure for the Earth's diameter was wrong by ten percent. Archimedes almost discovered calculus, but failed because Arabic numerals, invented by some nameless Hindu or group of Hindus, were unknown to him.

"For that matter, the mere existence of a slave society in ancient Greece and Rome meant that machines could scarcely attract much attention—slaves being so much cheaper and more adaptable. And men of true intellect could scarcely be expected to spend their energies on devices intended for manual labor. Even Archimedes, the greatest engineer of antiquity, refused to publish any of his practical inventions—only mathematic abstractions. And when a young man asked Plato of what use geometry was, he was forthwith expelled from the Academy as a man with a mean, unphilosophic soul.

"Science does not plunge forward—it inches along in the directions permitted by the greater forces that mold society and which are in turn molded by society. And no great man advances but on the shoulders of the society that surrounds him—"

The Boss interrupted him at that point "Suppose you tell us what your part in Tywood's work was, then. We'll take your word for it that history cannot be changed."

"Oh it can, but not purposefully—You see, when Tywood first requested my services in the matter of translating certain textbook passages into Greek, I agreed for the money involved. But he wanted the translation on parchment; he insisted on the use of ancient Greek terminology—the language of Plato, to use his words—regardless of how I had to twist the literal significance of passages, and he wanted it hand-written in rolls.

"I was curious. I, too, found his magazine article. It was difficult for me to jump to the obvious conclusion since the achievements of modern science transcend the imaginings of philosophy in so many ways. But I learned the truth eventually, and it was at once obvious that Tywood's theory of changing history was infantile. There are twenty million variables for every instant of time, and no system of mathematics—no mathematic psychohistory, to coin a phrase—has yet been developed to handle that ocean of varying functions.

"In short, any variation of events two thousand years ago would change all subsequent history but in *no predictable way*."

The Boss suggested, with a false quietness: "Like the pebble that starts the avalanche, right?"

"Exactly. You have some understanding of the situation, I see. I thought deeply for weeks before I proceeded, and then I realized how I must act—*must* act."

There was a low roar. The Boss stood up and his chair went over backward. He swung around his desk, and he had a hand on Boulder's throat. I was stepping out to stop him, but he waved me back—

He was only tightening the necktie a little. Boulder could still breathe. He had gone very white, and for all the time that the Boss talked, he restricted himself to just that—breathing.

And the Boss said: "Sure, I can see how you decided you must act. I know that some of you brain-sick philosophers think the world needs fixing. You want to throw the dice again and see what turns up. Maybe you don't even care if you're alive in the new setup—or that no one can possibly know what you've done. But you're going to create just the same. You're going to give God another chance so to speak.

"Maybe I just want to live—but the world could be worse. In twenty million different ways, it could be worse. A fellow named Wilder once wrote a play called *The Skin of Our Teeth*. Maybe you've read it. Its thesis was that Mankind survived by just that skin of their teeth. No, I'm not going to give you a speech about the Ice Age nearly wiping us out. I don't know enough. I'm not even going to talk about the Greeks winning at Marathon; the Arabs being defeated at Tours; the Mongols turning back at the last minute without even being defeated—because I'm no historian.

"But take the Twentieth Century. The Germans were stopped at the Marne twice in World War I. Dunkirk happened in World War II, and somehow the Germans were stopped at Moscow and Stalingrad. We could have used the atom bomb in the last war and we didn't, and just when it looked as if both sides would have to, the Great Compromise happened—just because General Bruce was delayed in taking off from the Ceylon airfield long enough to receive the message directly. One after the other, just like that, all through history—lucky breaks. For every 'if' that didn't come true, that would have made wonder-men of all of us, if it had, there were twenty 'ifs' that didn't come true, that would have brought disaster to all of us, if they had.

"You're gambling on that one-in-twenty chance—gambling every life on Earth. And you've succeeded, too, because Tywood *did* send that text back."

He ground out that last sentence, and opened his fist, so that Boulder could fall out and back into his chair.

And Boulder laughed.

"You fool," he gasped, bitterly, "How close you can be and yet how widely you can miss the mark. Tywood *did* send his book back, then? You are sure of that?"

"No chemical textbook in Greek was found on the scene," said the Boss, grimly, "and millions of calories of energy had disappeared. Which doesn't change the fact, however, that we have two and a half weeks in which to—make things interesting for you."

"Oh, nonsense. No foolish dramatics, please. Just listen to me, and try to understand. There were Greek philosophers once, named Leucippus and Democritus who evolved an atomic theory. All matter, they said was composed of atoms. Varieties of atoms were distinct and changeless and by their different combinations with each other formed the various substances found in nature. That theory was not the result of experiment or observation. It came into being, somehow, full-grown.

"The didactic Roman poet, Lucretius, in his '*De Rerum Natura*,'—'On the Nature of Things'—elaborated on that theory and throughout manages to sound startlingly modern.

"In Hellenistic times, Hero built a steam engine and weapons of war became almost mechanized. The period has been referred to as an abortive mechanical age, which came to nothing because somehow, it neither grew out of nor fitted into its social and economic milieu. Alexandrian science was a queer and rather inexplicable phenomenon.

"Then one might mention the old Roman legend about the books of the Sibyl that contained mysterious information direct from the gods—

"In other words, gentlemen, while you are right that any change in the course of past events, however trifling, would have incalculable consequences, and while I also believe that you are right in supposing that any random change is much more likely to be for the worst than for the better, I must point out that you are nevertheless wrong in your final conclusions.

"*Because* THIS *is the world in which the Greek chemistry text* WAS *sent back.*

"This has been a Red Queen's race, if you remember your *Through the Looking Glass*. In the Red Queen's country, one had to run as fast as one could merely to stay in the same place. And so it was in this case! Tywood may have thought he was creating a new world, but it was *I* who prepared the translations, and I took care that only such passages as would account for the queer scraps of knowledge the ancients apparently got from nowhere would be included.

"And my only intention, for all my racing, was to stay in the same place."

Three weeks passed; three months; three years. Nothing happened. When nothing happens, you have no proof. We gave up trying to explain, and we ended, the Boss and I, by doubting it ourselves.

The case never ended. Boulder could not be considered a criminal without being considered a world savior as well, and vice versa. He was ignored. And in the end, the case was neither solved, nor closed out; merely put in a file all by itself, under the designation "?" and buried in the deepest vault in Washington.

The Boss is in Washington now; a big wheel. And I'm Regional Head of the Bureau.

Boulder is still assistant professor, though. Promotions are slow at the University.

FLAW

John D. MacDonald (1916–   )

***Startling Stories*, January**

John D. MacDonald returns (see his two excellent stories in our 1948 volume) with this interesting and unusual piece of speculative fiction. MacDonald was tremendously prolific in the late 1940s, working in almost every genre that still had magazine markets available, in what was the twilight of the pulp era. He got published because he was a wonderful storyteller, but also because he developed an excellent working knowledge of genres and their conventions. However, like all great writers, he could successfully defy genre conventions and get away with it, as in this story, which is blatantly pessimistic and questions the very possibility of going to the stars—an attitude and point of view that most late 1940s science fiction writers and their readers certainly did not share.—M.H.G.

(Science fiction can be at its most amusing [and most useful, perhaps] when it challenges our assumptions. And that is true of straightforward scientific speculation, also.

Even when the challenge is doomed to failure [and in my opinion the one in this story is so doomed] or when scientific advance actually demonstrates, within a few years, the challenge to be doomed, the story is likely to remain interesting. —Thus, I once wrote a story in which I speculated that the Moon was only a false front and that on the other side were merely wooden supports. Within a few years the other side of the Moon was photographed and our satellite proved not to be a false front after all. But who cares? Anyone who reads the story is not likely to forget the speculation.

Read "Flaw," then, and ask yourself: With the rockets and probes of the last three decades, has the thesis of this story yet been demonstrated to be false? If so, how?—I.A.)

I rather imagine that I am quite mad. Nothing spectacular, you understand. Nothing calling for restraint, or shock therapy. I can live on, dangerous to no one but myself.

This beach house at La Jolla is comfortable. At night I sit on the rocks and watch the distant stars and think of Johnny. He probably wouldn't like the way I look now. My fingernails are cracked and broken and there are streaks of gray in my blonde hair. I no longer use makeup. Last night I looked at myself in the mirror and my eyes were dead.

It was then that I decided that it might help me to write all this down. I have no idea what I'll do with it.

You see, I shared Johnny's dreams.

And now I know that those dreams are no longer possible. I wonder if he learned how impossible they were in the few seconds before his flaming death.

There have always been people like Johnny and me. For a thousand years mankind has looked at the stars and thought of reaching them. The stars were to be the new frontier, the new worlds on which mankind could expand and find the full promise of the human soul.

I never thought much about it until I met Johnny. Five years ago. My name is Carol Adlar. At that time I was a government clerk working in the offices at the rocket station in Arizona. It was 1959. The year before the atomic drive was perfected.

Johnny Pritchard. I figured him out, I thought. A good-looking boy with dark hair and a careless grin and a swagger. That's all I saw in the beginning. The hot sun blazed down on the rocks and the evenings were cool and clear.

There were a lot of boys like Johnny at the rocket station—transferred from Air Corps work. Volunteers. You couldn't order a man off the surface of the earth in a rocket.

The heart is ever cautious. Johnny Pritchard began to hang around my desk, a warm look in his eyes. I was as cool as I could be. You don't give your heart to a man who soars up at the tip of a comet plume. But I did.

I told myself that I would go out with him one evening and I would be so cool to him that it would cure him and he would stop bothering me. I expected him to drive me to the city in his little car. Instead we drove only five miles from the compound, parked on the brow of a hill looking across the moon-silvered rock and sand.

At first I was defensive, until I found that all he wanted to do was talk. He talked about the stars. He talked in a low voice that was somehow tense with his visions. I found out that first evening that he wasn't like the others. He wasn't merely one of those young men with perfect coordination and high courage. Johnny had in him the blood of pioneers. And his frontier was the stars.

"You see, Carol," he said, "I didn't know a darn thing about the upstairs at the time of my transfer. I guess I don't know much right now. Less, probably than the youngest astronomer or physicist on the base. But I'm learning. I spend every minute I can spare studying about it. Carol, I'm going upstairs some day. Right out into space. And I want to know about it. I want to know all about it.

"We've made a pretty general mess of this planet. I sort of figure that the powers-that-be planned it that way. They said, 'We'll give this puny little fella called man a chance to mess up one planet and mess it up good. But we'll let him slowly learn how to travel to another. Then, by the time he can migrate, he will be smart enough to turn the next planet into the sort of a deal we wanted him to have in the beginning. A happy world with no wars, no disease, no starvation.' "

I should have said something flip at that point, but the words weren't in me. Like a fool, I asked him questions about the galaxies, about the distant stars. We drove slowly back. The next day he loaned me two of his books. Within a week I had caught his fervor, his sense of dedication.

After that it was, of course, too late.

All persons in love have dreams. This was ours. Johnny would be at the controls of one of the first interplanetary rockets. He would return to me and then we would become one of the first couples to become colonists for the new world.

Silly, wasn't it?

He told me of the problems that would be solved with that first interplanetary flight. They would take instruments far enough out into space so that triangulation could solve that tiresome bickering among the physicists and astronomers about the theory of the exploding universe as against the theory of "tired light" from the distant galaxies.

And now I am the only person in the world who can solve that problem. Oh, the others will find the answer soon enough. And then they, too, can go quietly mad.

They will find out that for years they have been in the position of the man at the table with his fingers almost touching the sugar bowl and who asks why there isn't any sugar on the table.

That year was the most perfect year of my life.

"When are you going to marry me, Johnny?" I asked him.

"This is so sudden," he said, laughing. Then he sobered. "Just as soon as I come back from the first one, honey. It isn't fair any other way. Don't you see?"

I saw with my mind, but not with my heart. We exchanged rings. All very sentimental. He gave me a diamond and I gave him my father's ring, the one that was sent home to my mother and me when Dad was killed in Burma in World War II. It fit him and he liked it. It was a star ruby in a heavy silver setting. The star was perfect, but by looking closely into the stone you could see the flaws. Two dark little dots and a tiny curved line which together gave the look of a small and smiling face.

With his arm around me, with the cool night air of Arizona touching our faces, we looked up at the sky and talked of the home we would make millions of miles away.

Childish, wasn't it?

Last night after looking in the mirror, I walked down to the rocks. The Government money was given to me when Johnny didn't come back. It is enough. It will last until I die and I hope it will not be too long before I die.

The sea, washing the rocks, asked me the soft, constant question. "Why? Why? Why?" I looked at the sky. The answer was not there.

Fourteen months after I met Johnny, a crew of two in the *Destiny I* made the famous circuit of the moon and landed safely. Johnny was not one of them. He had hoped to be.

"A test run," he called it. The first step up the long flight of stairs.

You certainly remember the headlines given that flight of *Destiny I*. Even the New York *Times* broke out a new and larger type face for the headlines. Korby and Sweeny became the heroes of the entire world.

The world was confident then. The intervening years have shaken that confidence. But the world does not know yet. I think some suspect, but they do not know. Only I know for a certainty. And I, of course, am quite mad. I know that now.

Call it a broken heart—or broken dreams.

* * *

Johnny was selected for *Destiny II*. After he told me and after the tears came, partly from fear, partly from the threat of loneliness, he held me tightly and kissed my eyes. I had not known that the flight of *Destiny II*, if successful, would take fourteen months. The fourteen months were to include a circuit of Mars and a return to the takeoff point. Fourteen months before I would see him again. Fourteen months before I would feel his arms around me.

A crew of four. The famous Korby and Sweeny, plus Anthony Marinetta and my Johnny. Each morning when I went to work I could see the vast silver ship on the horizon, the early sun glinting on the blunt nose. Johnny's ship.

Those last five months before takeoff were like the five months of life ahead of a prisoner facing execution. And Johnny's training was so intensified after his selection that I couldn't see him as often as before.

We were young and we were in love and we made our inevitable mistake. At least we called it a mistake. Now I know that it wasn't, because Johnny didn't come back.

With the usual sense of guilt we planned to be married, and then reverted to our original plan. I would wait for him. Nothing could go wrong.

Takeoff was in the cold dawn of a February morning. I stood in the crowd beside a girl who worked in the same office. I held her arm. She carried the bruises for over a week.

The silver hull seemed to merge with the gray of the dawn. The crowd was silent. At last there was the blinding, blue-white flare of the jets, the stately lift into the air, the moment when *Destiny II* seemed to hang motionless fifty feet in the air, and then the accelerating blast that arrowed it up and up into the dark-gray sky where a few stars still shone. I walked on leaden legs back to the administration building and sat slumped at my desk, my mouth dry, my eyes hot and burning.

The last faint radio signal came in three hours later.

"All well. See you next year."

From then on there would be fourteen months of silence.

I suppose that in a way I became accustomed to it.

I was numb, apathetic, stupefied. They would probably have got rid of me had they not known how it was between Johnny and me. I wouldn't have blamed them. Each morning I saw the silver form of *Destiny III* taking shape near where *Destiny II* had taken off. The brash young men made the same jokes, gave the office girls the same line of chatter.

But they didn't bother me. Word had got around.

I found a friend. The young wife of Tony Marienetta. We spent hours telling each other in subtle ways that everything would come out all right.

I remember one night when Marge grinned and said:

"Well anyway, Carol, nobody has ever had their men go quite so far away."

There is something helpless about thinking of the distance between two people in the form of millions of miles.

After I listened to the sea last night, I walked slowly back up the steep path to this beach house. When I clicked the lights on Johnny looked at me out of the silver frame on my writing desk. His eyes are on me as I write this. They are happy and confident eyes. I am almost glad that he didn't live to find out.

The fourteen months were like one single revolution of a gigantic Ferris wheel. You start at the top of the wheel, and through seven months the wheel carries you slowly down into the darkness and the fear. Then, after you are at your lowest point, the wheel slowly starts to carry you back up into the light.

Somewhere in space I knew that Johnny looked at the small screen built into the control panel and saw the small bright sphere of earth and thought of me. I knew all during that fourteen months that he wasn't dead. If he had died, no matter how many million miles away from me, I would have known it in the instant of his dying.

The world forgets quickly. The world had pushed *Destiny II* off the surface of consciousness a few months after takeoff. Two months before the estimated date of return, it began to creep back into the papers and onto the telescreens of the world.

Work had stopped on *Destiny III*. The report of the four crewmen might give a clue to alterations in the interior.

It was odd the way I felt. As though I had been frozen under the transparent ice of a small lake. Spring was coming and the ice grew thinner.

Each night I went to sleep thinking of Johnny driving down through the sky toward me at almost incalculable speed. Closer, closer, ever closer.

It was five weeks before the date when they were due to return. I was asleep in the barracks-like building assigned to the unmarried women of the base.

The great thud and jar woke me up and through the window I saw the night sky darkening in the afterglow of some brilliant light.

* * *

We gathered by the windows and talked for a long time about what it could have been. It was in all of our minds that it could have been the return of *Destiny II*, but we didn't put it into words, because no safe landing could have resulted in that deathly thud.

With the lights out again, I tried to sleep. I reached out into the night sky with my heart, trying to contact Johnny.

And the sky was empty.

I sat up suddenly, my lips numb, my eyes staring. No. It was imagination. It was illusion. Johnny was still alive. Of course. But when I composed myself for sleep it was as though dirges were softly playing. In all the universe there was no living entity called Johnny Pritchard. Nowhere.

The telescreens were busy the next morning and I saw the shape of fear. An alert operator had caught the fast shape as it had slammed flaming down through the atmosphere to land forty miles from the base in deserted country making a crater a half-mile across.

"It is believed that the object was a meteor," the voice of the announcer said. "Radar screens picked up the image and it is now known that it was far too large to be the *Destiny II* arriving ahead of a schedule."

It was then that I took a deep breath. But the relief was not real. I was only kidding myself. It was as though I was in the midst of a dream of terror and could not think of magic words to cause the spell to cease.

After breakfast I was ill.

The meteor had hit with such impact that the heat generated had fused the sand. Scientific instruments proved that the mass of the meteor itself, nine hundred feet under the surface was largely metallic. The telescreens began to prattle about invaders from an alien planet. And the big telescopes scanned the heavens for the first signs of the returning *Destiny II*.

The thought began as a small spot, glowing in some deep part of my mind. I knew that I had to cross the forty miles between the base and the crater. But I did not know why I had to cross it. I did not know why I had to stand at the lip of the crater and watch the recovery operations. I felt like a subject under post-hypnotic influence—compelled to do something without knowing the reason. But compelled, nevertheless.

One of the physicists took me to the crater in one of the base helicopters after I had made the request of him in such a way that he could not refuse.

Eleven days after the meteor had fallen, I stood on the lip of the crater and looked down into the heart of it to where the vast shaft had been sunk to the meteor itself. Dr. Rawlins handed me his binoculars and I watched the mouth of the shaft.

Men working down in the shaft had cut away large pieces of the body of the meteor and some of them had been hauled out and trucked away. They were blackened and misshapen masses of fused metal.

I watched the mouth of the shaft until my eyes ached and until the young physicist shifted restlessly and kept glancing at his watch and at the sun sinking toward the west. When he asked to borrow the binoculars, I gave them up reluctantly. I could hear the distant throb of the hoist motors. Something was coming up the shaft.

Dr. Rawlins made a sudden exclamation. I looked at the mouth of the shaft. The sun shone with red fire on something large. It dwarfed the men who stood near it.

Rudely I snatched the binoculars from Dr. Rawlins and looked, knowing even as I lifted them to my eyes what I would see.

Because at that moment I knew the answer to something that the astronomers and physicists had been bickering about for many years. There is no expanding universe. There is no tired light.

As I sit here at my writing desk, I can imagine how it was during those last few seconds. The earth looming up in the screen on the instrument panel, but not nearly large enough. Not large enough at all. Incredulity, then because of the error in size, the sudden application of the nose jets. Too late. Fire and oblivion and a thud that shook the earth for hundreds of miles.

No one else knows what I know. Maybe soon they will guess. And then there will be an end to the proud dreams of migration to other worlds. We are trapped here. There will be no other worlds for us. We have made a mess of this planet, and it is something that we cannot leave behind us. We must stay here and clean it up as best we can.

Maybe a few of them already know. Maybe they have guessed. Maybe they guessed, as I did, on the basis of the single object that was brought up out of that shaft on that bright, cold afternoon.

Yes, I saw the sun shining on the six-pointed star. With the binoculars I looked into the heart of it and saw the two dots and a curved line that made the flaws look like a smiling face. A ruby the size of a bungalow.

There is no expanding universe. There is no "tired light."

There is only a Solar system that, due to an unknown influence, is constantly shrinking.

For a little time the *Destiny II* avoided that influence. That is why they arrived too soon, why they couldn't avoid the crash, and why I am quite mad.

The ruby was the size of a bungalow, but it was, of course, quite unchanged. It was I and my world that had shrunk.

If Johnny had landed safely, I would be able to walk about on the palm of his hand.

It is a good thing that he died.

And it will not be long before I die also.

The sea whispers softly against the rocks a hundred yards from the steps of my beach house.

And *Destiny III* has not yet returned.

It is due in three months.

PRIVATE EYE

by "Lewis Padgett" (Henry Kuttner, 1914–1958 and C.L. Moore, 1911– ; this story is generally believed to have been written by Kuttner)

***Astounding Science Fiction*, January**

The Kuttners were so prolific that they made extensive use of pen names—in addition to Kuttner and Moore, singly and listed together, they wrote as "Lewis Padgett" and as "Lawrence O'Donnell," producing important stories under both of these pseudonyms. The present selection is the first of three in this book—the late 1940s were tremendously productive for this wonderful writing team.

As Isaac points out, "Private Eye" is a classic blend of mystery and science fiction and fully deserves the title of "classic." It is not now unusual for such combinations to see print; indeed, in the last twenty years dozens of stories incorporating a murder mystery with sf have appeared, and many have been collected in such anthologies as Miriam Allen deFord's Space, Time & Crime *(1964), Barry N. Malzberg and Bill Pronzini's wonderful* Dark Sins, Dark Crimes *(1978), and our own (along with Charles G. Waugh)* The 13 Crimes of Science Fiction *(1979).—M.H.G.*

(John Campbell, the greatest of all science fiction editors, was one of the most prescient people I have ever met—and yet he was given to peculiar blind spots. For instance, during the 1940's he frequently maintained that science fiction mysteries were impossible, because it was so easy to use futuristic gimmicks to help the detective crack his case.

I eventually showed, in 1953, that a classic mystery could be combined with science fiction if one simply set up the boundary conditions at the start and stuck to them. I resolutely allowed no futuristic gimmicks to appear suddenly and give the detective an unfair advantage.

In "Private Eye" however, Henry Kuttner [preceding me by four years] took the harder task of allowing a futuristic gimmick—one that would seem to make it impossible to get away with murder—and then labored to produce an honest murder mystery anyway. *The result was an undoubted classic—I.A.)*

The forensic sociologist looked closely at the image on the wall screen. Two figures were frozen there, one in the act of stabbing the other through the heart with an antique letter cutter, once used at Johns Hopkins for surgery. That was before the ultra-microtome, of course.

"As tricky a case as I've ever seen," the sociologist remarked. "If we can make a homicide charge stick on Sam Clay, I'll be a little surprised."

The tracer engineer twirled a dial and watched the figures on the screen repeat their actions. One—Sam Clay—snatched the letter cutter from a desk and plunged it into the other man's heart. The victim fell down dead. Clay started back in apparent horror. Then he dropped to his knees beside the twitching body and said wildly that he didn't mean it. The body drummed its heels upon the rug and was still.

"That last touch was nice," the engineer said.

"Well, I've got to make the preliminary survey," the sociologist sighed, settling in his dictachair and placing his fingers on the keyboard. "I doubt if I'll find any evidence. However, the analysis can come later. Where's Clay now?"

"His mouthpiece put in a *habeas mens*."

"I didn't think we'd be able to hold him. But it was worth trying. Imagine, just one shot of scop and he'd have told the truth. Ah, well. We'll do it the hard way, as usual. Start the tracer, will you? It won't make sense till we run it chronologically, but one must start somewhere. Good old Blackstone," the sociologist said, as, on the screen, Clay stood up, watching the corpse revive and arise, and then pulled the miraculously clean paper cutter out of its heart, all in reverse.

"Good old Blackstone," he repeated. "On the other hand, sometimes I wish I'd lived in Jeffreys' time. In those days, homicide was homicide."

Telepathy never came to much. Perhaps the developing faculty went underground in response to a familiar natural law after the new science appeared—omniscience. It wasn't really that, of course. It was a device for looking into the past. And it was limited to a fifty-year span; no chance of seeing the arrows at Agincourt or the homunculi of Bacon. It was sensitive enough to pick up the "fingerprints" of light and sound waves imprinted on matter, descramble and screen them, and reproduce the image of what had happened. After all, a man's shadow can be photographed on concrete, if he's unlucky enough to be caught in an atomic blast. Which is something. The shadow's about all here is left.

However, opening the past like a book didn't solve all problems. It took generations for the maze of complixties to iron itself out, though finally a tentative check-and-balance was reached. The right to kill has been sturdily defended by mankind since Cain rose up against Abel. A good many idealists quoted, "The voice of thy brother's blood crieth unto me from the ground," but that didn't stop the lobbyists and the pressure groups. Magna Carta was quoted in reply. The right to privacy was defended desperately.

And the curious upshot of this imbalance came when the act of homicide was declared nonpunishable, unless intent and forethought could be proved. Of course, it was considered at least naughty to fly in a rage and murder someone on impulse, and there was a nominal punishment—imprisonment, for example—but in practice this never worked, because so many defenses were possible. Temporary insanity. Undue provocation. Self-defense. Manslaughter, second-degree homicide, third degree, fourth degree—it went on like that. It was up to the State to prove that the killer had planned his killing in advance; only then would a jury convict. And the jury, of course, had to waive immunity and take a scop test, to prove the box hadn't been packed. But no defendant ever waived immunity.

A man's home wasn't his castle—not with the Eye able to enter it at will and scan his past. The device couldn't interpret, and it couldn't read his mind; it could only see and listen. Consequently the sole remaining fortress of privacy was defended to the last ditch. No truth-serum, no hypnoanalysis, no third-degree, no leading questions.

If, by viewing the prisoner's past actions, the prosecution could prove forethought and intent, O.K.

Otherwise, Sam Clay would go scot-free. Superficially, it appeared as though Andrew Vanderman had, during a quarrel, struck Clay across the face with a stingaree whip. Anyone who has been stung by a Portuguese man-of-war can understand that, at this point, Clay could plead temporary insanity and self-defense, as well as undue provocation and possible justification.

Only the curious cult of the Alaskan Flagellantes, who make the stingaree whips for their ceremonials, know how to endure the pain. The Flagellantes even like it, the pre-ritual drug they swallow transmutes pain into pleasure. Not having swallowed this drug, Sam Clay very naturally took steps to protect himself—irrational steps, perhaps, but quite logical and defensible ones.

Nobody but Clay knew that he had intended to kill Vanderman all along. That was the trouble. Clay couldn't understand why he felt so let down.

The screen flickered. It went dark. The engineer chuckled.

"My, my. Locked up in a dark closet at the age of four. What one of those old-time psychiatrists would have made of that. Or do I mean obimen? Shamans? I forget. They interpreted dreams, anyway."

"You're confused. It—"

"Astrologers! No, it wasn't either. The ones I mean went in for symbolism. They used to spin prayer wheels and say 'A rose is a rose is a rose,' didn't they? To free the unconscious mind?"

"You've got the typical layman's attitude toward antique psychiatric treatments."

"Well, maybe they had something, at that. Look at quinine and digitalis. The United Amazon natives used those long before science discovered them. But why use eye of newt and toe of frog? To impress the patient?"

"No, to convince themselves," the Sociologist said. "In those days the study of mental aberrations drew potential psychotics, so naturally there was unnecessary mumbo-jumbo. Those medicos were trying to fix their own mental imbalance while they treated their patients. But it's a science today, not a religion. We've found out how to allow for individual psychotic deviation in the psychiatrist himself, so we've got a better chance of finding true north. However, let's get on with this. Try ultraviolet. Oh, never mind. Somebody's letting him out of that closet. The devil with it. I think we've cut back far enough. Even if he was frightened by a thunderstorm at the age of three months, that can be filed under Gestalt and ignored. Let's run through this chronologically. Give it the screening for . . . let's see. Incidents involving these persons: Vanderman, Mrs. Vanderman, Josephine Wells—and these places: the office, Vanderman's apartment, Clay's place—"

"Got it."

"Later we can recheck for complicating factors. Right now

we'll run the superficial survey. Verdict first, evidence later," he added, with a grin. "All we need is a motive—"

"What about this?"

A girl was talking to Sam Clay. The background was an apartment, grade B-2.

"I'm sorry, Sam. It's just that . . . well, these things happen."

"Yeah. Vanderman's got something I haven't got, apparently."

"I'm in love with him."

"Funny. I thought all along you were in love with me."

"So did I . . . for a while."

"Well, forget it. No, I'm not angry, Bea. I'll even wish you luck. But you must have been pretty certain how I'd react to this."

"I'm sorry—"

"Come to think of it, I've always let you call the shots. Always."

Secretly—and this the screen could not show—he thought: Let her? I wanted it that way. It was so much easier to leave the decisions up to her. Sure, she's dominant, but I guess I'm just the opposite. And now it's happened again.

It always happens. I was loaded with weight-cloths from the start. And I always felt I had to toe the line, or else. Vanderman—that cocky, arrogant air of his. Reminds me of somebody. I was locked up in a dark place, I couldn't breathe. I forget. What . . . who . . . my father. No, I don't remember. But my life's been like that. He always watched me, and I always thought some day I'd do what I wanted—but I never did. Too late now. He's been dead quite a while.

He was always so sure I'd knuckle under. If I'd only defied him once—

Somebody's always pushing me in and closing the door. So I can't use my abilities. I can't prove I'm competent. Prove it to myself, to my father, to Bea, to the whole world. If only I could—I'd like to push Vanderman into a dark place and lock the door. A dark place, like a coffin. It would be satisfying to surprise him that way. It would be fine if I killed Andrew Vanderman.

"Well, that's the beginning of a motive," the sociologist said. "Still, lots of people get jilted and don't turn homicidal. Carry on."

"In my opinion, Bea attracted him because he wanted to be bossed," the engineer remarked. "He'd given up."

"Protective passivity."

The wire taps spun through the screening apparatus. A new scene showed on the oblong panel. It was the Paradise Bar.

Anywhere you sat in the Paradise Bar, a competent robot analyzer instantly studied your complexion and facial angles, and switched on lights, in varying tints and intensities, that showed you off to best advantage. The joint was popular for business deals. A swindler could look like an honest man there. It was also popular with women and slightly passé teleo talent. Sam Clay looked rather like an ascetic young saint. Andrew Vanderman looked noble, in a grim way, like Richard Coeur-de-Lion offering Saladin his freedom, though he knew it wasn't really a bright thing to do. *Noblesse oblige*, his firm jaw seemed to say, as he picked up the silver decanter and poured. In ordinary light, Vanderman looked slightly more like a handsome bulldog. Also, away from the Paradise Bar, he was redder around the chops, a choleric man.

"As to that deal we were discussing," Clay said, "you can go to—"

The censoring juke box blared out a covering bar or two.

Vanderman's reply was unheard as the music got briefly louder, and the lights shifted rapidly to keep pace with his sudden flush.

"It's perfectly easy to outwit these censors," Clay said. "They're keyed to familiar terms of profane abuse, not to circumlocutions. If I said that the arrangement of your chromosomes would have surprised your father . . . you see?" He was right. The music stayed soft.

Vanderman swallowed nothing. "Take it easy," he said. "I can see why you're upset. Let me say first of all—"

"Hijo—"

But the censor was proficient in Spanish dialects. Vanderman was spared hearing another insult.

"—that I offered you a job because I think you're a very capable man. You have potentialities. It's not a bribe. Our personal affairs should be kept out of this."

All the same, Bea was engaged to me."

"Clay, are you drunk?"

"Yes," Clay said, and threw his drink into Vanderman's face. The music began to play Wagner very, very loudly. A few minutes later, when the waiters interfered, Clay was supine and bloody, with a mashed nose and a bruised cheek. Vanderman had skinned his knuckles.

* * *

"That's a motive," the engineer said.

"Yes, it is, isn't it? But why did Clay wait a year and a half? And remember what happened later. I wonder if the murder itself was just a symbol? If Vanderman represented, say, what Clay considered the tyrannical and oppressive force of society in general—synthesized in the representative image . . . oh, nonsense. Obviously Clay was trying to prove something to himself though. Suppose you cut forward now. I want to see this in normal chronology, not backwards. What's the next selection?"

"Very suspicious. Clay got his nose fixed up and then went to a murder trial."

He thought: I can't breathe. Too crowded in here. Shut up in a box, a closet, a coffin, ignored by the spectators and the vested authority on the bench. What would I do if I were in the dock, like that chap? Suppose they convicted? That would spoil it all. Another dark place— If I'd inherited the right genes, I'd have been strong enough to beat up Vanderman. But I've been pushed around too long.

I keep remembering that song.

Stray in the herd and the boss said kill it,
So I shot him in the rump with the handle of a skillet.

A deadly weapon that's in normal usage wouldn't appear dangerous. But if it could be used homicidally—No, the Eye could check on that. All you can conceal these days is motive. But couldn't the trick be reversed. Suppose I got Vanderman to attack me with what he thought was the handle of a skillet, but which I knew was a deadly weapon—

The trial Sam Clay was watching was fairly routine. One man had killed another. Counsel for the defense contended that the homicide had been a matter of impulse, and that, as a matter of fact, only assault and battery plus culpable negligence, at worst, could be proved, and the latter was canceled by an Act of God. The fact that the defendant inherited the decedent's fortune, in Martial oil, made no difference. Temporary insanity was the plea.

The prosecuting attorney showed films of what had happened before the fact. True, the victim hadn't been killed by the blow, merely stunned. But the affair had occurred on an isolated beach, and when the tide came in—

Act of God, the defense repeated hastily.

The screen showed the defendant, some days before his crime, looking up the tide-table in a news tape. He also, it appeared, visited the site and asked a passing stranger if the beach was often crowded. "Nope," the stranger said, "it ain't crowded after sundown. Gits too cold. Won't do you no good, though. Too cold to swim then."

One side matched *Actus non facit reum, nisi mens sit rea*—"The act does not make a man guilty, unless the mind be also guilty"—against *Acta exteriora indicant interiora secreta*—"By the outward acts we are to judge of the inward thoughts." Latin legal basics were still valid, up to a point. A man's past remained sacrosanct, provided—and here was the joker—that he possessed the right of citizenship. And anyone accused of a capital crime was automatically suspended from citizenship until his innocence had been established.

Also, no past-tracing evidence could be introduced into a trial unless it could be proved that it had direct connection with the crime. The average citizen did have a right of privacy against tracing. Only if accused of a serious crime was that forfeit, and even then evidence uncovered could be used only in correlation with the immediate charge. There were various loopholes, of course, but theoretically a man was safe from espionage as long as he stayed within the law.

Now a defendant stood in the dock, his past opened. The prosecution showed recordings of a ginger blonde blackmailing him, and that clinched the motive and the verdict—guilty. The condemned man was led off in tears. Clay got up and walked out of the court. From his appearance, he seemed to be thinking.

He was. He had decided that there was only one possible way in which he could kill Vanderman and get away with it. He couldn't conceal the deed itself, nor the actions leading up to it, nor any written or spoken word. All he could hide were his own thoughts. And, without otherwise betraying himself, he'd have to kill Vanderman so that his act would appear justified. Which meant covering his tracks for yesterday as well as for tomorrow and tomorrow.

Now, thought Clay, this much can be assumed: If I stand to lose by Vanderman's death instead of gaining, that will help considerably. I must juggle that somehow. But I mustn't forget that at present I have an obvious motive. First, he stole Bea. Second, he beat me up.

So I must make it seem as though he's done me a favor—somehow.

I must have an opportunity to study Vanderman carefully, and it must be a normal, logical, waterproof opportunity. Private secretary. Something like that. The Eye's in the future now, after the fact, but it's watching me—

I must remember that. *It's watching me now!*

All right. Normally, I'd have thought of murder, at this point. That can't and shouldn't be disguised. I must work out of the mood gradually, but meanwhile—

He smiled.

Going off to buy a gun, he felt uncomfortable, as though that prescient Eye, years in the future, could with a wink summon the police. But it was separated from him by a barrier of time that only the natural processes could shorten. And, in fact, it had been watching him since his birth. You could look at it that way—

He could defy it. The Eye couldn't read thoughts.

He bought the gun and lay in wait for Vanderman in a dark alley. But first he got thoroughly drunk. Drunk enough to satisfy the Eye.

After that—

"Feel better now?" Vanderman asked, pouring another coffee.

Clay buried his face in his hands.

"I was crazy," he said, his voice muffled. "I must have been. You'd better t-turn me over to the police."

"We can forget about that end of it, Clay. You were drunk, that's all. And I . . . well, I—"

"I pull a gun on you . . . try to kill you . . . and you bring me up to your place and—"

"You didn't use that gun, Clay. Remember that. You're no killer. All this has been my fault. I needn't have been so blasted tough with you," Vanderman said, looking like Coeur-de-Lion in spite of uncalculated amber fluorescence.

"I'm no good. I'm a failure. Every time I try to do something, a man like you comes along and does it better. I'm a second-rater."

"Clay, stop talking like that. You're just upset, that's all. Listen to me. You're going to straighten up. I'm going to see that you do. Starting tomorrow, we'll work something out. Now drink your coffee."

"You know," Clay said, "you're quite a guy."

So the magnanimous idiot's fallen for it, Clay thought, as he was drifting happily off to sleep. Fine. That begins to take care of the Eye. Moreover, it starts the ball rolling with Vanderman. Let a man do you a favor and he's your pal. Well, Vanderman's going to do me a lot more favors. In fact, before I'm through, I'll have every motive for wanting to keep him alive.

Every motive visible to the naked Eye.

Probably Clay had not heretofore applied his talents in the right direction, for there was nothing second-rate about the way he executed his homicide plan. In that, he proved very capable. He needed a suitable channel for his ability, and perhaps he needed a patron. Vanderman fulfilled that function; probably it salved his conscience for stealing Bea. Being the man he was, Vanderman needed to avoid even the appearance of ignobility. Naturally strong and ruthless, he told himself he was sentimental. His sentimentality never reached the point of actually inconveniencing him, and Clay knew enough to stay within the limits.

Nevertheless it is nerve-racking to know you're living under the scrutiny of an extratemporal Eye. As he walked into the lobby of the V Building a month later, Clay realized that light-vibrations reflected from his own body were driving irretrievably into the polished onyx walls and floor, photographing themselves there, waiting for a machine to unlock them, some day, some time, for some man perhaps in this very city, who as yet didn't know even the name of Sam Clay. Then, sitting in his relaxer in the spiral lift moving swiftly up inside the walls, he knew that those walls were capturing his image, stealing it, like some superstition he remembered . . . ah?

Vanderman's private secretary greeted him. Clay let his gaze wander freely across that young person's neatly dressed figure and mildly attractive face. She said that Mr. Vanderman was out, and the appointment was for three, not two, wasn't it? Clay referred to a notebook. He snapped his fingers.

"Three—you're right, Miss Wells. I was so sure it was two I didn't even bother to check up. Do you think he might be back sooner? I mean, is he out, or in conference?"

"He's out, all right, Mr. Clay," Miss Wells said. "I don't think he'll be back much sooner than three. I'm sorry."

"Well, may I wait in here?"

She smiled at him efficiently. "Of course. There's a stereo and the magazine spools are in that case."

She went back to her work, and Clay skimmed through an article about the care and handling of lunar filchards. It gave him an opportunity to start a conversation by asking Miss Wells if she liked filchards. It turned out that she had no opinion whatsoever of filchards but the ice had been broken.

This is the cocktail acquaintance, Clay thought. I may have a broken heart, but, naturally, I'm lonesome.

The trick wasn't to get engaged to Miss Wells so much as to fall in love with her convincingly. The Eye never slept. Clay was beginning to wake at night with a nervous start, and lie there looking up at the ceiling. But darkness was no shield.

"The question is," said the sociologist at this point, "whether or not Clay was acting for an audience."

"You mean us?"

"Exactly. It just occurred to me. Do you think he's been behaving perfectly naturally?"

The engineer pondered.

"I'd say yes. A man doesn't marry a girl only to carry out some other plan, does he? After all, he'd get himself involved in a whole new batch of responsibilities."

"Clay hasn't married Josephine Wells yet, however," the sociologist countered. "Besides, that responsibility angle might have applied a few hundred years ago, but not now." He went off at random. "Imagine a society where, after divorce, a man was forced to support a perfectly healthy, competent woman! It was vestigial, I know—a throwback to the days when only males could earn a living—but imagine the sort of women who were willing to accept such support. That was reversion to infancy if I ever—"

The engineer coughed.

"Oh," the sociologist said. "Oh . . . yes. The question is, would Clay have got himself engaged to a woman unless he really—"

"Engagements can be broken."

"This one hasn't been broken yet, as far as we know. And *we know*."

A normal man wouldn't plan on marrying a girl he didn't care anything about, unless he had some stronger motive—I'll go along that far."

"But how normal is Clay?" the sociologist wondered. "Did he know in advance we'd check back on his past? Did you notice that he cheated at solitaire?"

"Proving?"

"There are all kinds of trivial things you don't do if you think people are looking. Picking up a penny in the street, drinking soup out of the bowl, posing before a mirror—the sort of foolish or petty things everyone does when alone. Either Clay's innocent, or he's a very clever man—"

* * *

He was a very clever man. He never intended the engagement to get as far as marriage, though he knew that in one respect marriage would be a precaution. If a man talks in his sleep, his wife will certainly mention the fact. Clay considered gagging himself at night if the necessity should arise. Then he realized that if he talked in his sleep at all, there was no insurance against talking too much the very first time he had an auditor. He couldn't risk such a break. But there was no necessity, after all. Clay's problem, when he thought it over, was simply: How can I be sure I don't talk in my sleep?

He solved that easily enough by renting a narcohypnotic supplementary course in common trade dialects. This involved studying while awake and getting the information repeated in his ear during slumber. As a necessary preparation for the course, he was instructed to set up a recorder and chart the depth of his sleep, so the narcohypnosis could be keyed to his individual rhythms. He did this several times, rechecked once a month thereafter, and was satisfied. There was no need to gag himself at night.

He was glad to sleep provided he didn't dream. He had to take sedatives after a while. At night, there was relief from the knowledge that an Eye watched him always, an Eye that could bring him to justice, an Eye whose omnipotence he could not challenge in the open. But he dreamed about the Eye.

Vanderman had given him a job in the organization, which was enormous. Clay was merely a cog, which suited him well enough, for the moment. He didn't want any more favors yet. Not till he had found out the extent of Miss Wells' duties—Josephine, her Christian name was. That took several months, but by that time friendship was ripening into affection. So Clay asked Vanderman for another job. He specified. It wasn't obvious, but he was asking for work that would, presently, fit him for Miss Wells' duties.

Vanderman probably still felt guilty about Bea; he'd married her and she was in Antarctica now, at the Casino. Vanderman was due to join her, so he scribbled a memorandum, wished Clay good luck, and went to Antarctica, bothered by no stray pangs of conscience. Clay improved the hour by courting Josephine ardently.

From what he had heard about the new Mrs. Vanderman, he felt secretly relieved. Not long ago, when he had been content to remain passive, the increasing dominance of Bea would have satisfied him, but no more. He was learning self-reliance, and liked it. These days, Bea was behaving rather badly. Given all the money and freedom she could use, she had too much time on her hands. Once in a while Clay heard rumors that made him smile secretly. Vanderman wasn't having an easy time of it. A dominant character, Bea—but Vanderman was no weakling himself.

After a while Clay told his employer he wanted to marry Josephine Wells. "I guess that makes us square," he said. "You took Bea away from me and I'm taking Josie away from you."

"Now wait a minute," Vanderman said. "I hope you don't—"

"My fiancée, your secretary. That's all. The thing is, Josie and I are in love." He poured it on, but carefully. It was easier to deceive Vanderman than the Eye, with its trained technicians and forensic sociologists looking through it. He thought, sometime, of those medieval pictures of an immense eye, and that reminded him of something vague and distressing, though he couldn't isolate the memory.

After all, what could Vanderman do? He arranged to have Clay given a raise. Josphine, always conscientious, offered to keep on working for a while, till office routine was straightened out, but it never did get straightened out, somehow. Clay deftly saw to that by keeping Josephine busy. She didn't have to bring work home to her apartment, but she brought it, and Clay gradually began to help her when he dropped by. His job, plus the narcohypnotic courses, had already trained him for this sort of tricky organizational work. Vanderman's business was highly specialized—planet-wide exports and imports, and what with keeping track of specific groups, seasonal trends, sectarian holidays, and so forth, Josephine, as a sort of animated memorandum book for Vanderman, had a more than full-time job.

She and Clay postponed marriage for a time. Clay—naturally enough—began to appear mildly jealous of Josephine's work, and she said she'd quit soon. But one night she stayed on at the office, and he went out in a pet and got drunk. It just happened to be raining that night, Clay got tight enough to walk unprotected through the drizzle, and to fall asleep at home in his wet clothes. He came down with influenza. As he was recovering, Josephine got it.

Under the circumstances, Clay stepped in—purely a temporary job—and took over his fiancée's duties. Office routine was extremely complicated that week, and only Clay knew the ins and outs of it. The arrangement saved Vanderman a certain amount of inconvenience, and, when the situation resolved itself, Josephine had a subsidiary job and Clay was Vanderman's private secretary.

"I'd better know more about him," Clay said to Josephine. "After all, there must be a lot of habits and foibles he's got that need to be catered to. If he wants lunch ordered up, I don't want to get smoked tongue and find out he's allergic to it. What about his hobbies?"

But he was careful not to pump Josephine too hard, because of the Eye. He still needed sedatives to sleep.

The sociologist rubbed his forehead.

"Let's take a break," he suggested. "Why does a guy want to commit murder anyway?"

"For profit, one sort or another."

"Only partly, I'd say. The other part is an unconscious desire to be punished—usually for something else. That's why you get accident prones. Ever think about what happens to murderers who feel guilty and yet who aren't punished by the Law? They must live a rotten sort of life—always stepping in front of speedsters, cutting themselves with an ax—accidentally; accidentally touching wires full of juice—"

"Conscience, eh?"

"A long time ago, people thought God sat in the sky with a telescope and watched everything they did. They really lived pretty carefully, in the Middle Ages—the first Middle Ages, I mean. Then there was the era of disbelief, where people had nothing to believe in very strongly—and finally we get this." He nodded toward the screen. "A universal memory. By extension, it's a universal social conscience, an externalized one. It's exactly the same as the medieval concept of God—omniscience."

"But not omnipotence."

"Mm."

All in all, Clay kept the Eye in mind for a year and a half. Before he said or did anything whatsoever, he reminded himself of the Eye, and made certain that he wasn't revealing his motive to the judging future. Of course, there was—would be—an Ear, too, but that was a little too absurd. One couldn't visualize a large, disembodied Ear decorating the wall like a plate in a plate holder. All the same, whatever he said would be as important evidence—some time—as what he did. So Sam Clay was very careful indeed, and behaved like Caesar's wife. He wasn't exactly defying authority, but he was certainly circumventing it.

Superficially Vanderman was more like Caesar, and his wife was not above reproach, these days. She had too much money to play with. And she was finding her husband too strong-willed a person to be completely satisfactory. There was enough of the matriarch in Bea to make her feel rebellion against Andrew Vanderman, and there was a certain lack of romance. Vanderman had little time for her. He was busy these days, involved with a whole string of deals which demanded much of his time. Clay, of course, had something to do with that. His interest in his new work was most laudable. He stayed up nights plotting and planning as though expecting Vanderman to make him a full partner. In fact, he even suggested this possibility to Josephine. He wanted it on the record. The marriage date had been set, and Clay wanted to move before then; he had no intention of being drawn into a marriage of convenience after the necessity had been removed.

One thing he did, which had to be handled carefully, was to get the whip. Now Vanderman was a fingerer. He liked to have something in his hands while he talked. Usually it was a crystalline paper weight, with a miniature thunderstorm in it, complete with lightning, when it was shaken. Clay put this where Vanderman would be sure to knock it off and break it. Meanwhile, he had plugged one deal with Callisto Ranches for the sole purpose of getting a whip for Vanderman's desk. The natives were proud of their leatherwork and their silversmithing, and a nominal makeweight always went with every deal they closed. Thus, presently, a handsome miniature whip, with Vanderman's initials on it, lay on the desk, coiled into a loop, acting as a paperweight except when he picked it up and played with it while he talked.

The other weapon Clay wanted was already there—an antique paper knife, once called a surgical scalpel. He never let his gaze rest on it too long, because of the Eye.

The other whip came. He absentmindedly put it in his desk and pretended to forget it. It was a sample of the whips made by the Alaskan Flagellantes for use in their ceremonies, and was wanted because of some research being made into the pain-neutalizing drugs the Flagellantes used. Clay, of course, had engineered this deal, too. There was nothing suspicious about that; the firm stood to make a sound profit. In fact, Vanderman had promised him a percentage bonus at the end of the year on every deal he triggered. It would be quite a lot. It was December, a year and a half had passed since Clay first recognized that the Eye would seek him out.

He felt fine. He was careful about the sedatives, and his nerves, though jangled, were nowhere near the snapping point. It had been a strain, but he had trained himself so that he would make no slips. He visualized the Eye in the walls, in the ceiling, in the sky, everywhere he went. It was the only way to play completely safe. And very soon now it would pay off. But he would have to do it soon; such a nervous strain could not be continued indefinitely.

A few details remained. He carefully arranged matters—under the Eye's very nose, so to speak—so that he was offered a well-paying position with another firm. He turned it down.

And one night an emergency happened to arise so that Clay, very logically, had to go to Vanderman's apartment.

Vanderman wasn't there; Bea was. She had quarreled violently with her husband. Moreover, she had been drinking. (This, too, he had expected.) If the situation had not worked out exactly as he wanted, he would have tried again—and again—but there was no need.

Clay was a little politer than necessary. Perhaps too polite, certainly Bea, that incipient matriarch, was led down the garden path, a direction she was not unwilling to take. After all, she had married Vanderman for his money, found him as dominant as herself, and now saw Clay as an exaggerated symbol of both romance and masculine submissiveness.

The camera eye hidden in the wall, in a decorative bas-relief, was grinding away busily, spooling up its wiretape in a way that indicated Vanderman was a suspicious as well as a jealous husband. But Clay knew about this gadget, too. At the suitable moment he stumbled against the wall in such a fashion that the device broke. Then, with only that other eye spying on him, he suddenly became so virtuous that it was a pity Vanderman couldn't witness his *volte face*.

"Listen, Bea," he said, "I'm sorry, but I didn't understand. It's no good. I'm not in love with you anymore. I was once, sure, but that was quite a while ago. There's somebody else, and you ought to know it by now."

"You still love me," Bea said with intoxicated firmness. "We belong together."

"Bea. Please. I hate to have to say this, but I'm grateful to Andrew Vanderman for marrying you. I . . . well, you got what you wanted, and I'm getting what I want. Let's leave it at that."

"I'm used to getting what I want, Sam. Opposition is something I don't like. Especially when I know you really—"

She said a good deal more, and so did Clay—he was perhaps unnecessarily harsh. But he had to make the point, for the Eye, that he was no longer jealous of Vanderman.

He made the point.

* * *

The next morning he got to the office before Vanderman, cleaned up his desk, and discovered the stingaree whip still in its box. "Oops," he said, snapping his fingers—the Eye watched, and this was the crucial period. Perhaps it would all be over within the hour. Every move from now on would have to be specially calculated in advance, and there could be no slightest deviation. The Eye was everywhere—literally everywhere.

He opened the box, took out the whip, and went into the inner sanctum. He tossed the whip on Vanderman's desk, so carelessly that a stylus rack toppled. Clay rearranged everything, leaving the stingaree whip near the edge of the desk, and placing the Callistan silver-leather whip at the back, half concealed behind the interoffice visor-box. He didn't allow himself more than a casual sweeping glance to make sure the paper knife was still there.

Then he went out for coffee.

Half an hour later he got back, picked up a few letters for signature from the rack, and walked into Vanderman's office. Vanderman looked up from behind his desk. He had changed a little in a year and a half; he was looking older, less noble, more like an aging bulldog. Once, Clay thought coldly, this man stole my fiancée and beat me up.

Careful. Remember the Eye.

There was no need to do anything but follow the plan and let events take their course. Vanderman had seen the spy films, all right, up to the point where they had gone blank, when Clay fell against the wall. Obviously he hadn't really expected Clay to show up this morning. But to see the louse grinning hello, walking across the room, putting some letters down on his desk—

Clay was counting on Vanderman's short temper, which had not improved over the months. Obviously the man had been simply sitting there, thinking unpleasant thoughts, and just as Clay had known would happen, he'd picked up the whip and begun to finger it. But it was the stingaree whip this time.

"Morning," Clay said cheerfully to his stunned employer. His smile became one-sided. "I've been waiting for you to check this letter to the Kirghiz kovar-breeders. Can we find a market for two thousand of those ornamental horns?"

It was at this point that Vanderman, bellowing, jumped to his feet, swung the whip, and sloshed Clay across the face. There is probably nothing more painful than the bite of a stingaree whip.

Clay staggered back. He had not known it would hurt so

much. For an instant the shock of the blow knocked every other consideration out of his head, and blind anger was all that remained.

Remember the Eye!

He remembered it. There were dozens of trained men watching everything he did just now. Literally he stood on an open stage surrounded by intent observers who made notes on every expression of his face, every muscular flection, every breath he drew.

In a moment Vanderman would be dead—but Sam Clay would not be alone. An invisible audience from the future was fixing him with cold, calculating eyes. He had one more thing to do and the job would be over. Do it—carefully, carefully!—while they watched.

Time stopped for him. *The job would be over*.

It was very curious. He had rehearsed this series of actions so often in the privacy of his mind that his body was going through with it now, without further instructions. His body staggered back from the blow, recovered balance, glared at Vanderman in shocked fury, poised for a dive at that paper knife in plain sight on the desk.

That was what the outward and visible Sam Clay was doing. But the inward and spiritual Sam Clay went through quite a different series of actions.

The job would be over.

And what was he going to do after that?

The inward and spiritual murderer stood fixed with dismay and surprise, staring at a perfectly empty future. He had never looked beyond this moment. He had made no plans for his life beyond the death of Vanderman. But now—he had no enemy but Vanderman. When Vanderman was dead, what would he fix upon to orient his life? What would he work at then? His job would be gone, too. And he liked his job.

Suddenly he knew how much he liked it. He was good at it. For the first time in his life, he had found a job he could do really well.

You can't live a year and a half in a new environment without acquiring new goals. The change had come imperceptibly. He was a good operator; he'd discovered that he could be successful. He didn't have to kill Vanderman to prove that to himself. He'd proved it already without committing murder.

In that time-stasis which had brought everything to a full stop he looked at Vanderman's red face and he thought of Bea, and of

Vanderman as he had come to know him—and he didn't want to be a murderer.

He didn't want Vanderman dead. He didn't want Bea. The thought of her made him feel a little sick. Perhaps that was because he himself had changed from passive to active. He no longer wanted or needed a dominant woman. He could make his own decisions. If he were choosing now, it would be someone more like Josephine—

Josephine. That image before his mind's stilled eye was suddenly very pleasant. Josephine with her mild, calm prettiness, her admiration for Sam Clay the successful businessman, the rising young importer in Vanderman, Inc. Josephine whom he was going to marry—Of course he was going to marry her. He loved Josephine. He loved his job. All he wanted was the status quo, exactly as he had achieved it. Everything was perfect right now—as of maybe thirty seconds ago.

But that was a long time ago—thirty seconds. A lot can happen in a half a minute. A lot had happened. Vanderman was coming at him again, the whip raised. Clay's nerves crawled at the anticipation of its burning impact across his face a second time. If he could get hold of Vanderman's wrist before he struck again—if he could talk fast enough—

The crooked smile was still on his face. It was part of the pattern, in some dim way he did not quite understand. He was acting in response to conditioned reflexes set up over a period of many months of rigid self-training. His body was already in action. All that had taken place in his mind had happened so fast there was no physical hiatus at all. His body knew its job and it was doing the job. It was lunging forward toward the desk and the knife, and he could not stop it.

All this had happened before. It had happened in his mind, the only place where Sam Clay had known real freedom in the past year and a half. In all that time he had forced himself to realize that the Eye was watching every outward move he made. He had planned each action in advance and schooled himself to carry it through. Scarcely once had he let himself act purely on impulse. Only in following the plan exactly was there safety. He had indoctrinated himself too successfully.

Something was wrong. This wasn't what he'd wanted. He was still afraid, weak, failing—

He lurched against the desk, clawed at the paper knife, and, knowing failure, drove it into Vanderman's heart.

* * *

"It's a tricky case," the forensic sociologist said to the engineer. "Very tricky."

"Want me to run it again?"

"No, not right now. I'd like to think it over. Clay . . . that firm that offered him another job. The offer's withdrawn now, isn't it? Yes, I remember—they're fussy about the morals of their employees. It's insurance or something, I don't know. Motive. Motive, now."

The sociologist looked at the engineer.

The engineer said: "A year and a half ago he had a motive. But a week ago he had everything to lose and nothing to gain. He's lost his job and that bonus, he doesn't want Mrs. Vanderman anymore, and as for that beating Vanderman once gave him . . . ah?"

"Well, he did try to shoot Vanderman once, and he couldn't, remember? Even though he was full of Dutch courage. But—something's wrong. Clay's been avoiding even the appearance of evil a little too carefully. Only I can't put my finger on anything, blast it."

"What about tracing back his life further? We only got to his fourth year."

"There couldn't be anything useful that long ago. It's obvious he was afraid of his father and hated him, too. Typical stuff, basic psych. The father symbolizes judgment to him. I'm very much afraid Sam Clay is going to get off scot-free."

"But if you think there's something haywire—"

"The burden of proof is up to us," the sociologist said.

The visor sang. A voice spoke softly.

"No, I haven't got the answer yet. Now? All right. I'll drop over."

He stood up.

"The D.A. wants a consultation. I'm not hopeful, though. I'm afraid the State's going to lose this case. That's the trouble with the externalized conscience—"

He didn't amplify. He went out, shaking his head, leaving the engineer staring speculatively at the screen. But within five minutes he was assigned to another job—the bureau was understaffed—and he didn't have a chance to investigate on his own until a week later. Then it didn't matter anymore.

For, a week later, Sam Clay was walking out of the court an acquitted man. Bea Vanderman was waiting for him at the foot of the ramp. She wore black, but obviously her heart wasn't in it.

"Sam," she said.

He looked at her.

He felt a little dazed. It was all over. Everything had worked out exactly according to plan. And nobody was watching him now. The Eye had closed. The invisible audience had put on its hats and coats and left the theater of Sam Clay's private life. From now on he could do and say precisely what he liked, with no censoring watcher's omnipresence to check him. He could act on impulse again.

He had outwitted society. He had outwitted the Eye and all its minions in all their technological glory. He, Sam Clay, private citizen. It was a wonderful thing, and he could not understand why it left him feeling so flat.

That had been a nonsensical moment, just before the murder. The moment of relenting. They say you get the same instant's frantic rejection on the verge of a good many important decisions—just before you marry, for instance. Or—what was it? Some other common instance he'd often heard of. For a second it eluded him. Then he had it. The hour before marriage—and the instant after suicide. After you've pulled the trigger, or jumped off the bridge. The instant of wild revulsion when you'd give anything to undo the irrevocable. Only, you can't. It's too late. The thing is done.

Well, he'd been a fool. Luckily, it *had* been too late. His body took over and forced him to success he'd trained it for. About the job—it didn't matter. He'd get another. He'd proved himself capable. If he could outwit the Eye itself, what job existed he couldn't lick if he tried? Except—nobody knew exactly how good he was. How could he prove his capabilities? It was infuriating to achieve such phenomenal success after a lifetime of failures, and never to get the credit for it. How many men must have tried and failed where he had tried and succeeded? Rich men, successful men, brilliant men who had yet failed in the final test of all—the contest with the Eye, their own lives at stake. Only Sam Clay had passed that most important test in the world—and he could never claim credit for it.

". . . knew they wouldn't convict," Bea's complacent voice was saying.

Clay blinked at her. "What?"

"I said I'm so glad you're free, darling. I knew they wouldn't convict you. I knew that from the very beginning." She smiled at him, and for the first time it occurred to him that Bea looked a little like a bulldog. It was something about her lower jaw. He thought that when her teeth were closed together the lower set probably rested just outside the upper. He had an instant's impulse to ask her about it. Then he decided he had better not.

"You knew, did you?" he said.

She squeezed his arm. What an ugly lower jaw that was. How odd he'd never noticed it before. And behind the heavy lashes, how small her eyes were. How mean.

"Let's go where we can be alone," Bea said, clinging to him. "There's such a lot to talk about."

"We *are* alone," Clay said, diverted for an instant to his original thoughts. "Nobody's watching," He glanced up at the sky and down at the mosaic pavement. He drew a long breath and let it out slowly. "Nobody," he said.

"My speeder's parked right over here. We can—"

"Sorry, Bea."

"What do you mean?"

"I've got business to attend to."

"Forget business. Don't you understand that we're free now, both of us?"

He had a horrible feeling he knew what she meant.

"Wait a minute," he said, because this seemed the quickest way to end it. "I killed your husband, Bea. Don't forget that."

"You were acquitted. It was self-defense. The court said so."

"It—" He paused, glanced up quickly at the high wall of the Justice Building, and began a one-sided, mirthless smile. It was all right; there was no Eye now. There never would be, again. He was unwatched.

"You mustn't feel guilty, even within yourself," Bea said firmly. "It wasn't your fault. It simply wasn't. You've got to remember that. You *couldn't* have killed Andrew except by accident, Sam, so—"

"What? What do you mean by that?"

"Well, after all. I know the prosecution kept trying to prove you'd planned to kill Andrew all along, but you mustn't let what they said put any ideas in your head. I know you, Sam. I knew Andrew. You couldn't have planned a thing like that, and even if you had, it wouldn't have worked."

The half-smile died.

"It wouldn't?"

She looked at him steadily.

"Why, you couldn't have managed it," she said. "Andrew was the better man, and we both know it. He'd have been too clever to fall for anything—"

"Anything a second-rater like me could dream up?" Clay swallowed. His lips tightened. "Even you— What's the idea?

What's your angle now—that we second-raters ought to get together?''

''Come on,'' she said, and slipped her arm through his. Clay hung back for a second. Then he scowled, looked back at the Justice Building, and followed Bea toward her speeder.

The engineer had a free period. He was finally able to investigate Sam Clay's early childhood. It was purely academic now, but he liked to indulge his curiosity. He traced Clay back to the dark closet, when the boy was four, and used ultraviolet. Sam was huddled in a corner, crying silently, staring up with frightened eyes at a top shelf.

What was on that shelf the engineer could not see.

He kept the beam focused on the closet and cast back rapidly through time. The closet often opened and closed, and sometimes Sam Clay was locked in it as punishment, but the upper shelf held its mystery until—

It was in reverse. A woman reached to that shelf, took down an object, walked backward out of the closet to Sam Clay's bedroom, and went to the wall by the door. This was unusual, for generally it was Sam's father who was warden of the closet.

She hung up a framed picture of a single huge staring eye floating in space. There was a legend under it. The letters spelled out: THOU GOD SEEST ME.

The engineer kept on tracing. After a while it was night. The child was in bed, sitting up wide-eyed, afraid. A man's footsteps sounded on the stair. The scanner told all secrets but those of the inner mind. The man was Sam's father, coming up to punish him for some childish crime committed earlier. Moonlight fell upon the wall beyond which the footsteps approached showing how the wall quivered a little to the vibrations of the feet, and the Eye in its frame quivered, too. The boy seemed to brace himself. A defiant half-smile showed on his mouth, crooked, unsteady.

This time he'd keep that smile, no matter what happened. When it was over he'd still have it, so his father could see it, and the Eye could see it and they'd know he hadn't given in. He hadn't . . . he—

The door opened.

He couldn't help it. The smile faded and was gone.

''Well, what was eating him?'' the engineer demanded.

The sociologist shrugged. ''You could say he never did really grow up. It's axiomatic that boys go through a phase of rivalry with their fathers. Usually that's sublimated; the child grows up and wins, in one way or another. But Sam Clay didn't. I suspect he developed an externalized conscience very early. Symbolizing partly his father, partly God, an Eye and society—which fulfills the role of protective, punishing parent, you know."

"It still isn't evidence."

"We aren't going to get any evidence on Sam Clay. But that doesn't mean he's got away with anything, you know. He's always been afraid to assume the responsibilities of maturity. He never took on an optimum challenge. He was afraid to succeed at anything because that symbolic Eye of his might smack him down. When he was a kid, he might have solved his entire problem by kicking his old man in the shins. Sure, he'd have got a harder whaling, but he'd have made some move to assert his individuality. As it is, he waited too long. And then he defied the wrong thing, and it wasn't really defiance, basically. Too late now. His formative years are past. The thing that might really solve Clay's problem would be his conviction for murder—but he's been acquitted. If he'd been convicted, then he could prove to the world that he'd hit back. He'd kicked his father in the shins, kept that defiant smile on his face, killed Andrew Vanderman. I think that's what he actually has wanted all along—recognition. Proof of his own ability to assert himself. He had to work hard to cover his tracks—if he made any—but that was part of the game. By winning it he's lost. The normal ways of escape are closed to him. He always had an Eye looking down at him."

"Then the acquittal stands?"

"There's still no evidence. The State's lost its case. But I . . . I don't think Sam Clay has won his. Something will happen." He sighed. "It's inevitable, I'm afraid. Sentence first, you see. Verdict afterward. The sentence was passed on Clay a long time ago."

Sitting across from him in the Paradise Bar, behind a silver decanter of brandy in the center of the table, Bea looked lovely and hateful. It was the lights that made her lovely. They even managed to cast their shadows over that bulldog chin, and under her thick lashes the small, mean eyes acquired an illusion of beauty. But she still looked hateful. The lights could do nothing about that. They couldn't cast shadows into Sam Clay's private mind or distort the images there.

He thought of Josephine. He hadn't made up his mind fully yet about that. But if he didn't quite know what he wanted, there was no shadow of doubt about what he *didn't* want—no possible doubt whatever.

"You need me, Sam," Bea told him over her brimming glass.

"I can stand on my own feet. I don't need anybody."

It was the indulgent way she looked at him. It was the smile that showed her teeth. He could see as clearly as if he had X-ray vision how the upper teeth would close down inside the lower when she shut her mouth. There would be a lot of strength in a jaw like that. He looked at her neck and saw the thickness of it, and thought how firmly she was getting her grip upon him, how she maneuvered for position and waited to lock her bulldog clamp deep into the fabric of his life again.

"I'm going to marry Josephine, you know," he said.

"No, you're not. You aren't the man for Josephine. I know that girl, Sam. For a while you may have had her convinced you were a go-getter. But she's bound to find out the truth. You'd be miserable together. You need me, Sam darling. You don't know what you want. Look at the mess you got into when you tried to act on your own. Oh, Sam, why don't you stop pretending? You know you never were a planner. You . . . what's the matter, Sam?"

His sudden burst of laughter had startled both of them. He tried to answer her, but the laughter wouldn't let him. He lay back in his chair and shook with it until he almost strangled. He had come so close, so desperately close to bursting out with a boast that would have been confession. Just to convince the woman. Just to shut her up. He must care more about her good opinion than he had realized until now. But that last absurdity was too much. It was only ridiculous now. Sam Clay, not a planner.

How good it was to let himself laugh, now. To let himself go, without having to think ahead. Acting on impulse again, after those long months of rigid repression. No audience from the future was clustering around this table, analyzing the quality of his laughter, observing that it verged on hysteria. Who cared? He deserved a little blow-off like this, after all he'd been through. He'd risked so much, and achieved so much—and in the end gained nothing, not even glory except in his own mind. He'd gained nothing, really, except the freedom to be hysterical if he felt like it. He laughed and laughed and laughed, hearing the shrill note of lost control in his own voice and not caring.

People were turning to stare. The bartender looked over at him uneasily, getting ready to move if this went on. Bea stood up, leaned across the table, shook him by the shoulder.

"Sam, what's the matter? Sam, do get hold of yourself!

You're making a spectacle of me, Sam! What *are* you laughing at?"

With a tremendous effort he forced the laughter back in his throat. His breath still came heavily and little bursts of merriment kept bubbling up so that he could hardly speak, but he got the words out somehow. They were probably the first words he had spoken without rigid consorship since he first put his plan into operation. And the words were these.

"I'm laughing at the way I fooled you. I fooled everybody! You think I didn't know what I was doing every minute of the time? You think I wasn't planning, every step of the way? It took me eighteen months to do it, but I killed Andrew Vanderman with malice aforethought, and nobody can ever prove I did it." He giggled foolishly. "I just wanted you to know," he added in a mild voice.

And it wasn't until he got his breath back and began to experience that feeling of incredible, delightful, incomparable relief that he knew what he had done.

She was looking at him without a flicker of expression on her face. Total blank was all that showed. There was a dead silence for a quarter of a minute. Clay had the feeling that his words must have rung from the roof, that in a moment the police would come in to hale him away. But the words had been quietly spoken. No one had heard but Bea.

And now, at last, Bea moved. She answered him, but not in words. The bulldog face convulsed suddenly and overflowed with laughter.

As he listened, Clay felt all that flood of glorious relief ebbing away. For he saw that she did not believe him. And there was no way he could prove the truth.

"Oh, you silly little man," Bea gasped when words came back to her. "You had me almost convinced for a minute. I almost believed you. I—" Laughter silenced her again, consciously silvery laughter that made heads turn. That conscious note in it warned him that she was up to something. Bea had had an idea. His own thoughts outran hers and he knew in an instant before she spoke exactly what the idea was and how she would apply it. He said: "I *am* going to marry Josephine," in the very instant that Bea spoke.

"You're going to marry me," she said flatly. "You've got to. You don't know your own mind, Sam. I know what's best for you and I'll see you do it. Do you understand me, Sam?"

"The police won't realize that was only a silly boast," she

told him. "They'll believe you. You wouldn't want me to tell them what you just said, would you, Sam?"

He looked at her in silence, seeing no way out. This dilemma had sharper horns than anything he could have imagined. For Bea did not and would not believe him, no matter how he yearned to convince her, while the police undoubtedly would believe him, to the undoing of his whole investment in time, effort, and murder. He had said it. It was engraved upon the walls and in the echoing air, waiting for that invisible audience in the future to observe. No one was listening now, but a word from Bea could make them reopen the case.

A word from Bea.

He looked at her, still in silence, but with a certain cool calculation beginning to dawn in the back of his mind.

For a moment Sam Clay felt very tired indeed. In that moment he encompassed a good deal of tentative future time. In his mind he said yes to Bea, married her, lived an indefinite period as her husband. And he saw what that life would be like. He saw the mean small eyes watching him, the relentlessly gripping jaw set, the tyranny that would emerge slowly or not slowly, depending on the degree of his subservience, until he was utterly at the mercy of the woman who had been Andrew Vanderman's widow.

Sooner or later, he thought clearly to himself, *I'd kill her.*

He'd have to kill. That sort of life, with that sort of woman, wasn't a life Sam Clay could live, indefinitely. And he'd proved his ability to kill and go free.

But what about Andrew Vanderman's death?

Because they'd have another case against him then. This time it had been qualitative; the next time, the balance would shift toward quantitative. If Sam Clay's wife died, Sam Clay would be investigated no matter how she died. Once a suspect, always a suspect in the eyes of the law. The Eye of the law. They'd check back. They'd return to this moment, while he sat here revolving thoughts of death in his mind. And they'd return to five minutes ago, and listen to him boast that he had killed Vanderman.

A good lawyer might get him off. He could claim it wasn't the truth. He could say he had been goaded to an idle boast by the things Bea said. He might get away with that, and he might not. Scop would be the only proof, and he couldn't be compelled to take scop.

But—no. That wasn't the answer. That wasn't the way out. He could tell by the sick, sinking feeling inside him. There had been just one glorious moment of release, after he'd made his confession to Bea, and from then on everything seemed to run downhill again.

But that moment had been the goal he'd worked toward all this time. He didn't know what it was, or why he wanted it. But he recognized the feeling when it came. He wanted it back.

This helpless feeling, this impotence—was this the total sum of what he had achieved? Then he'd failed, after all. Somehow, in some strange way he could only partly understand, he had failed; killing Vanderman hadn't been the answer at all. He wasn't a success. He was a second-rater, a passive, helpless worm whom Bea would manage and control and drive, eventually, to—

"What's the matter, Sam?" Bea asked solicitously.

"You think I'm a second-rater, don't you?" he said. "You'll never believe I'm not. You think I couldn't have killed Vanderman except by accident. You'll never believe I could possibly have defied—"

"What?" she asked, when he did not go on.

There was a new note of surprise in his voice.

"But it wasn't defiance," he said slowly. "I just hid and dodged. Circumvented. I hung dark glasses on an Eye, because I was afraid of it. But—that wasn't defiance. So—what I really was trying to prove—"

She gave him a startled, incredulous stare as he stood up.

"Sam! What are you doing?" Her voice cracked a little.

"Proving something," Clay said, smiling crookedly, and glancing up from Bea to the ceiling. "Take a good look," he said to the Eye as he smashed her skull with the decanter.

MANNA

by Peter Phillips (1921–   )

***Astounding Science Fiction*, February**

British newspaperman Peter Phillips (not to be confused with Rog Phillips, another good writer) returns—his incredible "Dreams are Sacred" is a very tough act to follow—with this fine story about other dimensions and religious beliefs. We know far less about Peter Phillips than we should, except that at his best he was very good indeed, and that like many (too many) other writers he seems to have only had one solid productive decade in his career, in this case 1948 to 1958. It is interesting to speculate on what kind of sf he would be writing if he began his career in 1978 instead of thirty years earlier.—M.H.G.

(It seems to me that science fiction writers tend to avoid religion. Surely, religion has permeated many societies at all times; all Western societies from ancient Sumeria on have had strong religious components. And yet—

Societies depicted in science fiction and fantasy often ignore religion. While the great Manichean battle of good and evil—God and Satan—seems to permeate Tolkien's "Lord of the Rings," there is no religious ritual anywhere mentioned. In my own "Foundation" series, the only religious element found is a purely secular fake—and that was put in only at the insistence of John Campbell, to my own enormous unease.

Still, there are exceptions. Religion does appear sometimes, usually in forms that appear [to me] to be somewhat Catholic in atmosphere, or else Fundamentalist. "Manna" by Peter Phillips is an example.—I.A.)

* * *

Take best-quality synthetic protein. Bake it, break it up, steam it, steep in in sucrose, ferment it, add nut oil, piquant spices from the Indies, fruit juices, new flavors from the laboratory, homogenize it, hydrolize it, soak it in brine; pump in glutamic acid, balanced proportions of A, B_1, B_2, C, D, traces of calcium, copper and iron salts, an unadvertised drop of benzedrine; dehydrate, peptonize, irradiate, reheat in malt vapor under pressure compress, cut into mouth-sized chunks, pack in liquor from an earlier stage of process—

Miracle Meal.

Everything the Body Needs to Sustain Life and Bounding Vitality, in the Most DEEE LISHUSSS *Food Ever Devised. It will Invigorate You, Build Muscle, Brain, Nerve. Better than the Banquets of Imperial Rome, Renaissance Italy, Eighteenth Century France—All in One Can. The Most Heavenly Taste Thrills You Have Ever Experienced. Gourmets' Dream and Housewives' Delight. You Can Live On It. Eat it for Breakfast, Lunch, Dinner. You'll Never Get Tired of MIRACLE MEAL.*

Ad cuts of Zeus contemptuously tossing a bowl of ambrosia over the edge of Mount Olympus and making a goggle-eyed grab for a can of Miracle Meal.

Studio fake-ups of Lucretia Borgia dropping a phial of poison and crying piously: "It Would Be a Sin to Spoil Miracle Meal."

Posters and night-signs of John Doe—or Bill Smith, or Henri Brun, or Hans Schmitt or Wei Lung—balancing precariously on a pyramided pile of empty M.M. cans, eyes closed, mouth pursed in slightly inane ecstasy as he finished the last mouthful of his hundred-thousandth can.

You could live on it, certainly.

The publicity co-ordinator of the Miracle Meal Corporation chose the victim himself—a young man named Arthur Adelaide from Greenwich Village.

For a year, under the closest medical supervision and observation, Arthur ate nothing but Miracle Meal.

From this Miracle Meal Marathon, as it was tagged by video-print newssheets, he emerged smiling, twice the weight—publicity omitted to mention that he'd been half-starved to begin with—he'd been trying to live off pure art and was a bad artist—perfectly fit, and ten thousand dollars richer.

He was also given a commercial art job with M.M., designing new labels for the cans.

His abrupt death at the end of an eighty-story drop from his office window a week or two later received little attention.

It would be unreasonable to blame the cumulative effect of M.M., for Arthur was probably a little unbalanced to begin with, whereas M.M. was Perfectly Balanced—a Kitchen in a Can.

Maybe you could get tired of it. But not very quickly. The flavor was the secret. It was delicious yet strangely and tantalizingly indefinable. It seemed to react progressively on the taste-buds so that the tastes subtly changed with each mouthful.

One moment it might be *omelette au fine herbes*, the next, turkey and cranberry, then buckwheat and maple. You'd be through the can before you could make up your mind. So you'd buy another.

Even the can was an improvement on the usual plastic self-heater—shape of a small, shallow pie-dish, with a pre-impressed crystalline fracture in the plastic lid.

Press the inset button on the preheating unit at one side, and when the food was good and hot, a secondary chemical reaction in the unit released a fierce little plunger just inside the perimeter fracture. Slight steam pressure finished the job. The lip flipped off.

Come and get it. You eat right out of the can it comes in. Keep your fingers out, Johnny. Don't you see the hygiplast spoon in its moisture- and heat-repellent wrapper fixed under the lid?

The Rev. Malachi Pennyhorse did not eat Miracle Meal. Nor was he impressed when Mr. Stephen Samson, Site Advisor to the Corporation, spoke in large dollar signs of the indirect benefits a factory would bring to the district.

"Why here? You already have one factory in England. Why not extend it?"

"It's our policy, Reverend—"

"Not 'Reverend' young man. Call me Vicar. Or Mr. Pennyhorse. Or merely Pennyhorse— Go on."

"It's our policy, sir, to keep our factories comparatively small, site them in the countryside for the health of employees, and modify the buildings to harmonize with the prevailing architecture of the district. There is no interference with local amenities. All transport of employees, raw materials, finished product is by silent copter."

Samson laid a triphoto on the vicar's desk. "What would you say that was?"

Mr. Pennyhorse adjusted his pince-nez, looked closely. "Byzantine. Very fine. Around 500 A.D."

"And this—"

"Moorish. Quite typical. Fifteenth century."

Samson said: "They're our factories at Istanbul and Tunis respectively. At Allahabad, India, we had to put up big notices saying: 'This is not a temple or place of worship' because natives kept wandering in and offering-up prayers to the processing machines."

Mr. Pennyhorse glanced up quickly. Samson kept his face straight, added: "The report may have been exaggerated, but—you get the idea?"

The vicar said: "I do. What shape do you intend your factory to take in this village?"

"That's why I came to you. The rural district council suggested that you might advise us."

"My inclination, of course, is to advise you to go away and not return."

The vicar looked out of his study window at the sleepy, sun-washed village street, gables of the ancient Corn Exchange, paved market-place, lichened spire of his own time-kissed church; and, beyond, rolling Wiltshire pastures cradling the peaceful community.

The vicar sighed: "We've held out here so long—I hoped we would remain inviolate in my time, at least. However, I suppose we must consider ourselves fortunate that your corporation has some respect for tradition and the feelings of the . . . uh . . . 'natives.' "

He pulled out a drawer in his desk. "It might help you to understand those feelings if I show you a passage from the very full diary of my predecessor here, who died fifty years ago at the age of ninety-five—we're a long-lived tribe, we clergy. It's an entry he made one hundred years ago—sitting at this very desk."

Stephen Samson took the opened volume.

The century-old handwriting was as readable as typescript.

"*May 3, 1943. Long, interesting discussion with young American soldier, one of those who are billeted in the village. They term themselves G.I.'s. Told me countryside near his home in Pennsylvania not unlike our Wiltshire downs. Showed him round church. Said he was leaving soon, and added: 'I love this place. Nothing like my home town in looks, but the atmosphere's the same—old, and kind of comfortable. And I guess if I came back here a hundred years from now, it wouldn't have changed one bit.' An engaging young man. I trust he is right.*"

Samson looked up. Mr. Pennyhorse said: "That young man may have been one of your ancestors."

Samson gently replaced the old diary on the desk. "He wasn't.

My family's Ohioan. But I see what you mean, and respect it. That's why I want you to help us. You will?"

"Do you fish?" asked the vicar, suddenly and irrelevantly.

"Yes, sir. Very fond of the sport."

"Thought so. You're the type. That's why I like you. Take a look at these flies. Seen anything like them? Make 'em myself. One of the finest trout streams in the country just outside the village. Help you? Of course I will."

"Presumption," said Brother James. He eased himself through a graystone wall by twisting his subexistential plane slightly, and leaned reflectively against a moonbeam that slanted through the branches of an oak.

A second habited and cowled figure materialized beside him. "Perhaps so. But it does my age-wearied heart a strange good to see those familiar walls again casting their shadows over the field."

"A mockery, Brother Gregory. A mere shell that simulates the outlines of our beloved Priory. Think you that even the stones are of that good, gray granite that we built with? Nay! As this cursed simulacrum was a-building, I warped two hands into the solid, laid hold of a mossy block, and by the saints, 'twas of such inconsequential weight I might have hurled it skyward with a finger. And within, is there aught which we may recognize? No chapel, no cloisters, no refectory—only long, geometrical rooms. And what devilries and unholy rites may not be centered about those strange mechanisms, with which the rooms are filled?"

At the tirade, Brother Gregory sighed and thrust back his cowl to let the gracious moonbeams play on his tonsured head. "For an Untranslated One of some thousand years' standing," he said, "you exhibit a mulish ignorance, Brother James. You would deny men all advancement. I remember well your curses when first we saw horseless carriages and flying machines."

"Idols!" James snapped. "Men worship them. Therefore are they evil."

"You are so good, Brother James," Gregory said, with the heaviest sarcasm. "So good, it is my constant wonderment that you have had to wait so long for Translation Upwards. Do you think that Dom Pennyhorse, the present incumbent of Selcor—a worthy man, with reverence for the past—would permit evil rites within his parish? You are a befuddled old anachronism, brother."

"That," said James, "is quite beyond sufferance. For you to speak thus of Translation, when it was your own self-indulgent pursuit of carnal pleasures that caused us to be bound here through the centuries!"

Brother Gregory said coldly: "It was not I who inveigled the daughter of Ronald the Wry-Neck into the kitchen garden, thus exposing the weak flesh of a brother to grievous temptation."

There was silence for a while, save for the whisper of a midnight breeze through the branches of the oak, and the muted call of a nightbird from the far woods.

Gregory extended a tentative hand and lightly touched the sleeve of James's habit. "The argument might proceed for yet another century and bring us no nearer Translation. Besides it is not such unbearable penance, my brother. Were we not both lovers of the earth, of this fair countryside?"

James shrugged. Another silence. Then he fingered his gaunt white cheeks. "What we do, Brother Gregory? Shall we—appear to them?"

Gregory said: "I doubt whether common warp manifestation would be efficacious. As dusk fell tonight, I overheard a conversation between Dom Pennyhorse and a tall, young-featured man who has been concerned in the building of this simulacrum. The latter spoke in one of the dialects of the Americas; and it was mentioned that several of the men who will superintend the working of the machines within will also be from the United States—for a time at least. It is not prudent to haunt Americans in the normal fashion. Their attitude towards such matters is notoriously—unseemly."

"We could polter," suggested Brother James.

Gregory replaced his cowl. "Let us review the possibilities, then," he said, "remembering that our subetheric energy is limited."

They walked slowly together over the meadow towards the resuscitated gray walls of the Selcor Prior. Blades of grass, positively charged by their passage, sprang suddenly upright, relaxed slowly into limpness as the charge leaked away.

They halted at the walls to adjust their planes of incidence and degree of tenuity, and passed inside.

The new Miracle Meal machines had had their first test run. The bearings on the dehydrator pumps were still warm as two black figures, who seemed to carry with them an air of vast and wistful loneliness, paced silently between rows of upright cylinders which shone dully in moonlight diffused through narrow windows.

"Here," said Gregory, the taller of the two, softly, "did we once walk the cloisters in evening meditation."

Brother James's broad features showed signs of unease. He felt more than mere nostalgia.

"Power—what are they using? Something upsets my bones. I am queasy, as when a thunderstorm is about to break. Yet there is no static."

Gregory stopped, looked at his hand. There was a faint blue aura at his fingertips. "Slight neutron escape," he said. "They have a small thorium-into-233 pile somewhere. It needs better shielding."

"You speak riddles."

Gregory said, with a little impatience: "You have the entire science section of the village library at your disposal at nightfall for the effort of a trifling polter, yet for centuries you have read nothing but the *Lives of the Saints*. So, of course, I speak riddles—to you. You are even content to remain in ignorance of the basic principles of your own structure and functioning, doing everything by traditional thought-rote and rule of thumb. But I am not so content; and of my knowledge, I can assure you that the radiation will not harm you unless you warp to solid and sit atop the pile when it is in full operation." Gregory smiled. "And then, dear brother, you would doubtless be so uncomfortable that you would dewarp before any harm could be done beyond the loss of a little energy that would be replaced in time. Let us proceed."

They went through three departments before Brother Gregory divined the integrated purpose of the vats, driers, conveyor-tubes, belts and containers.

"The end product, I'm sure, is a food of sorts," he said, "and by some quirk of fate, it is stored in approximately the position that was once occupied by our kitchen store—if my sense of orientation has not been bemused by these strange internal surroundings."

The test run of the assembly had produced a few score cans of Miracle Food. They were stacked on metal shelves which would tilt and gravity-feed them into the shaft leading up to the crating machine. Crated, they would go from there to the copter-loading bay on the roof.

Brother James reached out to pick up a loose can. His hand went through it twice.

"Polt, you dolt!" said Brother Gregory. "Or are you trying to be miserly with your confounded energy? Here, let me do it."

The telekineticized can sprang into his solid hands. He turned it about slightly increasing his infrared receptivity to read the label, since the storeroom was in darkness.

"Miracle Meal. Press here."

He pressed, pressed again, and was closely examining the can when, after thirty seconds, the lid flipped off, narrowly missing his chin.

Born, and living, in more enlightened times, Brother Gregory's inquiring mind and insatiable appetite for facts would have made him a research worker. He did not drop the can. His hands were quite steady. He chuckled. He said: "Ingenious, very ingenious. See—the food is hot."

He warped his nose and back-palate into solid and delicately inhaled vapors. His eyes widened. He frowned, inhaled again. A beatific smile spread over his thin face.

"Brother James—warp your nose!"

The injunction, in other circumstances, might have been considered both impolite and unnecessary. Brother James was no beauty, and his big, blunt, snoutlike nose, which had been a flaring red in life, was the least prepossessing of his features.

But he warped it, and sniffed.

M.M. Sales Leaflet Number 14: It Will Sell By Its Smell Alone.

Gregory said hesitantly: "Do you think Brother James, that we might—"

James licked his lips, from side to side, slowly. "It would surely take a day's accumulation of energy to hold digestive and alimentary in solid for a sufficient period. But—"

"Don't be a miser," said Gregory. "There's a spoon beneath the lid. Get a can for yourself. And don't bother with digestive. Teeth, palate and throat are sufficient. It would not digest in any case. It remains virtually unchanged. But going down—ah, bliss!"

It went down. Two cans.

"Do you remember, brother," said James, in a weak, reminiscing voice, "what joy it was to eat and be strengthened. And now to eat is to be weakened."

Brother Gregory's voice was faint but happy. "Had there been food of this character available before our First Translation, I doubt whether other desires of the flesh would have appealed to me. But what was our daily fare set on the refectory table: peas; lentils; cabbage soup; hard, tasteless cheese. Year after year—*ugh!*"

"Health-giving foods," murmured Brother James, striving to be righteous even in his exhaustion. "Remember when we bribed the kitchener to get extra portions. Good trenchermen, we. Had we not died of the plague before our Priory became rich and powerful, then, by the Faith, our present bodies would be of greater girth."

"Forms, not bodies," said Gregory, insisting even in *his* exhaustion on scientific exactitudes. "Variable fields, consisting of open lattices of energy foci resolvable into charged particles—and thus solid matter—when they absorb energy beyond a certain stage. In other words, my dear ignorant brother, when we polt. The foci themselves—or rather the spaces between them—act as a limited-capacity storage battery for the slow accretion of this energy from cosmic sources, which may be controlled and concentrated in the foci by certain thought-patterns."

Talking was an increasing effort in his energy-low state.

"When we polt," he went on slowly, "we take up heat, air cools, live people get cold shivers; de-polt, give up heat, live people get clammy, cold-hot feeling; set up 'lectrostatic field, live peoples' hair stan's on end"—his voice was trailing into deep, blurred inaudibility, like a mechanical phonograph running down, but James wasn't listening anyway—"an' then when we get Translated Up'ards by The Power That Is, all the energy goes back where it came from an' we jus' become thought. Thassall. Thought. Thought, thought, thought, thought—"

The phonograph ran down, stopped. There was silence in the transit storeroom of the Selcor Priory Factory branch of the Miracle Meal Corporation.

For a while.

Then—

"THOUGHT!"

The shout brought Brother James from his uneasy, uncontrolled repose at the nadir of an energy balance.

"What is it?" he grumbled. "I'm too weak to listen to any of your theorizing."

"Theorizing! I have it!"

"Conserve your energies, brother, else will you be too weak even to twist yourself from this place."

Both monks had permitted their forms to relax into a corner of the storeroom, supine, replete in disrepletion.

Brother Gregory sat up with an effort.

"Listen, you attenuated conserve of very nothingness, I have a way to thwart, bemuse, mystify and irritate these crass philistines—and nothing so simple that a psychic investigator could put a thumb on us. What are we, Brother James?"

It was a rhetorical question, and Brother James had barely formulated his brief repy—"Ghosts"—before Brother Gregory, energized in a way beyond his own understanding by his own enthusiasm, went on: "Fields, in effect. Mere lines of force, in our un-polted state. What happens if we whirl? A star whirls. It has mass, rate of angular rotation, degree of compactness—therefore, gravity. Why? Because it has a field to start with. But we are our own fields. We need neither mass nor an excessive rate of rotation to achieve the same effect. Last week I grounded a high-flying wood-pigeon by whirling. It shot down to me through the air, and I'd have been buffeted by its pinions had I not stood aside. It hit the ground—not too heavily, by the grace of St. Barbara—recovered and flew away."

The great nose of Brother James glowed pinkly for a moment. "You fuddle and further weaken me by your prating. Get to your point, if you have such. And explain how we may do anything in our present unenergized state, beyond removing ourselves to a nexus point for recuperation."

Brother Gregory warped his own nose into solid in order to scratch its tip. He felt the need of this reversion to a life habit, which had once aided him in marshaling his thoughts.

"You think only of personal energy," he said scornfully. "We do need that, to whirl. It is an accumulative process, yet we gain nothing, lose nothing. Matter is not the only thing we can warp. If you will only listen, you woof of unregenerate and forgotten flesh, I will try to explain without mathematics."

He talked.

After a while, Brother James's puzzled frown gave way to a faint smile. "Perhaps I understand," he said.

"Then forgive me for implying you were a moron," said Gregory. "Stand up, Brother James."

Calls on transatlantic tight-beam cost heavy. Anson Dewberry, Miracle Meal Overseas Division head, pointed this out to Mr. Stephen Samson three times during their conversation.

"Listen," said Samson at last, desperately, "I'll take no more delegation of authority. In my contract, it says I'm site adviser. That means I'm architect and negotiator, not detective or scientist or occulist. I offered to stay on here to supervise building because I happen to like the place. I like the pubs. I like the people. I like the fishing. But it wasn't in my contract. And I'm now standing on that contract. Building is finished to schedule, plant installed—your tech men, incidentally, jetted out of here without waiting to catch snags after the first runoff—and now I'm through. The machines are running, the cans are coming off—and if the copters don't collect, that's for you and the

London office to bat your brains out over. And the Lord forgive that mess of terminal propositions,'' he added in lower voice. Samson was a purist in the matter of grammar.

Anson Dewberry jerked his chair nearer the scanner in his New York office. His pink, round face loomed in Samson's screen like that of an avenging cherub.

''Don't you have no gendarmes around that place?'' Mr. Dewberry was no purist, in moments of stress. ''Get guards on, hire some militia, check employees. Ten thousand cans of M.M. don't just evaporate.''

''They do,'' Samson replied sadly. ''Maybe it's the climate. And for the seventh time, I tell you I've done all that. I've had men packed so tightly around the place that even an orphan neutron couldn't get by. This morning I had two men from Scotland Yard gumming around. They looked at the machines, followed the assembly through to the transit storeroom, examined the electrolocks and mauled their toe-caps trying to boot a dent in the door. Then the top one—that is, the one who only looked half-asleep—said, 'Mr. Samson, sir, do you think it's . . . uh . . . possible . . . that . . . uh . . . this machine of yours . . . uh . . . goes into reverse when your . . . uh . . . backs are turned and . . . uh . . . sucks the cans back again?' ''

Grating noises that might have been an incipient death rattle slid over the tight-beam from New York.

Samson nodded, a smirk of mock sympathy on his tanned, humor-wrinkled young face.

The noises ended with a gulp. The image of Dewberry thrust up a hesitant forefinger in interrogation. ''Hey! Maybe there's something to that, at that—would it be possible?''

Samson groaned a little. ''I wouldn't really know or overmuch care. But I have doubts. Meantime—''

''Right.'' Dewberry receded on the screen. ''I'll jet a man over tonight. The best. From Research. Full powers. Hand over to him. Take some of your vacation. Design some more blamed mosques or tabernacles. Go fishing.''

''A sensible suggestion,'' Samson said. ''Just what I was about to do. It's a glorious afternoon here, sun a little misted, grass green, stream flowing cool and deep, fish lazing in the pools where the willow-shadows fall—''

The screen blanked. Dewberry was no purist, and no poet either.

Samson made a schoolkid face. He switched off the fluor lamps that supplemented the illumination from a narrow window in the supervisor's office—which, after studying the ground-plan of the original Selcor Priory, he had sited in the space that was occupied centuries before by the business sanctum of the Prior—got up from his desk and walked through a Norman archway into the sunlight.

He breathed the meadow-sweet air deeply, with appreciation.

The Rev. Malachi Pennyhorse was squatting with loose-jointed ease against the wall. Two fishing rods in brown canvas covers lay across his lap. He was studying one of the trout-flies nicked into the band of his ancient hat. His balding, brown pate was bared to the sun. He looked up.

"What fortune, my dear Stephen?"

"I convinced him at last. He's jetting a man over tonight. He told me to go fishing."

"Injunction unnecessary, I should imagine. Let's go. We shan't touch a trout with the sky as clear as this, but I have some float tackle for lazier sport." They set off across a field. "Are you running the plant today?"

Samson nodded his head towards a faint hum. "Quarter-speed. That will give one copter-load for the seventeen hundred hours collection, and leave enough over to go in the transit store for the night and provide Dewberry's man with some data. Or rather, lack of it."

"Where do you think it's going?"

"I've given up guessing."

Mr. Pennyhorse paused astride a stile and looked back at the gray bulk of the Priory. "I could guess who's responsible," he said, and chuckled.

"Uh? Who?"

Mr. Pennyhorse shook his head. "Leave that to your investigator."

A few moments later he murmured as if to himself: "What a haunt! Ingenious devils."

But when Stephen Samson looked at him inquiringly, he added: "But I can't guess where your cans have been put."

And he would say nothing more on the subject.

Who would deny that the pure of heart are often simple-minded? (The obverse of the proposition need not be argued.) And that cause-effect relations are sometimes divined more readily by the intuition of simpletons than the logic of scholars?

Brother Simon Simplex—Simple Simon to later legends—looked open-mouthed at the array of strange objects on the stone shelves of the kitchen storeroom. He was not surprised—his mouth was always open, even in sleep.

He took down one of the objects and examined it with mild curiosity. He shook it, turned it round, thrust a forefinger into a small depression. Something gave slightly, but there was no other aperture. He replaced it on the shelf.

When his fellow-kitchener returned, he would ask him the purpose of the objects—if he could remember to do so. Simon's memory was poor. Each time the rota brought him onto kitchen duty for a week, he had to be instructed afresh in the business of serving meals in the refectory: platter so, napkin thus, spoon here, finger bowls half-filled, three water pitchers, one before the Prior, one in the center, one at the foot of the table—"and when you serve, tread softly and do not breathe down the necks of the brothers."

Even now could he hear the slight scrape of benches on stone as the monks, with bowed heads, freshly washed hands in the sleeves of their habits, filed slowly into the refectory and took their seats at the long, oak table. And still his fellow-kitchener had not returned from the errand. Food was prepared—dared he begin to serve alone?

It was a great problem for Simon, brother in the small House of Selcor, otherwise Selcor Priory, poor cell-relation to the rich monastery of the Cluniac Order at Battle, in the year 1139 A.D.

Steam pressure in the triggered can of Miracle Meal did its work. The lid flipped. The aroma issued.

Simon's mouth nearly shut as he sniffed.

The calm and unquestioning acceptance of the impossible is another concommitant of simplicity and purity of heart. To the good and simple Simon the rising of the sun each morning and the singing of birds were recurrent miracles. Compared with these, a laboratory miracle of the year 2143 A.D. was as nothing.

Here was a new style of platter, filled with hot food, ready to serve. Wiser minds than his had undoubtedly arranged matters. His fellow-kitchener, knowing the task was thus simplified, had left him to serve alone.

He had merely to remove the covers from these platters and carry them into the refectory. To remove the covers—cause—effect—the intuition of a simple mind.

Simon carried fourteen of the platters to the kitchen table, pressed buttons and waited.

He was gravely tempted to sample the food himself, but all-inclusive Benedictine rules forbade kitcheners to eat until their brothers had been served.

He carried a loaded tray into the refectory where the monks sat in patient silence except for the one voice of the Reader who stood at a raised lectern and intoned from the *Lives of the Saints*.

Pride that he had been thought fit to carry out the duty alone made Simon less clumsy than usual. He served the Prior, Dom Holland, first, almost deftly; then the other brothers, in two trips to the kitchen.

A spicy, rich, titillating fragrance filled the refectory. The intoning of the *Lives of the Saints* faltered for a moment as the mouth of the Reader filled with saliva, then he grimly continued.

At Dom Holland's signal, the monks ate.

The Prior spooned the last drops of gravy into his mouth. He sat back. A murmur arose. He raised a hand. The monks became quiet. The Reader closed his book.

Dom Holland was a man of faith; but he did not accept miracles or even the smallest departures from routine existence without questioning. He had sternly debated with himself whether he should question the new platters and the new food before or after eating. The aroma decided him. He ate first.

Now he got up, beckoned to a senior monk to follow him, and paced with unhurried calmness to the kitchen.

Simon had succumbed. He was halfway through his second tin.

He stood up, licking his fingers.

"Whence comes this food, my son?" asked Dom Holland, in sonorous Latin.

Simon's mouth opened wider. His knowledge of the tongue was confined to prayers.

Impatiently the Prior repeated the question in the English dialect of the district.

Simon pointed, and led them to the storeroom.

"I looked, and it was here," he said simply. The words were to become famed.

His fellow-kitchener was sought—he was found dozing in a warm corner of the kitchen garden—and questioned. He shook his head. The provisioner rather reluctantly disclaimed credit.

Dom Holland thought deeply, then gave instructions for a general assembly. The plastic "platters" and the hygiplast spoons were carefully examined. There were murmurs of wonderment at the workmanship. The discussion lasted two hours.

Simon's only contribution was to repeat with pathetic insistence: "I looked and it was there."

He realized dimly that he had become a person of some importance.

His face became a mask of puzzlement when the Prior summed up:

"Our simple but blessed brother, Simon Simplex, it seems to me, has become an instrument or vessel of some thaumaturgical manifestation. It would be wise, however, to await further demonstration before the matter is referred to higher authorities."

The storeroom was sealed and two monks were deputed as nightguards.

Even with the possibility of a miracle on his hands, Dom Holland was not prepared to abrogate the Benedictine rule of only one main meal a day. The storeroom wasn't opened until early afternoon of the following day.

It was opened by Simon, in the presence of the Prior, a scribe, the provisioner, and two senior monks.

Released, a pile of Miracle Meal cans toppled forward like a crumbling cliff, slithering and clattering in noisy profusion around Simon's legs, sliding over the floor of the kitchen.

Simon didn't move. He was either too surprised or cunningly aware of the effectiveness of the scene. He stood calf-deep in cans, pointed at the jumbled stack inside the storeroom, sloping up nearly to the stone roof, and said his little piece:

"I look, and it is here."

"Kneel, my sons," said Dom Holland gravely, and knelt.

Manna.

And at a time when the Priory was hard-pressed to maintain even its own low standard of subsistence, without helping the scores of dispossessed refugees encamped in wattle shacks near its protecting walls.

The countryside was scourged by a combination of civil and foreign war. Stephen of Normandy against Matilda of Anjou for the British throne. Neither could control his own followers. When the Flemish mercenaries of King Stephen were not chasing Queen Matilda's Angevins back over the borders of Wiltshire, they were plundering the lands and possessions of nominal supporters of Stephen. The Angevins and the barons who supported Matilda's cause quite impartially did the same, then pillaged each other's property, castle against castle, baron against baron.

It was anarchy and free-for-all—but nothing for the ignored serfs, bondmen, villeins and general peasantry, who fled from stricken homes and roamed the countryside in bands of starving thousands. Some built shacks in the inviolate shadow of churches and monasteries.

Selcor Priory had its quota of barefoot, raggedly men, women and children—twelfth century Displaced Persons.

They were a headache to the Prior, kindly Dom Holland—until Simple Simon's Miracle.

There were seventy recipients of the first hand-out of Miracle Meal cans from the small door in the Priory's walled kitchen garden.

The next day there were three hundred, and the day after that, four thousand. Good news doesn't need radio to get around fast.

Fourteen monks worked eight-hour shifts for twenty-four hours, hauling stocks from the capacious storeroom, pressing buttons, handing out steaming platters to orderly lines of refugees.

Two monks, shifting the last few cans from the store, were suddenly buried almost to their necks by the arrival of a fresh consignment, which piled up out of thin air.

Providence, it seemed, did not depend solely upon the intervention of Simon Simplex. The Priory itself and all its inhabitants were evidently blessed.

The Abbot of Battle, Dom Holland's superior, a man of great girth and great learning visited the Priory. He confirmed the miracle—by studying the label on the can.

After several hours' work in the Prior's office, he announced to Dom Holland:

"The script presented the greatest difficulty. It is an extreme simplification of letter-forms at present in use by Anglo-Saxon scholars. The pertinent text is a corruption—if I may be pardoned the use of such a term in the circumstances—of the Latin '*miraculum*' compounded with the word '*maél*' from our own barbarous tongue—so, clearly, Miracle Meal!"

Dom Holland murmured his awe of this learning.

The Abbot added, half to himself: "Although why the nature of the manifestation should be thus advertised in repetitive engraving, when it is self-evident—" He shrugged. "The ways of Providence are passing strange."

Brother Gregory, reclining in the starlight near his favorite oak, said:

"My only regret is that we cannot see the effect of our gift—the theoretical impact of a modern product—usually a weapon—on past ages is a well-tried topic of discussion and speculation among historians, scientists, economists and writers of fantasy."

Brother James, hunched in vague adumbration on a wall behind, said: "You are none of those things, else might you explain why it is that, if these cans have reached the period for which, according to your obtruse calculations, they were destined—an age in which we were both alive—we cannot remember such an event, or why it is not recorded in histories of the period."

"It was a time of anarchy, dear brother. Many records were destroyed. And as for your memories—well, great paradoxes of time are involved. One might as profitably ask how many angels may dance on the point of a pin. Now if you should wish to know how many atoms might be accommodated in a like position—"

Brother Gregory was adroit at changing the subject. He didn't wish to speculate aloud until he'd figured out all the paradox possibilities. He'd already discarded an infinity of time-streams as intellectually unsatisfying, and was toying with the concept of recurrent worlds—

"Dom Pennyhorse has guessed that it is our doing."

"What's that?"

Brother James repeated the information smugly.

Gregory said slowly: "Well, he is not—unsympathetic—to us."

"Assuredly, brother, we have naught to fear from him, nor from the pleasant young man with whom he goes fishing. But this young man was today in consultation with his superior, and an investigator is being sent from America."

"Psychic investigator, eh? Phooey. We'll tie him in knots," and Gregory complacently.

"I assume," said Brother James, with a touch of self-righteousness, "that these vulgar colloquialisms to which you sometimes have recourse are another result of your nocturnal reading. They offend my ear. 'Phooey,' indeed—No, this investigator is one with whom you will undoubtedly find an affinity. I gather that he is from a laboratory—a scientist of sorts."

Brother Gregory sat up and rubbed his tonsure thoughtfully. "That," he admitted, "is different." There was a curious mixture of alarm and eagerness in his voice. "There are means of detecting the field we employ."

An elementary electroscope was one of the means. An ionization indicator and a thermometer were others. They were all bolted firmly on a bench just inside the storeroom. Wires led from them under the door to a jury-rigged panel outside.

Sandy-haired Sidney Meredith of M.M. Research sat in front of the panel on a folding stool, watching dials with intense blue eyes, chin propped in hands.

Guards had been cleared from the factory. He was alone, on the advice of Mr. Pennyhorse, who had told him: "If, as I suspect, it's the work of two of my . . . uh . . . flock . . . two very ancient parishioners . . . they are more likely to play their tricks in the absence of a crowd."

"I get it," Meredith had said. "Should be interesting."

It was.

He poured coffee from a thermos without taking his eyes from the panel. The thermometer reading was dropping slowly. Ionization was rising. From inside the store came the faint rasp of moving objects.

Meredith smiled, sighted a thumb-size camera, recorded the panel readings. "This," he said softly, "will make a top feature in the *Journal*: 'The most intensive psychic and poltergeist phenomena ever recorded. M.M.'s top tech trouble-shooter spikes spooks.' "

There was a faint snap beyond the door. Dials swooped back to Zero. Meredith quit smiling and daydreaming.

"Hey—play fair!" he called.

The whisper of a laugh answered him, and a soft, hollow whine, as of a wind cycloning into outer space.

He grabbed the door, pulled. It resisted. It was like trying to break a vacuum. He knelt, lit a cigarette, held it near the bottom of the nearly flush-fitting door. A thin streamer of smoke curled down and was drawn swiftly through the barely perceptible crack.

The soft whine continued for a few seconds, began to die away.

Meredith yanked at the door again. It gave, to a slight ingush of air. He thrust his foot in the opening, said calmly into the empty blackness: "When you fellers have quite finished—I'm coming in. Don't go away. Let's talk."

He slipped inside, closed the door, stood silent for a moment. He sniffed. Ozone. His scalp prickled. He scratched his head, felt the hairs standing upright. And it was cold.

He said: "Right. No point in playing dumb or covering-up, boys." He felt curiously ashamed of the platitudes as he uttered them. "I must apologize for breaking in," he added—and meant it. "But this has got to finish. And if you're not willing to—co-operate—I think I know now how to finish it."

Another whisper of a laugh. And two words, faint, gently mocking: "Do you?"

Meredith strained his eyes against the darkness. He saw only the nerve-patterns in his own eyes. He shrugged.

"If you won't play—" He switched on a blaze of fluor lamps. The long steel shelves were empty. There was only one can of Miracle Meal left in the store.

He felt it before he saw it. It dropped on his head, clattered to the plastocrete floor. When he'd retrieved his breath, he kicked it savagely to the far end of the store and turned to his instruments.

The main input lead had been pulled away. The terminal had been loosened first.

He unclamped a wide-angle infrared camera, waited impatiently for the developrinter to act, pulled out the print.

And laughed. It wasn't a good line-caricature of himself, but it was recognizable, chiefly by the shock of unruly hair.

The lines were slightly blurred, as though written by a needle-point of light directly on the film. There was a jumble of writing over and under it.

"Old English, I suppose," he murmured. He looked closer. The writing above the caricature was a de Sitter version of the Reimann-Christoffel tensor, followed in crabbed but readable modern English by the words: "Why reverse the sign? Do we act like anti-particles?"

Underneath the drawing was an energy tensor and a comment: "You will notice that magnetic momenta contribute a negative density and pressure."

A string of symbols followed, ending with an equals sign and a query mark. And another comment: "You'll need to take time out to balance this one."

Meredith read the symbols, then sat down heavily on the edge of the instrument bench and groaned. Time *out*. But Time was already out, and there was neither matter nor radiation in a de Sitter universe.

Unless—

He pulled out a notebook, started to scribble.

An hour later Mr. Pennyhorse and Stephen Samson came in.

Mr. Pennyhorse said: "My dear young fellow, we were quite concerned. We thought—"

He stopped. Meredith's blue eyes were slightly out of focus. There were beads of sweat on his brow despite the coolness of the storeroom. Leaves from his notebook and cigarette stubs littered the floor around his feet.

He jumped like a pricked frog when the vicar gently tapped his shoulder, and uttered a vehement cuss-word that startled even the broad-minded cleric.

Samson tutted.

Meredith muttered: "Sorry, sir. But I think I nearly had it."

"What, my son?"

Meredith looked like a ruffle-haired schoolboy. His eyes came back into focus. "A crossword puzzle clue," he said. "Set by a spook with a super-I.Q. Two quite irreconcilable systems of mathematics lumped together, the signs in an extended energy tensor reversed, merry hell played with a temporal factor—and yet it was beginning to make sense."

He smiled wryly. "A ghost who unscrews terminals before he breaks connections and who can make my brain boil is a ghost worth meeting."

Mr. Pennyhorse eased his pince-nez. "Uh . . . yes. Now, don't you think it's time you came to bed? It's four A.M. My housekeeper has made up a comfortable place on the divan in the sitting room." He took Meredith's arm and steered him from the store.

As they walked across the dewy meadows towards the vicarage, with the first pale streaks of dawn showing in the sky, Samson said: "How about the cans?"

"Time," replied Meredith vaguely, "will tell."

"And the guards?"

"Pay them off. Send them away. Keep the plant rolling. Fill the transit store tonight. And I want a freighter copter to take me to London University this afternoon."

Back in the transit store, the discarded leaves from Meredith's notebook fluttered gently upwards in the still air and disappeared.

Brother James said: "He is alone again."

They looked down on the sandy head of Sidney Meredith from the vantage point of a dehydrating tower.

"So I perceive. And I fear this may be our last uh . . . consignment to our erstwhile brothers," said Gregory thoughtfully.

"Why?"

"You will see. In giving him the clue to what we were doing, I gave him the clue to what we are, essentially."

They drifted down towards the transit store.

"After you, Brother James," said Brother Gregory with excessive politeness.

James adjusted his plane of incidence, started through the wall, and—

Shot backwards with a voiceless scream of agony.

Brother Gregory laughed. "I'm sorry. But that's why it will be our last consignment. Heterodyning is painful. He is a very intelligent fellow. The next time, he will take care to screen both his ultra-short generator and controls so that I cannot touch them."

Brother James recovered. "You . . . you use me as a confounded guinea pig! By the saints, you appear to have more sympathy with the man than with me!"

"Not more sympathy, my beloved brother, but certainly much more in common," Brother Gregory replied frankly. "Wait."

He drifted behind Meredith's back and poltered the tip of one finger to flick a lightly soldered wire from a terminal behind a switch. Meredith felt his scalp tingle. A pilot light on his panel blinked out.

Meredith got up from his stool, stretched lazily, grinned into the empty air. He said aloud: "Right. Help yourselves. But I warn you—once you're in, you don't come out until you agree to talk. I have a duplicate set and a built-in circuit-tester. The only way you can spike them is by busting tubes. And I've a hunch you wouldn't do that."

"No," James muttered. "You wouldn't. Let us go."

"No," Gregory answered. "Inside quickly—and whirl. Afterwards I shall speak with him. He is a youth of acute sensibilities and gentleness, whose word is his bond."

Gregory urged his fellow-monk to the wall. They passed within.

Meredith heard nothing, until a faint whine began in the store. He waited until it died away, then knocked on the door. It seemed, crazily, the correct thing to do.

He went into the darkness. "You there?"

A low and pleasant voice, directionless: "Yes. Why didn't you switch on your duplicate generator?"

Meredith breathed deep. "I didn't think it would be necessary. I feel we understand each other. My name is Sidney Meredith."

"Mine is Gregory of Ramsbury."

"And your—friend?"

"James Brasenose. I may say that he disapproves highly of this conversation."

"I can understand that. It is unusual. But then, you're a very unusual . . . um—"

" 'Ghost' is the common term, Mr. Meredith. Rather inadequate, I think, for supranormal phenomena which are, nevertheless, subject to known laws. Most Untranslated spirits remain quite ignorant of their own powers before final Translation. It was only by intensive reading and thought that I determined the principles and potentialities of my construction."

"Anti-particles?"

"According to de Sitter," said Brother Gregory, "that is what we should be. But we are not mere mathematical experessions. I prefer the term 'energy foci.' From a perusal of the notes you left behind yesterday morning—and, of course, from your use of ultra-short waves tonight—it seems you struck the correct train of deduction immediately. Incidentally, where did you obtain the apparatus at such short notice?''

''London University.''

Brother Gregory sighed. ''I should like to visit their laboratories. But we are bound to this area by a form of moral compulsion that I cannot define or overcome. Only vicariously, through the achievements of others, may I experience the thrill of research.''

''You don't do so badly,'' Meredith said. He was mildly surprised that he felt quite so sane and at ease, except for the darkness. ''Would you mind if we had a light?''

''I must be semipolted—or warped—to speak with you. It's not a pleasant sight—floating lungs, larynx, palate, tongue and lips. I'd feel uncomfortable for you. We might appear for you later, if you wish.''

''Right. But keep talking. Give me the how and the why. I want this for my professional journal.''

''Will you see that the issue containing your paper is placed in the local library?''

''Surely,'' Meredith said. ''Two copies.''

''Brother James is not interested. Brother James, will you kindly stop whispering nonsense and remove yourself to a nexus point for a while. I intend to converse with Mr. Meredith. Thank you.''

The voice of Brother Gregory came nearer, took on a slightly professorial tone. ''Any massive and rotating body assumes the qualities of magnetism—or rather, gravitic, one-way flux—by virtue of its rotation, and the two quantities of magnetic momentum and angular momentum are always proportional to one another, as you doubtless know.''

Meredith smiled inwardly. A lecture on elementary physics from a ghost. Well—maybe not so elementary. He remembered the figures that he'd sweated over. But he could almost envisage the voice of Brother Gregory emananting from a black-gowned instructor in front of a classroom board.

''Take a star,'' the voice continued. ''Say 78 Virginis—from whose flaming promontories the effect was first deduced a hundred years ago—and put her against a counter-whirling star of similar mass. What happens? Energy warp, of the kind we use every time we polt. But something else happens—did you infer it from my incomplete expression?''

Meredith grinned. He said: ''Yes. Temporal warp.''

''Oh.'' There was a trace of disappointment in the voice.

Meredith added quickly: "But it certainly gave me a headache figuring it out."

Gregory was evidently mollified by the admission. "Solids through time," he went on. "Some weeks ago, calculating that my inherent field was as great in certain respects as that of 78 Virginis, I whirled against a longitudinal line, and forced a stone back a few days—the nearest I could get to laboratory confirmation. Knowing there would be a logical extension of the effect if I whirled against a field as strong as my own, I persuaded Brother James to co-operate with me—and you know the result."

"How far back?"

"According to my mathematics, the twelfth century, at a time when we were—alive. I would appreciate your views on the paradoxes involved."

Meredith said: "Certainly. Let's go over your math together first. If it fits in with what I've already figured, perhaps I'll have a suggestion to make. You appreciate, of course, that I can't let you have any more cans?"

"Quite. I must congratulate your company on manufacturing a most delicious comestible. If you will hand me the roll of infrared film from your camera, I can make my calculations visible to you on the emulsion in the darkness. Thank you. It is a pity," Gregory murmured, "that we could not see with our own eyes what disposal they made of your product in the days of our Priory."

When, on the morning of a certain bright summer day in 1139, the daily consignment of Miracle Meal failed to arrive at Selcor Priory, thousands of disappointed refugees went hungry.

The Prior, Dom Holland—who, fortunately for his sanity or at least his peace of mind, was not in a position to separate cause from effect—attributed the failure of supply to the lamentable departure from grace and moral standards of two of the monks.

By disgracing themselves in the kitchen garden with a female refugee, he said, they had obviously rendered the Priory unfit to receive any further miraculous bounty.

The abject monks, Brother Gregory and Brother James, were severely chastised and warned in drastic theological terms that it would probably be many centuries before they had sufficiently expiated their sins to attain blessedness.

On the morning of another bright summer day, the Rev. Malachi Pennyhorse and Stephen Samson were waiting for Sidney Meredith in the vicar's comfortable study.

Meredith came in, sank into a century-old leather easy-chair, stretched his shoes, damp with dew from the meadow grass, towards the flames. He accepted a glass of whiskey gratefully, sipped it.

He said: "The cans are there. And from now on, they stay in the transit store until the copters collect."

There was an odd note of regret in his voice.

Samson said: "Fine. Now maybe you'll tell us what happened yesterday."

Mr. Pennyhorse said: "You . . . uh . . . liked my parishioners, then?"

Meredith combined a smile and a sigh. "I surely did. That Brother Gregory had the most intense and dispassionate intellectual curiosity of anyone I ever met. He nearly grounded me on some aspects of energy mathematics. I could have used him in my department. He'd have made a great research man. Brother James wasn't a bad old guy, either. They appeared for me—"

"How did you get rid of them?" Samson interrupted.

"They got rid of themselves. Gregory told me how, by whirling against each other with gravitic fields cutting, they drew the cans into a vortex of negated time that threw them way back to the twelfth century. After we'd been through his math, I suggested they whirl together."

"What—and throw the cans ahead?"

"No. Themselves, in a sense, since they precipitated a future, hoped-for state. Gregory had an idea what would happen. So did I. He'd only discovered the effect recently. Curiosity got the better of him. He had to try it out straight away. They whirled together. The fields reinforced, instead of negated. Enough ingoing energy was generated to whoop their own charges well above capacity and equilibrium. They just—went. As Gregory would put it—they were Translated."

"Upwards, I trust," said Mr. Pennyhorse gently.

"Amen to that," said Samson.

Upwards—

Pure thought, unbound, Earth-rid, roaming free amid the wild bright stars—

Thought to Thought, over galactic vastness, wordless, yet swift and clear, before egos faded—

"Why didn't I think of this before? We might have Translated ourselves centuries ago."

"But then we would never have tasted Miracle Meal."

"That is a consideration," agreed the Thought that had been Brother Gregory.

"Remember our third can?" came the Thought that had been Brother James.

But there was no reply. Something of far greater urgency and interest than memories of Miracle Meal had occurred to the Thought that had been Brother Gregory.

With eager curiosity, it was spiraling down into the heart of a star to observe the integration of helium at first hand.

THE PRISONER IN THE SKULL

by "Lewis Padgett" (Henry Kuttner, 1914–1958 and C.L. Moore, 1911–)

***Astounding Science Fiction*, February**

The dream of every anthologist is to discover a major story that has never been reprinted. This is particularly difficult in science fiction because there have been more than 800 sf reprint anthologies published to date, the majority edited by men and women who were themselves central to the field and tremendously knowledgeable. We would therefore love to take credit for finding "The Prisoner in the Skull" and bringing it to your attention but alas, we cannot. Barry N. Malzberg (himself an excellent anthologist) brought it to us and deserves the honor. Thanks, Barry.—M.H.G.

(There are certain irrepressible yearnings in the human heart which are universal and which are, therefore, obvious material for stories that will hit home. Don't we all long, in the midst of confusion and frustration, for someone supremely competent to come in and take over?

Is not this why the typical "woman's romance" so often features the Prince Charming figure, the knight on the white horse; and why Westerns so often feature the tall, silent stranger who rides into town, defeats the desperados and then rides away? Or, for that matter, is it not why Bertie Wooster has Jeeves?

It is in fantasy that this reaches its peak, and that peak is surely "Aladdin and His Wonderful Lamp." Who of us has not at some time in his life longed for the services of just such an all-powerful and utterly subservient genie, whose response to all requests, however unreasonable, is a calm, "I hear and obey"?

If science fiction is too disciplined to allow itself the utter chaos of omnipotence, neither is it forced to restrict itself to something as dull and straightforward as a man with a gun and a fast draw. In "The Prisoner in the Skull," then, we have a science fictional Lamp, with its limits, its pity, and its irony.—I.A.)

He felt cold and weak, strangely, intolerably, inhumanly weak with a weakness of the blood and bone, of the mind and soul. He saw his surroundings dimly, but he saw—other things—with a swimming clarity that had no meaning to him. He saw causes and effects as tangible before him as he had once seen trees and grass. But remote, indifferent, part of another world.

Somehow there was a door before him. He reached vaguely—

It was almost wholly a reflex gesture that moved his finger toward the doorbell.

The chimes played three soft notes.

John Fowler was staring at a toggle switch. He felt baffled. The thing had suddenly spat at him and died. Ten minutes ago he had thrown the main switch, unscrewed the wall plate and made hopeful gestures with a screwdriver, but the only result was a growing suspicion that this switch would never work again. Like the house itself, it was architecturally extreme, and the wires were sealed in so that the whole unit had to be replaced if it went bad.

Minor irritations bothered Fowler unreasonably today. He wanted the house in perfect running order for the guest he was expecting. He had been chasing Veronica Wood for a long time, and he had an idea this particular argument might tip the balance in the right direction.

He made a note to keep a supply of spare toggle switches handy. The chimes were still echoing softly as Fowler went into the hall and opened the front door, preparing a smile. But it wasn't Veronica Wood on the doorstep. It was a blank man.

That was Fowler's curious impression, and it was to recur to him often in the year to come. Now he stood staring at the strange emptiness of the face that returned his stare without really seeming to see him. The man's features were so typical they might have been a matrix, without the variations that combine to make up the recognizable individual. But Fowler thought that even if he had known those features, it would be hard to recognize a man behind such utter emptiness. You can't recognize a man who isn't there. And there was nothing here. Some erasure, some expunging, had wiped out all trace of character and personality. *Empty*.

And empty of strength, too—for the visitant lurched forward and fell into Fowler's arms.

Fowler caught him automatically, rather horrified at the lightness of the body he found himself supporting. "Hey," he said, and, realizing the inadequacy of that remark, added a few pertinent questions. But there was no answer. Syncope had taken over.

Fowler grimaced and looked hopefully up and down the road. He saw nobody. So he lifted his guest across the threshold and carried him easily to a couch. *Fine*, he thought. *Veronica due any minute*, and this paperweight barging in.

Brandy seemed to help. It brought no color to the pale cheeks, but it pried the eyelids open to show a blank, wondering look.

"O.K. now?" Fowler asked, wanting to add, "Then go home."

There was only the questioning stare. Fowler stood up with some vague intention of calling a doctor, and then remembered that the televisor instrument hadn't yet been delivered. For this was a day when artificial shortages had begun to supplant real ones, when raw material was plentiful but consumers were wary, and were, therefore, put on a starvation diet to build their appetites and loosen their purse strings. The televisor would be delivered when the company thought Fowler had waited long enough.

Luckily he was versatile. As long as the electricity was on he could jury-rig anything else he needed, including facilities for first aid. He gave his patient the routine treatment, with satisfying results. Until, that is, the brandy suddenly hit certain nerve centers and emesis resulted.

Fowler lugged his guest back from the bathroom and left him on the bed in the room with the broken light switch to recuperate. Convalescence was rapid. Soon the man sat up, but all he did was look at Fowler hopefully. Questions brought no answers.

Ten minutes later the blank man was still sitting there, looking blank.

The door chimes sang again. Fowler, assured that his guest wasn't *in articulo mortis*, began to feel irritation. Why the devil did the guy have to barge in now, at this particular crucial moment? In fact, where had he come from? It was a mile to the nearest highway, along a dirt road, and there was no dust on the man's shoes. Moreover, there was something indefinably disturbing about the—*lack* in his appearance. There was no other word that fitted so neatly. Village idiots are popularly termed "wanting," and, while there was no question of idiocy here, the man did seem—

What?

For no reason at all Fowler shivered. The door chimes reminded him of Veronica. He said: "Wait here. You'll be all right. Just wait. I'll be back—"

There was a question in the soulless eyes.

Fowler looked around. "There're some books on the shelf. Or fix this—" He pointed to the wall switch. "If you want anything, call me." On that note of haphazard solicitude he went out, carefully closing the door. After all, he wasn't his brother's keeper. And he hadn't spent days getting the new house in shape to have his demonstration go haywire because of an unforseen interruption.

Veronica was waiting on the threshold. "Hello," Fowler said. "Have any trouble finding the place? Come in."

"It sticks up like a sore thumb," she informed him. "Hello. So this is the dream house, is it?"

"Right. After I figure out the right method of dream-analysis, it'll be perfect." He took her coat, led her into the livingroom, which was shaped like a fat comma and walled with triple-seal glass, and decided not to kiss her. Veronica seemed withdrawn. That was regrettable. He suggested a drink.

"Perhaps I'd better have one," she said, "before I look the joint over."

Fowler began battling with a functional bar. It should have poured and mixed drinks at the spin of a dial, but instead there came a tinkle of breaking glass. Fowler finally gave up and went back to the old-fashioned method. "Highball? Well, theoretically, this is a perfect machine for living. But the architect wasn't as perfect as his theoretical ideas. Methods of construction have to catch up with ideas, you know."

"This room's nice," Veronica acknowledged, relaxing on airfoam. With a glass in her hand, she seemed more cheerful. "Almost everything's curved, isn't it? And I like the windows."

"It's the little things that go wrong. If a fuse blows, a whole unit goes out. The windows—I insisted on those."

"Not much of a view."

"Unimproved. Building restrictions, you know. I wanted to build on the top of a hill a few miles away, but the township laws wouldn't allow it. This house is unorthodox. Not very, but enough. I might as well have tried to put up a Wright house in Williamsburg. This place is functional and convenient—"

"Except when you want a drink?"

"Trivia," Fowler said airily. "A house is complicated. You expect a few things to go wrong at first. I'll fix 'em as they come up. I'm a jerk of all trades. Want to look around?"

"Why not?" Veronica said. It wasn't quite the enthusiastic reaction for which Fowler had hoped, but he made the best of it. He showed her the house. It was larger than it had seemed from the outside. There was nothing super about it, but it was—theoretically—a functional unit, breaking away completely from the hidebound traditions that had made attics, cellars, and conventional bathrooms and kitchens as vestigially unfunctional as the vermiform appendix. "Anyway," Fowler said, "statistics show most accidents happen in kitchens and bathrooms. They can't happen here."

"What's this?" Veronica asked, opening a door. Fowler grimaced.

"The guest room," he said. "That was the single mistake. I'll use it for storage or something. The room hasn't any windows."

"The light doesn't work—"

"Oh, I forgot. I turned off the main switch. Be right back." He hurried to the closet that held the house controls, flipped the switch, and returned. Veronica was looking into a room that was pleasantly furnished as a bedroom, and, with tinted, concealed fluorescents, seemed light and airy despite the lack of windows.

"I called you," she said. "Didn't you hear me?"

Fowler smiled and touched a wall. "Sound-absorbent. The whole house is that way. The architect did a good job, but this room—"

"What's wrong with it?"

"Nothing—unless you're inside and the door should get stuck. I've a touch of claustrophobia."

"You should face these fears," said Veronica, who had read it somewhere. Fowler repressed a slight irritation. There were times when he had felt an impulse to slap Veronica across the chops, but her gorgeousness entirely outweighted any weakness she might have in other directions.

"Air conditioning, too," he said, touching another switch. "Fresh as spring breeze. Which reminds me. Does your drink want freshening?"

"Yes," Veronica said, and they turned to the comma-shaped room. It was appreciably darker. The girl went to the window and stared through the immense, wall-long pane.

"Storm coming up," she said. "The car radio said it'll be a bad one. I'd better go, Johnny."

"Must you? You just got here."

"I have a date. Anyway, I've got to work early tomorrow." She was a Korys model, much in demand.

Fowler turned from the recalcitrant bar and reached for her hand.

"I wanted to ask you to marry me," he said.

There was silence, while leaden grayness pressed down beyond the window, and yellow hills rippled under the gusts of unfelt wind. Veronica met his gaze steadily.

"I know you did. I mean—I've been expecting you to."

"Well?"

She moved her shoulders uneasily.

"Not now."

"But—Veronica. Why not? We've known each other for a couple of years—"

"The truth is—I'm not sure about you, Johnny. Sometimes I think I love you. But sometimes I'm not sure I even like you."

He frowned. "I don't get that."

"Well, I can't explain it. It's just that I think you could be either a very nice guy or a very nasty one. And I'd like to be quite certain first. Now I've got to go. It's starting to rain."

On that note she went out, leaving Fowler with a sour taste in his mouth. He mixed himself another drink and wandered over to his drawing board, where some sketches were sheafed up on a disorderly fashion. Nuts. He was making good dough at commercial art, he'd even got himself a rather special house—

One of the drawings caught his eye. It was a background detail, intended for incorporation later in a larger picture. It showed a gargoyle, drawn with painstaking care, and a certain quality of vivid precision that was very faintly unpleasant. Veronica—

Fowler suddenly remembered his guest and hastily set down his drink. He had avoided that room during the tour of inspection, managing to put the man completely out of his mind. That was too bad. He could have asked Veronica to send out a doctor from the village.

But the guest didn't seem to need a doctor. He was working on the wall-switch, at some danger, Fowler thought, of electrocuting himself. "Look out!" Fowler said sharply. "It's hot!" But the man merely gave him a mild, blank stare and passed his hand downward before the panel.

The light went out.

It came on again, to show the man finishing an upward gesture.

No toggle switch stub protruded from the slot in the center of the plate. Fowler blinked. "What—?" he said.

Gesture. Blackout. Another gesture.

"What did you do to that?" Fowler asked, but there was no audible reply.

Fowler drove south through the storm, muttering about ham electricians. Beside him the guest sat, smiling vacantly. The one thing Fowler wanted was to get the guy off his hands. A doctor, or a cop, in the village, would solve that particular problem. Or, rather, that would have been the solution, if a minor landslide hadn't covered the road at a crucial point.

With difficulty Fowler turned the car around and drove back home, cursing gently.

The blank man sat obediently at his side.

They were marooned for three days. Luckily the larder was well-stocked, and the power lines, which ran underground, weren't cut by the storm. The water-purifying unit turned the muddy stream from outside into crystalline nectar, the FM set wasn't much bothered by atmospheric disturbances, and Fowler had plenty of assignments to keep him busy at his drawing board. But he did no drawing. He was exploring a fascinating, though unbelievable, development.

The light switch his guest had rigged was unique. Fowler discovered that when he took the gadget apart. The sealed plastic had been broken open, and a couple of wires had been rewound in an odd fashion. The wiring didn't make much sense to Fowler. There was no photo-electric hookup that would have explained it. But the fact remained that he could turn on the lights in that room by moving his hand upward in front of the switch plate, and reverse the process with a downward gesture.

He made tests. It seemed as though an invisible fourteen-inch beam extended directly outward from the switch. At any rate, gestures, no matter how emphatic, made beyond that fourteen-inch distance had no effect on the lights at all.

Curious, he asked his guest to rig up another switch in the same fashion. Presently all the switches in the house were converted, but Fowler was no wiser. He could duplicate the hookup, but he didn't understand the principle. He felt a little frightened.

Locked in the house for three days, he had time to wonder and worry. He fed his guest—who had forgotten the use of knife and fork, if he had ever known it—and he tried to make the man talk. Not too successfully.

Once the man said: "Forgotten . . . forgotten—"

"You haven't forgotten how to be an electrician. Where did you come from?"

The blank face turned to him. "Where?" A pause. And then—

"When? Time . . . time—"

Once he picked up a newspaper and pointed questioningly at the date line—the year.

"That's right," Fowler said, his stomach crawling. "What year did you think it was?"

"Wrong—" the man said. "Forgotten—"

Fowler stared. On impulse, he got up to search his guest's pockets. But there were no pockets. The suit was ordinary, though slightly strange in cut, but it had no pockets.

"What's your name?"

"No answer.

"Where did you come from? Another—*time?*"

Still no answer.

Fowler thought of robots. He thought of a soulless world of the future peopled by automatons. But he knew neither was the right answer. The man sitting before him was horribly normal. And empty, somehow—drained. Normal?

The norm? That non-existant, figurative symbol which would be monstrous if it actually appeared? The closer an individual approaches the norm, the more colorless he is. Just as a contracting line becomes a point, which has few, if any, distinguishing characteristics. One point is exactly like another point. As though humans, in some unpleasant age to come, had been reduced to the lowest common denominator.

The norm.

"All right," Fowler said. "I'll call you Norman, till you remember your right name. But you can't be a . . . point. You're no moron. You've got a talent for electricity, anyhow."

Norman had other talents, too, as Fowler was to discover soon. He grew tired of looking through the window at the gray, pouring rain, pounding down over a drenched and dreary landscape, and when he tried to close the built-in Venetian shutters, of course they failed to work. "May that architect be forced to live in one of his own houses," Fowler said, and, noticing Norman made explanatory gestures toward the window.

Norman smiled blankly.

"The view," Fowler said. "I don't like to see all that rain. The shutters won't work. See if you can fix them. The view—"

He explained patiently, and presently Norman went out to the unit nominally called a kitchen, though it was far more efficient. Fowler shrugged and sat down at his drawing board. He looked up, some while later, in time to see Norman finish up with a few swabs of cloth. Apparently he had been painting the window with water.

Fowler snorted. "I didn't ask you to wash it," he remarked. "It was the shutters—"

Norman laid a nearly empty basin on a table and smiled expectantly. Fowler suffered a slight reorientation. "Time-traveling, ha," he said. "You probably crashed out of some booby hatch. The sooner I can get you back there the better I'll like it. If it'd only stop raining . . . I wonder if you could rig up the televisor? No, I forgot. We don't even have one yet. And I suspect you couldn't do it. That light switch business was a fluke."

He looked out at the rain and thought of Veronica. Then she was there before him, dark and slender, smiling a little.

"Wha—" Fowler said throatily.

He blinked. Hallucinations? He looked again, and she was still there, three-dimensionally, outside the window—

Norman smiled and nodded. He pointed to the apparition.

"Do you see it too?" Fowler asked madly. "It can't be. She's outside. She'll get wet. What in the name of—"

But it was only Fowler who got wet, dashing out bareheaded in the drenching rain. There was no one outside. He looked through the window and saw the familiar room, and Norman.

He came back. "Did you paint her on the window?" he asked. "But you've never seen Veronica. Besides, she's moving—three-dimensional. Oh, it can't be. My mind's snapping. I need peace and quiet. A green thought in a green shade." He focused on a green thought, and Veronica faded out slowly. A cool, quiet, woodland glade was visible through the window.

After a while Fowler figured it out. His window made thoughts visible.

It wasn't as simple as that, naturally. He had to experiment and brood for quite some time. Norman was no help. But the fact finally emerged that whenever Fowler looked at the window and visualized something with strong emphasis, an image of that thought appeared—a projective screen, so to speak.

It was like throwing a stone into calm water. The ripples moved out for a while, and then slowly quieted. The woodland scene wasn't static; there was a breeze there, and the leaves glittered and the branches swayed. Clouds moved softly across a blue sky. It was a scene Fowler finally recognized, a Vermont woodland he had seen years ago. Yet when did sequoias ever grow in Vermont?

A composite, then. And the original impetus of his thoughts set the scene into action along normal lines. When he visualized the forest, he had known that there would be a wind, and that the branches would move. So they moved. But slower and slower—though it took a long while for the action to run down.

He tried again. This time Chicago's lake shore. Cars rushed along the drive. He tried to make them run backwards, but got a sharp headache and a sense of watching a jerky film. Possibly he could reverse the normal course of events, but his mind wasn't geared to handle film running backward. Then he thought hard and watched a seascape appear through the glass. This time he waited to see how long it would take the image to vanish. The action stopped in an hour, but the picture did not face completely for another hour.

Only then did the possibilities strike him with an impact as violent as lightning.

Considerable poetry has been written about what happens when love rejected turns to hate. Psychology could explain the cause as well as the effect—the mechanism of displacement. Energy has to go somewhere, and if one channel is blocked, another will be found. Not that Veronica had definitely rejected Fowler, and certainly his emotion for the girl had not suffered an alchemic transformation, unless one wishes to delve into the abysses of psychology in which love is merely the other face of hatred—but on those levels of semantic confusion you can easily prove anything.

Call it reorientation. Fowler had never quite let himself believe that Veronica wouldn't fall into his arms. His ego was damaged. Consequently it had to find some other justification, some assurance—and it was unfortunate for Norman that the displacement had to occur when he was available as scapegoat. For the moment Fowler began to see the commercial possibilities of the magic windowpane, Norman was doomed.

Not at once; in the beginning, Fowler would have been shocked and horrified had he seen the end result of his plan. He was no villain, for there are no villains. There is a check-and-balance system, as inevitable in nature and mind as in politics, and the balance was beginning to tip when Fowler locked Norman in the windowless room for safekeeping and drove to New York to see a patent attorney. He was careful at first. He knew the formula for the telepathically-receptive window paint by now, but he merely arranged to patent the light-switch gadget that was operated by a gesture. Afterwards, he regretted his ignorance, for clever infringements appeared on the heels of his own device. He hadn't known enough about the matter to protect himself thoroughly in the patent.

By a miracle, he had kept the secret of the telepathic paint to himself. All this took time, naturally, and meanwhile Norman, urged on by his host, had made little repairs and improvements around the house. Some of them were impractical, but others were decidedly worth using—short-cuts, conveniences, clever methods of bridging difficulties that would be worth money in the open market. Norman's way of thinking seemed curiously alien. Given a problem, he could solve it, but he had no initiative on his own. He seemed satisfied to stay in the house—

Well, satisfied was scarcely the word. He was satisfied in the same sense that a jellyfish is satisfied to remain in its pool. If there were quivers of volition, slight directional stirrings, they were very feeble indeed. There were times when Fowler, studying his guest, decided that Norman was in a psychotic state—catatonic stupor seemed the most appropriate label. The man's will was submerged, if, indeed, he had ever had any.

No one has ever detailed the probable reactions of the man who owned the goose who laid the golden eggs. He brooded over a mystery, and presently took empirical steps, afterwards regretted. Fowler had a more analytical mind, and suspected that Norman might be poised at a precarious state of balance, during which—and only during which—he laid golden eggs. Metal can be pliable until pressure is used, after which it may become work-hardened and inflexible. Fowler was afraid of applying too much pressure. But he was equally afraid of not finding out all he could about the goose's unusual oviparity.

So he studied Norman. It was like watching a shadow. Norman seemed to have none of the higher reflexes; his activities were little more than tropism. Ego-consciouness was present, certainly, but—where had he come from? What sort of place or time had it been? Or was Norman simply a freak, a lunatic, a mutation? All that seemed certain was that part of his brain didn't know its own function. Without conscious will or volition, it was useless. Fowler had to supply the volition; he had to give orders. Between orders, Norman simply sat, occasionally quivering slightly.

It was bewildering. It was fascinating.

Also, it might be a little dangerous. Fowler had no intention of letting his captive escape if he could help it, but vague recollections of peonage disturbed him sometimes. Probably this was illegal. Norman ought to be in an institution, under medical care. But then, Norman had such unusual talents!

Fowler, to salve his uneasiness, ceased to lock the door of the windowless room. By now he had discovered it was unnecessary, anyhow. Norman was like a subject in deep hypnosis. He would obey when told not to leave the room. Fowler, with a layman's knowledge of law, thought that probably gave him an out. He pictured himself in the dock blandly stating that Norman had never been a prisoner, had always been free to leave the house if he chose.

Actually, only hunger would rouse Norman to disobey Fowler's commands to stay in his room. He would have to be almost famished, even then, before he would go to the kitchen and eat whatever he found, without discrimination and apparently without taste.

Time went by. Fowler was reorienting, though he scarcely knew it yet, toward a whole new set of values. He let his illustrating dwindle away until he almost ceased to accept orders. This was after an abortive experiment with Norman in which he tried to work out on paper an equivalent of the telepathic pictures on glass. If he could simply sit and *think* his drawings onto bristol board—

That was, however, one of Norman's failures.

It wasn't easy to refrain from sharing this wonderful new secret with Veronica. Fowler found himself time and again shutting his lips over the information just in time. He didn't invite her out to the house any more; Norman was too often working at odd jobs around the premises. Beautiful visions of the future were building up elaborately in Fowler's mind—Veronica wrapped in mink and pearls, himself commanding financial empires all based on Norman's extraordinary talents and Norman's truly extraordinary willingness to obey.

That was because of his physical weakness, Fowler felt sure. It seemed to take so much of Norman's energy simply to breathe and eat that nothing remained. And after the solution of a problem, a complete fatigue overcame him. He was useless for a day or two between jobs, recovering from the utter exhaustion that work seemed to induce. Fowler was quite willing to accept that. It made him even surer of his—guest. The worst thing that could happen, of course, would be Norman's recovery, his return to normal—

* * *

Money began to come in very satisfactorily, although Fowler wasn't really a good business man. In fact, he was a remarkably poor one. It didn't matter much. There was always more where the first had come from.

With some of the money Fowler started cautious inquiries about missing persons. He wanted to be sure no indignant relatives would turn up and demand an accounting of all this money. He questioned Norman futilely.

Norman simply could not talk. His mind was too empty for coherence. He could produce words, but he could not connect them. And this was a thing that seemed to give him his only real trouble. For he wanted desperately sometimes to speak. There was something he seemed frantic to tell Fowler, in the intervals when his strength was at its peak.

Fowler didn't want to know it. Usually when Norman reached this pitch he set him another exhausting problem. Fowler wondered for awhile just why he dreaded hearing the message. Presently he faced the answer.

Norman might be trying to explain how he could be cured.

Eventually, Fowler had to face an even more unwelcome truth. Norman did seem in spite of everything to be growing stronger.

He was working one day on a vibratory headset gimmick later to be known as a Hed-D-Acher, when suddenly he threw down his tools and faced Fowler over the table with a look that bordered on animation—for Norman.

"Sick—" he said painfully. "I . . . know . . . *work!*" It was an anathema. He made a defiant gesture and pushed the tools away.

Fowler, with a sinking sensation, frowned at the rebellious nonentity.

"All right, Norman," he said soothingly. "All right. You can rest when you finish this job. You must finish it first, though. You must finish this job, Norman. Do you understand that? You must finish—"

It was sheer accident, of course—or almost accident—that the job turned out to be much more complicated than Fowler had expected. Norman, obedient to the slow, repeated commands, worked very late and very hard.

The end of the job found him so completely exhausted he couldn't speak or move for three days.

As a matter of fact it was the Hed-D-Acher that turned out to be an important milestone in Fowler's progress. He couldn't recognize it at the time, but when he looked back, years later, he saw the occasion of his first serious mistake. His first, that is, unless you count the moment when he lifted Norman across his threshold at the very start of the thing.

Fowler had to go to Washington to defend himself in some question of patent infringement. A large firm had found out about the Hed-D-Acher and jumped in on the grounds of similar wiring—at least that was Fowler's impression. He was no technician. The main point was that the Hed-D-Acher couldn't be patented in its present form, and Fowler's rivals were trying to squeeze through a similar—and stolen—Hed-D-Acher of their own.

Fowler phoned the Korys Agency. Long distance television was not on the market yet and he was not able to see Veronica's face, but he knew what expression must be visible on it when he told her what he wanted.

"But I'm going out on a job, John. I can't just drop everything and rush out to your house."

"Listen, Veronica, there may be a hundred thousand bucks in it. I . . . there's no one else I can trust." He didn't add his chief reason for trusting her—the fact that she wasn't over-bright.

In the end, she went. Dramatic situations appealed to her, and he dropped dark hints of corporation espionage and bloody doings on Capitol Hill. He told her where to find the key and she hung up, leaving Fowler to gnaw his nails intermittently and try to limit himself to one whiskey-soda every half hour. He was paged, it seemed to him, some years later.

"Hello, Veronica?"

"Right. I'm at the house. The key was where you said. Now what?"

Fowler had had time to work out a plan. He put pencil and note pad on the jutting shelf before him and frowned slightly. This might be a risk, but—

But he intended to marry Veronica, so it was no great risk. And she wasn't smart enough to figure out the real answers.

He told her about the windowless room. "That's my house-boy's—Norman. He's slightly half-witted, but a good boy on mechanical stuff. Only he's a little deaf, and you've got to tell him a thing three times before he understands it."

"I think I'd better get out of here," Veronica remarked. "Next you'll be telling me he's a homicidal maniac."

Fowler laughed heartily. "There's a box in the kitchen—it's in that red cupboard with the blue handle. It's pretty heavy. But see if you can manage it. Take it in to Norman and tell him to make another Hed-D-Acher with a different wiring circuit.''

''Are you drunk?''

Fowler repressed an impulse to bite the mouthpiece off the telephone. His nerves were crawling under his skin. ''This isn't a gag, Veronica. I told you how important it is. A hundred thousand bucks isn't funny. Look, got a pencil? Write this down.'' He dictated some technical instructions he had gleaned by asking the right questions. ''Tell that to Norman. He'll find all the materials and tools he needs in the box.''

''If this is a gag—'' Veronica said, and there was a pause. ''Well, hang on.''

Silence drew on. Fowler tried to hear what was happening so many miles away. He caught a few vague sounds, but they were meaningless. Then voices rose in loud debate.

''Veronica!'' Fowler shouted. ''Veronica!'' There was no answer.

After that, voices again, but softer. And presently:

''Johnny,'' Veronica said, ''if you ever pull a trick like that on me again—''

''What happened?''

''Hiding a gibbering idiot in your house—'' She was breathing fast.

''He's . . . what did he do? *What happened?*''

''Oh, nothing. Nothing at all. Except when I opened the door your houseboy walked out and began running around the house like a . . . a bat. He was trying to talk—Johnny, he scared me!'' She was plaintive.

''Where is he now?''

''Back in his room. I . . . I was afraid of him. But I was trying not to show it. I thought if I could get him back in and lock the door—I spoke to him, and he swung around at me so fast I guess I let out a yell. And then he kept trying to say something—''

''What?''

''How should I know? He's in his room, but I couldn't find a key to it. I'm not staying here a minute longer. I . . . *here he comes!*''

''Verónica! Tell him to go back to his room. Loud and—like you mean it!''

She obeyed. Fowler could hear her saying it. She said it several times.

''It doesn't work. He's going out—''

"Stop him!"

"I won't! I had enough trouble coaxing him back the first time—"

"Let me talk to him," Fowler said suddenly. "He'll obey me. Hold the phone to his ear. Get him to listen to me." He raised his voice to a shout. "*Norman! Come here! Listen to me!*" Outside the booth people were turning to stare, but he ignored them.

He heard a faint mumble and recognized it.

"Norman," he said, more quietly but with equal firmness. "Do exactly what I tell you to do. Don't leave the house. Don't leave the house. *Don't leave the house.* Do you understand?"

Mumble. Then words: "Can't get out . . . can't—"

"Don't leave the house. Build another Hed-D-Acher. Do it now. Get the equipment you need and build it in the living room, on the table where the telephone is. Do it now."

A pause, and then Veronica said shakily: "He's gone back to his room. Johnny, I . . . he's coming back! With that box of stuff—"

"Let me talk to him again. Get yourself a drink. A couple of 'em." He needed Veronica as his interpreter, and the best way to keep her there would be with the aid of Dutch courage.

"Well—here he is."

Norman mumbled.

Fowler referred to his notes. He gave firm, incisive, detailed directions. He told Norman exactly what he wanted. He repeated his orders several times.

And it ended with Norman building a Hed-D-Acher, with a different type of circuit, while Veronica watched, made measurements as Fowler commanded, and relayed the information across the wire. By the time she got slightly high, matters were progressing more smoothly. There was the danger that she might make inaccurate measurements, but Fowler insisted on check and double-check of each detail.

Occasionally he spoke to Norman. Each time the man's voice was weaker. The dangerous surge of initiative was passing as energy drained out of Norman while his swift fingers flew.

In the end, Fowler had his information, and Norman, completely exhausted, was ordered back to his room. According to Veronica, he went there obediently and fell flat on the floor.

"I'll buy you a mink coat," Fowler said. "See you later."

"But—"

"I've got to hurry. Tell you all about it when I see you."

* * *

He got the patent, by the skin of his teeth. There was instant litigation, which was why he didn't clean up on the gadget immediately. He was willing to wait. The goose still laid golden eggs.

But he was fully aware of the danger now. He had to keep Norman busy. For unless the man's strength remained at a minimum, initiative would return. And there would be nothing to stop Norman from walking out of the house, or—

Or even worse. For Fowler could, after all, keep the doors locked. But he knew that locks wouldn't imprison Norman long once the man discovered how to pose a problem to himself. Once Norman thought: *Problem how to escape*—then his clever hands would construct a wall-melter or a matter-transmitter, and that would be the end for Fowler.

Norman had one specialized talent. To keep that operating efficiently—for Fowler's purpose—all Norman's other faculties had to be cut down to minimum operation speed.

The rosy light in the high-backed booth fell flatteringly upon Veronica's face. She twirled her martini glass on the table and said: "But John, I don't think I want to marry you." The martini glass shot pinpoints of soft light in his face as she turned it. She looked remarkably pretty, even for a Korys model. Fowler felt like strangling her.

"Why not?" he demanded.

She shrugged. She had been blowing hot and cold, so far as Fowler was concerned, ever since the day she had seen Norman. Fowler had been able to buy her back, at intervals, with gifts or moods that appealed to her, but the general drift had been toward estrangement. She wasn't intelligent, but she did have sensitivity of a sort, and it served its purpose. It was stopping her from marrying John Fowler.

"Maybe we're too much alike, Johnny," she said reflectively. "I don't know. I . . . how's that miserable house-boy of yours?"

"Is *that* still bothering you?" His voice was impatient. She had been showing too much concern over Norman. It had probably been a mistake to call her in at all, but what else could he have done? "I wish you'd forget about Norman. He's all right."

"Johnny, I honestly do think he ought to be under a doctor's care. He didn't look at all well that day. Are you sure—"

"Of course I'm sure! What do you take me for? As a matter of fact, he is under a doctor's care. Norman's just feeble-minded. "I've told you that a dozen times, Veronica. I wish you'd take my word for it. He . . . he sees a doctor regularly. It was just having you there that upset him. Strangers throw him off his balance. He's fine now. Let's forget about Norman. We were talking about getting married, remember?"

"You were. Not me. No, Johnny, I'm afraid it wouldn't work." She looked at him in the soft light, her face clouded with doubt and—was it suspicion? With a woman of Veronica's mentality, you never knew just where you stood. Fowler could reason her out of every objection she offered to him, but because reason meant so little to her, the solid substratum of her convictions remained unchanged.

"You'll marry me," he said, his voice confident.

"No." She gave him an uneasy look and then drew a deep breath and said: "You may as well know this now, Johnny—I've just about decided to marry somebody else."

"Who?" He wanted to shout the question, but he forced himself to be calm.

"No one you know. Ray Barnaby. I . . . I've pretty well made up my mind about it, John."

"I don't know the man," Fowler told her evenly, "but I'll make it my business to find out all I can."

"Now John, let's not quarrel. I—"

"You're going to marry me or nobody, Veronica." Fowler was astonished at the sudden violence of his own reaction. "Do you understand that?"

"Don't be silly, John. You don't own me."

"I'm not being silly! I'm just telling you."

"John, I'll do exactly as I please. Now, let's not quarrel about it."

Until now, until this moment of icy rage, he had never quite realized what an obsession Veronica had become. Fowler had got out of the habit of being thwarted. His absolute power over one individual and one unchanging situation was giving him a taste for tyranny. He sat looking at Veronica in the pink dimness of the booth, grinding his teeth together in an effort not to shout at her.

"If you go through with this, Veronica, I'll make it my business to see you regret it as long as you live," he told her in a harsh, low voice.

She pushed her half-emptied glass aside with sudden violence that matched his. "Don't get me started, John Fowler!" she said angrily. "I've got a temper, too! I've always known there was something I didn't like about you."

"There'll be a lot more you don't like if you—"

"That's enough, John!" She got up abruptly, clutching at her slipping handbag. Even in this soft light he could see the sudden hardening of her face, the lines of anger pinching downward along her nose and mouth. A perverse triumph filled him because at this moment she was ugly in her rage, but it did not swerve his determination.

"You're going to marry me," he told her harshly. "Sit down. You're going to marry me if I have to—" He paused.

"To what?" Her voice was goading. He shook his head. He couldn't finish the threat aloud.

Norman will help me, he was thinking in cold triumph. *Norman will find a way.*

He smiled thinly after her as she stalked in a fury out of the bar.

For a week Fowler heard no more from her. He made inquiries about the man Barnaby and was not surprised to learn that Veronica's intended—if she had really been serious about the fellow, after all—was a young broker of adequate income and average stupidity. A nonentity. Fowler told himself savagely that they were two of a kind and no doubt deserved each other. But his obsession still ruled him, and he was determined that no one but himself should marry Veronica.

Short of hypnosis, there seemed no immediate way to change her mind. But perhaps he could change Barnaby's. He believed he could, given enough time. Norman was at work on a rather ingenious little device involving the use of a trick lighting system. Fowler had been impressed, on consideration, by the effect of a rosy light in the bar on Veronica's appearance.

Another week passed, with no news about Veronica. Fowler told himself he could afford to remain aloof. He had the means to control her very nearly within his grasp. He would watch her, and wait his time in patience.

He was very busy, too, with other things. Two more devices were ready for patenting—the Magic Latch keyed to fingerprint patterns, and the Haircut Helmet that could be set for any sort of hair trimming and would probably wreak havoc among barbers. But litigation on the Hed-D-Acher was threatening to be expensive, and Fowler had learned already to live beyond his means. Far beyond. It seemed ridiculous to spend only what he took in each day, when such fortunes in royalties were just around the corner.

Twice he had to take Norman off the lighting device to perform small tasks in other directions. And Norman was in himself a problem.

The work exhausted him. It had to exhaust him. That was

necessary. An unpleasant necessity, of course, but there it was. Sometimes the exhaustion in Norman's eyes made one uncomfortable. Certainly Norman suffered. But because he was seldom able to show it plainly, Fowler could tell himself that perhaps he imagined the worst part of it. Casuistry, used to good purpose, helped him to ignore what he preferred not to see.

By the end of the second week, Fowler decided not to wait on Veronica any longer. He bought a dazzling solitaire diamond whose cost faintly alarmed even himself, and a wedding band that was a full circle of emerald-cut diamonds to complement it. With ten thousand dollars worth of jewelry in his pocket, he went into the city to pay her a call.

Barnaby answered the door.

Stupidly Fowler heard himself saying: "Miss Wood here?"

Barnaby, grinning, shook his head and started to answer. Fowler knew perfectly well what he was about to say. The fatuous grin would have told him even if some accurate sixth sense had not already made it clear. But he wouldn't let Barnaby say it. He thrust the startled bridegroom aside and shouldered angrily into the apartment, calling: "Veronica! Veronica, where are you?"

She came out of the kitchen in a ruffled apron, apprehension and defiance on her face.

"You can just get right out of here, John Fowler," she said firmly. Barnaby came up from behind him and began a blustering remonstrance, but she slipped past Fowler and linked her arm with Barnaby's, quieting him with a touch.

"We were married day before yesterday, John," she said.

Fowler was astonished to discover that the cliché about a red swimming maze of rage was perfectly true. The room and the bridal couple shimmered before him for an instant. He could hardly breathe in the suffocating fury that swam in his brain.

He took out the white velvet box, snapped it open and waved it under Veronica's nose. Liquid fire quivered in the myriad cut surfaces of the jewels and for an instant pure greed made Veronica's face as hard as the diamonds.

Barnaby said: "I think you'd better go, Fowler."

In silence, Fowler went.

The little light-device wouldn't do now. He would need something more powerful for his revenge. Norman put the completed gadget aside and began to work on something new. There would be a use for the thing later. Already plans were spinning themselves out in Fowler's mind.

They would be expensive plans. Fowler took council with himself and decided that the moment had come to put the magic window on the market.

Until now he had held this in reserve. Perhaps he had even been a little afraid of possible repercussions. He was artist enough to know that a whole new art-form might result from a practical telepathic projector. There were so many possibilities—

But the magic window failed.

Not wholly, of course. It was a miracle, and men always will buy miracles. But it wasn't the instant, overwhelming financial success Fowler had felt certain it would be. For one thing, perhaps this was too much of a miracle. Inventions can't become popular until the culture is ready for them. Talking films were made in Paris by Méliès around 1890, but perhaps because that was a double miracle, nobody took to the idea. As for a telepathic screen—

It was a specialized luxury item. And it wasn't as easy or as safe to enjoy as one might suppose. For one thing, few minds turned out to be disciplined enough to maintain a picture they deliberately set out to evoke. As a mass entertaining medium it suffered from the same faults as family motion pictures—other peoples' memories and dreams are notoriously boring unless one sees oneself in them.

Besides, this was too close to pure telepathy to be safe. Fowler had lived alone too long to remember the perils of exposing one's thoughts to a group. Whatever he wanted to project on his private window, he projected. But in the average family it wouldn't do. It simply wouldn't do.

Some Hollywood companies and some millionaires leased windows—Fowler refused to sell them outright. A film studio photographed a batch of projected ideations and cut them into a dream sequence for a modern Cinderella story. But trick photography had already done work so similar that it made no sensation whatever. Even Disney had done some of the stuff better. Until trained imaginative projective artists could be developed, the windows were simply not going to be a commercial success.

One ethnological group tried to use a window to project the memories of oldsters in an attempt to recapture everyday living customs of the recent past, but the results were blurred and inaccurate, full of anachronisms. They all had to be winnowed and checked so completely that little of value remained. The fact stood out that the ordinary mind is too undisciplined to be worth anything as a projector. Except as a toy, the window was useless.

It was useless commercially. But for Fowler it had one intrinsic usefulness more valuable than money—

One of the wedding presents Vernonica and Barnaby received was a telepathic window. It came anonymously. Their suspicions should have been roused. Perhaps they were, but they kept the window. After all, in her modeling work Veronica had met many wealthy people, and Barnaby also had moneyed friends, any of whom might in a generous mood have taken a window-lease for them as a goodwill gesture. Also, possession of a magic window was a social distinction. They did not allow themselves to look the gift-horse too closely in the mouth. They kept the window.

They could not have known—though they might have guessed—that this was a rather special sort of window. Norman had been at work on it through long, exhausting hours, while Fowler stood over him with the goading repetitious commands that kept him at his labor.

Fowler was not too disappointed at the commercial failure of the thing. There were other ways of making money. So long as Norman remained his to command the natural laws of supply and demand did not really affect him. He had by now almost entirely ceased to think in terms of the conventional mores. Why should he? They no longer applied to him. His supply of money and resources was limitless. He never really had to suffer for a failure. It would always be Norman, not Fowler, who suffered.

There was unfortunately no immediate way in which he could check how well his magic window was working. To do that you would have to be an invisible third person in the honeymoon apartment. But Fowler, knowing Veronica as he did, could guess.

The window was based on the principle that if you give a child a jackknife he'll probably cut himself.

Fowler's first thought had been to create a window on which he could project his own thoughts, disguised as those of the bride or groom. But he had realized almost immediately that a far more dangerous tool lay ready-made in the minds of the two whose marriage he meant to undermine.

"It isn't as if they wouldn't break up anyhow, in a year or two," he told himself as he speculated on the possibilities of his magic window. He was not justifying his intent. He didn't need to, any more. He was simply considering possibilities. "They're both stupid, they're both selfish. They're not material you could make a good marriage of. This ought to be almost too easy—"

Every man, he reasoned, has a lawless devil in his head. What filters through the censor-band from the unconscious mind is controllable. But the lower levels of the brain are utterly without morals.

Norman produced a telepathic window that would at times project images from the unconscious mind.

It was remotely controlled, of course; most of the time it operated on the usual principles of the magic window. But whenever Fowler chose he could throw a switch that made the glass twenty miles away hypersensitive.

Before he threw it for the first time, he televised Veronica. It was evening. When the picture dawned in the television he could see the magic window set up in its elegant frame within range of the televisor, so that everyone who called might be aware of the Barnaby's distinction.

Luckily it was Veronica who answered, though Barnaoy was visible in the background, turning toward the 'visor an interested glance that darkened when Fowler's face dawned upon the screen. Veronica's politely expectant look turned sullen as she recognized the caller.

"Well?"

Fowler grinned. "Oh, nothing. Just wondered how you were getting along."

"Beautifully, thanks. Is that all?"

Fowler shrugged. "If that's the way you feel, yes."

"Good-by," Veronica said firmly, and flicked the switch. The screen before Fowler went blank. He grinned. All he had wanted to do was remind her of himself. He touched the stud that would activate that magic window he had just seen, and settled down to wait.

What would happen now he didn't know. Something would. He hoped the sight of him had reminded Veronica of the dazzling jewelry he had carried when they last met. He hoped that upon the window now would be dawning a covetous image of those diamonds, clear as dark water and quivering with fiery light. The sight should be enough to rouse resentment in Barnaby's mind, and when two people quarrel wholeheartedly, there are impulses toward mayhem in even the most civilized mind. It should shock the bride and groom to see on a window that reflected their innermost thoughts a picture of hatred and wishful violence. Would Veronica see herself being strangled in effigy in the big wall-frame? Would Barnaby see himself bleeding from the deep scratches his bride would be yearning to score across his face?

Fowler sat back comfortably, luxuriating in speculation.

It might take a long time. It might take years. He was willing to wait.

It took even longer than Fowler had expected. Slowly the poison built up in the Barnaby household, very slowly. And in that time a different sort of toxicity developed in Fowler's. He scarcely realized it. He was too close.

He never recognized the moment when his emotional balance shifted and he began actively to hate Norman.

The owner of the golden goose must have lived under considerable strain. Every day when he went out to look in the nest he must have felt a quaking wonder whether this time the egg would be white, and valuable only for omelets or hatching. Also, he must have had to stay very close to home, living daily with the nightmare of losing his treasure—

Norman was a prisoner—but a prisoner handcuffed to his jailer. Both men were chained. If Fowler left him alone for too long, Norman might recover. It was the inevitable menace that made travel impossible. Fowler could keep no servants; he lived alone with his prisoner. Occasionally he thought of Norman as a venomous snake whose poison fangs had to be removed each time they were renewed. He dared not cut out the poison sacs themselves, for there was no way to do that without killing the golden goose. The mixed metaphors were indicative of the state of Fowler's mind by then.

And he was almost as much a prisoner in the house as Norman was.

Constantly now he had to set Norman problems to solve simply as a safety measure, whether or not they had commercial value. For Norman was slowly regaining his strength. He was never completely coherent, but he could talk a little more, and he managed to put across quite definitely his tremendous urge to give Fowler certain obscure information.

Fowler knew, of course, what it probably was. The cure. And Norman seemed to have a strangely touching confidence that if he could only frame his message intelligibly, Fowler would make arrangements for the mysterious cure.

Once Fowler might have been touched by the confidence. Not now. Because he was exploiting Norman so ruthlessly, he had to hate either Norman or himself. By a familiar process he was projecting his own fault upon his prisoner and punishing Norman for it. He no longer speculated upon Norman's mysterious origin or the source of his equally mysterious powers. There was obviously something in that clouded mind that gave forth flashes of a certain peculiar genius. Fowler accepted the fact and used it.

There was probably some set of rules that would govern what Norman could and could not do, but Fowler did not discover—until it was too late—what the rules were. Norman could produce inconceivably intricate successes, and then fail dismally at the simplest tasks.

Curiously, he turned out to be an almost infallible finder of lost articles, so long as they were lost in the confines of the house. Fowler discovered this by accident, and was gratified to learn that for some reason that kind of search was the most exhausting task he could set for his prisoner. When all else failed, and Norman still seemed too coherent or too strong for safekeeping, Fowler had only to remember that he had misplaced his wristwatch or a book or screwdriver, and to send Norman after it.

Then something very odd happened, and after that he stopped the practice, feeling bewildered and insecure. He had ordered Norman to find a lost folder of rather important papers. Norman had gone into his own room and closed the door. He was missing for a long time. Eventually Fowler's impatience built up enough to make him call off the search, and he shouted to Norman to come out.

There was no answer. When he had called a third time in vain, Fowler opened the door and looked in. The room was empty. There were no windows. The door was the only exit, and Fowler could have sworn Norman had not come out of it.

In a rising panic he ransacked the room, calling futilely. He went through the rest of the house in a fury of haste and growing terror. Norman was not in the kitchen or the living room or the cellar or anywhere in sight outside.

Fowler was on the verge of a nervous collapse when Norman's door opened and the missing man emerged, staggering a little, his face white and blank with exhaustion, and the folder of papers in his hand.

He slept for three days afterward. And Fowler never again used that method of keeping his prisoner in check.

After six uneventful months had passed Fowler put Norman to work on a supplementary device that might augment the Barnaby magic window. He was receiving reports from a bribed daily maid, and he took pains to hear all the gossip mutual friends were happy to pass on. The Barnaby marriage appeared to suffer from a higher than normal percentage of spats and disagreements, but so far it still held. The magic window was not enough.

Norman turned out a little gadget that produced supersonics guaranteed to evoke irritability and nervous tension. The maid smuggled it into the apartment. Thereafter, the reports Fowler received were more satisfactory, from his point of view.

All in all, it took three years.

And the thing that finally turned the trick was the lighting gadget which Fowler had conceived in that bar interlude when Veronica first told him about Barnaby.

Norman worked on the fixtures for some time. They were subtle. The exact tinting involved a careful study of Veronica's skin tones, the colors of the apartment, the window placement. Norman had a scale model of the rooms where the Barnabys were working out their squabbles toward divorce. He took a long time to choose just what angles of lighting he would need to produce the worst possible result. And of course it all had to be done with considerable care because the existing light fixtures couldn't be changed noticeably.

With the help of the maid, the job was finally done. And thereafter, Veronica in her own home was—ugly.

The lights made her look haggard. They brought out every line of fatigue and ill-nature that lurked anywhere in her face. They made her sallow. They caused Barnaby increasingly to wonder why he had ever thought the girl attractive.

"It's your fault!" Veronica said hysterically. "It's all your fault and you know it!"

"How could it be my fault?" Fowler demanded in a smug voice, trying hard to iron out the smile that kept pulling up the corners of his mouth.

The television screen was between them like a window. Veronica leaned toward it, the cords in her neck standing out as she shouted at him. He had never seen that particular phenomenon before. Probably she had acquired much practice in angry shouting in the past three years. There were thin vertical creases between her brows that were new to him, too. He had seen her face to face only a few times in the years of her marriage. It had been safer and pleasanter to create her in the magic window when he felt the need of seeing her.

This was a different face, almost a different woman. He wondered briefly if he was watching the effect of his own disenchanting lighting system, but a glimpse beyond her head of a crowded drugstore assured him that he was not. This was real, not illusory. This was a Verònica he and Norman had, in effect, created.

"You did it!" Veronica said accusingly. "I don't know how, but you did it."

Fowler glanced down at the morning paper he had just been reading, folded back to the gossip column that announced last night's spectacular public quarrel between a popular Korys model and her broker husband.

"What really happened?" Fowler asked mildly.

"None of your business," Veronica told him with fine illogic. "You ought to know! You were behind it—you know you were! You and that half-wit of yours, that Norman. You think I don't know? With all those fool inventions you two work out, I know perfectly well you must have done *something*—"

"Veronica, you're raving."

She was, of course. It was sheer hysteria, plus her normal conviction that no unpleasant thing that happened to her could possibly be her own fault. By pure accident she had hit upon the truth, but that was beside the point.

"Has he left you? Is that it?" Fowler demanded.

She gave him a look of hatred. But she nodded. "It's your fault and you've got to help me. I need money. I—"

"All right, all right! You're hysterical, but I'll help you. Where are you? I'll pick you up and we'll have a drink and talk things over. You're better off than you know, baby. He never was the man for you. You haven't got a thing to worry about. I'll be there in half an hour and we can pick up where we left off three years ago."

Part of what he implied was true enough, he reflected as he switched off the television screen. Curiously, he still meant to marry her. The changed face with its querulous lines and corded throat repelled him, but you don't argue with an obsession. He had worked three years toward this moment, and he still meant to marry Veronica Barnaby as he had originally meant to marry Veronica Wood. Afterward—well, things might be different.

One thing frightened him. She was not quite as stupid as he had gambled on that day years ago when he had been forced to call on her for help with Norman. She had seen too much, deduced too much—remembered much too much. She might be dangerous. He would have to find out just what she thought she knew about him and Norman.

It might be necessary to silence her, in one way or another.

* * *

Norman said with painful distinctness: "Must tell you . . . *must*—"

"No, Norman." Fowler spoke hastily. "We have a job to do. There isn't time now to discuss—"

"Can't work," Norman said. "No . . . *must* tell you—" He paused, lifted a shaking hand to his eyes, grimacing against his own palm with a look of terrible effort and entreaty. The strength that was mysteriously returning to him at intervals now had made him almost a human being again. The blankness of his face flooded sometimes with almost recognizable individuality.

"Not yet, Norman!" Fowler heard the alarm in his own voice. "I need you. Later we'll work out whatever it is you're trying to say. Not now. I . . . look, we've got to reverse that lighting system we made for Veronica. I want a set of lights that will flatter her. I need it in a hurry, Norman. You'll have to get to work on it right away."

Norman looked at him with hollow eyes. Fowler didn't like it. He would not meet the look. He focused on Norman's forehead as he repeated his instructions in a patient voice.

Behind that colorless forehead the being that was Norman must be hammering against its prison walls of bone, striving hard to escape. Fowler shook off the fanciful idea in distaste, repeated his orders once more and left the house in some haste. Veronica would be waiting.

But the look in Norman's eyes haunted him all the way into the city. Dark, hollow, desperate. The prisoner in the skull, shut into a claustrophobic cell out of which no sound could carry. He was getting dangerously strong, that prisoner. It would be a mercy in the long run if some task were set to exhaust him, throw him back into that catatonic state in which he no longer knew he was in prison.

Veronica was not there. He waited for an hour in the bar. Then he called her apartment, and got no answer. He tried his own house, and no one seemed to be there either. With unreasonably mounting uneasiness, he went home at last.

She met him at the door.

"Veronica! I waited for an hour! What's the idea?"

She only smiled at him. There was an almost frightening triumph in the smile, but she did not speak a word.

Fowler pushed past her, fighting his own sinking sensation of alarm. He called for Norman almost automatically, as if his unconscious mind recognized before the conscious knew just what the worst danger might be. For Veronica might be stupid but he had perhaps forgotten how cunning the stupid sometimes are. Veronica could put two and two together very well. She could reason from cause to effect quite efficiently, when her own welfare was at stake.

She had reasoned extremely well today.

Norman lay on the bed in his windowless room, his face as blank as paper. Some effort of the mind and will had exhausted him out of all semblance to a rational being. Some new, some overwhelming task, set him by—Veronica? Not by Fowler. The job he had been working on an hour ago was no such killing job as this.

But would Norman obey anyone except Fowler? He had defied Veronica on that other occasion when she tried to give him orders. He had almost escaped before Fowler's commanding voice ordered him back. Wait, though—she had coaxed him. Fowler remembered now. She could not command, but she had coaxed the blank creature into obedience. So there was a way. And she knew it.

But what had the task been?

With long strides Fowler went back into the drop-shaped living room. Veronica stood in the doorway where he had left her. She was waiting.

"What did you do?" he demanded.

She smiled. She said nothing at all.

"What happened?" Fowler cried urgently. "Veronica, answer me! What did you do?"

"I talked to Norman," she said. "I . . . got him to do a little job for me. That was all. Good-by, John."

"Wait! You can't leave like that. I've got to know what happened. I—"

"You'll find out," Veronica said. She gave him that thin smile again and then the door closed behind her. He heard her heels click once or twice on the walk and she was gone. There was nothing he could do about it.

He didn't know what she had accomplished. That was the terrifying thing. She had talked to Norman— And Norman had been in an almost coherent mood today. If she asked the right questions, she could have learned—almost anything. About the magic window and the supersonics and the lighting. About Norman himself. About—even about a weapon she could use against Fowler. Norman would make one if he were told to. He was an automaton. He could not reason; he could only comply.

Perhaps she had a weapon, then. But what? Fowler knew nothing at all of Veronica's mind. He had no idea what sort of revenge she might take if she had a field as limitless as Norman's talents offered her. Fowler had never been interested in Veronica's mind at all. He had no idea what sort of being crouched there behind her forehead as the prisoner crouched behind Norman's. He only knew that it would have a thin smile and that it hated him.

"You'll find out," Veronica had said. But it was several days before he did, and even then he could not be sure. So many things could have been accidental. Although he tried desperately he could not find Veronica anywhere in the city. But he kept thinking her eyes were on him, that if he could turn quickly enough he would catch her staring.

"That's what makes voodoo magic work," he told himself savagely. "A man can scare himself to death, once he knows he's been threatened—"

Death, of course, had nothing to do with it. Clearly it was no part of her plan that her enemy should die—and escape her. She knew what Fowler would hate most—ridicule.

Perhaps the things that kept happening were accidents. The time he tripped over nothing and did a foolishly clownish fall for the amusement of a long line of people waiting before a ticket window. His ears burned whenever he remembered that. Or the time he had three embarrassing slips of the tongue in a row when he was trying to make a good impression on a congressman and his pompous wife in connection with a patent. Or the time in the Biltmore dining room when he dropped every dish or glass he touched, until the whole room was staring at him and the head-waiter was clearly of two minds about throwing him out.

It was like a perpetual time bomb. He never knew what would happen next, or when or where. And it was certainly sheer imagination that made him think he could hear Veronica's clear, high, ironic laughter whenever his own body betrayed him into one of these ridiculous series of slips.

He tried shaking the truth out of Norman.

"What did you do?" he demanded of the blank, speechless face. "What did she make you do? Is there something wrong with my synapses now? Did you rig up something that would throw me out of control whenever she wants me to? *What did you do, Norman?*"

But Norman could not tell him.

On the third day she televised the house. Fowler went limp with relief when he saw her features taking shape in the screen. But before he could speak she said sharply: "All right, John. I only have a minute to waste on you. I just wanted you to know I'm *really* going to start to work on you beginning next week. That's all, John. Good-by."

The screen would not make her face form again no matter how sharply he rapped on it, no matter how furiously he jabbed the buttons to call her back. After awhile he relaxed limply in his chair and sat staring blankly at the wall. And now he began to be afraid—

It had been a long time since Fowler faced a crisis in which he could not turn to Norman for help. And Norman was no use to him now. He could not or would not produce a device that Fowler could use as protection against the nameless threat. He could give him no inkling of what weapon he had put in Veronica's hand.

It might be a bluff. Fowler could not risk it. He had changed a great deal in three years, far more than he had realized until this crisis arose. There had been a time when his mind was flexible enough to assess dangers coolly and resourceful enough to produce alternative measures to meet them. But not any more. He had depended too long on Norman to solve all his problems for him. Now he was helpless. Unless—

He glanced again at that stunning alternative and then glanced mentally away, impatient, knowing it for an impossibility. He had thought of it often in the past week, but of course it couldn't be done. Of course—

He got up and went into the windowless room where Norman sat quietly, staring at nothing. He leaned against the door frame and looked at Norman. There in that shuttered skull lay a secret more precious than any miracle Norman had yet produced. The brain, the mind, the source. The mysterious quirk that brought forth golden eggs.

"There's a part of your brain in use that normal brains don't have," Fowler said thoughtfully aloud. Norman did not stir. "Maybe you're a freak. Maybe you're a mutation. But there's something like a thermostat in your head. When it's activated, your mind's activated, too. You don't use the same brain-centers I do. You're an idling motor. When the supercharger cuts in *something* begins to work along lines of logic I don't understand. I see the result, but I don't know what the method is. If I could know that—"

He paused and stared piercingly at the bent head. "If I could only get that secret out of you, Norman! It's no good to you. But there isn't any limit to what *I* could do with it if I had your secret and my own brain."

If Norman heard he made no motion to show it. But some impulse suddenly goaded Fowler to action. "I'll do it!" he declared. "I'll try it! What have I got to lose, anyhow? I'm a prisoner here as long as this goes on, and Norman's no good to me the way things stand. It's worth a try."

He shook the silent man by the shoulder. "Norman, wake up. Wake up, wake up, wake up. Norman, do you hear me? Wake up, Norman, we have work to do."

Slowly, out of infinite distances, the prisoner returned to his cell, crept forward in the bone cage of the skull and looked dully at Fowler out of deep sockets.

And Fowler was seized with a sudden, immense astonishment that until now he had never really considered this most obvious of courses. Norman could do it. He was quite confident of that, suddenly. Norman could and must do it. This was the point toward which they had both been moving ever since Norman first rang the doorbell years ago. It had taken Veronica and a crisis to make the thing real. But now was the time—time and past time for the final miracle.

Fowler was going to become sufficient unto himself.

"You're going to get a nice long rest, Norman," he said kindly. "You're going to help me learn to . . . to think the way you think. Do you understand, Norman? Do you know what it is that makes your brain work the way it does? I want you to help my brain think that way, too. Afterward, you can rest, Norman. A nice, long rest. I won't be needing you any more after that, Norman."

Norman worked for twenty-four hours without a break. Watching him, forcing down the rising excitement in his mind, Fowler thought the blank man too seemed overwrought at this last and perhaps greatest of all his tasks. He mumbled a good deal over the intricate wiring of the thing he was twisting together. It looked rather like a tesseract, an open, interlocking framework which Norman handled with great care. From time to time he looked up and seemed to want to talk, to protest. Fowler ordered him sternly back to his task.

When it was finished it looked a little like the sort of turban a sultan might wear. It even had a jewel set in the front, like a headlight, except that this jewel really was light. All the wires came together there, and out of nowhere the bluish radiance sprang, shimmering softly in its little nest of wiring just above the forehead. It made Fowler think of an eye gently opening and closing. A thoughtful eye that looked up at him from between Norman's hands.

At the last moment Norman hesitated. His face was gray with exhaustion as he bent above Fowler, holding out the turban. Like Charlemagne, Fowler reached impatiently for the thing and set it on his own head. Norman bent reluctantly to adjust it.

There was a singing moment of anticipation—

The turban was feather-light on his head, but wherever it touched it made his scalp ache a bit, as if every hair had been pulled the wrong way. The aching grew. It wasn't only the hair that was going the wrong way, he realized suddenly—

It wasn't only his hair, but his mind—

It wasn't only—

Out of the wrenching blur that swallowed up the room he saw Norman's anxious face take shape, leaning close. He felt the crown of wire lifted from his head. Through a violent, blinding ache he watched Norman grimace with bewilderment.

"No," Norman said. "No . . . wrong . . . *you* . . . wrong—"

"I'm wrong?" Fowler shook his head a little and the pain subsided, but not the feeling of singing anticipation, nor the impatient disappointment at this delay. Any moment now might bring some interruption, might even bring some new, unguessable threat from Veronica that could ruin everything.

"What's wrong?" he asked, schooling himself to patience. "Me? How am I wrong, Norman? Didn't anything happen?"

"No. Wrong . . . *you*—"

"Wait, now." Fowler had had to help work out problems like this before. "O.K., I'm wrong. How?" He glanced around the room. "Wrong room?" he suggested at random. "Wrong chair? Wrong wiring? Do I have to co-operate somehow?" The last question seemed to strike a response. "Co-operate how? Do you need help with the wiring? Do I have to do something after the helmet's on?"

"Think!" Norman said violently.

"I have to think?"

"No. Wrong, wrong. Think wrong."

"I'm thinking wrong?"

Norman made a gesture of despair and turned away toward his room, carrying the wire turban with him.

Fowler, rubbing his forehead where the wires had pressed, wondered dizzily what had happened. *Think wrong*. It didn't make sense. He looked at himself in the television screen, which was a mirror when not in use, fingered the red line of the turban's pressure, and murmured, "Thinking, something to do with thinking. What?" Apparently the turban was designed to alter his patterns of thought, to open up some dazzling door through which he could perceive the new causalities that guided Norman's mind.

He thought that in some way it was probably connected with that moment when the helmet had seemed to wrench first his hair and then his skull and then his innermost thoughts in the wrong direction. But he couldn't work it out. He was too tired. All the emotional strain of the past days, the menace still hanging over him, the tremulous excitement of what lay in the immediate future—no, he couldn't be expected to reason things through very clearly just now. It was Norman's job. Norman would have to solve that problem for them both.

Norman did. He came out of his room in a few minutes, carrying the turban, twisted now into a higher, rounder shape, the gem of light glowing bluer than before. He approached Fowler with a firm step.

"You . . . thinking wrong," he said with great distinctness. "Too . . . too old. Can't change. Think wrong!"

He stared anxiously at Fowler and Fowler stared back, searching the deep-set eyes for some clue to the meaning hidden in the locked chambers of the skull behind them.

"Thinking wrong." Fowler echoed. "Too . . . old? I don't understand. Or—do I? You mean my mind isn't flexible enough any more?" He remembered the wrenching moment when every mental process had tried vainly to turn sidewise in his head. "But then it won't work at all!"

"Oh, yes," Norman said confidently.

"But if I'm too old—" It wasn't age, really. Fowler was not old in years. But the grooves of his thinking had worn themselves deep in the past years since Norman came. He had fixed inflexibly in the paths of his own self-indulgence and now his mind could not accept the answer the wire turban offered. "I can't change," he told Norman despairingly. "If I'd only made you do this when you first came, before my mind set in its pattern—"

Norman held out the turban, reversed so that the blue light bathed his face in blinking radiance. "This—will work," he said confidently.

Belated caution made Fowler dodge back a little. "Now wait. I want to know more before we . . . how *can* it work? You can't make me any younger, and I don't want any random tampering with my brain. I—"

Norman was not listening. With a swift, sure gesture he pressed the wired wreath down on Fowler's head.

There was the wrenching of hair and scalp, skull and brain. This first—and then very swiftly the shadows moved upon the floor, the sun gleamed for one moment through the eastern windows and the world darkened outside. The darkness winked and was purple, was dull red, was daylight—

Fowler could not stir. He tried furiously to snatch the turban from his head, but no impulse from his brain made any connection with the motionless limbs. He still stood facing the mirror, the blue light still winked thoughtfully back at him, but everything moved so fast he had no time to comprehend light or dark for what they were, or the blurred motions reflected in the glass, or what was happening to him.

This was yesterday, and the week before, and the year before, but he did not clearly know it. *You can't make me any younger*. Very dimly he remembered having said that to Norman at some remote interval of time. His thoughts moved sluggishly somewhere at the very core of his brain, whose outer layers were being peeled off one by one, hour by hour, day by day. But Norman could make him younger. Norman *was* making him younger. Norman was whisking him back and back toward the moment when his brain would regain flexibility enough for the magical turban to open that door to genius.

Those blurs in the mirror were people moving at normal time-speed—himself, Norman, Veronica going forward in time as he slipped backward through it, neither perceiving the other. But twice he saw Norman moving through the room at a speed that matched his own, walking slowly and looking for something. He saw him search behind a chair-cushion and pull out a creased folder, legal size—the folder he had last sent Norman to find, on that day when he vanished from his closed room!

Norman, then, had traveled in time before. Norman's powers must be more far-reaching, more dazzling, than he had ever guessed. As his own powers would be, when his mind cleared again and this blinding flicker stopped.

Night and day went by like the flapping of a black wing. That was the way Wells had put it. That was the way it looked. A hypnotic flapping. It left him dazed and dull—

Norman, holding the folder, lifted his head and for one instant looked Fowler in the face in the glass. Then he turned and went away through time to another meeting in another interval that would lead backward again to this meeting, and on and on around a closing spiral which no mind could fully comprehend.

It didn't matter. Only one thing really mattered. Fowler stood there shocked for an instant into almost total wakefulness, staring at his own face in the mirror, remembering Norman's face.

For one timeless moment, while night and day flapped around him, he stood helpless, motionless, staring appalled at his reflection in the gray that was the blending of time—and he knew who Norman was.

Then mercifully the hypnosis took over again and he knew nothing at all.

There are centers in the brain never meant for man's use today. Not until the race has evolved the strength to handle them. A man of today might learn the secret that would unlock those centers, and if he were a fool he might even turn the key that would let the door swing open.

But after that he would do nothing at all of his own volition.

For modern man is still too weak to handle the terrible energy that must pour forth to activate those centers. The grossly overloaded physical and mental connections could hold for only a fraction of a second. Then the energy flooding into the newly unlocked brain-center never meant for use until perhaps a thousand more years have remodeled mankind, would collapse the channels, fuse the connections, make every synapse falter in the moment when the gates of the mind swing wide.

On Fowler's head the turban of wires glowed incandescent and vanished. The thing that had once happened to Norman happened now to him. The dazzling revelation—the draining, the atrophy—

He had recognized Norman's face reflected in the mirror beside his own, both white with exhaustion, both stunned and empty. He knew who Norman was, what motives moved him, what corroding irony had made his punishing of Norman just. But by the time he knew, it was already far too late to alter the future or the past.

Time flapped its wings more slowly. That moment of times gone swung round again as the circle came to its close. Memories flickered more and more dimly in Fowler's mind, like day and night, like the vague, shapeless world which was all he could perceive now. He felt cold and weak, strangely, intolerably, inhumanly weak with a weakness of the blood and bone, of the mind and soul. He saw his surroundings dimly, but he saw—other things—with a swimming clarity that had no meaning to him. He saw causes and effects as tangible before him as he had once seen trees and grass. But remote, indifferent, part of another world.

Help was what he needed. There was something he must remember. Something of terrible import. He must find help, to focus his mind upon the things that would work his cure. Cure was possible; he knew it—he knew it. But he needed help.

Somehow there was a door before him. He reached vaguely, moving his hand almost by reflex toward his pocket. But he had no pocket. This was a suit of the new fashion, sleek in fabric, cut without pockets. He would have to knock, to ring. He remembered—

The face he had seen in the mirror. His own face? But even then it had been changing, as a cloud before the sun drains life and color and soul from a landscape. The expunging amnesia wiped across its mind had had its parallel physically, too; the traumatic shock of moving through time—*the dark wing flapping*—had sponged the recognizable characteristics from his face, leaving the matrix, the characterless basic. This was not his face. He had no face; he had no memory. He knew only that this familiar door before him was the door to the help he must have to save himself from a circling eternity.

It was almost wholly a reflex gesture that moved his finger toward the doorbell. The last dregs of memory and initiative drained from him with the motion.

Again the chimes played three soft notes. Again the circle closed.

Again the blank man waited for John Fowler to open the door.

ALIEN EARTH

by Edmond Hamilton (1904–1977)

***Thrilling Wonder Stories*, April**

Isaac mentions that Edmond Hamilton was known as the "Universe-saver," but he was also known to "wreck" a few in his day. Indeed, he was (and is, thank goodness) so well known for his space opera that his fine work in other areas of science fiction is not nearly as famous as it ought to be.

"Alien Earth" is an excellent example of this relative obscurity, a wonderful, moody story that is science fiction at its finest. Amazingly, it has only been reprinted twice—in The Best of Edmond Hamilton *(1977) and in the anthology* Alien Earth and Other Stories *(1969). It is a pleasure to reprint it again.—M.H.G.*

(There are "great dyings" in the course of biological evolution, periods when in a comparatively short interval of time, a large fraction of the species of living things on Earth die. The most recent example was the period at the end of the Cretaceous, 65,000,000 years ago.

I have often thought there are also "great dyings" in the history of science fiction, periods when large percentages of the established science fiction writers stopped appearing. The most dramatic example came in 1938, when John Campbell became editor of Astounding *and introduced an entirely new stable of writers, replacing the old.*

Some old-timers survived, of course (even as some species always survived the biological "great dyings"). To me, one of the most remarkable survivors was Edmond Hamilton. He was one of the great stars of the pre-Campbell era, so grandiose in his plots that he was known as the "Universe-saver." And yet he was able to narrow his focus and survive, whereas many others who seemed to require a smaller re-adaptation could not do so. In "Alien Earth" there is no Universe being saved; there is only a close look at the world of plants.—I.A.)

CHAPTER 1

Slowed-down Life

The dead man was standing in a little moonlit clearing in the jungle when Farris found him.

He was a small swart man in white cotton, a typical Laos tribesman of this Indo-China hinterland. He stood without support, eyes open, staring unwinkingly ahead, one foot slightly raised. And he was not breathing.

"But he can't be dead!" Farris exclaimed. "Dead men don't stand around in the jungle."

He was interrupted by Piang, his guide. That cocksure little Annamese had been losing his impudent self-sufficiency ever since they had wandered off the trail. And the motionless, standing dead man had completed his demoralization.

Ever since the two of them had stumbled into this grove of silk-cotton trees and almost run into the dead man, Piang had been goggling in a scared way at the still unmoving figure. Now he burst out volubly:

"The man is *hunati!* Don't touch him! We must leave here—we have strayed into a bad part of the jungle!"

Farris didn't budge. He had been a teak-hunter for too many years to be entirely skeptical of the superstitions of Southeast Asia. But, on the other hand, he felt a certain responsibility.

"If this man isn't really dead, then he's in bad shape somehow and needs help," he declared.

"No, no!" Piang insisted. "He is *hunati!* Let us leave here quickly!"

Pale with fright, he looked around the moonlit grove. They were on a low plateau where the jungle was monsoon-forest rather than rain-forest. The big silk-cotton and ficus trees were less choked with brush and creepers here, and they could see along dim forest aisles to gigantic distant banyans that loomed like dark lords of the silver silence.

Silence. There was too much of it to be quite natural. They could faintly hear the usual clatter of birds and monkeys from down in the lowland thickets, and the cough of a tiger echoed from the Laos foothills. But the thick forest here on the plateau was hushed.

Farris went to the motionless, staring tribesman and gently touched his thin brown wrist. For a few moments, he felt no pulse. Then he caught its throb—an incredibly slow beating.

"About one beat every two minutes," Farris muttered. "How the devil can he keep living?"

He watched the man's bare chest. It rose—but so slowly that his eye could hardly detect the motion. It remained expanded for minutes. Then, as slowly, it fell again.

He took his pocket-light and flashed it into the tribesman's eyes.

There was no reaction to the light, not at first. Then, slowly, the eyelids crept down and closed, and stayed closed, and finally crept open again.

"A wink—but a hundred times slower than normal!" Farris exclaimed. "Pulse, respiration, reactions—they're all a hundred times slower. The man has either suffered a shock, or been drugged."

Then he noticed something that gave him a little chill.

The tribesman's eyeball seemed to be turning with infinite slowness toward him. And the man's raised foot was a little higher now. As though he were walking—but walking at a pace a hundred times slower than normal.

The thing was eery. There came something more eery. A sound—the sound of a small stick cracking.

Piang exhaled breath in a sound of pure fright, and pointed off into the grove. In the moonlight Farris saw.

There was another tribesman standing a hundred feet away. He, too, was motionless. But his body was bent forward in the attitude of a runner suddenly frozen. And beneath his foot, the stick had cracked.

"They worship the great ones, by the Change!" said the Annamese in a hoarse undertone. "We must not interfere!"

That decided Farris. He had, apparently, stumbled on some sort of weird jungle rite. And he had had too much experience with Asiatic natives to want to blunder into their private religious mysteries.

His business here in easternmost Indo-China was teak-hunting. It would be difficult enough back in this wild hinterland without antagonizing the tribes. These strangely dead-alive men, whatever drug or compulsion they were suffering from, could not be in danger if others were near.

"We'll go on," Farris said shortly.

Piang led hastily down the slope of the forested plateau. He went through the brush like a scared deer, till they hit the trail again.

"This is it—the path to the Government station," he said, in great relief. "We must have lost it back at the ravine. I have not been this far back in Laos, many times."

Farris asked, "Piang, what is *hunati?* This Change that you were talking about?"

The guide became instantly less voluble. "It is a rite of worship." He added, with some return of his cocksureness, "These tribesmen are very ignorant. They have not been to mission school, as I have."

"Worship of what?" Farris asked. "The great ones, you said. Who are they?"

Piang shrugged and lied readily. "I do not know. In all the great forest, there are men who can become *hunati,* it is said. How, I do not know."

Farris pondered, as he tramped onward. There had been something uncanny about those tribesmen. It had been almost a suspension of animation—but not quite. Only an incredible slowing down.

What could have caused it? And what, possibly, could be the purpose of it?

"I should think," he said, "that a tiger or snake would make short work of a man in that frozen condition."

Piang shook his head vigorously. "No. A man who is *hunati* is safe—at least, from beasts. No beast would touch him."

Farris wondered. Was that because the extreme motionlessness made the beasts ignore them? He supposed that it was some kind of fear-ridden nature-worship. Such animistic beliefs were common in this part of the world. And it was small wonder, Farris thought a little grimly. Nature, here in the tropical forest, wasn't the smiling goddess of temperate lands. It was something, not to be loved, but to be feared.

He ought to know! He had had two days of the Laos jungle since leaving the upper Mekong, when he had expected that one would take him to the French Government botanic survey station that was his goal.

He brushed stinging winged ants from his sweating neck, and wished that they had stopped at sunset. But the map had showed them but a few miles from the Station. He had not counted on

Piang losing the trail. But he should have, for it was only a wretched track that wound along the forested slope of the plateau.

The hundred-foot ficus, dyewood and silk-cotton trees smothered the moonlight. The track twisted constantly to avoid impenetrable bamboo-hells or to ford small streams, and the tangle of creepers and vines had a devilish deftness at tripping one in the dark.

Farris wondered if they had lost their way again. And he wondered not for the first time, why he had ever left America to go into teak.

"That is the Station," said Piang suddenly, in obvious relief.

Just ahead of them on the jungled slope was a flat ledge. Light shone there, from the windows of a rambling bamboo bungalow.

Farris became conscious of all his accumulated weariness, as he went the last few yards. He wondered whether he could get a decent bed here, and what kind of chap this Berreau might be who had chosen to bury himself in such a Godforsaken post of the botanical survey.

The bamboo house was surrounded by tall, graceful dyewoods. But the moonlight showed a garden around it, enclosed by a low sappan hedge.

A voice from the dark veranda reached Farris and startled him. It startled him because it was a girl's voice, speaking in French.

"Please, Andre! Don't go again! It is madness!"

A man's voice rapped harsh answer, *"Lys, tais-toi! Je reviendrai—"*

Farris coughed diplomatically and then said up to the darkness of the veranda, "Monsieur Berreau?"

There was a dead silence. Then the door of the house was swung open so that light spilled out on Farris and his guide.

By the light, Farris saw a man of thirty, bareheaded, in whites—a thin, rigid figure. The girl was only a white blur in the gloom.

He climbed the steps. "I suppose you don't get many visitors. My name is Hugh Farris. I have a letter for you, from the Bureau at Saigon."

There was a pause. Then, "If you will come inside, M'sieu Farris—"

In the lamplit, bamboo-walled living room, Farris glanced quickly at the two.

Berreau looked to his experienced eye like a man who had stayed too long in the tropics—his blond handsomeness tarnished by a corroding climate, his eyes too feverishly restless.

"My sister, Lys," he said, as he took the letter Farris handed.

Farris' surprise increased. A wife, he had supposed until now. Why should a girl under thirty bury herself in this wilderness?

He wasn't surprised that she looked unhappy. She might have been a decently pretty girl, he thought, if she didn't have that woebegone anxious look.

"Will you have a drink?" she asked him. And then, glancing with swift anxiety at her brother, "You'll not be going now, Andre?"

Berreau looked out at the moonlit forest, and a queer, hungry tautness showed his cheekbones in a way Farris didn't like. But the Frenchman turned back.

"No, Lys. And drinks, please. Then tell Ahra to care for his guide."

He read the letter swiftly, as Farris sank with a sigh into a rattan chair. He looked up from it with troubled eyes.

"So you come for teak?"

Farris nodded. "Only to spot and girdle trees. They have to stand a few years then before cutting, you know."

Berreau said, "The Commissioner writes that I am to give you every assistance. He explains the necessity of opening up new teak cuttings."

He slowly folded the letter. It was obvious, Farris thought, that the man did not like it, but had to make the best of orders.

"I shall do everything possible to help," Berreau promised. "You'll want a native crew, I suppose. I can get one for you." Then a queer look filmed his eyes. "But there are some forests here that are impracticable for lumbering. I'll go into that later."

Farris, feeling every moment more exhausted by the long tramp, was grateful for the rum and soda Lys handed him.

"We have a small extra room—I think it will be comfortable," she murmured.

He thanked her. "I could sleep on a log, I'm so tired. My muscles are as stiff as though I were *hunati* myself."

Berreau's glass dropped with a sudden crash.

CHAPTER 2

Sorcery of Science

Ignoring the shattered glass, the young Frenchman strode quickly toward Farris.

"What do you know of *huanti?*" he asked harshly.

Farris saw with astonishment that the man's hands were shaking.

"I don't know anything except what we saw in the forest. We came upon a man standing in the moonlight who looked dead, and wasn't. He just seemed incredibly slowed down. Piang said he was *hunati*."

A flash crossed Berreau's eyes. He exclaimed, "I knew the Rite would be called! And the others are there—"

He checked himself. It was as though the unaccustomedness of strangers had made him for a moment forget Farris' presence.

Lys' blonde head drooped. She looked away from Farris.

"You were saying?" the American prompted.

But Berreau had tightened up. He chose his words now. "The Laos tribes have some queer beliefs, M'sieu Farris. They're a little hard to understand."

Farris shrugged. "I've seen some queer Asian witchcraft, in my time. But this is unbelievable!"

"It is science, not witchcraft," Berreau corrected. "Primitive science, born long ago and transmitted by tradition. That man you saw in the forest was under the influence of a chemical not found in our pharmacopeia, but nonetheless potent."

"You mean that these tribesmen have a drug that can slow the life-process to that incredibly slow tempo?" Farris asked skeptically. "One that modern science doesn't know about?"

"Is that so strange? Remember, M'sieu Farris, that a century ago an old peasant woman in England was curing heart-disease with foxglove, before a physician studied her cure and discovered digitalis."

"But why on earth would even a Laos tribesman want to live so much *slower?*" Farris demanded.

"Because," Berreau answered, "they believe that in that state they can commune with something vastly greater than themselves."

Lys interrupted. "M'sieu Farris must be very weary. And his bed is ready."

Farris saw the nervous fear in her face, and realized that she wanted to end this conversation.

He wondered about Berreau, before he dropped off to sleep. There was something odd about the chap. He had been too excited about this *hunati* business.

Yet that was weird enough to upset anyone, that incredible and uncanny slowing-down of a human being's life-tempo. "To commune with something vastly greater than themselves," Berreau had said.

What gods were so strange that a man must live a hundred times slower than normal, to commune with them?

Next morning, he breakfasted with Lys on the broad veranda. The girl told him that her brother had already gone out.

"He will take you later today to the tribal village down in the valley, to arrange for your workers," she said.

Farris noted the faint unhappiness still in her face. She looked silently at the great, green ocean of forest that stretched away below this plateau on whose slope they were.

"You don't like the forest?" he ventured.

"I hate it," she said. "It smothers one, here."

Why, he asked, didn't she leave? The girl shrugged.

"I shall, soon. It is useless to stay. Andre will not go back with me."

She explained. "He has been here five years too long. When he didn't return to France, I came out to bring him. But he won't go. He has ties here now."

Again, she became abruptly silent. Farris discreetly refrained from asking her what ties she meant. There might be an Annamese woman in the background—though Berreau didn't look that type.

The day settled down to the job of being stickily tropical, and the hot still hours of the morning wore on. Farris, sprawling in a chair and getting a welcome rest, waited for Berreau to return.

He didn't return. And as the afternoon waned, Lys looked more and more worried.

An hour before sunset, she came out onto the veranda, dressed in slacks and jacket.

"I am going down to the village—I'll be back soon," she told Farris.

She was a poor liar. Farris got to his feet. "You're going after your brother. Where is he?"

Distress and doubt struggled in her face. She remained silent.

"Believe me, I want to be a friend," Farris said quietly. "Your brother is mixed up in something here, isn't he?"

She nodded, white-faced. "It's why he wouldn't go back to France with me. He can't bring himself to leave. It's like a horrible fascinating vice."

"What is?"

She shook her head. "I can't tell you. Please wait here."

He watched her leave, and then realized she was not going down the slope but up it—up toward the top of the forested plateau.

He caught up to her in quick strides. "You can't go up into that forest alone, in a blind search for him."

"It's not a blind search. I think I know where he is," Lys whispered. "But you should not go there. The tribesmen wouldn't like it!"

Farris instantly understood. "That big grove up on top of the plateau, where we found the *hunati* natives?"

Her unhappy silence was answer enough. "Go back to the bungalow," he told her. "I'll find him."

She would not do that. Farris shrugged, and started forward. "Then we'll go together."

She hesitated, then came on. They went up the slope of the plateau, through the forest.

The westering sun sent spears and arrows of burning gold through chinks in the vast canopy of foliage under which they walked. The solid green of the forest breathed a rank, hot exhalation. Even the birds and monkeys were stifledly quiet at this hour.

"Is Berreau mixed up in that queer *hunati* rite?" Farris asked.

Lys looked up as though to utter a quick denial, but then dropped her eyes.

"Yes, in a way. His passion for botany got him interested in it. Now he's involved."

Farris was puzzled. "Why should botanical interest draw a man to that crazy drug-rite or whatever it is?"

She wouldn't answer that. She walked in silence until they reached the top of the forested plateau. Then she spoke in a whisper.

"We must be quiet now. It will be bad if we are seen here."

The grove that covered the plateau was pierced by horizontal bars of red sunset light. The great silk-cottons and ficus trees were pillars supporting a vast cathedral-nave of darkening green.

A little way ahead loomed up those huge, monster banyans he had glimpsed before in the moonlight. They dwarfed all the rest, towering bulks that were infinitely ancient and infinitely majestic.

Farris suddenly saw a Laos tribesman, a small brown figure, in the brush ten yards ahead of him. There were two others, farther in the distance. And they were all standing quite still, facing away from him.

They were *hunati*, he knew. In that queer state of slowed-down life, that incredible retardation of the vital processes.

Farris felt a chill. He muttered over his shoulder, "You had better go back down and wait."

"No," she whispered. "There is Andre."

He turned, startled. Then he too saw Berreau.

His blond head bare, his face set and white and masklike,

standing frozenly beneath a big wild-fig a hundred feet to the right.

Hunati!

Farris had expected it, but that didn't make it less shocking. It wasn't that the tribesmen mattered less as human beings. It was just that he had talked with a normal Berreau only a few hours before. And now, to see him like this!

Berreau stood in a position ludicrously reminiscent of the old-time "living statues." One foot was slightly raised, his body bent a little forward, his arms raised a little.

Like the frozen tribesmen ahead, Berreau was facing toward the inner recesses of the grove, where the giant banyans loomed.

Farris touched his arm. "Berreau, you have to snap out of this."

"It's no use to speak to him," whispered the girl. "He can't hear."

No, he couldn't hear. He was living at a tempo so low that no ordinary sound could make sense to his ears. His face was a rigid mask, lips slightly parted to breathe, eyes fixed ahead. Slowly, slowly, the lids crept down and veiled those staring eyes and then crept open again in the infinitely slow wink. Slowly, slowly, his slightly raised left foot moved down toward the ground.

Movement, pulse, breathing—all a hundred times slower than normal. Living, but not in a human way—not in a human way at all.

Lys was not so stunned as Farris was. He realized later that she must have seen her brother like this, before.

"We must take him back to the bungalow, somehow," she murmured. "I *can't* let him stay out here for many days and nights, again!"

Farris welcomed the small practical problem that took his thoughts for a moment away from this frozen, standing horror.

"We can rig a stretcher, from our jackets," he said. "I'll cut a couple of poles."

The two bamboos, through the sleeves of the two jackets, made a makeshift stretcher which they laid upon the ground.

Farris lifted Berreau. The man's body was rigid, muscles locked in an effort no less strong because it was infinitely slow.

He got the young Frenchman down on the stretcher, and then looked at the girl. "Can you help carry him? Or will you get a native?"

She shook her head. "The tribesmen mustn't know of this. Andre isn't heavy."

He wasn't. He was light as though wasted by fever, though the sickened Farris knew that it wasn't any fever that had done it.

Why should a civilized young botanist go out into the forest and partake of a filthy primitive drug of some kind that slowed him down to a frozen stupor? It didn't make sense.

Lys bore her share of their living burden through the gathering twilight, in stolid silence. Even when they put Berreau down at intervals to rest, she did not speak.

It was not until they reached the dark bungalow and had put him down on his bed, that the girl sank into a chair and buried her face in her hands.

Farris spoke with a rough encouragement he did not feel. "Don't get upset. He'll be all right now. I'll soon bring him out of this."

She shook her head. "No, you must not attempt that! He must come out of it by himself. And it will take many days."

The devil it would, Farris thought. He had teak to find, and he needed Berreau to arrange for workers.

Then the dejection of the girl's small figure got him. He patted her shoulder.

"All right, I'll help you take care of him. And together, we'll pound some sense into him and make him go back home. Now you see about dinner."

She lit a gasoline lamp, and went out. He heard her calling the servants.

He looked down at Berreau. He felt a little sick, again. The Frenchman lay, eyes staring toward the ceiling. He was living, breathing—and yet his retarded life-tempo cut him off from Farris as effectually as death would.

No, not quite. Slowly, so slowly that he could hardly detect the movement, Berreau's eyes turned toward Farris' figure.

Lys came back into the room. She was quiet, but he was getting to know her better, and he knew by her face that she was startled.

"The servants are gone! Ahra, and the girls—and your guide. They must have seen us bring Andre in."

Farris understood. "They left because we brought back a man who's *hunati?*"

She nodded. "All the tribespeople fear the rite. It's said there's only a few who belong to it, but they're dreaded."

Farris spared a moment to curse softly the vanished Annamese. "Piang would bolt like a scared rabbit, from something like this. A sweet beginning for my job here."

"Perhaps you had better leave," Lys said uncertainly. Then she added contradictorily, "No, I can't be heroic about it! Please stay!"

"That's for sure," he told her. "I can't go back down river and report that I shirked my job because of—"

He stopped, for she wasn't listening to him. She was looking past him, toward the bed.

Farris swung around. While they two had been talking, Berreau had been moving. Infinitely slowly—but moving.

His feet were on the floor now. He was getting up. His body straightened with a painful, dragging slowness, for many minutes.

Then his right foot began to rise almost imperceptibly from the floor. He was starting to walk, only a hundred times slower than normal.

He was starting to walk toward the door.

Lys' eyes had a yearning pity in them. "He is trying to go back up to the forest. He will try so long as he is *hunati*."

Farris gently lifted Berreau back to the bed. He felt a cold dampness on his forehead.

What was there up there that drew worshippers in a strange trance of slowed-down life?

CHAPTER 3

Unholy Lure

He turned to the girl and asked, "How long will he stay in this condition?"

"A long time," she answered heavily. "It may take weeks for the *hunati* to wear off."

Farris didn't like the prospect, but there was nothing he could do about it.

"All right, we'll take care of him. You and I."

Lys said, "One of us will have to watch him, all the time. He will keep trying to go back to the forest."

"You've had enough for a while," Farris told her. "I'll watch him tonight."

Farris watched. Not only that night but for many nights. The days went into weeks, and the natives still shunned the house, and he saw nobody except the pale girl and the man who was living in a different way than other humans lived.

Berreau didn't change. He didn't seem to sleep, nor did he

seem to need food or drink. His eyes never closed, except in that infinitely slow blinking.

He didn't sleep, and he did not quit moving. He was always moving, only it was in that weird, utterly slow-motion tempo that one could hardly see.

Lys had been right. Berreau wanted to go back to the forest. He might be living a hundred times slower than normal, but he was obviously still conscious in some weird way, and still trying to go back to the hushed, forbidden forest up there where they had found him.

Farris wearied of lifting the statue-like figure back into bed, and with the girl's permission tied Berreau's ankles. It did not make things much better. It was even more upsetting, in a way, to sit in the lamplit bedroom and watch Berreau's slow struggles for freedom.

The dragging slowness of each tiny movement made Farris' nerves twitch to see. He wished he could give Berreau some sedative to keep him asleep, but he did not dare to do that.

He had found, on Berreau's forearm, a tiny incision stained with sticky green. There were scars of other, old incisions near it. Whatever crazy drug had been injected into the man to make him *hunati* was unknown. Farris did not dare try to counteract its effect.

Finally, Farris glanced up one night from his bored perusal of an old *L'Illustration* and then jumped to his feet.

Berreau still lay on the bed, but he had just winked. Had winked with normal quickness, and not that slow, dragging blink.

"Berreau!" Farris said quickly. "Are you all right now? Can you hear me?"

Berreau looked up at him with a level, unfriendly gaze. "I can hear you. May I ask why you meddled?"

It took Farris aback. He had been playing nurse so long that he had unconsciously come to think of the other as a sick man who would be grateful to him. He realized now that Berreau was coldly angry, not grateful.

The Frenchman was untying his ankles. His movements were shaky, his hands trembling, but he stood up normally.

"Well?" he asked.

Farris shrugged. "Your sister was going up there after you. I helped her bring you back. That's all."

Berreau looked a little startled. "Lys did that? But it's a breaking of the Rite! It can mean trouble for her!"

Resentment and raw nerves made Farris suddenly brutal. "Why

should you worry about Lys now, when you've made her wretched for months by your dabbing in native wizardries?''

Berreau didn't retort angrily, as he had expected. The young Frenchman answered heavily.

''It's true. I've done that to Lys.''

Farris exclaimed, ''Berreau, why do you do it? Why this unholy business of going *hunati,* of living a hundred times slower? What can you gain by it?''

The other man looked at him with haggard eyes. ''By doing it, I've entered an alien world. A world that exists around us all our lives, but that we never live in or understand at all.''

''What world?''

''The world of green leaf and root and branch,'' Berreau answered. ''The world of plant life, which we can never comprehend because of the difference between its life-tempo and our life-tempo.''

Farris began dimly to understand. ''You mean, this *hunati* change makes you live at the same tempo as plants?''

Berreau nodded. ''Yes. And that simple difference in life-tempo is the doorway into an unknown, incredible world.''

''But how?''

The Frenchman pointed to the half-healed incision on his bare arm. ''The drug does it. A native drug, that slows down metabolism, heart-action, respiration, nerve-messages, everything.

''Chlorophyll is its basis. The green blood of plant-life, the complex chemical that enables plants to take their energy direct from sunlight. The natives prepare it directly from grasses, by some method of their own.''

''I shouldn't think,'' Farris said incredulously, ''that chlorophyll could have any effect on an animal organism.''

''Your saying that,'' Berreau retorted, ''shows that your biochemical knowledge is out of date. Back in March of Nineteen Forty-Eight, two Chicago chemists engaged in mass production or extraction of chlorophyll, announced that their injection of it into dogs and rats seemed to prolong life greatly by altering the oxidation capacity of the cells.

''Prolong life greatly—yes! But it prolongs it, by slowing it down! A tree lives longer than a man, because it doesn't live so fast. You can make a man live as long—*and as slowly*—as a tree, by injecting the right chlorophyll compound into his blood.''

Farris said, ''That's what you meant, by saying that primitive peoples sometimes anticipate modern scientific discoveries?''

Berreau nodded. ''This chlorophyll *hunati* solution may be an age-old secret. I believe it's always been known to a few among the primitive forest-folk of the world.''

He looked somberly past the American. ''Tree-worship is as old as the human race. The Sacred Tree of Sumeria, the groves of Dodona, the oaks of the Druids, the tree Ygdrasil of the Norse, even our own Christmas Tree—they all stem from primitive worship of that other, alien kind of life with which we share Earth.

''I think that a few secret worshippers have always known how to prepare the chlorophyll drug that enabled them to attain complete communion with that other kind of life, by living at the same slow rate for a time.''

Farris stared. ''But how did *you* get taken into this queer secret worship?''

The other man shrugged. ''The worshippers were grateful to me, because I had saved the forests here from possible death.''

He walked across to the corner of the room that was fitted as a botanical laboratory, and took down a test-tube. It was filled with dusty, tiny spores of a leprous, gray-green color.

''This is the Burmese Blight, that's withered whole great forests down south of the Mekong. A deadly thing, to tropical trees. It was starting to work up into this Laos country, but I showed the tribes how to stop it. The secret *hunati* sect made me one of them, in reward.''

''But I still can't understand why an educated man like you would want to join such a crazy mumbo-jumbo,'' Farris said.

''*Dieu,* I'm trying to make you understand why! To show you that it was my curiosity as a botanist that made me join the Rite and take the drug!''

Berreau rushed on. ''But you can't understand, any more than Lys could! You can't comprehend the wonder and strangeness and beauty of living that other kind of life!''

Something in Berreau's white, rapt face, in his haunted eyes, made Farris' skin crawl. His words seemed momentarily to lift a veil, to make the familiar vaguely strange and terrifying.

''Berreau, listen! You've got to cut this and leave here at once.''

The Frenchman smiled mirthlessly. ''I know. Many times, I have told myself so. But I do not go. How can I leave something that is a botanist's heaven?''

Lys had come into the room, was looking wanly at her brother's face.

''Andre, won't you give it up and go home with me?'' she appealed.

"Or are you too sunken in this uncanny habit to care whether your sister breaks her heart?" Farris demanded.

Berreau flared. "You're a smug pair! You treat me like a drug addict, without knowing the wonder of the experience I've had! I've gone into another world, an alien Earth that is around us every day of our lives and that we can't even see. And I'm going back again, and again."

"Use that chlorophyll drug and go *hunati* again?" Farris said grimly.

Berreau nodded defiantly.

"No," said Farris. "You're not. For if you do, we'll just go out there and bring you in again. You'll be quite helpless to prevent us, once you're *hunati*."

The other man raged. "There's a way I can stop you from doing that! Your threats are dangerous!"

"There's no way," Farris said flatly. "Once you've frozen yourself into that slower life-tempo, you're helpless against normal people. And I'm not threatening. I'm trying to save your sanity, man!"

Berreau flung out of the room without answer. Lys looked at the American, with tears glimmering in her eyes.

"Don't worry about it," he reassured her. "He'll get over it, in time."

"I fear not," the girl whispered. "It has become a madness in his brain."

Inwardly, Farris agreed. Whatever the lure of the unknown world that Berreau had entered by that change in life-tempo, it had caught him beyond all redemption.

A chill swept Farris when he thought of it—men out there, living at the same tempo as plants, stepping clear out of the plane of animal life to a strangely different kind of life and world.

The bungalow was oppressively silent that day—the servants gone, Berreau sulking in his laboratory, Lys moving about with misery in her eyes.

But Berreau didn't try to go out, though Farris had been expecting that and had been prepared for a clash. And by evening, Berreau seemed to have got over his sulks. He helped prepare dinner.

He was almost gay, at the meal—a febrile good humor that Farris didn't quite like. By common consent, none of the three spoke of what was uppermost in their minds.

Berreau retired, and Farris told Lys, "Go to bed—you've lost so much sleep lately you're half asleep now. I'll keep watch."

In his own room, Farris found drowsiness assailing him too.

He sank back in a chair, fighting the heaviness that weighed down his eyelids.

Then, suddenly, he understood. "Drugged!" he exclaimed, and found his voice little more than a whisper. "Something in the dinner!"

"Yes," said a remote voice. "Yes, Farris."

Berreau had come in. He loomed gigantic to Farris' blurred eyes. He came closer, and Farris saw in his hand a needle that dripped sticky green.

"I'm sorry, Farris." He was rolling up Farris' sleeve, and Farris could not resist. "I'm sorry to do this to you and Lys. But you *would* interfere. And this is the only way I can keep you from bringing me back."

Farris felt the sting of the needle. He felt nothing more, before drugged unconsciousness claimed him.

CHAPTER 4

Incredible World

Farris awoke, and for a dazed moment wondered what it was that so bewildered him. Then he realized.

It was the daylight. It came and went, every few minutes. There was the darkness of night in the bedroom, and then a sudden burst of dawn, a little period of brilliant sunlight, and then night again.

It came and went, as he watched numbly, like the slow, steady beating of a great pulse—a systole and diastole of light and darkness.

Days shortened to minutes? But how could that be? And then, as he awakened fully, he remembered.

"*Hunati!* He injected the chlorophyll drug into my bloodstream!"

Yes. He was *hunati*, now. Living at a tempo a hundred times slower than normal.

And that was why day and night seemed a hundred times faster than normal, to him. He had, already, lived through several days!

Farris stumbled to his feet. As he did so, he knocked his pipe from the arm of the chair.

It did not fall to the floor. It just disappeared instantly, and the next instant was lying on the floor.

"It fell. But it fell so fast I couldn't see it."

Farris felt his brain reel to the impact of the unearthly. He found that he was trembling violently.

He fought to get a grip on himself. This wasn't witchcraft. It was a secret and devilish science, but it wasn't supernatural.

He, himself, felt as normal as ever. It was his surroundings, the swift rush of day and night especially, that alone told him he was changed.

He heard a scream, and stumbled out to the living-room of the bungalow. Lys came running toward him.

She still wore her jacket and slacks, having obviously been too worried about her brother to retire completely. And there was terror in her face.

"What's happened?" she cried. "The light—"

He took her by the shoulders. "Lys, don't lose your nerve. What's happened is that we're *hunati* now. Your brother did it—drugged us at dinner, then injected the chlorophyll compound into us."

"But why?" she cried.

"Don't you see? He was going *hunati* himself again, going back up to the forest. And we could easily overtake and bring him back, if we remained normal. So he changed us too, to prevent that."

Farris went into Berreau's room. It was as he had expected. The Frenchman was gone.

"I'll go after him," he said tightly. "He's got to come back, for he may have an antidote to that hellish stuff. You wait here."

Lys clung to him. "No! I'd go mad, here by myself, like this."

She was, he saw, on the brink of hysterics. He didn't wonder. The slow, pulsing beat of day and night alone was enough to unseat one's reason.

He acceded. "All right. But wait till I get something."

He went back to Berreau's room and took a big bolo-knife he had seen leaning in a corner. Then he saw something else, something glittering in the pulsing light, on the botanist's laboratory-table.

Farris stuffed that into his pocket. If force couldn't bring Berreau back, the threat of this other thing might influence him.

He and Lys hurried out onto the veranda and down the steps. And then they stopped, appalled.

The great forest that loomed before them was now a nightmare sight. It seethed and stirred with unearthly life—great branches clawing and whipping at each other as they fought for the light, vines writhing through them at incredible speed, a rustling uproar of tossing, living plant-life.

Lys shrank back. "The forest is *alive* now!"

"It's just the same as always," Farris reassured. "It's we who have changed—who are living so slowly now that the plants seem to live faster."

"And Andre is out in that!" Lys shuddered. Then courage came back into her pale face. "But I'm not afraid."

They started up through the forest toward the plateau of giant trees. And now there was an awful unreality about this incredible world.

Farris felt no difference in himself. There was no sensation of slowing down. His own motions and perceptions appeared normal. It was simply that all around him the vegetation had now a savage motility that was animal in its swiftness.

Grasses sprang up beneath his feet, tiny green spears climbing toward the light. Buds swelled, burst, spread their bright petals on the air, breathed out their fragrance—and died.

New leaves leaped joyously up from every twig, lived out their brief and vital moment, withered and fell. The forest was a constantly shifting kaleidoscope of colors, from pale green to yellowed brown, that rippled as the swift tides of growth and death washed over it.

But it was not peaceful nor serene, that life of the forest. Before, it had seemed to Farris that the plants of the earth existed in a placid inertia utterly different from the beasts, who must constantly hunt or be hunted. Now he saw how mistaken he had been.

Close by, a tropical nettle crawled up beside a giant fern. Octopus-like, its tendrils flashed around and through the plant. The fern writhed. Its fronds tossed wildly, its stalks strove to be free. But the stinging death conquered it.

Lianas crawled like great serpents among the trees, encircling the trunks, twining themselves swiftly along the branches, striking their hungry parasitic roots into the living bark.

And the trees fought them. Farris could see how the branches lashed and struck against the killer vines. It was like watching a man struggle against the crushing coils of the python.

Very likely. Because the trees, the plants, knew. In their own strange, alien fashion, they were as sentient as their swifter brothers.

Hunter and hunted. The strangling lianas, the deadly, beautiful orchid that was like a cancer eating a healthy trunk, the leprous, crawling fungi—they were the wolves and the jackals of this leafy world.

Even among the trees, Farris saw, existence was a grim and never-ending struggle. Silk-cotton and bamboo and ficus trees—they too knew pain and fear and the dread of death.

He could hear them. Now, with his aural nerves slowed to an incredible receptivity, he heard the voice of the forest, the true voice that had nothing to do with the familiar sounds of wind in the branches.

The primal voice of birth and death that spoke before ever man appeared on Earth, and would continue to speak after he was gone.

At first he had been conscious only of that vast, rustling uproar. Now he could distinguish separate sounds—the thin screams of grass blades and bamboo-shoots thrusting and surging out of the earth, the lash and groan of enmeshed and dying branches, the laughter of young leaves high in the sky, the stealthy whisper of the coiling vines.

And almost, he could hear thoughts, speaking in his mind. The age-old thoughts of the trees.

Farris felt a freezing dread. He did not want to listen to the thoughts of the trees.

And the slow, steady pulsing of darkness and light went on. Days and nights, rushing with terrible speed over the *hunati*.

Lys, stumbling along the trail beside him, uttered a little cry of terror. A snaky black vine had darted out of the bush at her with cobra swiftness, looping swiftly to encircle her body.

Farris swung his bolo, slashed through the vine. But it struck out again, growing with that appalling speed, its tip groping for him.

He slashed again with sick horror, and pulled the girl onward, on up the side of the plateau.

"I am afraid!" she gasped. "I can hear the thoughts—the thoughts of the forest!"

"It's your own imagination!" he told her. "Don't listen!"

But he too could hear them! Very faintly, like sounds just below the threshold of hearing. It seemed to him that every minute—or every minute-long day—he was able to get more clearly the telepathic impulses of these organisms that lived an undreamed-of life of their own, side by side with man, yet forever barred from him, except when man was *hunati*.

It seemed to him that the temper of the forest had changed, that his slaying of the vine had made it aware of them. Like a crowd aroused to anger, the massed trees around them grew wrathful. A tossing and moaning rose among them.

Branches struck at Farris and the girl, lianas groped with blind heads and snakelike grace toward them. Brush and bramble clawed them spitefully, reaching out thorny arms to rake their flesh. The slender saplings lashed them like leafy whips, the swift-growing bamboo spears sought to block their path, canes clattering together as if in rage.

"It's only in our own minds!" he said to the girl. "Because the forest is living at the same rate as we, we imagine it's aware of us."

He had to believe that, he knew. He had to, because when he quit believing it there was only black madness.

"No!" cried Lys. "No! The forest knows we are here."

Panic fear threatened Farris' self-control, as the mad uproar of the forest increased. He ran, dragging the girl with him, sheltering her with his body from the lashing of the raging forest.

They ran on, deeper into the mighty grove upon the plateau, under the pulsing rush of day and darkness. And now the trees about them were brawling giants, great silk-cotton and ficus that struck crashing blows at each other as their branches fought for clear sky—contending and terrible leafy giants beneath which the two humans were pigmies.

But the lesser forest beneath them still tossed and surged with wrath, still plucked and tore at the two running humans. And still, and clearer, stronger, Farris' reeling mind caught the dim impact of unguessable telepathic impulses.

Then, drowning all those dim and raging thoughts, came vast and dominating impulses of greater majesty, thought-voices deep and strong and alien as the voice of primal Earth.

"Stop them!" they seemed to echo in Farris' mind. "Stop them! Slay them! For they are our enemies!"

Lys uttered a trembling cry. "Andre!"

Farris saw him, then. Saw Berreau ahead, standing in the shadow of the monster banyans there. His arms were upraised toward those looming colossi, as though in worship. Over him towered the leafy giants, dominating all the forest.

"Stop them! Slay them!"

They thundered, now, those majestic thought-voices that Farris' mind could barely hear. He was closer to them—closer—

He knew, then, even though his mind refused to admit the knowledge. Knew whence those mighty voices came, and why Berreau worshipped the banyans.

And surely they were godlike, these green colossi who had

lived for ages, whose arms reached skyward and whose aerial roots drooped and stirred and groped like hundreds of hands!

Farris forced that thought violently away. He was a man, of the world of men, and he must not worship alien lords.

Berreau had turned toward them. The man's eyes were hot and raging, and Farris knew even before Berreau spoke that he was no longer altogether sane.

"Go, both of you!" he ordered. "You were fools, to come here after me! You killed as you came through the forest, and the forest knows!"

"Berreau, listen!" Farris appealed. "You've got to go back with us, forget this madness!"

Berreau laughed shrilly. "Is it madness that the Lords even now voice their wrath against you? You hear it in your mind, but you are afraid to listen! Be afraid, Farris! There is reason! You have slain trees, for many years, as you have just slain here—and the forest knows you for a foe."

"Andre!" Lys was sobbing, her face half-buried in her hands.

Farris felt his mind cracking under the impact of the crazy scene. The ceaseless, rushing pulse of light and darkness, the rustling uproar of the seething forest around them, the vines creeping snakelike and branches whipping at them and giant banyans rocking angrily overhead.

"*This* is the world that man lives in all his life, and never sees or senses!" Berreau was shouting. "I've come into it, again and again. And each time, I've heard more clearly the voices of the Great Ones!

"The oldest and mightiest creatures on our planet! Long ago, men knew that and worshipped them for the wisdom they could teach. Yes, worshipped them as Ygdrasil and the Druid Oak and the Sacred Tree! But modern men have forgotten this other Earth. Except me, Farris—except me! I've found wisdom in this world such as you never dreamed. And your stupid blindness is not going to drag me out of it!"

Farris realized then that it was too late to reason with Berreau. The man had come too often and too far into this other Earth that was as alien to humanity as thought it lay across the universe.

It was because he had feared that, that he had brought the little thing in his jacket pocket. The one thing with which he might force Berreau to obey.

Farris took it out of his pocket. He held it up so that the other could see it.

"You know what it is, Berreau! And you know what I can do with it, if you force me to!"

Wild dread leaped into Berreau's eyes as he recognized that glittering little vial from his own laboratory.

"The Burmese Blight! You wouldn't, Farris! You wouldn't turn that loose *here!*"

"I will!" Farris said hoarsely. "I will, unless you come out of here with us, now!"

Raging hate and fear were in Berreau's eyes as he stared at that innocent corked glass vial of gray-green dust.

He said thickly, "For this, I will kill!"

Lys screamed. Black lianas had crept upon her as she stood with her face hidden in her hands. They had writhed around her legs like twining serpents, they were pulling her down.

The forest seemed to roar with triumph. Vine and branch and bramble and creeper surged toward them. Dimly thunderous throbbed the strange telepathic voices.

"Slay them!" said the trees.

Farris leaped into that coiling mass of vines, his bolo slashing. He cut loose the twining lianas that held the girl, sliced fiercely at the branches that whipped wildly at them.

Then, from behind, Berreau's savage blow on his elbow knocked the bolo from his hand.

"I told you not to kill, Farris! I told you!"

"Slay them!" pulsed the alien thought.

Berreau spoke, his eyes not leaving Farris. "Run, Lys. Leave the forest. This—murderer must die."

He lunged as he spoke, and there was death in his white face and clutching hands.

Farris was knocked back, against one of the giant banyan trunks. They rolled, grappling. And already the vines were sliding around them—looping and enmeshing them, tightening upon them!

It was then that the forest shrieked.

A cry telepathic and auditory at the same time—and dreadful. An utterance of alien agony beyond anything human.

Berreau's hands fell away from Farris. The Frenchman, enmeshed with him by the coiling vines, looked up in horror.

Then Farris saw what had happened. The little vial, the vial of the blight, had smashed against the banyan trunk as Berreau charged.

And that little splash of gray-green mould was rushing through the forest faster than flame! The blight, the gray-green killer from far away, propagating itself with appalling rapidity! "*Dieu!*" screamed Berreau. "*Non—non—*"

Even normally, a blight seems to spread swiftly. And to Farris and the other two, slowed down as they were, this blight was a raging cold fire of death.

It flashed up trunks and limbs and aerial roots of the majestic banyans, eating leaf and spore and bud. It ran triumphantly across the ground, over vine and grass and shrub, bursting up other trees, leaping along the airy bridges of lianas.

And it leaped among the vines that enmeshed the two men! In mad death-agonies the creepers writhed and tightened.

Farris felt the musty mould in his mouth and nostrils, felt the construction as of steel cables crushing the life from him. The world seemed to darken—

Then a steel blade hissed and flashed, and the pressure loosened. Lys' voice was in his ears, Lys' hand trying to drag him from the dying, tightening creepers that she had partly slashed through. He wrenched free. "My brother!" she gasped.

With the bolo he sliced clumsily through the mass of dying writhing snake-vines that still enmeshed Berreau.

Berreau's face appeared, as he tore away the slashed creepers. It was dark purple, rigid, his eyes staring and dead. The tightening vines had caught him around the throat, strangling him.

Lys knelt beside him, crying wildly. But Farris dragged her to her feet.

"We have to get out of here! He's dead—but I'll carry his body!"

"No, leave it," she sobbed. "Leave it here, in the forest."

Dead eyes, looking up at the death of the alien world of life into which he had now crossed, forever! Yes, it was fitting.

Farris' heart quailed as he stumbled away with Lys through the forest that was rocking and raging in its death-throes.

Far away around them, the gray-green death was leaping on. And fainter, fainter, came the strange telepathic cries that he would never be sure he had really heard.

"We die, brothers! We die!"

And then, when it seemed to Farris that sanity must give way beneath the weight of alien agony, there came a sudden change.

The pulsing rush of alternate day and night lengthened in tempo. Each period of light and darkness was longer now, and longer—

Out of a period of dizzying semi-consciousness, Farris came

back to awareness. They were standing unsteadily in the blighted forest, in bright sunlight.

And they were no longer *hunati*.

The chlorophyll drug had spent its force in their bodies, and they had come back to the normal tempo of human life.

Lys looked up dazedly, at the forest that now seemed static, peaceful, immobile—and in which the gray-green blight now crept so slowly they could not see it move.

"The same forest, and it's still writhing in death!" Farris said huskily. "But now that we're living at normal speed again, we can't see it!"

"Please, let us go!" choked the girl. "Away from here, at once!"

It took but an hour to return to the bungalow and pack what they could carry, before they took the trail toward the Mekong.

Sunset saw them out of the blighted area of the forest, well on their way toward the river.

"Will it kill all the forest?" whispered the girl.

"No. The forest will fight back, come back, conquer the blight, in time. A long time, by our reckoning—years, decades. But to *them*, that fierce struggle is raging on even now."

And as they walked on, it seemed to Farris that still in his mind there pulsed faintly from far behind that alien, throbbing cry.

"We die, brothers!"

He did not look back. But he knew that he would not come back to this or any other forest, and that his profession was ended, and that he would never kill a tree again.

HISTORY LESSON

by Arthur C. Clarke (1917–   )

***Startling Stories*, May**

Trivia contests have become quite popular at science fiction conventions large and small. Sf fans pride themselves on their knowledge of the field and don't hesitate to engage in determined contests to show off their ability to retrieve information. One exciting category of question involves identifying the author and title of a work based on the opening sentence; more rarely, closing lines are used in a similar fashion. "History Lesson" contains one of the most famous closing lines in science fiction—but if you are approaching the story for the first time, don't you dare take a peek!

*Arthur C. Clarke's "The Forgotten Enemy" (*New Worlds*, England, May) just missed inclusion in this volume.—M.H.G.*

(During the New York World's Fair of 1939, a "time capsule" was buried and the plan was to have it dug up five thousand years later so that our long-distant descendants could see what life was like in the United States in the 20th Century. For that reason, a wide variety of objects were included, all sealed under an inert atmosphere to preserve them, as far as possible, from deterioration.

Among the objects included was a copy of Amazing Stories *so that our descendants might be amused by our primitive science fictional speculations. —And I was devastated. The issue they included was that of February, 1939. Had they waited one more month for the March, 1939 issue they would have had the one with my first published story. By that much did I miss immortality! (Or at least so it seemed to me at the time, since I had no way of knowing then that I would become so prolific that I might survive—for some time, at least—without the help of a time capsule.)*

But that is personal and unimportant. What do we have left over to tell us about daily life in ancient Sumeria, Egypt, or Rome? What trivia just happens to survive? What laundry bills? What letters written home by students in need of money?

In "History Lesson," Arthur Clarke tackles that subject for Earth as a whole.—I.A.)

No one could remember when the tribe had begun its long journey. The land of great rolling plains that had been its first home was now no more than a half-forgotten dream.

For many years Shann and his people had been fleeing through a country of low hills and sparkling lakes, and now the mountains lay ahead. This summer they must cross them to the southern lands. There was little time to lose. The white terror that had come down from the Poles, grinding continents to dust and freezing the very air before it, was less than a day's march behind.

Shann wondered if the glaciers could climb the mountains ahead, and within his heart he dared to kindle a little flame of hope. This might prove a barrier against which even the remorseless ice would batter in vain. In the southern lands of which the legends spoke, his people might find refuge at last.

It took weeks to discover a pass through which the tribe and the animals could travel. When midsummer came, they had camped in a lonely valley where the air was thin and the stars shone with a brilliance no one had ever seen before.

The summer was waning when Shann took his two sons and went ahead to explore the way. For three days they climbed, and for three nights slept as best they could on the freezing rocks. And on the fourth morning there was nothing ahead but a gentle rise to a cairn of gray stones built by other travelers, centuries ago.

Shann felt himself trembling, and not with cold, as they walked toward the little pyramid of stones. His sons had fallen behind. No one spoke, for too much was at stake. In a little while they would know if all their hopes had been betrayed.

To east and west, the wall of mountains curved away as if embracing the land beneath. Below lay endless miles of undulating plain, with a great river swinging across it in tremendous loops. It was a fertile land, one in which the tribe could raise crops knowing that there would be no need to flee before the harvest came.

Then Shann lifted his eyes to the south, and saw the doom of all his hopes. For there at the edge of the world glimmered that deadly light he had seen so often to the north—the glint of ice below the horizon.

There was no way forward. Through all the years of flight, the glaciers from the south had been advancing to meet them. Soon they would be crushed beneath the moving walls of ice. . . .

Southern glaciers did not reach the mountains until a generation later. In the last summer the sons of Shann carried the sacred treasures of the tribe to the lonely cairn overlooking the plain. The ice that had once gleamed below the horizon was now almost at their feet. By spring it would be splintering against the mountain walls.

No one understood the treasures now. They were from a past too distant for the understanding of any man alive. Their origins were lost in the mists that surrounded the Golden Age, and how they had come at last into the possession of this wandering tribe was a story that now would never be told. For it was the story of a civilization that had passed beyond recall.

Once, all these pitiful relics had been treasured for some good reason and now they had become sacred though their meaning had long been lost. The print in the old books had faded centuries ago though much of the lettering was still visible—if there had been any to read it. But many generations had passed since anyone had had a use for a set of seven-figure logarithms, an atlas of the world, and the score of Sibelius' Seventh Symphony, printed, according to the flyleaf, by H. K. Chu and Sons. At the City of Pekin in the year A.D. 2371.

The old books were placed reverently in the little crypt that had been made to receive them. There followed a motley collection of fragments—gold and platinum coins, a broken telephoto lens, a watch, a cold-light lamp, a microphone, the cutter from an electric shaver, some midget radio tubes, the flotsam that had been left behind when the great tide of civilization had ebbed forever.

All these treasures were carefully stowed away in their resting place. Then came three more relics, the most sacred of all because the least understood.

The first was a strangely shaped piece of metal, showing the coloration of intense heat. It was, in its way, the most pathetic of all these symbols from the past, for it told of man's greatest achievement and of the future he might have known. The mahogany stand on which it was mounted bore a silver plate with the inscription:

Auxiliary igniter from Starboard Jet
Spaceship *Morning Star*
Earth-Moon, A.D. 1985

Next followed another miracle of the ancient science—a sphere of transparent plastic with strangely shaped pieces of metal embedded in it. At its center was a tiny capsule of synthetic radio-element, surrounded by the converting screens that shifted its radiation far down the spectrum. As long as the material remained active, the sphere would be a tiny radio transmitter, broadcasting power in all directions. Only a few of these spheres had ever been made. They had been designed as perpetual beacons to mark the orbits of the asteroids. But man had never reached the asteroids and the beacons had never been used.

Last of all was a flat, circular tin, wide in comparison with its depth. It was heavily sealed, and rattled when shaken. The tribal lore predicted that disaster would follow if it were ever opened, and no one knew that it held one of the great works of art of nearly a thousand years before.

The work was finished. The two men rolled the stones back into place and slowly began to descend the mountainside. Even to the last, man had given some thought to the future and had tried to preserve something for posterity.

That winter the great waves of ice began their first assault on the mountains, attacking from north and south. The foothills were overwhelmed in the first onslaught, and the glaciers ground them into dust. But the mountains stood firm, and when the summer came the ice retreated for a while.

So, winter after winter, the battle continued, and the roar of the avalanches, the grinding of rock and the explosions of splintering ice filled the air with tumult. No war of man's had been fiercer than this, and even man's battles had not quite engulfed the globe as this had done.

At last the tidal waves of ice began to subside and to creep slowly down the flanks of the mountains they had never quite subdued. The valleys and passes were still firmly in their grip. It was stalemate. The glaciers had met their match, but their defeat was too late to be of any use to Man.

So the centuries passed, and presently there happened something that must occur once at least in the history of every world in the universe, no matter how remote and lonely it may be.

The ship from Venus came five thousand years too late, but its crew knew nothing of this. While still many millions of miles away, the telescopes had seen the great shroud of ice that made Earth the most brilliant object in the sky next to the sun itself.

Here and there the dazzling sheet was marred by black specks that revealed the presence of almost buried mountains. That was all. The rolling oceans, the plains and forests, the deserts and lakes—all that had been the world of Man was sealed beneath the ice, perhaps forever.

The ship closed in to Earth and established an orbit less than a thousand miles away. For five days it circled the planet, while cameras recorded all that was left to see and a hundred instruments gathered information that would give the Venusian scientists many years of work.

An actual landing was not intended. There seemed little purpose in it. But on the sixth day the picture changed. A panoramic monitor, driven to the limit of its amplification, detected the dying radiation of the five-thousand-year-old beacon. Through all the centuries, it had been sending out its signals with ever-failing strength as its radioactive heart steadily weakened.

The monitor locked on the beacon frequency. In the control room, a bell clamored for attention. A little later, the Venusian ship broke free from its orbit and slanted down toward Earth, toward a range of mountains that still towered proudly above the ice, and to a cairn of gray stones that the years had scarcely touched. . . .

The great disc of the Sun blazed fiercely in a sky no longer veiled with mist, for the clouds that had once hidden Venus had now completely gone. Whatever force had caused the change in the Sun's radiation had doomed one civilization, but had given birth to another. Less than five thousand years before, the half-savage people of Venus had seen Sun and stars for the first time. Just as the science of Earth had begun with astronomy, so had that of Venus, and on the warm, rich world that man had never seen progress had been incredibly rapid.

Perhaps the Venusians had been lucky. They never knew the Dark Ages that held Man enchained for a thousand years. They missed the long detour into chemistry and mechanics but came at once to the more fundamental laws of radiation physics. In the time that man had taken to progress from the Pyramids to the rocket-propelled spaceship, the Venusians had passed fróm the discovery of agriculture to antigravity itself—the ultimate secret that Man had never learned.

The warm ocean that still bore most of the young planet's life rolled its breakers languidly against the sandy shore. So new was this continent that the very sands were coarse and gritty. There had not yet been time enough for the sea to wear them smooth.

The scientists lay half in the water, their beautiful reptilian bodies gleaming in the sunlight. The greatest minds of Venus had gathered on this shore from all the islands of the planet. What they were going to hear they did not yet know, except that it concerned the Third World and the mysterious race that had peopled it before the coming of the ice.

The Historian was standing on the land, for the instruments he wished to use had no love of water. By his side was a large machine which attracted many curious glances from his colleagues. It was clearly concerned with optics, for a lens system projected from it toward a screen of white material a dozen yards away.

The Historian began to speak. Briefly he recapitulated what little had been discovered concerning the third planet and its people.

He mentioned the centuries of fruitless research that had failed to interpret a single word of the writings of Earth. The planet had been inhabited by a race of great technical ability. That, at least, was proved by the few pieces of machinery that had been found in the cairn upon the mountain.

"We do not know why so advanced a civilization came to an end," he observed. "Almost certainly, it had sufficient knowledge to survive an Ice Age. There must have been some factor of which we know nothing. Possibly disease or racial degeneration may have been responsible. It has even been suggested that the tribal conflicts endemic to our own species in prehistoric times may have continued on the third planet after the coming of technology.

"Some philosophers maintain that knowledge of machinery does not necessarily imply a high degree of civilization, and it is theoretically possible to have wars in a society possessing mechanical power, flight, and even radio. Such a conception is alien to our thoughts, but we must admit its possibility. It would certainly account for the downfall of the lost race.

"It has always been assumed that we should never know anything of the physical form of the creatures who lived in Planet Three. For centuries our artists have been depicting scenes from the history of the dead world, peopling it with all manner of fantastic beings. Most of the creations have resembled us more or less closely, though it has often been pointed out that because *we* are reptiles it does not follow that all intelligent life must necessarily be reptilian.

"We now know the answer to one of the most baffling problems of history. At last, after a hundred years of research, we have discovered the exact form and nature of the ruling life on the Third Planet."

There was a murmur of astonishment from the assembled scientists. Some were so taken aback that they disappeared for a while into the comfort of the ocean, as all Venusians were apt to do in moments of stress. The Historian waited until his colleagues reemerged into the element they so disliked. He himself was quite comfortable, thanks to the tiny sprays that were continually playing over his body. With their help he could live on land for many hours before having to return to the ocean.

The excitement slowly subsided and the lecturer continued:

"One of the most puzzling of the objects found on Planet Three was a flat metal container holding a great length of transparent plastic material, perforated at the edges and wound tightly into a spool. This transparent tape at first seemed quite featureless, but an examination with the new subelectronic microscope has shown that this is not the case. Along the surface of the material, invisible to our eyes but perfectly clear under the correct radiation, are literally thousands of tiny pictures. It is believed that they were imprinted on the material by some chemical means, and have faded with the passage of time.

"These pictures apparently form a record of life as it was on the Third Planet at the height of its civilization. They are not independent. Consecutive pictures are almost identical, differing only in the detail of movement. The purpose of such a record is obvious. It is only necessary to project the scenes in rapid succession to give an illusion of continuous movement. We have made a machine to do this, and I have here an exact reproduction of the picture sequence.

"The scenes you are now going to witness take us back many thousands of years, to the great days of our sister planet. They show a complex civilization, many of whose activities we can only dimly understand. Life seems to have been very violent and energetic, and much that you will see is quite baffling.

"It is clear that the Third Planet was inhabited by a number of different species, none of them reptilian. That is a blow to our pride, but the conclusion is inescapable. The dominant type of life appears to have been a two-armed biped. It walked upright and covered its body with some flexible material, possibly for protection against the cold, since even before the Ice Age the planet was at a much lower temperature than our own world. But I will not try your patience any further. You will now see the record of which I have been speaking.''

A brilliant light flashed from the projector. There was a gentle whirring, and on the screen appeared hundreds of strange beings moving rather jerkily to and fro. The picture expanded to embrace one of the creatures, and the scientists could see that the Historian's description had been correct.

The creature possessed two eyes, set rather close together, but the other facial adornaments were a little obscure. There was a large orifice in the lower portion of the head that was continually opening and closing. Possibly it had something to do with the creature's breathing.

The scientists watched spellbound as the strange being became involved in a series of fantastic adventures. There was an incredibly violent conflict with another, slightly different creature. It seemed certain that they must both be killed, but when it was all over neither seemed any the worse.

Then came a furious drive over miles of country in a four-wheeled mechanical device which was capable of extraordinary feats of locomotion. The ride ended in a city packed with other vehicles moving in all directions at breathtaking speeds. No one was surprised to see two of the machines meet head on with devastating results.

After that, events became even more complicated. It was now quite obvious that it would take many years of research to analyze and understand all that was happening. It was also clear that the record was a work of art, somewhat stylized, rather than an exact reproduction of life as it actually had been on the Third Planet.

Most of the scientists felt themselves completely dazed when the sequence of pictures came to an end. There was a final flurry of motion, in which the creature that had been the center of interest became involved in some tremendous but incomprehensible catastrophe. The picture contracted to a circle, centered on the creature's head.

The last scene of all was an expanded view of its face, obviously expressing some powerful emotion. But whether it was rage, grief, defiance, resignation or some other feeling could not be guessed. The picture vanished. For a moment some lettering appeared on the screen, then it was all over.

For several minutes there was complete silence, save the

lapping of the waves upon the sand. The scientists were too stunned to speak. The fleeting glimpse of Earth's civilization had had a shattering effect on their minds. Then little groups began to start talking together, first in whispers and then more and more loudly as the implications of what they had seen became clearer. Presently the Historian called for attention and addressed the meeting again.

"We are now planning," he said, "a vast program of research to extract all available knowledge from this record. Thousands of copies are being made for distribution to all workers. You will appreciate the problems involved. The psychologists in particular have an immense task confronting them.

"But I do not doubt that we shall succeed. In another generation, who can say what we many not have learned of this wonderful race? Before we leave, let us look again at our remote cousins, whose wisdom may have surpassed our own but of whom so little has survived."

Once more the final picture flashed on the screen, motionless this time, for the projector had been stopped. With something like awe, the scientists gazed at the still figure from the past, while in turn the little biped stared back at them with its characteristic expression of arrogant bad temper.

For the rest of time it would symbolize the human race. The psychologists of Venus would analyze its actions and watch its every movement until they could reconstruct its mind. Thousands of books would be written about it. Intricate philosophies would be contrived to account for its behavior.

But all this labor, all this research, would be utterly in vain. Perhaps the proud and lonely figure on the screen was smiling sardonically at the scientists who were starting on their agelong fruitless quest.

Its secret would be safe as long as the universe endured, for no one now would ever read the lost language of Earth. Millions of times in the ages to come those last few words would flash across the screen, and none could ever guess their meaning:

A Walt Disney Production.

ETERNITY LOST

by Clifford D. Simak (1904–   )

***Astounding Science Fiction*, July**

As Isaac points out, this fine story is about immortality, one of the most important themes in modern science fiction. However, it is also about personal and political corruption, *which in modern science fiction is a common assumption, if not a theme. The corruptibility of human beings in positions of power in sf stories is the rule, not the exception, and directly parallels attitudes in American society, which views politicians with great distrust, ranking them last out of twenty occupational types in a recent poll (used car salesman was nineteenth). However, it should be pointed out that these attitudes are almost universal across human cultures.*

We have discussed the impressive career of Clifford D. Simak in earlier volumes of this series, but for the record let it be stated again that he has been working productively in this field for some fifty-five *years, and is still near the top of his form.—M.H.G.*

(Immortality is the oldest dream of human beings. Death is the ultimate outrage; the ultimate disappointment. Why should people die?

Surely, that was not the original plan. Human beings were meant to live forever and it was only through some small miscalculation or misstep that death entered the world. In Gilgamesh, *the oldest surviving epic in the world, Gilgamesh searched for immortality and attained it and then lost it when, while he was asleep, a snake filched the plant that contained the secret.*

In the story of Adam and Eve, with which the Bible begins, Adam and Eve had immortality, until a snake— But you know that *one.*

And even today, so many people, so many *people [even that supreme rationalist, Martin Gardner, to my astonishment] can't accept death but believe that something about us must remain eternal. Personally, I don't know why. Considering how few people find any happiness in this wonderful world of ours, why should human beings, generally, feel anything but relief at the thought that life is only temporary?*

Science fiction writers sometimes play with the possibility of physical immortality attained through technological advance, but you can't cheat drama. The excitement comes, as with Gilgamesh and Adam, with the chance that immortality may be lost, as in "Eternity Lost," by Clifford D. Simak.—I.A.)

Mr. Reeves: *The situation, as I see it, calls for well defined safeguards which would prevent continuation of life from falling under the patronage of political parties or other groups in power.*

Chairman Leonard: *You mean you are afraid it might become a political football?*

Mr. Reeves: *Not only that, sir, I am afraid that political parties might use it to continue beyond normal usefulness the lives of certain so-called elder statesmen who are needed by the party to maintain prestige and dignity in the public eye.*

From the Records of a hearing before the science subcommittee of the public policy committee of the World House of Representatives.

Senator Homer Leonard's visitors had something on their minds. They fidgeted mentally as they sat in the senator's office and drank the senator's good whiskey. They talked, quite importantly, as was their wont, but they talked around the thing they had come to say. They circled it like a hound dog circling a coon, waiting for an opening, circling the subject to catch an opportunity that might make the message sound just a bit offhanded—as if they had just thought of it in passing and had not called purposely on the senator to say it.

It was queer, the senator told himself. For he had known these two for a good while now. And they had known him equally as long. There should be nothing they should hesitate to tell him.

They had, in the past, been brutally frank about many things in his political career.

It might be, he thought, more bad news from North America, but he was as well acquainted with that bad news as they. After all, he told himself philosophically, a man cannot reasonably expect to stay in office forever. The voters, from sheer boredom if nothing else, would finally reach the day when they would vote against a man who had served them faithfully and well. And the senator was candid enough to admit, at least to himself, that there had been times when he had served the voters of North America neither faithfully nor well.

Even at that, he thought, he had not been beaten yet. It was still several months until election time and there was a trick or two that he had never tried, political dodges that even at this late date might save the senatorial hide. Given the proper time and the proper place and he would win out yet. Timing, he told himself—proper timing is the thing that counts.

He sat quietly in his chair, a great hulk of a man, and for a single instant he closed his eyes to shut out the room and the sunlight in the window. Timing, he thought. Yes, timing and a feeling for the public, a finger on the public pulse, the ability to know ahead of time what the voter eventually will come to think—those were the ingredients of good strategy. To know ahead of time, to be ahead in thinking, so that in a week or a month or year, the voters would say to one another: "You know, Bill, old Senator Leonard had it right. Remember what he said last week—or month or year—over there in Geneva. Yes, sir, he laid it on the line. There ain't much that gets past that old fox of a Leonard."

He opened his eyes a slit, keeping them still half closed so his visitors might think he'd only had them half closed all the time. For it was impolite and a political mistake to close one's eyes when one had visitors. They might get the idea one wasn't interested. Or they might seize the opportunity to cut one's throat.

It's because I'm getting old again, the senator told himself. Getting old and drowsy. But just as smart as ever. Yes, sir, said the senator, talking to himself, just as smart and slippery as I ever was.

He saw by the tight expressions on the faces of the two that they finally were set to tell him the thing they had come to tell. All their circling and sniffing had been of no avail. Now they had to come out with it, on the line, cold turkey.

"There has been a certain matter," said Alexander Gibbs,

"which has been quite a problem for the party for a long time now. We had hoped that matters would so arrange themselves that we wouldn't need to call it to your attention, senator. But the executive committee held a meeting in New York the other night and it seemed to be the consensus that we communicate it to you."

It's bad, thought the senator, even worse than I thought it might be—for Gibbs is talking in his best double-crossing manner.

The senator gave them no help. He sat quietly in his chair and held the whiskey glass in a steady hand and did not ask what it was all about, acting as if he didn't really care.

Gibbs floundered slightly. "It's a rather personal matter, senator," he said.

"It's this life continuation business," blurted Andrew Scott.

They sat in shocked silence, all three of them, for Scott should not have said it in that way. In politics, one is not blunt and forthright, but devious and slick.

"I see," the senator said finally. "The party thinks the voters would like it better if I were a normal man who would die a normal death."

Gibbs smoothed his face of shocked surprise.

"The common people resent men living beyond their normal time," he said. "Especially—"

"Especially," said the senator, "those who have done nothing to deserve it."

"I wouldn't put it exactly that way," Gibbs protested.

"Perhaps not," said the senator. "But no matter how you say it, that is what you mean."

They sat uncomfortably in the office chairs, with the bright Geneva sunlight pouring through the windows.

"I presume," said the senator, "that the party, having found I am no longer an outstanding asset, will not renew my application for life continuation. I suppose that is what you were sent to tell me."

Might as well get it over with, he told himself grimly. Now that it's out in the open, there's no sense in beating around the bush.

"That's just about it, senator," said Scott.

"That's exactly it," said Gibbs.

The senator heaved his great body from the chair, picked up the whiskey bottle, filled their glasses and his own.

"You delivered the death sentence very deftly," he told them. "It deserves a drink."

He wondered what they had thought that he would do. Plead

with them, perhaps. Or storm around the office. Or denounce the party.

Puppets, he thought. Errand boys. Poor, scared errand boys.

They drank, their eyes on him, and silent laughter shook inside him from knowing that the liquor tasted very bitter in their mouths.

Chairman Leonard: *You are agreed then, Mr. Chapman, with the other witnesses, that no person should be allowed to seek continuation of life for himself, that it should be granted only upon application by someone else, that—*

Mr. Chapman: *It should be a gift of society to those persons who are in the unique position of being able to materially benefit the human race.*

Chairman Leonard: *That is very aptly stated, sir.*

> From the Records of a hearing before the science subcommittee of the public policy committee of the World House of Representatives.

The senator settled himself carefully and comfortably into a chair in the reception room of the Life Continuation Institute and unfolded his copy of the *North American Tribune*.

Column one said that system trade was normal, according to a report by the World Secretary of Commerce. The story went on at length to quote the secretary's report. Column two was headed by an impish box that said a new life form may have been found on Mars, but since the discoverer was a spaceman who had been more than ordinarily drunk, the report was being viewed with some skepticism. Under the box was a story reporting a list of boy and girl health champions selected by the state of Finland to be entered later in the year in the world health contest. The story in column three gave the latest information on the unstable love life of the world's richest woman.

Column four asked a question:

WHAT HAPPENED TO DR. CARSON:
NO RECORD OF REPORTED DEATH

The story, the senator saw, was by-lined Anson Lee and the senator chuckled dryly. Lee was up to something. He was always up to something, always ferreting out some fact that eventually was sure to prove embarrassing to someone. Smart as a steel trap, that Lee, but a bad man to get into one's hair.

There had been, for example, that matter of the spaceship contract.

Anson Lee, said the senator underneath his breath, is a pest. Nothing but a pest.

But Dr. Carson? Who was Dr. Carson?

The senator played a little mental game with himself, trying to remember, trying to identify the name before he read the story.

Dr. Carson?

Why, said the senator, I remember now. Long time ago. A biochemist or something of the sort. A very brilliant man. Did something with colonies of soil bacteria, breeding the things for therapeutic work.

Yes, said the senator, a very brilliant man. I remember that I met him once. Didn't understand half the things he said. But that was long ago. A hundred years or more.

A hundred years ago—maybe more than that.

Why, bless me, said the senator, he must be one of us.

The senator nodded and the paper slipped from his hands and fell upon the floor. He jerked himself erect. There I go again, he told himself. Dozing. It's old age creeping up again.

He sat in his chair, very erect and quiet, like a small scared child that won't admit it's scared, and the old, old fear came tugging at his brain. Too long, he thought. I've already waited longer than I should. Waiting for the party to renew my application and now the party won't. They've thrown me overboard. They've deserted me just when I needed them the most.

Death sentence, he had said back in the office, and that was what it was—for he couldn't last much longer. He didn't have much time. It would take a while to engineer whatever must be done. One would have to move most carefully and never tip one's hand. For there was a penalty—a terrible penalty.

The girl said to him: "Dr. Smith will see you now."

"Eh?" said the senator.

"You asked to see Dr. Dana Smith," the girl reminded him. "He will see you now."

"Thank you, miss," said the senator. "I was sitting here half dozing."

He lumbered to his feet.

"That door," said the girl.

"I know," the senator mumbled testily. "I know. I've been here many times before."

Dr. Smith was waiting.

"Have a chair, senator," he said. "Have a drink? Well, then, a cigar, maybe. What is on your mind?"

The senator took his time, getting himself adjusted to the chair. Grunting comfortably, he clipped the end off the cigar, rolled it in his mouth.

"Nothing particular on my mind," he said. "Just dropped around to pass the time of day. Have a great and abiding interest in your work here. Always have had. Associated with it from the very start."

The director nodded. "I know. You conducted the original hearings on life continuation."

The senator chuckled. "Seemed fairly simple then. There were problems, of course, and we recognized them and we tried the best we could to meet them."

"You did amazingly well," the director told him. "The code you drew up five hundred years ago has never been questioned for its fairness and the few modifications which have been necessary have dealt with minor points which no one could have anticipated."

"But it's taken too long," said the senator.

The director stiffened. "I don't understand," he said.

The senator lighted the cigar, applying his whole attention to it, flaming the end carefully so it caught even fire.

He settled himself more solidly in the chair. "It was like this," he said. "We recognized life continuation as a first step only, a rather blundering first step toward immortality. We devised the code as an interim instrument to take care of the period before immortality was available—not to a selected few, but to everyone. We viewed the few who could be given life continuation as stewards, persons who would help to advance the day when the race could be granted immortality."

"That still is the concept," Dr. Smith said, coldly.

"But the people grow impatient."

"That is just too bad," Smith told him. "The people will simply have to wait."

"As a race, they may be willing to," explained the senator. "As individuals, they're not."

"I fail to see your point, senator."

"There may not be a point," said the senator. "In late years I've often debated with myself the wisdom of the whole procedure. Life continuation is a keg of dynamite if it fails of immortality. It will breed, system-wide revolt if the people wait too long."

"Have you a solution, senator?"

"No," confessed the senator. "No, I'm afraid I haven't. I've often thought that it might have been better if we had taken the people into our confidence, let them know all that was going on. Kept them up with all developments. An informed people are a rational people."

The director did not answer and the senator felt the cold weight of certainty seep into his brain.

He knows, he told himself. He knows the party has decided not to ask that I be continued. He knows that I'm a dead man. He knows I'm almost through and can't help him any more—and he's crossed me out. He won't tell me a thing. Not the thing I want to know.

But he did not allow his face to change. He knew his face would not betray him. His face was too well trained.

"I know there is an answer," said the senator. "There's always been an answer to any question about immortality. You can't have it until there's living space. Living space to throw away, more than we ever think we'll need, and a fair chance to find more of it if it's ever needed."

Dr. Smith nodded. "That's the answer, senator. The only answer I can give."

He sat silent for a moment, then he said: "Let me assure you on one point, senator. When Extrasolar Research finds the living space, we'll have the immortality."

The senator heaved himself out of the chair, stood planted solidly on his feet.

"It's good to hear you say that, doctor," he said. "It is very heartening. I thank you for the time you gave me."

Out on the street, the senator thought bitterly:

They have it now. They have immortality. All they're waiting for is the living space and another hundred years will find that. Another hundred years will simply have to find it.

Another hundred years, he told himself, just one more continuation, and I would be in for good and all.

Mr. Andrews: *We must be sure there is a divorcement of life continuation from economics. A man who has money must not be allowed to purchase additional life, either through the payment of money or the pressure of influence, while another man is doomed to die a natural death simply because he happens to be poor.*

Chairman Leonard: *I don't believe that situation has ever been in question.*

Mr. Andrews: *Nevertheless, it is a matter which must be emphasized again and again. Life continuation must not be a commodity to be sold across the counter at so many dollars for each added year of life.*

> From the Records of a hearing before the science subcommittee of the public policy committee of the World House of Representatives.

The senator sat before the chessboard and idly worked at the problem. Idly, since his mind was on other things than chess.

So they had immortality, had it and were waiting, holding it a secret until there was assurance of sufficient living space. Holding it a secret from the people and from the government and from the men and women who had spent many lifetimes working for the thing which already had been found.

For Smith had spoken, not as a man who was merely confident, but as a man who knew. When Extrasolar Research finds the living space, he'd said, we'll have immortality. Which meant they had it now. Immortality was not predictable. You would not know you'd have it; you would only know if and when you had it.

The senator moved a bishop and saw that he was wrong. He slowly pulled it back.

Living space was the key, and not living space alone, but economic living space, self-supporting in terms of food and other raw materials, but particularly in food. For if living space had been all that mattered, Man had it in Mars and Venus and the moons of Jupiter. But not one of those worlds was self-supporting. They did not solve the problem.

Living space was all they needed and in a hundred years they'd have that. Another hundred years was all that anyone would need to come into possession of the common human heritage of immortality.

Another continuation would give me that hundred years, said the senator, talking to himself. A hundred years and some to spare, for this time I'll be careful of myself. I'll lead a cleaner life. Eat sensibly and cut out liquor and tobacco and the woman-chasing.

There were ways and means, of course. There always were. And he would find them, for he knew all the dodges. After five hundred years in world government, you got to know them all. If you didn't know them, you simply didn't last.

Mentally he listed the possibilities as they occurred to him.

ONE: A person could engineer a continuation for someone

else and then have that person assign the continuation to him. It would be costly, of course, but it might be done.

You'd have to find someone you could trust and maybe you couldn't find anyone you could trust that far—for life continuation was something hard to come by. Most people, once they got it, wouldn't give it back.

Although on second thought, it probably wouldn't work. For there'd be legal angles. A continuation was a gift of society to one specific person to be used by him alone. It would not be transferable. It would not be legal property. It would not be something that one owned. It could not be bought or sold, it could not be assigned.

If the person who had been granted a continuation died before he got to use it—died of natural causes, of course, of wholly natural causes that could be provable—why, maybe, then— But still it wouldn't work. Not being property, the continuation would not be part of one's estate. It could not be bequeathed. It most likely would revert to the issuing agency.

Cross that one off, the senator told himself.

TWO: He might travel to New York and talk to the party's executive secretary. After all, Gibbs and Scott were mere messengers. They had their orders to carry out the dictates of the party and that was all. Maybe if he saw someone in authority—

But, the senator scolded himself, that is wishful thinking. The party's through with me. They've pushed their continuation racket as far as they dare push it and they have wrangled about all they figure they can get. They don't dare ask for more and they need my continuation for someone else most likely—someone who's a comer; someone who has vote appeal.

And I, said the senator, am an old has-been.

Although I'm a tricky old rascal, and ornery if I have to be, and slippery as five hundred years of public life can make one.

After that long, said the senator, parenthetically, you have no more illusions, not even of yourself.

I couldn't stomach it, he decided. I couldn't live with myself if I went crawling to New York—and a thing has to be pretty bad to make me feel like that. I've never crawled before and I'm not crawling now, not even for an extra hundred years and a shot at immortality.

Cross that one off, too, said the senator.

THREE: Maybe someone could be bribed.

Of all the possibilities, that sounded the most reasonable. There always was someone who had a certain price and always someone else who could act as intermediary. Naturally, a world senator could not get mixed up directly in a deal of that sort.

It might come a little high, but what was money for? After all, he reconciled himself, he'd been a frugal man of sorts and had been able to lay away a wad against such a day as this.

The senator moved a rook and it seemed to be all right, so he left it there.

Of course, once he managed the continuation, he would have to disappear. He couldn't flaunt his triumph in the party's face. He couldn't take a chance of someone asking how he'd been continuated. He'd have to become one of the people, seek to be forgotten, live in some obscure place and keep out of the public eye.

Norton was the man to see. No matter what one wanted, Norton was the man to see. An appointment to be secured, someone to be killed, a concession on Venus or a spaceship contract—Norton did the job. All quietly and discreetly and no questions asked. That is, if you had the money. If you didn't have the money, there was no use of seeing Norton.

Otto came into the room on silent feet.

"A gentleman to see you, sir," he said.

The senator stiffened upright in his chair.

"What do you mean by sneaking up on me?" he shouted. "Always pussyfooting. Trying to startle me. After this you cough or fall over a chair or something so I'll know that you're around."

"Sorry, sir," said Otto. "There's a gentleman here. And there are those letters on the desk to read."

"I'll read the letters later," said the senator.

"Be sure you don't forget," Otto told him, stiffly.

"I never forget," said the senator. "You'd think I was getting senile, the way you keep reminding me."

"There's a gentleman to see you," Otto said patiently. "A Mr. Lee."

"Anson Lee, perhaps."

Otto sniffed. "I believe that was his name. A newspaper person, sir."

"Show him in," said the senator.

He sat stolidly in his chair and thought: Lee's found out about it. Somehow he's ferreted out the fact the party's thrown me over. And he's here to crucify me.

He may suspect, but he cannot know. He may have heard a rumor, but he can't be sure. The party would keep mum, must necessarily keep mum, since it can't openly admit its traffic in life continuation. So Lee, having heard a rumor, had come to blast it out of me, to catch me by surprise and trip me up with words.

I must not let him do it, for once the thing is known, the wolves will come in packs knee deep.

Lee was walking into the room and the senator rose and shook his hand.

"Sorry to disturb you, senator," Lee told him, "but I thought maybe you could help me."

"Anything at all," the senator said, affably. "Anything I can. Sit down, Mr. Lee."

"Perhaps you read my story in the morning paper," said Lee. "The one on Dr. Carson's disappearance."

"No," said the senator. "No, I'm afraid I—"

He rumbled to a stop, astounded.

He hadn't read the paper!

He had forgotten to read the paper!

He always read the paper. He never failed to read it. It was a solemn rite, starting at the front and reading straight through to the back, skipping only those sections which long ago he'd found not to be worth the reading.

He'd had the paper at the institute and he had been interrupted when the girl told him that Dr. Smith would see him. He had come out of the office and he'd left the paper in the reception room.

It was a terrible thing. Nothing, absolutely nothing, should so upset him that he forgot to read the paper.

"I'm afraid I didn't read the story," the senator said lamely. He simply couldn't force himself to admit that he hadn't read the paper.

"Dr. Carson," said Lee, "was a biochemist, a fairly famous one. He died ten years or so ago, according to an announcement from a little village in Spain, where he had gone to live. But I have reason to believe, senator, that he never died at all, that he may still be living."

"Hiding?" asked the senator.

"Perhaps," said Lee. "Although there seems no reason that he should. His record is entirely spotless."

"Why do you doubt he died, then?"

"Because there's no death certificate. And he's not the only one who died without benefit of certificate."

"Hm-m-m," said the senator.

"Galloway, the anthropologist, died five years ago. There's no certificate. Henderson, the agricultural expert, died six years ago. There's no certificate. There are a dozen more I know of and probably many that I don't."

"Anything in common?" asked the senator. "Any circumstances that might link these people?"

"Just one thing," said Lee. "They were all continuators."

"I see," said the senator. He clasped the arms of his chair with a fierce grip to keep his hands from shaking.

"Most interesting," he said. "Very interesting."

"I know you can't tell me anything officially," said Lee, "but I thought you might give me a fill-in, an off-the-record background. You wouldn't let me quote you, of course, but any clues you might give me, any hint at all—"

He waited hopefully.

"Because I've been close to the Life Continuation people?" asked the senator.

Lee nodded. "If there's anything to know, you know it, senator. You headed the committee that held the original hearings on life continuation. Since then you've held various other congressional posts in connection with it. Only this morning you saw Dr. Smith."

"I can't tell you anything," mumbled the senator. "I don't know anything. You see, it's a matter of policy—"

"I had hoped you would help me, senator."

"I can't," said the senator. "You'll never believe it, of course, but I really can't."

He sat silently for a moment and then he asked a question: "You say all these people you mention were continuators. You checked, of course, to see if their applications had been renewed?"

"I did," said Lee. "There are no renewals for any one of them—at least no records of renewals. Some of them were approaching death limit and they actually may be dead by now, although I doubt that any of them died at the time or place announced."

"Interesting," said the senator. "And quite a mystery, too."

Lee deliberately terminated the discussion. He gestured at the chessboard. "Are you an expert, senator?"

The senator shook his head. "The game appeals to me. I fool around with it. It's a game of logic and also a game of ethics. You are perforce a gentleman when you play it. You observe certain rules of correctness of behavior."

"Like life, senator?"

"Like life should be," said the senator. "When the odds are

too terrific, you resign. You do not force your opponent to play out to the bitter end. That's ethics. When you see that you can't win, but that you have a fighting chance, you try for the next best thing—a draw. That's logic."

Lee laughed, a bit uncomfortably. "You've lived according to those rules, senator?"

"I've done my best," said the senator, trying to sound humble.

Lee rose. "I must be going, senator."

"Stay and have a drink."

Lee shook his head. "Thanks, but I have work to do."

"I owe you a drink," said the senator. "Remind me of it sometime."

For a long time after Lee left, Senator Homer Leonard sat unmoving in his chair.

Then he reached out a hand and picked up a knight to move it, but his fingers shook so that he dropped it and it clattered on the board.

Any person who gains the gift of life continuation by illegal or extralegal means, without bona fide recommendation or proper authorization through recognized channels, shall be, in effect, excommunicated from the human race. The facts of that person's guilt, once proved, shall be published by every means at humanity's command throughout the Earth and to every corner of the Earth so that all persons may know and recognize him. To further insure such recognition and identification, said convicted person must wear at all times, conspicuously displayed upon his person, a certain badge which shall advertise his guilt. While he may not be denied the ordinary basic requirements of life, such as food, adequate clothing, a minimum of shelter and medical care, he shall not be allowed to partake of or participate in any of the other refinements of civilization. He will not be allowed to purchase any item in excess of the barest necessities for the preservation of life, health and decency; he shall be barred from all endeavors and normal associations of humankind; he shall not have access to nor benefit of any library, lecture hall, amusement place or other facility, either private or public, designed for instruction, recreation or entertainment. Nor may any person, under certain penalties hereinafter set forth, knowingly converse with him or establish any human relationship whatsoever with him. He will be suffered to live out his life within the framework of the human community, but to all intent and purpose he will be denied all the privileges and obligations of a human being. And the same provisions as are listed above shall apply in full and equal force to any person or persons who shall in any way knowingly aid such a person to obtain life continuation by other than legal means.

From The Code of Life Continuation.

"What you mean," said J. Barker Norton, "is that the party all these years has been engineering renewals of life continuation for you. Paying you off for services well rendered."

The senator nodded miserably.

"And now that you're on the verge of losing an election, they figure you aren't worth it any longer and have refused to ask for a renewal."

"In curbstone language," said the senator, "that sums it up quite neatly."

"And you come running to me," said Norton. "What in the world do you think I can do about it?"

The senator leaned forward. "Let's put it on a business basis, Norton. You and I have worked together before."

"That's right," said Norton. "Both of us cleaned up on that spaceship deal."

The senator said: "I want another hundred years and I'm willing to pay for it. I have no doubt you can arrange it for me."

"How?"

"I wouldn't know," said the senator. "I'm leaving that to you. I don't care how you do it."

Norton leaned back in his chair and made a tent out of his fingers.

"You figure I could bribe someone to recommend you. Or bribe some continuation technician to give you a renewal without authorization."

"Those are a pair of excellent ideas," agreed the senator.

"And face excommunication if I were found out," said Norton. "Thanks, senator, I'm having none of it."

The senator sat impassively, watching the face of the man across the desk.

"A hundred thousand," the senator said quietly.

Norton laughed at him.

"A half million, then."

"Remember that excommunication, senator. It's got to be worth my while to take a chance like that."

"A million," said the senator. "And that's absolutely final."

"A million now," said Norton. "Cold cash. No receipt. No record of the transaction. Another million when and if I can deliver."

The senator rose slowly to his feet, his face a mask to hide the excitement that was stirring in him. The excitement and the naked surge of exultation. He kept his voice level.

"I'll deliver that million before the week is over."

Norton said: "I'll start looking into things."

On the street outside, the senator's step took on a jauntiness it had not known in years. He walked along briskly, flipping his cane.

Those others, Carson and Galloway and Henderson, had disappeared, exactly as he would have to disappear once he got his extra hundred years. They had arranged to have their own deaths announced and then had dropped from sight, living against the day when immortality would be a thing to be had for the simple asking.

Somewhere, somehow, they had got a new continuation, an unauthorized continuation, since a renewal was not listed in the records. Someone had arranged it for them. More than likely Norton.

But they had bungled. They had tried to cover up their tracks and had done no more than call attention to their absence.

In a thing like this, a man could not afford to blunder. A wise man, a man who took the time to think things out, would not make a blunder.

The senator pursed his flabby lips and whistled a snatch of music.

Norton was a gouger, of course. Pretending that he couldn't make arrangements, pretending he was afraid of excommunication, jacking up the price.

The senator grinned wryly. It would take almost every dime he had, but it was worth the price.

He'd have to be careful, getting together that much money. Some from one bank, some from another, collecting it piecemeal by withdrawals and by cashing bonds, floating a few judicious loans so there'd not be too many questions asked.

He bought a paper at the corner and hailed a cab. Settling back in the seat, he creased the paper down its length and startd in on column one. Another health contest. This time in Australia.

Health, thought the senator, they're crazy on this health business. Health centers. Health cults. Health clinics.

He skipped the story, moved on to column two.

The head said:

SIX SENATORS POOR BETS FOR RE-ELECTION

The senator snorted in disgust. One of the senators, of course, would be himself.

He wadded up the paper and jammed it in his pocket.

Why should he care? Why knock himself out to retain a senate seat he could never fill? He was going to grow young again, get another chance at life. He would move to some far part of the earth and be another man.

Another man. He thought about it and it was refreshing. Dropping all the old dead wood of past association, all the ancient accumulation of responsibilities.

Norton had taken on the job. Norton would deliver.

Mr. Miller: *What I want to know is this: Where do we stop? You give this life continuation to a man and he'll want his wife and kids to have it. And his wife will want her Aunt Minnie to have it and the kids will want the family dog to have it and the dog will want—*

Chairman Leonard: *You're facetious, Mr. Miller.*

Mr. Miller: *I don't know what that big word means, mister. You guys here in Geneva talk fancy with them six-bit words and you get the people all balled up. It's time the common people got in a word of common sense.*

> From the Records of a hearing before the science subcommittee of the public policy committee of the World House of Representatives.

"Frankly," Norton told him, "it's the first time I ever ran across a thing I couldn't fix. Ask me anything else you want to, senator, and I'll rig it up for you."

The senator sat stricken. "You mean you couldn't— But, Norton, there was Dr. Carson and Galloway and Henderson. Someone took care of them."

Norton shook his head. "Not I. I never heard of them."

"But someone did," said the senator. "They disappeared—"

His voice trailed off and he slumped deeper in the chair and the truth suddenly was plain—the truth he had failed to see.

A blind spot, he told himself. A blind spot!

They had disappeared and that was all he knew. They had published their own deaths and had not died, but had disappeared.

He had assumed they had disappeared because they had got an illegal continuation. But that was sheer wishful thinking. There was no foundation for it, no fact that would support it.

There could be other reasons, he told himself, many other

reasons why a man would disappear and seek to cover up his tracks with a death report.

But it had tied in so neatly!

They were continuators whose applications had not been renewed. Exactly as he was a continuator whose application would not be renewed.

They had dropped out of sight. Exactly as he would have to drop from sight once he gained another lease on life.

It had tied in so neatly—and it had been all wrong.

"I tried every way I knew," said Norton. "I canvassed every source that might advance your name for continuation and they laughed at me. It's been tried before, you see, and there's not a chance of getting it put through. Once your original sponsor drops you, you're automatically cancelled out.

"I tried to sound out technicians who might take a chance, but they're incorruptible. They get paid off in added years for loyalty and they're not taking any chance of trading years for dollars."

"I guess that settles it," the senator said wearily. "I should have known."

He heaved himself to his feet and faced Norton squarely. "You are telling me the truth," he pleaded. "You aren't just trying to jack up the price a bit."

Norton stared at him, almost unbelieving. "Jack up the price! Senator, if I had put this through, I'd have taken your last penny. Want to know how much you're worth? I can tell you within a thousand dollars."

He waved a hand at a row of filing cases ranged along the wall.

"It's all there, senator. You and all the other big shots. Complete files on every one of you. When a man comes to me with a deal like yours, I look in the files and strip him to the bone."

"I don't suppose there's any use of asking for some of my money back?"

Norton shook his head. "Not a ghost. You took your gamble, senator. You can't even prove you paid me. And, beside, you still have plenty left to last you the few years you have to live."

The senator took a step toward the door, then turned back.

"Look, Norton, I can't die! Not now. Just one more continuation and I'd be—"

The look on Norton's face stopped him in his tracks. The look he'd glimpsed on other faces at other times, but only glimpsed. Now he stared at it—at the naked hatred of a man whose life is short for the man whose life is long.

"Sure, you can die," said Norton. "You're going to. You can't live forever. Who do you think you are!"

The senator reached out a hand and clutched the desk.

"But you don't understand."

"You've already lived ten times as long as I have lived," said Norton, coldly, measuring each word, "and I hate your guts for it. Get out of here, you sniveling old fool, before I throw you out."

Dr. Barton: *You may think that you would confer a boon on humanity with life continuation, but I tell you, sir, that it would be a curse. Life would lose its value and its meaning if it went on forever, and if you have life continuation now, you eventually must stumble on immortality. And when that happens, sir, you will be compelled to set up boards of review to grant the boon of death. The people, tired of life, will storm your hearing rooms to plead for death.*

Chairman Leonard: *It would banish uncertainty and fear.*

Dr. Barton: *You are talking of the fear of death. The fear of death, sir, is infantile.*

Chairman Leonard: *But there are benefits—*

Dr. Barton: *Benefits, yes. The benefit of allowing a scientist the extra years he needs to complete a piece of research; a composer an additional lifetime to complete a symphony. Once the novelty wore off, men in general would accept added life only under protest, only as a duty.*

Chairman Leonard: *You're not very practical-minded, doctor.*

Dr. Barton: *But I am. Extremely practical and down to earth. Man must have newness. Man cannot be bored and live. How much do you think there would be left to look forward to after the millionth woman, the billionth piece of pumpkin pie?*

From the Records of the hearing before the science subcommittee of the public policy committee of the World House of Representatives.

So Norton hated him.

As all people of normal lives must hate, deep within their souls, the lucky ones whose lives went on and on.

A hatred deep and buried, most of the time buried. But sometimes breaking out, as it had broken out of Norton.

Resentment, tolerated because of the gently, skillfully fostered hope that those whose lives went on might some day make it possible that the lives of all, barring violence or accident or incurable disease, might go on as long as one would wish.

I can understand it now, thought the senator, for I am one of them. I am one of those whose lives will not continue to go on, and I have even fewer years than the most of them.

He stood before the window in the deepening dusk and saw the lights come out and the day die above the unbelievably blue waters of the far-famed lake.

Beauty came to him as he stood there watching, beauty that had gone unnoticed through all the later years. A beauty and a softness and a feeling of being one with the city lights and the last faint gleam of day above the darkening waters.

Fear? The senator admitted it.

Bitterness? Of course.

Yet, despite the fear and bitterness, the window held him with the scene it framed.

Earth and sky and water, he thought. I am one with them. Death has made me one with them. For death brings one back to the elementals, to the soil and trees, to the clouds and sky and the sun dying in the welter of its blood in the crimson west.

This is the price we pay, he thought, that the race must pay, for its life eternal—that we may not be able to assess in their true value the things that should be dearest to us; for a thing that has no ending, a thing that goes on forever, must have decreasing value.

Rationalization, he accused himself. Of course, you're rationalizing. You want another hundred years as badly as you ever did. You want a chance at immortality. But you can't have it and you trade eternal life for a sunset seen across a lake and it is well you can. It is a blessing that you can.

The senator made a rasping sound within his throat.

Behind him the telephone came to sudden life and he swung around. It chirred at him again. Feet pattered down the hall and the senator called out: "I'll get it, Otto."

He lifted the receiver. "New York calling," said the operator. "Senator Leonard, please."

"This is Leonard."

Another voice broke in. "Senator, this is Gibbs."

"Yes," said the senator. "The executioner."

"I called you," said Gibbs, "to talk about the election."

"What election?"

"The one here in North America. The one you're running in. Remember?"

"I am an old man," said the senator, "and I'm about to die. I'm not interested in elections."

Gibbs practically chattered. "But you have to be. What's the matter with you, senator? You have to do something. Make some speeches, make a statement, come home and stump the country. The party can't do it all alone. You have to do some of it yourself."

"I will do something," declared the senator. "Yes, I think that finally I'll do something."

He hung up and walked to the writing desk, snapped on the light. He got paper out of a drawer and took a pen out of his pocket.

The telephone went insane and he paid it no attention. It rang on and on and finally Otto came and answered.

"New York calling, sir," he said.

The senator shook his head and he heard Otto talking softly and the phone did not ring again.

The senator wrote:

To Whom It May Concern:

Then crossed it out.

He wrote:

A Statement to the World:

And crossed it out.

He wrote:

A Statement by Senator Homer Leonard:

He crossed that out, too.

He wrote:

Five centuries ago the people of the world gave into the hands of a few trusted men and women the gift of continued life in the hope and belief that they would work to advance the day when longer life spans might be made possible for the entire population.

From time to time, life continuation has been granted additional men and women, always with the implied understanding that the gift was made under the same conditions—that the persons so favored should work against the day when each inhabitant of the entire world might enter upon a heritage of near-eternity.

Through the years some of us have carried that trust forward and have lived with it and cherished it and bent every effort toward its fulfillment.

Some of us have not.

Upon due consideration and searching examination of my own status in this regard, I have at length decided that I no longer can accept further extension of the gift.

Human dignity requires that I be able to meet my fellow man upon the street or in the byways of the world without flinching from him. This I could not do should I continue to accept a gift to which I have no claim and which is denied to other men.

The senator signed his name, neatly, carefully, without the usual flourish.

"There," he said, speaking aloud in the silence of the night-filled room, "that will hold them for a while."

Feet padded and he turned around.

"It's long past your usual bedtime, sir," said Otto.

The senator rose clumsily and his aching bones protested. Old, he thought. Growing old again. And it would be so easy to start over, to regain his youth and live another lifetime. Just the nod of someone's head, just a single pen stroke and he would be young again.

"This statement, Otto," he said. "Please give it to the press."

"Yes, sir," said Otto. He took the paper, held it gingerly.

"Tonight," said the senator.

"Tonight, sir? It is rather late."

"Nevertheless, I want to issue it tonight."

"It must be important, sir."

"It's my resignation," said the senator.

"Your resignation! From the senate, sir!"

"No," said the senator. "From life."

Mr. Michaelson: *As a churchman, I cannot think otherwise than that the proposal now before you gentlemen constitutes a perversion of God's law. It is not within the province of man to say a man may live beyond his allotted time.*

Chairman Leonard: *I might ask you this: How is one to know when a man's allotted time has come to an end? Medicine has prolonged the lives of many persons. Would you call a physician a perverter of God's law?*

Mr. Michaelson: It has become apparent through the testimony given here that the eventual aim of continuing research is immortality. Surely you can see that physical immortality does not square with the Christian concept. I tell you this, sir: You can't fool God and get away with it.

From the Records of a hearing before the science subcommittee of the public policy committee of the World House of Representatives.

Chess is a game of logic.

But likewise a game of ethics.

You do not shout and you do not whistle, nor bang the pieces on the board, nor twiddle your thumbs, nor move a piece then take it back again. When you're beaten, you admit it. You do not force your opponent to carry on the game to absurd lengths. You resign and start another game if there is time to play one. Otherwise, you just resign and you do it with all the good grace possible. You do not knock all the pieces to the floor in anger. You do not get up abruptly and stalk out of the room. You do not reach across the board and punch your opponent in the nose.

When you play chess you are, or you are supposed to be, a gentleman.

The senator lay wide-awake, staring at the ceiling.

You do not reach across the board and punch your opponent in the nose. You do not knock the pieces to the floor.

But this isn't chess, he told himself, arguing with himself. This isn't chess; this is life and death. A dying thing is not a gentleman. It does not curl up quietly and die of the hurt inflicted. It backs into a corner and it fights, it lashes back and does all the hurt it can.

And I am hurt. I am hurt to death.

And I have lashed back. I have lashed back, most horribly.

They'll not be able to walk down the street again, not ever again, those gentlemen who passed the sentence on me. For they have no more claim to continued life than I and the people now will know it. And the people will see to it that they do not get it.

I will die, but when I go down I'll pull the others with me. They'll know I pulled them down, down with me into the pit of death. That's the sweetest part of all—they'll know who pulled them down and they won't be able to say a word about it. They can't even contradict the noble things I said.

Someone in the corner said, some voice from some other time and place: *You're no gentleman, senator. You fight a dirty fight.*

Sure I do, said the senator. They fought dirty first. And politics always was a dirty game.

Remember all that fine talk you dished out to Lee the other day?

That was the other day, snapped the senator.

You'll never be able to look a chessman in the face again, said the voice in the corner.

I'll be able to look my fellow men in the face, however, said the senator.

Will you? asked the voice.

And that, of course, was the question. Would he?

I don't care, the senator cried desperately. I don't care what happens. They played a lousy trick on me. They can't get away with it. I'll fix their clocks for them. I'll—

Sure, you will, said the voice, mocking.

Go away, shrieked the senator. Go away and leave me. Let me be alone.

You are alone, said the thing in the corner. *You are more alone than any man has ever been before.*

Chairman Leonard: *You represent an insurance company, do you not, Mr. Markely? A big insurance company.*

Mr. Markely: *That is correct.*

Chairman Leonard: *And every time a person dies, it costs your company money?*

Mr. Markely: *Well, you might put it that way if you wished, although it is scarcely the case—*

Chairman Leonard: *You do have to pay out benefits on deaths, don't you?*

Mr. Markely: *Why, yes, of course we do.*

Chairman Leonard: *Then I can't understand your opposition to life continuation. If there were fewer deaths, you'd have to pay fewer benefits.*

Mr. Markely: *All very true, sir. But if people had reason to believe they would live virtually forever, they'd buy no life insurance.*

Chairman Leonard: *Oh, I see. So that's the way it is*

> From the Records of a hearing before the science subcommittee of the public policy committee of the World House of Representatives.

The senator awoke. He had not been dreaming, but it was almost as if he had awakened from a bad dream—or awakened to a bad dream—and he struggled to go back to sleep again, to gain the Nirvana of unawareness, to shut out the harsh reality of existence, to dodge the shame of knowing who and what he was.

But there was someone stirring in the room, and someone spoke to him and he sat upright in bed, stung to wakefulness by the happiness and something else that was almost worship which the voice held.

"It's wonderful, sir," said Otto. "There have been phone calls all night long. And the telegrams and radiograms still are stacking up."

The senator rubbed his eyes with pudgy fists.

"Phone calls, Otto? People sore at me?"

"Some of them were, sir. Terribly angry, sir. But not too many of them. Most of them were happy and wanted to tell you what a great thing you'd done. But I told them you were tired and I could not waken you."

"Great thing?" said the senator. "What great thing have I done?"

"Why, sir, giving up life continuation. One man said to tell you it was the greatest example of moral courage the world had ever known. He said all the common people would bless you for it. Those were his very words. He was very solemn, sir."

The senator swung his feet to the floor, sat on the edge of the bed, scratching at his ribs.

It was strange, he told himself, how a thing would turn out sometimes. A heel at bedtime and a hero in the morning.

"Don't you see, sir," said Otto, "you have made yourself one of the common people, one of the short-lived people. No one has ever done a thing like that before."

"I was one of the common people," said the senator, "long before I wrote that statement. And I didn't make myself one of them. I was forced to become one of them, much against my will."

But Otto, in his excitement, didn't seem to hear.

He rattled on: "The newspapers are full of it, sir. It's the biggest news in years. The political writers are chuckling over it. They're calling it the smartest political move that was ever pulled. They say that before you made the announcement you didn't have a chance of being re-elected senator and now, they say, you can be elected president if you just say the word."

The senator sighed. "Otto," he said, "please hand me my pants. It is cold in here."

Otto handed him his trousers. "There's a newspaperman waiting in the study, sir. I held all the others off, but this one sneaked in the back way. You know him, sir, so I let him wait. He is Mr. Lee."

"I'll see him," said the senator.

So it was a smart political move, was it? Well, maybe so, but after a day or so, even the surprised political experts would begin to wonder about the logic of a man literally giving up his life to be re-elected to a senate seat.

Of course the common herd would love it, but he had not done it for applause. Although, so long as the people insisted upon thinking of him as great and noble, it was all right to let them go on thinking so.

The senator jerked his tie straight and buttoned his coat. He went into the study and Lee was waiting for him.

"I suppose you want an interview," said the senator. "Want to know why I did this thing."

Lee shook his head. "No, senator, I have something else. Something you should know about. Remember our talk last week? About the disappearances."

The senator nodded.

"Well, I have something else. You wouldn't tell me anything last week, but maybe now you will. I've checked, senator, and I've found this—the health winners are disappearing, too. More than eighty percent of those who participated in the finals of the last ten years have disappeared."

"I don't understand," said the senator.

"They're going somewhere," said Lee. "Something's happening to them. Something's happening to two classes of our people—the continuators and the healthiest youngsters."

"Wait a minute," gasped the senator. "Wait a minute, Mr. Lee."

He groped his way to the desk, grasped its edge and lowered himself into a chair.

"There is something wrong, senator?" asked Lee.

"Wrong?" mumbled the senator. "Yes, there must be something wrong."

"They've found living space," said Lee, triumphantly. "That's it, isn't it? They've found living space and they're sending out the pioneers."

The senator shook his head. "I don't know, Lee. I have not been informed. Check Extrasolar Research. They're the only ones who know—and they wouldn't tell you."

Lee grinned at him. "Good day, senator," he said. "Thanks so much for helping."

Dully, the senator watched him go.

Living space? Of course, that was it.

They had found living space and Extrasolar Research was sending out handpicked pioneers to prepare the way. It would take years of work and planning before the discovery could be announced. For once announced, world government must be ready to confer immortality on a mass production basis, must have ships available to carry out the hordes to the far, new worlds. A premature announcement would bring psychological and economic disruption that would make the government a shambles. So they would work very quietly, for they must work quietly.

His eyes found the little stack of letters on one corner of the desk and he remembered, with a shock of guilt, that he had meant to read them. He had promised Otto that he would and then he had forgotten.

I keep forgetting all the time, said the senator. I forget to read my paper and I forget to read my letters and I forget that some men are loyal and morally honest instead of slippery and slick. And I indulge in wishful thinking and that's the worst of all.

Continuators and health champions disappearing. Sure, they're disappearing. They're headed for new worlds and immortality.

And I . . . I . . . if only I had kept my big mouth shut—

The phone chirped and he picked it up.

"This is Sutton at Extrasolar Research," said an angry voice.

"Yes, Dr. Sutton," said the senator. "It's nice of you to call."

"I'm calling in regard to the invitation that we sent you last week," said Sutton. "In view of your statement last night, which we feel very keenly is an unjust criticism, we are withdrawing it."

"Invitation," said the senator. "Why, I didn't—"

"What I can't understand," said Sutton, "is why, with the invitation in your pocket, you should have acted as you did."

"But," said the senator, "but, doctor—"

"Good-by, senator," said Sutton.

Slowly the senator hung up. With a fumbling hand, he reached out and picked up the stack of letters.

It was the third one down. The return address was Extrasolar Research and it had been registered and sent special delivery and it was marked both PERSONAL and IMPORTANT.

The letter slipped out of the senator's trembling fingers and fluttered to the floor. He did not pick it up.

It was too late now, he knew, to do anything about it.

THE ONLY THING WE LEARN

by C.M. Kornbluth (1923-1958)

***Startling Stories*, July**

One of the great things about Cyril Kornbluth is that his stories stand the test of time, and this little gem is a perfect example of this virtue. It also conveys the essence of the attitude he brought to almost all his fiction—an intense cynicism that was an extension of himself. When he died at the age of thirty-five he had been a professional writer for nearly twenty years. What would he have said about the 1960s and beyond? It is a tragedy that we will never know. However, he left us a great deal, and will begin to appear frequently in future volumes in this series.—M.H.G.

(I like to use quotations or well-known phrases, or parts of them, for titles, and so do others.

In Philosophy of History, *published in 1832, and written by the German philosopher, Georg W. F. Hegel, it is stated, "What experience and history teach is this—that people and governments never have learned anything from history, or acted on principles deduced from it."*

And in 1903, George Bernard Shaw, in The Revolutionist's Handbook, *deliberately paraphrasing Hegel, said, "We learn from history that we learn nothing from history." The usual form the quotation takes today is "The only thing we learn from history is that we don't learn anything from history."*

This is just a little bit of pedantry on my part. Now go ahead and read "The Only Thing We Learn" by C. M. Kornbluth.—I.A.)

The Professor, though he did not know the actor's phrase for it, was counting the house—peering through a spyhole in the door through which he would in a moment appear before the class. He was pleased with what he saw. Tier after tier of young people, ready with notebooks and styli, chattering tentatively, glancing at the door against which his nose was flattened, waiting for the pleasant interlude known as "Archaeo-Literature 203" to begin.

The professor stepped back, smoothed his tunic, crooked four books in his left elbow and made his entrance. Four swift strides brought him to the lectern and, for the thousandth-odd time, he impassively swept the lecture hall with his gaze. Then he gave a wry little smile. Inside, for the thousandth-odd time, he was nagged by the irritable little thought that the lectern really ought to be a foot or so higher.

The irritation did not show. He was out to win the audience, and he did. A dead silence, the supreme tribute, gratified him. Imperceptibly, the lights of the lecture hall began to dim and the light on the lectern to brighten.

He spoke.

"Young gentlemen of the Empire, I ought to warn you that this and the succeeding lectures will be most subversive."

There was a little rustle of incomprehension from the audience—but by then the lectern light was strong enough to show the twinkling smile about his eyes that belied his stern mouth, and agreeable chuckles sounded in the gathering darkness of the tiered seats. Glow-lights grew bright gradually at the students' tables, and they adjusted their notebooks in the narrow ribbons of illumination. He waited for the small commotion to subside.

"Subversive—" He gave them a link to cling to. "Subversive because I shall make every effort to tell both sides of our ancient beginnings with every resource of archaeology and with every clue my diligence has discovered in our epic literature.

"There *were* two sides, you know—difficult though it may be to believe that if we judge by the Old Epic alone—such epics as the noble and tempestuous *Chant of Remd,* the remaining fragments of *Krall's Voyage,* or the gory and rather out-of-date *Battle for the Ten Suns*." He paused while styli scribbled across the notebook pages.

"The Middle Epic is marked, however, by what I might call the rediscovered ethos." From his voice, every student knew that that phrase, surer than death and taxes, would appear on an examination paper. The styli scribbled. "By this I mean an awakening of fellow-feeling with the Home Suns People, which had once been filial loyalty to them when our ancestors were few and pioneers, but which turned into contempt when their numbers grew.

"The Middle Epic writers did not despise the Home Suns People, as did the bards of the Old Epic. Perhaps this was because they did not have to—since their long war against the Home Suns was drawing to a victorious close.

"Of the New Epic I shall have little to say. It was a literary fad, a pose, and a silly one. Written within historic times, the some two score pseudo-epics now moulder in their cylinders, where they belong. Our ripening civilization could not with integrity work in the epic form, and the artistic failures produced so indicate. Our genius turned to the lyric and to the unabashedly romantic novel.

"So much, for the moment, of literature. What contribution, you must wonder, have archaeological studies to make in an investigation of the wars from which our ancestry emerged?

"Archaeology offers—one—a check in historical matter in the epics—confirming or denying. Two—it provides evidence glossed over in the epics—for artistic or patriotic reasons. Three—it provides evidence which has been lost, owing to the fragmentary nature of some of the early epics."

All this he fired at them crisply, enjoying himself. Let them not think him a dreamy litterateur, nor, worse, a flat precisionist, but let them be always a little off-balance before him, never knowing what came next, and often wondering, in class and out. The styli paused after heading Three.

"We shall examine first, by our archaeo-literary technique, the second book of the *Chant of Remd*. As the selected youth of the Empire, you know much about it, of course—much that is false, some that is true and a great deal that is irrelevant. You know that Book One hurls us into the middle of things, aboard ship with Algan and his great captain, Remd, on their way from the triumph over a Home Suns stronghold, the planet Telse. We watch Remd on his diversionary action that splits the Ten Suns Fleet into two halves. But before we see the destruction of those halves by the Horde of Algan, we are told in Book Two of the battle for Telse."

He opened one of his books on the lectern, swept the amphitheater again and read sonorously.

"Then battle broke
And high the blinding blast
Sight-searing leaped
While folk in fear below
Cowered in caverns
From the wrath of Remd—

"Or, in less sumptuous language, one fission bomb—or a stick of time-on-target bombs—was dropped. An unprepared and disorganized populace did not take the standard measure of dispersing, but huddled foolishly to await Algan's gunfighters and the death they brought.

"One of the things you believe because you have seen them in notes to elementary-school editions of *Remd* is that Telse was the fourth planet of the star, Sol. Archaeology denies it by establishing that the fourth planet—actually called Marse, by the way—was in those days weather-roofed at least, and possibly atmosphere-roofed as well. As potential warriors, you know that one does not waste fissionable material on a roof, and there is no mention of chemical explosives being used to crack the roof. Marse, therefore, was not the locale of *Remd*, Book Two.

"Which planet was? The answer to that has been established by X-radar, differential decay analyses, video-coring and every other resource of those scientists still quaintly called 'diggers.' We know and can prove that Telse was the *third* planet of Sol. So much for the opening of the attack. Let us jump to Canto Three, the Storming of the Dynastic Palace.

> "Imperial purple wore they
> Fresh from the feast
> Grossly gorged
> They sought to slay—

"And so on. Now, as I warned you, Remd is of the Old Epic, and makes no pretense at fairness. The unorganized huddling of Telse's population was read as cowardice instead of poor A.R.P. The same is true of the Third Canto. Video-cores show on the site of the palace a hecatomb of dead in once-purple livery, but also shows impartially that they were not particularly gorged and that digestion of their last meals had been well advanced. They didn't give such a bad accounting of themselves, either. I hesitate to guess, but perhaps they accounted for one of our ancestors apiece and were simply outnumbered. The study is not complete.

"That much we know." The professor saw they were tiring of the terse scientist and shifted gears. "But if the veil of time were rent that shrouds the years between us and the Home Suns People, how much more would we learn? Would we despise the Home Suns People as our frontiersman ancestors did, or would we cry: '*This* is our spiritual home—this world of rank and order, this world of formal verse and exquisitely patterned arts'?"

If the veil of time were rent—?

We can try to rend it . . .

Wing Commander Arris heard the clear jangle of the radar net alarm as he was dreaming about a fish. Struggling out of his too-deep, too-soft bed, he stepped into a purple singlet, buckled on his Sam Browne belt with its holstered .45 automatic and tried to read the radar screen. Whatever had set it off was either too small or too distant to register on the five-inch C.R.T.

He rang for his aide, and checked his appearance in a wall-mirror while waiting. His space tan was beginning to fade, he saw, and made a mental note to get it renewed at the parlor. He stepped into the corridor as Evan, his aide, trotted up—younger, browner, thinner, but the same officer type that made the Service what it was, Arris thought with satisfaction.

Evan gave him a bone-cracking salute, which he returned. They set off for the elevator that whisked them down to a large, chilly, dark underground room where faces were greenly lit by radar screens and the lights of plotting tables. Somebody yelled "Attention!" and the tecks snapped. He gave them "At ease" and took the brisk salute of the senior teck, who reported to him in flat, machine-gun delivery:

"Object-becoming-visible-on-primary-screen-sir."

He studied the sixty-inch disk for several seconds before he spotted the intercepted particle. It was coming in fast from zenith, growing while he watched.

"Assuming it's now traveling at maximum, how long will it be before it's within striking range?" he asked the teck.

"Seven hours, sir."

"The interceptors at Idlewild alerted?"

"Yessir."

Arris turned on a phone that connected with Interception. The boy at Interception knew the face that appeared on its screen, and was already capped with a crash helmet.

"Go ahead and take him, Efrid," said the wing commander.

"Yessir!" and a punctilious salute, the boy's pleasure plain at being known by name and a great deal more at being on the way to a fight that might be first-class.

Arris cut him off before the boy could detect a smile that was forming on his face. He turned from the pale lunar glow of the sixty-incher to enjoy it. Those kids—when every meteor was an invading dreadnaught, when every ragged scouting ship from the rebels was an armada!

He watched Efrid's squadron soar off on the screen and then he retreated to a darker corner. This was his post until the meteor or scout or whatever it was got taken care of. Evan joined him, and they silently studied the smooth, disciplined functioning of the plot room, Arris with satisfaction and Evan doubtless with the same. The aide broke silence, asking:

"Do you suppose it's a Frontier ship, sir?" He caught the wing commander's look and hastily corrected himself: "I mean rebel ship, sir, of course."

"Then you should have said so. Is that what the junior officers generally call those scoundrels?"

Evan conscientiously cast his mind back over the last few junior messes and reported unhappily: "I'm afraid we do, sir. We seem to have got into the habit."

"I shall write a memorandum about it. How do you account for that very peculiar habit?"

"Well, sir, they do have something like a fleet, and they did take over the Regulus Cluster, didn't they?"

What had got into this incredible fellow, Arris wondered in amazement. Why, the thing was self-evident! They had a few ships—accounts differed as to how many—and they had, doubtless by raw sedition, taken over some systems temporarily.

He turned from his aide, who sensibly became interested in a screen and left with a murmured excuse to study it very closely.

The brigands had certainly knocked together some ramshackle league or other, but— The wing commander wondered briefly if it could last, shut the horrid thought from his head, and set himself to composing mentally a stiff memorandum that would be posted in the junior officer's mess and put an end to this absurd talk.

His eyes wandered to the sixty-incher, where he saw the interceptor squadron climbing nicely toward the particle—which, he noticed, had become three particles. A low crooning distracted him. Was one of the tecks singing at work? It couldn't be!

It wasn't. An unsteady shape wandered up in the darkness, murmuring a song and exhaling alcohol. He recognized the Chief Archivist, Glen.

"This is Service country, mister," he told Glen.

"Hullo, Arris," the round little civilian said, peering at him.

"I come down here regularly—regularly against regulations—to wear off my regular irregularities with the wine bottle. That's all right, isn't it?"

He was drunk and argumentative. Arris felt hemmed in. Glen couldn't be talked into leaving without loss of dignity to the wing commander, and he couldn't be chucked out because he was writing a biography of the chamberlain and could, for the time being, have any head in the palace for the asking. Arris sat down unhappily, and Glen plumped down beside him.

The little man asked him.

"Is that a fleet from the Frontier League?" He pointed to the big screen. Arris didn't look at his face, but felt that Glen was grinning maliciously.

"I know of no organization called the Frontier League," Arris said. "If you are referring to the brigands who have recently been operating in Galactic East, you could at least call them by their proper names." Really, he thought—civilians!

"So sorry. But the brigands should have the Regulus Cluster by now, shouldn't they?" he asked, insinuatingly.

This was serious—a grave breach of security. Arris turned to the little man.

"Mister, I have no authority to command you," he said measuredly. "Furthermore, I understand you are enjoying a temporary eminence in the non-service world which would make it very difficult for me to—ah—tangle with you. I shall therefore refer only to your altruism. How did you find out about the Regulus Cluster?"

"Eloquent!" murmured the little man, smiling happily. "I got it from Rome."

Arris searched his memory. "You mean Squadron Commander Romo broke security? I can't believe it!"

"No, commander. I mean Rome—a place—a time—a civilization. I got it also from Babylon, Assyria, the Mogul Raj—every one of them. You don't understand me, of course."

"I understand that you're trifling with Service security and that you're a fat little, malevolent, worthless drone and scribbler!"

"Oh, commander!" protested the archivist. "I'm not so little!" He wandered away, chuckling.

Arris wished he had the shooting of him, and tried to explore the chain of secrecy for a weak link. He was tired and bored by this harping on the Fron—on the brigands.

His aide tentatively approached him. "Interceptors in striking range, sir," he murmured.

"Thank you," said the wing commander, genuinely grateful to be back in the clean, etched-line world of the Service and out of that blurred, water-color, civilian land where long-dead Syrians apparently retailed classified matter to nasty little drunken warts who had no business with it. Arris confronted the sixty-incher. The particle that had become three particles was now—he counted—eighteen particles. Big ones. Getting bigger.

He did not allow himself emotion, but turned to the plot on the interceptor squadron.

"Set up Lunar relay," he ordered.

"Yessir."

Half the plot room crew bustled silently and efficiently about the delicate job of applied relativistic physics that was 'lunar relay.' He knew that the palace power plant could take it for a few minutes, and he wanted to *see*. If he could not believe radar pips, he might believe a video screen.

On the great, green circle, the eighteen—now twenty-four—particles neared the thirty-six smaller particles that were interceptors, led by the eager young Efrid.

"Testing Lunar relay, sir," said the chief teck.

The wing commander turned to a twelve-inch screen. Unobtrusively, behind him, tecks jockeyed for position. The picture on the screen was something to see. The chief let mercury fill a thick-walled, ceramic tank. There was a sputtering and contact was made.

"Well done," said Arris. "Perfect seeing."

He saw, upper left, a globe of ships—what ships! Some were Service jobs, with extra turrets plastered on them wherever there was room. Some were orthodox freighters, with the same porcupine-bristle of weapons. Some were obviously home-made crates, hideously ugly—and as heavily armed as the others.

Next to him, Arris heard his aide murmur, "It's all wrong, sir. They haven't got any pick-up boats. They haven't got any hospital ships. What happens when one of them gets shot up?"

"Just what ought to happen, Evan," snapped the wing commander. "They float in space until they desiccate in their suits. Or if they get grappled inboard with a boat hook, they don't get any medical care. As I told you, they're brigands, without decency even to care for their own." He enlarged on the theme. "Their morale must be insignificant compared with our men's. When the Service goes into action, every rating and teck knows he'll be cared for if he's hurt. Why, if we didn't have pick-up boats and hospital ships the men wouldn't—'' He almost finished it with ''fight,'' but thought, and lamely ended—''wouldn't like it.''

Evan nodded, wonderingly, and crowded his chief a little as he craned his neck for a look at the screen.

''Get the hell away from here!'' said the wing commander in a restrained yell, and Evan got.

The interceptor squadron swam into the field—a sleek, deadly needle of vessels in perfect alignment, with its little cloud of pick-ups trailing, and farther astern a white hospital ship with the ancient red cross.

The contact was immediate and shocking. One of the rebel ships lumbered into the path of the interceptors, spraying fire from what seemed to be as many points as a man has pores. The Service ships promptly riddled it and it should have drifted away—but it didn't. It kept on fighting. It rammed an interceptor with a crunch that must have killed every man before the first bulwark, but aft of the bulwark the ship kept fighting.

It took a torpedo portside and its plumbing drifted through space in a tangle. Still the starboard side kept squirting fire. Isolated weapon blisters fought on while they were obviously cut off from the rest of the ship. It was a pounded tangle of wreckage, and it had destroyed two interceptors, crippled two more, and kept fighting.

Finally, it drifted away, under feeble jets of power. Two more of the fantastic rebel fleet wandered into action, but the wing commander's horrified eyes were on the first pile of scrap. It was going *somewhere*—

The ship neared the thin-skinned, unarmored, gleaming hospital vessel, rammed it amidships, square in one of the red crosses, and then blew itself up, apparently with everything left in its powder magazine, taking the hospital ship with it.

The sickened wing commander would never have recognized what he had seen as it was told in a later version, thus:

''The crushing course they took
And nobly knew
Their death undaunted
By heroic blast
The hospital's host
They dragged to doom
Hail! Men without mercy
From the far frontier!''

Lunar relay flickered out as overloaded fuses flashed into vapor. Arris distractedly paced back to the dark corner and sank into a chair.

"I'm sorry," said the voice of Glen next to him, sounding quite sincere. "No doubt it was quite a shock to you."

"Not to you?" asked Arris bitterly.

"Not to me."

"Then how did they do it?" the wing commander asked the civilian in a low, desperate whisper. "They don't even wear .45's. Intelligence says their enlisted men have hit their officers and got away with it. They *elect* ship captains! Glen, what does it all mean?"

"It means," said the fat little man with a timbre of doom in his voice, "that they've returned. They always have. They always will. You see, commander, there is always somewhere a wealthy, powerful city, or nation, or world. In it are those whose blood is not right for a wealthy, powerful place. They must seek danger and overcome it. So they go out—on the marshes, in the desert, on the tundra, the planets, or the stars. Being strong, they grow stronger by fighting the tundra, the planets or the stars. They—they change. They sing new songs. They know new heroes. And then, one day, they return to their old home.

"They return to the wealthy, powerful city, or nation or world. They fight its guardians as they fought the tundra, the planets or the stars—a way that strikes terror to the heart. Then they sack the city, nation or world and sing great, ringing sagas of their deeds. They always have. Doubtless they always will."

"But what shall we do?"

"We shall cower, I suppose, beneath the bombs they drop on us, and we shall die, some bravely, some not, defending the palace within a very few hours. But you will have your revenge."

"How?" asked the wing commander, with haunted eyes.

The fat little man giggled and whispered in the officer's ear. Arris irritably shrugged it off as a bad joke. He didn't believe it. As he died, drilled through the chest a few hours later by one of Algan's gunfighters he believed it even less.

The professor's lecture was drawing to a close. There was time for only one more joke to send his students away happy. He was about to spring it when a messenger handed him two slips of paper. He raged inwardly at his ruined exit and poisonously read from them:

"I have been asked to make two announcements. One, a bulletin from General Sleg's force. He reports that the so-called Outland Insurrection is being brought under control and that there is no cause for alarm. Two, the gentlemen who are members of the S.O.T.C. will please report to the armory at 1375 hours—whatever that may mean—for blaster inspection. The class is dismissed."

Petulantly, he swept from the lectern and through the door.

PRIVATE—KEEP OUT

by Philip MacDonald (1896–1981?)

The Magazine of Fantasy*, Fall later known as *The Magazine of Fantasy and Science Fiction

The late Philip MacDonald was the grandson of the famous Scottish poet George MacDonald and a highly regarded Hollywood screenwriter and detective novelist. Perhaps his most famous film work was his script for Daphne du Maurier's Rebecca *(1940), but he also wrote a number of Mr. Moto and Charlie Chan films. His detective character Anthony Gethryn, introduced in 1924, appeared in some ten novels.*

MacDonald's work was partially lost in the large shadows of the two other great writers with the same last name—John D. and Ross MacDonald—which is a shame, because he was a major talent. Mystery critics maintain that his short stories are even better than his novels; "Private—Keep Out" was unfortunately one of only a handful of works he published in the sf field.

And we can't allow another moment to go by without welcoming The Magazine of Fantasy and Science Fiction *to this series. Few realized it at the time, but Anthony Boucher and J. Francis McComas had launched what many* believe to be the finest sf magazine of all time, one that is happily still with us today. —M.H.G.*

*Not *all*, Marty. (I.A.)

(They say that earthquakes are extremely terrifying, even if you are in no immediate danger of having anything fall on you; even if you are in an open field and no fissures form; even if it only lasts for a minute or so.

I have never experienced an earthquake, but I think I can imagine the sensation and can appreciate what it is that is so terrifying. It is the fact that the solid earth is moving, shaking, vibrating. We are so used to the ground we walk upon being the motionless substratum on which all exists, we take it so for granted, that when that basic assumption is negated for even a short time, we feel the terror of chaos.

And yet there are assumptions that are more basic still, and if we were to get the notion that these, too, might vanish, our terror would be past description. "Private—Keep Out" by Philip MacDonald deals with such a disruption and you will not be human if you don't feel a frisson of horror at the last sentence.

Marty, by the way, wondered if this story was really science fiction. My response was that it most certainly was; and not only that but that I liked it better than I did any other story in the book—including mine.—I.A.)

The world goes mad—and people tend to put the cause of its sickness down to Man; sometimes even to one particular little man. Perhaps, only a few months ago, I would have thought like this myself about the existing outbreak of virulent insanity—but now I can't.

I can't because of something which happened to me a little while ago. I was in Southern California, working at Paramount. Most days, I used to get to the studio about ten and leave at five forty-five, but on this particular evening—it was Wednesday, the 18th of June—I was a little late getting away.

I went out through the front hall and hurried across the street to the garage. The entrance is a tunnelled archway. It was fairly dark in there—and I bumped square into a man who'd either been on his way out or standing there in the deepest part of the shadow. The latter didn't seem probable, but I had an odd sort of feeling that that was just what he had been doing.

"Sorry," I said. "I was . . ." I cut myself off short and stared. I recognized him, but what with the semi-darkness and the funny, stiff way he was standing and looking at me, I couldn't place him. It wasn't one of those half-memories of having once met someone somewhere. It was a definite, full-fledged memory which told me this man had been a friend closely knit into my particular life-pattern, and not so long ago.

He turned away—and something about the movement slipped the loose memory-cog back into place. It was Charles Moffat—Charles who'd been a friend for fifteen years; Charles whom I hadn't seen or heard about since he'd gone east in a mysterious hurry two years ago; Charles whom I was delighted to see again; Charles who'd changed amazingly; Charles, as I realized with a shock, who must have been very ill.

I shouted his name and leapt after him and grabbed him by the arm and swung him around to face me.

"You old sucker!" I said. "Don't you know me?"

He smiled with his mouth but nothing happened to his eyes. He said:

"How are you? I thought you'd forgotten me."

It should have been a jest—but it wasn't. I felt . . . *uncomfortable*.

"It's so damn' dark in here!" I said, and dragged him out into the sunshine of the street. His arm felt very thin.

"Straight over to Lucey's for a drink!" I was prattling and knew it. "We can talk there. Listen, Charles; you've been ill, haven't you? I can see it. Why didn't you let me know?"

He didn't answer, and I went on babbling rubbish; trying to talk myself out of the . . . the *apprehensiveness* which seemed to be oozing out of him and wrapping itself around the pair of us like a grey fog. I kept looking at him as we walked past the barber's and reached the corner and turned towards Melrose and its rushing river of traffic. He was looking straight ahead of him. He was extraordinarily thin: he must have lost twenty pounds—and he'd never been fat. I kept wishing I could see his eyes again, and then being glad I couldn't.

We stood on the curb by the auto-park and waited a chance to cross Melrose. The sun was low now, and I was shading my eyes from it when Charles spoke for the first time.

"I can use that drink," he said, but he still didn't look at me.

I half-turned, to get the sun out of my eyes—and noticed the briefcase for the first time. It was tucked firmly under his left arm and clamped tightly to his side. Even beneath his sleeve I could see an unusual tensing of the wasted muscles. I was going to say something, but a break came in the traffic and Charles plunged out into the road ahead of me.

It was cool in Lucey's bar, and almost empty. I wondered if the barman would remember Charles, then recalled that he'd only been here a couple of months. We ordered—a gin-and-tonic for me and a whiskey-sour for Charles which he put down in a couple of gulps.

"Another?" he said. He was looking at the pack of cigarettes in his hand.

"Mine's long," I said. "Miss me this time."

While I finished my tall glass, he had two more whiskey-sours, the second with an absinthe float. I chatted, heavily. Charles didn't help: with the briefcase tucked under his arm and clamped against his side, he looked like a starving bird with one wing.

I bought another round—and began to exchange my uneasiness for a sort of anger. I said:

"Look here! This is damn ridiculous!" I swivelled around on my stool and stared at him.

He gave a small barking sound which I suppose was meant to be a laugh. He said:

"*Ridiculous!* . . . Maybe that's not *quite* the word, my boy."

He barked again—and I remembered his old laugh, a Gargantuan affair which would make strangers smile at thirty paces. My anger went and the other feeling came back.

"Look," I said, dropping my voice. "Tell me what's wrong, Charles. There's something awfully wrong. What *is* it?"

He stood up suddenly and clicked his fingers at the barman. "Two more," he said. "And don't forget the absinthe on mine."

He looked at me fully. His eyes were brighter now, but that didn't alter the look in them. I couldn't kid myself any more: it was fear—and, even to me who have seen many varieties of this unpleasant ailment, a new mixture. Not, in fact, as before, but a *new* fear; a fear which transcended all known variations upon the fear theme.

I supposed I sat there gaping at him. But he didn't look at me any more. He clamped the briefcase under his arm and turned away.

" 'Phone," he said. "Back in a minute."

He took a step and then halted, turning his head to speak to me over his shoulder. He said:

"Seen the Archers lately?" and then was gone.

That's exactly what he said, but at the time, I thought I must have mis-heard him—because I didn't know any Archers. Twenty-five years before, there'd been a John Archer at school with me but I hadn't known him well and hadn't liked what I did know.

I puzzled over this for a moment; then went back to my problem. What was the matter with Charles? Where had he been all this time? Why didn't anyone hear from or about him? Above all, what was he afraid of? And why should I be feeling, in the most extraordinary way, that life was a thin crust upon which we all moved perilously?

The barman, a placid crust-walker, set a new drink down in front of me and said something about the weather. I answered him eagerly, diving into a sunny sanctuary of platitude.

It did me good—until Charles came back. I watched him cross the room—and didn't like it. His clothes hung loose about him, with room for another Charles inside them. He picked up his drink and drained it. He drank with his left hand, because the briefcase was under his right arm now. I said:

"Why don't you put that thing down? What's in it, anyway—nuggets?"

He shifted it under the other arm and looked at me for a moment. He said:

"Just some papers. Where're you dining?"

"With you." I made a quick mental cancellation. "Or you are with me, rather."

"Good!" He nodded jerkily. "Let's get a booth now. One of the end ones."

I stood up. "Okay. But if we're going to drink any more, I'll switch to a martini."

He gave the order and we left the bar and in a minute were facing each other in a far corner booth. Charles looked right at me now, and I couldn't get away from his eyes and what was in them. A waiter came with the drinks and put them in front of us and went away. I looked down at mine and began to fool with the toothpick which speared the olive.

"You're not a moron," he said suddenly. "Nor a cabbage. Ever wake up in the morning and know you know the Key—but when you reach for it, you can't remember it? It was just *there* . . ." He made a vague, sharp gesture in the air, close to his head. "But it's gone the minute your waking mind reaches for it. Ever do that? Ever feel that? Not only when you wake maybe; perhaps at some other sort of time?"

He was looking down at the table now and I didn't have to see his eyes. He was looking down at his hands, claw-like as they fiddled with brass locks on the briefcase. I said:

"What're you talking about? What key?" I was deliberately dense.

His eyes blazed at me with some of the old Carolian fire.

"Listen, numbskull!" He spoke without opening his teeth. "Have you, at any moment in your wretched existence, ever felt that you knew, only a moment before, the answer to . . . to *everything?* To the colossal WHY of the Universe? To the myriad questions entailed by the elaborate creation of Man? To . . . to *Everything*, you damned fool!"

I stopped pretending. "Once or twice," I said. "Maybe more than that. You mean that awful sensation that you're on the verge of knowing the . . . the Universal Answer: and know it's amazingly simple and you wonder why you never thought of it before—and then you find you don't know it at all. It's gone; snatched away. And you go practically out of your mind trying to get it back but you never succeed. That's it, isn't it? I've had the feeling several times, notably coming out of ether. Everyone has. Why?''

He was fiddling with the briefcase again. ''Why what?'' he said dully. The momentary flash of the old fire had died away.

But I kept at him. I said:

''You can't start something like that and then throw it away. Why did you bring the subject up? Did you finally grab the Key this morning—or did it bite you—or what?''

He still didn't look up. He went on fiddling with the brass locks on the case.

''For God's sake, leave that thing alone!'' My irritation was genuine enough. ''It's getting on my nerves. Sit on it or something, if it's so precious. But quit *fiddling*!''

He stood up suddenly. He didn't seem to hear me.

'' 'Phone again,'' he said. ''Sorry. Forgot something. Won't be long.'' He started away; then turned and slapped the case down in front of me. ''Have a look through it. Might interest you.''

And he was gone. I put my hands on the case and was just going to slip the locks back with my thumbs, when a most extraordinary sensation . . . *permeated* me is the only word I can think of. I was suddenly extremely loath to open the thing. I pushed it away from me with a quick involuntary gesture, as if it were hot to the touch.

And immediately I was ashamed of this childish behavior and took myself in hand and in a moment had it open and the contents spread in front of me.

They were mostly papers, and all completely innocuous and unrelated. If you tried for a year you couldn't get together a less alarming collection.

There was a program from the Frohman Theatre, New York, for a play called ''Every Other Friday'' which I remembered seeing in '31. There was a letter from the Secretary to the Dean of Harvard, with several pages of names attached to it, saying that in answer to Mr. Moffat's letter he would find attached the list he had requested of the Alumni of 1925. There was a letter from the Manager of a Fifth Avenue apartment house, courteously replying to Mr. Moffat's request for a list of the tenants of his penthouse during the years 1933 to 1935. There were several old bills from a strange miscellany of stores, a folded page from an old school magazine containing the photograph of the football team of C.M.I. in the year 1919, and a page torn from "Who's Who" around one entry of which heavy blue pencil lines had been drawn.

And that finished the papers. There were only three other things—an empty, much-worn photograph frame of leather, a small silver plate (obviously unscrewed from the base of some trophy) with the names *Charles Moffat* and *T. Perry Devonshire* inscribed upon it, and an old briar pipe with a charred bowl and broken mouthpiece but a shiny new silver band.

The photograph frame stared up at me from the white tablecloth. I picked it up—and, as I did so, was struck by a sudden but undefinable familiarity. I turned it over in my hands, struggling with the elusive memory-shape, and I saw that, although the front of it bore every sign of considerable age and usage, it had never in fact been used. It was one of those frames which you undo at the back to insert the photograph, and pasted across the joint between the body of the frame and the movable part was the original price tag, very old and very dirty, but still bearing the dim figures $5.86.

I was still looking at it when Charles came back.

"Remember it?" he said.

I twisted the thing about, trying to find a new angle to look at it from. He said:

"It used to be on my desk. You've seen it hundreds of times."

I began to remember. I could see it sitting beside a horseshoe inkpot—but I couldn't see what was inside it. I said:

"I can't think what was in it." And then I remembered. "But there can't have been anything." I turned the thing over and showed him the price tag. I was suddenly conscious of personal fear.

"Charles!" I said. "What the hell *is* all this?"

He spoke—but he didn't answer me. He picked up the collection of nonsense and put it back into the briefcase.

"Did you look at all the stuff?" he said.

I nodded, watching him. It seemed that we never looked at each other squarely, for his eyes were upon his hands.

"Did it suggest anything?" he said.

"Not a thing. How could it?" I saw that the knuckles of his interlocked fingers were white. "Look here, Charles, if you don't tell me what all this is about I'll go out of my mind."

And then the head waiter came. He smiled at me and bowed gravely to Charles and asked whether we wished to order.

I was going to tell him to wait, but Charles took the menu and looked at it and ordered something, so I did the same.

It was nearly dark outside now and they'd put on the lights. People were beginning to come in and there was quite a murmur of talk from the bar. I held my tongue: the moment had passed—I must wait for another.

They brought cocktails and we sipped them and smoked and didn't speak until Charles broke the silence. He said then, much too casually:

"So you haven't been seeing much of the Archers?"

"Charles," I said carefully, "I don't know anyone called Archer. I never have—except an unpleasant little tick at school."

Our eyes met now, and he didn't look away. But a waiter came with hors d'oeuvres. I refused them, but Charles heaped his plate and began to eat with strange voracity.

"These Archers?" I said at last. "Who are they? Anything to do with this . . . this . . . trouble you seem to have?"

He looked at me momentarily; then down at his plate again. He finished what was on it and leaned back and gazed at the wall over my right shoulder. He said:

"Adrian Archer was a great friend of mine." He took a cigarette from the pack on the table and lit it. "He was also a friend of yours."

The waiter came again and took away my full plate and Charles's empty one.

"*What* did you say?" I wasn't trusting my ears.

He took the briefcase from the seat beside him and groped in it and brought his hand out holding the extract from "Who's Who."

"Look at this." He handed me the sheet. "That's Adrian's father."

I took the paper, but went on staring at him. His eyes were glittering.

"Go on!" he said. "Read it."

The marked entry was short and prosaic. It was the history, in seven lines, of an Episcopalian minister named William Archibald Archer.

I read it carefully. I ought to have been feeling, I suppose, that Charles was a sick man. But I wasn't feeling anything of the sort. I can't describe what I was feeling.

I read the thing again.

"Look here, Charles," I said. "This man had three daughters. There's no mention of a son."

"Yes," said Charles. "I know."

He twiched the paper out of my hand and fished in the briefcase again and brought out the little silver plate. He said:

"In '29 I won the doubles in the Lakeside tennis tournament. Adrian Archer was my partner." His voice was flat, and the words without any emphasis. He handed the piece of metal across to me and once more I read *Charles Moffet—T. Perry Devonshire*. . . .

And then the waiter was with us again and for the longest half hour of my life I watched Charles devour his food while I pushed mine aside and drank a glass of wine. I watched him eat. I couldn't help myself. He ate with a sort of desperate determination; like a man clutching at the one reality.

Then, at last, the meal was over, with even the coffee gone and just brandy glasses before us. He began to talk. Not in the guarded, jerky way he had been using, but with words pouring out of him. He said:

"I'm going to tell you the story of Adrian Archer—straight. He was a contemporary of ours—in fact, I was at C.M.I. and Harvard with him. It was settled he should be a lawyer, but a year after he left Harvard he suddenly went on the stage. His father and all his friends—*you* included—advised him not to. But Adrian didn't pay attention. He just smiled, with that odd, *secret* smile he'd use sometimes. He just smiled—and his rise to what they call fame was what they call meteoric. In three years he was a big name on Broadway. In four he was another in London. In six they were billing his name before the title of the play—and in the eighth Hollywood grabbed him and made what they call a star out of him in a period they call overnight. That was four years ago—same year that you and I first came out here. We were both at RKO when he made his terrific hit in *Judgment Day*, playing the blind man. . . ."

For the first time I interrupted.

"Charles!" I said. "Charles! I saw *Judgment Day*. Spencer Tracy played . . ."

"Yes," said Charles. "I know. . . . When Adrian came to Hollywood, you and I were awfully glad to see him—and when Margaret came to join him and brought the kid and we'd installed them comfortably in a house on the Santa Monica Palisades, everything was fine."

He drained the brandy in his glass and tipped some more into it from the bottle. The single lamp on the table threw sharp-angled shadows across his face. He said:

"Well, there they were. Adrian went from success to success

in things like *The Key Above the Door, Fit for Heroes* and *Sunday's Children.*''

He stopped again—and looked directly at me.

''I'm sorry for you,'' he said suddenly. ''It's a bad spot to be in—meeting an old friend and finding he's gone out of his mind. And pretending to listen while your mind's busy with doctors' names and 'phone numbers.''

I said: ''I don't know what I think—except that I'm not doubting your sanity. And I can't understand why I'm not.''

I wished he'd stop looking at me now. But his eyes didn't leave my face. He said:

''Seen the Mortimers lately?''

I jumped as if he'd hit me. But I answered in a minute.

''Of course I have,'' I said. ''I see 'em all the time. Frank and I have been working together. Matter of fact, I had dinner there only last night.''

His mouth twisted into the shape of a smile. ''Still living on the Palisades, are they? 107 Paloma Drive?''

''Yes.'' I tried to keep my voice steady. ''They bought that place, you know.''

''Yes,'' said Charles, ''I know. The Archers had the next house, 109. You found it actually. Adrian liked it all right and Margaret and the boy were crazy about it, especially the pool.''

He drank some more brandy—and there was a long, sharp-edged silence. But I wouldn't say anything, and he began again. He said:

''D'you remember when you were at MGM two years ago? You were revamping that *Richard The Lion-Heart* job and you had to go to Del Monte on location?''

I nodded. I remembered very well.

''That,'' said Charles, ''was when it happened. The Mortimers gave a cocktail party. At least, that's what it started out to be, but it was after midnight when I left—with the Archers. I'd parked my car at the corner of Paloma and Palisade, right outside their house, so I walked along with them and went in for a nightcap. It was pretty hot, and we sat on the patio, looking over the swimming pool. There weren't any servants up and Adrian went into the house for the drinks. He'd been very quiet all night and not, I thought, looking particularly fit. I said something casual about this to Margaret—and then was surprised when she took me up, very seriously. She said: 'Charles: he's worried—and so am I!'' I remember looking at her and finding that her eyes were grave and troubled as I'd never seen them. 'Charles,' she said, 'he's . . . *frightened*—and so am I!' ''

Charles broke off again. He pulled out a handkerchief and I saw that sweat was glistening on his forehead. He said:

"Before I could say anything Adrian came out with a tray and put it down and began mixing drinks. He looked at Margaret—and asked what we'd been talking about and wouldn't be put off. She looked apprehensive when I told him, but he didn't seem to mind. He gave us both drinks and took one himself—and suddenly asked me a question I asked you earlier this evening."

"About the Key?" My voice surprised me: I hadn't told it to say anything.

Charles nodded. But he didn't go on.

"Then what?" said my voice. "Then what?"

"It's funny," he said. "But this is the first time I've told all this—and I've just realized I should've begun at the other end and said *I* was worried and frightened. Because I was—had been for weeks. . . ."

A frightful feeling of verification swept over me. I said excitedly:

"By God, I remember. About the time I went on location you were sort of down. You'd had a polo spill. I was a bit worried about you, but you said you were O.K. . . ."

For a moment I thought he was going to break. He looked—*Charles Moffat* looked—as if he were going to weep. But he took hold of himself, and the jaw-muscles in his face stood out like wire rope. He said:

"The doctor said I was all right. But I wasn't. Not by a mile! There was only one thing wrong with me—but that was plenty. I wasn't sleeping. It may have been something to do with the crack on the head or it may not. But, whatever it was, it was bad. Very bad. And dope made no difference—except, perhaps, for the worse. I'd *go* to sleep all right—but then I'd keep waking up. And that was the bad part. Because every time I'd wake, that God-damned Key would be a little nearer. . . . At first, it wasn't so worrying—merely an irritation. But as it went on, stronger and stronger, three and four and six times a night—well, it was *bad*!"

He stopped abruptly. His tongue seemed to be trying to moisten his lips. He took a swallow of brandy and then, incredibly, a long draught of water. The film of sweat was over his forehead again, and he mopped at it absentmindedly, with the back of his hand. He said:

"So there you are: and we're back again—half in moonlight, half in shadow—on Adrian's patio, and he's just asked me the question and Margaret is leaning forward, her chin cupped in her hands and I can feel her eyes on my face and I'm staring at Adrian in amazement that *he* should ask *me* whether *I* know what it's like to feel that you're coming nearer and nearer to the Answer—that simple, A.B.C. *answer* which has always eluded Man; the Answer which is forbidden to Man but which, when it's dangled in front of his nose like a donkey's carrot, he's bound to clutch for desperately. . . .

"We were pretty full of drink—you know what the Mortimer hospitality's like—and once I'd got over the awful shock of egotistical surprise at finding that another man, and my greatest friend to boot, was being ridden by a demon I'd considered my own personal property, we began to talk thirty to the dozen, while Margaret turned those great dark eyes upon us in turn. There was fear in them, but we went on, theorizing to reduce *our* fear, and traced the *Key-awareness* back to our adolescence and wondered why we'd never told each other about it at school and gradually—with the decanter getting lower and lower and the impossible California moon beginning to pale—began to strive to put into words what we *thought* might be the *shape* of the Key. . . .

"We didn't get very far and we didn't make much sense: who can when they're talking about things for which there are no words. But we frightened ourselves badly—and Margaret. We began to talk—or Adrian did, rather because he was much *nearer* than I'd ever been—we began to talk about the feeling that made it all the more essential to grasp the thing; the feeling that the knowledge wasn't *allowed*. And Margaret suddenly jumped to her feet, and a glass fell from the wicker table and smashed on the tiles with a thin, shivering ring. I can remember what she said. I can hear her say it any time I want to and many times when I don't. She looked down at us—and she seemed, I remember, to look very tall although she was a little woman. She said: 'Look at it all! *Look*!' and she made a great sweeping gesture with her arms towards everything in the world outside this little brick place where we were sitting. And then she said: "Leave it there—*leave* it! . . ."

Charles shivered—like a man with ague. And then he took hold of himself. I could see the jaw-muscles again, and the shine of the sweat on his forehead. He said at last:

"Margaret sort of crumpled up and fell back into her chair. She looked small again, and tears were rolling slowly down her cheeks. I know she didn't know there were any tears. She sat with her head up and her arms on the edge of the table and stared out at the world beyond the swimming pool; the world which was turning from solid, moon-shot darkness to vague and nebulous and unhappy grey. Adrian got up. He sat on the arm of her chair and put an arm around her shoulders and laid his cheek against her hair. They were very still and absolutely silent. I couldn't stand it and went into the house and found Adrian's cellar and a couple of bottles of Perrier Jouet—it was '28, I remember—and put some ice in a pail and found some glasses and took my loot back to the patio. They were still exactly as I'd left them and I shouted at them to break that immobility: I didn't like it. . . .

"It broke all right—and I fooled around with the pail and the bottles and began talking a streak and at last shoved some wine down their throats and put away half a pint at a swallow myself and started in to be very funny. . . .

"Adrian began to help me—and we played the fool and drank the second bottle and he found a third and at last we got Margaret laughing and then he stole the curtain with a very nice swan dive from the patio-wall into the pool, ruining a good dinner-jacket in the process. . . .

"It was nearly dawn when I left—and they both came around to the front of the house to see me off. And Margaret asked me to come to lunch. And I said I would and waved at them and started the car. And . . . that was all."

He didn't stop abruptly this time. His voice and words just trailed softly into silence. He sat looking straight at me, absolutely still. I wanted to get away from his eyes—but I couldn't. The silence went on too long. I said:

"Go on! I don't understand. What d'you *mean*—'that was all'?"

He said: "I didn't see the Archers any more. They weren't there. They . . . weren't. I heard Margaret's voice again—but it only said one word."

And then more silence. I said, finding some words:

"I don't understand. Tell me."

He dropped his eyes while he found a cigarette and lit it. He said:

"There's a lot in slang. As Chesterton once pointed out, the greatest poet of 'em all is Demos. The gag-man or gangster or rewrite man who first used the phrase *'rub him out'*, said a whole lot more than he knew. . . . Because that's what happened to Adrian. He was *rubbed out*—erased—deleted in all three dimensions of Time—cancelled—made not!"

"You can't stop in the middle like that! Tell me what you're talking about. What d'you mean?"

He still looked at me. "I mean what I said. After that morning, there was no more Adrian. . . . He was—*rubbed out*. Remember the things in the briefcase? Well, they'll help to explain. After . . . it happened, I was—sort of ill. I've no idea for how long—but when I could *think* again, I set out on a sort of crusade: to prove to myself that I was the only living thing which remembered—which knew there'd ever been such an entity as Adrian Archer. Mind you, I hoped to *disprove* it, though I felt all the time I never would. And I haven't. You saw those papers and things—they're just an infinitesimal fraction of my proof. There *was* an Adrian Archer—but now there never has been. That photograph frame used to have his and Margaret's picture in it—but now there's the old price-tag to show it's never been opened. That pipe: Adrian gave it to me and my initials were on it in facsimile of his writing—but now the band's plain and bare and new. . . . Adrian Archer was at school and college with me—but no records show the name and no contemporary mind remembers. I've known his father since I was a pup—but his father *knows* he never had a son. There were pictures—photographs—in which Adrian and I both were, sometimes together—and now those same pictures show me with someone whom every one knows but me. On the programmes of all his plays there's another man listed for his part—and that man is a known and living man in every case; a man who *knows* he played the part and remembers doing it as well as other people—you, for instance—remember his playing it. The pictures he made are all available to be seen—but there's no Adrian in them: there's some other star—who remembers everything about playing the part and has the weeks he took in shooting intricately woven into his life-pattern. Adrian—and everything that was Adrian's—have been removed and replaced: he *isn't* and *won't be* and *never has been;* he was cancelled in *esse* and *posse;* taken out of our little life and time and being like a speck out of yeast. And over the hole which the speck made the yeast has bubbled and seethed and closed—and there never was any speck—except to the knowledge of another speck; a speck who was almost as near to the danger-point of accidental knowledge as the one which was removed; a speck whose punishment and warning are memory!"

"Tell me!" I said. "Tell me what *happened*—after you drove away. . . ."

"My God!" said Charles, and there seemed to be tears in his eyes. "My God! You're believing me! . . . I'll tell you: I drove home. I was so tired I thought I might really sleep. I tore off my clothes and rolled into bed after I'd pulled the blinds tight down against the sun which would be up in a few minutes. And I *did* sleep. I'd put a note on the door for my servant not to wake me, and he didn't. But the telephone did—and I cursed and rolled over and groped for it without opening my eyes. . . .

"And then I heard Margaret's voice, calling my name. I knew it was her voice—though it was shrill and harsh with wild, incredible terror. It called my name, over and over again. And then, when I answered, it said 'Adrian's . . .' And then, without any other sound—without any click or noise or any sound at all—she wasn't there.

"I didn't waste any time. I slammed the phone down—and in nothing flat I was in the car and racing up Sunset, past the Riviera.

"I took the turn into Paloma Drive on two wheels and went on, around those endless curves, at well over sixty. And I came, past the Mortimers' house, to the corner of Paloma and Palisade. . . ."

I interrupted again, in that voice which didn't feel like mine.

"Wait! I've remembered something. You say this house was on the corner of Palisade Avenue and Paloma Drive, next the Mortimers'? Well, *there isn't any house there!* There's a little park-place there—a garden. . . ."

"Yes," said Charles, "I know. That's what *you* know; what everyone knows; what the Urban records would prove. . . . But there, right on that corner, *had been* a white colonial house, which *you* got for the Archers, and out of which I had come only a few hours before. . . .

"It was glaring, monstrous impossibility—and a brutal, inescapable fact! The green grass and the red flowers blazed at me with appalling reality, flaunting neat and well-tended and matured beauty—and the little white railings and the odd-shaped green seats and the yellow gravel paths and the spraying fountain all stared at me with smug actuality. . . .

"I stopped the car somehow. I knew I was on the right road because I'd seen Mary Mortimer talking to a gardener in front of their house. I was shaking all over—and Fear had me by the guts with a cold claw which twisted. I fumbled at the car door. I had to have air. The sunshine was bright and golden but it was . . . *filthy* somehow; it was like the light which might be shed by some huge, undreamt-of reptile. I had to have air, though. I stumbled out onto the sidewalk and staggered across it towards one of the seats by the fountain. And my foot caught against something and there was a sharp pain in my leg and I looked down. I'd run my shin onto one of those little metal signs they stick up on lawns, and the plate was bent back so that the white printing on the green background was staring up at me. It said: 'KEEP OFF THE GRASS'!"

The crust felt thin beneath my feet. I knew he wasn't going to say any more—but I kept expecting him to. We sat for a long time, while a waiter came and cleared away and spread a clean cloth and finally went.

"Just a minute," said Charles suddenly. "Have to 'phone again."

He walked away—and I went on sitting.

In half an hour, the waiter came back. I asked him where Mr. Moffat was; surely not still in the 'phone-booth?

He stared. "Mr. Who, sir?"

I said after a long pause but very sharply:

"Mr. Moffat. The gentleman who was dining with me."

He didn't seem to know what I was talking about.

I wonder how much longer there is for me.

THE HURKLE IS A HAPPY BEAST

by Theodore Sturgeon (1918–   )

***The Magazine of Fantasy and Science Fiction*, Fall**

Alien beings are one of the staples of modern science fiction, appearing in countless stories and novels. They come in all sizes, shapes and colors; they are sometimes very intelligent, sometimes not; some can handle our atmosphere and some cannot; sometimes we visit them and on occasion they visit us—the variations are endless. However, in the early history of American genre sf, aliens were mean*—they wanted our planet because their own was dying or because it was overpopulated; they wanted our resources; and they frequently (beyond all biological possibility) seemed to want our women (there were very few stories in which they wanted our men in the same way). Sometimes they wanted* all of us *for dinner.*

Things did change after a time, thanks to writers like Stanley G. Weinbaum, and friendly *aliens began to appear and then humans often mistreated them or took advantage of them and they became surrogates for colonized native peoples, American Indians, and minority group members. Currently another type of alien appears frequently—the cuddly, cutesy aliens of* Close Encounters of the Third Kind *and especially* E.T. *Personally, I like my aliens without many redeeming qualities, but I have an open mind and I know a great cutesy alien story when I read one.*

So here is "The Hurkle is a Happy Beast," one of the best of its sub-type, and also one (it's only fair to warn you) that's not all that it appears to be.—M.H.G.

(A woman, recently, told me that she never read science fiction because it frightened her so. I realized that she was

thinking of science fiction purely in terms of horror stories such as those written by Stephen King. Seeing a chance to educate her and, at the same time, do myself a bit of good, I said, "Buy one of my science fiction books. It won't frighten you. If it does, let me know, and I'll refund your money."

After a few days, she wrote me, quite enthusiastically, that my book had not frightened her at all, but had greatly interested her, and that she had now discovered a new and particularly suitable sort of reading material. I was delighted.

As a matter of fact, science fiction can not only be non-frightening; it can be downright light and happy. "The Hurkle Is a Happy Beast" by Theodore Sturgeon is an example. It is a very pleasant story involving a very pleasant alien beast whom any one of us would gladly hug to his (or her) bosom.

And if that makes you happy, then perhaps you had better not read the last eight lines.—I.A.)

Lirht is either in a different universal plane or in another island galaxy. Perhaps these terms mean the same thing. The fact remains that Lirht is a planet with three moons (one of which is unknown) and a sun, which is as important in its universe as is ours.

Lirht is inhabited by gwik, its dominant race, and by several less highly developed species which, for purposes of this narrative, can be ignored. Except, of course, for the hurkle. The hurkle are highly regarded by the gwik as pets, in spite of the fact that a hurkle is so affectionate that it can have no loyalty.

The prettiest of the hurkle are blue.

Now, on Lirht, in its greatest city, there was trouble, the nature of which does not matter to us, and a gwik named Hvov, whom you may immediately forget, blew up a building which was important for reasons we cannot understand. This event caused great excitement, and gwik left their homes and factories and strubles and streamed toward the center of town, which is how a certain laboratory door was left open.

In times of such huge confusion, the little things go on. During the "Ten Days that Shook the World" the cafes and theaters of Moscow and Petrograd remained open, people fell in love, sued each other, died, shed sweat and tears; and some of these were tears of laughter. So on Lirht, while the decisions on the fate of the miserable Hvov were being formulated, gwik still fardled, funted, and fupped. The great central hewton still beat out its mighty pulse, and in the anams the corsons grew . . .

Into the above-mentioned laboratory, which had been left open through the circumstances described, wandered a hurkle kitten. It was very happy to find itself there; but then, the hurkle is a happy beast. It prowled about fearlessly—it could become invisible if frightened—and it glowed at the legs of the tables and at the glittering, racked walls. It moved sinuously, humping its back and arching along on the floor. Its front and rear legs were stiff and straight as the legs of a chair; the middle pair had two sets of knees, one bending forward, one back. It was engineered as ingeniously as a scorpion, and it was exceedingly blue.

Occupying almost a quarter of the laboratory was a huge and intricate machine, unhoused, showing the signs of development projects the galaxies over—temporary hookups from one component to another, cables terminating in spring clips, measuring devices standing about on small tables near the main work. The kitten regarded the machine with curiosity and friendly intent, sending a wave of radiations outward which were its glow or purr. It arched daintily around to the other side, stepping delicately but firmly on a floor switch.

Immediately there was a rushing, humming sound, like small birds chasing large mosquitoes, and parts of the machine began to get warm. The kitten watched curiously, and saw, high up inside the clutter of coils and wires, the most entrancing muzziness it had ever seen. It was like heat-flicker over a fallow field; it was like a smoke-vortex; it was like red neon lights on a wet pavement. To the hurkle kitten's senses, that red-orange flicker was also like the smell of catnip to a cat, or anise to a terrestrial terrier.

It reared up toward the glow, hooked its forelegs over a busbar—fortunately there was no ground potential—and drew itself upward. It climbed from transformer to powerpack, skittered up a variable condenser—the setting of which was changed thereby—disappeared momentarily as it felt the bite of a hot tube, and finally teetered on the edge of the glow.

The glow hovered in midair in a sort of cabinet, which was surrounded by heavy coils embodying tens of thousands of turns of small wire and great loops of bus. One side, the front, of the cabinet was open, and the kitten hung there fascinated, rocking back and forth to the rhythm of some unheard music it made to contrast this sourceless flame. Back and forth, back and forth it rocked and wove, riding a wave of delicious, compelling sensation. And once, just once, it moved its center of gravity too far from its point of support. Too far—far enough. It tumbled into the cabinet, into the flame.

* * *

One muggy, mid-June day a teacher, whose name was Stott and whose duties were to teach seven subjects to forty moppets in a very small town, was writing on a blackboard. He was writing the word Madagascar, and the air was so sticky and warm that he could feel his undershirt pasting and unpasting itself on his shoulder blade with each round "a" he wrote.

Behind him there was a sudden rustle from the moist seventh-graders. His schooled reflexes kept him from turning from the board until he had finished what he was doing, by which time the room was in a young uproar. Stott about-faced, opened his mouth, closed it again. A thing like this would require more than a routine reprimand.

His forty-odd charges were writhing and squirming in an extraordinary fashion, and the sound they made, a sort of whimpering giggle, was unique. He looked at one pupil after another. Here a hand was busily scratching a nape; there a boy was digging guiltily under his shirt; yonder a scrubbed and shining damsel violently worried her scalp.

Knowing the value of individual attack, Stott intoned, "Hubert, what seems to be the trouble?"

The room immediately quieted, though diminished scrabblings continued. "Nothin', Mister Stott," quavered Hubert.

Stott flicked his gaze from side to side. Wherever it rested, the scratching stopped and was replaced by agonized control. In its wake was rubbing and twitching. Stott glared, and idly thumbed a lower left rib. Someone snickered. Before he could identify the source, Stott was suddenly aware of an intense itching. He checked the impulse to go after it, knotted his jaw, and swore to himself that he wouldn't scratch as long as he was out there, front and center. "The class will—" he began tautly, and then stopped.

There was a—a *something* on the sill of the open window. He blinked and looked again. It was a translucent, bluish cloud which was almost nothing at all. It was less than a something should be, but it was indeed more than a nothing. If he stretched his imagination just a little, he might make out the outlines of an arched creature with too many legs; but of course that was ridiculous.

He looked away from it and scowled at his class. He had had two unfortunate experiences with stink bombs, and in the back of his mind was the thought of having seen once, in a trick-store window, a product called "itching powder." Could this be it, this terrible itch? He knew better, however, than to accuse anyone yet; if he were wrong, there was no point in giving the little geniuses any extracurricular notions.

He tried again. "The cl—" He swallowed. This itch was . . . "The class will—" He noticed that one head, then another and another, were turning toward the window. He realized that if the class got too interested in what he thought he saw on the window sill, he'd have a panic on his hands. He fumbled for his ruler and rapped twice on the desk. His control was not what it should have been at the moment; he struck far too hard, and the reports were like gunshots. The class turned to him as one; and behind them the thing on the window sill appeared with great distinctness.

It was blue—a truly beautiful blue. It had a small spherical head and an almost identical knob at the other end. There were four stiff, straight legs, a long sinuous body, and two central limbs with a boneless look about them. On the side of the head were four pairs of eyes, of graduated sizes. It teetered there for perhaps ten seconds, and then, without a sound, leapt through the window and was gone.

Mr. Stott, pale and shaking, closed his eyes. His knees trembled and weakened, and a delicate, dewy mustache of perspiration appeared on his upper lip. He clutched at the desk and forced his eyes open; and then, flooding him with relief, pealing into his terror, swinging his control back to him, the bell rang to end the class and the school day.

"Dismissed," he mumbled, and sat down. The class picked up and left, changing itself from a twittering pattern of rows to a rowdy kaleidoscope around the bottleneck doorway. Mr. Stott slumped down in his chair, noticing that the dreadful itch was gone, had been gone since he had made that thunderclap with the ruler.

Now, Mr. Stott was a man of method. Mr. Stott prided himself on his ability to teach his charges to use their powers of observation and all the machinery of logic at their command. Perhaps, then, he had more of both at his command—after he recovered himself—than could be expected of an ordinary man.

He sat and stared at the open window, not seeing the sunswept lawns outside. And after going over these events a half-dozen times, he fixed on two important facts:

First, that the animal he had seen, or thought he had seen, had six legs.

Second, that the animal was of such nature as to make anyone who had not seen it believe he was out of his mind.

These two thoughts had their corollaries:

First, that every animal he had ever seen which had six legs was an insect, and

Second, that if anything were to be done about this fantastic creature, he had better do it by himself. And whatever action he took must be taken immediately. He imagined the windows being kept shut to keep the thing out—in this heat—and he cowered away from the thought. He imagined the effect of such a monstrosity if it bounded into the midst of a classroom full of children in their early teens, and he recoiled. No; there could be no delay in this matter.

He went to the window and examined the sill. Nothing. There was nothing to be seen outside, either. He stood thoughtfully for a moment, pulling on his lower lip and thinking hard. Then he went downstairs to borrow five pounds of DDT powder from the janitor for an "experiment." He got a wide, flat wooden box and an electric fan, and set them up on a table he pushed close to the window. Then he sat down to wait, in case, just in case the blue beast returned.

When the hurkle kitten fell into the flame, it braced itself for a fall at least as far as the floor of the cabinet. Its shock was tremendous, then, when it found itself so braced and already resting on a surface. It looked around, panting with fright, its invisibility reflex in full operation.

The cabinet was gone. The flame was gone. The laboratory with its windows, lit by the orange Lirhtian sky, its ranks of shining equipment, its hulking, complex machine—all were gone.

The hurkle kitten sprawled in an open area, a sort of lawn. No colors were right; everything seemed half-lit, filmy, out-of-focus. There were trees, but not low and flat and bushy like honest Lirhtian trees, but with straight naked trunks and leaves like a portle's tooth. The different atomospheric gases had colors; clouds of fading, changing faint colors obscured and revealed everything. The kitten twitched its cafmors and ruddled its kump, right there where it stood; for no amount of early training could overcome a shock like this.

It gathered itself together and tried to move; and then it got its second shock. Instead of arching over inchwormwise, it floated into the air and came down three times as far as it had ever jumped in its life.

It cowered on the dreamlike grass, darting glances all about, under, and up. It was lonely and terrified and felt very much put upon. It saw its shadow through the shifting haze, and the sight terrified it even more, for it had no shadow when it was frightened on Lirht. Everything here was all backwards and wrong way up; it got more visible, instead of less, when it was frightened; its legs didn't work right, it couldn't see properly, and there wasn't a single, solitary malapek to be throdded anywhere. It thought it heard some music; happily, that sounded all right inside its round head, though somehow it didn't resonate as well as it had.

It tried, with extreme caution, to move again. This time its trajectory was shorter and more controlled. It tried a small, grounded pace, and was quite successful. Then it bobbed for a moment, seesawing on its flexible middle pair of legs, and, with utter abandon, flung itself skyward. It went up perhaps fifteen feet, turning end over end, and landed with its stiff forefeet in the turf.

It was completely delighted with this sensation. It gathered itself together, gryting with joy, and leapt up again. This time it made more distance than altitude, and bounced two long, happy bounces as it landed.

Its fears were gone in the exploration of this delicious new freedom of motion. The hurkle, as has been said before, is a happy beast. It curvetted and sailed, soared and somersaulted, and at last brought up against a brick wall with stunning and unpleasant results. It was learning, the hard way, a distinction between weight and mass. The effect was slight but painful. It drew back and stared forlornly at the bricks. Just when it was beginning to feel friendly again . . .

It looked upward, and saw what appeared to be an opening in the wall some eight feet above the ground. Overcome by a spirit of high adventure, it sprang upward and came to rest on a window sill—a feat of which it was very proud. It crouched there, preening itself, and looked inside.

It saw a most pleasing vista. More than forty amusingly ugly animals, apparently imprisoned by their lower extremities in individual stalls, bowed and nodded and mumbled. At the far end of the room stood a taller, more slender monster with a naked head—naked compared with those of the trapped ones, which were covered with hair like a mawson's egg. A few moments' study showed the kitten that in reality only one side of the heads was hairy; the tall one turned around and began making tracks in the end wall, and its head proved to be hairy on the other side too.

The hurkle kitten found this vastly entertaining. It began to radiate what was, on Lirht, a purr, or glow. In this fantastic place it was not visible; instead, the trapped animals began to respond with most curious writhings and squirmings and susurrant rubbings of their hides with their claws. This pleased the kitten even more, for it loved to be noticed, and it redoubled the glow. The receptive motions of the animals became almost frantic.

Then the tall one turned around again. It made a curious sound or two. Then it picked up a stick from the platform before it and brought it down with a horrible crash.

The sudden noise frightened the hurkle kitten half out of its wits. It went invisible; but its visibility system was reversed here, and it was suddenly outstandingly evident. It turned and leapt outside, and before it reached the ground, a loud metallic shrilling pursued it. There were gabblings and shufflings from the room which added force to the kitten's consuming terror. It scrambled to a low growth of shrubbery and concealed itself among the leaves.

Very soon, however, its irrepressible good nature returned. It lay relaxed, watching the slight movement of the stems and leaves—some of them may have been flowers—in a slight breeze. A winged creature came humming and dancing about one of the blossoms. The kitten rested on one of its middle legs, shot the other out and caught the creature in flight. The thing promptly jabbed the kitten's foot with a sharp black probe. This the kitten ignored. It ate the thing, and belched. It lay still for a few minutes, savoring the sensation of the bee in its clarfel. The experiment was suddenly not a success. It ate the bee twice more and then gave it up as a bad job.

It turned its attention again to the window, wondering what those racks of animals might be up to now. It seemed very quiet up there . . . Boldly the kitten came from hiding and launched itself at the window again. It was pleased with itself; it was getting quite proficient at precision leaps in this mad place. Preening itself, it balanced on the window sill and looked inside.

Surprisingly, all the smaller animals were gone. The larger one was huddled behind the shelf at the end of the room. The kitten and the animal watched each other for a long moment. The animal leaned down and stuck something into the wall.

Immediately there was a mechanical humming sound and something on a platform near the window began to revolve. The next thing the kitten knew it was enveloped in a cloud of pungent dust.

It choked and became as visible as it was frightened, which was very. For a long moment it was incapable of motion; gradually, however, it became conscious of a poignant, painfully penetrating sensation which thrilled it to the core. It gave itself up to the feeling. Wave after wave of agonized ecstasy rolled over it, and it began to dance to the waves. It glowed brilliantly, though the emanation served only to make the animal in the room scratch hysterically.

The hurkle felt strange, transported. It turned and leapt high into the air, out from the building.

Mr. Stott stopped scratching. Disheveled indeed, he went to the window and watched the odd sight of the blue beast, quite invisible now, but coated with dust, so that it was like a bubble in a fog. It bounced across the lawn in huge floating leaps, leaving behind it diminishing patches of white powder in the grass. He smacked his hands, one on the other, and smirking, withdrew to straighten up. He had saved the earth from battle, murder, and bloodshed, forever, but he did not know that. No one ever found out what he had done. So he lived a long and happy life.

And the hurkle kitten?

It bounded off through the long shadows, and vanished in a copse of bushes. There it dug itself a shallow pit, working drowsily, more and more slowly. And at last it sank down and lay motionless, thinking strange thoughts, making strange music, and racked by strange sensations. Soon even its slightest movements ceased, and it stretched out stiffly, motionless . . .

For about two weeks. At the end of that time, the hurkle, no longer a kitten, was possessed of a fine, healthy litter of just under two hundred young. Perhaps it was the DDT, and perhaps it was the new variety of radiation that the hurkle received from the terrestrial sky, but they were all parthenogenetic females, even as you and I.

And the humans? Oh, we *bred* so! And how happy we were!

But the humans had the slidy itch, and the scratchy itch, and the prickly or tingly or titillative paraesthetic formication. And there wasn't a thing they could do about it.

So they left.

Isn't this a lovely place?

KALEIDOSCOPE

by Ray Bradbury (1920–   )

***Thrilling Wonder Stories*, October**

Thrilling Wonder Stories, *like its sister magazine,* Startling Stories, *was one of the Standard Magazines group of publications. From 1945 to 1951 both magazines were edited by Sam Merwin (1910–   ), who has to be one of the most criminally neglected editors in the history of science fiction.* Thrilling *and* Startling *existed in the shadow of* Astounding, *which in many cases was the preferred market for sf writers. However, under Merwin and then under Samuel Mines they achieved a high level of excellence, providing badly needed alternatives for writers who would not submit to John W. Campbell, Jr., or for whatever reason would not be published by him. The Kuttners were regulars (although they also published heavily in ASF), as was Ray Bradbury, for whom they, along with* Planet Stories, *were major markets in the late 1940s. Fully one-third of the stories in this book first appeared in the pages of those two magazines.*

The late 1940s were very productive years for Ray Bradbury, and two other stories, "The Naming of Names" (Thrilling, *August) and "The Man"* (Thrilling, *February), just missed inclusion in this volume.—M.H.G.*

(I've never been able to figure out Ray Bradbury's writing. If I were to describe the plot of one of his stories, I think it would seem to you to be impossible to make a story out of it that would be any good at all, let alone memorable. And you would be right!

—Unless the story was written by Ray Bradbury.

He can write vignettes in which he creates a powerful

emotion out of the simplest situation, and "Kaleidoscope" is an example.

It is unrelievedly grim, yet it reads quickly, matter-of-factly, and is unforgettable. And, at the end, there is one quick sub-vignette only four lines long that makes it seem—

But I'll let you figure out the "moral." Yours may be different from mine.

I've only met Ray Bradbury twice in my life. He lives on the west coast; I live on the east coast; and neither of us flies. That makes the process of life-intersection a difficult one for us.—I.A.)

The first concussion cut the ship up the side like a giant can opener. The men were thrown into space like a dozen wriggling silverfish. They were scattered into a dark sea; and the ship, in a million pieces, went on like a meteor swarm seeking a lost sun.

'Barkley, Barkley, where are you?'

The sound of voices calling like lost children on a cold night.

'Woode, Woode!'

'Captain!'

'Hollis, Hollis, this is Stone.'

'Stone, this is Hollis. Where are you?'

'I don't know, how can I? Which way is up? I'm falling. Good gosh, I'm falling.'

They fell. They fell as pebbles fall in the long autumns of childhood, silver and thin. They were scattered as jack-stones are scattered from a gigantic throw. And now instead of men there were only voices—all kinds of voices, disembodied and impassioned, in varying degrees of terror and resignation.

'We're going away from each other.'

This was true. Hollis, swinging head over heels, knew this was true. He knew it with a vague acceptance. They were parting to go their separate ways, and nothing could bring them back. They were wearing their sealed-tight space suits with the glass tubes over their pale faces, but they hadn't had time to lock on their force units. With them, they could be small lifeboats in space, saving themselves, saving others, collecting together, finding each other until they were an island of men with some plan. But without the force units snapped to their shoulders they were meteors, senseless, each going to a separate and irrecoverable fate.

A period of perhaps ten minutes elapsed while the first terror died and a metallic calm took its place. Space began to weave their strange voices in and out, on a great dark loom, crossing, recrossing, making a final pattern.

'Stone to Hollis. How long can we talk by phone?'

'It depends on how fast you're going your way and I'm going mine.'

'An hour, I make it.'

'That should do it,' said Hollis, abstracted and quiet.

'What happened?' said Hollis, a minute later.

'The rocket blew up, that's all. Rockets do blow up.'

'Which way are you going?'

'It looks like I'll hit the sun.'

'It's Earth for me. Back to old Mother Earth at ten thousand miles per hour. I'll burn like a match.' Hollis thought of it with a queer abstraction of mind. He seemed to be removed from his body, watching it fall down and down through space, as objective as he had been in regard to the first falling snowflakes of a winter season long gone.

The others were silent, thinking of the destiny that had brought them to this, falling, falling, and nothing they could do to change it. Even the captain was quiet, for there was no command or plan he knew that could put things back together again.

'Oh, it's a long way down, oh it's a long way down, a long, long, long, way down,' said a voice. 'I don't want to die. I don't want to die, it's a long way down.'

'Who's that?'

'I don't know.'

'Stimson, I think. Stimson, is that you?'

'It's a long long way and I don't like it, oh God, I don't like it.'

'Stimson, this is Hollis, Stimson, you hear me?'

A pause while they fell separate from one another.

'Stimson?'

'Yes.'' He replied at last.

'Stimson, take it easy, we're all in the same fix.'

'I don't want to be here, I want to be somewhere else.'

'There's a chance we'll be found.'

'I must be, I must be,' said Stimson. 'I don't believe this, I don't believe any of this is happening.'

'It's a bad dream,' said someone.

'Shut up!' said Hollis.

'Come and make me,' said the voice. It was Applegate. He laughed easily, with a similar objectivity. 'Come and shut me up.'

Hollis for the first time felt the impossibility of his position. A great anger filled him, for he wanted more than anything in existence at this moment to be able to do something to Applegate. He had wanted for many years to do something and now it was too late. Applegate was only a telephonic voice.

Falling, falling, falling!

Now, as if they had discovered the horror, two of the men began to scream. In a nightmare, Hollis saw one of them float by, very near, screaming and screaming.

'Stop it!' The man was almost at his fingertips, screaming insanely. He would never stop. He would go on screaming for a million miles, as long as he was in radio range, disturbing all of them, making it impossible for them to talk to one another.

Hollis reached out. It was best this way. He made the extra effort and touched the man. He grasped the man's ankle and pulled himself up along the body until he reached the head. The man screamed and clawed frantically, like a drowning swimmer. The screaming filled the universe.

One way or the other, thought Hollis. The sun or Earth or meteors will kill him, so why not now?

He smashed the man's glass mask with his iron fist. The screaming stopped. He pushed off from the body and let it spin away on its own course, falling, falling.

Falling, falling down space went Hollis and the rest of them in the long, endless dropping and whirling of silent terror.

'Hollis, you still there?'

Hollis did not speak, but felt the rush of heat in his face.

'This is Applegate again.'

'All right, Applegate.'

'Let's talk. We haven't anything else to do.'

The captain cut in. 'That's enough of that. We've got to figure a way out of this.'

'Captain, why don't you shut up?' said Applegate.

'What!'

'You heard me, Captain. Don't pull your rank on me, you're ten thousand miles away by now, and let's not kid ourselves. As Stimson puts it, it's a long way down.'

'See here, Applegate!'

'Can it. This a mutiny of one. I haven't a damn thing to lose. Your ship was a bad ship and you were a bad captain and I hope you roast when you hit the sun.'

'I'm ordering you to stop!'

'Go on, order me again.' Applegate smiled across ten thousand miles. The captain was silent. Applegate continued, 'Where were we, Hollis? Oh, yes, I remember. I hate you, too. But you know that. You've known it for a long time.'

Hollis clenched his fists, helplessly.

'I want to tell something,' said Applegate. 'Make you happy. I was the one who blackballed you with the Rocket Company five years ago.'

A meteor flashed by. Hollis looked down and his left hand was gone. Blood spurted. Suddenly there was no air in his suit. He had enough air in his lungs to move his right hand over and twist a knob at his left elbow, tightening the joint and sealing the leak. It had happened so quickly that he was not surprised. Nothing surprised him any more. The air in the suit came back to normal in an instant now that the leak was sealed. And the blood that had flowed so swiftly was pressured as he fastened the knob yet tighter, until it made a tourniquet.

All of this took place in a terrible silence on his part. And the other men chatted. That one man, Lespere, went on and on with his talk about his wife on Mars, his wife on Venus, his wife on Jupiter, his money, his wondrous times, his drunkenness, his gambling, his happiness. On and on, while they all fell, fell. Lespere reminisced on the past, happy, while he fell to his death.

It was so very odd. Space, thousands of miles of space, and these voices vibrating in the center of it. No one visible at all, and only the radio waves quivering and trying to quicken other men into emotion.

'Are you angry, Hollis?'

'No.' And he was not. The abstraction had returned and he was a thing of dull concrete, forever falling nowhere.

'You wanted to get to the top all your life, Hollis. And I ruined it for you. You always wondered what happened. I put the black mark on you just before I was tossed out myself.'

'That isn't important,' said Hollis. And it was not. It was gone. When life is over it is like a flicker of bright film, an instant on the screen, all of its prejudices and passions condensed and illumined for an instant on space, and before you could cry out. There was a happy day, there a bad one, there an evil face, there a good one, the film burned to a cinder, the screen went dark.

From this outer edge of his life, looking back, there was only one remorse, and that was only that he wished to go on living. Did all dying people feel this way, as if they had never lived? Does life seem that short, indeed, over and down before you took a breath? Did it seem this abrupt and impossible to everyone, or only to himself, here, now, with a few hours left to him for thought and deliberation?

One of the other men was talking. 'Well, I had me a good life. I had a wife on Mars and one on Venus and one on Earth and one on Jupiter. Each of them had money and they treated me swell. I had a wonderful time. I got drunk and once I gambled away twenty thousand dollars.'

But you're here now, thought Hollis. I didn't have any of those things. When I was living I was jealous of you, Lespere, when I had another day ahead of me I envied you your women and your good times. Women frightened me and I went into space, always wanting them, and jealous of you for having them, and money, and as much happiness as you could have in your own wild way. But now, falling here, with everything over, I'm not jealous of you any more, because it's over for you as it is over for me, and right now it's like it never was. Hollis craned his face forward and shouted into the telephone.

'It's all over, Lespere!'

Silence.

'It's just as if it never was, Lespere!'

'Who's that?' Lespere's faltering voice.

'This is Hollis.'

He was being mean. He felt the meanness, the senseless meanness of dying. Applegate had hurt him, now he wanted to hurt another. Applegate and space had both wounded him.

'You're out here, Lespere. It's all over. It's just as if it had never happened, isn't it?'

'No.'

'When anything's over, it's just like it never happened. Where's your life any better than mine, now? While it was happening, yes, but now? Now is what counts. Is it any better, is it?'

'Yes, it's better!'

'How!'

'Because I got my thoughts; I remember!' cried Lespere, far away, indignant, holding his memories to his chest with both hands.

And he was right. With a feeling of cold water gushing through his head and his body, Hollis knew he was right. There were differences between memories and dreams. He had only dreams of things he had wanted to do, while Lespere had memories of things done and accomplished. And this knowledge began to pull Hollis apart, with a slow, quivering precision.

'What good does it do you?' he cried to Lespere. 'Now? When a thing's over it's not good any more. You're no better off than me.'

'I'm resting easy,' said Lespere. 'I've had my turn. I'm not getting mean at the end, like you.'

'Mean?' Hollis turned the word on his tongue. He had never been mean, as long as he could remember, in his life. He had never dared to be mean. He must have saved it all of these years for such a time as this. 'Mean.' He rolled the word into the back of his mind. He felt tears start into his eyes and roll down his face. Someone must have heard his gasping voice.

'Take it easy, Hollis.'

It was, of course, ridiculous. Only a minute before he had been giving advice to others, to Stimson, he had felt a braveness which he had thought to be the genuine thing, and now he knew that it had been nothing but shock and the objectivity possible in shock. Now he was trying to pack a lifetime of suppressed emotion into an interval of minutes.

'I know how you feel, Hollis,' said Lespere, now twenty thousand miles away, his voice fading. 'I don't take it personally.'

But aren't we equal, his wild mind wondered. Lespere and I? Here, now? If a thing's over it's done, and what good is it? You die anyway. But he knew he was rationalizing, for it was like trying to tell the difference between a live man and a corpse. There was a spark in one, and not in the other, an aura, a mysterious element.

So it was with Lespere and himself; Lespere had lived a good full life, and it made him a different man now, and he, Hollis, had been as good as dead for many years. They came to death by separate paths and, in all likelihood, if there were kinds of deaths, their kinds would be as different as night from day. The quality of death, like that of life, must be of infinite variety, and if one has already died once, then what is there to look for in dying for once and all, as he was now?

It was a second later that he discovered his right foot was cut sheer away. It almost made him laugh. The air was gone from his suit again, he bent quickly, and there was blood, and the meteor had taken flesh and suit away to the ankle. Oh, death in space was most humorous, it cut you away, piece by piece, like a black and invisible butcher. He tightened the valve at the knee, his head whirling into pain, fighting to remain aware, and with the valve tightened, the blood retained, the air kept, he straightened up and went on falling, falling, for that was all there was left to do.

'Hollis?'

Hollis nodded sleepily, tired of waiting for death.

'This is Applegate again,' said the voice.

'Yes.'

'I've had time to think. I listened to you. This isn't good. It makes us mean. This is a bad way to die. It brings all the bile out. You listening, Hollis?'

'Yes.'

'I lied. A minute ago. I lied. I didn't blackball you. I don't know why I said that. Guess I wanted to hurt you. You seemed the one to hurt. We've always fought. Guess I'm getting old fast and repenting fast, I guess listening to you be mean made me ashamed. Whatever the reason, I want you to know I was an idiot, too. There's not an ounce of truth in what I said. To heck with you.'

Hollis felt his heart begin to work again. It seemed as if it hadn't worked for five minutes, but now all of his limbs began to take color and warmth. The shock was over, and the successive shocks of anger and terror and loneliness were passing. He felt like a man emerging from a cold shower in the morning, ready for breakfast and a new day.

'Thanks, Applegate.'

'Don't mention it. Up your nose, you slob.'

'Where's Stimson, how is he?'

'Stimson?'

They listened.

No answer.

'He must be gone.'

'I don't think so. Stimson!'

They listened again.

They could hear a long, slow, hard breathing in their phones.

'That's him. Listen.'

'Stimson!'

No reply.

Only the slow, hard breathing.

'He won't answer.'

'He's gone insane, God help him.'

'That's it. Listen.'

The silent breathing, the quiet.

'He's closed up like a clam. He's in himself, making a pearl. Listen to the poet, will you. He's happier than us now, anyway.'

They listened to Stimson float away.

'Hey,' said Stone.

'What?' Hollis called across space, for Stone, of all of them, was a good friend.

'I've got myself into a meteor swarm, some little asteroids.'

'Meteors?'

'I think it's the Myrmidone cluster that goes out past Mars and in toward Earth once every five years. I'm right in the middle. It's like a big kaleidoscope. You get all kinds of colors and shapes and sizes. God, it's beautiful, all the metal.'

Silence.

'I'm going with them,' said Stone. 'They're taking me off with them. I'll be damned.' He laughed tightly.

Hollis looked to see, but saw nothing. There were only the great jewelries of space, the diamonds and sapphires and emerald mists and velvet inks of space, with God's voice mingling among the crystal fires. There was a kind of wonder and imagination in the thought of Stone going off in the meteor swarm, out past Mars for years and coming in toward Earth every five years, passing in and out of the planet's ken for the next million years, Stone and the Myrmidone cluster eternal and unending, shifting and shaping like the kaleidoscope colours when you were a child and held the long tube to the sun and gave it a twirl.

'So long, Hollis.' Stone's voice, very faint now. 'So long.'

'Good luck,' shouted Hollis across thirty thousand miles.

'Don't be funny,' said Stone, and was gone.

The stars closed in.

Now all the voices were fading, each on their own trajectories, some to the sun, others into farthest space. And Hollis himself. He looked down. He, of all the others, was going back to Earth alone.

'So long.'

'Take it easy.'

'So long, Hollis.' That was Applegate.

The many goodbyes. The short farewells. And now the great loose brain was disintegrating. The components of the brain which had worked so beautifully and efficiently in the skull case of the rocket ship racing through space, were dying one by one, the meaning of their life together was falling apart. And as a body dies when the brain ceases functioning, so the spirit of the ship and their long time together and what they meant to one another was dying. Applegate was now no more than a finger blown from the parent body, no longer to be despised and worked against. The brain was exploded, and the senseless, useless fragments of it were far-scattered. The voices faded and now all of space was silent. Hollis was alone, falling.

They were all alone. Their voices had died like echoes of the words of God spoken and vibrating in the starred space. There went the captain to the sun; there Stone with the meteor swarm; there Stimson, tightened and unto himself; there Applegate toward Pluto; there Smith and Turner and Underwood and all the rest, the shards of the kaleidoscope that had formed a thinking pattern for so long, now hurled apart.

And I? thought Hollis. What can I do? Is there anything I can do now to make up for a terrible and empty life? If I could do one good thing to make up for the meanness I collected all these years and didn't even know was in me? But there's no one here, but myself, and how can you do good all alone? You can't. Tomorrow night I'll hit Earth's atmosphere.

I'll burn, he thought, and be scattered in ashes all over the continental lands. I'll be put to use. Just a little bit, but ashes are ashes and they'll add to the land.

He fell swiftly, like a bullet, like a pebble, like an iron weight, objective, objective all of the time now, not sad or happy or anything, but only wishing he could do a good thing now that everyone was gone, a good thing for just himself to know about.

When I hit the atmosphere, I'll burn like a meteor.

'I wonder,' he said. 'If anyone'll see me?'

The small boy on the country road looked up and screamed. 'Look, Mom, look! A falling star!'

The blazing white star fell down the sky of dusk in Illinois.

'Make a wish,' said his mother. 'Make a wish.'

DEFENSE MECHANISM

by Katherine MacLean (1925–   )

***Astounding Science Fiction*, October**

The number of notable first stories in the history of science fiction is truly impressive. In fact, at least two anthologies of these stories have been published, First Flight *(1963), and* First Voyages *(greatly expanded version of the previous book, 1981), and one could easily fill up several additional volumes. "Defense Mechanism" was Katharine MacLean's first published story, and began a career that, while filled with excellent stories and some recognition, never attained the heights she was capable of. Like Ray Bradbury and Harlan Ellison, she is primarily a short story writer, but unlike them she is not very prolific. She won a Nebula Award for "The Missing Man" (1971), a part of her novel* Missing Man *(1975). The best of her early stories can be found in* The Diploids *(1962), while* Cosmic Checkmate *(1962, written with Charles de Vet) is an interesting first, and so far, only novel* (Missing Man *consists of previously published linked stories).—M.H.G.*

(Telepathy is something we all apparently have a hankering for. At least, any report of the existence of telepathy is eagerly accepted, and any story dealing with telepathy has a great big point in its favor from the start.

Why this interest? I suppose an obvious answer is that it would be so convenient to be able to communicate as easily as we think.

Isn't talking almost as convenient and easy as thinking? Well, maybe, but the possibility of lying turns speech sour. As the saying goes, "Speech was invented so that we might conceal our thoughts."

In that case, might it not be very convenient to be tele-

pathic and to see beyond the lies? Convenient for whom? Not for the liar, certainly. —And that means all of us.

If you're not a liar, tell the truth! Do you want all your thoughts out in the open? Isn't it convenient, even necessary, to let your words mismatch the facts now and then?

Actually, there are all sorts of quirks to telepathy and, in "Defense Mechanism," Katherine Maclean thinks up a nice one. And if her speculation were correct, to how many of us might something like this have happened?—I.A.)

The article was coming along smoothly, words flowing from the typewriter in pleasant simple sequence, swinging to their predetermined conclusion like a good tune. Ted typed contentedly, adding pages to the stack at his elbow.

A thought, a subtle modification of the logic of the article began to glow in his mind; but he brushed it aside impatiently. This was to be a short article, and there was no room for subtlety. His articles sold, not for depth, but for an oddly individual quirk that he could give to commonplaces.

While he typed a little faster, faintly in the echoes of his thought the theme began to elaborate itself richly with correlations, modifying qualifications, and humorous parenthetical remarks. An eddy of especially interesting conclusions tried to insert itself into the main stream of his thoughts. Furiously he typed along the dissolving thread of his argument.

"Shut up," he snarled. "Can't I have any privacy around here?"

The answer was not a remark, it was merely a concept; two electro-chemical calculators pictured with the larger in use as a control mech, taking a dangerously high inflow, and controlling it with high resistance and blocs, while the smaller one lay empty and unblocked, its unresistant circuits ramifying any impulses received along the easy channels of pure calculation. Ted recognized the diagram from his amateur concepts of radio and psychology.

"All right. So I'm doing it myself. So you can't help it!" He grinned grudgingly. "Answering back at your age!"

Under the impact of a directed thought the small circuits of the idea came in strongly, scorching their reception and rapport diagram into his mind in flashing repetitions, bright as small lightning strokes. Then it spread and the small other brain flashed into brightness, reporting and repeating from every center. Ted even received a brief kinesthetic sensation of lying down, before it was all cut off in a hard bark of thought that came back in exact echo of his own irritation.

"Tune down!" It ordered furiously. "You're blasting in too loud and jamming everything up! What do you want, an idiot child?"

Ted blanketed down desperately, cutting off all thoughts, relaxing every muscle; but the angry thoughts continued coming in strongly a moment before fading.

"Even when I take a nap," they said, "he starts thinking at me! Can't I get any peace and privacy around here?"

Ted grinned. The kid's last remark sounded like something a little better than an attitude echo. It would be hard to tell when the kid's mind grew past a mere selective echoing of outside thoughts and became true personality, but that last remark was a convincing counterfeit of a sincere kick in the shin. Conditioned reactions can be efficient.

All the luminescent streaks of thought faded and merged with the calm meaningless ebb and flow of waves in the small sleeping mind. Ted moved quietly into the next room and looked down into the blue-and-white crib. The kid lay sleeping, his thumb in his mouth and his chubby face innocent of thought. Junior—Jake.

It was an odd stroke of luck that Jake was born with this particular talent. Because of it they would have to spend the winter in Connecticut, away from the mental blare of crowded places. Because of it Ted was doing free lance in the kitchen, instead of minor editing behind a New York desk. The winter countryside was wide and windswept, as it had been in Ted's own childhood, and the warm contacts with the stolid personalities of animals through Jake's mind were already a pleasure. Old acquaintances—Ted stopped himself skeptically. He was no telepath. He decided that it reminded him of Ernest Thompson Seton's animal biographies, and went back to typing, dismissing the question.

It was pleasant to eavesdrop on things through Jake, as long as the subject was not close enough to the article to interfere with it.

Five small boys let out of kindergarten came trooping by on the road, chattering and throwing pebbles. Their thoughts came in jumbled together in distracting cross currents, but Ted stopped typing for a moment, smiling, waiting for Jake to show his latest trick. Babies are hypersensitive to conditioning. The burnt hand learns to yank back from fire, the unresisting mind learns automatically to evade too many clashing echoes of other minds.

Abruptly the discordant jumble of small boy thoughts and sensations delicately untangled into five compartmented strands of thoughts, then one strand of little boy thoughts shoved the others out, monopolizing and flowing easily through the blank baby mind, as a dream flows by without awareness, leaving no imprint of memory, fading as the children passed over the hill. Ted resumed typing, smiling. Jake had done the trick a shade faster than he had yesterday. He was learning reflexes easily enough to demonstrate normal intelligences. At least he was to be more than a gifted moron.

A half hour later, Jake had grown tired of sleeping and was standing up in his crib, shouting and shaking the bars. Martha hurried in with a double armload of groceries.

"Does he want something?"

"Nope. Just exercising his lungs." Ted stubbed out his cigarette and tapped the finished stack of manuscript contentedly. "Got something here for you to proofread."

"Dinner first," she said cheerfully, unpacking food from the bags. "Better move the typewriter and give us some elbow room."

Sunlight came in the windows and shone on the yellow table top, and glinted on her dark hair as she opened packages.

"What's the local gossip?" he asked, clearing off the table. "Anything new?"

"Meat's going up again," she said, unwrapping peas and fillets of mackerel. "Mrs. Watkins' boy, Tom, is back from the clinic. He can see fine now, she says."

He put water on to boil and began greasing a skillet while she rolled the fillets in cracker crumbs. "If I'd had to run a flame thrower during the war, I'd have worked up a nice case of hysteric blindness myself," he said. "I call that a legitimate defense mechanism. Sometimes it's better to be blind."

"But not all the time," Martha protested, putting baby food in the double boiler. In five minutes lunch was cooking.

"Whaaaa—" wailed Jake.

Martha went into the baby's room, and brought him out, cuddling him and crooning. "What do you want, Lovekins? Baby just wants to be cuddled, doesn't baby."

"Yes," said Ted.

She looked up, startled, and her expression changed, became withdrawn and troubled, her dark eyes clouded in difficult thought.

Concerned, he asked: "What is it, Honey?"

"Ted, you shouldn't—" She struggled with words. "I know, it is handy to know what he wants, whenever he cries. It's handy having you tell me, but I don't— It isn't right somehow. It isn't *right*."

Jake waved an arm and squeaked randomly. He looked unhappy. Ted took him and laughed, making an effort to sound confident and persuasive. It would be impossible to raise the kid in a healthy way if Martha began to feel he was a freak. "Why isn't it right? It's normal enough. Look at E. S. P. Everybody has that according to Rhine."

"E. S. P. is different," she protested feebly, but Jake chortled and Ted knew he had her. He grinned, bouncing Jake up and down in his arms.

"Sure it's different," he said cheerfully. "E. S. P. is queer. E. S. P. comes in those weird accidental little flashes that contradict time and space. With clairvoyance you can see through walls, and read pages from a closed book in France. E. S. P., when it comes, is so ghastly precise it seems like tips from old Omniscience himself. It's enough to drive a logical man insane, trying to explain it. It's illogical, incredible, and random. But what Jake has is limited telepathy. It is starting out fuzzy and muddled and developing towards accuracy by plenty of trial and error—like sight, or any other normal sense. You don't mind communicating by English, so why mind communicating by telepathy?"

She smiled wanly. "But he doesn't weigh much, Ted. He's not growing as fast as it says he should in the baby book."

"That's all right. I didn't really start growing myself until I was about two. My parents thought I was sickly."

"And look at you now." She smiled genuinely. "All right, you win. But when does he start talking English? I'd like to understand him, too. After all, I'm his mother."

"Maybe this year, maybe next year," Ted said teasingly. "I didn't start talking until I was three."

"You mean that you don't want him to learn," she told him indignantly, and then smiled coaxingly at Jake. "You'll learn English soon for Mommy, won't you, Lovekins?"

Ted laughed annoyingly. "Try coaxing him next month or the month after. Right now he's not listening to all these thoughts. He's just collecting associations and reflexes. His cortex might organize impressions on a logic pattern he picked up from me, but it doesn't know what it is doing any more than this fist knows that it is in his mouth. That right, bud?'' There was no demanding thought behind the question, but instead, very delicately, Ted introspected to the small world of impression and sensation that flickered in what seemed a dreaming corner of his own mind. Right then it was a fragmentary world of green and brown that murmured with the wind.

''He's out eating grass with the rabbit,'' Ted told her.

Not answering, Martha started putting out plates. ''I like animal stories for children,'' she said determinedly. ''Rabbits are nicer than people.''

Putting Jake in his pen, Ted began to help. He kissed the back of her neck in passing. ''Some people are nicer than rabbits.''

Wind rustled tall grass and tangled vines where the rabbit snuffled and nibbled among the sun-dried herbs, moving on habit, ignoring the abstract meaningless contact of minds, with no thought but deep comfort.

Then for a while Jake's stomach became aware that lunch was coming, and the vivid business of crying and being fed drowned the gentler distant neural flow of the rabbit.

Ted ate with enjoyment, toying with an idea fantastic enough to keep him grinning, as Martha anxiously spooned food into Jake's mouth. She caught him grinning and indignantly began justifying herself. ''But he only gained four pounds, Ted. I have to make sure he eats something.''

''Only!'' he grinned. ''At that rate he'd be thirty feet high by the time he reaches college.''

''So would any baby.'' But she smiled at the idea, and gave Jake his next spoonful still smiling. Ted did not tell his real thought, that if Jake's abilities kept growing in a straight-line growth curve, by the time he was old enough to vote he would be God; but he laughed again, and was rewarded by an answering smile from both of them.

The idea was impossible, of course. Ted knew enough biology to know that there could be no sudden smooth jumps in evolution. Smooth changes had to be worked out gradually through generations of trial and selection. Sudden changes were not smooth, they crippled and destroyed. Mutants were usually monstrosities.

Jake was no sickly freak, so it was certain that he would not turn out very different from his parents. He could be only a little better. But the contrary idea had tickled Ted and he laughed again. "Boom food," he told Martha. "Remember those straight-line growth curves in the story?"

Martha remembered, smiling, "Redfern's dream—sweet little man, dreaming about a growth curve that went straight up." She chuckled, and fed Jake more spoonfuls of strained spinach, saying, "Open wide. Eat your boom food, darling. Don't you want to grow up like King Kong?"

Ted watched vaguely, toying now with a feeling that these months of his life had happened before, somewhere. He had felt it before, but now it came back with a sense of expectancy, as if something were going to happen.

It was while drying the dishes that Ted began to feel sick. Somewhere in the far distance at the back of his mind a tiny phantom of terror cried and danced and gibbered. He glimpsed it close in a flash that entered and was cut off abruptly in a vanishing fragment of delirium. It had something to do with a tangle of brambles in a field, and it was urgent.

Jake grimaced, his face wrinkled as if ready either to smile or cry. Carefully Ted hung up the dish towel and went out the back door, picking up a billet of wood as he passed the woodpile. He could hear Jake whimpering, beginning to wail.

"Where to?" Martha asked, coming out the back door.

"Dunno," Ted answered. "Gotta go rescue Jake's rabbit. It's in trouble."

Feeling numb, he went across the fields through an outgrowth of small trees, climbed a fence into a field of deep grass and thorny tangles of raspberry vines, and started across.

A few hundred feet into the field there was a hunter sitting on an outcrop of rock, smoking, with a successful bag of two rabbits dangling near him. He turned an inquiring face to Ted.

"Sorry," the hunter said. He was quiet-looking man with a sagging, middle-aged face. "It can't understand being upside down with its legs tied." Moving with shaky urgency he took his penknife and cut the small animal's pulsing throat, then threw the wet knife out of his hand into the grass. The rabbit kicked once more, staring still at the tangled vines of refuge. Then its nearsighted baby eyes lost their glazed bright stare and became meaningless.

"That's all right," Ted replied, "but be a little more careful next time, will you? You're out of season anyhow." He looked up from the grass to smile stiffly at the hunter. It was difficult.

There was a crowded feeling in his head, like a coming headache, or a stuffy cold. It was difficult to breathe, difficult to think.

It occurred to Ted then to wonder why Jake had never put him in touch with the mind of an adult. After a frozen stoppage of thought he laboriously started the wheels again and realized that something had put him in touch with the mind of the hunter, and that was what was wrong. His stomach began to rise. In another minute he would retch.

Ted stepped forward and swung the billet of wood in a clumsy sidewise sweep. The hunter's rifle went off and missed as the middle-aged man tumbled face first into the grass.

Wind rustled the long grass and stirred the leafless branches of trees. Ted could hear and think again, standing still and breathing in deep, shuddering breaths of air to clean his lungs. Briefly he planned what to do. He would call the sheriff and say that a hunter hunting out of season had shot at him and he had been forced to knock the man out. The sheriff would take the man away, out of thought range.

Before he started back to telephone he looked again at the peaceful, simple scene of field and trees and sky. It was safe to let himself think now. He took a deep breath and let himself think. The memory of horror came into clarity.

The hunter had been psychotic.

Thinking back, Ted recognized parts of it, like faces glimpsed in writhing smoke. The evil symbols of psychiatry, the bloody poetry of the Golden Bough, that had been the law of mankind in the five hundred thousand lost years before history. Torture and sacrifice, lust and death, a mechanism in perfect balance, a short circuit of conditioning through a glowing channel of symbols, an irreversible and perfect integration of traumas. It is easy to go mad, but it is not easy to go sane.

"Shut up!" Ted had been screaming inside his mind as he struck. "Shut up."

It had stopped. It had shut up. The symbols were fading without having found root in his mind. The sheriff would take the man away out of thought reach, and there would be no danger. It had stopped.

The burned hand avoids the fire. Something else had stopped. Ted's mind was queerly silent, queerly calm and empty, as he walked home across the winter fields, wondering how it had happened at all, kicking himself with humor for a suggestible fool, not yet missing—Jake.

And Jake lay awake in his pen, waving his rattle in random motions, and crowing ''glaglagla gla—'' in a motor sensory cycle, closed and locked against outside thoughts.

He would be a normal baby, as Ted had been, and as Ted's father before him.

And as all mankind was ''normal.''

COLD WAR

by Henry Kuttner (1914—1958)

***Thrilling Wonder Stories*, October**

The third selection by the terrific Kuttners (and to some extent all they published under whatever name after their marriage owed something to both) is this charming tale about "just plain folks" who happen to be mutants. "Cold War" is the last of a series of four stories about the Hogbens, all of which appeared in Thrilling Wonder Stories*—"Exit the Professor" (October, 1947), "Pile of Trouble" (April, 1948), and "See You Later" (June, 1949). It's a shame that they didn't write a few more, because they would have made a fine collection.—M.H.G.*

(When I first started to write, I attempted, in a few stories, to present a dialect by means of specialized spelling. No doubt I wasn't skillful enough to carry it off, so that I found the stories embarrassing to reread when I was done, and even more embarrassing to reread if they happened to get published (as a few did.) Quite early in the game I therefore stopped and had every character I dealt with speak cultured English or, at least, correctly spelled English.

There are advantages to dialect, however. If you tell a story in the first person and in dialect, you make it plain to the reader that you are dealing with a culture quite distinct from that of the American establishment. It gives odd events and odd outlooks a greater verisimilitude, and it also serves as a source of humor. Of two narratives, all things being otherwise equal, *the one in dialect is funnier.*

If, that is, it is done right. Henry Kuttner does it right in Cold War *as I'm sure you will very quickly decide for yourself.* I *couldn't do it.—I.A.)*

Chapter I. Last of the Pughs

I'll never have a cold in the haid again without I think of little Junior Pugh. Now there was a repulsive brat if ever I saw one. Built like a little gorilla, he was. Fat, pasty face, mean look, eyes so close together you could poke 'em both out at once with one finger. His paw thought the world of him though. Maybe that was natural, seeing as how little Junior was the image of his pappy.

"The last of the Pughs," the old man used to say stickin' his chest out and beamin' down at the little gorilla. "Finest little lad that ever stepped."

It made my blood run cold sometimes to look at the two of 'em together. Kinda sad, now, to think back to those happy days when I didn't know either of 'em. You may not believe it but them two Pughs, father and son, between 'em came within *that* much of conquerin' the world.

Us Hogbens is quiet folks. We like to keep our heads down and lead quiet lives in our own little valley, where nobody comes near withouten we say so. Our neighbors and the folks in the village are used to us by now. They know we try hard not to act conspicuous. They make allowances.

If Paw gets drunk, like last week, and flies down the middle of Main Street in his red underwear most people make out they don't notice, so's not to embarrass Maw. They know he'd walk like a decent Christian if he was sober.

The thing that druv Paw to drink that time was Little Sam, which is our baby we keep in a tank down-cellar, startin' to teethe again. First time since the War Between the States. We'd figgered he was through teething, but with Little Sam you never can tell. He was mighty restless, too.

A perfesser we keep in a bottle told us once Little Sam e-mitted subsonic somethings when he yells but that's just his way of talking. Don't mean a thing. It makes your nerves twiddle, that's all. Paw can't stand it. This time it even woke up Grandpaw in the attic and he hadn't stirred since Christmas. First thing after he got his eyes open he bust out madder'n a wet hen at Paw.

"I see ye, wittold knave that ye are!" he howled. "Flying again, is it? Oh, sic a reowfule sigte! I'll ground ye, ywis!" There was a far-away thump.

"You made me fall a good ten feet!" Paw hollered from away down the valley. "It ain't fair. I could of busted something!"

"Ye'll bust us all, with your dronken carelessness," Grandpaw said. "Flying in full sight of the neighbors! People get burned at the stake for less. You want mankind to find out all about us? Now shut up and let me tend to Baby."

Grandpaw can always quiet the baby if nobody else can. This time he sung him a little song in Sanskrit and after a bit they was snoring a duet.

I was fixing up a dingus for Maw to sour up some cream for sour-cream biscuits. I didn't have much to work with but an old sled and some pieces of wire but I didn't need much. I was trying to point the top end of the wire north-northeast when I seen a pair of checked pants rush by in the woods.

It was Uncle Lem. I could hear him thinking. "It *ain't* me!" he was saying, real loud, inside his haid. "Git back to yer work, Saunk. I ain't within a mile of you. Yer Uncle Lem's a fine old feller and never tells lies. Think I'd fool ye, Saunkie boy?"

"You shore would," I thunk back. "If you could. What's up, Uncle Lem?"

At that he slowed down and started to saunter back in a wide circle.

"Oh, I just had an idy yer Maw might like a mess of blackberries," he thunk, kicking a pebble very nonchalant. "If anybody asks you say you ain't seen me. It's no lie. You ain't."

"Uncle Lem," I thunk, real loud, "I gave Maw my bounden word I wouldn't let you out of range without me along, account of the last time you got away—"

"Now, now, my boy," Uncle Lem thunk fast. "Let bygones be bygones."

"You just can't say no to a friend, Uncle Lem," I reminded him, taking a last turn of the wire around the runner. "So you wait a shake till I get this cream soured and we'll both go together, wherever it is you have in mind."

I saw the checked pants among the bushes and he come out in the open and give me a guilty smile. Uncle Lem's a fat little feller. He means well, I guess, but he can be talked into most anything by most anybody, which is why we have to keep a close eye on him.

"How you gonna do it?" he asked me, looking at the creamjug. "Make the little critters work faster?"

"Uncle Lem!" I said. "You know better'n that. Cruelty to dumb animals is something I can't abide. Them there little critters work hard enough souring milk the way it is. They're such teentsy-weentsy fellers I kinda feel sorry for 'em. Why, you can't even see 'em without you go kinda crosseyed when you look. Paw says they're enzymes. But they can't be. They're too teeny."

"Teeny is as teeny does," Uncle Lem said. "How you gonna do it, then?"

"This here gadget," I told him, kinda proud, "will send Maw's cream-jug ahead into next week some time. This weather, don't take cream more'n a couple of days but I'm giving it plenty of time. When I bring it back—bingo, it's sour." I set the jug on the sled.

"I never seen such a dö-lass brat," Uncle Lem said, stepping forward and bending a wire crosswise. "You better do it thataway, on account of the thunderstorm next Tuesday. All right now, shoot her off."

So I shot her off. When she come back, sure enough, the cream was sour enough to walk a mouse. Crawling up the can there was a hornet from next week, which I squashed. Now that was a mistake. I knowed it the minute I touched the jug. Dang Uncle Lem, anyhow.

He jumped back into the underbrush, squealing real happy.

"Fooled you that time, you young stinker," he yelled back. "Let's see you get your thumb outa the middle of next week!"

It was the time-lag done it. I mighta knowed. When he crossed that wire he didn't have no thunderstorm in mind at all. Took me nigh onto ten minutes to work myself loose, account of some feller called Inertia, who mixes in if you ain't careful when you fiddle around with time. I don't understand much about it myself. I ain't got my growth yet. Uncle Lem says he's already forgot more'n I'll ever know.

With that head start I almost lost him. Didn't even have time to change into my store-bought clothes and I knowed by the way he was all dressed up fit to kill he was headed for somewheres fancy.

He was worried, too. I kept running into little stray worrisome thoughts he'd left behind him, hanging like teeny little mites of clouds on the bushes. Couldn't make out much on account of they was shredding away by the time I got there but he'd shore done something he shouldn't. That much *anybody* coulda told. They went something like this:

"Worry, worry—wish I hadn't done it—oh, heaven help me if Grandpaw ever finds out—oh, them nasty Pughs, how could I a-been such a fool? Worry, worry—pore ole feller, such a good soul, too, never done nobody no harm and look at me now.

"That Saunk, too big for his britches, teach him a thing or two, ha-ha. Oh, worry, worry—never mind, brace up, you good ole boy, everything's bound to turn out right in the end. You deserve the best, bless you, Lemuel. Grandpaw'll never find out."

Well, I seen his checkered britches high-tailing through the woods after a bit, but I didn't catch up to him until he was down the hill, across the picnic grounds at the edge of town and pounding on the sill of the ticket-window at the railroad station with a Spanish dubloon he snitched from Paw's seachest.

It didn't surprise me none to hear him asking for a ticket to State Center. I let him think I hadn't caught up. He argued something turrible with the man behind the window but finally he dug down in his britches and fetched up a silver dollar, and the man calmed down.

The train was already puffing up smoke behind the station when Uncle Lem darted around the corner. Didn't leave me much time but I made it too—just. I had to fly a little over the last half-dozen yards but I don't think anybody noticed.

Once when I was just a little shaver there was a Great Plague in London, where we were living at the time, and all us Hogbens had to clear out. I remember the hullabaloo in the city but looking back now it don't seem a patch on the hullabaloo in State Center station when the train pulled in. Times have changed, I guess.

Whistles blowing, horns honking, radios yelling bloody murder—seems like every invention in the last two hundred years had been noisier than the one before it. Made my head ache until I fixed up something Paw once called a raised decibel threshold, which was pure showing-off.

Uncle Lem didn't know I was anywhere around. I took care to think real quiet but he was so wrapped up in his worries he wasn't paying no mind to nothing. I followed him through the crowds in the station and out onto a wide street full of traffic. It was a relief to get away from the trains.

I always hate to think what's going on inside the boiler, with all the little bitty critters so small you can't hardly see 'em, pore things, flying around all hot and excited and bashing their heads together. It seems plumb pitiable.

Of course, it just don't do to think what's happening inside the automobiles that go by.

Uncle Lem knowed right where he was headed. He took off down the street so fast I had to keep reminding myself not to fly, trying to keep up. I kept thinking I ought to get in touch with the folks at home, in case this turned into something I couldn't handle, but I was plumb stopped everywhere I turned. Maw was at the church social that afternoon and she whopped me the last time I spoke to her outa thin air right in front of the Reverend Jones. He ain't used to us Hogbens yet.

Paw was daid drunk. No good trying to wake him up. And I was scared to death I *would* wake the baby if I tried to call on Grandpaw.

Uncle Lem scuttled right along, his checkered legs a-twinkling. He was worrying at the top of his mind, too. He'd caught sight of a crowd in a side-street gathered around a big truck, looking up at a man standing on it and waving bottles in both hands.

He seemed to be making a speech about headaches. I could hear him all the way to the corner. There was big banners tacked along the sides of the truck that said, PUGH HEADACHE CURE.

"Oh, worry, worry!" Uncle Lem thunk. "Oh, bless my toes, what *am* I going to do? I never *dreamed* anybody'd marry Lily Lou Mutz. Oh, worry!"

Well, I reckon we'd all been surprised when Lily Lou Mutz up and got herself a husband awhile back—around ten years ago, I figgered. But what it had to do with Uncle Lem I couldn't think. Lily Lou was just about the ugliest female that ever walked. Ugly ain't no word for her, pore gal.

Grandpaw said once she put him in mind of a family name of Gorgon he used to know. Not that she wasn't a goodhearted critter. Being so ugly, she put up with a lot in the way of rough acting-up from the folks in the village—the riff-raff lot, I mean.

She lived by herself in a little shack up the mountain and she musta been close onto forty when some feller from the other side of the river come along one day and rocked the whole valley back on its heels by asking her to marry up with him. Never saw the feller myself but I heard tell he wasn't no beauty-prize winner neither.

Come to think of it, I told myself right then, looking at the truck—come to think of it, feller's name was Pugh.

Chapter 2. A Fine Old Feller

Next thing I knowed, Uncle Lem had spotted somebody under a lamp-post on the sidewalk, at the edge of the crowd. He trotted over. It seemed to be a big gorilla and a little gorilla, standing there watching the feller on the truck selling bottles with both hands.

"Come and get it," he was yelling. "Come and get your bottle of Pugh's Old Reliable Headache Cure while they last!"

"Well, Pugh, here I am," Uncle Lem said, looking up at the big gorilla. "Hello, Junior," he said right afterward, glancing down at the little gorilla. I seen him shudder a little.

You shore couldn't blame him for that. Two nastier specimens of the human race I never did see in all my born days. If they hadn't been *quite* so pasty-faced or just the least mite slimmer, maybe they wouldn't have put me so much in mind of two well-fed slugs, one growed-up and one baby-sized. The paw was all dressed up in a Sunday-meeting suit with a big gold watch-chain across his front and the way he strutted you'd a thought he'd never had a good look in a mirror.

"Howdy, Lem," he said, casual-like. "Right on time, I see. Junior, say howdy to Mister Lem Hogben. You owe Mister Hogben a lot, sonny." And he laughed a mighty nasty laugh.

Junior paid him no mind. He had his beady little eyes fixed on the crowd across the street. He looked about seven years old and mean as they come.

"Shall I do it now, paw?" he asked in a squeaky voice. "Can I let 'em have it now, paw? Huh, paw?" From the tone he used, I looked to see if he'd got a machine-gun handy. I didn't see none but if looks was ever mean enough to kill Junior Pugh could of mowed the crowd right down.

"Manly little feller, ain't he, Lem?" Paw Pugh said, real smug. "I tell you, I'm mighty proud of this youngster. Wish his dear grandpaw coulda lived to see him. A fine old family line, the Pughs is. Nothing like it anywhere. Only trouble is, Junior's the last of his race. You see why I got in touch with you, Lem."

Uncle Lem shuddered again. "Yep," he said. "I see, all right. But you're wasting your breath, Pugh. I ain't a-gonna do it."

Young Pugh spun around in his tracks.

"Shall I let him have it, paw?" he squeaked, real eager. "Shall I, paw? Now, paw? Huh?"

"Shaddup, sonny," the big feller said and he whammed the little feller across the side of the haid. Pugh's hands was like hams. He shore was built like a gorilla.

The way his great big arms swung down from them big hunched shoulders, you'd of thought the kid would go flying across the street when his paw whopped him one. But he was a burly little feller. He just staggered a mite and then shook his haid and went red in the face.

He yelled out, loud and squeaky, "Paw, I warned you! The

last time you whammed me I warned you! Now I'm gonna let you have it!''

He drew a deep breath and his two little teeny eyes got so bright I coulda sworn they was gonna touch each other across the middle of his nose. His pasty face got bright red.

''Okay, Junior,'' Paw Pugh said, real hasty. ''The crowd's ready for you. Don't waste your strength on me, sonny. Let the crowd have it!''

Now all this time I was standing at the edge of the crowd, listening and watching Uncle Lem. But just then somebody jiggled my arm and a thin kinda voice said to me, real polite, ''Excuse me, but may I ask a question?''

I looked down. It was a skinny man with a kind-hearted face. He had a notebook in his hand.

''It's all right with me,'' I told him, polite. ''Ask away, mister.''

''I just wondered how you feel, that's all,'' the skinny man said, holding his pencil over the notebook ready to write down something.

''Why, peart,'' I said. ''Right kind of you to inquire. Hope you're feeling well too, mister.''

He shook his head, kind of dazed. ''That's the trouble,'' he said. ''I just don't understand it. I feel fine.''

''Why not?'' I asked. ''Fine day.''

''Everybody here feels fine,'' he went right on, just like I hadn't spoke. ''Barring normal odds, everybody's in average good health in this crowd. But in about five minutes or less, as I figure it—'' He looked at his wristwatch.

Just then somebody hit me right on top of the haid with a red-hot sledge-hammer.

Now you shore can't hurt a Hogben by hitting him on the haid. Anybody's a fool to try. I felt my knees buckle a little but I was all right in a couple of seconds and I looked around to see who'd whammed me.

Wasn't a soul there. But oh my, the moaning and groaning that was going up from that there crowd! People was a-clutching at their foreheads and a-staggering around the street, clawing at each other to get to that truck where the man was handing out the bottles of headache cure as fast as he could take in the dollar bills.

The skinny man with the kind face rolled up his eyes like a duck in thunder.

''Oh, my head!'' he groaned. ''What did I tell you? Oh, my

head!" Then he sort of tottered away, fishing in his pocket for money.

Well, the family always did say I was slow-witted but you'd have to be downright feeble-minded if you didn't know there was something mighty peculiar going on around here. I'm no ninny, no matter what Maw says. I turned around and looked for Junior Pugh.

There he stood, the fat-faced little varmint, red as a turkey-gobbler, all swole up and his mean little eyes just a-flashing at the crowd.

"It's a hex," I thought to myself, perfectly calm. "I'd never have believed it but it's a real hex. Now how in the world—"

Then I remembered Lily Lou Mutz and what Uncle Lem had been thinking to himself. And I began to see the light.

The crowd had gone plumb crazy, fighting to get at the headache cure. I purty near had to bash my way over toward Uncle Lem. I figured it was past time I took a hand, on account of him being so soft in the heart and likewise just about as soft in the haid.

"Nosirree," he was saying, firm-like. "I won't do it. Not by no manner of means I won't."

"Uncle Lem," I said.

I bet he jumped a yard into the air.

"Saunk!" he squeaked. He flushed up and grinned sheepish and then he looked mad, but I could tell he was kinda relieved, too. "I told you not to foller me," he said.

"Maw told me not to let you out of my sight," I said. "I promised Maw and us Hogbens never break a promise. What's going on here, Uncle Lem?"

"Oh, Saunk, everything's gone dead wrong!" Uncle Lem wailed out. "Here I am with a heart of gold and I'd just as soon be dead! Meet Mister Ed Pugh, Saunk. He's trying to get me kilt."

"Now Lem," Ed Pugh said. "You know that ain't so. I just want my rights, that's all. Pleased to meet you, young fellow. Another Hogben, I take it. Maybe you can talk your uncle into—"

"Excuse me for interrupting, Mister Pugh," I said, real polite. "But maybe you'd better explain. All this is purely a mystery to me."

He cleared his throat and threw his chest out, important-like. I could tell this was something he liked to talk about. Made him feel pretty big, I could see.

"I don't know if you was acquainted with my dear departed

wife, Lily Lou Mutz that was,'' he said. ''This here's our little child, Junior. A fine little lad he is too. What a pity we didn't have eight or ten more just like him.'' He sighed real deep.

''Well, that's life. I'd hoped to marry young and be blessed with a whole passel of younguns, being as how I'm the last of a fine old line. I don't mean to let it die out, neither.'' Here he gave Uncle Lem a mean look. Uncle Lem sorta whimpered.

''I ain't a-gonna do it,'' he said. ''You can't make me do it.''

''We'll see about that,'' Ed Pugh said, threatening. ''Maybe your young relative here will be more reasonable. I'll have you know I'm getting to be a power in this state and what I says goes.''

''Paw,'' little Junior squeaked out just then, ''Paw, they're kinda slowing down. Kin I give it to 'em double-strength this time, Paw? Betcha I could kill a few if I let myself go. Hey, Paw—''

Ed Pugh made as if he was gonna clonk the little varmint again, but I guess he thought better of it.

''Don't interrupt your elders, sonny,'' he said. ''Paw's busy. Just tend to your job and shut up.'' He glanced out over the moaning crowd. ''Give that bunch over beyond the truck a little more treatment,'' he said. ''They ain't buying fast enough. But no double-strength, Junior. You gotta save your energy. You're a growing boy.''

He turned back to me. ''Junior's a talented child,'' he said, very proud. ''As you can see. He inherited it from his dear dead-and-gone mother, Lily Lou. I was telling you about Lily Lou. It was my hope to marry young, like I said, but the way things worked out, somehow I just didn't get around to wifin' till I'd got well along into the prime of life.''

He blew out his chest like a toadfrog, looking down admiring. I never did see a man that thought better of himself. ''Never found a woman who'd look at—I mean, never found the right woman,'' he went on, ''till the day I met Lily Lou Mutz.''

''I know what you mean,'' I said, polite. I did, too. He musta searched a long, long ways before he found somebody ugly enough herself to look twice at him. Even Lily Lou, pore soul, musta thunk a long time afore she said yes.

''And that,'' Ed Pugh went on, ''is where your Uncle Lem comes in. It seems like he'd give Lily Lou a bewitchment quite some while back.''

''I never!'' Uncle Lem squealed. ''And anyway, how'd I know she'd get married and pass it on to her child? Who'd ever think Lily Lou would—''

"He gave her a bewitchment," Ed Pugh went right on talking. "Only she never told me till she was a-layin' on her death-bed a year ago. Lordy, I sure woulda whopped her good if I'd knowed how she held out on me all them years! It was the hex Lemuel gave her and she inherited it on to her little child."

"I only done it to protect her," Uncle Lem said, right quick. "You know I'm speaking the truth, Saunk boy. Pore Lily Lou was so pizon ugly, people used to up and heave a clod at her now and then afore they could help themselves. Just automatic-like. Couldn't blame 'em. I often fought down the impulse myself.

"But pore Lily Lou, I shore felt sorry for her. You'll never know how long I fought down my good impulses, Saunk. But my heart of gold does get me into messes. One day I felt so sorry for the pore hideous critter I gave her the hexpower. Anybody'd have done the same, Saunk."

"How'd you do it?" I asked, real interested, thinking it might come in handy someday to know. I'm young yet, and I got lots to learn.

Well, he started to tell me and it was kinda mixed up. Right at first I got a notion some furrin feller named Gene Chromosome had done it for him and after I got straight on that part he'd gone cantering off into a rigamarole about the alpha waves of the brain.

Shucks, I knowed that much my own self. Everybody musta noticed the way them little waves go a-sweeping over the tops of people's haids when they're thinking. I've watched Grandpaw sometimes when he had as many as six hundred different thoughts follering each other up and down them little paths where his brain is. Hurts my eyes to look too close when Grandpaw's thinking.

"So that's how it is, Saunk," Uncle Lem wound up. "And this here little rattlesnake's inherited the whole shebang."

"Well, why don't you get this here Gene Chromosome feller to unscramble Junior and put him back the way other people are?" I asked. "I can see how easy you could do it. Look here, Uncle Lem." I focused down real sharp on Junior and made my eyes go funny the way you have to when you want to look inside a person.

Sure enough, I seen just what Uncle Lem meant. There was teensy-weensy little chains of fellers, all hanging onto each other for dear life, and skinny little rods jiggling around inside them awful teensy cells everybody's made of—except maybe Little Sam, our baby.

"Look here, Uncle Lem," I said. "All you did when you gave Lily Lou the hex was to twitch these here little rods over *that-away* and patch 'em onto them little chains that wiggle so fast. Now why can't you switch 'em back again and make Junior behave himself? It oughta be easy."

"It would be easy," Uncle Lem kinda sighed at me. "Saunk, you're a scatterbrain. You wasn't listening to what I said. I can't switch 'em back without I kill Junior."

"The world would be a better place," I said.

"I know it would. But you know what we promised Grandpaw? No more killings."

"But Uncle Lem!" I bust out. "This is turrible! You mean this nasty little rattlesnake's gonna go on all his life hexing people?"

"Worse than that, Saunk," pore Uncle Lem said, almost crying. "He's gonna pass the power on to his descendants, just like Lily Lou passed it on to him."

For a minute it sure did look like a dark prospect for the human race. Then I laughed.

"Cheer up, Uncle Lem," I said. "Nothing to worry about. Look at the little toad. There ain't a female critter alive who'd come within a mile of him. Already he's as repulsive as his daddy. And remember, he's Lily Lou Mutz's child, too. Maybe he'll get even horribler as he grows up. One thing's sure—he ain't never gonna get married."

"Now there's where you're wrong," Ed Pugh busted in, talking real loud. He was red in the face and he looked mad. "Don't think I ain't been listening," he said. "And don't think I'm gonna forget what you said about my child. I told you I was a power in this town. Junior and me can go a long way, using his talent to help us.

"Already I've got on to the board of aldermen here and there's gonna be a vacancy in the state senate come next week—unless the old coot I have in mind's a lot tougher than he looks. So I'm warning you, young Hogben, you and your family's gonna pay for them insults."

"Nobody oughta get mad when he hears the gospel truth about himself," I said. "Junior *is* a repulsive specimen."

"He just takes getting used to," his paw said. "All us Pughs is hard to understand. Deep, I guess. But we got our pride. And I'm gonna make sure the family line never dies out. Never, do you hear that, Lemuel?"

Uncle Lem just shut his eyes up tight and shook his head fast.

''Nosirree,'' he said. ''I'll never do it. Never, never, never, never—''

''Lemuel,'' Ed Pugh said, real sinister. ''Lemuel, do you want me to set Junior on you?''

''Oh, there ain't no use in that,'' I said. ''You seen him try to hex me along with the crowd, didn't you? No manner of use, Mister Pugh. Can't hex a Hogben.''

''Well—'' He looked around, searching his mind. ''Hm-m. I'll think of something. I'll—soft-hearted, aren't you? Promised your Grandpappy you wouldn't kill nobody, hey? Lemuel, open your eyes and look over there across the street. See that sweet old lady walking with the cane? How'd you like it if I had Junior drop her dead in her tracks?''

Uncle Lemuel just squeezed his eyes tighter shut.

''I won't look. I don't know the sweet old thing. If she's that old, she ain't got much longer anyhow. Maybe she'd be better off dead. Probably got rheumatiz something fierce.''

''All right, then, how about that purty young girl with the baby in her arms? Look, Lemuel. Mighty sweet-looking little baby. Pink ribbon in its bonnet, see? Look at them dimples. Junior, get ready to blight them where they stand. Bubonic plague to start with maybe. And after that—''

''Uncle Lem,'' I said, feeling uneasy. ''I dunno what Grandpaw would say to this. Maybe—''

Uncle Lem popped his eyes wide open for just a second. He glared at me, frantic.

''I can't help it if I've got a heart of gold,'' he said. ''I'm a fine old feller and everybody picks on me. Well, I won't stand for it. You can push me just so far. Now I don't care if Ed Pugh kills off the whole human race. I don't care if Grandpaw *does* find out what I done. I don't care a hoot about nothing no more.'' He gave a kind of wild laugh.

''I'm gonna get out from under. I won't know nothing about nothing. I'm gonna snatch me a few winks, Saunk.''

And with that he went rigid all over and fell flat on his face on the sidewalk, stiff as a poker.

Chapter 3. Over a Barrel

Well, worried as I was, I had to smile. Uncle Lem's kinda cute sometimes. I knowed he'd put hisself to sleep again, the way he always does when trouble catches up with him. Paw says it's catalepsy but cats sleep a lot lighter than that.

Uncle Lem hit the sidewalk flat and kinda bounced a little. Junior give a howl of joy. I guess maybe he figgered he'd had something to do with Uncle Lem falling over. Anyhow, seeing somebody down and helpless, Junior naturally rushed over and pulled his foot back and kicked Uncle Lem in the side of the haid.

Well, like I said, us Hogbens have got pretty tough haids. Junior let out a howl. He started dancing around nursing his foot in both hands.

"I'll hex you good!" he yelled at Uncle Lem. "I'll hex you good, you—you ole Hogben, you!" He drew a deep breath and turned purple in the face and—

And then it happened.

It was like a flash of lightning. I don't take no stock in hexes, and I had a fair idea of what was happening, but it took me by surprise. Paw tried to explain to me later how it worked and he said it just stimulated the latent toxins inherent in the organism. It made Junior into a catalytoxic agent on account of the way the rearrangement of the desoxyribonucleic acid his genes was made of worked on the kappa waves of his nasty little brain, stepping them up as much as thirty microvolts. But shucks, you know Paw. He's too lazy to figger the thing out in English. He just steals them fool words out of other folks' brains when he needs 'em.

What really happened was that all the pizon that little varmint had bottled up in him, ready to let go on the crowd, somehow seemed to r'ar back and smack Uncle Lem right in the face. I never seen such a hex. And the awful part was—it worked.

Because Uncle Lem wasn't resisting a mite now he was asleep. Red-hot pokers wouldn't have waked him up and I wouldn't put red-hot pokers past little Junior Pugh. But he didn't need 'em this time. The hex hit Uncle Lem like a thunderbolt.

He turned pale green right before our eyes.

Somehow it seemed to me a turrible silence fell as Uncle Lem went green. I looked up, surprised. Then I realized what was happening. All that pitiful moaning and groaning from the crowd had stopped.

People was swigging away at their bottles of headache cure, rubbing their foreheads and kinda laughing weak-like with relief. Junior's whole complete hex had gone into Uncle Lem and the crowd's headaches had naturally stopped right off.

"What's happened here?" somebody called out in a kinda familiar voice. "Has that man fainted? Why don't you help him? Here, let me by—I'm a doctor."

It was the skinny man with the kind-looking face. He was still drinking out of the headache bottle as he pushed his way through the crowd toward us but he'd put his notebook away. When he saw Ed Pugh he flushed up angrylike.

"So it's you, is it, Alderman Pugh?" he said. "How is it you're always around when trouble starts? What did you do to this poor man, anyhow? Maybe this time you've gone too far."

"I didn't do a thing," Ed Pugh said. "Never touched him. You watch your tongue, Dr. Brown, or you'll regret it. I'm a powerful man in this here town."

"Look at that!" Dr. Brown yells, his voice going kinda squeaky as he stares down at Uncle Lem. "The man's dying! Call an ambulance, somebody, quick!"

Uncle Lem was changing color again. I had to laugh a little, inside my haid. I knowed what was happening and it was kinda funny. Everybody's got a whole herd of germs and viruses and suchlike critters swarming through them all the time, of course.

When Junior's hex hit Uncle Lem it stimulated the entire herd something turrible, and a flock of little bitty critters Paw calls antibodies had to get to work pronto. They ain't really as sick as they look, being white by nature.

Whenever a pizon starts chawing on you these pale little fellers grab up their shooting-irons and run like crazy to the battlefield in your insides. Such fighting and yelling and swearing you never seen. It's a regular Bull Run.

That was going on right then inside Uncle Lem. Only us Hogbens have got a special militia of our own inside us. And they got called up real fast.

They was swearing and kicking and whopping the enemy so hard Uncle Lem had gone from pale green to a sort of purplish color, and big yeller and blue spots was beginning to bug out all over him where it showed. He looked oncommon sick. Course it didn't do him no real harm. The Hogbens militia can lick any germ that breathes.

But he sure looked revolting.

The skinny doctor crouched down beside Uncle Lem and felt his pulse.

"Now you've done it," he said, looking up at Ed Pugh. "I don't know how you've worked this, but for once you've gone too far. This man seems to have bubonic plague. I'll see you're put under control this time and that young Kallikak of yours, too."

Ed Pugh just laughed a little. But I could see he was mad.

"Don't you worry about me, Dr. Brown," he said, mean.

"When I get to be governor—and I got my plans all made—that there hospital you're so proud of ain't gonna operate on state funds no more. A fine thing!

"Folks laying around in hospitals eating their fool heads off! Make 'em get out and plough, that's what I say. Us Pughs never gets sick. I got lots of better uses for state money than paying folks to lay around in bed when I'm governor."

All the doctor said was, "Where's that ambulance?"

"If you mean that big long car making such a noise," I said, "it's about three miles off but coming fast. Uncle Lem don't need no help, though. He's just having an attack. We get 'em in the family all the time. It don't mean nothing."

"Good heavens!" the doc said, staring down at Uncle Lem. "You mean he's had this before and lived?" Then he looked up at me and smiled all of a sudden. "Oh, I see," he said. "Afraid of hospitals, are you? Well, don't worry. We won't hurt him."

That surprised me some. He was a smart man. I'd fibbed a little for just that reason. Hospitals is no place for Hogbens. People in hospitals are too danged nosy. So I called Uncle Lem real loud, inside my head.

"Uncle Lem!" I hollered, only thinking it, not out loud. "Uncle Lem, wake up quick! Grandpaw'll nail your hide to the barn door if'n you let yourself get took to a hospital. You want 'em to find out about them two hearts you got in your chest? And the way your bones are fixed and the shape of your gizzard? Uncle Lem! Wake up!"

It wasn't no manner of use. He never even twitched.

Right then I began to get really scared. Uncle Lem had sure landed me in the soup. There I was with all that responsibility on my shoulders and I didn't have the least idea how to handle it. I'm just a young feller after all. I can hardly remember much farther back than the great fire of London, when Charles II was king, with all them long curls a-hanging on his shoulders. On him, though, they looked good.

"Mister Pugh," I said, "you've got to call off Junior. I can't let Uncle Lem get took to the hospital. You know I can't."

"Junior, pour it on," Mister Pugh said, grinning real nasty. "I want a little talk with young Hogben here." The doctor looked up, puzzled, and Ed Pugh said, "Step over here a mite, Hogben. I want a private word with you. Junior, bear down!"

Uncle Lem's yellow and blue spots got green rings around their outside edges. The doctor sorta gasped and Ed Pugh took my arm and pulled me back. When we was out of earshot he said to me, confidential, fixing me with his tiny little eyes:

"I reckon you know what I want, Hogben. Lem never did say he *couldn't*, he only said he wouldn't, so I know you folks can do it for me."

"Just exactly what is it you want, Mister Pugh?" I asked him.

"You know. I want to make sure our fine old family line goes on. I want there should always be Pughs. I had so much trouble getting married off myself and I know Junior ain't going to be easy to wife. Women don't have no taste nowadays.

"Since Lily Lou went to glory there hasn't been a woman on earth ugly enough to marry a Pugh and I'm skeered Junior'll be the last of a great line. With his talent I can't bear the thought. You just fix it so our family won't never die out and I'll have Junior take the hex off Lemuel."

"If I fixed it so your line didn't die out," I said, "I'd be fixing it so everybody else's line *would* die out, just as soon as there was enough Pughs around."

"What's wrong with that?" Ed Pugh asked, grinning. "Way I see it we're good strong stock." He flexed his gorilla arms. He was taller than me, even. "No harm in populatin' the world with good stock, is there? I figger given time enough us Pughs could conquer the whole danged world. And you're gonna help us do it, young Hogben."

"Oh, no," I said. "Oh, no! Even if I knowed how—"

There was a turrible noise at the end of the street and the crowd scattered to make way for the ambulance, which drawed up at the curb beside Uncle Lem. A couple of fellers in white coats jumped out with a sort of pallet on sticks. Dr. Brown stood up, looking real relieved.

"Thought you'd never get here," he said. "This man's a quarantine case, I think. Heaven knows what kind of results we'll find when we start running tests on him. Hand me my bag out of the back there, will you? I want my stethoscope. There's something funny about this man's heart."

Well, *my* heart sunk right down into my boots. We was goners and I knowed it—the whole Hogben tribe. Once them doctors and scientists find out about us we'll never know a moment's peace again as long as we live. We won't have no more privacy than a corncob.

Ed Pugh was watching me with a nasty grin on his pasty face.

"Worried, huh?" he said. "You gotta right to be worried. I know about you Hogbens. All witches. Once they get Lem in the hospital, no telling what they'll find out. Against the law to be witches, probably. You've got about half a minute to make up your mind, young Hogben. What do you say?"

Well, what could I say? I couldn't give him a promise like he was asking, could I? Not and let the whole world be overrun by hexing Pughs. Us Hogbens live a long time. We've got some pretty important plans for the future when the rest of the world begins to catch up with us. But if by that time the rest of the world is all Pughs, it won't hardly seem worth while, somehow. I couldn't say yes.

But if I said no Uncle Lem was a goner. Us Hogbens was doomed either way, it seemed to me.

Looked like there was only one thing to do. I took a deep breath, shut my eyes, and let out a desperate yell inside my head.

"*Grandpaw!*" I hollered.

"Yes, my boy?" said a big deep voice in the middle of my brain. You'd athought he'd been right alongside me all the time, just waiting to be called. He was a hundred-odd miles off, and sound asleep. But when a Hogben calls in the tone of voice *I* called in he's got a right to expect an answer—quick. I got it.

Mostly Grandpaw woulda dithered around for fifteen minutes, asking cross questions and not listening to the answers, and talking in all kinds of queer old-fashioned dialects, like Sanskrit, he's picked up through the years. But this time he seen it was serious.

"Yes, my boy?" was all he said.

I flapped my mind wide open like a school-book in front of him. There wasn't no time for questions and answers. The doc was getting out his dingus to listen to Uncle Lem's two hearts beating out of tune and once he heard that the jig would be up for us Hogbens.

"Unless you let me kill 'em, Grandpaw," I added. Because by that time I knowed he'd read the whole situation from start to finish in one fast glance.

It seemed to me he was quiet an awful long time after that. The doc had got the dingus out and he was fitting its little black arms into his ears. Ed Pugh was watching me like a hawk. Junior stood there all swole up with pizon, blinking his mean little eyes around for somebody to shoot it at. I was half hoping he'd pick on me. I'd worked out a way to make it bounce back in his face and there was a chance it might even kill him.

I heard Grandpaw give a sorta sigh in my mind.

"They've got us over a barrel, Saunk," he said. I remember being a little surprised he could speak right plain English when he wanted to. "Tell Pugh we'll do it."

"But Grandpaw—" I said.

"Do as I say!" It gave me a headache, he spoke so firm. "Quick, Saunk! Tell Pugh we'll give him what he wants."

Well, I didn't dare disobey. But this once I really came close to defying Grandpaw.

It stands to reason even a Hogben has got to get senile someday, and I thought maybe old age had finally set in with Grandpaw at last.

What I thunk at him was, "All right, if you say so, but I sure hate to do it. Seems like if they've got us going and coming, the least we can do is take our medicine like Hogbens and keep all that pizon bottled up in Junior stead of spreading it around the world." But out loud I spoke to Mister Pugh.

"All right, Mister Pugh," I said, real humble. "You win. Only, call off your hex. Quick, before it's too late."

Chapter 4. Pughs A-Coming

Mister Pugh had a great big yellow automobile, low-slung, without no top. It went awful fast. And it was sure awful noisy. Once I'm pretty sure we run over a small boy in the road but Mister Pugh paid him no mind and I didn't dare say nothing. Like Grandpaw said, the Pughs had us over a barrel.

It took quite a lot of palaver before I convinced 'em they'd have to come back to the homestead with me. That was part of Grandpaw's orders.

"How do I know you won't murder us in cold blood once you get us out there in the wilderness?" Mister Pugh asked.

"I could kill you right here if I wanted," I told him. "I would too but Grandpaw says no. You're safe if Grandpaw says so, Mister Pugh. The word of a Hogben ain't never been broken yet."

So he agreed, mostly because I said we couldn't work the spells except on home territory. We loaded Uncle Lem into the back of the car and took off for the hills. Had quite an argument with the doc, of course. Uncle Lem sure was stubborn.

He wouldn't wake up nohow but once Junior took the hex off Uncle Lem faded out fast to a good healthy color again. The doc just didn't believe it coulda happened, even when he saw it. Mister Pugh had to threaten quite a lot before we got away. We left the doc sitting on the curb, muttering to himself and rubbing his haid dazed like.

I could feel Grandpaw a-studying the Pughs through my mind all the way home. He seemed to be sighing and kinda shaking his haid—such as it is—and working out problems that didn't make no manner of sense to me.

When we drawed up in front of the house there wasn't a soul in sight. I could hear Grandpaw stirring and muttering on his gunnysack in the attic but Paw seemed to have went invisible and he was too drunk to tell me where he was when I asked. The baby was asleep. Maw was still at the church sociable and Grandpaw said to leave her be.

"We can work this out together, Saunk," he said as soon as I got outa the car. "I've been thinking. You know that sled you fixed up to sour your Maw's cream this morning? Drag it out, son. Drag it out."

I seen in a flash what he had in mind. "Oh, no, Grandpaw!" I said, right out loud.

"Who you talking to?" Ed Pugh asked, lumbering down outa the car. "I don't see nobody. This your homestead? Ratty old dump, ain't it? Stay close to me, Junior. I don't trust these folks any farther'n I can see 'em."

"Get the sled, Saunk," Grandpaw said, very firm. "I got it all worked out. We're gonna send these two gorillas right back through time, to a place they'll really fit."

"But Grandpaw!" I hollered, only inside my head this time. "Let's talk this over. Lemme get Maw in on it anyhow. Paw's right smart when he's sober. Why not wait till he wakes up? I think we oughta get the Baby in on it too. I don't think sending 'em back through time's a good idea at all, Grandpaw."

"The Baby's asleep," Grandpaw said. "You leave him be. He read himself to sleep over his Einstein, bless his little soul."

I think the thing that worried me most was the way Grandpaw was talking plain English. He never does when he's feeling normal. I thought maybe his old age had all caught up with him at one bank, and knocked all the sense outa his—so to speak—haid.

"Grandpaw," I said, trying to keep calm. "Don't you see? If we send 'em back through time and give 'em what we promised it'll make everything a million times worse than before. You gonna strand 'em back there in the year one and break your promise to 'em?"

"Saunk!" Grandpaw said.

"I know. If we promised we'd make sure the Pugh line won't die out, then we gotta make sure. But if we send 'em back to the year one that'll mean all the time before then and now they'll spend spreading out and spreading out. More Pughs every generation.

"Grandpaw, five seconds after they hit the year one, I'm liable to feel my two eyes rush together in my haid and my face go all fat and pasty like Junior. Grandpaw, everybody in the world may be Pughs if we give 'em that much time to spread out in!"

"Cease thy chirming, thou chilce dolt," Grandpaw hollered. "Do my bidding, young fool!"

That made me feel a little better but not much. I went and dragged out the sled. Mister Pugh put up quite a argument about that.

"I ain't rid on a sled since I was so high," he said. "Why should I git on one now? This is some trick. I won't do it."

Junior tried to bite me.

"Now Mister Pugh," I said, "you gotta cooperate or we won't get nowheres. I know what I'm doing. Just step up here and set down. Junior, there's room for you in front. That's fine."

If he hadn't seen how worried I was I don't think he'd a-done it. But I couldn't hide how I was feeling.

"Where's your Grandpaw?" he asked, uneasy. "You're not going to do this whole trick by yourself, are you? Young ignorant feller like you? I don't like it. Suppose you made a mistake?"

"We give our word," I reminded him. "Now just kindly shut up and let me concentrate. Or maybe you don't want the Pugh line to last forever?"

"That was the promise," he says, settling himself down. "You gotta do it. Lemme know when you commence."

"All right, Saunk," Grandpaw says from the attic, right brisk. "Now you watch. Maybe you'll learn a thing or two. Look sharp. Focus your eyes down and pick out a gene. Any gene."

Bad as I felt about the whole thing I couldn't help being interested. When Grandpaw does a thing he does it up brown. Genes are mighty slippery little critters, spindle-shaped and awful teensy. They're partners with some skinny guys called chromosomes, and the two of 'em show up everywhere you look, once you've got your eyes focused just right.

"A good dose of ultraviolet ought to do the trick," Grandpaw muttered. "Saunk, you're closer."

I said, "All right, Grandpaw," and sort of twiddled the light as it sifted down through the pines above the Pughs. Ultraviolet's the color at the *other* end of the line, where the colors stop having names for most people.

Grandpaw said, "Thanks, son. Hold it for a minute."

The genes began to twiddle right in time with the light waves. Junior said, "Paw, something's tickling me."

Ed Pugh said, "Shut up."

Grandpaw was muttering to himself. I'm pretty sure he stole the words from that perfesser we keep in the bottle, but you can't tell, with Grandpaw. Maybe he was the first person to make 'em up in the beginning.

"The euchromatin," he kept muttering. "That ought to fix it. Ultraviolet gives us hereditary mutation and the euchromatin contains the genes that transmit heredity. Now that other stuff's heterochromatin and *that* produces evolutionary change of the cataclysmic variety.

"Very good, very good. We can always use a new species. Hum-m-m. About six bursts of heterochromatinic activity ought to do it." He was quiet for a minute. Then he said, "Ich am eldre and ek magti! Okay, Saunk, take it away."

I let the ultraviolet go back where it came from.

"The year one, Grandpaw?" I asked, very doubtful.

"That's close enough," he said. "Wite thou the way?"

"Oh yes, Grandpaw," I said. And I bent over and give them the necessary push.

The last thing I heard was Mister Pugh's howl.

"What's that you're doin'?" he hollered at me. "What's the idea? Look out, there, young Hogben or—what's this? Where we goin'? Young Saunk, I warn you, if this is some trick I'll set Junior on you! I'll send you such a hex as even you-u . . ."

Then the howl got real thin and small and far away until it wasn't no more than the noise a mosquito makes. After that it was mighty quiet in the dooryard.

I stood there all braced, ready to stop myself from turning into a Pugh if I could. Them little genes is tricky fellers.

I knowed Grandpaw had made a turrible mistake.

The minute them Pughs hit the year one and started to bounce back through time toward now I knowed what would happen.

I ain't sure how long ago the year one was, but there was plenty of time for the Pughs to populate the whole planet. I put two fingers against my nose to keep my eyes from banging each other when they started to rush together in the middle like all us Pughs' eyes do—

"You ain't a Pugh yet, son," Grandpaw said, chuckling. "Kin ye see 'em?"

"No," I said. "What's happening?"

"The sled's starting to slow down," he said. "Now it's

stopped. Yep, it's the year one, all right. Look at all them men and women flockin' outa the caves to greet their new company! My, my, what great big shoulders the men have got. Bigger even than Paw Pugh's.

"An' ugh—just look at the women! I declare, little Junior's positively handsome alongside them folks! He won't have no trouble finding a wife when the time comes."

"But Grandpaw, that's turrible!" I said.

"Don't sass your elders, Saunk," Grandpaw chuckled. "Looka there now. Junior's just pulled a hex. Another little child fell over flat on his ugly face. Now the little child's mother is knocking Junior endwise. Now his pappy's sailing into Paw Pugh. Look at that fight! Just look at it! Oh, I guess the Pugh family's well took care of, Saunk."

"But what about our family?" I said, almost wailing.

"Don't you worry," Grandpaw said. "Time'll take care of that. Wait a minute, let me watch. Hm-m. A generation don't take long when you know how to look. My, my, what ugly little critters the ten baby Pughs was! They was just like their pappy and their grandpappy.

"I wish Lily Lou Mutz could see her grandbabies. I shorely do. Well, now, ain't that cute? Every one of them babies growed up in a flash, seems like, and each of 'em has got ten babies of their own. I like to see my promises working out, Saunk. I said I'd do this, and I done it."

I just moaned.

"All right," Grandpaw said. "Let's jump ahead a couple of centuries. Yep, still there and spreading like crazy. Family likeness is still strong, too. Hum-m. Another thousand years and—well, I declare! If it ain't Ancient Greece! Hasn't changed a bit, neither. What do you know, Saunk!" He cackled right out, tickled pink.

"Remember what I said once about Lily Lou putting me in mind of an old friend of mine named Gorgon? No wonder! Perfectly natural. You ought to see Lily Lou's great-great-great-grandbabies! No, on second thought, it's lucky you can't. Well, well, this is shore interesting."

He was still about three minutes. Then I heard him laugh.

"Bang," he said. "First heterochromatinic burst. Now the changes start."

"What changes, Grandpaw?" I asked, feeling pretty miserable.

"The changes," he said, "that show your old Grandpaw ain't such a fool as you thought. I know what I'm doing. They go fast, once they start. Look there now, that's the second change. Look at them little genes mutate!"

"You mean," I said, "I ain't gonna turn into a Pugh after all? But Grandpaw, I thought we'd promised the Pughs their line wouldn't die out."

"I'm keeping my promise," Grandpaw said, dignified. "The genes will carry the Pugh likeness right on to the toot of the judgment horn, just like I said. And the hex power goes right along with it."

Then he laughed.

"You better brace yourself, Saunk," he said. "When Paw Pugh went sailing off into the year one seems like he uttered a hex threat, didn't he? Well, he wasn't fooling. It's a-coming at you right now."

"Oh, Lordy!" I said. "There'll be a million of 'em by the time they get here! Grandpaw! What'll I do?"

"Just brace yourself," Grandpaw said, real unsympathetic. "A million, you think? Oh, no, lots more than a million."

"How many?" I asked him.

He started in to tell me. You may not believe it but he's *still* telling me. It takes that long. There's that many of 'em.

You see, it was like with that there Jukes family that lived down south of here. The bad ones was always a mite worse than their children and the same dang thing happened to Gene Chromosome and his kin, so to speak. The Pughs stayed Pughs and they kept the hex power—and I guess you might say the Pughs conquered the whole world, after all.

But it could of been worse. The Pughs could of stayed the same size down through the generations. Instead they got smaller—a whole lot smaller. When I knowed 'em they was bigger than most folks—Paw Pugh, anyhow.

But by the time they'd done filtering the generations from the year one, they'd shrunk so much them little pale fellers in the blood was about their size. And many a knock-down drag-out fight they have with 'em, too.

Them Pugh genes took such a beating from the heterochromatinic bursts Grandpaw told me about that they got whopped all outa their proper form. You might call 'em a virus now—and of course a virus is exactly the same thing as a gene, except the virus is friskier. But heavens above, that's like saying the Jukes boys is exactly the same as George Washington!

The hex hit me—hard.

I sneezed something turrible. Then I heard Uncle Lem sneezing in his sleep, lying back there in the yaller car. Grandpaw was still droning on about how many Pughs was a-coming at me right that minute, so there wasn't no use asking questions. I fixed my eyes different and looked right down into the middle of that sneeze to see what had tickled me—

Well, you never seen so many Junior Pughs in all your born days! It was the hex, all right. Likewise, them Pughs is still busy, hexing everybody on earth, off and on. They'll do it for quite a time, too, since the Pugh line has got to go on forever, account of Grandpaw's promise.

They tell me even the microscopes ain't never yet got a good look at certain viruses. The scientists are sure in for a surprise someday when they focus down real close and see all them pasty-faced little devils, ugly as sin, with their eyes set real close together, wiggling around hexing everybody in sight.

It took a long time—since the year one, that is—but Gene Chromosome fixed it up, with Grandpaw's help. So Junior Pugh ain't a pain in the neck no more, so to speak.

But I got to admit he's an awful cold in the haid.

THE WITCHES OF KARRES

by James H. Schmitz (1911–1981)

***Astounding Science Fiction*, December**

The late James Schmitz was the creator of Telzey Amberton, a female secret agent who starred in such exciting novels as The Universe Against Her *(1964) and* The Lion Game *(1973) as well as the story collection* The Telzey Toy *(1973). Telzey was certainly ahead of her time—her adventurous and amorous escapades were fully worthy of male protaganists, and she is frequently referred to in defenses of science fiction's earlier anti-female bias.*

Telzey is also a telepath, like the three Witches of Karres. This was no accident, because John Campbell's postwar Astounding *was a center for "psi" stories of all types, one of several seeming obsessions of this great editor.* Astounding *began to enter a period of slow decline as the 1940s ended, brought on in no small measure by the magazine boom which saw the creation of powerful competition in the form of* Galaxy *and* The Magazine of Fantasy and Science Fiction. *It is also possible that by this time Campbell had done as much for science fiction as he could.*

Astounding *accounts for less than half of the stories in this book.—M.H.G.*

(Witches come in all sorts. During the European witch-hunting mania, witches were unredeemably evil, and in league with the Devil.

It depends on your definition, of course. All through the Christian centuries there was the survival of remnants of pre-Christian ritual which had not been absorbed into Christianity. The practitioners of such archaic rites were members of a competing religion, and the only competing religion that Christian enthusiasts recognized was devil-worship. From which it followed—

For those who don't take witchcraft seriously, but who write stories about witches, witches (and their male counterparts, the wizards or warlocks) are only practitioners of magic. And like the practitioners of technology, they can do so for good or for evil. Thus, in The Wizard of Oz *we have the Wicked Witch of the West, immortalized forever by Margaret Hamilton, while we also have the Good Witch, Glinda, much less convincingly played by Billie Burke.*

In the running, however, for the most charming witches are the three little girls who are "The Witches of Karres" as portrayed by James H. Schmitz.—I.A.)

I.

It was around the hub of the evening on the planet of Porlumma that Captain Pausert, commercial traveler from the Republic of Nikkeldepain, met the first of the witches of Karres.

It was just plain fate, so far as he could see.

He was feeling pretty good as he left a high-priced bar on a cobbly street near the spaceport, with the intention of returning straight to his ship. There hadn't been an argument, exactly. But someone grinned broadly, as usual, when the captain pronounced the name of his native system; and the captain had pointed out then, with considerable wit, how much more ridiculous it was to call a planet Porlumma, for instance, then to call it Nikkeldepain.

He proceeded to collect a gradually increasing number of pained stares by a detailed comparison of the varied, interesting and occasionally brilliant role Nikkeldepain had played in history with Porlumma's obviously dull and dumpy status as a sixth-rate Empire outpost.

In conclusion, he admitted frankly that he wouldn't care to be found dead on Porlumma.

Somebody muttered loudly in Imperial Universum that in that case it might be better if he didn't hang around Porlumma too long. But the captain only smiled politely, paid for his two drinks and left.

There was no point in getting into a rhubarb on one of these border planets. Their citizens still had an innocent notion that they ought to act like frontiersmen—but then the Law always showed up at once.

He felt pretty good. Up to the last four months of his young life, he had never looked on himself as being particularly patriotic. But compared to most of the Empire's worlds, Nikkeldepain was downright attractive in its stuffy way. Besides, he was returning there solvent—would they ever be surprised!

And awaiting him, fondly and eagerly, was Illyla, the Miss Onswud, fair daughter of the mighty Councilor Onswud, and the captain's secretly affianced for almost a year. She alone had believed in him!

The captain smiled and checked at a dark cross-street to get his bearings on the spaceport beacon. Less than half a mile away— He set off again. In about six hours, he'd be beyond the Empire's space borders and headed straight for Illyla.

Yes, she alone had believed! After the prompt collapse of the captain's first commercial venture—a miffel-fur farm, largely on capital borrowed from Councilor Onswud—the future had looked very black. It had even included a probable ten-year stretch of penal servitude for "willful and negligent abuse of intrusted monies." The laws of Nikkeldepain were rough on debtors.

"But you've always been looking for someone to take out the old *Venture* and get her back into trade!" Illyla reminded her father tearfully.

"Hm-m-m, yes! But it's in the blood, my dear! His great-uncle Threbus went the same way! It would be far better to let the law take its course," Councilor Onswud said, glaring at Pausert who remained sulkily silent. He had *tried* to explain that the mysterious epidemic which suddenly wiped out most of the stock of miffels wasn't his fault. In fact, he more than suspected the tricky hand of young Councilor Rapport who had been wagging futilely around Illyla for the last couple of years!

"The *Venture,* now—!" Councilor Onswud mused, stroking his long, craggy chin. "Pausert can handle a ship, at least," he admitted.

That was how it happened. Were they ever going to be surprised! For even the captain realized that Councilor Onswud was unloading all the dead fish that had gathered the dust of his warehouses for the past fifty years on him and the *Venture,* in a last, faint hope of getting *some* return on those half-forgotten investments. A value of eighty-two thousand maels was placed on the cargo; but if he'd brought even three-quarters of it back in cash, all would have been well.

Instead—well, it started with that lucky bet on a legal point with an Imperial Official at the Imperial capitol itself. Then came a six-hour race fairly won against a small, fast private yacht—the old *Venture* 7333 had been a pirate-chaser in the last century and could still produce twice as much speed as her looks suggested. From there on, the captain was socially accepted as a sporting man and was in on a long string of jovial parties and meets.

Jovial and profitable—the wealthier Imperials just couldn't resist a gamble; and the penalty he always insisted on was that they had to buy!

He got rid of the stuff right and left! Inside of twelve weeks, nothing remained of the original cargo except two score bundles of expensively-built but useless tinklewood fishing poles and one dozen gross bales of useful but unattractive allweather cloaks. Even on a bet, nobody would take them! But the captain had a strong hunch those items had been hopefully added to the cargo from his own stocks by Councilor Rapport; so his failure to sell them didn't break his heart.

He was a neat twenty percent net ahead, at that point—

And finally came this last-minute rush-delivery of medical supplies to Porlumma on the return route. That haul alone would have repaid the miffle-farm losses three times over!

The captain grinned broadly into the darkness. Yes, they'd be surprised—but just where was he now?

He checked again in the narrow street, searching for the port-beacon in the sky. There it was—off to his left and a little behind him. He'd got turned around somehow!

He set off carefully down an excessively dark little alley. It was one of those towns where everybody locked their front doors at night and retired to lit-up, inclosed courtyards at the backs of the houses. There were voices and the rattling of dishes nearby, and occasional whoops of laughter and singing all around him; but it was all beyond high walls which let little or no light into the alley.

It ended abruptly in a cross-alley and another wall. After a moment's debate, the captain turned to his left again. Light spilled out on his new route a few hundred yards ahead, where a courtyard was opened on the alley. From it, as he approached, came the sound of doors being violently slammed, and then a sudden, loud mingling of voices.

"Yeeee-eep!" shrilled a high, childish voice. It could have been mortal agony, terror, or even hysterical laughter. The captain broke into an apprehensive trot.

"Yes, I see you up there!" a man shouted excitedly in Universum. "I caught you now—you get down from those boxes! I'll skin you alive! Fifty-two customers sick of the stomachache—YOW!"

The last exclamation was accompanied by a sound as of a small, loosely-built wooden house collapsing, and was followed by a succession of squeals and an angry bellowing, in which the only distinguishable words were: ". . . .threw the boxes on me!" Then more sounds of splintering wood.

"Hey!" yelled the captain indignantly from the corner of the alley.

All action ceased. The narrow courtyard, brightly illuminated under its single overhead bulb, was half covered with a tumbled litter of what appeared to be empty wooden boxes. Standing with his foot temporarily caught in one of them was a very large, fat man dressed all in white and waving a stick. Momentarily cornered between the wall and two of the boxes, over one of which she was trying to climb, was a smallish, fair-haired girl dressed in a smock of some kind, which was also white. She might be about fourteen, the captain thought—a helpless kid, anyway.

"What *you* want?" grunted the fat man, pointing the stick with some dignity at the captain.

"Lay off the kid!" rumbled the captain, edging into the courtyard.

"Mind your own business!" shouted the fat man, waving his stick like a club. "I'll take care of her! She—"

"I never did!" squealed the girl. She burst into tears.

"Try it, Fat and Ugly!" the captain warned. "I'll ram the stick down your throat!"

He was very close now. With a sound of grunting exasperation, the fat man pulled his foot free of the box, wheeled suddenly and brought the end of the stick down on the top of the captain's cap. The captain hit him furiously in the middle of the stomach.

There was a short flurry of activity, somewhat hampered by shattering boxes everywhere. Then the captain stood up, scowling and breathing hard. The fat man remained sitting on the ground, gasping about ". . . the law!"

Somewhat to his surprise, the captain discovered the girl standing just behind him. She caught his eye and smiled.

"My name's Maleen," she offered. She pointed at the fat man. "Is he hurt bad?"

"Huh—no!" panted the captain. "But maybe we'd better—"

It was too late! A loud, self-assured voice became audible now at the opening to the alley:

"Here, here, here, here, here!" it said in the reproachful, situation-under-control tone that always seemed the same to the captain, on whatever world and in whichever language he heard it.

"What's all this about?" it inquired rhetorically.

"You'll all have to come along!" it replied.

Police Court on Porlumma appeared to be a business conducted on a very efficient, around-the-clock basis. They were the next case up.

Nikkeldepain was an odd name, wasn't it, the judge smiled. He then listened attentively to the various charges, countercharges, and denials.

Bruth the Baker was charged with having struck a citizen of a foreign government on the head with a potentially lethal instrument—produced in evidence. Said citizen had admittedly attempted to interfere as Bruth was attempting to punish his slave Maleen—also produced in evidence—whom he suspected of having added something to a batch of cakes she was working on that afternoon, resulting in illness and complaints from fifty-two of Bruth's customers.

Said foreign citizen had also used insulting language—the captain admitted under pressure to "Fat and Ugly."

Some provocation could be conceded for the action taken by Bruth, but not enough. Bruth paled.

Captain Pausert, of the Republic of Nikkeldepain—everybody but the prisoners smiled this time—was charged (a) with said attempted interference, (b) with said insult, (c) with having frequently and severely struck Bruth the Baker in the course of the subsequent dispute.

The blow on the head was conceded to have provided a provocation for charge (c)—but not enough.

Nobody seemed to be charging the slave Maleen with anything. The judge only looked at her curiously, and shook his head.

"As the Court considers this regrettable incident," he remarked, "it looks like two years for you, Bruth; and about three for you, captain. Too bad!"

The captain had an awful sinking feeling. He had seen something and heard a lot of Imperial court methods in the fringe systems. He could probably get out of this three-year rap; but it would be expensive.

He realized that the judge was studying him reflectively.

"The Court wishes to acknowledge," the judge continued, "that the captain's chargeable actions were due largely to a natural feeling of human sympathy for the predicament of the slave Maleen. The Court, therefore, would suggest a settlement as follows—subsequent to which all charges could be dropped:

''That Bruth the Baker resell Maleen of Karres—with whose services he appears to be dissatisfied—for a reasonable sum to Captain Pausert of the Republic of Nikkeldepain.''

Bruth the Baker heaved a gusty sigh of relief. But the captain hesitated. The buying of human slaves by private citizens was a very serious offense in Nikkeldepain! Still, he didn't have to make a record of it. If they weren't going to soak him too much—

At just the right moment, Maleen of Karres introduced a barely audible, forlorn, sniffling sound.

''How much are you asking for the kid?'' the captain inquired, looking without friendliness at his recent antagonist. A day was coming when he would think less severely of Bruth; but it hadn't come yet.

Bruth scowled back but replied with a certain eagerness: ''A hundred and fifty m—'' A policeman standing behind him poked him sharply in the side. Bruth shut up.

''Seven hundred maels,'' the judge said smoothly. ''There'll be Court charges, and a fee for recording the transaction—'' He appeared to make a swift calculation. ''Fifteen hundred and forty-two maels—'' He turned to a clerk: ''You've looked him up?''

The clerk nodded. ''He's right!''

''And we'll take your check,'' the judge concluded. He gave the captain a friendly smile. ''Next case.''

The captain felt a little bewildered.

There was something peculiar about this! He was getting out of it much too cheaply. Since the Empire had quit its wars of expansion, young slaves in good health were a high-priced article. Furthermore, he was practically positive that Bruth the Baker had been willing to sell for a tenth of what the captain actually had to pay!

Well, he wouldn't complain. Rapidly, he signed, sealed and thumb-printed various papers shoved at him by a helpful clerk; and made out a check.

''I guess,'' he told Maleen of Karres, ''we'd better get along to the ship.''

And now what was he going to do with the kid, he pondered, padding along the unlighted streets with his slave trotting quietly behind him. If he showed up with a pretty girl-slave in Nikkeldepain, even a small one, various good friends there would toss him into ten years or so of penal servitude—immediately after Illyla had personally collected his scalp. They were a moral lot.

Karres—?

"How far off is Karres, Maleen?" he asked into the dark.

"It takes about two weeks," Maleen said tearfully.

Two weeks! The captain's heart sank again.

"What are you blubbering about?" he inquired uncomfortably.

Maleen choked, sniffed, and began sobbing openly.

"I have two little sisters!" she cried.

"Well, well," the captain said encouragingly. "That's nice—you'll be seeing them again soon. I'm taking you home, you know!"

Great Patham—now he'd said it! But after all—

But this piece of good news seemed to be having the wrong effect on his slave! Her sobbing grew much more violent.

"No, I won't," she wailed. "They're here!"

"Huh?" said the captain. He stopped short. "Where?"

"And the people they're with are mean to them, too!" wept Maleen.

The captain's heart dropped clean through his boots. Standing there in the dark, he helplessly watched it coming:

"You could buy them awfully cheap!" she said.

II.

In times of stress, the young life of Karres appeared to take to the heights. It might be a mountainous place.

The Leewit sat on the top shelf of the back wall of the crockery and antiques store, strategically flanked by two expensive-looking vases. She was a doll-sized edition of Maleen; but her eyes were cold and gray instead of blue and tearful. About five or six, the captain vaguely estimated. He wasn't very good at estimating them around that age.

"Good evening," he said, as he came in through the door. The Crockery and Antiques Shop had been easy to find. Like Bruth the Baker's, it was the one spot in the neighborhood that was all lit up.

"Good evening, sir!" said what was presumably the store owner, without looking around. He sat with his back to the door, in a chair approximately at the center of the store and facing the Leewit at a distance of about twenty feet.

". . . and there you can stay without food or drink till the

Holy Man comes in the morning!'' he continued immediately, in the taut voice of a man who has gone through hysteria and is sane again. The captain realized he was addressing the Leewit

''Your other Holy Man didn't stay very long!'' the diminutive creature piped, also ignoring the captain. Apparently, she had not yet discovered Maleen behind him.

''This is a stronger denomination—much stronger!'' the store owner replied, in a shaking voice but with a sort of relish. ''*He'll* exorcise you, all right, little demon—you'll whistle no buttons off him! Your time is up! Go on and whistle all you want! Bust every vase in the place—''

The Leewit blinked her gray eyes thoughtfully at him.

''Might!'' she said.

''But if you try to climb down from there,'' the store owner went on, on a rising note, ''I'll chop you into bits—into little, little bits!''

He raised his arm as he spoke and weakly brandished what the captain recognized with a start of horror as a highly ornamented but probably still useful antique battle-ax.

''Ha!'' said the Leewit.

''Beg your pardon, sir!'' the captain said, clearing his throat.

''Good evening, sir!'' the store owner repeated, without looking around. ''What can I do for you?''

''I came to inquire,'' the captain said hesitantly, ''about that child.''

The store owner shifted about in his chair and squinted at the captain with red-rimmed eyes.

''You're not a Holy Man!'' he said.

''Hello, Maleen!'' the Leewit said suddenly. ''That him?''

''We've come to buy you,'' Maleen said. ''Shut up!''

''Good!'' said the Leewit.

''Buy it? Are you mocking me, sir?'' the store owner inquired.

''Shut up, Moonell!'' A thin, dark, determined-looking woman had appeared in the doorway that led through the back wall of the store. She moved out a step under the shelves; and the Leewit leaned down from the top shelf and hissed. The woman moved hurriedly back into the doorway.

''Maybe he means it,'' she said in a more subdued voice.

''I can't sell to a citizen of the Empire,'' the store owner said defeatedly.

''I'm not a citizen,'' the captain said shortly. This time, he wasn't going to name it.

''No, he's from Nikkel—'' Maleen began.

''Shut up, Maleen!'' the captain said helplessly in turn.

"I never heard of Nikkel," the store owner muttered doubtfully.

"Maleen!" the woman called shrilly. "That's the name of one of the others—Bruth the Baker got her. He means it, all right! He's buying them—"

"A hundred and fifty maels!" the captain said craftily, remembering Bruth the Baker. "In cash!"

The store owner looked dazed.

"Not enough, Moonell!" the woman called. "Look at all it's broken! Five hundred maels!"

There was a sound then, so thin the captain could hardly hear it. It pierced at his eardrums like two jabs of a delicate needle. To right and left of him, two highly glazed little jugs went "*Clink-clink!*", showed a sudden veining of cracks, and collapsed.

A brief silence settled on the store. And now that he looked around more closely, the captain could spot here and there other little piles of shattered crockery—and places where similar ruins apparently had been swept up, leaving only traces of colored dust.

The store owner laid the ax down carefully beside his chair, stood up, swaying a little, and came towards the captain.

"You offered me a hundred and fifty maels!" he said rapidly as he approached. "I accept it here, now, see—before witnesses!" He grabbed the captain's right hand in both of his and pumped it up and down vigorously. "Sold!" he yelled.

Then he wheeled around in a leap and pointed a shaking hand at the Leewit.

"And NOW," he howled, "break something! Break anything! You're his! I'll sue him for every mael he ever made and ever will!"

"Oh, do come help me down, Maleen!" the Leewit pleaded prettily.

For a change, the store of Wansing, the jeweler, was dimly lit and very quiet. It was a sleek, fashionable place in a fashionable shopping block near the spaceport. The front door was unlocked, and Wansing was in.

The three of them entered quietly, and the door sighed quietly shut behind them. Beyond a great crystal display-counter, Wansing was moving about among a number of opened shelves, talking softly to himself. Under the crystal of the counter, and in close-packed rows on the satin-covered shelves, reposed a many-colored array gleaming and glittering and shining. Wansing was no piker.

"Good evening, sir!" the captain said across the counter.

"It's morning!" the Leewit remarked from the other side of Maleen.

"Maleen!" said the captain.

"We're keeping out of this," Maleen said to the Leewit.

"All right," said the Leewit.

Wansing had come around jerkily at the captain's greeting, but had made no other move. Like all the slave owners the captain had met on Porlumma so far, Wansing seemed unhappy. Otherwise, he was a large, dark, sleek-looking man with jewels in his ears and a smell of expensive oils and perfumes about him.

"This place is under constant visual guard, of course!" he told the captain gently. "Nothing could possibly happen to me here. Why am I so frightened?"

"Not of me, I'm sure!" the captain said with an uncomfortable attempt at geniality. "I'm glad your store's still open," he went on briskly. "I'm here on business—"

"Oh, yes, it's still open, of course," Wansing said. He gave the captain a slow smile and turned back to his shelves. "I'm making inventory, that's why! I've been making inventory since early yesterday morning. I've counted them all seven times—"

"You're very thorough," the captain said.

"Very, very thorough!" Wansing nodded to the shelves. "The last time I found I had made a million maels. But twice before that, I had lost approximately the same amount. I shall have to count them again, I suppose!" He closed a shelf softly. "I'm sure I counted those before. But they move about constantly. Constantly! It's horrible."

"You've got a slave here called Goth," the captain said, driving to the point.

"Yes, I have!" Wansing said, nodding. "And I'm sure she understands by now I meant no harm! I do, at any rate. It was perhaps a little—but I'm sure she understands now, or will soon!"

"Where is she?" the captain inquired, a trifle uneasily.

"In her room perhaps," Wansing suggested. "It's not so bad when she's there in her room with the door closed. But often she sits in the dark and looks at you as you go past—" He opened another drawer, and closed it quietly again. "Yes, they do move!" he whispered, as if confirming an earlier suspicion. "Constantly—"

"Look, Wansing," the captain said in a loud, firm voice. "I'm not a citizen of the Empire. I want to buy this Goth! I'll pay you a hundred and fifty maels, cash."

Wansing turned around completely again and looked at the

captain. "Oh, you do?" he said. "You're not a citizen?" He walked a few steps to the side of the counter, sat down at a small desk and turned a light on over it. Then he put his face in his hands for a moment.

"I'm a wealthy man," he muttered. "An influential man! The name of Wansing counts for a great deal on Porlumma. When the Empire suggests you buy, you buy, of course—but it need not have been I who bought her! I thought she would be useful in the business—and then, even I could not sell her again within the Empire. She has been here for a week!"

He looked up at the captain and smiled. "One hundred and fifty maels!" he said. "Sold! There are records to be made out—" He reached into a drawer and took out some printed forms. He began to write rapidly. The captain produced identifications.

Maleen said suddenly: "Goth?"

"Right here," a voice murmured. Wansing's hand jerked sharply, but he did not look up. He kept on writing.

Something small and lean and bonelessly supple, dressed in a dark jacket and leggings, came across the thick carpets of Wansing's store and stood behind the captain. This one might be about nine or ten.

"I'll take your check, captain!" Wansing said politely. "You must be an honest man. Besides, I want to frame it."

"And now," the captain heard himself say in the remote voice of one who moves through a strange dream, "I suppose we could go to the ship."

The sky was gray and cloudy; and the streets were lightening. Goth, he noticed, didn't resemble her sisters. She had brown hair cut short a few inches below her ears, and brown eyes with long, black lashes. Her nose was short and her chin was pointed. She made him think of some thin, carnivorous creature, like a weasel.

She looked up at him briefly, grinned, and said: "Thanks!"

"What was wrong with *him*?" chirped the Leewit, walking backwards for a last view of Wansing's store.

"Tough crook," muttered Goth. The Leewit giggled.

"You premoted this just dandy, Maleen!" she stated next.

"Shut up," said Maleen.

"All right," said the Leewit. She glanced up at the captain's face. "You been fighting!" she said virtuously. "Did you win?"

"Of course, the captain won!" said Maleen.

"Good for you!" said the Leewit.

* * *

"What about the take-off?" Goth asked the captain. She seemed a little worried.

"Nothing to it!" the captain said stoutly, hardly bothering to wonder how she'd guessed the take-off was the one operation on which he and the old *Venture* consistently failed to co-operate.

"No," said Goth, "I meant when?"

"Right now," said the captain. "They've already cleared us. We'll get the sign any second."

"Good," said Goth. She walked off slowly down the hall towards the back of the ship.

The take-off was pretty bad, but the *Venture* made it again. Half an hour later, with Porlumma dwindling safely behind them, the captain switched to automatic and climbed out of his chair. After considerable experimentation, he got the electric butler adjusted to four breakfasts, hot, with coffee. It was accomplished with a great deal of advice and attempted assistance from the Leewit, rather less from Maleen, and no comments from Goth.

"Everything will be coming along in a few minutes now!" he announced. Afterwards, it struck him there had been a quality of grisly prophecy about the statement.

"If you'd listened to me," said the Leewit, "we'd have been done eating a quarter of an hour ago!" She was perspiring but triumphant—she had been right all along.

"Say, Maleen," she said suddenly, "you premoting again?"

Premoting? The captain looked at Maleen. She seemed pale and troubled.

"Spacesick?" he suggested. "I've got some pills—"

"No, she's premoting," the Leewit said scowling. "What's up, Maleen?"

"Shut up," said Goth.

"All right," said the Leewit. She was silent a moment, and then began to wriggle. "Maybe we'd better—"

"Shut up," said Maleen.

"It's all ready," said Goth.

"What's all ready?" asked the captain.

"All right," said the Leewit. She looked at the captain. "Nothing," she said.

He looked at them then, and they looked at him—one set each of gray eyes, and brown, and blue. They were all sitting around the control room floor in a circle, the fifth side of which was occupied by the electric butler.

What peculiar little waifs, the captain thought. He hadn't

perhaps really realized until now just how *very* peculiar. They were still staring at him.

"Well, well!" he said heartily. "So Maleen 'premotes' and gives people stomach-aches."

Maleen smiled dimly and smoothed back her yellow hair.

"They just thought they were getting them," she murmured.

"Mass history," explained the Leewit, offhandedly.

"Hysteria," said Goth. "The Imperials get their hair up about us every so often."

"I noticed that," the captain nodded. "And little Leewit here—she whistles and busts things."

"It's *the* Leewit," the Leewit said, frowning.

"Oh, I see," said the captain. "Like *the* captain, eh?"

"That's right," said the Leewit. She smiled.

"And what does little Goth do?" the captain addressed the third witch.

Little Goth appeared pained. Maleen answered for her.

"Goth teleports mostly," she said.

"Oh, she does?" said the captain. "I've heard about that trick, too," he added lamely.

"Just small stuff really!" Goth said abruptly. She reached into the top of her jacket and pulled out a cloth-wrapped bundle the size of the captain's two fists. The four ends of the cloth were knotted together. Goth undid the knot. "Like this," she said and poured out the contents on the rug between them. There was a sound like a big bagful of marbles being spilled.

"Great Patham!" the captain swore, staring down at what was a cool quarter-million in jewel stones, or he was still a miffel-farmer.

"Good gosh," said the Leewit, bouncing to her feet. "Maleen, we better get at it right away!"

The two blondes darted from the room. The captain hardly noticed their going. He was staring at Goth.

"Child," he said, "don't you realize they hang you without trial on places like Porlumma, if you're caught with stolen goods?"

"We're not on Porlumma," said Goth. She looked slightly annoyed. "They're for you. You spent money on us, didn't you?"

"Not that kind of money," said the captain. "If Wansing noticed— They're Wansing's, I suppose?"

"Sure!" said Goth. "Pulled them in just before take-off!"

"If he reported, there'll be police ships on our tail any—"

"Goth!" Maleen shrilled.

Goth's head came around and she rolled up on her feet in one motion. "Coming," she shouted. "Excuse me," she murmured to the captain. Then she, too, was out of the room.

But again, the captain scarcely noticed her departure. He had rushed to the control desk with a sudden awful certainty and ʼitched on all screens.

There they were! Two sleek, black ships coming up fast from ʼhind, and already almost in gun-range! They weren't regular police boats, the captain recognized, but auxiliary craft of the Empire's frontier fleets. He rammed the *Venture*'s drives full on. Immediately, red-and-black fire blossoms began to sprout in space behind him—then a finger of flame stabbed briefly past, not a hundred yards to the right of the ship.

But the communicator stayed dead. Porlumma preferred risking the sacrifice of Wansing's jewels to giving them a chance to surrender! To do the captain justice, his horror was due much more to the fate awaiting his three misguided charges than to the fact that he was going to share it.

He was putting the *Venture* through a wildly erratic and, he hoped, aim-destroying series of sideways hops and forward lunges with one hand, and trying to unlimber the turrets of the nova guns with the other, when suddenly—!

No, he decided at once, there was no use trying to understand it— There were just no more Empire ships around. The screens all blurred and darkened simultaneously; and, for a short while, a darkness went flowing and coiling lazily past the *Venture*. Light jumped out of it at him once, in a cold, ugly glare, and receded again in a twisting, unnatural fashion. The *Venture*'s drives seemed dead.

Then, just as suddenly, the old ship jerked, shivered, roared aggrievedly, and was hurling herself along on her own power again!

But Porlumma's sun was no longer in evidence. Stars gleamed and shifted distantly against the blackness of deep space all about. The patterns seemed familiar, but he wasn't a good enough navigator to be sure.

The captain stood up stiffly, feeling a heavy cloud. And at that moment, with a wild, hilarious clacking like a metallic hen, the electric butler delivered four breakfasts, hot, one after the other, right onto the center of the control room floor.

The first voice said distinctly: "Shall we just leave it on?"

A second voice, considerably more muffled, replied: "Yes, let's! You never know when you need it—"

The third voice, tucked somewhere in between them, said simply: "*Whew!*"

Peering about the dark room in bewilderment, the captain realized suddenly that the voices had come from the speaker of an intership communicator, leading to what had once been the *Venture*'s captain's cabin.

He listened; but only a dim murmuring came from it now, and then nothing at all. He started towards the hall, then returned and softly switched off the communicator. He went quietly down the hall until he came to the captain's cabin. Its door was closed.

He listened a moment, and opened it suddenly.

There was a trio of squeals:

"Oh, don't! You spoiled it!"

The captain stood motionless. Just one glimpse had been given him of what seemed to be a bundle of twisted black wires arranged loosely like the frame of a truncated cone on—or was it just above?—a table in the center of the cabin. Where the tip of the cone should have been burned a round, swirling, orange fire. About it, their faces reflecting its glow, stood the three witches.

Then the fire vanished; the wires collapsed. There was only ordinary light in the room. They were looking up at him variously—Maleen with smiling regret, the Leewit in frank annoyance, Goth with no expression at all.

"What out of Great Patham's Seventh Hell was that?" inquired the captain, his hair bristling slowly.

The Leewit looked at Goth; Goth looked at Maleen. Maleen said doubtfully: "We can just tell you its name—"

"That was the Sheewash Drive," said Goth.

"The what-drive?" asked the captain.

"Sheewash," repeated Maleen.

"The one you have to do it with yourself," the Leewit said helpfully.

"Shut up," said Maleen.

There was a long pause. The captain looked down at the handful of thin, black, twelve-inch wires scattered about the table top. He touched one of them. It was dead-cold.

"I see," he said. "I guess we're all going to have a long talk." Another pause. "Where are we now?"

"About three light-years down the way you were going," said Goth. "We only worked it thirty seconds."

"Twenty-eight!" corrected Maleen, with the authority of her years. "The Leewit was getting tired."

"I see," said Captain Pausert carefully. "Well, let's go have some breakfast."

III.

They ate with a silent voraciousness, dainty Maleen, the exquisite Leewit, supple Goth, all alike. The captain, long finished, watched them with amazement and—now at last—with something like awe.

"It's the Sheewash Drive," explained Maleen finally, catching his expression.

"Takes it out of you!" said Goth.

The Leewit grunted affirmatively and stuffed on.

"Can't do too much of it," said Maleen. "Or too often. It kills you sure!"

"What," said the captain, "*is* the Sheewash Drive?"

They became reticent. People did it on Karres, said Maleen, when they had to go somewhere else fast. Everybody knew how there.

"But of course," she added, "we're pretty young to do it right!"

"We did it pretty good!" the Leewit contradicted positively. She seemed to be finished at last.

"But how?" said the captain.

Reticence thickened almost visibly. If you couldn't do it, said Maleen, you couldn't understand it either.

He gave it up, for the time being.

"I guess I'll have to take you home next," he said; and they agreed.

Karres, it developed, was in the Iverdahl System. He couldn't find any planet of that designation listed in his maps of the area, but that meant nothing. The maps were old and often inaccurate, and local names changed a lot.

Barring the use of weird and deadly miracle-drives, that detour was going to cost him almost a month in time—and a good chunk of his profits in power used up. The jewels Goth had illegally teleported must, of course, be returned to their owner, he explained. He'd intended to look severely at the culprit at that point; but she'd meant well, after all! They were extremely peculiar children, but still children—they couldn't really understand.

He would stop off en route to Karres at an Empire planet with banking facilities to take care of that matter, the captain added.

A planet far enough off so the police wouldn't be likely to take any particular interest in the *Venture*.

A dead silence greeted this schedule. It appeared that the representatives of Karres did not think much of his logic.

"Well," Maleen sighed at last, "we'll see you get your money back some other way then!"

The junior witches nodded coldly.

"How did you three happen to get into this fix?" the captain inquired, with the intention of changing the subject.

They'd left Karres together on a jaunt of their own, they explained. No, they hadn't run away—he got the impression that such trips were standard procedure for juveniles in that place. They were on another planet, a civilized one but beyond the borders and law of Empire, when the town they were in was raided by a small fleet of slavers. They were taken along with most of the local youngsters.

"It's a wonder," he said reflectively, "you didn't take over the ship."

"Oh, brother!" exclaimed the Leewit.

"Not that ship!" said Goth.

"That was an Imperial Slaver!" Maleen informed him. "You behave yourself every second on those crates."

Just the same, the captain thought as he settled himself to rest in the control room on a couch he had set up there, it was no longer surprising that the Empire wanted no young slaves from Karres to be transported into the interior! Oddest sort of children—But he ought to be able to get his expenses paid by their relatives. Something very profitable might even be made of this deal—

Have to watch the record-entries though! Nikkeldepain's laws were explicit about the penalties invoked by anything resembling the purchase and sale of slaves.

He'd thoughtfully left the intership communicator adjusted so he could listen in on their conversation in the captain's cabin. However, there had been nothing for some time beyond frequent bursts of childish giggling. Then came a succession of piercing shrieks from the Leewit. It appeared she was being forcibly washed behind the ears by Maleen and obliged to brush her teeth, in preparation for bedtime.

It had been agreed that he was not to enter the cabin, because—for reasons not given—they couldn't keep the Sheewash Drive on in his presence; and they wanted to have it ready, in case of an emergency. Piracy was rife beyond the Imperial borders, and the *Venture* would keep beyond the border for a good part of the trip, to avoid the more pressing danger of police pursuit instigated by Porlumma. The captain had explained the potentialities of the nova guns the *Venture* boasted, or tried to. Possibly, they hadn't understood. At any rate, they seemed unimpressed.

The Sheewash Drive! Boy, he thought in sudden excitement, if he could just get the principles of that. Maybe he would!

He raised his head suddenly. The Leewit's voice had lifted clearly over the communicator:

". . . .not such a bad old dope!" the childish treble remarked.

The captain blinked indignantly.

"He's not so old," Maleen's soft voice returned. "And he's certainly no dope!"

He smiled. Good kid, Maleen.

"Yeah, yeah!" squeaked the Leewit offensively. "Maleen's sweet onthu-ulp!"

A vague commotion continued for a while, indicating, he hoped, that someone he could mention was being smothered under a pillow.

He drifted off to sleep before it was settled.

If you didn't happen to be thinking of what they'd done, they seemed more or less like normal children. Right from the start, they displayed a flattering interest in the captain and his background; and he told them all about everything and everybody in Nikkeldepain. Finally, he even showed them his treasured pocket-sized picture of Illyla—the one with which he'd held many cozy conversations during the earlier part of his trip.

Almost at once, though, he realized that was a mistake. They studied it intently in silence, their heads crowded close together.

"Oh, brother!" the Leewit whispered then, with entirely the wrong kind of inflection.

"Just what did you mean by that?" the captain inquired coldly.

"Sweet!" murmured Goth. But it was the way she closed her eyes briefly, as though gripped by a light spasm of nausea.

"Shut up, Goth!" Maleen said sharply. "I think she's very swee . . . I mean, she looks very nice!" she told the captain.

The captain was disgruntled. Silently, he retrieved the maligned Illyla and returned her to his breast pocket. Silently, he went off and left them standing there.

But afterwards, in private, he took it out again and studied it worriedly. His Illyla! He shifted the picture back and forth under the light. It wasn't really a very good picture of her, he decided.

It had been bungled! From certain angles, one might even say that Illyla did look the least bit insipid.

What was he thinking, he thought, shocked.

He unlimbered the nova gun turrets next and got in a little firing practice. They had been sealed when he took over the *Venture* and weren't supposed to be used, except in absolute emergencies. They were somewhat uncertain weapons, though very effective, and Nikkeldepain had turned to safer forms of armament many decades ago. But on the third day out from Nikkeldepain, the captain made a brief notation in his log:

"Attacked by two pirate craft. Unsealed nova guns. Destroyed one attacker; survivor fled—"

He was rather pleased by that crisp, hard-bitten description of desperate space-adventure, and enjoyed rereading it occasionally. It wasn't true, though. He had put in an interesting four hours at the time pursuing and annihilating large, craggy chunks of substance of a meteorite-cloud he found the *Venture* plowing through. Those nova guns were fascinating stuff! You'd sight the turrets on something; and so long as it didn't move after that, it was all right. If it did move, it got it—unless you relented and deflected the turrets first. They were just the thing for arresting a pirate in midspace.

The *Venture* dipped back into the Empire's borders four days later and headed for the capitol of the local province. Police ships challenged them twice on the way in; and the captain found considerable comfort in the awareness that his passengers foregathered silently in their cabin on these occasions. They didn't tell him they were set to use the Sheewash Drive—somehow it had never been mentioned since that first day; but he knew the queer orange fire was circling over its skimpy framework of twisted wires there and ready to act.

However, the space police waved him on, satisfied with routine identification. Apparently, the *Venture* had not become generally known as a criminal ship, to date.

Maleen accompanied him to the banking institution that was to return Wansing's property to Porlumma. Her sisters, at the captain's definite request, remained on the ship.

The transaction itself went off without a visible hitch. The jewels would reach their destination in Porlumma within a month. But he had to take out a staggering sum in insurance—"Piracy, thieves!" smiled the clerk. "Even summary capital punishment won't keep the rats down." And, of course, he had to register name, ship, home planet, and so on. But since they already had all that information in Porlumma, he gave it without hesitation.

On the way back to the spaceport, he sent off a sealed message by radio-relay to the bereaved jeweler, informing him of the action taken, and regretting the misunderstanding.

He felt a little better after that, though the insurance payment had been a severe blow! If he didn't manage to work out a decent profit on Karres somehow, the losses on the miffel farm would hardly be covered now.

Then he noticed that Maleen was getting uneasy.

"We'd better hurry!" was all she would say, however. Her face grew pale.

The captain understood. She was having another premonition! The hitch to this premoting business was, apparently, that when something was brewing you were informed of the bare fact but had to guess at most of the details. They grabbed an aircab and raced back to the spaceport.

They had just been cleared there when he spotted a small group of uniformed men coming along the dock on the double. They stopped short and then scattered, as the *Venture* lurched drunkenly sideways into the air. Everyone else in sight was scattering, too.

That was a very bad take-off—one of the captain's worst! Once afloat, however, he ran the ship promptly into the nightside of the planet and turned her nose towards the border. The old pirate-chaser had plenty of speed when you gave her the reins; and throughout the entire next sleep-period, he let her use it all.

The Sheewash Drive was not required that time.

Next day, he had a lengthy private talk with Goth on the Golden Rule and the Law, with particular reference to individual property rights. If Councilor Onswud had been monitoring the sentiments expressed by the captain, he could not have failed to rumble surprised approval. The delinquent herself listened impassively; but the captain fancied she showed distinct signs of being rather impressed by his earnestness.

It was two days after that—well beyond the borders again—when they were obliged to make an unscheduled stop at a mining moon. For the captain discovered he had already miscalculated the extent to which the prolonged run on overdrive after leaving the capitol was going to deplete the *Venture*'s reserves. They would have to juice up—

A large, extremely handsome Sirian freighter lay beside them at the Moon station. It was half a battlecraft really, since it dealt regularly beyond the borders. They had to wait while it was being serviced; and it took a long time. The Sirians turned out to be as unpleasant as their ship was good-looking—a snooty, conceited, hairy lot who talked only their own dialect and pretended to be unfamiliar with Imperial Universum.

The captain found himself getting irked by their bad manners—particularly when he discovered they were laughing over his argument with the service superintendent about the cost of repowering the *Venture*.

"You're out in deep space, captain!" said the superintendent. "And you haven't juice enough left even to travel back to the Border. You can't expect Imperial prices here!"

"It's not what you charged *them*!" The captain angrily jerked his thumb at the Sirian.

"Regular customers!" the superintendent shrugged. "You start coming by here every three months like they do, and we can make an arrangement with you, too."

It was outrageous—it actually put the *Venture* back in the red! But there was no help for it.

Nor did it improve the captain's temper when he muffed the take-off once more—and then had to watch the Sirian floating into space, as sedately as a swan, a little behind him!

An hour later, as he sat glumly before the controls, debating the chance of recouping his losses before returning to Nikkeldepain, Maleen and the Leewit hurriedly entered the room. They did something to a port screen.

"They sure are!" the Leewit exclaimed. She seemed childishly pleased.

"Are what?" the captain inquired absently.

"Following us," said Maleen. She did not sound pleased. "It's that Sirian ship, Captain Pausert—"

The captain stared bewilderedly at the screen. There *was* a ship in focus there. It was quite obviously the Sirian and, just as obviously, it was following them.

"What do they want?" he wondered. "They're stinkers but they're not pirates. Even if they were, they wouldn't spend an hour running after a crate like the *Venture*!"

Maleen said nothing. The Leewit observed: "Oh, brother! Got their bow-turrets out now—better get those nova guns ready!"

"But it's all nonsense!" the captain said, flushing angrily. He turned suddenly towards the communicators. "What's that Empire general beam-length?"

".0044," said Maleen.

A roaring, abusive voice flooded the control room immediately.

The one word understandable to the captain was *"Venture."* It was repeated frequently, sometimes as if it were a question.

"Sirian!" said the captain. "Can you understand them?" he asked Maleen.

She shook her head. "The Leewit can—"

The Leewit nodded, her gray eyes glistening.

"What are they saying?"

"They says you're for stopping," the Leewit translated rapidly, but apparently retaining much of the original sentence-structure. "They says you're for skinning alive . . . ha! They says you're for stopping right now and for only hanging. They says—"

Maleen scuttled from the control room. The Leewit banged the communicator with one small fist.

"Beak-Wock!" she shrieked. It sounded like that, anyway. The loud voice paused a moment.

"Beak-Wock?" it returned in an aggrieved, demanding roar.

"Beak-Wock!" the Leewit affirmed with apparent delight. She rattled off a string of similar-sounding syllables. She paused.

A howl of inarticulate wrath responded.

The captain, in a whirl of outraged emotions, was yelling at the Leewit to shut up, at the Sirian to go to Great Patham's Second Hell—the worst—and wrestling with the nova gun adjustors at the same time. He'd had about enough! He'd—

SSS-whoosh!

It was the Sheewash Drive.

"And where are we now?" the captain inquired, in a voice of unnatural calm.

"Same place, just about," said the Leewit. "Ship's still on the screen. Way back though—take them an hour again to catch up." She seemed disappointed; then brightened. "You got lots of time to get the guns ready!"

The captain didn't answer. He was marching down the hall towards the rear of the *Venture*. He passed the captain's cabin and noted the door was shut. He went on without pausing. He was mad clean through—he knew what had happened!

After all he'd told her, Goth had teleported again.

It was all there, in the storage. Items of half a pound in weight seemed to be as much as she could handle. But amazing quantities of stuff had met that one requirement—bottles filled with what might be perfume or liquor or dope, expensive-looking garments and cloths in a shining variety of colors, small boxes, odds, ends and, of course, jewelry!

He spent half an hour getting it loaded into a steel space crate.

He wheeled the crate into the rear lock, sealed the inside lock and pulled the switch that activated the automatic launching device.

The outside lock clicked shut. He stalked back to the control room. The Leewit was still in charge, fiddling with the communicators.

"I could try a whistle over them," she suggested, glancing up. She added: "But they'd bust somewheres, sure."

"Get them on again!" the captain said.

"Yes, sir," said the Leewit surprised.

The roaring voice came back faintly.

"SHUT UP!" the captain shouted in Imperial Universum.

The voice shut up.

"Tell them they can pick up their stuff—it's been dumped out in a crate!" the captain told the Leewit. "Tell them I'm proceeding on my course. Tell them if they follow me one light-minute beyond that crate, I'll come back for them, shoot their front end off, shoot their rear end off, and ram 'em in the middle."

"Yes, SIR!" the Leewit sparkled. They proceeded on their course.

Nobody followed.

"Now I want to speak to Goth," the captain announced. He was still at a high boil. "Privately," he added. "Back in the storage—"

Goth followed him expressionlessly into the storage. He closed the door to the hall. He'd broken off a two-foot length from the tip of one of Councilor Rapport's overpriced tinklewood fishing poles. It made a fair switch.

But Goth looked terribly small just now! He cleared his throat. He wished for a moment he were back on Nikkeldepain.

"I warned you," he said.

Goth didn't move. Between one second and the next, however, she seemed to grow remarkably. Her brown eyes focused on the captain's Adam's apple; her lip lifted at one side. A slightly hungry look came into her face.

"Wouldn't try that!" she murmured.

Mad again, the captain reached out quickly and got a handful of leathery cloth. There was a blur of motion, and what felt like a small explosion against his left kneecap. He grunted with anguished surprise and fell back on a bale of Councilor Rapport's all-weather cloaks. But he had retained his grip—Goth fell half on top of him, and that was still a favorable position. Then her head snaked around, her neck seemed to extend itself; and her teeth snapped his wrist.

Weasels don't let go—

* * *

"Didn't think he'd have the nerve!" Goth's voice came over the communicator. There was a note of grudging admiration in it. It seemed that she was inspecting her bruises.

All tangled up in the job of bandaging his freely bleeding wrist, the captain hoped she'd find a good plenty to count. His knee felt the size of a sofa pillow and throbbed like a piston engine.

"The captain is a brave man," Maleen was saying reproachfully. "You should have known better—"

"He's not very *smart*, though!" the Leewit remarked suggestively.

There was a short silence.

"Is he? Goth? Eh?" the Leewit urged.

"Perhaps not very," said Goth.

"You two lay off him!" Maleen ordered. "Useless," she added meaningly, "you want to *swim* back to Karres—on the Egger Route!"

"Not me," the Leewit said briefly.

"You could still do it, I guess," said Goth. She seemed to be reflecting. "All right—we'll lay off him. It was a fair fight, anyway."

IV.

They raised Karres the sixteenth day after leaving Porlumma. There had been no more incidents; but then, neither had there been any more stops or other contacts with the defenseless Empire. Maleen had cooked up a poultice which did wonders for his knee. With the end of the trip in sight, all tensions had relaxed; and Maleen, at least, seemed to grow hourly more regretful at the prospect of parting.

After a brief study, Karres could be distinguished easily enough by the fact that it moved counterclockwise to all the other planets of the Iverdahl System.

Well, it would, the captain thought.

They came soaring into its atmosphere on the dayside without arousing any visible interest. No communicator signals reached them; and no other ships showed up to look them over. Karres, in fact, had all the appearance of a completely uninhabited world. There were a larger number of seas, too big to be called lakes and too small to be oceans, scattered over its surface. There was one enormously towering ridge of mountains that ran from pole to pole, and any number of lesser chains. There were two good-sized ice caps; and the southern section of the planet was speckled with intermittent stretches of snow. Almost all of it seemed to be dense forest.

It was a handsome place, in a wild, somber way.

They went gliding over it, from noon through morning and into the dawn fringe—the captain at the controls, Goth and the Leewit flanking him at the screens, and Maleen behind him to do the directing. After a few initial squeals, the Leewit became oddly silent. Suddenly the captain realized she was blubbering.

Somehow, it startled him to discover that her homecoming had affected the Leewit to that extent. He felt Goth reach out behind him and put her hand on the Leewit's shoulder. The smallest witch sniffled happily.

" 'S beautiful!" she growled.

He felt a resurge of the wondering, protective friendliness they had aroused in him at first. They must have been having a rough time of it, at that. He sighed; it seemed a pity they hadn't got along a little better!

"Where's everyone hiding?" he inquired, to break up the mood. So far, there hadn't been a sign of human habitation.

"There aren't many people on Karres," Maleen said from behind his shoulder. "But we're going to The Town—you'll meet about half of them there!"

"What's that place down there?" the captain asked with sudden interest. Something like an enormous lime-white bowl seemed to have been set flush into the floor of the wide valley up which they were moving.

"That's the Theater where . . . *ouch*!" the Leewit said. She fell silent then but turned to give Maleen a resentful look.

"Something strangers shouldn't be told about, eh?" the captain said tolerantly. Goth glanced at him from the side.

"We've got rules," she said.

He let the ship down a little as they passed over "the Theater where—" It was a sort of large, circular arena, with numerous steep tiers of seats running up around it. But all was bare and deserted now.

On Maleen's direction, they took the next valley fork to the right and dropped lower still. He had his first look at Karres animal life then. A flock of large, creamy-white birds, remarkably Terrestrial in appearance, flapped by just below them, apparently unconcerned about the ship. The forest underneath had opened out into a long stretch of lush meadow land, with small creeks winding down into its center. Here a herd of several hundred head of beasts was grazing—beasts of mastodonic size and build, with hairless, shiny black hides. The mouths of their long, heavy heads were twisted up into sardonic, crocodilian grins as they blinked up at the passing *Venture*.

"Black Bollems," said Goth, apparently enjoying the captain's expression. "Lots of them around; they're tame. But the gray mountain ones are good hunting."

"Good eating, too!" the Leewit said. She licked her lips daintily. "Breakfast—!" she sighed, her thoughts diverted to a familiar track. "And we ought to be just in time!"

"There's the field!" Maleen cried, pointing. "Set her down there, captain!"

The "field" was simply a flat meadow of close-trimmed grass running smack against the mountainside to their left. One small vehicle, bright blue in color, was parked on it; and it was bordered on two sides by very tall, blue-black trees.

That was all.

The captain shook his head. Then he set her down.

The town of Karres was a surprise to him in a good many ways. For one thing, there was much more of it than you would have thought possible after flying over the area. It stretched for miles through the forest, up the flanks of the mountain and across the valley—little clusters of houses or individual ones, each group screened from all the rest and from the sky overhead by the trees.

They liked color on Karres; but then they hid it away! The houses were bright as flowers, red and white, apple-green, golden-brown—all spick and span, scrubbed and polished and aired with that brisk, green forest-smell. At various times of the day, there was also the smell of remarkably good things to eat. There were brooks and pools and a great number of shaded vegetable gardens to the town. There were risky-looking treetop playgrounds, and treetop platforms and galleries which seemed to have no particular purpose. On the ground was mainly an enormously confusing maze of paths—narrow trails of sandy soil snaking about among great brown tree roots and chunks of gray mountain rock, and half covered with fallen needle leaves. The first six times the captain set out unaccompanied, he'd lost his way hopelessly within minutes, and had to be guided back out of the forest.

But the most hidden of all were the people! About four thousand of them were supposed to live in the town, with as many more scattered about the planet. But you never got to see more than three or four at any one time—except when now and then a pack of children, who seemed to the captain to be uniformly of the Leewit's size, would burst suddenly out of the undergrowth across a path before you, and vanish again.

As for the others, you did hear someone singing occasionally; or there might be a whole muted concert going on all about, on a large variety of wooden musical instruments which they seemed to enjoy tootling with, gently.

But it wasn't a real town at all, the captain thought. They didn't live like people, these Witches of Karres—it was more like a flock of strange forest birds that happened to be nesting in the same general area. Another thing: they appeared to be busy enough—but what was their business?

He discovered he was reluctant to ask Toll too many questions about it. Toll was the mother of his three witches; but only Goth really resembled her. It was difficult to picture Goth becoming smoothly matured and pleasantly rounded; but that was Toll. She had the same murmuring voice, the same air of sideways observation and secret reflection. And she answered all the captain's questions with apparent frankness; but he never seemed to get much real information out of what she said.

It was odd, too! Because he was spending several hours a day in her company, or in one of the next rooms at any rate, while she went about her housework. Toll's daughters had taken him home when they landed; and he was installed in the room that belonged to their father—busy just now, the captain gathered, with some sort of research of a geological nature elsewhere on Karres. The arrangement worried him a little at first, particularly since Toll and he were mostly alone in the house. Maleen was going to some kind of school; she left early in the morning and came back late in the afternoon; and Goth and the Leewit were just plain running wild! They usually got in long after the captain had gone to bed and were off again before he turned out for breakfast.

It hardly seemed like the right way to raise them! One afternoon, he found the Leewit curled up and asleep in the chair he usually occupied on the porch before the house. She slept there for four solid hours, while the captain sat nearby and leafed gradually through a thick book with illuminated pictures called "Histories of Ancient Yarthe." Now and then, he sipped at a cool, green, faintly intoxicating drink Toll had placed quietly beside him some while before, or sucked an aromatic smoke from the enormous pipe with a floor rest, which he understood was a favorite of Toll's husband.

* * *

Then the Leewit woke up suddenly, uncoiled, gave him a look between a scowl and a friendly grin, slipped off the porch and vanished among the trees.

He couldn't quite figure that look! It might have meant nothing at all in particular, but—

The captain laid down his book then and worried a little more. It was true, of course, that nobody seemed in the least concerned about his presence. All of Karres appeared to know about him, and he'd met quite a number of people by now in a casual way. But nobody came around to interview him or so much as dropped in for a visit. However, Toll's husband presumably would be returning presently, and—

How long had he been here, anyway?

Great Patham, the captain thought, shocked. He'd lost count of the days!

Or was it weeks?

He went in to find Toll.

"It's been a wonderful visit," he said, "but I'll have to be leaving, I guess. Tomorrow morning, early—"

Toll put some fancy sewing she was working on back in a glass basket, laid her thin, strong witch's hands in her lap, and smiled up at him.

"We thought you'd be thinking that," she said, "and so we— You know, captain, it was quite difficult to find a way to reward you for bringing back the children?"

"It was?" said the captain, suddenly realizing he'd also clean forgotten he was broke! And now the wrath of Onswud lay close ahead.

"Gold and jewel stones would have been just right, of course!" she said, "but unfortunately, while there's no doubt a lot of it on Karres somewhere, we never got around to looking for it. And we haven't money—none that you could use, that is!"

"No, I don't suppose you do," the captain agreed sadly.

"However," said Toll, "we've all been talking about it in the town, and so we've loaded a lot of things aboard your ship that we think you can sell at a fine profit!"

"Well now," the captain said gratefully, "that's fine of—"

"There are furs," said Toll, "the very finest furs we could fix up—two thousand of them!"

"Oh!" said the captain, bravely keeping his smile. "Well, that's wonderful!"

"And essences of perfume!" said Toll. "Everyone brought

one bottle of their own, so that's eight thousand three hundred and twenty-three bottles of perfume essences—all different!''

''Perfume!'' said the captain. ''Fine, fine—but you really shouldn't—''

''And the rest of it,'' Toll concluded happily, ''is the green Lepti liquor you like so much, and the Wintenberry jellies!'' She frowned. ''I forgot just how many jugs and jars,'' she admitted, ''but there were a lot. It's all loaded now. And do you think you'll be able to sell all that?'' she smiled.

''I certainly can!'' the captain said stoutly. ''It's wonderful stuff, and there's nothing like it in the Empire.''

Which was very true. They wouldn't have considered miffel-furs for lining on Karres. But if he'd been alone he would have felt like he wanted to burst into tears.

The witches couldn't have picked more completely unsalable items if they'd tried! Furs, cosmetics, food and liquor—he'd be shot on sight if he got caught trying to run that kind of merchandise into the Empire. For the same reason that they couldn't use it on Nikkeldepain—they were that scared of contamination by goods that came from uncleared worlds!

He breakfasted alone next morning. Toll had left a note beside his plate, which explained in a large, not too legible script that she had to run off and fetch the Leewit; and that if he was gone before she got back she was wishing him good-by and good luck.

He smeared two more buns with Wintenberry jelly, drank a large mug of cone-seed coffee, finished every scrap of the omelet of swan hawk eggs and then, in a state of pleasant repletion, toyed around with his slice of roasted Bollem liver. Boy, what food! He must have put on fifteen pounds since he landed on Karres.

He wondered how Toll kept that sleek figure.

Regretfully, he pushed himself away from the table, pocketed her note for a souvenir, and went out on the porch. There a tear-stained Maleen hurled herself into his arms.

''Oh, captain!'' she sobbed. ''You're leaving—''

''Now, now!'' the captain murmured, touched and surprised by the lovely child's grief. He patted her shoulders soothingly. ''I'll be back,'' he said rashly.

''Oh, yes, do come back!'' cried Maleen. She hesitated and added: ''I become marriageable two years from now. Karres time—''

''Well, well,'' said the captain, dazed. ''Well, now—''

He set off down the path a few minutes later, with a strange melody tinkling in his head. Around the first curve, it changed abruptly to a shrill keening which seemed to originate from a spot some two hundred feet before him. Around the next curve, he entered a small, rocky clearing full of pale, misty, early-morning sunlight and what looked like a slow-motion fountain of gleaming rainbow globes. These turned out to be clusters of large, vari-hued soap bubbles which floated up steadily from a wooden tub full of hot water, soap and the Leewit. Toll was bent over the tub; and the Leewit was objecting to a morning bath, with only that minimum of interruptions required to keep her lungs pumped full of a fresh supply of air.

As the captain paused beside the little family group, her red, wrathful face came up over the rim of the tub and looked at him.

"Well, Ugly," she squealed, in a renewed outburst of rage, "who you staring at?" Then a sudden determination came into her eyes. She pursed her lips.

Toll up-ended her promptly and smacked the Leewit's bottom.

"She was going to make some sort of a whistle at you," she explained hurriedly. "Perhaps you'd better get out of range while I can keep her head under. And good luck, captain!"

Karres seemed even more deserted than usual this morning. Of course, it was quite early. Great banks of fog lay here and there among the huge dark trees and the small bright houses. A breeze sighed sadly far overhead. Faint, mournful bird-cries came from still higher up—it could have been swan hawks reproaching him for the omelet.

Somewhere in the distance, somebody tootled on a wood-instrument, very gently.

He had gone halfway up the path to the landing field, when something buzzed past him like an enormous wasp and went *CLUNK*! into the bole of a tree just before him.

It was a long, thin, wicked-looking arrow. On its shaft was a white card; and on the card was printed in red letters:

STOP, MAN OF NIKKELDEPAIN!

The captain stopped and looked around slowly and cautiously. There was no one in sight. What did it mean?

He had a sudden feeling as if all of Karres were rising up silently in one stupendous, cool, foggy trap about him. His skin began to crawl. What was going to happen?

"Ha-ha!" said Goth, suddenly visible on a rock twelve feet to his left and eight feet above him. "You did stop!"

The captain let his breath out slowly.

"What else did you think I'd do?" he inquired. He felt a little faint.

She slid down from the rock like a lizard and stood before him. "Wanted to say good-by!" she told him.

Thin and brown, in jacket, breeches, boots, and cap of gray-green rock-lichen color, Goth looked very much in her element. The brown eyes looked up at him steadily; the mouth smiled faintly; but there was no real expression on her face at all. There was a quiverful of those enormous arrows slung over her shoulder, and some arrow-shooting gadget—not a bow—in her left hand.

She followed his glance.

"Bollem hunting up the mountain," she explained. "The wild ones. They're better meat—"

The captain reflected a moment. That's right, he recalled; they kept the tame Bollem herds mostly for milk, butter, and cheese. He'd learned a lot of important things about Karres, all right!

"Well," he said, "good-by, Goth!"

They shook hands gravely. Goth was the real Witch of Karres, he decided—more so than her sisters, more so even than Toll. But he hadn't actually learned a single thing about any of them. Peculiar people!

He walked on, rather glumly.

"Captain!" Goth called after him. He turned.

"Better watch those take-offs," Goth called, "or you'll kill yourself yet!"

The captain cussed softly all the way up to the *Venture*.

And the take-off was terrible! A few swan hawks were watching but, he hoped, no one else.

V.

There wasn't the remotest possibility, of course, of resuming direct trade in the Empire with the cargo they'd loaded for him. But the more he thought about it now, the less likely it seemed that Councilor Onswud was going to let a genuine fortune slip through his hands on a mere technicality of embargoes. Nikkeldepain knew all the tricks of interstellar merchandising; and the councilor himself was undoubtedly the slickest unskinned miffel in the Republic.

More hopefully, the captain began to wonder whether some

sort of trade might not be made to develop eventually between Karres and Nikkeldepain. Now and then, he also thought of Maleen growing marriageable two years hence, Karres time. A handful of witch-notes went tinkling through his head whenever that idle reflection occurred.

The calendric chronometer informed him he'd spent three weeks there. He couldn't remember how their year compared with the standard one.

He found he was getting remarkably restless on this homeward run; and it struck him for the first time that space travel could also be nothing much more than a large hollow period of boredom. He made a few attempts to resume his sessions of small-talk with Illyla, via her picture; but the picture remained aloof.

The ship seemed unnaturally quiet now—that was the trouble! The captain's cabin, particularly, and the hall leading past it had become as dismal as a tomb.

But at long last, Nikkeldepain II swam up on the screen ahead. The captain put the *Venture* 7333 on orbit, and broadcast the ship's identification number. Half an hour later, Landing Control called him. He repeated the identification number, and added the ship's name, his name, owner's name, place of origin and nature of cargo.

The cargo had to be described in detail.

''Assume Landing Orbit 21,203 on your instruments,'' Landing Control instructed him. ''A customs ship will come out to inspect.''

He went on the assigned orbit and gazed moodily from the vision ports at the flat continents and oceans of Nikkeldepain II as they drifted by below. A sense of equally flat depression overcame him unexpectedly. He shook it off and remembered Illyla.

Three hours later, a ship ran up next to him; and he shut off the orbital drive. The communicator began buzzing. He switched it on.

''Vision, please!'' said an official-sounding voice. The captain frowned, located the vision-stud of the communicator screen and pushed it down. Four faces appeared in vague outline on the screen, looking at him.

''Illyla!'' the captain said.

''At least,'' young Councilor Rapport said unpleasantly, ''he's brought back the ship, Father Onswud!''

''Illyla!'' said the captain.

Councilor Onswud said nothing. Neither did Illyla. They both seemed to be staring at him, but the screen wasn't good enough to permit the study of expression in detail.

The fourth face, an unfamiliar one above a uniform collar, was the one with the official-sounding voice.

"You are instructed to open the forward lock, Captain Pausert," it said, "for an official investigation."

It wasn't till he was releasing the outer lock to the control room that the captain realized it wasn't Customs who had sent a boat out to him, but the police of the Republic.

However, he hesitated for only a moment. Then the outer lock gaped wide.

He tried to explain. They wouldn't listen. They had come on board in contamination-proof repulsor suits, all four of them; and they discussed the captain as if he weren't there. Illyla looked pale and angry and beautiful, and avoided looking at him.

However, he didn't want to speak to her before the others anyway.

They strolled back to the storage and gave the Karres cargo a casual glance.

"Damaged his lifeboat, too!" Councilor Rapport remarked.

They brushed past him down the narrow hallway and went back to the control room. The policeman asked to see the log and commercial records. The captain produced them.

The three men studied them briefly. Illyla gazed stonily out at Nikkeldepain II.

"Not too carefully kept!" the policeman pointed out.

"Surprising he bothered to keep them at all!" said Councilor Rapport.

"But it's all clear enough!" said Councilor Onswud.

They straightened up then and faced him in a line. Councilor Onswud folded his arms and projected his craggy chin. Councilor Rapport stood at ease, smiling faintly. The policeman became officially rigid.

Illyla remained off to one side, looking at the three.

"Captain Pausert," the policeman said, "the following charges—substantiated in part by this preliminary investigation—are made against you—"

"Charges?" said the captain.

"Silence, please!" rumbled Councilor Onswud.

"First: material theft of a quarter-million value of maels of jewels and jeweled items from a citizen of the Imperial Planet of Porlumma—"

"They were returned!" the captain protested.

"Restitution, particularly when inspired by fear of retribution, does not affect the validity of the original charge," Councilor Rapport quoted, gazing at the ceiling.

"Second," continued the policeman. "Purchase of human slaves, permitted under Imperial law but prohibited by penalty of ten years to lifetime penal servitude by the laws of the Republic of Nikkeldepain—"

"I was just taking them back where they belonged!" said the captain.

"We shall get to that point presently," the policeman replied. "Third, material theft of sundry items in the value of one hundred and eighty thousand maels from a ship of the Imperial Planet of Lepper, accompanied by threats of violence to the ship's personnel—"

"I might add in explanation of the significance of this particular charge," added Councilor Rapport, looking at the floor, "that the Regency of Sirius, containing Lepper, is allied to the Republic of Nikkeldepain by commercial and military treaties of considerable value. The Regency has taken the trouble to point out that such hostile conduct by a citizen of the Republic against citizens of the Regency is likely to have an adverse effect on the duration of the treaties. The charge thereby becomes compounded by the additional charge of a treasonable act against the Republic—"

He glanced at the captain. "I believe we can forestall the accused's plea that these pilfered goods also were restored. They were, in the face of superior force!"

"Fourth," the policeman went on patiently, "depraved and licentious conduct while acting as commercial agent, to the detriment of your employer's business and reputation—"

"WHAT?" choked the captain.

"—involving three of the notorious Witches of the Prohibited Planet of Karres—"

"Just like his great-uncle Threbus!" nodded Councilor Onswud gloomily. "It's in the blood, I always say!"

"—and a justifiable suspicion of a prolonged stay on said Prohibited Planet of Karres—"

"I never heard of that place before this trip!" shouted the captain.

"Why don't you read your Instructions and Regulations then?" shouted Councilor Rapport. "It's all there!"

"Silence, please!" shouted Councilor Onswud.

"Fifth," said the policeman quietly, "general willful and

negligent actions resulting in material damage and loss to your employer to the value of eighty-two thousand maels."

"I've still got fifty-five thousand. And the stuff in the storage," the captain said, also quietly, "is worth half a million, at least!"

"Contraband and hence legally valueless!" the policeman said. Councilor Onswud cleared his throat.

"It will be impounded, of course," he said. "Should a method of resale present itself, the profits, if any, will be applied to the cancellation of your just debts. To some extent, that might reduce your sentence." He paused. "There is another matter—"

"The sixth charge," the policeman said, "is the development *and* public demonstration of a new type of space drive, which should have been brought promptly and secretly to the attention of the Republic of Nikkeldepain!"

They all stared at him—alertly and quite greedily.

So *that* was it—the Sheewash Drive!

"Your sentence may be greatly reduced, Pausert," Councilor Onswud said wheedlingly, "if you decide to be reasonable now. What have you discovered?"

"Look out, father!" Illyla said sharply.

"Pausert," Councilor Onswud inquired in a fading voice, "what is that in your hand?"

"A Blythe gun," the captain said, boiling.

There was a frozen stillness for an instant. Then the policeman's right hand made a convulsive movement.

"Uh-uh!" said the captain warningly.

Councilor Rapport started a slow step backwards.

"Stay where you are!" said the captain.

"Pausert!" Councilor Onswud and Illyla cried out together.

"Shut up!" said the captain.

There was another stillness.

"If you'd looked," the captain said, in an almost normal voice, "you'd have seen I've got the nova gun turrets out. They're fixed on that boat of yours. The boat's lying still and keeping its little yap shut. You do the same—"

He pointed a finger at the policeman. "You got a repulsor suit on," he said. "Open the inner port lock and go squirt yourself back to your boat!"

The inner port lock groaned open. Warm air left the ship in a long, lazy wave, scattering the sheets of the *Venture*'s log and commercial records over the floor. The thin, cold upper atmosphere of Nikkeldepain II came eddying in.

"You next, Onswud!" the captain said.

And a moment later: "Rapport, you just turn around—"

Young Councilor Rapport went through the port at a higher velocity than could be attributed reasonably to his repulsor units. The captain winced and rubbed his foot. But it had been worth it.

"Pausert," said Illyla in justifiable apprehension, "you are stark, staring mad!"

"Not at all, my dear," the captain said cheerfully. "You and I are now going to take off and embark on a life of crime together."

"But, Pausert—"

"You'll get used to it," the captain assured her, "just like I did. It's got Nikkeldepain beat every which way."

"Pausert," Illyla said, whitefaced, "we told them to bring up revolt ships!"

"We'll blow them out through the stratosphere," the captain said belligerently, reaching for the port-control switch. He added, "But they won't shoot anyway while I've got you on board!"

Illyla shook her head. "You just don't understand," she said desperately. "You can't make me stay!"

"Why not?" asked the captain.

"Pausert," said Illyla, "I am Madame Councilor Rapport."

"Oh!" said the captain. There was a silence. He added, crestfallen: "Since when?"

"Five months ago, yesterday," said Illyla.

"Great Patham!" cried the captain, with some indignation. "I'd hardly got off Nikkeldepain then! We were engaged!"

"Secretly . . . and I guess," said Illyla, with a return of spirit, "that I had a right to change my mind!"

There was another silence.

"Guess you had, at that," the captain agreed. "All right—the port's still open, and your husband's waiting in the boat. Beat it!"

He was alone. He let the ports slam shut and banged down the oxygen release switch. The air had become a little thin.

He cussed.

The communicator began rattling for attention. He turned it on.

"Pausert!" Councilor Onswud was calling in a friendly but shaking voice. "May we not depart, Pausert? Your nova guns are still fixed on this boat!"

"Oh, that—" said the captain. He deflected the turrets a trifle. "They won't go off now. Scram!"

The police boat vanished.

There was other company coming, though. Far below him but climbing steadily, a trio of revolt ships darted past on the screen, swung around and came back for the next turn of their spiral. They'd have to get a good deal closer before they started shooting; but they'd try to stay under him so as not to knock any stray chunks out of Nikkeldepain.

He sat a moment, reflecting. The revolt ships went by once more. The captain punched in the *Venture*'s secondary drives, turned her nose towards the planet and let her go. There were some scattered white puffs around as he cut through the revolt ships' plane of flight. Then he was below them, and the *Venture* groaned as he took her out of the dive.

The revolt ships were already scattering and nosing over for a counter-maneuver. He picked the nearest one and swung the nova guns towards it.

"—and ram them in the middle!" he muttered between his teeth.

SSS-whoosh!

It was the Sheewash Drive—but, like a nightmare now, it kept on and on!

VI.

"Maleen!" the captain bawled, pounding at the locked door of the captain's cabin. "Maleen—shut it off! Cut it off! You'll kill yourself, Maleen!"

The *Venture* quivered suddenly throughout her length, then shuddered more violently, jumped and coughed; and commenced sailing along on her secondary drives again. He wondered how many light-years from everything they were by now. It didn't matter!

"Maleen!" he yelled. "Are you all right?"

There was a faint *thump-thump* inside the cabin, and silence. He lost almost a minute finding the right cutting tool in the storage. A few seconds later, a section of door panel sagged inwards; he caught it by one edge and came tumbling into the cabin with it.

He had the briefest glimpse of a ball of orange-colored fire swirling uncertainly over a cone of oddly bent wires. Then the fire vanished, and the wires collapsed with a loose rattling to the table top.

The crumpled small shape lay behind the table, which was

why he didn't discover it at once. He sagged to the floor beside it, all the strength running out of his knees.

Brown eyes opened and blinked at him blearily.

"Sure takes it out of you!" Goth grunted. "Am I hungry?"

"I'll whale the holy, howling tar out of you again," the captain roared, "if you ever—"

"Quit your bawling!" snarled Goth. "I got to eat."

She ate for fifteen minutes straight, before she sank back in her chair, and sighed.

"Have some more Wintenberry jelly," the captain offered anxiously. She looked pretty pale.

Goth shook her head. "Couldn't—and that's about the first thing you've said since you fell through the door, howling for Maleen. Ha-ha! Maleen's *got* a boyfriend!"

"Button your lip, child," the captain said. "I was thinking." He added, after a moment: "Has she really?"

"Picked him out last year," Goth nodded. "Nice boy from town—they get married as soon as she's marriageable. She just told you to come back because she was upset about you. Maleen had a premonition you were headed for awful trouble!"

"She was quite right, little chum," the captain said nastily.

"What were you thinking about?" Goth inquired.

"I was thinking," said the captain, "that as soon as we're sure you're going to be all right, I'm taking you straight back to Karres!"

"I'll be all right now," Goth said. "Except, likely, for a stomach-ache. But you can't take me back to Karres."

"Who will stop me, may I ask?" the captain asked.

"Karres is gone," Goth said.

"Gone?" the captain repeated blankly, with a sensation of not quite definable horror bubbling up in him.

"Not blown up or anything," Goth reassured him. "They just moved it! The Imperialists got their hair up about us again. But this time, they were sending a fleet with the big bombs and stuff, so everybody was called home. But they had to wait then till they found out where we were—me and Maleen and the Leewit. Then you brought us in; and they had to wait again, and decide about you. But right after you'd left . . . *we'd* left, I mean . . . they moved it."

"Where?"

"Great Patham!" Goth shrugged. "How'd I know? There's lots of places!"

* * *

There probably were, the captain admitted silently. A scene came suddenly before his eyes—that lime-white, arenalike bowl in the valley, with the steep tiers of seats around it, just before they'd reached the town of Karres—"the Theater where—"

But now there was unnatural night-darkness all over and about that world; and the eight thousand-some Witches of Karres sat in circles around the Theater, their heads bent towards one point in the center, where orange fire washed hugely about the peak of a cone of curiously twisted girders.

And a world went racing off at the speeds of the Sheewash Drive! There'd be lots of places, all right. What peculiar people!

"Anyway," he sighed, "if I've got to start raising you—don't say 'Great Patham' any more. That's a cuss word!"

"I learned it from you!" Goth pointed out.

"So you did, I guess," the captain acknowledged. "I won't say it either. Aren't they going to be worried about you?"

"Not very much," said Goth. "We don't get hurt often—especially when we're young. That's when we can do all that stuff like teleporting, and whistling, like the Leewit. We lose it mostly when we get older—they're working on that now so we won't. About all Maleen can do right now is premote!"

"She premotes just dandy, though," the captain said. "The Sheewash Drive—they can all do that, can't they?"

"Uh-huh!" Goth nodded. "But that's learned stuff. That's one of the things they already studied out." She added, a trace uncomfortably: "I can't tell you about that till you're one yourself."

"Till I'm what myself?" the captain asked, becoming puzzled again.

"A witch, like us," said Goth. "We got our rules. And that won't be for four years, Karres time."

"It won't, eh?" said the captain. "What happens then?"

"That's when I'm marriageable age," said Goth, frowning at the jar of Wintenberry jelly. She pulled it towards her and inspected it carefully. "I got it all fixed," she told the jelly firmly, "as soon as they started saying they ought to pick out a wife for you on Karres, so you could stay. I said it was me, right away; and everyone else said finally that was all right then—even Maleen, because she had this boy friend."

"You mean?" said the captain, stunned, "this was all planned out on Karres?"

"Sure," said Goth. She pushed the jelly back where it had been standing, and glanced up at him again. "For three weeks, that's about all everyone talked about in the town! It set a perceedent—''

She paused doubtfully.

''That would explain it,'' the captain admitted.

''Uh-huh,'' Goth nodded relieved, settling back in her chair. ''But it was my father who told us how to do it so you'd break up with the people on Nikkeldepain. He said it was in the blood.''

''What was in the blood?'' the captain said patiently.

''That you'd break up with them. That's Threbus, my father,'' Goth informed him. ''You met him a couple of times in the town. Big man with a blond beard—Maleen and the Leewit take after him.''

''You wouldn't mean my great-uncle Threbus?'' the captain inquired. He was in a state of strange calm by now.

''That's right,'' said Goth. ''He liked you a lot.''

''It's a small Galaxy,'' said the captain philosophically. ''So that's where Threbus wound up! I'd like to meet him again some day.''

''We'll start after Karres four years from now, when you learn about those things,'' Goth said. ''We'll catch up with them all right. That's still thirteen hundred and seventy-two Old Sidereal days,'' she added, ''but there's a lot to do in between. You want to pay the money you owe back to those people, don't you? I got some ideas—''

''None of those teleporting tricks now!'' the captain warned.

''Kid stuff!'' Goth said scornfully. ''I'm growing up. This'll be fair swapping. But we'll get rich.''

''I wouldn't be surprised,'' the captain admitted. He thought a moment. ''Seeing we've turned out to be distant relatives, I suppose it is all right, too, if I adopt you meanwhile—''

''Sure,'' said Goth. She stood up.

''Where you going?'' the captain asked.

''Bed,'' said Goth. ''I'm tired.'' She stopped at the hall door. ''About all I can tell you about us till then,'' she said, ''you can read in those Regulations, like the one man said—the one you kicked off the ship. There's a lot about us in there. Lots of lies, too, though!''

''And when did you find out about the communicator between here and the captain's cabin?'' the captain inquired.

Goth grinned. ''A while back,'' she admitted. ''The others never noticed!''

"All right," the captain said. "Good night, witch—if you get a stomach-ache, yell and I'll bring the medicine."

"Good night," Goth yawned. "I will, I think."

"And wash behind your ears!" the captain added, trying to remember the bedtime instructions he'd overheard Maleen giving the junior witches.

"All right," said Goth sleepily. The hall door closed behind her—but half a minute later, it was briskly opened again. The captain looked up startled from the voluminous stack of "General Instructions and Space Regulations of the Republic of Nikkeldepain" he'd just discovered in one of the drawers of the control desk. Goth stood in the doorway, scowling and wide-awake.

"And you wash behind yours!" she said.

"Huh?" said the captain. He reflected a moment. "All right," he said. "We both will, then."

"Right," said Goth, satisfied.

The door closed once more.

The captain began to run his finger down the lengthy index of K's—or could it be under W?

NOT WITH A BANG

Damon Knight (1922–   )

THE MAGAZINE OF FANTASY AND SCIENCE FICTION
Winter

The extinction of the human species has interested and frightened science fiction writers since at least Mary Shelley's The Last Man *of 1826. It is a subject that has produced moving, nostalgic, and powerful stories. Here, the urbane Damon Knight tackles the subject with somewhat different results.*

—M.H.G.

T. S. Eliot in 1925 published a poem called "The Hollow Men" of which the most famous lines are:

This is the way the world ends
Not with a bang but a whimper.

People who don't read science fiction think of T. S. Eliot when those lines are quoted. I think of Damon Knight because he composed "Not With a Bang," which expresses those lines perfectly.

Only one thing bothers me. How did Damon mean the phrase "Not With a Bang"? If we consider it as a vulgarism, the story illustrates that perfectly, too. Is that just a coincidence? Is it possible that Damon never thought of the other meaning?

And if Damon missed it, I cannot conceive that Tony Boucher, the editor of the magazine in which it appeared, missed it. I knew Tony too well in those old days to believe that for a minute.

—I. A.

Ten months after the last plane passed over, Rolf Smith knew beyond doubt that only one other human being had survived. Her name was Louise Oliver, and he was sitting opposite her in a department-store cafe in Salt Lake City. They were eating canned Vienna sausages and drinking coffee.

Sunlight struck through a broken pane, lying like a judgment on the cloudy air of the room. Inside and outside, there was no sound; only a stifling rumor of absence. The clatter of dishware in the kitchen, the heavy rumble of streetcars: never again. There was sunlight; and silence; and the watery, astonished eyes of Louise Oliver.

He leaned forward, trying to capture the attention of those fishlike eyes for a second. "Darling," he said, "I respect your views, naturally. But I've got to make you see that they're impractical."

She looked at him with faint surprise, then away again. Her head shook slightly: No. *No, Rolf. I will not live with you in sin.*

Smith thought of the women of France, of Russia, of Mexico, of the South Seas. He had spent three months in the ruined studios of a radio station in Rochester, listening to the voices until they stopped. There had been a large colony in Sweden, including an English cabinet minister. They reported that Europe was gone. Simply gone; there was not an acre that had not been swept clean by radioactive dust. They had two planes and enough fuel to take them anywhere on the Continent; but there was nowhere to go. Three of them had the plague; then eleven; then all.

There was a bomber pilot who had fallen near a government radio in Palestine. He did not last long, because he had broken some bones in the crash; but he had seen the vacant waters where the Pacific Islands should have been. It was his guess that the Arctic ice-fields had been bombed. He did not know whether that had been a mistake or not.

There were no reports from Washington, from New York, from London, Paris, Moscow, Chungking, Sydney. You could not tell who had been destroyed by disease, who by the dust, who by bombs.

Smith himself had been a laboratory assistant in a team that was trying to find an antibiotic for the plague. His superiors had found one that worked sometimes, but it was a little too late. When he left, Smith took along with him all there was of it—forty ampoules, enough to last him for years.

Louise had been a nurse in a genteel hospital near Denver. According to her, something rather odd had happened to the hospital as she was approaching it the morning of the attack. She was quite calm when she said this, but a vague look came into her eyes and her shattered expression seemed to slip a little more. Smith did not press her for an explanation.

Like himself, she had found a radio station which still functioned, and when Smith discovered that she had not contracted the plague, he agreed to meet her. She was, apparently, naturally immune. There must have been others, a few at least; but the bombs and the dust had not spared them.

It seemed very awkward to Louise that not one Protestant minister was left alive.

The trouble was, she really meant it. It had taken Smith a long time to believe it, but it was true. She would not sleep in the same hotel with him, either; she expected, and received, the utmost courtesy and decorum. Smith had learned his lesson. He walked on the outside of the rubble-heaped sidewalks; he opened doors for her, when there were still doors; he held her chair; he refrained from swearing. He courted her.

Louise was forty or thereabouts, at least five years older than Smith. He often wondered how old she thought she was. The shock of seeing whatever it was that had happened to the hospital, the patients she had cared for, had sent her mind scuttling back to her childhood. She tacitly admitted that everyone else in the world was dead, but she seemed to regard it as something one did not mention.

A hundred times in the last three weeks, Smith had felt an almost irresistible impulse to break her thin neck and go his own way. But there was no help for it; she was the only woman in the world, and he needed her. If she died, or left him, he died. *Old bitch!* he thought to himself furiously, and carefully kept the thought from showing on his face.

"Louise, honey," he told her gently, "I want to spare your feelings as much as I can. You know that."

"Yes, Rolf," she said, staring at him with the face of a hypnotized chicken.

Smith forced himself to go on. "We've got to face the facts, unpleasant as they may be. Honey, we're the only man and the only woman there are. We're like Adam and Eve in the Garden of Eden."

Louise's face took on a slightly disgusted expression. She was obviously thinking of fig-leaves.

"Think of the generations unborn," Smith told her, with a tremor in his voice. *Think about me for once. Maybe you're good for another ten years, maybe not.* Shuddering, he thought of the second stage of the disease—the helpless rigidity, striking without warning. He'd had one such attack already, and Louise had helped him out of it. Without her, he would have stayed like that till he died, the hypodermic that would save him within inches of his rigid hand. He thought desperately, *If I'm lucky, I'll get at least two kids out of you before you croak. Then I'll be safe.*

He went on, "God didn't mean for the human race to end like this. He spared us, you and me, to—" He paused; how could he say it without offending her? "Parents" wouldn't do—too suggestive. "—to carry on the torch of life," he ended. There. That was sticky enough.

Louise was staring vaguely over his shoulder. Her eyelids blinked regularly, and her mouth made little rabbit-like motions in the same rhythm.

Smith looked down at his wasted thighs under the tabletop. *I'm not strong enough to force her,* he thought. *Christ, if I were strong enough!*

He felt the futile rage again, and stifled it. He had to keep his head, because this might be his last chance. Louise had been talking lately, in the cloudy language she used about everything, of going up in the mountains to pray for guidance. She had not said, "alone," but it was easy enough to see that she pictured it that way. He had to argue her around before her resolve stiffened. He concentrated furiously, and tried once more.

The pattern of words went by like a distant rumbling. Louise heard a phrase here and there; each of them fathered chains of thought, binding her reverie tighter. "Our duty to humanity . . ." Mama had often said—that was in the old house on Waterbury Street of course, before Mama had taken sick—she had said, "Child, your duty is to be clean, polite, and God-fearing. Pretty doesn't matter. There's a plenty of plain women that have got themselves good, Christian husbands."

Husbands . . . To have and to hold . . . Orange blossoms, and the bridesmaids; the organ music. Through the haze, she saw Rolf's lean, wolfish face. Of course, he was the only one she'd ever get; *she* knew that well enough. Gracious, when a girl was past twenty-five, she had to take what she could get.

But I sometimes wonder if he's really a nice man, she thought. ". . . in the eyes of God . . ." She remembered the stained glass windows in the old First Episcopalian Church, and how she always thought God was looking down at her through that brilliant transparency. Perhaps He was still looking at her, though it seemed sometimes that He had forgotten. Well, of course she realized that marriage customs changed, and if you couldn't have a regular minister. . . . But it was really a shame, an outrage almost, that if she were actually going to marry this man, she couldn't have all those nice things . . . There wouldn't even be any wedding presents. Not even that. But of course Rolf would give her anything she wanted. She saw his face again, noticed the narrow black eyes staring at her with ferocious purpose, the thin mouth that jerked in a slow, regular tic, the hairy lobes of the ears below the tangle of black hair.

He oughtn't to let his hair grow so long, she thought, *it isn't quite decent.* Well, she could change all that. If she did marry him, she'd certainly make him change his ways. It was no more than her duty.

He was talking now about a farm he'd seen outside town—a good big house and a barn. There was no stock, he said, but they could get some later. And they'd plant things, and have their own food to eat, not go to restaurants all the time.

She felt a touch on her hand, lying pale before her on the table. Rolf's brown, stubby fingers, black-haired above and below the knuckles, were touching hers. He had stopped talking for a moment, but now he was speaking again, still more urgently. She drew her hand away.

He was saying, ". . . and you'll have the finest wedding dress you ever saw, with a bouquet. Everything you want, Louise, everything . . ."

A wedding dress! And flowers, even if there couldn't be any minister! Well, why hadn't the fool said so before?

Rolf stopped halfway through a sentence, aware that Louise had said quite clearly, "Yes, Rolf, I will marry you if you wish."

Stunned, he wanted her to repeat it, but dared not ask, "What did you say?" for fear of getting some fantastic answer, or none at all. He breathed deeply. He said, "Today, Louise?"

She said, "Well, *today* . . . I don't know quite . . . Of course, if you think you can make all the arrangements in time, but it does seem . . ."

Triumph surged through Smith's body. He had the advantage now, and he'd ride it. "Say you will, dear," he urged her; "say yes, and make me the happiest man . . ."

Even then, his tongue balked at the rest of it; but it didn't matter. She nodded submissively. "Whatever you think best, Rolf."

He rose, and she allowed him to kiss her pale, sapless cheek. "We'll leave right away," he said. "If you'll excuse me for just a minute, dear?"

He waited for her "Of course" and then left her, making footprints in the furred carpet of dust down toward the end of the room. Just a few more hours he'd have to speak to her like that, and then, in her eyes, she'd be committed to him forever. Afterwards, he could do with her as he liked—beat her when he pleased, submit her to any proof of his scorn and revulsion, use her. Then it would not be too bad, being the last man on Earth—not bad at all. She might even have a daughter . . .

He found the washroom door and entered. He took a step inside, and froze, balanced by a trick of motion, upright but helpless. Panic struck at his throat as he tried to turn his head and failed; tried to scream, and failed. Behind him, he was aware of a tiny click as the door, cushioned by the hydraulic check, shut forever. It was not locked; but its other side bore the warning: MEN.

SPECTATOR SPORT

John D. MacDonald

THRILLING WONDER STORIES
February

For those of you new to this series, this is the same John D. MacDonald responsible for the Travis Magee novels and several dozen other terrific suspense tales. Although he left the science fiction field (for the most part) in the early 1950s, he still has great affection for sf and the people who write and read it. His book-length science fiction is confined to the novels Wine of the Dreamers *(1951),* Ballroom of the Skies *(1952),* The Girl, The Gold Watch, and Everything *(1962) and the collection* Other Times, Other Worlds *(1978).*

"Spectator Sport" is a minor classic, a story with strong political overtones as well as some important observations on the nature of reality.

—M.H.G.

Science fiction, though usually dealing with the future, can't help but be rooted in its present.

In 1950, for instance, Americans began to realize that television was not just a fad, not just an oddity, but was going to alter society as deeply and permanently as the automobile had. Many intellectuals viewed it with a kind of horrified despair and began to foresee an unbearable future, as MacDonald does in "Spectator Sport."

Oddly enough, I think we fear television less now than we did a third of a century ago. (Heavens, is television that *old?)*

Custom hardens us. Nevertheless, we are still capable of being devastated by novelty. Ask people over forty what they think of video games.

—I.A.

Dr. Rufus Maddon was not generally considered to be an impatient man—or addicted to physical violence.

But when the tenth man he tried to stop on the street brushed by him with a mutter of annoyance Rufus Maddon grabbed the eleventh man, swung him around and held him with his shoulders against a crumbling wall.

He said, "You will listen to me, sir! I am the first man to travel into the future and I will not stand—"

The man pushed him away, turned around and said, "You got this dust on my suit. Now brush it off."

Rufus Maddon brushed mechanically. He said, with a faint uncontrollable tremble in his voice, "But nobody seems to care."

The man peered back over his shoulder. "Good enough, chum. Better go get yourself lobed. The first time I saw the one on time travel it didn't get to me at all. Too hammy for me. Give me those murder jobs. Every time I have one of those I twitch for twenty hours."

Rufus made another try. "Sir, I am physical living proof that the future is predetermined. I can explain the energy equations, redesign the warp projector, send myself from your day further into the future—"

The man walked away. "Go get a lobe job," he said.

"But don't I look different to you?" Rufus called after him, a plaintive note in his voice.

The man, twenty feet away, turned and grinned at him. "How?"

When the man had gone Rufus Maddon looked down at his neat grey suit, stared at the men and women in the street. It was not fair of the future to be so—so dismally normal.

Four hundred years of progress? The others had resented the experience that was to be his. In those last few weeks there had been many discussions of how the people four hundred years in the future would look on Rufus Maddon as a barbarian.

Once again he continued his aimless walk down the streets of the familiar city. There was a general air of disrepair. Shops were boarded up. The pavement was broken and potholed. A few automobiles traveled on the broken streets. They, at least, appeared to be of a slightly advanced design but they were dented, dirty and noisy.

The man who had spoken to him had made no sense. "Lobe job?" And what was "the one on time travel"?

He stopped in consternation as he reached the familiar park. His consternation arose from the fact that the park was all too familiar. Though it was a tangle of weeds the equestrian statue of General Murdy was still there in deathless bronze, liberally decorated by pigeons.

Clothes had not changed nor had common speech. He wondered if the transfer had gone awry, if this world were something he was dreaming.

He pushed through the knee-high tangle of grass to a wrought-iron bench. Four hundred years before he had sat on that same bench. He sat down again. The metal powdered and collapsed under his weight, one end of the bench dropping with a painful thump.

Dr. Rufus Maddon was not generally considered to be a man subject to fits of rage. He stood up, rubbing his bruised elbow, and heartily kicked the offending bench. The part he kicked was all too solid.

He limped out of the park, muttering, wondering why the park wasn't used, why everyone seemed to be in a hurry.

It appeared that in four hundred years nothing at all had been accomplished. Many familiar buildings had collapsed. Others still stood. He looked in vain for a newspaper or a magazine.

One new element of this world of the future bothered him considerably. That was the number of low-slung white-panel delivery trucks. They seemed to be in better condition than the other vehicles. Each bore in fairly large gilt letters the legend WORLD SENSEWAYS. But he noticed that the smaller print underneath the large inscription varied. Some read, *Feeder Division*—others, *Hookup Division*.

The one that stopped at the curb beside him read, *Lobotomy Division*. Two husky men got out and smiled at him and one said, "You've been taking too much of that stuff, Doc."

"How did you know my title?" Rufus asked, thoroughly puzzled.

The other man smiled wolfishly, patted the side of the truck.

"Nice truck, pretty truck. Climb in, bud. We'll take you down and make you feel wonderful, hey?"

Dr. Rufus Maddon suddenly had a horrid suspicion that he knew what a lobe job might be. He started to back away. They grabbed him quickly and expertly and dumped him into the truck.

The sign on the front of the building said WORLD SENSEWAYS. The most luxurious office inside was lettered, *Regional Director—Roger K. Handriss*.

Roger K. Handriss sat behind his handsome desk. He was a florid grey-haired man with keen grey eyes. He was examining his bank book thinking that in another year he'd have enough money to retire and buy a permanent hookup. Permanent was so much better than the Temp stuff you could get on the home sets. The nerve ends was what did it, of course.

The girl came in and placed several objects on the desk in front of him. She said, "Mr. Handriss, these just came up from LD. They took them out of the pockets of a man reported as wandering in the street in need of a lobe job."

She had left the office door open. Cramer, deputy chief of LD, sauntered in and said, "The guy was really off. He was yammering about being from the past and not to destroy his mind."

Roger Handriss poked the objects with a manicured finger. He said, "Small pocket change from the twentieth century, Cramer. Membership cards in professional organizations of that era. Ah, here's a letter."

As Cramer and the girl waited, Roger Handriss read the letter through twice. He gave Cramer an uncomfortable smile and said, "This appears to be a letter from a technical publishing house telling Mr.—ah—Maddon that they intend to reprint his book, Suggestions on Time Focus in February of nineteen hundred and fifty. Miss Hart, get on the phone and see if you can raise anyone at the library who can look this up for us. I want to know if such a book was published."

Miss Hart hastened out of the office.

As they waited, Handriss motioned to a chair. Cramer sat down. Handriss said, "Imagine what it must have been like in those days, Al. They had the secrets but they didn't begin to use them until—let me see—four years later. Aldous Huxley had already given them their clue with his literary invention of the Feelies. But they ignored them.

"All their energies went into wars and rumors of wars and random scientific advancement and sociological disruptions. Of course, with Video on the march at that time, they were beginning to get a little preview. Millions of people were beginning to sit in front of the Video screens, content even with that crude excuse for entertainment."

Cramer suppressed a yawn. Handriss was known to go on like that for hours.

"Now," Handriss continued, "all the efforts of a world society are channeled into World Senseways. There is no waste of effort changing a perfectly acceptable status quo. Every man can have Temp and if you save your money you can have Permanent, which they say is as close to heaven as man can get. Uh—what was that, Miss Hart?"

"There is such a book, Mr. Handriss, and it was published at that time. A Dr. Rufus Maddon wrote it."

Handriss sighed and clucked. "Well," he said, "have Maddon brought up here."

Maddon was brought into the office by an attendant. He wore a wide foolish smile and a tiny bandage on his temple. He walked with the clumsiness of an overgrown child.

"Blast it, Al," Handriss said, "why couldn't your people have been more careful! He looks as if he might have been intelligent."

Al shrugged. "Do they come here from the past every couple of minutes? He didn't look any different than any other lobey to me."

"I suppose it couldn't be helped," Handriss said. "We've done this man a great wrong. We can wait and reeducate, I suppose. But that seems to be treating him rather shabbily."

"We can't send him back," Al Cramer said.

Handriss stood up, his eyes glowing. "But it is within my authority to grant him one of the Perm setups given me. World Senseways knows that Regional Directors make mistakes. This will rectify any mistake to an individual."

"Is it fair he should get it for free?" Cramer asked. "And besides, maybe the people who helped send him up here into the future would like to know what goes on."

Handriss smiled shrewdly. "And if they knew, what would stop them from flooding in on us? Have Hookup install him immediately."

The subterranean corridor had once been used for underground trains. But with the reduction in population it had ceased to pay its way and had been taken over by World Senseways to house the sixty-five thousand Perms.

Dr. Rufus Maddon was taken, in his new shambling walk, to the shining cubicle. His name and the date of installation were written on a card and inserted in the door slot. Handriss stood enviously aside and watched the process.

The bored technicians worked rapidly. They stripped the unprotesting Rufus Maddon, took him inside his cubicle, forced him down onto the foam couch. They rolled him over onto his side, made the usual incision at the back of his neck, carefully slit the main motor nerves, leaving the senses, the heart and lungs intact. They checked the air conditioning and plugged him into the feeding schedule for that bank of Perms.

Next they swung the handrods and the footplates into position, gave him injections of local anesthetic, expertly flayed the palms of his hands and the soles of his feet, painted the raw flesh with the sticky nerve graft and held his hands closed around the rods, his feet against the plates until they adhered in the proper position.

Handriss glanced at his watch.

"Guess that's all we can watch, Al. Come along."

The two men walked back down the long corridor. Handriss said, "The lucky so and so. We have to work for it. I get my Perm in another year—right down here beside him. In the meantime we'll have to content ourselves with the hand sets, holding onto those blasted knobs that don't let enough through to hardly raise the hair on the back of your neck."

Al sighed enviously. "Nothing to do for as long as he lives except twenty-four hours a day of being the hero of the most adventurous and glamorous and exciting stories that the race has been able to devise. No memories. I told them to dial him in on the Cowboy series. There's seven years of that now. It'll be more familiar to him. I'm electing Crime and Detection. Eleven years of that now, you know."

Roger Handriss chuckled and jabbed Al with his elbow. "Be smart, Al. Pick the Harem series."

Back in the cubicle the technicians were making the final adjustments. They inserted the sound buttons in Rufus Maddon's ears, deftly removed his eyelids, moved his head into just the right position and then pulled down the deeply concave shining screen so that Rufus Maddon's staring eyes looked directly into it.

The elder technician pulled the wall switch. He bent and peered into the screen. "Color okay, three dimensions okay. Come on, Joe, we got another to do before quitting."

They left, closed the metal door, locked it.

Inside the cubicle, Dr. Rufus Maddon was riding slowly down the steep trail from the mesa to the cattle town on the plains. He was trail-weary and sun-blackened. There was an old score to settle. Feeney was about to foreclose on Mary Ann's spread and Buck Hoskie, Mary Ann's crooked foreman, had threatened to shoot on sight.

Rufus Maddon wiped the sweat from his forehead on the back of a lean hard brown hero's hand.

THERE WILL COME SOFT RAINS

Ray Bradbury

COLLIER'S
May

1950 was a banner year for the thirty-year-old Bradbury. It saw the publication of The Martian Chronicles, *the work for which he is still famous. The stories that comprise it were partly written in the second half of the 40s while others appeared in the volume for the first time. In spite of its impossible astronomy, it remains a landmark work in the history of modern science fiction. Obviously influenced by American history and the movement of the frontier westward as well as Bradbury's own midwestern childhood, the book established his reputation as a major American literary figure.*

"There Will Come Soft Rains" contains some of the most haunting scenes in sf, images that I have retained for more than thirty years. It was published in Collier's, *a* Saturday Evening Post*-like family magazine of beloved memory—Bradbury, along with Robert A. Heinlein, brought science fiction to its slick pages.*

—M.H.G.

One of the turning points of modern science fiction came in late 1949. Doubleday and Co., the largest of the trade publishers, actually decided to put out a line of hard-cover science fiction books.

This was unheard-of. For twenty-three years, American science fiction existed almost entirely in the magazines. There were some hard-cover books put out by fans, but they were curios more than anything else. There were also a couple of paperbacks put out, and one or two anthologies, but these were all exceptional.

Doubleday planned to put out science fiction books on a regular basis and use their expertise and facilities to publicize and sell them. Wow!

The first book they published was The Big Eye *by Max Ehrlich (who died recently). The second book—the first by a recognized science fiction writer—was* Pebble in the Sky *by Isaac Asimov (my first book). But what really established Doubleday's line and made a permanent thing of it (it still exists a third of a century later) was the third book, which was* The Martian Chronicles *by Ray Bradbury. It was an instant classic.*

But was I jealous?

Of course.

—I.A.

In the living room the voice-clock sang, *Tick-tock, seven o'clock, time to get up, time to get up, seven o'clock!* as if it were afraid that nobody would. The morning house lay empty. The clock ticked on, repeating and repeating its sounds into the emptiness. *Seven-nine, breakfast time, seven-nine!*

In the kitchen the breakfast stove gave a hissing sigh and ejected from its warm interior eight pieces of perfectly browned toast, eight eggs sunnyside up, sixteen slices of bacon, two coffees, and two cool glasses of milk.

"Today is August 4, 2026," said a second voice from the kitchen ceiling, "in the city of Allendale, California." It repeated the date three times for memory's sake. "Today is Mr. Featherstone's birthday. Today is the anniversary of Tilita's marriage. Insurance is payable, as are the water, gas, and light bills."

Somewhere in the walls, relays clicked, memory tapes glided under electric eyes.

Eight-one, tick-tock, eight-one o'clock, off to school, off to work, run, run, eight-one! But no doors slammed, no carpets took the soft tread of rubber heels. It was raining outside. The weather box on the front door sang quietly: "Rain, rain, go away; rubbers, raincoats for today . . ." And the rain tapped on the empty house, echoing.

Outside, the garage chimed and lifted its door to reveal the waiting car. After a long wait the door swung down again.

At eight-thirty the eggs were shriveled and the toast was like stone. An aluminum wedge scraped them into the sink, where hot water whirled them down a metal throat which digested and flushed them away to the distant sea. The dirty dishes were dropped into a hot washer and emerged twinkling dry.

Nine-fifteen, sang the clock, *time to clean.*

Out of warrens in the wall, tiny robot mice darted. The rooms were acrawl with the small cleaning animals, all rubber and metal. They thudded against chairs, whirling their mustached runners, kneading the rug nap, sucking gently at hidden dust. Then, like mysterious invaders, they popped into their burrows. Their pink electric eyes faded. The house was clean.

Ten o'clock. The sun came out from behind the rain. The house stood alone in a city of rubble and ashes. This was the one house left standing. At night the ruined city gave off a radioactive glow which could be seen for miles.

Ten-fifteen. the garden sprinklers whirled up in golden founts, filling the soft morning air with scatterings of brightness. The water pelted windowpanes, running down the charred west side where the house had been burned evenly free of its white paint. The entire west face of the house was black, save for five places. Here the silhouette in paint of a man mowing a lawn. Here, as in a photograph, a woman bent to pick flowers. Still farther over, their images burned on wood in one titanic instant, a small boy, hands flung into the air; higher up, the image of a thrown ball, and opposite him a girl, hands raised to catch a ball which never came down.

The five spots of paint—the man, the woman, the children, the ball—remained. The rest was a thin charcoaled layer.

The gentle sprinkler rain filled the garden with falling light.

Until this day, how well the house had kept its peace. How carefully it had inquired, "Who goes there? What's the password?" and, getting no answer from lonely foxes and whining cats, it had shut up its windows and drawn shades in an old-maidenly preoccupation with self-protection which bordered on a mechanical paranoia.

It quivered at each sound, the house did. If a sparrow brushed a window, the shade snapped up. The bird, startled, flew off! No, not even a bird must touch the house!

The house was an altar with ten thousand attendants, big,

small, servicing, attending, in choirs. But the gods had gone away, and the ritual of the religion continued senselessly, uselessly.

Twelve noon.

A dog whined, shivering, on the front porch.

The front door recognized the dog voice and opened. The dog, once huge and fleshy, but now gone to bone and covered with sores, moved in and through the house, tracking mud. Behind it whirred angry mice, angry at having to pick up mud, angry at inconvenience.

For not a leaf fragment blew under the door but what the wall panels flipped open and the copper scrap rats flashed swiftly out. The offending dust, hair, or paper, seized in miniature steel jaws, was raced back to the burrows. There, down tubes which fed into the cellar, it was dropped into the sighing vent of an incinerator which sat like a evil Baal in a dark corner.

The dog ran upstairs, hysterically yelping to each door, at last realizing, as the house realized, that only silence was here.

It sniffed the air and scratched the kitchen door. Behind the door, the stove was making pancakes which filled the house with a rich baked odor and the scent of maple syrup.

The dog frothed at the mouth, lying at the door, sniffing, its eyes turned to fire. It ran wildly in circles, biting at its tail, spun in a frenzy, and died. It lay in the parlor for an hour.

Two o'clock, sang a voice.

Delicately sensing decay at last, the regiments of mice hummed out as softly as blown gray leaves in an electrical wind.

Two-fifteen.

The dog was gone.

In the cellar, the incinerator glowed suddenly and a whirl of sparks leaped up the chimney.

Two thirty-five.

Bridge tables sprouted from patio walls. Playing cards fluttered onto pads in a shower of pips. Martinis manifested on an oaken bench with egg-salad sandwiches. Music played.

But the tables were silent and the cards untouched.

At four o'clock the tables folded like great butterflies back through the paneled walls.

Four-thirty.

The nursery walls glowed.

Animals took shape: yellow giraffes, blue lions, pink antelopes, lilac panthers cavorting in crystal substance. The walls were glass. They looked out upon color and fantasy. Hidden films clocked through well-oiled sprockets, and the walls lived. The nursery floor was woven to resemble a crisp, cereal meadow. Over this ran aluminum roaches and iron crickets, and in the hot still air butterflies of delicate red tissue wavered among the sharp aroma of animal spoors! There was the sound like a great matted yellow hive of bees within a dark bellows, the lazy bumble of a purring lion. And there was the patter of okapi feet and the murmur of a fresh jungle rain, like other hoofs, falling upon the summer-starched grass. Now the walls dissolved into distances of parched weed, mile on mile, and warm endless sky. The animals drew away into thorn brakes and water holes.

It was the children's hour.

Five o'clock. The bath filled with clear hot water.

Six, seven, eight o'clock. The dinner dishes manipulated like magic tricks, and in the study a *click*. In the metal stand opposite the hearth where a fire now blazed up warmly, a cigar popped out, half an inch of soft gray ash on it, smoking, waiting.

Nine o'clock. The beds warmed their hidden circuits, for nights were cool here.

Nine-five. A voice spoke from the study ceiling:

"Mrs. McClellan, which poem would you like this evening?"

The house was silent.

The voice said at last, "Since you express no preference, I shall select a poem at random." Quiet music rose to back the voice. "Sara Teasdale. As I recall, your favorite. . . .

"There will come soft rains and the smell of the ground,
And swallows circling with their shimmering sound;

And frogs in the pools singing at night,
And wild plum trees in tremulous white;

Robins will wear their feathery fire,
Whistling their whims on a low fence-wire;

And not one will know of the war, not one
Will care at last when it is done.

Not one would mind, neither bird nor tree,
If mankind perished utterly;

And Spring herself, when she woke at dawn
Would scarcely know that we were gone.''

The fire burned on the stone hearth and the cigar fell away into a mound of quiet ash on its tray. The empty chairs faced each other between the silent walls, and the music played.

At ten o'clock the house began to die.

The wind blew. A falling tree bough crashed through the kitchen window. Cleaning solvent, bottled, shattered over the stove. The room was ablaze in an instant!

''Fire!'' screamed a voice. The house lights flashed, water pumps shot water from the ceilings. But the solvent spread on the linoleum, licking, eating, under the kitchen door, while the voices took it up in chorus: ''Fire, fire, fire!''

The house tried to save itself. Doors sprang tightly shut, but the windows were broken by the heat and the wind blew and sucked upon the fire.

The house gave ground as the fire in ten billion angry sparks moved with flaming ease from room to room and then up the stairs. While scurrying water rats squeaked from the walls, pistoled their water, and ran for more. And the wall sprays let down showers of mechanical rain.

But too late. Somewhere, sighing, a pump shrugged to a stop. The quenching rain ceased. The reserve water supply which had filled baths and washed dishes for many quiet days was gone.

The fire crackled up the stairs. It fed upon Picassos and Matisses in the upper halls, like delicacies, baking off the oily flesh, tenderly crisping the canvases into black shavings.

Now the fire lay in beds, stood in windows, changed the colors of drapes!

And then, reinforcements.

From attic trapdoors, blind robot faces peered down with faucet mouths gushing green chemical.

The fire backed off, as even an elephant must at the sight of a dead snake. Now there were twenty snakes whipping over the floor, killing the fire with a clear cold venom of green froth.

But the fire was clever. It had sent flame outside the house, up through the attic to the pumps there. An explosion! The attic brain which directed the pumps was shattered into bronze shrapnel on the beams.

The fire rushed back into every closet and felt of the clothes hung there.

The house shuddered, oak bone on bone, its bared skeleton cringing from the heat, its wire, its nerves revealed as if a surgeon had torn the skin off to let the red veins and capillaries quiver in the scalded air. Help, help! Fire! Run, run! Heat snapped mirrors like the first brittle winter ice. And the voices wailed Fire, fire, run, run, like a tragic nursery rhyme, a dozen voices, high, low, like children dying in a forest, alone, alone. And the voices fading as the wires popped their sheathings like hot chestnuts. One, two, three, four, five voices died.

In the nursery the jungle burned. Blue lions roared, purple giraffes bounded off. The panthers ran in circles, changing color, and ten million animals, running before the fire, vanished off toward a distant steaming river. . . .

Ten more voices died. In the last instant under the fire avalanche, other chorusus, oblivious, could be heard announcing the time, playing music, cutting the lawn by remote-control mower, or setting an umbrella frantically out and in the slamming and opening front door, a thousand things happening, like a clock shop when each clock strikes the hour insanely before or after the other, a scene of maniac confusion, yet unity; singing, screaming, a few last cleaning mice darting bravely out to carry the horrid ashes away! And one voice, with sublime disregard for the situation, read poetry aloud in the fiery study, until all the film spools burned, until all the wires withered and the circuits cracked.

The fire burst the house and let it slam flat down, puffing out skirts of spark and smoke.

In the kitchen, an instant before the rain of fire and timber, the stove could be seen making breakfasts at a psychopathic rate, ten dozen eggs, six loaves of toast, twenty dozen bacon strips, which, eaten by fire, started the stove working again, hysterically hissing!

The crash. The attic smashing into kitchen and parlor. The parlor into cellar, cellar into sub-cellar. Deep freeze, armchair, film tapes, circuits, beds, and all like skeletons thrown in a cluttered mound deep under.

Smoke and silence. A great quantity of smoke.

Dawn showed faintly in the east. Among the ruins, one wall stood alone. Within the wall, a last voice said, over and over again and again, even as the sun rose to shine upon the heaped rubble and steam:

"Today is August 5, 2026, today is August 5, 2026, today is . . ."

DEAR DEVIL

Eric Frank Russell (1905–1978)

OTHER WORLDS
May

The wonderful and underrated Eric Frank Russell returns to this series with one of his best stories (and that is very high praise). It concerns one of his favorite themes, Earthman against alien. Russell could write almost any kind of science fiction—he excelled at adventure and action—but he seemed to really enjoy the automatic dramatic tension of encounters between two different intelligent species. "Dear Devil" contains the warmth and compassion that he often brought to his work, attributes not commonly found in the science fiction of his day. The title character in this story should remain in your mind for a long time—if he doesn't, you may need some professional help.

—M.H.G.

In the earliest tales of interplanetary travel, natives of other worlds were usually presented as reasonably friendly. Earthmen visited them as inquisitive travelers; they visited us likewise. The first case of a hostile encounter was The War of the Worlds, *by H. G. Wells, published in 1898.*

That did it. The tale of interplanetary warfare was so dramatic that it set the fashion for what followed. Interplanetary warfare and nothing but interplanetary warfare. And Mars was always particularly demonic; partly because of Wells's tale, partly because of the association with the god of war.

It took some courage, then, for Russell to reverse this, but the result was a terrific story, and a moving one. And a recipe for success, as well, as Steven Spielberg recently demonstrated with the motion picture E.T.

And there's a moral, too. I hate pointing out morals, but this one is so important I don't want anyone to miss it. If the great difference between Martian and Earthman could be bridged, did it make sense to destroy a planet over much smaller differences?

—I.A.

The first Martian vessel descended upon Earth with the slow, stately fall of a grounded balloon. It did resemble a large balloon in that it was spherical and had a strange buoyance out of keeping with its metallic construction. Beyond this superficial appearance all similarity to anything Terrestrial ceased.

There were no rockets, no crimson venturis, no external projections other than several solaradiant distorting grids which boosted the ship in any desired direction through the cosmic field. There were no observation ports. All viewing was done through a transparent band running right around the fat belly of the sphere. The bluish, nightmarish crew was assembled behind that band, surveying the world with great multifaceted eyes.

They gazed through the band in utter silence as they examined this world which was Terra. Even if they had been capable of speech they would have said nothing. But none among them had a talkative facility in any sonic sense. At this quiet moment none needed it.

The scene outside was one of the untrammeled desolation. Scraggy blue-green grass clung to tired ground right away to the horizon scarred by ragged mountains. Dismal bushes struggled for life here and there, some with the pathetic air of striving to become trees as once their ancestors had been. To the right, a long, straight scar through the grass betrayed the sterile lumpiness of rocks at odd places. Too rugged and too narrow ever to have been a road, it suggested no more than the desiccating remnants of a long-gone wall. And over all this loomed a ghastly sky.

Captain Skhiva eyed his crew, spoke to them with his sign-talking tentacle. The alternative was contact-telepathy which required physical touch.

"It is obvious that we are out of luck. We could have done no worse had we landed on the empty satellite. However, it is safe to go out. Anyone who wishes to explore a little while may do so."

One of them gesticulated back at him. "Captain, don't you wish to be the first to step upon this world?"

"It is of no consequence. If anyone deems it an honor, he is welcome to it." He pulled the lever opening both air-lock doors. Thicker, heavier air crowded in and pressure went up a little. "Beware of overexertion," he warned as they went out.

Poet Fander touched him, tentacles tip to tip as he sent his thoughts racing through their nerve ends. "This confirms all that we saw as we approached. A stricken planet far gone in its death throes. What do you suppose caused it?"

"I have not the remotest idea. I would like to know. If it has been smitten by natural forces, what might they do to Mars?" His troubled mind sent its throb of worry up Fander's contacting tentacle. "A pity that this planet had not been farther out instead of closer in; we might then have observed the preceding phenomena from the surface of Mars. It is so difficult properly to view this one against the Sun."

"That applies still more to the next world, the misty one," observed Poet Fander.

"I know it. I am beginning to fear what we may find there. If it proves to be equally dead, then we are stalled until we can make the big jump outward."

"Which won't be in our lifetimes."

"I doubt it," agreed Captain Skhiva. "We might move fast with the help of friends. We shall be slow—alone." He turned to watch his crew writhing in various directions across the grim landscape. "They find it good to be on firm ground. But what is a world without life and beauty? In a short time they will grow tired of it."

Fander said thoughtfully, "Nevertheless, I would like to see more of it. May I take out the lifeboat?"

"You are a songbird, not a pilot," reproved Captain Skhiva. "Your function is to maintain morale by entertaining us, not to roam around in a lifeboat."

"But I know how to handle it. Every one of us was trained to handle it. Let me take it that I may see more."

"Haven't we seen enough, even before we landed? What else is there to see? Cracked and distorted roads about to dissolve into nothingness. Ages-old cities, torn and broken, crumbling into dust. Shattered mountains and charred forests and craters little smaller than those upon the Moon. No sign of any superior lifeform still surviving. Only the grass, the shrubs, and various animals, two- or four-legged, that flee at our approach. Why do you wish to see more?''

''There is poetry even in death,'' said Fander.

''Even so, it remains repulsive.'' Skhiva gave a little shiver. ''All right. Take the lifeboat. Who am I to question the weird workings of the nontechnical mind?''

''Thank you, Captain.''

''It is nothing. See that you are back by dusk.'' Breaking contact, he went to the lock, curled snakishly on its outer rim and brooded, still without bothering to touch the new world. So much attempted, so much done—for so poor reward.

He was still pondering it when the lifeboat soared out of its lock. Expressionlessly, his multifaceted eyes watched the energized grids change angle as the boat swung into a curve and floated away like a little bubble. Skhiva was sensitive to futility.

The crew came back well before darkness. A few hours were enough. Just grass and shrubs and child-trees straining to grow up. One had discovered a grassless oblong that once might have been the site of a dwelling. He brought back a small piece of its foundation, a lump of perished concrete which Skhiva put by for later analysis.

Another had found a small, brown, six-legged insect, but his nerve ends had heard it crying when he picked it up, so hastily he had put it down and let it go free. Small, clumsily moving animals had been seen hopping in the distance, but all had dived down holes in the ground before any Martian could get near. All the crew were agreed upon one thing: the silence and solemnity of a people's passing was unendurable.

Fander beat the sinking of the sun by half a time-unit. His bubble drifted under a great, black cloud, sank to ship level, came in. The rain started a moment later, roaring down in frenzied torrents while they stood behind the transparent band and marveled at so much water.

After a while, Captain Skhiva told them, ''We must accept what we find. We have drawn a blank. The cause of this world's condition is a mystery to be solved by others with more time and better equipment. It is for us to abandon this graveyard and try the misty planet. We will take off early in the morning.''

None commented, but Fander followed him to his room, made contact with a tentacle-touch.

"One could live here, Captain."

"I am not so sure of that." Skhiva coiled on his couch, suspending his tentacles on the various limb-rests. The blue sheen of him was reflected by the back wall. "In some places are rocks emitting alpha sparks. They are dangerous."

"Of course, Captain. But I can sense them and avoid them."

"You?" Skhiva stared up at him.

"Yes, Captain. I wish to be left here."

"What? In this place of appalling repulsiveness?"

"It has an all-pervading air of ugliness and despair," admitted Poet Fander. "All destruction is ugly. But by accident I have found a little beauty. It heartens me. I would like to seek its source."

"To what beauty do you refer?" Skhiva demanded.

Fander tried to explain the alien in nonalien terms.

"Draw it for me," ordered Skhiva.

Fander drew it, gave him the picture, said, "There!"

Gazing at it for a long time, Skhiva handed it back, mused awhile, then spoke along the other's nerves. "We are individuals with all the rights of individuals. As an individual, I don't think that picture sufficiently beautiful to be worth the tail-tip of a domestic *arlan*. I will admit that it is not ugly, even that it is pleasing."

"But, Captain—"

"As an individual," Skhiva went on, "you have an equal right to your opinions, strange though they may be. If you really wish to stay I cannot refuse you. I am entitled only to think you a little crazy." He eyed Fander again. "When do you hope to be picked up?"

"This year, next year, sometime, never."

"It may well be never," Skhiva reminded him. "Are you prepared to face that prospect?"

"One must always be prepared to face the consequences of his own actions," Fander pointed out.

"True." Skhiva was reluctant to surrender. "But have you given the matter serious thought?"

"I am a nontechnical component. I am not guided by thought."

"Then by what?"

"By my desires, emotions, instincts. By my inward feelings."

Skhiva said fervently, "The twin moons preserve us!"

"Captain, sing me a song of home and play me the tinkling harp."

"Don't be silly. I have not the ability."

"Captain, if it required no more than careful thought you would be able to do it?"

"Doubtlessly," agreed Skhiva, seeing the trap but unable to avoid it.

"There you are!" said Fander pointedly.

"I give up. I cannot argue with someone who casts aside the accepted rules of logic and invents his own. You are governed by notions that defeat me."

"It is not a matter of logic or illogic," Fander told him. "It is merely a matter of viewpoint. You see certain angles; I see others."

"For example?"

"You won't pin me down that way. I can find examples. For instance, do you remember the formula for determining the phase of a series tuned circuit?"

"Most certainly."

"I felt sure you would. You are a technician. You have registered it for all time as a matter of technical utility." He paused, staring at Skhiva. "I know that formula, too. It was mentioned to me, casually, many years ago. It is of no use to me—yet I have never forgotten it."

"Why?"

"Because it holds the beauty of rhythm. It is a poem," Fander explained.

Skhiva sighed and said, "I don't get it."

"One upon R into omega L minus one upon omega C," recited Fander. "A perfect hexameter." He showed his amusement as the other rocked back.

After a while Skhiva remarked, "It could be sung. One could dance to it."

"Same with this." Fander exhibited his rough sketch. "This holds beauty. Where there is beauty there once was talent—may still be talent for all we know. Where talent abides is also greatness. In the realms of greatness we may find powerful friends. We *need* such friends."

"You win." Skhiva made a gesture of defeat. "We leave you to your self-chosen fate in the morning."

"Thank you, Captain."

* * *

That same streak of stubbornness which made Skhiva a worthy commander induced him to take one final crack at Fander shortly before departure. Summoning him to his room, he eyed the poet calculatingly.

"You are still of the same mind?"

"Yes, Captain."

"Then does it not occur to you as strange that I should be so content to abandon this planet if indeed it does hold the remnants of greatness?"

"No."

"Why not?" Skhiva stiffened slightly.

"Captain, I think you are a little afraid because you suspect what I suspect—that there was no natural disaster. They did it themselves, to themselves."

"We have no proof of it," said Skhiva uneasily.

"No, Captain." Fander paused there without desire to add more.

"*If* this is their own sad handiwork," Skhiva commented at length, "what are our chances of finding friends among people so much to be feared?"

"Poor," admitted Fander. "But that—being the product of cold thought—means little to me. I am animated by warm hopes."

"There you go again, blatantly discarding reason in favor of an idle dream. Hoping, hoping, hoping—to achieve the impossible."

Fander said, "The difficult can be done at once; the impossible takes a little longer."

"Your thoughts make my orderly mind feel lopsided. Every remark is a flat denial of something that makes sense." Skhiva transmitted the sensation of a lugubrious chuckle. "Oh, well, we live and learn." He came forward, moving closer to the other. "All your supplies are assembled outside. Nothing remains but to bid you goodby."

They embraced in the Martian manner. Leaving the lock, Poet Fander watched the big sphere shudder and glide up. It soared without sound, shrinking steadily until it was a mere dot entering a cloud. A moment later it had gone.

He remained there, looking at the cloud, for a long, long time. Then he turned his attention to the load-sled holding his supplies. Climbing onto its tiny, exposed front seat, he shifted the control which energized the flotation-grids, let it rise a few feet. The higher the rise the greater the expenditure of power.

He wished to conserve power; there was no knowing how long he might need it. So at low alttude and gentle pace he let the sled glide in the general direction of the thing of beauty.

Later, he found a dry cave in the hill on which his objective stood. It took him two days of careful, cautious raying to square its walls, ceiling and floor, plus half a day with a powered fan driving out silicate dust. After that, he stowed his supplies at the back, parked the sled near the front, set up a curtaining force-screen across the entrance. The hole in the hill was now home.

Slumber did not come easily that first night. He lay within the cave, a ropy, knotted thing of glowing blue with enormous, beelike eyes, and found himself listening for harps that played sixty million miles away. His tentacle-ends twitched in involuntary search of the telepathic-contact songs that would go with the harps, and twitched in vain. Darkness grew deep, and all the world a monstrous stillness held. His hearing organs craved for the eventide flip-flop of sand-frogs, but there were no frogs. He wanted the homely drone of night beetles, but none droned. Except for once when something faraway howled its heart at the Moon, there was nothing, nothing.

In the morning he washed, ate, took out the sled and explored the site of a small town. He found little to satisfy his curiosity, no more than mounds of shapeless rubble on ragged, faintly oblong foundations. It was a graveyard of long-dead domiciles, rotting, weedy, near to complete oblivion. A view from five hundred feet up gave him only one piece of information: the orderliness of outlines showed that these people had been tidy, methodical.

But tidiness is not beauty in itself. He came back to the top of his hill and sought solace with the thing that was beauty.

His explorations continued, not systematically as Skhiva would have performed them, but in accordance with his own mercurial whims. At times he saw many animals, singly or in groups, none resembling anything Martian. Some scattered at full gallop when his sled swooped over them. Some dived into groundholes, showing a brief flash of white, absurd tails, Others, four-footed, long-faced, sharp-toothed, hunted in gangs and bayed at him in concert with harsh, defiant voices.

On the seventieth day, in a deep, shadowed glade to the north, he spotted a small group of new shapes slinking along in single file. He recognized them at a glance, knew them so well that his searching eyes sent an immediate thrill of triumph into his mind.

They were ragged, dirty, and no more than half grown, but the thing of beauty had told him what they were.

Hugging the ground low, he swept around in a wide curve that brought him to the farther end of the glade. His sled sloped slightly into the drop as it entered the glade. He could see them better now, even the soiled pinkishness of their thin legs. They were moving away from him, with fearful caution, but the silence of his swoop gave them no warning.

The rearmost one of the stealthy file fooled him at the last moment. He was hanging over the side of the sled, tentacles outstretched in readiness to snatch the end one with the wild mop of yellow hair when, responding to some sixth sense, his intended victim threw itself flat. His grasp shot past a couple of feet short, and he got a glimpse of frightened gray eyes two seconds before a dexterous side-tilt of the sled enabled him to make good his loss by grabbing the less wary next in line.

This one was dark-haired, a bit bigger, and sturdier. It fought madly at his holding limbs while he gained altitude. Then suddenly, realizing the queer nature of its bonds, it writhed around and looked straight at him. The result was unexpected; it closed its eyes and went completely limp.

It was still limp when he bore it into the cave, but its heart continued to beat and its lungs to draw. Laying it carefully on the softness of his bed, he moved to the cave's entrance and waited for it to recover. Eventually it stirred, sat up, gazed confusedly at the facing wall. Its black eyes moved slowly around, taking in the surroundings. Then they saw Fander. They widened tremendously, and their owner began to make high-pitched, unpleasant noises as it tried to back away through the solid wall. It screamed so much, in one rising throb after another, that Fander slithered out of the cave, right out of sight, and sat in the cold winds until the noises had died down.

A couple of hours later he made cautious reappearance to offer it food, but its reaction was so swift, hysterical, and heartrending that he dropped his load and hid himself as though the fear were his own. The food remained untouched for two full days. On the third, a little of it was eaten. Fander ventured within.

Although the Martian did not go near, the boy cowered away, murmuring, "Devil! Devil!" His eyes were red, with dark discoloration beneath them.

"Devil!" thought Fander, totally unable to repeat the alien word, but wondering what it meant. He used his sign-talking tentacle in valiant effort to convey something reassuring. The attempt was wasted. The other watched its writhings half in fear, half with distaste, and showed complete lack of comprehension. He let the tentacle gently slither forward across the floor, hoping to make thought-contact. The other recoiled from it as from a striking snake.

"Patience," he reminded himself. "The impossible takes a little longer."

Periodically he showed himself with food and drink, and nighttimes he slept fitfully on the coarse, damp grass beneath lowering skies—while the prisoner who was his guest enjoyed the softness of the bed, the warmth of the cave, the security of the force-screen.

Time came when Fander betrayed an unpoetic shrewdness by using the other's belly to estimate the ripeness of the moment. When, on the eighth day, he noted that his food-offerings were now being taken regularly, he took a meal of his own at the edge of the cave, within plain sight, and observed that the other's appetite was not spoiled. That night he slept just within the cave, close to the force-screen, and as far from the boy as possible. The boy stayed awake late, watching him, always watching him, but gave way to slumber in the small hours.

A fresh attempt at sign-talking brought no better results than before, and the boy still refused to touch his offered tentacle. All the same, he was gaining ground slowly. His overtures still were rejected, but with less revulsion. Gradually, ever so gradually, the Martian shape was becoming familiar, almost acceptable.

The sweet savor of success was Fander's in the middle of the next day. The boy had displayed several spells of emotional sickness during which he lay on his front with shaking body and emitted low noises while his eyes watered profusely. At such times the Martian felt strangely helpless and inadequate. On this occasion, during another attack, he took advantage of the sufferer's lack of attention and slid near enough to snatch away the box by the bed.

From the box he drew his tiny electroharp, plugged its connectors, switched it on, touched its strings with delicate affection. Slowly he began to play, singing an accompaniment deep inside himself. For he had no voice with which to sing out loud, but the harp sang it for him. The boy ceased his quiverings, sat up, all his attention upon the dexterous play of the tentacles and the music they conjured forth. And when he judged that at last the listener's mind was captured, Fander ceased with easy, quieting strokes, gently offered him the harp. The boy registered interest and reluctance. Careful not to move nearer, not an inch nearer, Fander offered it at full tentacle length. The boy had to take four steps to get it. He took them.

That was the start. They played together, day after day and sometimes a little into the night, while almost imperceptibly the distance between them was reduced. Finally they sat together, side by side, and the boy had not yet learned to laugh but no longer did he show unease. He could now extract a simple tune from the instrument and was pleased with his own aptitude in a solemn sort of way.

One evening as darkness grew, and the things that sometimes howled at the moon were howling again, Fander offered his tentacle-tip for the hundredth time. Always the gesture had been unmistakable even if its motive was not clear, yet always it had been rebuffed. But now, now, five fingers curled around it in shy desire to please.

With a fervent prayer that human nerves would function just like Martian ones, Fander poured his thoughts through, swiftly, lest the warm grip be loosened too soon.

"Do not fear me. I cannot help my shape any more than you can help yours. I am your friend, your father, your mother. I need you as much as you need me."

The boy let go of him, began quiet, half-stifled whimpering noises. Fander put a tentacle on his shoulder, made little patting motions that he imagined were wholly Martian. For some inexplicable reason, this made matters worse. At his wits' end what to do for the best, what action to take that might be understandable in Terrestrial terms, he gave the problem up, surrendered to his instinct, put a long, ropy limb around the boy and held him close until the noises ceased and slumber came. It was then he realized the child he had taken was much younger than he had estimated. He nursed him through the night.

Much practice was necessary to make conversation. The boy had to learn to put mental drive behind his thoughts, for it was beyond Fander's power to suck them out of him.

"What is your name?"

Fander got a picture of thin legs running rapidly.

He returned it in question form. "Speedy?"

An affirmative.

"What name do you call me?"

An unflattering montage of monsters.

"Devil?"

The picture whirled around, became confused. There was a trace of embarrassment.

"Devil will do," assured Fander. He went on. "Where are your parents?"

More confusion.

"You must have had parents. Everyone has a father and mother, haven't they? Don't you remember yours?"

Muddled ghost-pictures. Grown-ups leaving children. Grown-ups avoiding children, as if they feared them.

"What is the first thing you remember?"

"Big man walking with me. Carried me a bit. Walked again."

"What happened to him?"

"Went away. Said he was sick. Might make me sick too."

"Long ago?"

Confusion.

Fander changed his aim. "What of those other children—have they no parents either?"

"All got nobody."

"But you've got somebody now, haven't you, Speedy?"

Doubtfully. "Yes."

Fander pushed it further. "Would you rather have me, or those other children?" He let it rest a moment before he added, "Or both?"

"Both," said Speedy with no hesitation. His fingers toyed with the harp.

"Would you like to help me look for them tomorrow and bring them here? And if they are scared of me will you help them not to be afraid?"

"Sure!" said Speedy, licking his lips and sticking his chest out.

"Then," said Fander, "perhaps you would like to go for a walk today? You've been too long in this cave. Will you come for a walk with me?"

"Y'betcha!"

Side by side they went for a short walk, one trotting rapidly along, the other slithering. The child's spirits perked up with this trip in the open; it was as if the sight of the sky and the feel of the grass made him realize at last that he was not exactly a prisoner. His formerly solemn features became animated, he made exclamations that Fander could not understand, and once he laughed at nothing for the sheer joy of it. On two occasions he grabbed a tentacle-tip in order to tell Fander something, performing the action as if it were in every way as natural as his own speech.

They got out the load-sled in the morning. Fander took the front seat and the controls; Speedy squatted behind him with hands gripping his harness-belt. With a shallow soar, they headed for the glade. Many small, white-tailed animals bolted down holes as they passed over.

"Good for dinner," remarked Speedy, touching him and speaking through the touch.

Fander felt sickened. Meat-eaters! It was not until a queer feeling of shame and apology came back at him that he knew the other had felt his revulsion. He wished he'd been swift to blanket that reaction before the boy could sense it, but he could not be blamed for the effect of so bald a statement taking him so completely unaware. However, it had produced another step forward in their mutual relationship—Speedy desired his good opinion.

Within fifteen minutes they struck it lucky. At a point half a mile south of the glade Speedy let out a shrill yell and pointed downward. A small, golden-haired figure was standing there on a slight rise, staring fascinatedly upward at the phenomenon in the sky. A second tiny shape, with red but equally long hair, was at the bottom of the slope gazing in similar wonderment. Both came to their senses and turned to flee as the sled tilted toward them.

Ignoring the yelps of excitement close behind him and the pulls upon his belt, Fander swooped, got first one, then the other. This left him with only one limb to right the sled and gain height. If the victims had fought he would have had his work cut out to make it. They did not fight. They shrieked as he snatched them and then relaxed with closed eyes.

The sled climbed, glided a mile at five hundred feet. Fander's attention was divided between his limp prizes, the controls and the horizon when suddenly a thunderous rattling sounded on the metal base on the sled, the entire framework shuddered, a strip of metal flew from its leading edge and things made whining sounds toward the clouds.

"Old Graypate," bawled Speedy, jigging around but keeping away from the rim. "He's shooting at us."

The spoken words meant nothing to the Martian, and he could not spare a limb for the contact the other had forgotten to make. Grimly righting the sled, he gave it full power. Whatever damage it had suffered had not affected its efficiency; it shot forward at a pace that set the red and golden hair of the captives streaming in the wind. Perforce his landing by the cave was clumsy. The sled bumped down and lurched across forty yards of grass.

First things first. Taking the quiet pair into the cave, he made them comfortable on the bed, came out and examined the sled. There were half a dozen deep dents in its flat underside, two bright furrows angling across one rim. He made contact with Speedy.

"What were you trying to tell me?"

"Old Graypate shot at us."

The mind-picture burst upon him vividly and with electrifying effect: a vision of a tall, white-haired, stern-faced old man with a tubular weapon propped upon his shoulder while it spat fire upward. A white-haired old man! An adult!

His grip was tight on the other's arm. "What is this oldster to you?"

"Nothing much. He lives near us in the shelters."

Picture of a long, dusty concrete burrow, badly damaged, its ceiling marked with the scars of a lighting system which had rotted away to nothing. The old man living hermitlike at one end; the children at the other. The old man was sour, taciturn, kept the children at a distance, spoke to them seldom but was quick to respond when they were menaced. He had guns. Once, he had killed many wild dogs that had eaten two children.

"People left us near shelters because Old Graypate was there, and had guns," informed Speedy.

"But why does he keep away from children? Doesn't he like children?"

"Don't know." He mused a moment. "Once told us that old people could get very sick and make young ones sick—and then we'd all die. Maybe he's afraid of making us die." Speedy wasn't very sure about it.

So there was some much-feared disease around, something

contagious, to which adults were peculiarly susceptible. Without hesitation they abandoned their young at the first onslaught, hoping that at least the children would live. Sacrifice after sacrifice that the remnants of the race might survive. Heartbreak after heartbreak as elders chose death alone rather than death together.

Yet Graypate himself was depicted as very old. Was this an exaggeration of the child-mind?

"I must meet Graypate."

"He will shoot," declared Speedy positively. "He knows by now that you took me. He saw you take the others. He will wait for you and shoot."

"We will find some way to avoid that."

"How?"

"When these two have become my friends, just as you have become my friend, I will take all three of you back to the shelters. You can find Graypate for me and tell him that I am not as ugly as I look."

"I don't think you're ugly," denied Speedy.

The picture Fander got along with that gave him the weirdest sensation of pleasure. It was of a vague, shadowy but distorted body with a clear human face.

The new prisoners were female. Fander knew it without being told because they were daintier than Speedy and had the warm, sweet smell of females. That meant complications. Maybe they were mere children, and maybe they lived together in the shelter, but he was permitting none of that while they were in his charge. Fander might be outlandish by other standards but he had a certain primness. Forthwith he cut another and smaller cave for Speedy and himself.

Neither of the girls saw him for two days. Keeping well out of their sight, he let Speedy take them food, talk to them, prepare them for the shape of the thing to come. On the third day he presented himself for inspection at a distance. Despite forewarnings they went sheet-white, clung together, but uttered no distressing sounds. He played his harp a little while, withdrew, came back in the evening and played for them again.

Encouraged by Speedy's constant and self-assured flow of propaganda, one of them grasped a tentacle-tip next day. What came along the nerves was not a picture so much as an ache, a desire, a childish yearning. Fander backed out of the cave, found wood, spent the whole night using the sleepy Speedy as a model, and fashioned the wood into a tiny, jointed semblance of a human being. He was no sculptor, but he possessed a natural delicacy of touch, and the poet in him ran through his limbs and expressed itself in the model. Making a thorough job of it, he clothed it in Terrestrial fashion, colored its face, fixed upon its features the pleasure-grimace which humans call a smile.

He gave her the doll the moment she awakened in the morning. She took it eagerly, hungrily, with wide, glad eyes. Hugging it to her unformed bosom, she crooned over it—and he knew that the strange emptiness within her was gone.

Though Speedy was openly contemptuous of this manifest waste of effort, Fander set to and made a second mannikin. It did not take quite as long. Practice on the first had made him swifter, more dexterous. He was able to present it to the other child by midafternoon. Her acceptance was made with shy grace, she held the doll close as if it meant more than the whole of her sorry world. In her thrilled concentration upon the gift, she did not notice his nearness, his closeness, and when he offered a tentacle, she took it.

He said, simply, "I love you."

Her mind was too untrained to drive a response, but her great eyes warmed.

Fander sat on the grounded sled at a point a mile east of the glade and watched the three children walk hand in hand toward the hidden shelters. Speedy was the obvious leader, hurrying them onward, bossing them with the noisy assurance of one who has been around and considers himself sophisticated. In spite of this, the girls paused at intervals to turn and wave to the ropy, bee-eyed thing they'd left behind. And Fander dutifully waved back, always using his signal-tentacle because it had not occurred to him that any tentacle would serve.

They sank from sight behind a rise of ground. He remained on the sled, his multifaceted gaze going over his surroundings or studying the angry sky now threatening rain. The ground was a dull, dead gray-green all the way to the horizon. There was no relief from that drab color, not one shining patch of white, gold, or crimson such as dotted the meadows of Mars. There was only the eternal gray-green and his own brilliant blueness.

Before long a sharp-faced, four-footed thing revealed itself in the grass, raised its head and howled at him. The sound was an eerily urgent wail that ran across the grasses and moaned into the distance. It brought others of its kind, two, ten, twenty. Their defiance increased with their numbers until there was a large band of them edging toward him with lips drawn back, teeth exposed. Then there came a sudden and undetectable flock-command which caused them to cease their slinking and spring forward like one, slavering as they came. They did it with the hungry, red-eyed frenzy of animals motivated by something akin to madness.

Repulsive though it was, the sight of creatures craving meat—even strange blue meat—did not bother Fander. He slipped a control a notch, the flotation grids radiated, the sled soared twenty feet. So calm and easy an escape so casually performed infuriated the wild dog pack beyond all measure. Arriving beneath the sled, they made futile springs upward, fell back upon one another, bit and slashed each other, leaped again and again. The pandemonium they set up was a compound of snarls, yelps, barks, and growls, the ferocious expressions of extreme hate. They exuded a pungent odor of dry hair and animal sweat.

Reclining on the sled in a maddening pose of disdain, Fander let the insane ones rave below. They raced around in tight circles, shrieking insults at him and biting each other. This went on for some time and ended with a spurt of ultra-rapid cracks from the direction of the glade. Eight dogs fell dead. Two flopped and struggled to crawl away. Ten yelped in agony, made off on three legs. The unharmed ones flashed away to some place where they could make a meal of the escaping limpers. Fander lowered the sled.

Speedy stood on the rise with Graypate. The latter restored his weapon to the crook of his arm, rubbed his chin thoughtfully, ambled forward.

Stopping five yards from the Martian, the old Earthman again massaged his chin whiskers, then said, "It sure is the darnedest thing, just the darnedest thing!"

"No use talking *at* him," advised Speedy. "You've got to touch him, like I told you."

"I know, I know." Graypate betrayed a slight impatience. "All in good time. I'll touch him when I'm ready." He stood there, gazing at Fander with eyes that were very pale and very sharp. "Oh, well, here goes." He offered a hand.

Fander placed a tentacle end in it.

"Jeepers, he's cold," commented Graypate, closing his grip. "Colder than a snake."

"He isn't a snake," Speedy contradicted fiercely.

"Ease up, ease up—I didn't say he is." Graypate seemed fond of repetitive phrases.

"He doesn't feel like one, either," persisted Speedy, who had never felt a snake and did not wish to.

Fander boosted a thought through. "I come from the fourth planet. Do you know what that means?"

"I ain't ignorant," snapped Graypate aloud.

"No need to reply vocally. I receive your thoughts exactly as you receive mine. Your responses are much stronger than the boy's, and I can understand you easily."

"Humph!" said Graypate to the world at large.

"I have been anxious to find an adult because the children can tell me little. I would like to ask questions. Do you feel inclined to answer questions?"

"It depends," answered Graypate, becoming leery.

"Never mind. Answer them if you wish. My only desire is to help you."

"Why?" asked Graypate, searching around for a percentage.

"We need intelligent friends."

"Why?"

"Our numbers are small, our resources poor. In visiting this world and the misty one we've come near to the limit of our ability. But with assistance we could go farther. I think that if we could help you a time might come when you could help us."

Graypate pondered it cautiously, forgetting that the inward workings of his mind were wide open to the other. Chronic suspicion was the keynote of his thoughts, suspicion based on life experiences and recent history. But inward thoughts ran both ways, and his own mind detected the clear sincerity in Fander's.

So he said. "Fair enough. Say more."

"What caused all this?" inquired Fander, waving a limb at the world.

"War," said Graypate. "The last war we'll ever have. The entire place went nuts."

"How did that come about?"

"You've got me there." Graypate gave the problem grave consideration. "I reckon it wasn't just any one thing; it was a multitude of things sort of piling themselves up."

"Such as?"

"Differences in people. Some were colored differently in their bodies, others in their ideas, and they couldn't get along. Some bred faster than others, wanted more room, more food. There wasn't any more room or more food. The world was full, and nobody could shove in except by pushing another out. My old man told me plenty before he died, and he always maintained that if folk had had the hoss-sense to keep their numbers down, there might not—"

"Your old man?" interjected Fander. "Your father? Didn't all this occur in your own lifetime?"

"It did not. I saw none of it. I am the son of the son of a survivor."

"Let's go back to the cave," put in Speedy, bored with the silent contact-talk. "I want to show him our harp."

They took no notice, and Fander went on, "Do you think there might be a lot of others still living?"

"Who knows?" Graypate was moody about it. "There isn't any way of telling how many are wandering around the other side of the globe, maybe still killing each other, or starving to death, or dying of the sickness."

"What sickness is this?"

"I couldn't tell what it is called." Graypate scratched his head confusedly. "My old man told me a few times, but I've long forgotten. Knowing the name wouldn't do me any good, see? He said his father told him that it was part of the war, it got invented and was spread deliberately—and it's still with us."

"What are its symptoms?"

"You go hot and dizzy. You get black swellings in the armpits. In forty-eight hours you're dead. Old ones get it first. The kids then catch it unless you make away from them mighty fast."

"It is nothing familiar to me," said Fander, unable to recognize cultured bubonic. "In any case, I'm not a medical expert." He eyed Graypate. "But you seem to have avoided it."

"Sheer luck," opined Graypate. "Or maybe I can't get it. There was a story going around during the war that some folk might develop immunity to it, durned if I know why. Could be that I'm immune, but I don't count on it."

"So you keep your distance from these children?"

"Sure." He glanced at Speedy. "I shouldn't really have come along with this kid. He's got a lousy chance as it is without me increasing the odds."

"That is thoughtful of you," Fander put over softly. "Especially seeing that you must be lonely."

Graypate bristled and his thought-flow became aggressive. "I ain't grieving for company. I can look after myself, like I have done since my old man went away to curl up by himself. I'm on my own feet. So's every other guy."

"I believe that," said Fander. "You must pardon me—I'm a stranger here myself. I judged you by my own feelings. Now and again I get pretty lonely."

"How come?" demanded Graypate, staring at him. "You ain't telling me they dumped you and left you, on your own?"

"They did."

"Man!" exclaimed Graypate fervently.

Man! It was a picture resembling Speedy's conception, a vision elusive in form but firm and human in face. The oldster was reacting to what he considered a predicament rather than a choice, and the reaction came on a wave of sympathy.

Fander struck promptly and hard. "You see how I'm fixed. The companionship of wild animals is nothing to me. I need someone intelligent enough to like my music and forget my looks, someone intelligent enough to—"

"I ain't so sure we're that smart," Graypate chipped in. He let his gaze swing morbidly around the landscape. "Not when I see this graveyard and think of how it looked in granpop's days."

"Every flower blooms from the dust of a hundred dead ones," answered Fander.

"What are flowers?"

It shocked the Martian. He had projected a mind-picture of a trumpet lily, crimson and shining, and Graypate's brain had juggled it around, uncertain whether it was fish, flesh, or fowl.

"Vegetable growths, like these." Fander plucked half a dozen blades of blue-green grass. "But more colorful, and sweet-scented." He transmitted the brilliant vision of a mile-square field of trumpet lilies, red and glowing.

"Glory be!" said Graypate. "We've nothing like those."

"Not here," agreed Fander. "Not here." He gestured toward the horizon. "Elsewhere may be plenty. If we got together we could be company for each other, we could learn things from each other. We could pool our ideas, our efforts, and search for flowers far away—also for more people."

"Folk just won't get together in large bunches. They stick to each other in family groups until the plague breaks them up. Then they abandon the kids. The bigger the crowd, the bigger the risk of someone contaminating the lot." He leaned on his gun, staring at the other, his thought-forms shaping themselves in dull solemnity. "When a guy gets hit, he goes away and takes it on his own. The end is a personal contract between him and his God, with no witnesses. Death's a pretty private affair these days."

"What, after all these years? Don't you think that by this time the disease may have run its course and exhausted itself?"

"Nobody knows—and nobody's gambling on it."

"I would gamble," said Fander.

"You ain't like us. You mightn't be able to catch it."

"Or I might get it worse, and die more painfully."

"Mebbe," admitted Graypate, doubtfully. "Anyway, you're looking at it from a different angle. You've been dumped on your own some. What've you got to lose?"

"My life," said Fander.

Graypate rocked back on his heels, then said, "Yes, sir, that is a gamble. A guy can't bet any heavier than that." He rubbed his chin whiskers as before. "All right, all right, I'll take you up on that. You come right here and live with us." His grip tightened on his gun, his knuckles showing white. "On this understanding: The moment you feel sick you get out fast, and for keeps. If you don't, I'll bump you and drag you away myself, even if that makes me get it too. The kids come first, see?"

The shelters were far roomier than the cave. There were eighteen children living in them, all skinny with their prolonged diet of roots, edible herbs, and an occasional rabbit. The youngest and most sensitive of them ceased to be terrified of Fander after ten days. Within four months his slithering shape of blue ropiness had become a normal adjunct to their small, limited world.

Six of the youngsters were males older than Speedy, one of them much older but not yet adult. He beguiled them with his harp, teaching them to play, and now and again giving them ten-minute rides on the load-sled as a special treat. He made dolls for the girls and queer, cone-shaped little houses for the dolls, and fan-backed chairs of woven grass for the houses. None of these toys was truly Martian in design, and none was Terrestrial.

They represented a pathetic compromise within his imagination; the Martian notion of what Terrestrial models might have looked like had there been any in existence.

But surreptitiously, without seeming to give any less attention to the younger ones, he directed his main efforts upon the six older boys and Speedy. To his mind, these were the hope of the world—and of Mars. At no time did he bother to ponder that the nontechnical brain is not without its virtues, or that there are times and circumstances when it is worth dropping the short view of what is practicable for the sake of the long view of what is remotely possible. So as best he could he concentrated upon the elder seven, educating them through the dragging months, stimulating their minds, encouraging their curiosity, and continually impressing upon them the idea that fear of disease can become a folk-separating dogma unless they conquered it within their souls.

He taught them that death is death, a natural process to be accepted philosophically and met with dignity—and there were times when he suspected that he was teaching them nothing, he was merely reminding them, for deep within their growing minds was the ancestral strain of Terrestrialism which had mulled its way to the same conclusions ten or twenty thousands of years before. Still, he was helping to remove this disease-block from the path of the stream, and was driving child-logic more rapidly toward adult outlook. In that respect he was satisfied. He could do little more.

In time, they organized group concerts, humming or making singing noises to the accompaniment of the harp, now and again improvising lines to suit Fander's tunes, arguing out the respective merits of chosen words until by process of elimination they had a complete song. As songs grew to a repertoire and singing grew more adept, more polished, Old Graypate displayed interest, came to one performance, then another, until by custom he had established his own place as a one-man audience.

One day the eldest boy, who was named Redhead, came to Fander and grasped a tentacle-tip. "Devil, may I operate your food-machine?"

"You mean you would like me to show you how to work it?"

"No, Devil, I know how to work it." The boy gazed self-assuredly into the other's great bee-eyes.

"Then how is it operated?"

"You fill its container with the tenderest blades of grass,

being careful not to include roots. You are equally careful not to turn a switch before the container is full and its door completely closed. You then turn the red switch for a count of two hundred eighty, reverse the container, turn the green switch for a count of forty-seven. You then close both switches, empty the container's warm pulp into the end molds and apply the press until the biscuits are firm and dry."

"How have you discovered all this?"

"I have watched you make biscuits for us many times. This morning, while you were busy, I tried it myself." He extended a hand. It held a biscuit. Taking it from him, Fander examined it. Firm, crisp, well-shaped. He tasted it. Perfect.

Redhead became the first mechanic to operate and service a Martian lifeboat's emergency premasticator. Seven years later, long after the machine had ceased to function, he managed to repower it, weakly but effectively, with dust that gave forth alpha sparks. In another five years he had improved it, speeded it up. In twenty years he had duplicated it and had all the know-how needed to turn out premasticators on a large scale. Fander could not have equalled this performance for, as a nontechnician, he'd no better notion than the average Terrestrial of the principles upon which the machine worked, neither did he know what was meant by radiant digestion or protein enrichment. He could do little more than urge Redhead along and leave the rest to whatever inherent genius the boy possessed—which was plenty.

In similar manner, Speedy and two youths named Blacky and Bigears took the load-sled out of his charge. On rare occasions, as a great privilege, Fander had permitted them to take up the sled for one-hour trips, alone. This time they were gone from dawn to dusk. Graypate mooched around, gun under arm, another smaller one stuck in his belt, going frequently to the top of a rise and scanning the skies in all directions. The delinquents swooped in at sunset, bringing with them a strange boy.

Fander summoned them to him. They held hands so that his touch would give him simultaneous contact with all three.

"I am a little worried. The sled has only so much power. When it is all gone there will be no more."

They eyed each other aghast.

"Unfortunately, I have neither the knowledge nor the ability to energize the sled once its power is exhausted. I lack the wisdom of the friends who left me here—and that is my shame."

He paused, watching them dolefully, then went on, "All I do know is that its power does not leak away. If not used much, the reserves will remain for many years." Another pause before he added, "And in a few years you will be men."

Blacky said, "But, Devil, when we are men we'll be much heavier, and the sled will use so much more power."

"How do you know that?" Fander put it sharply.

"More weight, more power to sustain it," opined Blacky with the air of one whose logic is incontrovertible. "It doesn't need thinking out. *It's obvious.*"

Very slowly and softly, Fander told him, "You'll do. May the twin moons shine upon you someday, for I know you'll do."

"Do what, Devil?"

"Build a thousand sleds like this one, or better—and explore the whole world."

From that time onward they confined their trips strictly to one hour, making them less frequently than of yore, spending more time poking and prying around the sled's innards.

Graypate changed character with the slow reluctance of the aged. Leastways, as two years then three rolled past, he came gradually out of his shell, was less taciturn, more willing to mix with those swiftly growing up to his own height. Without fully realizing what he was doing he joined forces with Fander, gave the children the remnants of Earthly wisdom passed down from his father's father. He taught the boys how to use the guns of which he had as many as eleven, some maintained mostly as a source of spares for others. He took them shell-hunting; digging deep beneath rotting foundations into stale, half-filled cellars in search of ammunition not too far corroded for use.

"Guns ain't no use without shells, and shells don't last forever."

Neither do buried shells. They found not one.

Of his own wisdom Graypate stubbornly withheld but a single item until the day when Speedy and Redhead and Blacky chivvied it out of him. Then, like a father facing the hangman, he gave them the truth about babies. He made no comparative mention of bees because there were no bees, nor of flowers because there were no flowers. One cannot analogize the nonexistent. Nevertheless he managed to explain the matter more or less to their satisfaction, after which he mopped his forehead and went to Fander.

"These youngsters are getting too nosy for my comfort. They've been asking me how kids come along."

"Did you tell them?"

"I sure did." He sat down, staring at the Martian, his pale gray eyes bothered. "I don't mind giving in to the boys when I can't beat 'em off any longer, but I'm durned if I'm going to tell the girls."

Fander said, "I have been asked about this many a time before. I could not tell much because I was by no means certain whether you breed precisely as we breed. But I told them how *we* breed."

"The girls too?"

"Of course."

"Jeepers!" Graypate mopped his forehead again. "How did they take it?"

"Just as if I'd told them why the sky is blue or why water is wet."

"Must've been something in the way you put it to them," opined Graypate.

"I told them it was poetry between persons."

Throughout the course of history, Martian, Venusian, or Terrestrial, some years are more noteworthy than others. The twelfth one after Fander's marooning was outstanding for its series of events, each of which was pitifully insignificant by cosmic standards but loomed enormously in this small community life.

To start with, on the basis of Redhead's improvements to the premasticator, the older seven—now bearded men—contrived to repower the exhausted sled and again took to the air for the first time in forty months. Experiments showed that the Martian load-carrier was now slower, could bear less weight, but had far longer range. They used it to visit the ruins of distant cities in search of metallic junk suitable for the building of more sleds, and by early summer they had constructed another, larger than the original, clumsy to the verge of dangerousness, but still a sled.

On several occasions they failed to find metal but did find people, odd families surviving in under-surface shelters, clinging grimly to life and passed-down scraps of knowledge. Since all these new contacts were strictly human to human, with no weirdly tentacled shape to scare off the parties of the second part, and since many were finding fear of plague more to be endured than their terrible loneliness, many families returned with the explorers, settled in the shelters, accepted Fander, added their surviving skills to the community's riches.

Thus local population grew to seventy adults and four hundred children. They compounded with their plague-fear by spreading through the shelters, digging through half-wrecked and formerly unused expanses, and moving apart to form twenty or thirty lesser communities each one of which could be isolated should death reappear.

Growing morale born of added strength and confidence in numbers soon resulted in four more sleds, still clumsy but slightly less dangerous to manage. There also appeared the first rock house above ground, standing four-square and solidly under the gray skies, a defiant witness that mankind still considered itself a cut above the rats and rabbits. The community presented the house to Blacky and Sweetvoice, who had announced their desire to associate. An adult who claimed to know the conventional routine spoke solemn words over the happy couple before many witnesses, while Fander attended the groom as best Martian.

Toward summer's end Speedy returned from a solo sled trip of many days, brought with him one old man, one boy and four girls, all of strange, outlandish countenance. They were yellow in complexion, had black hair, black, almond-shaped eyes, and spoke a language that none could understand. Until these newcomers had picked up the local speech, Fander had to act as interpreter, for his mind-pictures and theirs were independent of vocal sounds. The four girls were quiet, modest, and very beautiful. Within a month Speedy had married one of them whose name was a gentle clucking sound which meant Precious Jewel Ling.

After this wedding, Fander sought Graypate, placed a tentacle-tip in his right hand. "There were differences between the man and the girl, distinctive features wider apart than any we know upon Mars. Are these some of the differences which caused your war?"

"I dunno. I've never seen one of these yellow folk before. They must live mighty far off." He rubbed his chin to help his thoughts along. "I only know what my old man told me and his old man told him. There were too many folk of too many different sorts."

"They can't be all that different if they can fall in love."

"Mebbe not," agreed Graypate.

"Supposing most of the people still in this world could assemble here, breed together, and have less different children; the children breed others still less different. Wouldn't they eventually become all much the same—just Earth-people?"

"Mebbe so."

"All speaking the same language, sharing the same culture? If they spread out slowly from a central source, always in contact by sled, continually sharing the same knowledge, same progress, would there be any room for new differences to arise?"

"I dunno," said Graypate evasively. "I'm not so young as I used to be, and I can't dream as far ahead as I used to do."

"It doesn't matter so long as the young ones can dream it." Fander mused a moment. "If you're beginning to think yourself a back number, you're in good company. Things are getting somewhat out of hand as far as I'm concerned. The onlooker sees the most of the game, and perhaps that's why I'm more sensitive than you to a certain peculiar feeling."

"To what feeling?" inquired Graypate, eyeing him.

"That Terra is on the move once more. There are now many people where there were few. A house is up and more are to follow. They talk of six more. After the six they will talk of sixty, then six hundred, then six thousand. Some are planning to haul up sunken conduits and use them to pipe water from the northward lake. Sleds are being built. Premasticators will soon be built, and force-screens likewise. Children are being taught. Less and less is being heard of your plague, and so far no more have died of it. I feel a dynamic surge of energy and ambition and genius which may grow with appalling rapidity until it becomes a mighty flood. I feel that I, too, am a back number."

"Bunk!" said Graypate. He spat on the ground. "If you dream often enough, you're bound to have a bad one once in a while."

"Perhaps it is because so many of my tasks have been taken over and done better than I was doing them. I have failed to seek new tasks. Were I a technician I'd have discovered a dozen by now. Reckon this is as good a time as any to turn to a job with which you can help me."

"What is that?"

"A long, long time ago I made a poem. It was for the beautiful thing that first impelled me to stay here. I do not know exactly what its maker had in mind, nor whether my eyes see it as he wished it to be seen, but I have made a poem to express what I feel when I look upon his work."

"Humph!" said Graypate, not very interested.

"There is an outcrop of solid rock beneath its base which I can shave smooth and use as a plinth on which to inscribe my words. I would like to put them down twice—in the script of Mars and the script of Earth." Fander hesitated a moment, then went on. "Perhaps this is presumptuous of me, but it is many years since I wrote for all to read—and my chance may never come again."

Graypate said, "I get the idea. You want me to put down your notions in our writing so you can copy it."

"Yes."

"Give me your stylus and pad." Taking them, Graypate squatted on a rock, lowering himself stiffly, for he was feeling the weight of his years. Resting the pad on his knees, he held the writing instrument in his right hand while his left continued to grasp a tentacle-tip. "Go ahead."

He started drawing thick, laborious marks as Fander's mind-pictures came through, enlarging the letters and keeping them well separated. When he had finished he handed the pad over.

"Asymmetrical," decided Fander, staring at the queer letters and wishing for the first time that he had taken up the study of Earth-writing. "Cannot you make this part balance with that, and this with this?"

"It's what you said."

"It is your own translation of what I said. I would like it better balanced. Do you mind if we try again?"

They tried again. They made fourteen attempts before Fander was satisfied with the perfunctory appearance of letters and words he could not understand.

Taking the paper, he found his ray-gun, went to the base-rock of the beautiful thing and sheared the whole front to a flat, even surface. Adjusting his beam to cut a V-shaped channel one inch deep, he inscribed his poem on the rock in long, unpunctuated lines of neat Martian curlicues. With less confidence and much greater care, he repeated the verse in Earth's awkward, angular hieroglyphics. The task took him quite a time, and there were fifty people watching him when he finished. They said nothing. In utter silence they looked at the poem and at the beautiful thing, and were still standing there brooding solemnly when he went away.

One by one the rest of the community visited the site next day, going and coming with the air of pilgrims attending an ancient shrine. All stood there a long time, returned without comment.

Nobody praised Fander's work, nobody damned it, nobody reproached him for alienizing something wholly Earth's. The only effect—too subtle to be noteworthy—was a greater and still growing grimness and determination that boosted the already swelling Earth-dynamic.

In that respect, Fander wrought better than he knew.

A plague-scare came in the fourteenth year. Two sleds had brought back families from afar, and within a week of their arrival the children sickened, became spotted.

Metal gongs sounded the alarm, all work ceased, the affected section was cut off and guarded, the majority prepared to flee. It was a threatening reversal of all the things for which many had toiled so long; a destructive scattering of the tender roots of new civilization.

Fander found Graypate, Speedy, and Blacky, armed to the teeth, facing a drawn-faced and restless crowd.

"There's most of a hundred folk in that isolated part," Graypate was telling them. "They ain't all got it. Maybe they won't get it. If they don't it ain't so likely you'll go down either. We ought to wait and see. Stick around a bit."

"Listen who's talking," invited a voice in the crowd. "If you weren't immune you'd have been planted thirty-forty years ago."

"Same goes for near everybody," snapped Graypate. He glared around, his gun under one arm, his pale blue eyes bellicose. "I ain't much use at speechifying, so I'm just saying flatly that nobody goes before we know whether this really is the plague." He hefted his weapon in one hand, held it forward. "Anyone fancy himself at beating a bullet?"

The heckler in the audience muscled his way to the front. He was a swarthy man of muscular build, and his dark eyes looked belligerently into Graypate's. "While there's life there's hope. If we beat it, we live to come back, when it's safe to come back, if ever—and you know it. So I'm calling your bluff, see?" Squaring his shoulders, he began to walk off.

Graypate's gun already was halfway up when he felt the touch of Fander's tentacle on his arm. He lowered the weapon, called after the escapee.

"I'm going into that cut-off section and the Devil is going with me. We're running into things, not away from them. I never did like running away." Several of the audience fidgeted, murmuring approval. He went on, "We'll see for ourselves just what's wrong. We mightn't be able to put it right, but we'll find out what's the matter."

The walker paused, turned, eyed him, eyed Fander, and said, "You can't do that."

"Why not?"

"You'll get it yourself—and a heck of a lot of use you'll be dead and stinking."

"What, and me immune?" cracked Graypate grinning.

"The Devil will get it," hedged the other.

Graypate was about to retort, "What do *you* care?" but altered it slightly in response to Fander's contacting thoughts. He said, more softly, "Do you *care?*"

It caught the other off-balance. He fumbled embarrassedly within his own mind, avoided looking at the Martian, said lamely, "I don't see reason for any guy to take risks."

"He's taking them, because *he* cares," Graypate gave back. "And I'm taking them because I'm too old and useless to give a darn."

With that, he stepped down, marched stubbornly toward the isolated section, Fander slithered by his side, tentacle in hand. The one who wished to flee stayed put, staring after them. The crowd shuffled uneasily, seemed in two minds whether to accept the situation and stick around, or to rush Graypate and Fander and drag them away. Speedy and Blacky made to follow the pair but were ordered off.

No adult sickened; nobody died. Children in the affected sector went one after another through the same routine of liverishness, high temperature, and spots, until the epidemic of measles had died out. Not until a month after the last case had been cured by something within its own constitution did Graypate and Fander emerge.

The innocuous course and eventual disappearance of this suspected plague gave the pendulum of confidence a push, swinging it farther. Morale boosted itself almost to the verge of arrogance. More sleds appeared, more mechanics serviced them, more pilots rode them. More people flowed in; more oddments of past knowledge came with them.

Humanity was off to a flying start with the salvaged seeds of past wisdom and the urge to do. The tormented ones of Earth were not primitive savages, but surviving organisms of a greatness nine-tenths destroyed but still remembered, each contributing his mite of know-how to restore at least some of those things which had been boiled away in atomic fires.

When, in the twentieth year, Redhead duplicated the premasticator, there were eight thousand stone houses standing around the hill. A community hall seventy times the size of a house, with a great green dome of copper, reared itself upon the eastward fringe. A dam held the lake to the north. A hospital was going up in the west. The nuances and energies and talents of fifty races had built this town and were still building it. Among them were ten Polynesians and four Icelanders and one lean, dusky child who was the last of the Seminoles.

Farms spread wide. One thousand heads of Indian corn rescued from a sheltered valley in the Andes had grown to ten thousand acres. Water buffaloes and goats had been brought from afar to serve in lieu of the horses and sheep that would never be seen again—and no man knew why one species survived while another did not. The horses had died; the water buffaloes lived. The canines hunted in ferocious packs; the felines had departed from existence. The small herbs, some tubers, and a few seedy things could be rescued and cultivated for hungry bellies; but there were no flowers for the hungry mind. Humanity carried on, making do with what was available. No more than that could be done.

Fander was a back-number. He had nothing left for which to live but his songs and the affection of the others. In everthing but his harp and his songs the Terrans were way ahead of him. He could do no more than give of his own affection in return for theirs and wait with the patience of one whose work is done.

At the end of that year they buried Graypate. He died in his sleep, passing with the undramatic casualness of one who ain't much use at speechifying. They put him to rest on a knoll behind the community hall, and Fander played his mourning song, and Precious Jewel, who was Speedy's wife, planted the grave with sweet herbs.

In the spring of the following year Fander summoned Speedy and Blacky and Redhead. He was coiled on a couch, blue and shivering. They held hands so that his touch would speak to them simultaneously.

"I am about to undergo my *amafa*."

He had great difficulty in putting it over in understandable thought forms, for this was something beyond their Earthly experience.

"It is an unavoidable change of age during which my kind must sleep undisturbed." They reacted as if the casual reference to his kind was a strange and startling revelation, a new aspect previously unthought-of. He continued, "I must be left alone until this hibernation has run its natural course."

"For how long, Devil?" asked Speedy, with anxiety.

"It may stretch from four of your months to a full year, or—"

"Or what?" Speedy did not wait for a reassuring reply. His agile mind was swift to sense the spice of danger lying far back in the Martian's thoughts. "Or it may never end?"

"It may never," admitted Fander, reluctantly. He shivered again, drew his tentacles around himself. The brilliance of his blueness was fading visibly. "The possibility is small, but it is there."

Speedy's eyes widened and his breath was taken in a short gasp. His mind was striving to readjust itself and accept the appalling idea that Fander might not be a fixture, permanent, established for all time. Blacky and Redhead were equally aghast.

"We Martians do not last forever," Fander pointed out, gently. "All are mortal, here and there. He who survives his *amafa* has many happy years to follow, but some do not survive. It is a trial that must be faced as everything from beginning to end must be faced."

"But—"

"Our numbers are not large," Fander went on. "We breed slowly and some of us die halfway through the normal span. By cosmic standards we are a weak and foolish people much in need of the support of the clever and the strong. You are clever and strong. Whenever my people visit you again, or any other still stranger people come, always remember that you are clever and strong."

"We are strong," echoed Speedy, dreamily. His gaze swung around to take in the thousands of roofs, the copper dome, the thing of beauty on the hill. "We are strong."

A prolonged shudder went through the ropy, bee-eyed creature on the couch.

"I do not wish to be left here, an idle sleeper in the midst of life, posing like a bad example to the young. I would rather rest within the little cave where first we made friends and grew to know and understand each other. Wall it up and fix a door for me. Forbid anyone to touch me or let the light of day fall upon me until such time as I emerge of my own accord." Fander stirred sluggishly, his limbs uncoiling with noticeable lack of sinuousness. "I regret I must ask you to carry me there. Please forgive me; I have left it a little late and cannot . . . cannot . . . make it by myself."

Their faces were pictures of alarm, their minds bells of sorrow. Running for poles, they made a stretcher, edged him onto it, bore him to the cave. A long procession was following by the time they reached it. As they settled him comfortably and began to wall up the entrance, the crowd watched in the same solemn silence with which they had looked upon his verse.

He was already a tightly rolled ball of dull blueness, with filmed eyes, when they fitted the door and closed it, leaving him to darkness and slumber. Next day a tiny, brown-skinned man with eight children, all hugging dolls, came to the door. While the youngsters stared huge-eyed at the door, he fixed upon it a two-word name in metal letters, taking great pains over his self-imposed task and making a neat job of it.

The Martian vessel came from the stratosphere with the slow, stately fall of a grounding balloon. Behind the transparent band its bluish, nightmarish crew were assembled and looking with great, multifaceted eyes at the upper surface of the clouds. The scene resembled a pink-tinged snowfield beneath which the planet still remained concealed.

Captain Rdina could feel this as a tense, exciting moment even though his vessel had not the honor to be the first with such an approach. One Captain Skhiva, now long retired, had done it many years before. Nevertheless, this second venture retained its own exploratory thrill.

Someone stationed a third of the way around the vessel's belly came writhing at top pace toward him as their drop brought them near to the pinkish clouds. The oncomer's signaling tentacle was jiggling at a seldom-used rate.

"Captain, we have just seen an object swoop across the horizon."

"What sort of an object?"

"It looked like a gigantic load-sled."

"It couldn't have been."

"No, Captain, of course not—but that is exactly what it appeared to be."

"Where is it now?" demanded Rdina, gazing toward the side from which the other had come.

"It dived into the mists below."

"You must have been mistaken. Long-standing anticipation can encourage the strangest delusions." He stopped a moment as the observation band became shrouded in the vapor of a cloud. Musingly, he watched the gray wall of fog slide upward as his vessel continued its descent. "That old report says definitely that there is nothing but desolation and wild animals. There is no intelligent life except some fool of a minor poet whom Skhiva left behind, and twelve to one he's dead by now. The animals may have eaten him."

"Eaten him? Eaten *meat?*" exclaimed the other, thoroughly revolted.

"Anything is possible," assured Rdina, pleased with the extreme to which his imagination could be stretched. "Except a load-sled. That was plain silly."

At which point he had no choice but to let the subject drop for the simple and compelling reason that the ship came out of the base of the cloud, and the sled in question was floating alongside. It could be seen in complete detail, and even their own instruments were responding to the powerful output of its numerous flotation-grids.

The twenty Martians aboard the sphere sat staring bee-eyed at this enormous thing which was half the size of their own vessel, and the forty humans on the sled stared back with equal intentness. Ship and sled continued to descend side by side, while both crews studied each other with dumb fascination which persisted until simultaneously they touched ground.

It was not until he felt the slight jolt of landing that Captain Rdina recovered sufficiently to look elsewhere. He saw the houses, the green-domed building, the thing of beauty poised upon its hill, the many hundreds of Earth-people streaming out of their town and toward his vessel.

None of these queer, two-legged life forms, he noted, betrayed the slightest sign of revulsion or fear. They galloped to the tryst with a bumptious self-confidence which would still be evident any place the other side of the cosmos.

It shook him a little, and he kept saying to himself, again and again, "They're not scared—why should you be? They're not scared—why should you be?"

He went out personally to meet the first of them, suppressing his own apprehensions and ignoring the fact that many of them bore weapons. The leading Earthman, a big-built, spade-bearded two-legger, grasped his tentacle as to the manner born.

There came a picture of swiftly moving limbs. "My name is Speedy."

The ship emptied itself within ten minutes. No Martian would stay inside who was free to smell new air. Their first visit, in a slithering bunch, was to the thing of beauty. Rdina stood quietly looking at it, his crew clustered in a half-circle around him, the Earth-folk a silent audience behind.

It was a great rock statue of a female of Earth. She was broad-shouldered, full-bosomed, wide-hipped, and wore voluminous skirts that came right down to her heavy-soled shoes. Her back was a little bent, her head a little bowed, and her face was hidden in her hands, deep in her toilworn hands. Rdina tried in vain to gain some glimpse of the tired features behind those hiding hands. He looked at her a long while before his eyes lowered to read the script beneath, ignoring the Earth-lettering, running easily over the flowing Martian curlicues:

Weep, my country, for your sons asleep,
The ashes of your homes, your tottering towers.
Weep, my country, O, my country, weep!
For birds that cannot sing, for vanished flowers,
    The end of everything,
    The silenced hours.
    Weep! my country.

There was no signature. Rdina mulled it through many minutes while the others remained passive. Then he turned to Speedy, pointed to the Martian script.

"Who wrote this?"

"One of your people. He is dead."

"Ah!" said Rdina. "That songbird of Skhiva's. I have forgotten his name. I doubt whether many remember it. He was only a very small poet. How did he die?"

"He ordered us to enclose him for some long and urgent sleep he must have, and—"

"The *amafa,*" put in Rdina, comprehendingly. "And then?"

"We did as he asked. He warned us that he might never come out." Speedy gazed at the sky, unconscious that Rdina was picking up his sorrowful thoughts. "He has been there nearly two years and has not emerged." The eyes came down to Rdina.

"I don't know whether you can understand me, but he was one of us."

"I think I understand." Rdina was thoughtful. He asked, "How long is this period you call nearly two years?"

They managed to work it out between them, translating it from Terran to Martian time-terms.

"It is long," pronounced Rdina. "Much longer than the usual *amafa,* but not unique. Occasionally, for no known reason, someone takes even longer. Besides, Earth is Earth and Mars is Mars." He became swift, energetic as he called to one of his crew. "Physician Traith, we have a prolonged-*amafa* case. Get your oils and essences and come with me." When the other had returned, he said to Speedy, "Take us to where he sleeps."

Reaching the door to the walled-up cave, Rdina paused to look at the names fixed upon it in neat but incomprehensible letters. They read: DEAR DEVIL.

"What do those mean?" asked Physician Traith, pointing.

"Do not disturb," guessed Rdina carelessly. Pushing open the door, he let the other enter first, closed it behind him to keep all others outside.

They reappeared an hour later. The total population of the city had congregated outside the cave to see the Martians. Rdina wondered why they had not permitted his crew to satisfy their natural curiosity, since it was unlikely that they would be more interested in other things—such as the fate of one small poet. Ten thousand eyes were upon them as they came into the sunlight and fastened the cave's door. Rdina made contact with Speedy, gave him the news.

Stretching himself in the light as if reaching toward the sun, Speedy shouted in a voice of tremendous gladness which all could hear.

"He will be out again within twenty days."

At that, a mild form of madness seemed to overcome the two-leggers. They made pleasure-grimaces, piercing mouth-noises, and some went so far as to beat each other.

Twenty Martians felt like joining Fander that same night. The Martian constitution is peculiarly susceptible to emotion.

SCANNERS LIVE IN VAIN

Cordwainer Smith
(Paul M. A. Linebarger, 1913–1966)

FANTASY BOOK

June

"Cordwainer Smith" makes his debut in this series with one of the most famous first stories in the history of science fiction. "Smith's" true identity was a closely guarded secret for many years; the author was Professor of Asiatic Politics at the Johns Hopkins University School of Advanced International Studies and one of the leading experts in the world on political propaganda, a man who moved somewhat mysteriously through the Middle East and Southeast Asia during and after World War II. As a science fiction writer his work was poetic, imaginative, and mind-bending. Most of it is set in his own universe, a civilization called the "Instrumentality of Mankind," a wonderful creation that has attracted the notice of critics and readers since his too-early death in 1966. Its incomplete story can be found in about ten books, all collections or fix-ups of previously published material. The Best of Cordwainer Smith *is a treasure that should be on the shelf of every sf reader.*

"Scanners Live in VAin." contains a stunning first line that opened the sf career of a remarkable man and a remarkable writer. Fantasy Book *appeared irregularly over a five year period, with a total of only eight issues.*

—M.H.G.

Let me tell you a little story. In 1940, Frederik Pohl wrote a story called "Little Man on the Subway." He couldn't sell it anywhere (he was only 20 years old at the time). So he asked me to try to revise it. In January 1941 (I had just turned 21), I rewrote the story. It still couldn't sell anywhere.

Years later, we managed to sell it to Fantasy Book, *a semi-professional science fiction magazine. There it appeared as the lead novelette because by that time my name and Fred's meant something.*

Would you like to know the third story in that same issue of that same magazine? I'll tell you. It was "Scanners Live in Vain" which is now universally recognized as a classic and which obviously must have been as unable to find a home as my stinkeroo had.

I tell you this just in case you think that editors always know what they're doing.

—I.A.

Martel was angry. He did not even adjust his blood away from anger. He stamped across the room by judgment, not by sight. When he saw the table hit the floor, and could tell by the expression on Luci's face that the table must have made a loud crash, he looked down to see if his leg was broken. It was not. Scanner to the core, he had to scan himself. The action was reflex and automatic. The inventory included his legs, abdomen, chestbox of instruments, hands, arms, face and back with the mirror. Only then did Martel go back to being angry. He talked with his voice, even though he knew that his wife hated its blare and preferred to have him write.

"I tell you, I must cranch. I have to cranch. It's my worry, isn't it?"

When Luci answered, he saw only a part of her words as he read her lips: "Darling . . . you're my husband . . . right to love you . . . dangerous . . . do it . . . dangerous . . . wait . . ."

He faced her, but put sound in his voice, letting the blare hurt her again: "I tell you, I'm going to cranch."

Catching her expression, he became rueful and a little tender: "Can't you understand what it means to me? To get out of this horrible prison in my own head? To be a man again—hearing your voice, smelling smoke? To *feel* again—to feel my feet on the ground, to feel the air move against my face? Don't you know what it means?"

Her wide-eyed worrisome concern thrust him back into pure annoyance. He read only a few words as her lips moved: ". . . love you . . . your own good . . . don't you think I want you to be human? . . . your own good . . . too much . . . he said . . . they said . . ."

When he roared at her, he realized that his voice must be particularly bad. He knew that the sound hurt her no less than did the words: "Do you think I wanted you to marry a scanner? Didn't I tell you we're almost as low as the habermans? We're dead, I tell you. We've got to be dead to do our work. How can anybody go to the up-and-out? Can you dream what raw space is? I warned you. But you married me. All right, you married a man. Please, darling, let me be a man. Let me hear your voice, let me feel the warmth of being alive, of being human. Let me!"

He saw by her look of stricken assent that he had won the argument. He did not use his voice again. Instead, he pulled his tablet up from where it hung against his chest. He wrote on it, using the pointed fingernail of his right forefinger—the talking nail of a scanner—in quick cleancut script: *Pls, drlng, whrs crnching wire?*

She pulled the long gold-sheathed wire out of the pocket of her apron. She let its field sphere fall to the carpeted floor. Swiftly, dutifully, with the deft obedience of a scanner's wife, she wound the cranching wire around his head, spirally around his neck and chest. She avoided the instruments set in his chest. She even avoided the radiating scars around the instruments, the stigmata of men who had gone up and into the out. Mechanically he lifted a foot as she slipped the wire between his feet. She drew the wire taut. She snapped the small plug into the high-burden control next to his heart-reader. She helped him to sit down, arranging his hands for him, pushing his head back into the cup at the top of the chair. She turned then, full-face toward him, so that he could read her lips easily. Her expression was composed.

She knelt, scooped up the sphere at the other end of the wire, stood erect calmly, her back to him. He scanned her, and saw nothing in her posture but grief which would have escaped the eye of anyone but a scanner. She spoke: he could see her chest-muscles moving. She realized that she was not facing him, and turned so that he could see her lips.

"Ready at last?"

He smiled a *yes*.

She turned her back to him again. (Luci could never bear to

watch him go under the wire.) She tossed the wire-sphere into the air. It caught in the force-field, and hung there. Suddenly it glowed. That was all. All—except for the sudden red stinking roar of coming back to his senses. Coming back, across the wild threshold of pain.

When he awakened, under the wire, he did not feel as though he had just cranched. Even though it was the second cranching within the week, he felt fit. He lay in the chair. His ears drank in the sound of air touching things in the room. He heard Luci breathing in the next room, where she was hanging up the wire to cool. He smelt the thousand and one smells that are in anybody's room: the crisp freshness of the germ-burner, the sour-sweet tang of the humidifier, the odor of the dinner they had just eaten, the smells of clothes, furniture, of people themselves. All these were pure delight. He sang a phrase or two of his favorite song:

> *"Here's to the haberman, up-and-out!*
> *"Up—oh!—and out—oh!—up-and-out! . . ."*

He heard Luci chuckle in the next room. He gloated over the sounds of her dress as she swished to the doorway.

She gave him her crooked little smile. "You sound all right. Are you all right, really?"

Even with this luxury of senses, he scanned. He took the flash-quick inventory which constituted his professional skill. His eyes swept in the news of the instruments. Nothing showed off scale, beyond the nerve compression hanging in the edge of *Danger*. But he could not worry about the nerve-box. That always came through cranching. You couldn't get under the wire without having it show on the nerve-box. Some day the box would go to *Overload* and drop back down to *Dead*. That was the way a haberman ended. But you couldn't have everything. People who went to the up-and-out had to pay the price for space.

Anyhow, he should worry! He was a scanner. A good one, and he knew it. If he couldn't scan himself, who could? This cranching wasn't too dangerous. Dangerous, but not too dangerous.

Luci put out her hand and ruffled his hair as if she had been reading his thoughts, instead of just following them: "But you know you shouldn't have! You shouldn't!"

"But I did!" He grinned at her.

Her gaiety still forced, she said: "Come on, darling, let's have a good time. I have almost everything there is in the icebox—all your favorite tastes. And I have two new records just full of smells. I tried them out myself, and even I liked them. And you know me—"

"Which?"

"Which what, you old darling?"

He slipped his hand over her shoulders as he limped out of the room. (He could never go back to feeling the floor beneath his feet, feeling the air against his face, without being bewildered and clumsy. As if cranching was real, and being a haberman was a bad dream. But he *was* a haberman, and a scanner.) "You know what I meant, Luci . . . the smells, which you have. Which one did you like, on the record?"

"Well-l-l," said she, judiciously, "there were some lamb chops that were the strangest things—"

He interrupted: "What are lambtchots?"

"Wait till you smell them. Then guess. I'll tell you this much. It's a smell hundreds and hundreds of years old. They found out about it in the old books."

"Is a bambtchot a Beast?"

"I won't tell you. You've got to wait," she laughed, as she helped him sit down and spread his tasting dishes before him. He wanted to go back over the dinner first, sampling all the pretty things he had eaten, and savoring them this time with his now-living lips and tongue.

When Luci had found the music wire and had thrown its sphere up into the force-field, he reminded her of the new smells. She took out the long glass records and set the first one into a transmitter.

"Now sniff!"

A queer, frightening, exciting smell came over the room. It seemed like nothing in this world, nor like anything from the up-and-out. Yet it was familiar. His mouth watered. His pulse beat a little faster; he scanned his heartbox. (Faster, sure enough.) But that smell, what was it? In mock perplexity, he grabbed her hands, looked into her eyes, and growled:

"Tell me, darling! Tell me, or I'll eat you up!"

"That's just right!"

"What?"

"You're right. It should make you want to eat me. It's meat."

"Meat. Who?"

"Not a person," said she, knowledgeably, "a Beast. A Beast

which people used to eat. A lamb was a small sheep—you've seen sheep out in the Wild, haven't you?—and a chop is part of its middle—here!" She pointed at her chest.

Martel did not hear her. All his boxes had swung over toward *Alarm*, some to *Danger*. He fought against the roar of his own mind, forcing his body into excess excitement. How easy it was to be a scanner when you really stood outside your own body, haberman-fashion, and looked back into it with your eyes alone. Then you could manage the body, rule it coldly even in the enduring agony of space. But to realize that you *were* a body, that this thing was ruling you, that the mind could kick the flesh and send it roaring off into panic! That was bad.

He tried to remember the days before he had gone into the haberman device, before he had been cut apart for the up-and-out. Had he always been subject to the rush of his emotions from his mind to his body, from his body back to his mind, confounding him so that he couldn't scan? But he hadn't been a scanner then.

He knew what had hit him. Amid the roar of his own pulse, he knew. In the nightmare of the up-and-out, that smell had forced its way through to him, while their ship burned off Venus and the habermans fought the collapsing metal with their bare hands. He had scanned then: all were in *Danger*. Chestboxes went up to *Overload* and dropped to *Dead* all around him as he had moved from man to man, shoving the drifting corpses out of his way as he fought to scan each man in turn, to clamp vises on unnoticed broken legs, to snap the sleeping valve on men whose instruments showed they were hopelessly near *Overload*. With men trying to work and cursing him for a scanner while he, professional zeal aroused, fought to do his job and keep them alive in the great pain of space, he had smelled that smell. It had fought its way along his rebuilt nerves, past the haberman cuts, past all the safeguards of physical and mental discipline. In the wildest hour of tragedy, he had smelled aloud. He remembered it was like a bad cranching, connected with the fury and nightmare all around him. He had even stopped his work to scan himself, fearful that the first effect might come, breaking past all haberman cuts and ruining him with the pain of space. But he had come through. His own instruments stayed and stayed at *Danger*, without nearing *Overload*. He had done his job, and won a commendation for it. He had even forgotten the burning ship.

All except the smell.

And here the smell was all over again—the smell of meat-with-fire . . .

Luci looked at him with wifely concern. She obviously thought he had cranched too much, and was about to haberman back. She tried to be cheerful: "You'd better rest, honey."

He whispered to her: "Cut—off—that—smell."

She did not question his word. She cut the transmitter. She even crossed the room and stepped up the room controls until a small breeze flitted across the floor and drove the smells up to the ceiling.

He rose, tired and stiff. (His instruments were normal, except that heart was fast and nerves still hanging on the edge of *Danger*.) He spoke sadly:

"Forgive me, Luci. I suppose I shouldn't have cranched. Not so soon again. But darling, I have to get out from being a haberman. How can I ever be near you? How can I be a man—not hearing my own voice, not even feeling my own life as it goes through my veins? I love you, darling. Can't I ever be near you?"

Her pride was disciplined and automatic: "But you're a scanner!"

"I know I'm a scanner. But so what?"

She went over the words, like a tale told a thousand times to reassure herself: "You are the bravest of the brave, the most skillful of the skilled. All mankind owes most honor to the scanner, who unites the Earths of mankind. Scanners are the protectors of the habermans. They are the judges in the up-and-out. They make men live in the place where men need desperately to die. They are the most honored of mankind, and even the chiefs of the Instrumentality are delighted to pay them homage!"

With obstinate sorrow he demurred: "Luci, we've heard that all before. But does it pay us back—"

" 'Scanners work for more than pay. They are the strong guards of mankind.' Don't you remember that?"

"But our lives, Luci. What can you get out of being the wife of a scanner? Why did you marry me? I'm human only when I cranch. The rest of the time—you know what I am. A machine. A man turned into a machine. A man who has been killed and kept alive for duty. Don't you realize what I miss?"

"Of course, darling, of course—"

He went on: "Don't you think I remember my childhood?

Don't you think I remember what it is to be a man and not a haberman? To walk and feel my feet on the ground? To feel a decent clean pain instead of watching my body every minute to see if I'm alive? How will I know if I'm dead? Did you ever think of that, Luci? How will I know if I'm dead?''

She ignored the unreasonableness of his outburst. Pacifyingly, she said: ''Sit down, darling. Let me make you some kind of a drink. You're overwrought.''

Automatically, he scanned. ''No I'm not! Listen to me. How do you think it feels to be in the up-and-out with the crew tied-for-space all around you? How do you think it feels to watch them sleep? How do you think I like scanning, scanning, scanning month after month, when I can feel the pain of space beating against every part of my body, trying to get past my haberman blocks? How do you think I like to wake the men when I have to, and have them hate me for it? Have you ever seen habermans fight—strong men fighting, and neither knowing pain, fighting until one touches *Overload?* Do you think about that, Luci?'' Triumphantly he added: ''Can you blame me if I cranch, and come back to being a man, just two days a month?''

''I'm not blaming you, darling. Let's enjoy your cranch. Sit down now, and have a drink.''

He was sitting down, resting his face in his hands, while she fixed the drink, using natural fruits out of bottles in addition to the secure alkaloids. He watched her restlessly and pitied her for marrying a scanner; and then, though it was unjust, resented having to pity her.

Just as she turned to hand him the drink, they both jumped a little as the phone rang. It should not have rung. They had turned it off. It rang again, obviously on the emergency circuit. Stepping ahead of Luci, Martel strode over to the phone and looked into it. Vomact was looking at him.

The custom of scanners entitled him to be brusque, even with a senior scanner, on certain given occasions. This was one.

Before Vomact could speak, Martel spoke two words into the plate, not caring whether the old man could read lips or not:

''Cranching. Busy.''

He cut the switch and went back to Luci.

The phone rang again.

Luci said, gently, ''I can find out what it is, darling. Here, take your drink and sit down.''

''Leave it alone'' said her husband. ''No one has a right to call when I'm cranching. He knows that. He ought to know that."

The phone rang again. In a fury, Martel rose and went to the plate. He cut it back on. Vomact was on the screen. Before Martel could speak, Vomact held up his talking nail in line with his heartbox. Martel reverted to discipline:

"Scanner Martel present and waiting, sir."

The lips moved solemnly: "Top emergency."

"Sir, I am under the wire."

"Top emergency."

"Sir, don't you understand?" Martel mouthed his words, so he could be sure that Vomact followed. "I . . . am . . . under . . . the . . . wire. Unfit . . . for . . . Space!"

Vomact repeated: "Top emergency. Report to Central Tie-in."

"But, sir, no emergency like this—"

"Right, Martel. No emergency like this, ever before. Report to Tie-in." With a faint glint of kindliness, Vomact added: "No need to decranch. Report as you are."

This time it was Martel whose phone was cut out. The screen went gray.

He turned to Luci. The temper had gone out of his voice. She came to him. She kissed him, and rumpled his hair. All she could say was,

"I'm sorry."

She kissed him again, knowing his disappointment. "Take good care of yourself, darling. I'll wait."

He scanned, and slipped into his transparent aircoat. At the window he paused, and waved. She called, "Good luck!" As the air flowed past him he said to himself,

"This is the first time I've felt flight in—eleven years. Lord, but it's easy to fly if you can feel yourself live!"

Central Tie-in glowed white and austere far ahead. Martel peered. He saw no glare of incoming ships from the up-and-out, no shuddering flare of space-fire out of control. Everything was quiet, as it should be on an off-duty night.

And yet Vomact had called. He had called an emergency higher than space. There was no such thing. But Vomact had called it.

When Martel got there, he found about half the scanners present, two dozen or so of them. He lifted the talking finger. Most of the scanners were standing face to face, talking in pairs as they read lips. A few of the old, impatient ones were scribbling on their tablets and then thrusting the tablets into other people's faces. All the faces wore the dull dead relaxed look of a haberman. When Martel entered the room, he knew that most of the others laughed in the deep isolated privacy of their own minds, each thinking things it would be useless to express in formal words. It had been a long time since a scanner showed up at a meeting cranched.

Vomact was not there; probably, thought Martel, he was still on the phone calling others. The light of the phone flashed on and off; the bell rang. Martel felt odd when he realized that of all those present, he was the only one to hear that loud bell. It made him realize why ordinary people did not like to be around groups of habermans or scanners. Martel looked around for company.

His friend Chang was there, busy explaining to some old and testy scanner that he did not know why Vomact had called. Martel looked farther and saw Parizianski. He walked over, threading his way past the others with a dexterity that showed he could feel his feet from the inside, and did not have to watch them. Several of the others stared at him with their dead faces, and tried to smile. But they lacked full muscular control and their faces twisted into horrid masks. (Scanners usually knew better than to show expression on faces which they could no longer govern. Martel added to himself, *I swear I'll never smile again unless I'm cranched.*)

Parizianski gave him the sign of the talking finger. Looking face to face, he spoke:

"You come here cranched?"

Parizianski could not hear his own voice, so the words roared like the words on a broken and screeching phone; Martel was startled, but knew that the inquiry was well meant. No one could be better-natured than the burly Pole.

"Vomact called. Top emergency."

"You told him you were cranched?"

"Yes."

"He still made you come?"

"Yes."

"Then all this—it is not for Space? You could not go up-and-out? You are like ordinary men?"

"That's right."

"Then why did he call us?" Some pre-haberman habit made Parizianski wave his arms in inquiry. The hand struck the back of the old man behind them. The slap could be heard throughout the room, but only Martel heard it. Instinctively, he scanned Parizianski and the old scanner, and they scanned him back. Only then did the old man ask why Martel had scanned him. When Martel explained that he was under the wire, the old man moved swiftly away to pass on the news that there was a cranched scanner present at the tie-in.

Even this minor sensation could not keep the attention of most of the scanners from the worry about the top emergency. One young man, who had scanned his first transit just the year before, dramatically interposed himself between Parizianski and Martel. He dramatically flashed his tablet at them:

Is Vmct mad?

The older men shook their heads. Martel, remembering that it had not been too long that the young man had been haberman, mitigated the dead solemnity of the denial with a friendly smile. He spoke in a normal voice, saying:

"Vomact is the senior of scanners. I am sure that he could not go mad. Would he not see it on his boxes first?"

Martel had to repeat the question, speaking slowly and mouthing his words before the young scanner could understand the comment. The young man tried to make his face smile, and twisted it into a comic mask. But he took up his tablet and scribbled:

Yr rght.

Chang broke away from his friend and came over, his half-Chinese face gleaming in the warm evening. (It's strange, thought Martel, that more Chinese don't become scanners. Or not so strange perhaps, if you think that they never fill their quota of habermans. Chinese love good living too much. The ones who do scan are all good ones.) Chang saw that Martel was cranched, and spoke with voice:

"You break precedents. Luci must be angry to lose you?"

"She took it well. Chang, that's strange."

"What?"

"I'm cranched, and I can hear. Your voice sounds all right. How did you learn to talk like—like an ordinary person?"

"I practiced with soundtracks. Funny you noticed it. I think I am the only scanner in or between the Earths who can pass for an ordinary man. Mirrors and soundtracks. I found out how to act."

"But you don't . . .?"

"No, I don't feel, or taste, or hear, or smell things, any more than you do. Talking doesn't do me much good. But I notice that it cheers up the people around me."

"It would make a difference in the life of Luci."

Chang nodded sagely. "My father insisted on it. He said, 'You may be proud of being a scanner. I am sorry you are not a man. Conceal your defects.' So I tried. I wanted to tell the old boy about the up-and-out, and what we did there, but it did not matter. He said, 'Airplanes were good enough for Confucius, and they are for me too.' The old humbug! He tries so hard to be a Chinese when he can't even read Old Chinese. But he's got wonderful good sense, and for somebody going on two hundred he certainly gets around."

Martel smiled at the thought: "In his airplane?"

Chang smiled back. This discipline of his facial muscles was amazing; a bystander would not think that Chang was a haberman, controlling his eyes, cheeks, and lips by cold intellectual means. The expression had the spontaneity of life. Martel felt a flash of envy for Chang when he looked at the dead cold faces of Parizianski and the others. He knew that he himself looked fine: but why shouldn't he? He was cranched. Turning to Parizianski he said,

"Did you see what Chang said about his father? The old boy uses an airplane."

Parizianski made motions with his mouth, but the sounds meant nothing. He took up his tablet and showed it to Martel and Chang.

Bzz bzz. Ha ha. Gd ol' boy.

At that moment, Martel heard steps out in the corridor. He could not help looking toward the door. Other eyes followed the direction of his glance.

Vomact came in.

The group shuffled to attention in four parallel lines. They scanned one another. Numerous hands reached across to adjust the electrochemical controls on chestboxes which had begun to load up. One scanner held out a broken finger which his counter-scanner had discovered, and submitted it for treatment and splinting.

Vomact had taken out his staff of office. The cube at the top flashed red light through the room, the lines reformed, and all scanners gave the sign meaning, *Present and ready!*

Vomact countered with the stance signifying, *I am the senior and take command.*

Talking fingers rose in the counter-gesture, *We concur and commit ourselves.*

Vomact raised his right arm, dropped the wrist as though it were broken, in a queer searching gesture, meaning: *Any men around? Any habermans not tied? All clear for the scanners?*

Alone of all those present, the cranched Martel heard the queer rustle of feet as they all turned completely around without leaving position, looking sharply at one another and flashing their beltlights into the dark corners of the great room. When again they faced Vomact, he made a further sign:

All clear. Follow my words.

Martel noticed that he alone relaxed. The others could not know the meaning of relaxation with the minds blocked off up there in their skulls, connected only with the eyes, and the rest of the body connected with the mind only by controlling non-sensory nerves and the instrument boxes on their chests. Martel realized that, cranched as he was, he had expected to hear Vomact's voice: the senior had been talking for some time. No sound escaped his lips. (Vomact never bothered with sound.)

". . . and when the first men to go up-and-out went to the moon, what did they find?"

"Nothing," responded the silent chorus of lips.

"Therefore they went farther, to Mars and to Venus. The ships went out year by year, but they did not come back until the Year One of Space. Then did a ship come back with the first effect. Scanners, I ask you, what is the first effect?"

"No one knows. No one knows."

"No one will ever know. Too many are the variables. By what do we know the first effect?"

"By the great pain of space," came the chorus.

"And by what further sign?"

"By the need, oh the need for death."

Vomact again: "And who stopped the need for death?"

"Henry Haberman conquered the first effect, in the Year Eighty-three of Space."

"And, Scanners, I ask you, what did he do?"

"He made the habermans."

"How, O Scanners, are habermans made?"

"They are made with the cuts. The brain is cut from the heart, the lungs. The brain is cut from the ears, the nose. The brain is cut from the mouth, the belly. The brain is cut from desire, and pain. The brain is cut from the world. Save for the eyes. Save for the control of the living flesh."

"And how, O Scanners, is flesh controlled?"

"By the boxes set in the flesh, the controls set in the chest, the signs made to rule the living body, the signs by which the body lives."

"How does a haberman live and live?"

"The haberman lives by control of the boxes."

"Whence come the habermans?"

Martel felt in the coming response a great roar of broken voices echoing through the room as the scanners, habermans themselves, put sound behind their mouthings:

"Habermans are the scum of mankind. Habermans are the weak, the cruel, the credulous, and the unfit. Habermans are the sentenced-to-more-than-death. Habermans live in the mind alone. They are killed for space but they live for space. They master the ships that connect the Earths. They live in the great pain while ordinary men sleep in the cold, cold sleep of the transit."

"Brothers and Scanners, I ask you now: are we habermans or are we not?"

"We are habermans in the flesh. We are cut apart, brain and flesh. We are ready to go to the up-and-out. All of us have gone through the haberman device."

"We are habermans then?" Vomact's eyes flashed and glittered as he asked the ritual question.

Again the chorused answer was accompanied by a roar of voices heard only by Martel: "Habermans we are, and more, and more. We are the chosen who are habermans by our own free will. We are the agents of the Instrumentality of Mankind."

"What must the others say to us?"

"They must say to us, 'You are the bravest of the brave, the most skillful of the skilled. All mankind owes most honor to the scanner, who unites the Earths of mankind. Scanners are the protectors of the habermans. They are the judges in the up-and-out. They make men live in the place where men need desperately to die. They are the most honored of mankind, and even the chiefs of the Instrumentality are delighted to pay them homage!"

Vomact stood more erect: "What is the secret duty of the scanner?"

"To keep secret our law, and to destroy the acquirers thereof."

"How to destroy?"

"Twice to the *Overload*, back and *Dead*."

"If habermans die, what the duty then?"

The scanners all compressed their lips for answer. (Silence was the code.) Martel, who—long familiar with the code—was a little bored with the proceedings, noticed that Chang was breathing too heavily; he reached over and adjusted Chang's lung-control and received the thanks of Chang's eyes. Vomact observed the interruption and glared at them both. Martel relaxed, trying to imitate the dead cold stillness of the others. It was so hard to do, when you were cranched.

"If others die, what the duty then?" asked Vomact.

"Scanners together inform the Instrumentality. Scanners together accept the punishment. Scanners together settle the case."

"And if the punishment be severe?"

"Then no ships go."

"And if scanners be not honored?"

"Then no ships go."

"And if a scanner goes unpaid?"

"Then no ships go."

"And if the Others and the Instrumentality are not in all ways at all times mindful of their proper obligation to the scanners?"

"Then no ships go."

"And what, O Scanners, if no ships go?"

"The Earths fall apart. The Wild comes back in. The Old Machines and the Beasts return."

"What is the first known duty of a scanner?"

"Not to sleep in the up-and-out."

"What is the second duty of a scanner?"

"To keep forgotten the name of fear."

"What is the third duty of a scanner?"

"To use the wire of Eustace Cranch only with care, only with moderation." Several pairs of eyes looked quickly at Martel before the mouthed chorus went on. "To cranch only at home, only among friends, only for the purpose of remembering, of relaxing, or of begetting."

"What is the word of the scanner?"

"Faithful though surrounded by death."

"What is the motto of the scanner?"

"Awake though surrounded by silence."

"What is the work of the scanner?"

"Labor even in the heights of the up-and-out, loyalty even in the depths of the Earths."

"How do you know a scanner?"

"We know ourselves. We are dead though we live. And we talk with the tablet and the nail."

"What is this code?"

"This code is the friendly ancient wisdom of scanners; briefly put, that we may be mindful and be cheered by our loyalty to one another."

At this point the formula should have run: "We complete the code. Is there work or word for the scanners?" But Vomact said, and he repeated:

"Top emergency. Top emergency."

They gave him the sign, *Present and ready!*

He said, with every eye straining to follow his lips:

"Some of you know the work of Adam Stone?"

Martel saw lips move, saying: "The Red Asteroid. The Other who lives at the edge of Space."

"Adam Stone has gone to the Instrumentality, claiming success for his work. He says that he has found how to screen out the pain of space. He says that the up-and-out can be made safe for ordinary men to work in, to stay awake in. He says that there need be no more scanners."

Beltlights flashed on all over the room as scanners sought the right to speak. Vomact nodded to one of the older men. "Scanner Smith will speak."

Smith stepped slowly up into the light, watching his own feet. He turned so that they could see his face. He spoke: "I say that this is a lie. I say that Stone is a liar. I say that the Instrumentality must not be deceived."

He paused. Then, in answer to some question from the audience which most of the others did not see, he said:

"I invoke the secret duty of the scanners."

Smith raised his right hand for emergency attention:

"I say that Stone must die."

Martel, still cranched, shuddered as he heard the boos, groans, shouts, squeaks, grunts and moans which came from the scanners who forgot noise in their excitement and strove to make their dead bodies talk to one another's deaf ears. Beltlights flashed wildly all over the room. There was a rush for the rostrum and scanners milled around at the top, vying for attention until Parizianski—by sheer bulk—shoved the others aside and down, and turned to mouth at the group.

"Brother Scanners, I want your eyes."

The people on the floor kept moving, with their numb bodies jostling one another. Finally Vomact stepped up in front of Parizianski, faced the others, and said:

"Scanners, be scanners! Give him your eyes."

Parizianski was not good at public speaking. His lips moved too fast. He waved his hands, which took the eyes of the others away from his lips. Nevertheless, Martel was able to follow most of the message:

". . . can't do this. Stone may have succeeded. If he has succeeded, it means the end of the scanners. It means the end of the habermans, too. None of us will have to fight in the up-and-out. We won't have anybody else going under the wire for a few hours or days of being human. Everybody will be Other. Nobody will have to cranch, never again. Men can be men. The habermans can be killed decently and properly, the way men were killed in the old days, without anybody keeping them alive. They won't have to work in the up-and-out! There will be no more great pain—think of it! No . . . more . . . great . . . pain! How do we know that Stone is a liar—" Lights began flashing directly into his eyes. (The rudest insult of scanner to scanner was this.)

Vomact again exercised authority. He stepped in front of Parizianski and said something which the others could not see. Parizianski stepped down from the rostrum. Vomact again spoke:

"I think that some of the scanners disagree with our brother Parizianski. I say that the use of the rostrum be suspended till we have had a chance for private discussion. In fifteen minutes I will call the meeting back to order."

Martel looked around for Vomact when the senior had rejoined the group on the floor. Finding the senior, Martel wrote swift script on his tablet, waiting for a chance to thrust the tablet before the senior's eyes. He had written:

Am crnchd. Rspctfly requst prmissn lv now, stnd by fr orders.

Being cranched did strange things to Martel. Most meetings that he attended seemed formal, hearteningly ceremonial, lighting up the dark inward eternities of habermanhood. When he was not cranched, he noticed his body no more than a marble bust notices its marble pedestal. He had stood with them before. He had stood with them effortless hours, while the long-winded ritual broke through the terrible loneliness behind his eyes, and made him feel that the scanners, though a confraternity of the damned, were none the less forever honored by the professional requirements of their mutilation.

This time, it was different. Coming cranched, and in full possession of smell-sound-taste-feeling, he reacted more or less as a normal man would. He saw his friends and colleagues as a lot of cruelly driven ghosts, posturing out the meaningless ritual of their indefeasible damnation. What difference did anything make, once you were a haberman? Why all this talk about habermans and scanners? Habermans were criminals or heretics, and scanners were gentlemen-volunteers, but they were all in the same fix—except that scanners were deemed worthy of the short-time return of the cranching wire, while habermans were simply disconnected while the ships lay in port and were left suspended until they should be awakened, in some hour of emergency or trouble, to work out another spell of their damnation. It was a rare haberman that you saw on the street—someone of special merit or bravery, allowed to look at mankind from the terrible prison of his own mechanified body. And yet, what scanner ever pitied a haberman? What scanner ever honored a haberman except perfunctorily in the line of duty? What had the scanners as a guild and a class ever done for the habermans, except to murder them with a twist of the wrist whenever a haberman, too long beside a scanner, picked up the tricks of the scanning trade and learned how to live at his own will, not the will the scanners imposed? What could the Others, the ordinary men, know of what went on inside the ships? The Others slept in their cylinders, mercifully unconscious until they woke up on whatever other Earth they had consigned themselves to. What could the Others know of the men who had to stay alive within the ship?

What could any Other know of the up-and-out? What Other could look at the biting acid beauty of the stars in open space? What could they tell of the great pain, which started quietly in the marrow, like an ache, and proceeded by the fatigue and nausea of each separate nerve cell, brain cell, touchpoint in the body, until life itself became a terrible aching hunger for silence and for death?

He was a scanner. All right, he *was* a scanner. He had been a scanner from the moment when, wholly normal, he had stood in the sunlight before a subchief of the Instrumentality, and had sworn:

"I pledge my honor and my life to mankind. I sacrifice myself willingly for the welfare of mankind. In accepting the perilous austere honor, I yield all my rights without exception to the honorable chiefs of the Instrumentality and to the honored Confraternity of Scanners."

He had pledged.

He had gone into the haberman device.

He had remembered his hell. He had not had such a bad one, even though it had seemed to last a hundred-million years, all of them without sleep. He had learned to feel with his eyes. He had learned to see despite the heavy eyeplates set back of his eyeballs to insulate his eyes from the rest of him. He had learned to watch his skin. He still remembered the time he had noticed dampness on his shirt, and had pulled out his scanning mirror only to discover that he had worn a hole in his side by leaning against a vibrating machine. (A thing like that could not happen to him now; he was too adept at reading his own instruments.) He remembered the way that he had gone up-and-out, and the way that the great pain beat into him, despite the fact that his touch, smell, feeling, and hearing were gone for all ordinary purposes. He remembered killing habermans, and keeping others alive, and standing for months beside the honorable scanner-pilot while neither of them slept. He remembered going ashore on Earth Four, and remembered that he had not enjoyed it, and had realized on that day that there was no reward.

Martel stood among the other scanners. He hated their awkwardness when they moved, their immobility when they stood still. He hated the queer assortment of smells which their bodies yielded unnoticed. He hated the grunts and groans and squawks which they emitted from their deafness. He hated them, and himself.

How could Luci stand him? He had kept his chestbox reading *Danger* for weeks while he courted her, carrying the cranch wire about with him most illegally, and going direct from one cranch to the other without worrying about the fact his indicators all crept up to the edge of *Overload*. He had wooed her without thinking of what would happen if she did say, "Yes." She had.

"And they lived happily ever after." In old books they did, but how could they, in life? He had had eighteen days under the wire in the whole of the past year! Yet she had loved him. She still loved him. He knew it. She fretted about him through the long months that he was in the up-and-out. She tried to make home mean something to him even when he was haberman, make food pretty when it could not be tasted, make herself lovable when she could not be kissed—or might as well not, since a haberman body meant no more than furniture. Luci was patient.

And now, Adam Stone! (He let his tablet fade: how could he leave, now?)

God bless Adam Stone?

Martel could not help feeling a little sorry for himself. No longer would the high keen call of duty carry him through two hundred or so years of the Others' time, two million private eternities of his own. He could slouch and relax. He could forget high space, and let the up-and-out be tended by Others. He could cranch as much as he dared. He could be almost normal—almost—for one year or five years or no years. But at least he could stay with Luci. He could go with her into the Wild, where there were Beasts and Old Machines still roving the dark places. Perhaps he would die in the excitement of the hunt, throwing spears at an ancient manshonyagger as it leapt from its lair, or tossing hot spheres at the tribesmen of the Unforgiven who still roamed the Wild. There was still life to live, still a good normal death to die, not the moving of a needle out in the silence and agony of space!

He had been walking about restlessly. His ears were attuned to the sounds of normal speech, so that he did not feel like watching the mouthings of his brethren. Now they seemed to have come to a decision. Vomact was moving to the rostrum. Martel looked about for Chang, and went to stand beside him. Chang whispered.

"You're as restless as water in mid-air! What's the matter? Decranching?"

They both scanned Martel, but the instruments held steady and showed no sign of the cranch giving out.

The great light flared in its call to attention. Again they formed ranks. Vomact thrust his lean old face into the glare, and spoke:

"Scanners and Brothers, I call for a vote." He held himself in the stance which meant: *I am the senior and take command.*

A beltlight flashed in protest.

It was old Henderson. He moved to the rostrum, spoke to Vomact, and—with Vomact's nod of approval—turned full-face to repeat his question:

"Who speaks for the scanners out in space?"

No beltlight or hand answered.

Henderson and Vomact, face to face, conferred for a few moments. Then Henderson faced them again:

"I yield to the senior in command. But I do not yield to a meeting of the Confraternity. There are sixty-eight scanners, and only forty-seven present of whom one is cranched and U. D. I have therefore proposed that the senior in command assume authority only over an emergency committee of the Confraternity, not over a meeting. Is that agreed and understood by the honorable scanners?"

Hands rose in assent.

Chang murmured in Martel's ear, "Lot of difference that makes! Who can tell the difference between a meeting and a committee?" Martel agreed with the words, but was even more impressed with the way that Chang, while haberman, could control his own voice.

Vomact resumed chairmanship: "We now vote on the question of Adam Stone.

"First, we can assume that he has not succeeded, and that his claims are lies. We know that from our practical experience as scanners. The pain of space is only part of scanning," (*But the essential part, the basis of it all,* thought Martel.) "and we can rest assured that Stone cannot solve the problem of space discipline."

"That tripe again," whispered Chang, unheard save by Martel.

"The space discipline of our confraternity has kept high space clean of war and dispute. Sixty-eight disciplined men control all high space. We are removed by our oath and our haberman status from all Earthly passions.

"Therefore, if Adam Stone has conquered the pain of space, so that Others can wreck our confraternity and bring to space the trouble and ruin which afflicts Earths, I say that Adam Stone is wrong. If Adam Stone succeeds, scanners live in vain!

"Secondly, if Adam Stone has not conquered the pain of space, he will cause great trouble in all the Earths. The Instrumentality and the subchiefs may not give us as many habermans as we need to operate the ships of mankind. There will be wild stories, and fewer recruits, and, worst of all, the discipline of the Confraternity may relax if this kind of nonsensical heresy is spread around.

"Therefore, if Adam Stone has succeeded, he threatens the ruin of the Confraternity and should die.

"I move the death of Adam Stone."

And Vomact made the sign, *The honorable scanners are pleased to vote.*

Martel grabbed wildly for his beltlight. Chang, guessing ahead, had his light out and ready; its bright beam, voting *No,* shone straight up at the ceiling. Martel got his light out and threw its beam upward in dissent. Then he looked around. Out of the forty-seven present, he could see only five or six glittering.

Two more lights went on. Vomact stood as erect as a frozen corpse. Vomact's eyes flashed as he stared back and forth over the group, looking for lights. Several more went on. Finally Vomact took the closing stance:

May it please the scanners to count the vote.

Three of the older men went up on the rostrum with Vomact. They looked over the room. (Martel thought; *These damned ghosts are voting on the life of a real man, a live man! They have no right to do it. I'll tell the Instrumentality!* But he knew that he would not. He thought of Luci and what she might gain by the triumph of Adam Stone: the heart-breaking folly of the vote was then almost too much for Martel to bear.)

All three of the tellers held up their hands in unanimous agreement on the sign of the number: *Fifteen against.*

Vomact dismissed them with a bow of courtesy. He turned and again took the stance: *I am the senior and take command.*

Marveling at his own daring, Martel flashed his beltlight on. He knew that any one of the bystanders might reach over and twist his heartbox to *Overload* for such an act. He felt Chang's hand reaching to catch him by the aircoat. But he eluded Chang's grasp and ran, faster than a scanner should, to the platform. As he ran, he wondered what appeal to make. It was no use talking common sense. Not now. It had to be law.

He jumped up on the rostrum beside Vomact, and took the stance: *Scanners, a Illegality!*

He violated good custom while speaking, still in the stance: "A committee has no right to vote death by a majority vote. It takes two-thirds of a full meeting."

He felt Vomact's body lunge behind him, felt himself falling from the rostrum, hitting the floor, hurting his knees and his touch-aware hands. He was helped to his feet. He was scanned. Some scanner he scarcely knew took his instruments and toned him down.

Immediately Martel felt more calm, more detached, and hated himself for feeling so.

He looked up at the rostrum. Vomact maintained the stance signifying: *Order!*

The scanners adjusted their ranks. The two scanners next to Martel took his arms. He shouted at them, but they looked away, and cut themselves off from communication altogether.

Vomact spoke again when he saw the room was quiet: "A scanner came here cranched. Honorable Scanners, I apologize for this. It is not the fault of our great and worthy scanner and friend, Martel. He came here under orders. I told him not to de-cranch. I hoped to spare him an unnecessary haberman. We all know how happily Martel is married, and we wish his brave experiment well. I like Martel. I respect his judgment. I wanted him here. I knew you wanted him here. But he is cranched. He is in no mood to share in the lofty business of the scanners. I therefore propose a solution which will meet all the requirements of fairness. I propose that we rule Scanner Martel out of order for his violation of rules. This violation would be inexcusable if Martel were not cranched.

"But at the same time, in all fairness to Martel, I further propose that we deal with the points raised so improperly by our worthy but disqualified brother."

Vomact gave the sign, *The honorable scanners are pleased to vote*. Martel tried to reach his own beltlight; the dead strong hands held him tightly and he struggled in vain. One lone light shone high: Chang's, no doubt.

Vomact thrust his face into the light again: "Having the approval of our worthy scanners and present company for the general proposal, I now move that this committee declare itself to have the full authority of a meeting, and that this committee further make me responsible for all misdeeds which this committee may enact, to be held answerable before the next full meeting, but not before any other authority beyond the closed and secret ranks of scanners."

Flamboyantly this time, his triumph evident, Vomact assumed the *vote* stance.

Only a few lights shone: far less, patently, than a minority of one-fourth.

Vomact spoke again. The light shone on his high calm forehead, on his dead relaxed cheekbones. His lean cheeks and chin were half-shadowed, save where the lower light picked up and spotlighted his mouth, cruel even in repose. (Vomact was said to be a descendant of some ancient lady who had traversed, in an illegitimate and inexplicable fashion, some hundreds of years of time in a single night. Her name, the Lady Vomact, had passed into legend; but her blood and her archaic lust for mastery lived on in the mute masterful body of her descendant. Martel could believe the old tales as he stared at the rostrum, wondering what untraceable mutation had left the Vomact kin as predators among mankind.) Calling loudly with the movement of his lips, but still without sound, Vomact appealed:

"The honorable committee is now pleased to reaffirm the sentence of death issued against the heretic and enemy, Adam Stone." Again the *vote* stance.

Again Chang's light shone lonely in its isolated protest.

Vomact then made his final move:

"I call for the designation of the senior scanner present as the manager of the sentence. I call for authorization to him to appoint executioners, one or many, who shall make evident the will and majesty of scanners. I ask that I be accountable for the deed, and not for the means. The deed is a noble deed, for the protection of mankind and for the honor of the scanners; but of the means it must be said that they are to be the best at hand, and no more. Who knows the true way to kill an Other, here on a crowded and watchful Earth? This is no mere matter of discharging a cylindered sleeper, no mere question of upgrading the needle of a haberman. When people die down here, it is not like the up-and-out. They die reluctantly. Killing within the Earth is not our usual business, O Brothers and Scanners, as you know well. You must choose me to choose my agent as I see fit. Otherwise the common knowledge will become the common betrayal whereas if I alone know the responsibility, I alone could betray us, and you will not have far to look in case the Instrumentality comes searching." (*What about the killer you choose?* thought Martel. *He too will know unless—unless you silence him forever.*)

Vomact went into the stance: *The honorable scanners are pleased to vote.*

One light of protest shone; Chang's, again.

Martel imagined that he could see a cruel joyful smile on Vomact's dead face—the smile of a man who knew himself righteous and who found his righteousness upheld and affirmed by militant authority.

Martel tried one last time to come free.

The dead hands held. They were locked like vises until their owners' eyes unlocked them; how else could they hold the piloting month by month?

Martel then shouted: "Honorable Scanners, this is judicial murder."

No ear heard him. He was cranched, and alone.

Nonetheless, he shouted again: "You endanger the Confraternity."

Nothing happened.

The echo of his voice sounded from one end of the room to the other. No head turned. No eyes met his.

Martel realized that as they paired for talk, the eyes of the scanners avoided him. He saw that no one desired to watch his speech. He knew that behind the cold faces of his friends there lay compassion or amusement. He knew that they knew him to be cranched—absurd, normal, manlike, temporarily no scanner. But he knew that in this matter the wisdom of scanners was nothing. He knew that only a cranched scanner could feel with his very blood the outrage and anger which deliberate murder would provoke among the Others. He knew that the Confraternity endangered itself, and knew that the most ancient prerogative of law was the monopoly of death. Even the ancient nations, in the times of the Wars, before the Beasts, before men went into the up-and-out—even the ancients had known this. How did they say it? *Only the state shall kill.* The states were gone but the Instrumentality remained, and the Instrumentality could not pardon things which occurred within the Earths but beyond its authority. Death in space was the business, the right of the scanners: how could the Instrumentality enforce its laws in a place where all men who wakened, wakened only to die in the great pain? Wisely did the Instrumentality leave space to the scanners, wisely had the Confraternity not meddled inside the Earths. And now the Confraternity itself was going to step forth as a outlaw band, as a gang of rogues as stupid and reckless as the tribes of the Unforgiven!

Martel knew this because he was cranched. Had he been haberman, he would have thought only with his mind, not with his heart and guts and blood. How could the other scanners know?

Vomact returned for the last time to the rostrum: *The committee has met and its will shall be done.* Verbally he added: "Senior among you, I ask your loyalty and your silence."

At that point, the two scanners let his arms go. Martel rubbed his numb hands, shaking his fingers to get the circulation back into the cold fingertips. With real freedom, he began to think of what he might still do. He scanned himself; the cranching held. He might have a day. Well, he could go on even if haberman, but it would be inconvenient, having to talk with finger and tablet. He looked about for Chang. He saw his friend standing patient and immobile in a quiet corner. Martel moved slowly, so as not to attract any more attention to himself than could be helped. He faced Chang, moved until his face was in the light, and then articulated:

"What are we going to do? You're not going to let them kill Adam Stone, are you? Don't you realize what Stone's work will mean to us, if it succeeds? No more scanners. No more habermans. No more pain in the up-and-out. I tell you, if the others were all cranched, as I am, they would see it in a human way, not with the narrow crazy logic which they used in the meeting. We've got to stop them. How can we do it? What are we going to do? What does Parizianski think? Who has been chosen?"

"Which question do you want me to answer?"

Martel laughed. (It felt good to laugh, even then; it felt like being a man.) "Will you help me?"

Chang's eyes flashed across Martel's face as Chang answered: "No. No. No."

"You won't help?"

"No."

"Why not, Chang? Why not?"

"I am a scanner. The vote has been taken. You would do the same if you were not in this unusual condition."

"I'm not in an unusual condition. I'm cranched. That merely means that I see things the way that the Others would. I see the stupidity. The recklessness. The selfishness. It is murder."

"What is murder? Have you not killed? You are not one of the Others. You are a scanner. You will be sorry for what you are about to do, if you do not watch out."

"But why did you vote against Vomact then? Didn't you too see what Adam Stone means to all of us? Scanners will live in vain. Thank God for that! Can't you see it?"

"No."

"But you talk to me, Chang. You are my friend?"

"I talk to you. I am your friend. Why not?"

"But what are you going to do?"

"Nothing, Martel. Nothing."

"Will you help me?"

"No."

"Not even to save Stone?"

"No."

"Then I will go to Parizianski for help."

"It will do you no good."

"Why not? He's more human than you, right now."

"He will not help you, because he has the job. Vomact designated him to kill Adam Stone."

Martel stopped speaking in mid-movement. He suddenly took the stance: *I thank you, Brother, and I depart.*

At the window he turned and faced the room. He saw that Vomact's eyes were upon him. He gave the stance, *I thank you, Brother, and I depart,* and added the flourish of respect which is shown when seniors are present. Vomact caught the sign, and Martel could see the cruel lips move. He thought he saw the words ". . . take good care of yourself . . ." but did not wait to inquire. He stepped backward and dropped out the window.

Once below the window and out of sight, he adjusted his aircoat to a maximum speed. He swam lazily in the air, scanning himself thoroughly, and adjusting his adrenal intake down. He then made the movement of release, and felt the cold air rush past his face like running water.

Adam Stone had to be at Chief Downport.

Adam Stone had to be there.

Wouldn't Adam Stone be surprised in the night? Surprised to meet the strangest of beings, the first renegade among scanners. (Martel suddenly appreciated that it was of himself he was thinking. Martel the Traitor to Scanners! That sounded strange and bad. But what of Martel, the Loyal to Mankind? Was that not compensation? And if he won, he won Luci. If he lost, he lost nothing—an unconsidered and expendable haberman. It happened to be himself. But in contrast to the immense reward, to mankind, to the Confraternity, to Luci, what did that matter?)

Martel thought to himself: "Adam Stone will have two visitors tonight. Two scanners, who are the friends of one another." He hoped that Parizianski was still his friend.

"And the world," he added, "depends on which of us gets there first."

Multifaceted in their brightness, the lights of Chief Downport began to shine through the mist ahead. Martel could see the outer towers of the city and glimpsed the phosphorescent periphery which kept back the Wild, whether Beasts, Machines, or the Unforgiven.

Once more Martel invoked the lords of his chance: "Help me to pass for an Other!"

Within the Downport, Martel had less trouble than he thought. He draped his aircoat over his shoulder so that it concealed the instruments. He took up his scanning mirror, and made up his face from the inside, by adding tone and animation to his blood and nerves until the muscles of his face glowed and the skin gave out a healthy sweat. That way he looked like an ordinary man who had just completed a long night flight.

After straightening out his clothing, and hiding his tablet within his jacket, he faced the problem of what to do about the talking finger. If he kept the nail, it would show him to be a scanner. He would be respected, but he would be identified. He might be stopped by the guards whom the Instrumentality had undoubtedly set around the person of Adam Stone. If he broke the nail— But he couldn't! No scanner in the history of the Confraternity had ever willingly broken his nail. That would be resignation, and there was no such thing. The only way *out*, was in the up-and-out! Martel put his finger to his mouth and bit off the nail. He looked at the now-queer finger, and sighed to himself.

He stepped toward the city gate, slipping his hand into his jacket and running up his muscular strength to four times normal. He started to scan, and then realized that his instruments were masked. *Might as well take all the chances at once,* he thought.

The watcher stopped him with a searching wire. The sphere thumped suddenly against Martel's chest.

"Are you a man?" said the unseen voice. (Martel knew that as a scanner in haberman condition, his own field-charge would have illuminated the sphere.)

"I am a man." Martel knew that the timbre of his voice had been good; he hoped that it would not be taken for that of a manshonyagger or a Beast or an Unforgiven one, who with mimicry sought to enter the cities and ports of mankind.

"Name, number, rank, purpose, function, time departed."

"Martel." He had to remember his old number, not Scanner 34. "Sunward 4234, 782nd Year of Space. Rank, rising subchief." That was no lie, but his substantive rank. "Purpose, personal and lawful within the limits of this city. No function of the Instrumentality. Departed Chief Outport 2019 hours." Everything now depended on whether he was believed, or would be checked against Chief Outport.

The voice was flat and routine: "Time desired within the city."

Martel used the standard phrase: "Your honorable sufference is requested."

He stood in the cool night air, waiting. Far above him, through a gap in the mist, he could see the poisonous glittering in the sky of scanners. *The stars are my enemies,* he thought: *I have mastered the stars but they hate me. Ho, that sounds ancient! Like a book. Too much cranching.*

The voice returned: "Sunward 4234 dash 782 rising subchief Martel, enter the lawful gates of the city. Welcome. Do you desire food, raiment, money, or companionship?" The voice had no hospitality in it, just business. This was certainly different from entering a city in a scanner's role! Then the petty officers came out, and threw their beltlights on their fretful faces, and mouthed their words with preposterous deference, shouting against the stone deafness of scanner's ears. So that was the way that a subchief was treated: matter of fact, but not bad. Not bad.

Martel replied: "I have that which I need, but beg of the city a favor. My friend Adam Stone is here. I desire to see him, on urgent and personal lawful affairs."

The voice replied: "Did you have an appointment with Adam Stone?"

"No."

"The city will find him. What is his number?"

"I have forgotten it."

"You have forgotten it? Is not Adam Stone a magnate of the Instrumentality? Are you truly his friend?"

"Truly." Martel let a little annoyance creep into his voice. "Watcher, doubt me and call your subchief."

"No doubt implied. Why do you not know the number? This must go into the record," added the voice.

"We were friends in childhood. He has crossed the—" Martel started to say "the up-and-out" and remembered that the phrase was current only among scanners. "He has leapt from Earth to Earth, and has just now returned. I knew him well and I seek him out. I have word of his kith. May the Instrumentality protect us!"

"Heard and believed. Adam Stone will be searched."

At a risk, though a slight one, of having the sphere sound an alarm for *nonhuman,* Martel cut in on his scanner speaker within his jacket. He saw the trembling needle of light await his words and he started to write on it with his blunt finger. *That won't work,* he thought, and had a moment's panic until he found his comb, which had a sharp enough tooth to write. He wrote: "Emergency none. Martel Scanner calling Parizianski Scanner."

The needle quivered and the reply glowed and faded out: "Parizianski Scanner on duty and D.C. Calls taken by Scanner Relay."

Martel cut off his speaker.

Parizianski was somewhere around. Could he have crossed the direct way, right over the city wall, setting off the alert, and invoking official business when the petty officers overtook him in mid-air? Scarcely. That meant that a number of other scanners must have come in with Parizianski, all of them pretending to be in search of a few of the tenuous pleasures which could be enjoyed by a haberman, such as the sight of the newspictures or the viewing of beautiful women in the Pleasure Gallery. Parizianski was around, but he could not have moved privately, because Scanner Central registered him on duty and recorded his movements city by city.

The voice returned. Puzzlement was expressed in it. "Adam Stone is found and awakened. He has asked pardon of the Honorable, and says he knows no Martel. Will you see Adam Stone in the morning? The city will bid you welcome."

Martel ran out of resources. It was hard enough mimicking a man without having to tell lies in the guise of one. Martel could only repeat: "Tell him I am Martel. The husband of Luci."

"It will be done."

Again the silence, and the hostile stars, and the sense that Parizianski was somewhere near and getting nearer; Martel felt his heart beating faster. He stole a glimpse at his chestbox and set his heart down a point. He felt calmer, even though he had not been able to scan with care.

The voice this time was cheerful, as though an annoyance had been settled: "Adam Stone consents to see you. Enter Chief Downport, and welcome."

The little sphere dropped noiselessly to the ground and the wire whispered away into the darkness. A bright arc of narrow light rose from the ground in front of Martel and swept through the city to one of the higher towers—apparently a hostel, which Martel had never entered. Martel plucked his aircoat to his chest for ballast, stepped heel-and-toe on the beam, and felt himself whistle through the air to an entrance window which sprang up before him as suddenly as a devouring mouth.

A tower guard stood in the doorway. "You are awaited, sir. Do you bear weapons, sir?"

"None," said Martel, grateful that he was relying on his own strength.

The guard led him past the check-screen. Martel noticed the quick flight of a warning across the screen as his instruments registered and identified him as a scanner. But the guard had not noticed it.

The guard stopped at a door. "Adam Stone is armed. He is lawfully armed by authority of the Instrumentality and by the liberty of this city. All those who enter are given warning."

Martel nodded in understanding at the man and went in.

Adam Stone was a short man, stout and benign. His gray hair rose stiffly from a low forehead. His whole face was red and merry-looking. He looked like a jolly guide from the Pleasure Gallery, not like a man who had been at the edge of the up-and-out, fighting the great pain without haberman protection.

He stared at Martel. His look was puzzled, perhaps a little annoyed, but not hostile.

Martel came to the point. "You do not know me. I lied. My name is Martel, and I mean you no harm. But I lied. I beg the honorable gift of your hospitality. Remain armed. Direct your weapon against me—"

Stone smiled: "I am doing so," and Martel noticed the small wirepoint in Stone's capable, plump hand.

"Good. Keep on guard against me. It will give you confidence in what I shall say. But do, I beg of you, give us a screen of privacy. I want no casual lookers. This is a matter of life and death."

"First: whose life and death?" Stone's face remained calm, his voice even.

"Yours, and mine, and the worlds'."

"You are cryptic but I agree." Stone called through the doorway: "Privacy please." There was a sudden hum, and all the little noises of the night quickly vanished from the air of the room.

Said Adam Stone: "Sir, who are you? What brings you here?"

"I am Scanner 34."

"You a scanner? I don't believe it."

For an answer, Martel pulled his jacket open, showing his chestbox. Stone looked up at him, amazed. Martel explained:

"I am cranched. Have you never seen it before?"

"*Not with men*. On animals. Amazing! But—what do you want?"

"The truth. Do you fear me?"

"Not with this," said Stone, grasping the wirepoint. "But I shall tell you the truth."

"Is it true that you have conquered the great pain?"

Stone hesitated, seeking words for an answer.

"Quick, can you tell me how you have done it, so that I may believe you?"

"I have loaded the ships with life."

"Life?"

"Life. I don't know what the great pain is, but I did find that in the experiments, when I sent out masses of animals or plants, the life in the center of the mass lived longest. I built ships—small ones, of course—and sent them out with rabbits, with monkeys—"

"Those are Beasts?"

"Yes. With small Beasts. And the Beasts came back unhurt. They came back because the walls of the ships were filled with life. I tried many kinds, and finally found a sort of life which lives in the waters. Oysters. Oyster-beds. The outermost oysters died in the great pain. The inner ones lived. The passengers were unhurt."

"But they were Beasts?"

"Not only Beasts. Myself."

"You!"

"I came through space alone. Through what you call the up-and-out, alone. Awake and sleeping. I am unhurt. If you do not believe me, ask your brother scanners. Come and see my ship in the morning. I will be glad to see you then, along with your brother scanners. I am going to demonstrate before the chiefs of the Instrumentality."

Martel repeated his question: "You came here alone?"

Adam Stone grew testy: "Yes, alone. Go back and check your scanner's register if you do not believe me. You never put me in a bottle to cross Space."

Martel's face was radiant. "I believe you now. It is true. No more scanners. No more habermans. No more cranching."

Stone looked significantly toward the door.

Martel did not take the hint. "I must tell you that—"

"Sir, tell me in the morning. Go enjoy your cranch. Isn't it supposed to be pleasure? Medically I know it well. But not in practice."

"It is pleasure. It's normality—for a while. But listen. The scanners have sworn to destroy you, and your work."

"What!"

"They have met and have voted and sworn. You will make scanners unnecessary, they say. You will bring the ancient wars back to the world, if scanning is lost and the scanners live in vain!"

Adam Stone was nervous but kept his wits about him: "You're a scanner. Are you going to kill me—or try?"

"No, you fool. I have betrayed the Confraternity. Call guards the moment I escape. Keep guards around you. I will try to intercept the killer."

Martel saw a blur in the window. Before Stone could turn, the wirepoint was whipped out of his hand. The blur solidified and took form as Parizianski.

Martel recognized what Parizianski was doing: *High speed.*

Without thinking of his cranch, he thrust his hand to his chest, set himself up to *High speed* too. Waves of fire, like the great pain, but hotter, flooded over him. He fought to keep his face readable as he stepped in front of Parizianski and gave the sign, *Top emergency.*

Parizianski spoke, while the normally moving body of Stone stepped away from them as slowly as a drifting cloud: "Get out of my way. I am on a mission."

"I know it. I stop you here and now. Stop. Stop. Stop. Stone is right."

Parizianski's lips were barely readable in the haze of pain which flooded Martel. (He thought: *God, God, God of the ancients! Let me hold on! Let me live under* Overload *just long enough!)* Parizianski was saying: "Get out of my way. By order of the Confraternity, get out of my way!" And Parizianski gave the sign, *Help I demand in the name of my duty!*

Martel choked for breath in the syruplike air. He tried one last time: "Parizianski, friend, friend, my friend. Stop. Stop." (No scanner had ever murdered scanner before.)

Parizianski made the sign: *You are unfit for duty, and I will take over.*

Martel thought, *For the first time in the world!* as he reached over and twisted Parizianski's brainbox up to *Overload*. Parizianski's eyes glittered in terror and understanding. His body began to drift down toward the floor.

Martel had just strength to reach his own chestbox. As he faded into haberman or death, he knew not which, he felt his fingers turning on the control of speed, turning down. He tried to speak, to say, "Get a scanner, I need help, get a scanner . . ."

But the darkness rose about him, and the numb silence clasped him.

Martel awakened to see the face of Luci near his own.

He opened his eyes wider, and found that he was hearing—hearing the sound of her happy weeping, the sound of her chest as she caught the air back into her throat.

He spoke weakly: "Still cranched? Alive?"

Another face swam into the blur beside Luci's. It was Adam Stone. His deep voice rang across immensities of space before coming to Martel's hearing. Martel tried to read Stone's lips, but could not make them out. He went back to listening to the voice:

". . . not cranched. Do you understand me? Not cranched!"

Martel tried to say: "But I can hear! I can feel!" The others got his sense if not his words.

Adam Stone spoke again:

"You have gone back through the haberman. I put you back first. I didn't know how it would work in practice, but I had the theory all worked out. You don't think the Instrumentality would waste the scanners, do you? You go back to normality. We are letting the habermans die as fast as the ships come in. They don't need to live anymore. But we are restoring the scanners. You are the first. Do you understand? You are the first. Take it easy, now."

Adam Stone smiled. Dimly behind Stone, Martel thought that he saw the face of one of the chiefs of the Instrumentality. That face, too, smiled at him, and then both faces disappeared upward and away.

Martel tried to lift his head, to scan himself. He could not. Luci stared at him, calming herself, but with an expression of loving perplexity. She said,

"My darling husband! You're back again, to stay!"

Still, Martel tried to see his box. Finally he swept his hand across his chest with a clumsy motion. There was nothing there.

The instruments were gone. He was back to normality but still alive.

In the deep weak peacefulness of his mind, another troubling thought took shape. He tried to write with his finger, the way that Luci wanted him to, but he had neither pointed fingernail nor scanner's tablet. He had to use his voice. He summoned up his strength and whispered:

"Scanners?"

"Yes, darling? What is it?"

"Scanners?"

"Scanners. Oh, yes, darling, they're all right. They had to arrest some of them for going into *High speed* and running away. But the Instrumentality caught them all—all those on the ground—and they're happy now. Do you know, darling," she laughed, "some of them didn't want to be restored to normality. But Stone and the chiefs persuaded them."

"Vomact?"

"He's fine, too. He's staying cranched until he can be restored. Do you know, he has arranged for scanners to take new jobs. You're all to be deputy chiefs for Space. Isn't that nice? But he got himself made chief for Space. You're all going to be pilots, so that your fraternity and guild can go on. And Chang's getting changed right now. You'll see him soon."

Her face turned sad. She looked at him earnestly and said: "I might as well tell you now. You'll worry otherwise. There has been one accident. Only one. When you and your friend called on Adam Stone, your friend was so happy that he forgot to scan, and he let himself die of *Overload*."

"Called on Stone?"

"Yes. Don't you remember? Your friend."

He still looked surprised, so she said:

"Parizianski."

BORN OF MAN AND WOMAN

Richard Matheson (1926–)

THE MAGAZINE OF FANTASY AND SCIENCE FICTION
Summer

"Born of Man and Woman" was Richard Matheson's first sf story, and opened a rich career that includes such novels as I Am Legend *(1954) and* The Shrinking Man *(1956), both of which were filmed (the former twice, as* The Last Man on Earth *and* The Omega Man, *neither doing justice to the book). Matheson's connections with filmed sf and fantasy are considerable—he did many of the screenplays for Roger Corman's Poe movies, as well as for such television productions as the memorable* Duel *(later released theatrically),* The Night Stalker *series, and* The Enemy Within, *one of the best* Star Trek *scripts. His peers in the industry have recognized his talent with two Writers Guild of America Awards. He also has won a Hugo (for best screenplay) and the World Fantasy Award. Although he is often compared with Ray Bradbury and Charles Beaumont, his is a singular voice, and his early work was influential in the development of both science fiction and the contemporary horror story. His best short stories are scattered through six collections, and a definitive* Best of *book awaits publication.*

—M.H.G.

I'm ambivalent about first stories that are instantly recognized as classics. On the one hand, I turn slightly green, because my first published story was not a classic. (My fourteenth story was my first classic.) On the other hand, who wants to spend the rest of his life trying to repeat that first smash, though, as it turned out, Matheson didn't have much trouble with that.

Let me say this about "Born of Man and Woman": There are many stories I read thirty years ago and more, that I've liked and admired and felt I remembered. Usually, though, in preparing thses anthologies, I don't feel safe about it and must re-read it to make sure *what I remember is actually so and that the story does hold up over the years. Not so in the case of "Born of Man and Woman"; I remembered every word and was never in any doubt it belonged here. Read it and you'll see.*

—I.A.

X—— This day when it had light mother called me a retch. You retch she said. I saw in her eyes the anger. I wonder what is a retch.

This day it had water falling from upstairs. It fell all around. I saw that. The ground of the back I watched from the little window. The ground it sucked up the water like thirsty lips. It drank too much and it got sick and runny brown. I didn't like it.

Mother is a pretty I know. In my bed place with cold walls around I have a paper things that was behind the furnace. It says on it SCREENSTARS. I see in the pictures faces like of mother and father. Father says they are pretty. Once he said it.

And also mother he said. Mother so pretty and me decent enough. Look at you he said and didn't have the nice face. I touched his arm and said it is all right father. He shook and pulled away where I couldn't reach.

Today mother let me off the chain a little so I could look out the little window. That's how I saw the water falling from upstairs.

XX—— This day it had goldness in the upstairs. As I know, when I looked at it my eyes hurt. After I look at it the cellar is red.

I think this was church. They leave the upstairs. The big machine swallows them and rolls out past and is gone. In the back part is the *little* mother. She is much small than me. I am big. It is a secret but I have pulled the chain out of the wall. I can see out the little window all I like.

In this day when it got dark I had eat my food and some bugs.

I hear laughs upstairs. I like to know why there are laughs for. I took the chain from the wall and wrapped it around me. I walk squish to the stairs. They creak when I walk on them. My legs slip on them because I don't walk on stairs. My feet stick to the wood.

I went up and opened a door. It was a white place. White as white jewels that come from upstairs sometime. I went in and stood quiet. I hear the laughing some more. I walk to the sound and look through to the people. More people than I thought was. I thought I should laugh with them.

Mother came out and pushed the door in. It hit me and hurt. I fell back on the smooth floor and the chain made noise. I cried. She made a hissing noise into her and put her hand on her mouth. Her eyes got big.

She looked at me. I heard father call. What fell he called. She said an iron board. Come help pick it up she said. He came and said now is *that* so heavy you need. He saw me and grew big. The anger came in his eyes. He hit me. I spilled some of the drip on the floor from one arm. It was not nice. It made ugly green on the floor.

Father told me to go to the cellar. I had to go. The light it hurt some now in my eyes. It is not so like that in the cellar.

Father tied my legs and arms up. He put me on my bed. Upstairs I heard laughing while I was quiet there looking on a black spider that was swinging down to me. I thought what father said. Ohgod he said. And only eight.

XXX—— This day father hit in the chain again before it had light. I have to try pull it out again. He said I was bad to come upstairs. He said never do that again or he would beat me hard. That hurts.

I hurt. I slept the day and rested my head against the cold wall. I thought of the white place upstairs.

XXXX—— I got the chain from the wall out. Mother was upstairs. I heard little laughs very high. I looked out the window. I saw all little people like the little mother and little fathers too. They are pretty.

They were making nice noise and jumping around the ground. Their legs was moving hard. They are like mother and father. Mother says all right people look like they do.

One of the little fathers saw me. He pointed at the window. I let go and slid down the wall in the dark. I curled up as they would not see. I heard their talks by the window and foots running. Upstairs there was a door hitting. I heard the little mother call upstairs. I heard heavy steps and I rushed to my bed place. I hit the chain in the wall and lay down on my front.

I heard mother come down. Have you been at the window she said. I heard the anger. *Stay* away from the window. You have pulled the chain out again.

She took the stick and hit me with it. I didn't cry. I can't do that. But the drip ran all over the bed. She saw it and twisted away and made a noise. Oh mygod mygod she said why have you *done* this to me? I heard the stick go bounce on the stone floor. She ran upstairs. I slept the day.

XXX—— This day it had water again. When mother was upstairs I heard the little one come slow down the steps. I hidded myself in the coal bin for mother would have anger if the little mother saw me.

She had a little live thing with her. It walked on the arms and had pointy ears. She said things to it.

It was all right except the live thing smelled me. It ran up the coal and looked down at me. The hairs stood up. In the throat it made an angry noise. I hissed but it jumped on me.

I didn't want to hurt it. I got fear because it bit me harder than the rat does. I hurt and the little mother screamed. I grabbed the live thing tight. It made sounds I never heard. I pushed it all together. It was all lumpy and red on the black coal.

I hid there when mother called. I was afraid of the stick. She left. I crept over the coal with the thing. I hid it under my pillow and rested on it. I put the chain in the wall again.

X—— This is another times. Father chained me tight. I hurt because he beat me. This time I hit the stick out of his hands and made noise. He went away and his face was white. He ran out of my bed place and locked the door.

I am not so glad. All day it is cold in here. The chain comes slow out of the wall. And I have a bad anger with mother and father. I will show them. I will do what I did that once.

I will screech and laugh loud. I will run on the walls. Last I will hang head down by all my legs and laugh and drip green all over until they are sorry they didn't be nice to me.

If they try to beat me again I'll hurt them. I will.

THE LITTLE BLACK BAG

C. M. Kornbluth

ASTOUNDING SCIENCE FICTION

July

Until his tragic death in 1958 at the age of 35, Cyril M. Kornbluth was one of the finest craftmen working in the science fiction field. He was also one of the most sardonic, both in real life and in his fiction, a man who had little faith in the ability of average people to understand the forces affecting their lives. He liked *the masses in his stories, but his cynical views didn't permit him to respect them. Kornbluth is most famous for his very successful collaborative novels with Frederik Pohl, especially* The Space Merchants *(1953),* Gladiator-at-Law *(1955), and* Wolfbane *(1959).*

Although he had published in the sf magazines in the 1940–42 period, World War II and other concerns kept him silent until 1949. However, once he resumed writing he returned in a major way, and we will meet him many times as this series works its way through the 1950s. 1950 was a particularly notable year for him, and "The Little Black Bag" is the first of three of his stories in this book.

—M.H.G.

The C. stands for Cyril and I met him in 1938, when the Futurians came into being. He was the youngest of us, being only 15 (three years younger than I was at the time) and the most brilliant and erratic of us all. I always seemed quite staid and normal by comparison when I was in his presence.

We didn't get along. I didn't know this at the time because I liked him. (I liked everybody. Still do.) The trouble is that I don't think he liked me. I never really found out why, but I think it may have been that I am always very noisy and happy at gatherings, and he may well have thought I hurt his ears.

Anyway, about the time it began to dawn on me that he disapproved of me, he died—precocious in that as in everything else—and it was too late to get to the bottom of the matter and to make up. I've always regretted that. Especially when I read stories like "The Little Black Bag."

—I.A.

Old Dr. Full felt the winter in his bones as he limped down the alley. It was the alley and the back door he had chosen rather than the sidewalk and the front door because of the brown paper bag under his arm. He knew perfectly well that the flat-faced, stringy-haired women of his street and their gap-toothed, sour-smelling husbands did not notice if he brought a bottle of cheap wine to his room. They all but lived on the stuff themselves, varied with whiskey when pay checks were boosted by overtime. But Dr. Full, unlike them, was ashamed. One of the neighborhood dogs—a mean little black one he knew and hated, with its teeth always bared and always snarling with menace—hurled at his legs through a hole in the board fence that lined his path. Dr. Full flinched, then swung his leg in what was to have been a satisfying kick to the animal's gaunt ribs. But the winter in his bones weighed down the leg. His foot failed to clear a half-buried brick, and he sat down abruptly, cursing. When he smelled unbottled wine and realized his brown paper package had slipped from under his arm and smashed, his curses died on his lips. The snarling black dog was circling him at a yard's distance, tensely stalking, but he ignored it in the greater disaster.

With stiff fingers as he sat on the filth of the alley, Dr. Full unfolded the brown paper bag's top, which had been crimped over, grocer-wise. The early autumnal dusk had come; he could not see plainly what was left. He lifted out the jug-handled top of his half gallon, and some fragments, and then the bottom of the bottle. Dr. Full was far too occupied to exult as he noted that there was a good pint left. He had a problem, and emotions could be deferred until the fitting time.

The dog closed in, its snarl rising in pitch. He set down the bottom of the bottle and pelted the dog with the curved triangular glass fragments of its top. One of them connected, and the dog ducked back through the fence, howling. Dr. Full then placed a razor-like edge of the half-gallon bottle's foundation to his lips and drank from it as though it were a giant's cup. Twice he had to put it down to rest his arms, but in one minute he had swallowed the pint of wine.

He thought of rising to his feet and walking through the alley to his room, but a flood of well-being drowned the notion. It was, after all, inexpressibly pleasant to sit there and feel the frost-hardened mud of the alley turn soft, or seem to, and to feel the winter evaporating from his bones under a warmth which spread from his stomach through his limbs.

A three-year-old girl in a cut-down winter coat squeezed through the same hole in the board fence from which the black dog had sprung its ambush. Gravely she toddled up to Dr. Full and inspected him with her dirty forefinger in her mouth. Dr. Full's happiness had been providentially made complete; he had been supplied with an audience.

"Ah, my dear," he said hoarsely. And then: "Preposserous accusation. 'If that's what you call evidence,' I should have told them, 'you better stick to your doctoring.' I should have told them: 'I was here before your County Medical Society. And the License Commissioner never proved a thing on me. So, gennulmen, doesn't it stand to reason? I appeal to you as fellow memmers of a great profession—' "

The little girl, bored, moved away, picking up one of the triangular pieces of glass to play with as she left. Dr. Full forgot her immediately, and continued to himself earnestly: "But so help me, they *couldn't* prove a thing. Hasn't a man got any *rights?*" He brooded over the question, of whose answer he was so sure, but on which the Committee on Ethics of the County Medical Society had been equally certain. The winter was creeping into his bones again, and he had no money and no more wine.

Dr. Full pretended to himself that there was a bottle of whiskey somewhere in the fearful litter of his room. It was an old and cruel trick he played on himself when he simply had to be galvanized into getting up and going home. He might freeze there in the alley. In his room he would be bitten by bugs and would cough at the moldy reek from his sink, but he would not freeze and be cheated of the hundreds of bottles of wine that he still might drink, the thousands of hours of glowing content he still might feel. He thought about that bottle of whiskey—was it back of a mounded heap of medical journals? No; he had looked there last time. Was it under the sink, shoved well to the rear, behind the rusty drain? The cruel trick began to play itself out again. Yes, he told himself with mounting excitement, yes, it might be! Your memory isn't so good nowadays, he told himself with rueful good fellowship. You know perfectly well you might have bought a bottle of whiskey and shoved it behind the sink drain for a moment just like this.

The amber bottle, the crisp snap of the sealing as he cut it, the pleasurable exertion of starting the screw cap on its threads, and then the refreshing tangs in his throat, the warmth in his stomach, the dark, dull happy oblivion of drunkenness—they became real to him. You *could* have, you know! You *could* have! he told himself. With the blessed conviction growing in his mind—It *could* have happened, you know! It *could* have!—he struggled to his right knee. As he did, he heard a yelp behind him, and curiously craned his neck around while resting. It was the little girl, who had cut her hand quite badly on her toy, the piece of glass. Dr. Full could see the rilling bright blood down her coat, pooling at her feet.

He almost felt inclined to defer the image of the amber bottle for her, but not seriously. He knew that it was there, shoved well to the rear under the sink, behind the rusty drain where he had hidden it. He would have a drink and then magnanimously return to help the child. Dr. Full got to his other knee and then his feet, and proceeded at a rapid totter down the littered alley toward his room, where he would hunt with calm optimism at first for the bottle that was not there, then with anxiety, and then with frantic violence. He would hurl books and dishes about before he was done looking for the amber bottle of whiskey, and finally would beat his swollen knuckles against the brick wall until old scars on them opened and his thick old blood oozed over his hands. Last of all, he would sit down somewhere on the floor, whimpering, and would plunge into the abyss of purgative nightmare that was his sleep.

After twenty generations of shilly-shallying and "we'll cross that bridge when we come to it," genus homo had bred himself into an impasse. Dogged biometricians had pointed out with irrefutable logic that mental subnormals were outbreeding mental normals and supernormals, and that the process was occurring on an exponential curve. Every fact that could be mustered in the argument proved the biometricians' case, and led inevitably to the conclusion that genus homo was going to wind up in a preposterous jam quite soon. If you think that had any effect on breeding practices, you do not know genus homo.

There was, of course, a sort of masking effect produced by that other exponential function, the accumulation of technological devices. A moron trained to punch an adding machine seems to be a more skillful computer than a medieval mathematician trained to count on his fingers. A moron trained to operate the twenty-first century equivalent of a linotype seems to be a better typographer than a Renaissance printer limited to a few fonts of movable type. This is also true of medical practice.

It was a complicated affair of many factors. The supernormals "improved the product" at greater speed than the subnormals degraded it, but in smaller quantity because elaborate training of their children was practiced on a custom-made basis. The fetish of higher education had some weird avatars by the twentieth generation: "colleges" where not a member of the student body could read words of three syllables; "universities" where such degrees as "Bachelor of Typewriting," "Master of Shorthand" and "Doctor of Philosophy (Card Filing)" were conferred with the traditional pomp. The handful of supernormals used such devices in order that the vast majority might keep some semblance of a social order going.

Some day the supernormals would mercilessly cross the bridge; at the twentieth generation they were standing irresolutely at its approaches wondering what had hit them. And the ghosts of twenty generations of biometricians chuckled malignantly.

It is a certain Doctor of Medicine of this twentieth generation that we are concerned with. His name was Hemingway—John Hemingway, B.Sc., M.D. He was a general practitioner, and did not hold with running to specialists with every trifling ailment. He often said as much, in approximately these words: "Now, uh, what I mean is you got a good old G.P. See what I mean? Well, uh, now a good old G.P. don't claim he knows all about lungs and glands and them things, get me? But you got a G.P., you got, uh, you got a, well, you got a . . . *all-around man!* That's what you got when you got a G.P.—you got a all-around man."

But from this, do not imagine that Dr. Hemingway was a poor

doctor. He could remove tonsils or appendixes, assist at practically any confinement and deliver a living, uninjured infant, correctly diagnose hundreds of ailments, and prescribe and administer the correct medication or treatment for each. There was, in fact, only one thing he could not do in the medical line, and that was violate the ancient canons of medical ethics. And Dr. Hemingway knew better than to try.

Dr. Hemingway and a few friends were chatting one evening when the event occurred that precipitates him into our story. He had been through a hard day at the clinic, and he wished his physicist friend Walter Gillis, B.Sc., M.Sc., Ph.D., would shut up so he could tell everybody about it. But Gillis kept rambling on, in his stilted fashion: "You got to hand it to old Mike; he don't have what we call the scientific method, but you got to hand it to him. There this poor little dope is, puttering around with some glassware and I come up and I ask him, kidding of course, 'How's about a time-travel machine, Mike?' "

Dr. Gillis was not aware of it, but "Mike" had an I.Q. six times his own, and was—to be blunt—his keeper. "Mike" rode herd on the pseudo-physicists in the pseudo-laboratory, in the guise of a bottle washer. It was a social waste—but as has been mentioned before, the supernormals were still standing at the approaches to a bridge. Their irresolution led to many such preposterous situations. And it happens that "Mike," having grown frantically bored with his task, was malevolent enough to—but let Dr. Gillis tell it:

"So he gives me these here tube numbers and says, 'Series circuit. Now stop bothering me. Build your time machine, sit down at it and turn on the switch. That's all I ask, Dr. Gillis—that's all I ask.' "

"Say," marveled a brittle and lovely blond guest, "you remember real good, don't you, doc.?" She gave him a melting smile.

"Heck," said Gillis modestly, "I always remember good. It's what you call an inherent facility. And besides I told it quick to my secretary, so she wrote it down. I don't read so good, but I sure remember good, all right. Now, where was I?"

Everybody thought hard, and there were various suggestions:

"Something about bottles, doc?"

"You was starting a fight. You said 'time somebody was traveling.' "

"Yeah—you called somebody a swish. Who did you call a swish?"

"Not swish—*switch*."

Dr. Gillis's noble brow grooved with thought, and he declared: "Switch is right. It was about time travel. What we call travel through time. So I took the tube numbers he gave me and I put them into the circuit builder; I set it for 'series' and there it is—my time-traveling machine. It travels things through time real good." He displayed a box.

"What's in the box?" asked the lovely blonde.

Dr. Hemingway told her: "Time travel. It travels things through time."

"Look," said Gillis, the physicist. He took Dr. Hemingway's little black bag and put in on the box. He turned on the switch and the little black bag vanished.

"Say," said Dr. Hemingway, "that was, uh, swell. Now bring it back."

"Huh?"

"Bring back my little black bag."

"Well," said Dr. Gillis, "they don't come back. I tried it backwards and they don't come back. I guess maybe that dummy Mike give me a bum steer."

There was wholesale condemnation of "Mike" but Dr. Hemingway took no part in it. He was nagged by a vague feeling that there was something he would have to do. He reasoned: "I am a doctor, and a doctor has got to have a little black bag. I ain't got a little black bag—so ain't I a doctor no more?" He decided that this was absurd. He *knew* he was a doctor. So it must be the bag's fault for not being there. It was no good, and he would get another one tomorrow from that dummy Al, at the clinic. Al could find things good, but he was a dummy—never liked to talk sociable to you.

So the next day Dr. Hemingway remembered to get another little black bag from his keeper—another little black bag with which he could perform tonsillectomies, appendectomies, and the most difficult confinements, and with which he could diagnose and cure his kind until the day when the supernormals could bring themselves to cross that bridge. Al was kinda nasty about the missing little black bag, but Dr. Hemmingway didn't exactly remember what had happened, so no tracer was sent out, so—

* * *

Old Dr. Full awoke from the horrors of the night to the horrors of the day. His gummy eyelashes pulled apart convulsively. He was propped against a corner of his room, and something was making a little drumming noise. He felt very cold and cramped. As his eyes focused on his lower body, he croaked out a laugh. The drumming noise was being made by his left heel, agitated by fine tremors against the bare floor. It was going to be the D.T.'s again, he decided dispassionately. He wiped his mouth with his bloody knuckles, and the fine tremor coarsened; the snare-drum beat became louder and slower. He was getting a break this fine morning, he decided sardonically. You didn't get the horrors until you had been tightened like a violin string, just to the breaking point. He had a reprieve, if a reprieve into his old body with the blazing, endless headache just back of the eyes and the screaming stiffness in the joints was anything to be thankful for.

There was something or other about a kid, he thought vaguely. He was going to doctor some kid. His eyes rested on a little black bag in the center of the room, and he forgot about the kid. "I could have sworn," said Dr. Full, "I hocked that two years ago!" He hitched over and reached the bag, and then realized it was some stranger's kit, arriving here he did not know how. He tentatively touched the lock and it snapped open and lay flat, rows and rows of instruments and medications tucked into loops in its four walls. It seemed vastly larger open than closed. He didn't see how it could possibly fold up into that compact size again, but decided it was some stunt of the instrument makers. Since his time—that made it worth more at the hock shop, he thought with satisfaction.

Just for old times' sake, he let his eyes and fingers rove over the instruments before he snapped the bag shut and headed for Uncle's. More than a few were a little hard to recognize—exactly that is. You could see the things with blades for cutting, the forceps for holding and pulling, the retractors for holding fast, the needles and gut for suturing, the hypos—a fleeting thought crossed his mind that he could peddle the hypos separately to drug addicts.

Let's go, he decided, and tried to fold up the case. It didn't fold until he happened to touch the lock, and then it folded all at once into a little black bag. Sure have forged ahead, he thought, almost able to forget that what he was primarily interested in was its pawn value.

With a definite objective, it was not too hard for him to get to his feet. He decided to go down the front steps, out the front door, and down the sidewalk. But first—

He snapped the bag open again on his kitchen table, and pored through the medication tubes. "Anything to sock the autonomic nervous system good and hard," he mumbled. The tubes were numbered, and there was a plastic card which seemed to list them. The left margin of the card was a run-down of the systems—vascular, muscular, nervous. He followed the last entry across to the right. There were columns for "stimulant," "depressant," and so on. Under "nervous system" and "depressant" he found the number 17, and shakily located the little glass tube which bore it. It was full of pretty blue pills and he took one.

It was like being struck by a thunderbolt.

Dr. Full had so long lacked any sense of well-being except the brief glow of alcohol that he had forgotten its very nature. He was panic-stricken for a long moment at the sensation that spread through him slowly, finally tingling in his fingertips. He straightened up, his pains gone and his leg tremor stilled.

That was great, he thought. He'd be able to *run* to the hock shop, pawn the little black bag, and get some booze. He started down the stairs. Not even the street, bright with mid-morning sun, into which he emerged, made him quail. The little black bag in his left hand had a satisfying, authoritative weight. He was walking erect, he noted, and not in the somewhat furtive crouch that had grown on him in recent years. A little self-respect, he told himself, that's what I need. Just because a man's down doesn't mean—

"Docta, please-a come wit'!" somebody yelled at him, tugging his arm. "Da litt-la girl, she's-a burn' up!" It was one of the slum's innumerable flat-faced, stringy-haired women, in a slovenly wrapper.

"Ah, I happen to be retired from practice—" he began hoarsely, but she would not be put off.

"In by here, Docta!" she urged, tugging him to a doorway. "You come look-a da litt-la girl. I got two dolla, you come look!" That put a different complexion on the matter. He allowed himself to be towed through the doorway into a mussy, cabbage-smelling flat. He knew the woman now, or rather knew who she must be—a new arrival who had moved in the other night. These people moved at night, in motorcades of battered cars supplied by friends and relations, with furniture lashed to the tops, swearing and drinking until the small hours. It explained why she had stopped him: she did not yet know he was old Dr. Full, a drunken reprobate whom nobody would trust. The little black bag had been his guarantee, outweighing his whiskery face and stained black suit.

He was looking down on a three-year-old girl who had, he rather suspected, just been placed in the mathematical center of a freshly changed double bed. God knew what sour and dirty mattress she usually slept on. He seemed to recognize her as he noted a crusted bandage on her right hand. Two dollars, he thought— An ugly flush had spread up her pipe-stem arm. He poked a finger into the socket of her elbow, and felt little spheres like marbles under the skin and ligaments roll apart. The child began to squall thinly; beside him, the woman gasped and began to weep herself.

"Out," he gestured briskly at her, and she thudded away, still sobbing.

Two dollars, he thought— Give her some mumbo jumbo, take the money and tell her to go to a clinic. Strep, I guess, from that stinking alley. It's a wonder any of them grow up. He put down the little black bag and forgetfully fumbled for his key, then remembered and touched the lock. It flew open, and he selected a bandage shears, with a blunt wafer for the lower jaw. He fitted the lower jaw under the bandage, trying not to hurt the kid by its pressure on the infection, and began to cut. It was amazing how easily and swiftly the shining shears snipped through the crusty rag around the wound. He hardly seemed to be driving the shears with fingers at all. It almost seemed as though the shears were driving his fingers instead as they scissored a clean, light line through the bandage.

Certainly have forged ahead since my time, he thought—sharper than a microtome knife. He replaced the shears in their loop on the extraordinarily big board that the little black bag turned into when it unfolded, and leaned over the wound. He whistled at the ugly gash, and the violent infection which had taken immediate root in the sickly child's thin body. Now what can you do with a thing like that? He pawed over the contents of the little black bag, nervously. If he lanced it and let some of the pus out, the old woman would think he'd done something for her and he'd get the two dollars. But at the clinic they'd want to know who did it and if they got sore enough they might send a cop around. Maybe there was something in the kit—

He ran down the left edge of the card to "lymphatic" and read across to the column under "infection." It didn't sound right at all to him; he checked again, but it still said that. In the square to which the line and column led were the symbols: "IV-g-3cc." He couldn't find any bottles marked with Roman numerals, and then noticed that that was how the hypodermic needles were designated. He lifted number IV from its loop, noting that it was fitted with a needle already and even seemed to be charged. What a way to carry those things around! So—three cc. of whatever was in hypo number IV ought to do something or other about infections settled in the lymphatic system—which, God knows, this one was. What did the lower-case "g" mean, though? He studied the glass hypo and saw letters engraved on what looked like a rotating disk at the top of the barrel. They ran from "a" to "i," and there was an index line engraved on the barrel on the opposite side from the calibrations.

Shrugging, old Dr. Full turned the disk until "g" coincided with the index line, and lifted the hypo to eye level. As he pressed in the plunger he did not see the tiny thread of fluid squirt from the tip of the needle. There was a sort of dark mist for a moment about the tip. A closer inspection showed that the needle was not even pierced at the tip. It had the usual slanting cut across the bias of the shaft, but the cut did not expose an oval hole. Baffled, he tried pressing the plunger again. Again *something* appeared around the tip and vanished. "We'll settle this," said the doctor. He slipped the needle into the skin of his forearm. He thought at first that he had missed—that the point had glided over the top of his skin instead of catching and slipping under it. But he saw a tiny blood-spot and realized that somehow he just hadn't felt the puncture. Whatever was in the barrel, he decided, couldn't do him any harm if it lived up to its billing—and if it could come out through a needle that had no hole. He gave himself three cc. and twitched the needle out. There was the swelling—painless, but otherwise typical.

Dr. Full decided it was his eyes or something, and gave three cc. of "g" from hypodermic IV to the feverish child. There was no interruption to her wailing as the needle went in and the swelling rose. But a long instant later, she gave a final gasp and was silent.

Well, he told himself, cold with horror, you did it that time. You killed her with that stuff.

Then the child sat up and said: "Where's my mommy?"

Incredulously, the doctor seized her arm and palpated the

elbow. The gland infection was zero, and the temperature seemed normal. The blood-congested tissues surrounding the wound were subsiding as he watched. The child's pulse was stronger and no faster than a child's should be. In the sudden silence of the room he could hear the little girl's mother sobbing in her kitchen, outside. And he also heard a girl's insinuating voice:

"She gonna be O.K., doc?"

He turned and saw a gaunt-faced, dirty-blond sloven of perhaps eighteen leaning in the doorway and eyeing him with amused contempt. She continued: "I heard about you, *Doc-tor* Full. So don't go try and put the bite on the old lady. You couldn't doctor up a sick cat."

"Indeed?" he rumbled. This young person was going to get a lesson she richly deserved. "Perhaps you would care to look at my patient?"

"Where's my mommy?" insisted the little girl, and the blonde's jaw fell. She went to the bed and cautiously asked: "You O.K. now, Teresa? You all fixed up?"

"Where's my mommy?" demanded Teresa. Then, accusingly, she gestured with her wounded hand at the doctor. "You *poke* me!" she complained, and giggled pointlessly.

"Well—" said the blond girl, "I guess I got to hand it to you, doc. These loud-mouth women around here said you didn't know your . . . I mean, didn't know how to cure people. They said you ain't a real doctor."

"I *have* retired from practice," he said. "But I happened to be taking this case to a colleague as a favor, your good mother noticed me, and—" a deprecating smile. He touched the lock of the case and it folded up into the little black bag again.

"You stole it," the girl said flatly.

He sputtered.

"Nobody'd trust you with a thing like that. It must be worth plenty. You stole that case. I was going to stop you when I come in and saw you working over Teresa, but it looked like you wasn't doing her any harm. But when you give me that line about taking that case to a colleague I know you stole it. You gimme a cut or I go to the cops. A thing like that must be worth twenty—thirty dollars."

The mother came timidly in, her eyes red. But she let out a whoop of joy when she saw the little girl sitting up and babbling to herself, embraced her madly, fell on her knees for a quick prayer, hopped up to kiss the doctor's hand, and then dragged him into the kitchen, all the while rattling in her native language while the blond girl let her eyes go cold with disgust. Dr. Full allowed himself to be towed into the kitchen, but flatly declined a cup of coffee and a plate of anise cakes and St. John's Bread.

"Try him on some wine, ma," said the girl sardonically.

"Hyass! Hyass!" breathed the woman delightedly. "You like-a wine, docta?" She had a carafe of purplish liquid before him in an instant, and the blond girl snickered as the doctor's hand twitched out at it. He drew his hand back, while there grew in his head the old image of how it would smell and then taste and then warm his stomach and limbs. He made the kind of calculation at which he was practiced; the delighted woman would not notice as he downed two tumblers, and he could overawe her through two tumblers more with his tale of Teresa's narrow brush with the Destroying Angel, and then—why, then it would not matter. He would be drunk.

But for the first time in years, there was a sort of counter-image: a blend of the rage he felt at the blond girl to whom he was so transparent, and of pride at the cure he had just effected. Much to his own surprise, he drew back his hand from the carafe and said, luxuriating in the words: "No, thank you. I don't believe I'd care for any so early in the day." He covertly watched the blond girl's face, and was gratified at her surprise. Then the mother was shyly handing him two bills and saying: "Is no much-a money, docta—but you come again, see Teresa?"

"I shall be glad to follow the case through," he said. "But now excuse me—I really must be running along." He grasped the little black bag firmly and got up; he wanted very much to get away from the wine and the older girl.

"Wait up, doc," said she, "I'm going your way." She followed him out and down the street. He ignored her until he felt her hand on the black bag. Then old Dr. Full stopped and tried to reason with her:

"Look, my dear. Perhaps you're right. I might have stolen it. To be perfectly frank, I don't remember how I got it. But you're young and you can earn your own money—"

"Fifty-fifty," she said, "or I go to the cops. And if I get another word outta you, it's sixty-forty. And you know who gets the short end, don't you, doc?"

Defeated, he marched to the pawnshop, her impudent hand still on the handle with his, and her heels beating out a tattoo against his stately tread.

In the pawnshop, they both got a shock.

"It ain't standard," said Uncle, unimpressed by the ingenious lock. "I ain't nevva seen one like it. Some cheap Jap stuff, maybe? Try down the street. This I nevva could sell."

Down the street they got an offer of one dollar. The same complaint was made: "I ain't a collecta, mista—I buy stuff that got resale value. Who could I sell this to, a Chinaman who don't know medical instruments? Every one of them looks funny. You sure you didn't make these yourself?" They didn't take the one-dollar offer.

The girl was baffled and angry; the doctor was baffled too, but triumphant. He had two dollars, and the girl had a half-interest in something nobody wanted. But, he suddenly marveled, the thing had been all right to cure the kid, hadn't it?

"Well," he asked her, "do you give up? As you see, the kit is practically valueless."

She was thinking hard. "Don't fly off the handle, doc. I don't get this, but something's going on all right . . . would those guys know good stuff if they saw it?"

"They would. They make a living from it. Wherever this kit came from—"

She seized on that, with a devilish faculty she seemed to have of eliciting answers without asking questions. "I thought so. You don't know either, huh? Well, maybe I can find out for you. C'mon in here. I ain't letting go of that thing. There's money in it—some way, I don't know how, there's money in it." He followed her into a cafeteria and to an almost-empty corner. She was oblivious to stares and snickers from the other customers as she opened the little black bag—it almost covered a cafeteria table—and ferreted through it. She picked out a retractor from a loop, scrutinized it, contemptuously threw it down, picked out a speculum, threw it down, picked out the lower half of an O.B. forceps, turned it over, close to her sharp young eyes—and saw what the doctor's dim old ones could not have seen.

All old Dr. Full knew was that she was peering at the neck of the forceps and then turned white. Very carefully, she placed the half of the forceps back in its loop of cloth and then replaced the retractor and the speculum. "Well?" he asked. "What did you see?"

" 'Made in U.S.A.,' " she quoted hoarsely. " 'Patent Applied for July 2450.' "

He wanted to tell her she must have misread the inscription, that it must be a practical joke, that—

But he knew she had read correctly. Those bandage shears: they *had* driven his fingers, rather than his fingers driving them. The hypo needle that had no hole. The pretty blue pill that had struck him like a thunderbolt.

"You know what I'm going to do?" asked the girl, with sudden animation. "I'm going to go to charm school. You'll like that, won't ya, doc? Because we're sure going to be seeing a lot of each other."

Old Dr. Full didn't answer. His hands had been playing idly with that plastic card from the kit on which had been printed the rows and columns that had guided him twice before. The card had a slight convexity; you could snap the convexity back and forth from one side to the other. He noted, in a daze, that with each snap a different text appeared on the cards. *Snap*. "The knife with the blue dot in the handle is for tumors only. Diagnose tumors with your Instrument Seven, the Swelling Tester. Place the Swelling Tester—" *Snap*. "An overdose of the pink pills in Bottle 3 can be fixed with one white pill from Bottle—" *Snap*. "Hold the suture needle by the end without the hole in it. Touch it to one end of the wound you want to close and let go. After it has made the knot, touch it—" *Snap*. "Place the top half of the O.B. Forceps near the opening. Let go. After it has entered and conformed to the shape of—" *Snap*.

The slot man saw "FLANNERY 1—MEDICAL" in the upper left corner of the hunk of copy. He automatically scribbled "trim to .75" on it and skimmed it across the horseshoe-shaped copy desk to Piper, who had been handling Edna Flannery's quack-exposé series. She was a nice youngster, he thought, but like all youngsters she overwrote. Hence, the "trim."

Piper dealt back a city hall story to the slot, pinned down Flannery's feature with one hand and began to tap his pencil across it, one tap to a word, at the same steady beat as a teletype carriage traveling across the roller. He wasn't exactly reading it this first time. He was just looking at the letters and words to find out whether, as letters and words, they conformed to *Herald* style. The steady tap of his pencil ceased at intervals as it drew a black line ending with a stylized letter "d" through the word "breast" and scribbled in "chest" instead, or knocked down the capital "E" in "East" to lower case with a diagonal, or closed up a split word—in whose middle Flannery had bumped the space bar of her typewriter—with two curved lines like parentheses rotated through ninety degrees. The thick black pencil zipped a ring around the "30," which, like all youngsters, she put at the end of her stories. He turned back to the first page for the second reading. This time the pencil drew lines with the stylized "d's" at the end of them through adjectives and whole phrases, printed big "L's" to mark paragraphs, hooked some of Flannery's own paragraphs together with swooping recurved lines.

At the bottom of "FLANNERY ADD 2—MEDICAL" the pencil slowed down and stopped. The slot man, sensitive to the rhythm of his beloved copy desk, looked up almost at once. He saw Piper squinting at the story, at a loss. Without wasting words, the copy reader skimmed it back across the Masonite horseshoe to the chief, caught a police story in return and buckled down, his pencil tapping. The slot man read as far as the fourth add, barked at Howard, on the rim: "Sit in for me," and stumped through the clattering city room toward the alcove where the managing editor presided over his own bedlam.

The copy chief waited his turn while the make-up editor, the pressroom foreman, and the chief photographer had words with the M.E. When his turn came, he dropped Flannery's copy on his desk and said: "She says this one isn't a quack."

The M.E. read:

"FLANNERY 1—MEDICAL, by Edna Flannery, *Herald* Staff Writer.

"The sordid tale of medical quackery which the *Herald* has exposed in this series of articles undergoes a change of pace today which the reporter found a welcome surprise. Her quest for the facts in the case of today's subject started just the same way that her exposure of one dozen shyster M.D.'s and faith-healing phonies did. But she can report for a change that Dr. Bayard Full is, despite unorthodox practices which have drawn the suspicion of the rightly hypersensitive medical associations, a true healer living up to the highest ideals of his profession.

"Dr. Full's name was given to the *Herald's* reporter by the ethical committee of a county medical association, which reported that he had been expelled from the association on July 18, 1941, for allegedly 'milking' several patients suffering from trivial complaints. According to sworn statements in the committee's files, Dr. Full had told them they suffered from cancer, and that he had a treatment which would prolong their lives. After his expulsion from the association, Dr. Full dropped out of their sight—until he opened a midtown 'sanitarium' in a brownstone front which had for years served as a rooming house.

"The *Herald's* reporter went to that sanitarium, on East 89th Street, with the full expectation of having numerous imaginary ailments diagnosed and of being promised a sure cure for a flat sum of money. She expected to find unkempt quarters, dirty instruments, and the mumbo-jumbo paraphernalia of the shyster M.D. which she had seen a dozen times before.

"She was wrong.

"Dr. Full's sanitarium is spotlessly clean, from its tastefully furnished entrance hall to its shining, white treatment rooms. The attractive, blond receptionist who greeted the reporter was soft-spoken and correct, asking only the reporter's name, address, and the general nature of her complaint. This was given, as usual, as 'nagging backache.' The receptionist asked the *Herald's* reporter to be seated, and a short while later conducted her to a second-floor treatment room and introduced her to Dr. Full.

"Dr. Full's alleged past, as described by the medical society spokesman, is hard to reconcile with his present appearance. He is a clear-eyed, white-haired man in his sixties, to judge by his appearance—a little above middle height and apparently in good physical condition. His voice was firm and friendly, untainted by the ingratiating whine of the shyster M.D. which the reporter has come to know too well.

"The receptionist did not leave the room as he began his examination after a few questions as to the nature and location of the pain. As the reporter lay face down on a treatment table the doctor pressed some instrument to the small of her back. In about one minute he made this astounding statement: 'Young woman, there is no reason for you to have any pain where you say you do. I understand they're saying nowadays that emotional upsets cause pains like that. You'd better go to a psychologist or psychiatrist if the pain keeps up. There is no physical cause for it, so I can do nothing for you.'

"His frankness took the reporter's breath away. Had he guessed she was, so to speak, a spy in his camp? She tried again: 'Well, doctor, perhaps you'd give me a physical checkup, I feel run down all the time, besides the pains. Maybe I need a tonic.' This is never-failing bait to shyster M.D.'s—an invitation for them to find all sorts of mysterious conditions wrong with a patient, each of which 'requires' an expensive treatment. As explained in the first article of this series, of course, the reporter underwent a thorough physical checkup before she embarked on her quack hunt, and was found to be in one hundred percent perfect condition, with the exception of a 'scarred' area at the bottom tip of her left lung resulting from a childhood attack of tuberculosis and a tendency toward 'hyperthyroidism'—overactivity of the thyroid gland which makes it difficult to put on weight and sometimes causes a slight shortness of breath.

"Dr. Full consented to perform the examination, and took a number of shining, spotlessly clean instruments from loops in a large board literally covered with instruments—most of them unfamiliar to the reporter. The instrument with which he approached first was a tube with a curved dial in its surface and two wires that ended on flat disks growing from its ends. He placed one of the disks on the back of the reporter's right hand and the other on the back of her left. 'Reading the meter,' he called out some number which the attentive receptionist took down on a ruled form. The same procedure was repeated several times, thoroughly covering the reporter's anatomy and thoroughly convincing her that the doctor was a complete quack. The reporter had never seen any such diagnostic procedure practiced during the weeks she put in preparing for this series.

"The doctor then took the ruled sheet from the receptionist, conferred with her in low tones, and said: 'You have a slightly overactive thyroid, young woman. And there's something wrong with your left lung—not seriously, but I'd like to take a closer look.'

"He selected an instrument from the board which, the reporter knew, is called a 'speculum'—a scissorlike device which spreads apart body openings such as the orifice of the ear, the nostril, and so on, so that a doctor can look in during an examination. The instrument was, however, too large to be an aural or nasal speculum but too small to be anything else. As the *Herald's* reporter was about to ask further questions, the attending receptionist told her: 'It's customary for us to blindfold our patients during lung examinations—do you mind?' The reporter, bewildered, allowed her to tie a spotlessly clean bandage over her eyes, and waited nervously for what would come next.

"She still cannot say exactly what happened while she was blindfolded—but X rays confirm her suspicions. She felt a cold sensation at her ribs on the left side—a cold that seemed to enter inside her body. Then there was a snapping feeling, and the cold sensation was gone. She heard Dr. Full say in a matter-of-fact voice: 'You have an old tubercular scar down there. It isn't doing any particular harm, but an active person like you needs all the oxygen she can get. Lie still and I'll fix it for you.'

"Then there was a repetition of the cold sensation, lasting for a longer time. 'Another batch of alveoli and some more vascular glue,' the *Herald's* reporter heard Dr. Full say, and the receptionist's crisp response to the order. Then the strange sensation departed and the eye bandage was removed. The reporter saw no scar on her ribs, and yet the doctor assured her: 'That did it. We took out the fibrosis—and a good fibrosis it was, too; it walled off the infection so you're still alive to tell the tale. Then we planted a few clumps of alveoli—they're the little gadgets that get the oxygen from the air you breathe into your blood. I won't monkey with your thyroxin supply. You've got used to being the kind of person you are, and if you suddenly found yourself easygoing and all the rest of it, chances are you'd only be upset. About the backache: just check with the county medical society for the name of a good psychologist or psychiatrist. And look out for quacks; the woods are full of them.'

"The doctor's self-assurance took the reporter's breath away. She asked what the charge would be, and was told to pay the receptionist fifty dollars. As usual, the reporter delayed paying until she got a receipt signed by the doctor himself, detailing the services for which it paid. Unlike most, the doctor cheerfully wrote: 'For removal of fibrosis from left lung and restoration of alveoli,' and signed it.

"The reporter's first move when she left the sanitarium was to head for the chest specialist who had examined her in preparation for this series. A comparison of X rays taken on the day of the 'operation' and those taken previously would, the *Herald's* reporter then thought, expose Dr. Full as a prince of shyster M.D.'s and quacks.

"The chest specialist made time on his crowded schedule for the reporter, in whose series he has shown a lively interest from the planning stage on. He laughed uproariously in his staid Park Avenue examining room as she described the weird procedure to which she had been subjected. But he did not laugh when he took a chest X ray of the reporter, developed it, dried it, and compared it with the ones he had taken earlier. The chest specialist took six more X rays that afternoon, but finally admitted that they all told the same story. The *Herald's* reporter has it on his authority that the scar she had eighteen days ago from her tuberculosis is now gone and has been replaced by healthy lung tissue. He declared that this is a happening unparalleled in medical history. He does not go along with the reporter in her firm conviction that Dr. Full is responsible for the change.

"The *Herald's* reporter, however, sees no two ways about it. She concludes that Dr. Bayard Full—whatever his alleged past may have been—is now an unorthodox but highly successful practitioner of medicine, to whose hands the reporter would trust herself in any emergency.

"Not so is the case of 'Rev.' Annie Dimsworth—a female harpy who, under the guise of 'faith' preys on the ignorant and suffering who come to her sordid 'healing parlor' for help and remain to feed 'Rev.' Annie's bank account, which now totals up to $53,238.64. Tomorrow's article will show, with photostats of bank statements and sworn testimony that—"

The managing editor turned down "FLANNERY LAST ADD—MEDICAL" and tapped his front teeth with a pencil, trying to think straight. He finally told the copy chief: "Kill the story. Run the teaser as a box." He tore off the last paragraph—the "teaser" about "Rev." Annie—and handed it to the desk man, who stumped back to his Masonite horseshoe.

The make-up editor was back, dancing with impatience as he tried to catch the M.E.'s eye. The interphone buzzed with the red light which indicated that the editor and publisher wanted to talk to him. The M.E. thought briefly of a special series on this Dr. Full, decided nobody would believe it and that he probably was a phony anyway. He spiked the story on the "dead" hook and answered his interphone.

Dr. Full had become almost fond of Angie. As his practice had grown to engross the neighborhood illnesses, and then to a corner suite in an uptown taxpayer building, and finally to the sanitarium, she seemed to have grown with it. Oh, he thought, we have our little disputes—

The girl, for instance, was too much interested in money. She had wanted to specialize in cosmetic surgery—removing wrinkles from wealthy old women and whatnot. She didn't realize, at first, that a thing like this was in their trust, that they were the stewards and not the owners of the little black bag and its fabulous contents.

He had tried, ever so cautiously, to analyze them, but without success. All the instruments were slightly radioactive, for instance, but not quite so. They would make a Geiger-Mueller counter indicate, but they would not collapse the leaves of an electroscope. He didn't pretend to be up on the latest developments, but as he understood it, that was just plain *wrong*. Under the highest magnification there were lines on the instruments' superfinished surfaces: incredibly fine lines, engraved in random hatchments which made no particular sense. Their magnetic properties were preposterous. Sometimes the instruments were strongly attracted to magnets, sometimes less so, and sometimes not at all.

Dr. Full had taken X rays in fear and trembling lest he disrupt whatever delicate machinery worked in them. He was *sure* they were not solid, that the handles and perhaps the blades must be mere shells filled with busy little watchworks—but the X rays showed nothing of the sort. Oh, yes—and they were always sterile, and they wouldn't rust. Dust *fell* off them if you shook them: now, that was something he understood. They ionized the dust, or were ionized themselves, or something of the sort. At any rate, he had read of something similar that had to do with phonograph records.

She wouldn't know about that, he proudly thought. She kept the books well enough, and perhaps she gave him a useful prod now and then when he was inclined to settle down. The move from the neighborhood slum to the uptown quarters had been her idea, and so had the sanitarium. Good, good, it enlarged his sphere of usefulness. Let the child have her mink coats and her convertible, as they seemed to be calling roadsters nowadays. He himself was too busy and too old. He had so much to make up for.

Dr. Full thought happily of his Master Plan. She would not like it much, but she would have to see the logic of it. This marvelous thing that had happened to them must be handed on. She was herself no doctor; even though the instruments practically ran themselves, there was more to doctoring than skill. There were the ancient canons of the healing art. And so, having seen the logic of it, Angie would yield; she would assent to his turning over the little black bag to all humanity.

He would probably present it to the College of Surgeons, with as little fuss as possible—well, perhaps a *small* ceremony, and he would like a souvenir of the occasion, a cup or a framed testimonial. It would be a relief to have the thing out of his hands, in a way; let the giants of the healing art decide who was to have its benefits. No, Angie would understand. She was a goodhearted girl.

It was nice that she had been showing so much interest in the surgical side lately—asking about the instruments, reading the instruction card for hours, even practicing on guinea pigs. If something of his love for humanity had been communicated to her, old Dr. Full sentimentally thought, his life would not have been in vain. Surely she would realize that a greater good would be served by surrendering the instruments to wiser hands than theirs, and by throwing aside the cloak of secrecy necessary to work on their small scale.

Dr. Full was in the treatment room that had been the brownstone's front parlor; through the window he saw Angie's yellow convertible roll to a stop before the stoop. He liked the way she looked as she climbed the stairs; neat, not flashy, he thought. A sensible girl like her, she'd understand. There was somebody with her—a fat woman, puffing up the steps, overdressed and petulant. Now, what could she want?

Angie let herself in and went into the treatment room, followed by the fat woman. "Doctor," said the blond girl gravely, "may I present Mrs. Coleman?" Charm school had not taught her everything, but Mrs. Coleman, evidently *nouveau riche*, thought the doctor, did not notice the blunder.

"Miss Aquella told me *so* much about you, doctor, and your remarkable system!" she gushed.

Before he could answer, Angie smoothly interposed: "Would you excuse us for just a moment, Mrs. Coleman?"

She took the doctor's arm and led him into the reception hall. "Listen," she said swiftly, "I know this goes against your grain, but I couldn't pass it up. I met this old thing in the exercise class at Elizabeth Barton's. Nobody else'll talk to her there. She's a widow. I guess her husband was a black marketeer or something, and she has a pile of dough. I gave her a line about how you had a system of massaging wrinkles out. My idea is, you blindfold her, cut her neck open with the Cutaneous Series knife, shoot some Firmol into the muscles, spoon out some of that blubber with an Adipose Series curette and spray it all with Skintite. When you take the blindfold off she's got rid of a wrinkle and doesn't know what happened. She'll pay five hundred dollars. Now, don't say 'no,' doc. Just this once, let's do it my way, can't you? I've been working on this deal all along too, haven't I?"

"Oh," said the doctor, "very well." He was going to have to tell her about the Master Plan before long anyway. He would let her have it her way this time.

Back in the treatment room, Mrs. Coleman had been thinking things over. She told the doctor sternly as he entered: "Of course, your system is permanent, isn't it?"

"It is, madam," he said shortly. "Would you please lie down there? Miss Aquella, get a sterile three-inch bandage for Mrs. Coleman's eyes." He turned his back on the fat woman to avoid conversation, and pretended to be adjusting the lights. Angie blindfolded the woman, and the doctor selected the instruments he would need. He handed the blond girl a pair of retractors, and told her: "Just slip the corners of the blades in as I cut—" She gave him an alarmed look, and gestured at the reclining woman. He lowered his voice: "Very well. Slip in the corners and rock them along the incision. I'll tell you when to pull them out."

Dr. Full held the Cutaneous Series knife to his eyes as he adjusted the little slide for three centimeters depth. He sighed a little as he recalled that its last use had been in the extirpation of an "inoperable" tumor of the throat.

"Very well," he said, bending over the woman. He tried a tentative pass through her tissues. The blade dipped in and flowed through them, like a finger through quicksilver, with no wound left in the wake. Only the retractors could hold the edges of the incision apart.

Mrs. Coleman stirred and jabbered: "Doctor, that felt so peculiar! Are you sure you're rubbing the right way?"

"Quite sure, madam," said the doctor wearily. "Would you please try not to talk during the massage?"

He nodded at Angie, who stood ready with the retractors. The blade sank in to its three centimeters, miraculously cutting only the dead horny tissues of the epidermis and the live tissue of the dermis, pushing aside mysteriously all major and minor blood vessels and muscular tissue, declining to affect any system or organ except the one it was—tuned to, could you say? The doctor didn't know the answer, but he felt tired and bitter at this prostitution. Angie slipped in the retractor blades and rocked them as he withdrew the knife, then pulled to separate the lips of the incision. It bloodlessly exposed an unhealthy string of muscle, sagging in a dead-looking loop from blue-gray ligaments. The doctor took a hypo. Number IX, pre-set to "g," and raised it to his eye level. The mist came and went; there probably was no possibility of an embolus with one of these gadgets, but why take chances? He shot one cc. of "g"—identified as "Firmol" by the card—into the muscle. He and Angie watched as it tightened up against the pharynx.

He took the Adipose Series curette, a small one, and spooned out yellowish tissue, dropping it into the incinerator box, and then nodded to Angie. She eased out the retractors and the gaping incision slipped together into unbroken skin, sagging now. The doctor had the atomizer—dialed to "Skintite"—ready. He sprayed, and the skin shrank up into the new firm throat line.

As he replaced the instruments, Angie removed Mrs. Coleman's bandage and gaily announced: "We're finished! And there's a mirror in the reception hall—"

Mrs. Coleman didn't need to be invited twice. With incredulous fingers she felt her chin, and then dashed for the hall. The doctor grimaced as he heard her yelp of delight, and Angie turned to him with a tight smile. "I'll get the money and get her out," she said. "You won't have to be bothered with her any more."

He was grateful for that much.

She followed Mrs. Coleman into the reception hall, and the doctor dreamed over the case of instruments. A ceremony, certainly—he was *entitled* to one. Not everybody, he thought, would turn such a sure source of money over to the good of humanity. But you reached an age when money mattered less, and when you thought of these things you had done that *might* be open to misunderstanding if, just if, there chanced to be any of that, well, that judgment business. The doctor wasn't a religious man, but you certainly found yourself thinking hard about some things when your time drew near—

Angie was back, with a bit of paper in her hands. "Five hundred dollars," she said matter-of-factly. "And you realize, don't you, that we could go over her an inch at a time—at five hundred dollars an inch?"

"I've been meaning to talk to you about that," he said.

There was bright fear in her eyes, he thought—but why?

"Angie, you've been a good girl and an understanding girl, but we can't keep this up forever, you know."

"Let's talk about it some other time," she said flatly. "I'm tired now."

"No—I really feel we've gone far enough on our own. The instruments—"

"Don't say it, doc!" she hissed. "Don't say it, or you'll be sorry!" In her face there was a look that reminded him of the hollow-eyed, gaunt-faced, dirty-blond creature she had been. From under the charm-school finish there burned the guttersnipe whose infancy had been spent on a sour and filthy mattress, whose childhood had been play in the littered alley, and whose adolescence had been the sweat-shops and the aimless gatherings at night under the glaring street lamps.

He shook his head to dispel the puzzling notion. "It's this way," he patiently began. "I told you about the family that invented the O.B. forceps and kept them a secret for so many generations, how they could have given them to the world but didn't?"

"They knew what they were doing," said the guttersnipe flatly.

"Well, that's neither here nor there," said the doctor, irritated. "My mind is made up about it. I'm going to turn the instruments over to the College of Surgeons. We have enough money to be comfortable. You can even have the house. I've been thinking of going to a warmer climate, myself." He felt peeved with her for making the unpleasant scene. He was unprepared for what happened next.

Angie snatched the little black bag and dashed for the door, with panic in her eyes. He scrambled after her, catching her arm, twisting it in a sudden rage. She clawed at his face with her free hand, babbling curses. Somehow, somebody's finger touched the little black bag, and it opened grotesquely into the enormous board, covered with shining instruments, large and small. Half a dozen of them joggled loose and fell to the floor.

"*Now* see what you've done!" roared the doctor, unreasonably. Her hand was still viselike on the handle, but she was standing still, trembling with choked-up rage. The doctor bent stiffly to pick up the fallen instruments. Unreasonable girl! he thought bitterly. Making a scene—

Pain drove in between his shoulderblades and he fell face down. The light ebbed. "Unreasonable girl!" he tried to croak. And then: "They'll know I tried, anyway—"

Angie looked down on his prone body, with the handle of the

Number Six Cautery Series knife protruding from it. "—will cut through all tissues. Use for amputations before you spread on the Re-Gro. Extreme caution should be used in the vicinity of vital organs and major blood vessels or nerve trunks—"

"I didn't mean to do that," said Angie, dully, cold with horror. Now the detective would come, the implacable detective who would reconstruct the crime from the dust in the room. She would run and turn and twist, but the detective would find her out and she would be tried in a courtroom before a judge and jury; the lawyer would make speeches, but the jury would convict her anyway, and the headlines would scream: "BLOND KILLER GUILTY!" and she'd maybe get the chair, walking down a plain corridor where a beam of sunlight struck through the dusty air, with an iron door at the end of it. Her mink, her convertible, her dresses, the handsome man she was going to meet and marry—

The mist of cinematic clichés cleared, and she knew what she would do next. Quite steadily, she picked the incinerator box from its loop in the board—a metal cube with a different-textured spot on one side. "—to dispose of fibroses or other unwanted matter, simply touch the disk—" You dropped something in and touched the disk. There was a sort of soundless whistle, very powerful and unpleasant if you were too close, and a sort of lightless flash. When you opened the box again, the contents were gone. Angie took another of the Cautery Series knives and went grimly to work. Good thing there wasn't any blood to speak of— She finished the awful task in three hours.

She slept heavily that night, totally exhausted by the wringing emotional demands of the slaying and the subsequent horror. But in the morning, it was as though the doctor had never been there. She ate breakfast, then dressed with care. Nothing out of the ordinary, she told herself. Don't do one thing different from the way you would have done it before. After a day or two, you can phone the cops. Say he walked out spoiling for a drunk, and you're worried. But don't rush it, baby—*don't rush it*.

Mrs. Coleman was due at 10:00 a.m. Angie had counted on being able to talk the doctor into at least one more five-hundred-dollar session. She'd have to do it herself now—but she'd have to start sooner or later.

The woman arrived early. Angie explained smoothly: "The doctor asked me to take care of the massage today. Now that he has the tissue-firming process beginning, it only requires somebody trained in his methods—'' As she spoke, her eyes swiveled to the instrument case—open! She cursed herself for the single flaw as the woman followed her gaze and recoiled.

''What are those things!'' she demanded. ''Are you going to cut me with them? I *thought* there was something fishy—''

''Please, Mrs. Coleman,'' said Angie, ''please, *dear* Mrs. Coleman—you don't understand about the . . . the massage instruments!''

''Massage instruments, my foot!'' squabbled the woman shrilly. ''That doctor *operated* on me. Why, he might have killed me!''

Angie wordlessly took one of the smaller Cutaneous Series knives and passed it through her forearm. The blade flowed like a finger through quicksilver, leaving no wound in its wake. *That* should convince the old cow!

It didn't convince her, but it did startle her. ''What did you do with it? The blade folds up into the handle—that's it!''

''Now look closely, Mrs. Coleman,'' said Angie, thinking desperately of the five hundred dollars. ''Look very closely and you'll see that the, uh, the sub-skin massager simply slips beneath the tissues without doing any harm, tightening and firming the muscles themselves instead of having to work through layers of skin and adipose tissue. It's the secret of the doctor's method. Now, how can outside massage have the effect that we got last night?''

Mrs. Coleman was beginning to calm down. ''It *did* work, all right,'' she admitted, stroking the new line of her neck. But your arm's one thing and my neck's another! Let me see you do that with your neck!''

Angie smiled—

Al returned to the clinic after an excellent lunch that had almost reconciled him to three more months he would have to spend on duty. And then, he thought, and then a blessed year at the blessedly super-normal South Pole working on his specialty—which happened to be telekinesis exercises for ages three to six. Meanwhile, of course, the world had to go on and of course he had to shoulder his share in the running of it.

Before settling down to desk work he gave a routine glance at the bag board. What he saw made him stiffen with shocked surprise. A red light was on next to one of the numbers—the first since he couldn't think when. He read off the number and murmured ''O.K., 674,101. That fixes *you*.'' He put the number on a card sorter and in a moment the record was in his hand. Oh, yes—Hemingway's bag. The big dummy didn't remember how or where he had lost it; none of them ever did. There were hundreds of them floating around.

Al's policy in such cases was to leave the bag turned on. The things practically ran themselves, it was practically impossible to do harm with them, so whoever found a lost one might as well be allowed to use it. You turn it off, you have a social loss—you leave it on, it may do some good. As he understood it, and not very well at that, the stuff wasn't "used up." A temporalist had tried to explain it to him with little success that the prototypes in the transmitter *had been transducted* through a series of point-events of transfinite cardinality. Al had innocently asked whether that meant prototypes had been stretched, so to speak, through all time, and the temporalist had thought he was joking and left in a huff.

"Like to see him do this," thought Al darkly, as he telekinized himself to the combox, after a cautious look to see that there were no medics around. To the box he said: "Police chief," and then to the police chief: "There's been a homicide committed with Medical Instrument Kit 674,101. It was lost some months ago by one of my people, Dr. John Hemingway. He didn't have a clear account of the circumstances."

The police chief groaned and said: "I'll call him in and question him." He was to be astonished by the answers, and was to learn that the homicide was well out of his jurisdiction.

Al stood for a moment at the bag board by the glowing red light that had been sparked into life by a departing vital force giving, as its last act, the warning that Kit 674,101 was in homicidal hands. With a sigh, Al pulled the plug and the light went out.

"Yah," jeered the woman. "You'd fool around with my neck, but you wouldn't risk your own with that thing!"

Angie smiled with serene confidence a smile that was to shock hardened morgue attendants. She set the Cutaneous Series knife to three centimeters before drawing it across her neck. Smiling, knowing the blade would cut only the dead horny tissue of the epidermis and the live tissue of the dermis, mysteriously push aside all major and minor blood vessels and muscular tissue—

Smiling, the knife plunging in and its microtomesharp metal

shearing through major and minor blood vessels and muscular tissue and pharynx, Angie cut her throat.

In the few minutes it took the police, summoned by the shrieking Mrs. Coleman, to arrive, the instruments had become crusted with rust, and the flasks which had held vascular glue and clumps of pink, rubbery alveoli and spare gray cells and coils of receptor nerves held only black slime, and from them when opened gushed the foul gases of decomposition.

ENCHANTED VILLAGE

A. E. van Vogt (1913–   )

OTHER WORLDS

July

The May 1950 issue of Astounding Science Fiction *contained an article by veteran sf writer L. Ron Hubbard called "Dianetics, The Evolution of a Science," which was destined to spawn one of the most controversial "movements" in American history. Initially championed by John W. Campbell, Jr., its pseudo-scientific claims of self-therapy found a willing audience, including several members of the science fiction community. Hubbard's 1950 book,* Dianetics: The Modern Science of Mental Health, *eventually sold in the millions. The movement was to cost A. E. van Vogt, one of the major figures of "Golden Age" sf, many potentially productive years away from his writing, and although he later returned, he never achieved the same level of fame and excellence.*

In 1950, however, van Vogt was still going strong, as "Enchanted Village" indicates—it was also the year that his The Voyage of the Space Beagle *(consisting of earlier stories with linking material) was published to excellent reviews.*

—M.H.G.

The advance of science does kill some romance. In 1950, it was still possible to think of a barely habitable Mars. There was still the possibility of canals, of liquid water, of a high civilization either alive or recently dead—at least there was no definite scientific evidence to the contrary.

Therefore we had the Mars of Edgar Rice Burroughs and of

Ray Bradbury, and to it, "Enchanted Village" is a worthy addition. Notice that the Earthman on Mars has no trouble breathing and he is not suffering unduly from cold. Notice that there is plant life on Mars and the remnants of an advanced technology.

It was only in 1969 that the Mars-probe, Mariner 4, gave the first hint that this was all wrong. Now we know that the Martian atmosphere is far too thin to breathe and lacks oxygen anyway, that the surface temperature is reminiscent of Antarctica, and that there is no sign of life.

Too bad, but in this book it's still 1950 so cling to the romance.

—I.A.

"Explorers of a new frontier" they had been called before they left for Mars.

For a while after the ship crashed into a Martian desert, killing all on board except—miraculously—this one man, Bill Jenner spat the words occasionally into the constant, sand-laden wind. He despised himself for the pride he had felt when he first heard them.

His fury faded with each mile that he walked, and his black grief for his friends became a gray ache. Slowly he realized that he had made a ruinous misjudgment.

He had underestimated the speed at which the rocketship had been traveling. He'd guessed that he would have to walk three hundred miles to reach the shallow, polar sea he and the others had observed as they glided in from outer space. Actually, the ship must have flashed an immensely greater distance before it hurtled down out of control.

The days stretched behind him, seemingly as numberless as the hot, red, alien sand that scorched through his tattered clothes. This huge scarecrow of a man kept moving across the endless, arid waste—he would not give up.

By the time he came to the mountain, his food had long been gone. Of his four water bags, only one remained, and that was so close to being empty that he merely wet his cracked lips and swollen tongue whenever his thirst became unbearable.

Jenner climbed high before he realized that it was not just

another dune that had barred his way. He paused, and as he gazed up at the mountain that towered above him, he cringed a little. For an instant he felt the hopelessness of this mad race he was making to nowhere—but he reached the top. He saw that below him was a depression surrounded by hills as high as or higher than the one on which he stood. Nestled in the valley they made was a village.

He could see trees and the marble floor of a courtyard. A score of buildings were clustered around what seemed to be a central square. They were mostly low-constructed, but there were four towers pointing gracefully into the sky. They shone in the sunlight with a marble luster.

Faintly, there came to Jenner's ears a thin, high-pitched whistling sound. It rose, fell, faded completely, then came up again clearly and unpleasantly. Even as Jenner ran toward it, the noise grated on his ears, eerie and unnatural.

He kept slipping on smooth rock, and bruised himself when he fell. He rolled halfway down into the valley. The buildings remained new and bright when seen from nearby. Their walls flashed with reflections. On every side was vegetation—reddish-green shrubbery, yellow-green trees laden with purple and red fruit.

With ravenous intent, Jenner headed for the nearest fruit tree. Close up, the tree looked dry and brittle. The large red fruit he tore from the lowest branch, however, was plump and juicy.

As he lifted it to his mouth, he remembered that he had been warned during his training period to taste nothing on Mars until it had been chemically examined. But that was meaningless advice to a man whose only chemical equipment was in his own body.

Nevertheless, the possibility of danger made him cautious. He took his first bite gingerly. It was bitter to his tongue, and he spat it out hastily. Some of the juice which remained in his mouth seared his gums. He felt the fire of it, and he reeled from nausea. His muscles began to jerk, and he lay down on the marble to keep himself from falling. After what seemed like hours to Jenner, the awful trembling finally went out of his body and he could see again. He looked up despisingly at the tree.

The pain finally left him, and slowly he relaxed. A soft breeze rustled the dry leaves. Nearby trees took up that gentle clamor, and it struck Jenner that the wind here in the valley was only a whisper of what it had been on the flat desert beyond the mountain.

There was no other sound now. Jenner abruptly remembered the high-pitched, ever-changing whistle he had heard. He lay very still, listening intently, but there was only the rustling of the leaves. The noisy shrilling had stopped. He wondered if it had been an alarm, to warn the villagers of his approach.

Anxiously he climbed to his feet and fumbled for his gun. A sense of disaster shocked through him. It wasn't there. His mind was a blank, and then he vaguely recalled that he had first missed the weapon more than a week before. He looked around him uneasily, but there was not a sign of creature life. He braced himself. He couldn't leave, as there was nowhere to go. If necessary, he would fight to the death to remain in the village.

Carefully Jenner took a sip from his water bag, moistening his cracked lips and his swollen tongue. Then he replaced the cap and started through a double line of trees toward the nearest building. He made a wide circle to observe it from several vantage points. On one side a low, broad archway opened into the interior. Through it, he could dimly make out the polished gleam of a marble floor.

Jenner explored the buildings from the outside, always keeping a respectful distance between him and any of the entrances. He saw no sign of animal life. He reached the far side of the marble platform on which the village was built, and turned back decisively. It was time to explore interiors.

He chose one of the four tower buildings. As he came within a dozen feet of it, he saw that he would have to stoop low to get inside.

Momentarily, the implications of that stopped him. These buildings had been constructed for a life form that must be very different from human beings.

He went forward again, bent down, and entered reluctantly, every muscle tensed.

He found himself in a room without furniture. However, there were several low marble fences projecting from one marble wall. They formed what looked like a group of four wide, low stalls. Each stall had an open trough carved out of the floor.

The second chamber was fitted with four inclined planes of marble, each of which slanted up to a dais. Altogether there were four rooms on the lower floor. From one of them a circular ramp mounted up, apparently to a tower room.

Jenner didn't investigate the upstairs. The earlier fear that he would find alien life was yielding to the deadly conviction that he wouldn't. No life meant no food or chance of getting any. In frantic haste he hurried from building to building, peering into the silent rooms, pausing now and then to shout hoarsely.

Finally there was no doubt. He was alone in a deserted village on a lifeless planet, without food, without water—except for the pitiful supply in his bag—and without hope.

He was in the fourth and smallest room of one of the tower buildings when he realized that he had come to the end of his search. The room had a single stall jutting out from one wall. Jenner lay down wearily in it. He must have fallen asleep instantly.

When he awoke he became aware of two things, one right after the other. The first realization occurred before he opened his eyes—the whistling sound was back; high and shrill, it wavered at the threshold of audibility.

The other was that a fine spray of liquid was being directed down at him from the ceiling. It had an odor, of which technician Jenner took a single whiff. Quickly he scrambled out of the room, coughing, tears in his eyes, his face already burning from chemical reaction.

He snatched his handkerchief and hastily wiped the exposed parts of his body and face.

He reached the outside and there paused, striving to understand what had happened.

The village seemed unchanged.

Leaves trembled in a gentle breeze. The sun was poised on a mountain peak. Jenner guessed from its position that it was morning again and that he had slept at least a dozen hours. The glazing white light suffused the valley. Half hidden by trees and shrubbery, the buildings flashed and shimmered.

He seemed to be in an oasis in a vast desert. It was an oasis, all right, Jenner reflected grimly, but not for a human being. For him, with its poisonous fruit, it was more like a tantalizing mirage.

He went back inside the building and cautiously peered into the room where he had slept. The spray of gas had stopped, not a bit of odor lingered, and the air was fresh and clean.

He edged over the threshold, half-inclined to make a test. He had a picture in his mind of a long-dead Martian creature lazing on the floor in the stall while a soothing chemical sprayed down on its body. The fact that the chemical was deadly to human beings merely emphasized how alien to man was the life that had spawned on Mars. But there seemed little doubt of the reason for the gas. The creature was accustomed to taking a morning shower.

Inside the "bathroom," Jenner eased himself feet first into the stall. As his hips came level with the stall entrance, the solid ceiling sprayed a jet of yellowish gas straight down upon his legs. Hastily Jenner pulled himself clear of the stall. The gas stopped as suddenly as it had started.

He tried it again, to make sure it was merely an automatic process. It turned on, then shut off.

Jenner's thirst-puffed lips parted with excitement. He thought, "If there can be one automatic process, there may be others."

Breathing heavily, he raced into the outer room. Carefully he shoved his legs into one of the two stalls. The moment his hips were in, a steaming gruel filled the trough beside the wall.

He stared at the greasy-looking stuff with a horrified fascination—food—and drink. He remembered the poison fruit and felt repelled, but he forced himself to bend down and put his finger into the hot, wet substance. He brought it up, dripping, to his mouth.

It tasted flat and pulpy, like boiled wood fiber. It trickled viscously into his throat. His eyes began to water and his lips drew back convulsively. He realized he was going to be sick, and ran for the outer door—but didn't quite make it.

When he finally got outside, he felt limp and unutterably listless. In that depressed state of mind, he grew aware again of the shrill sound.

He felt amazed that he could have ignored its rasping even for a few minutes. Sharply he glanced about, trying to determine its source, but it seemed to have none. Whenever he approached a point where it appeared to be loudest, then it would fade or shift, perhaps to the far side of the village.

He tried to imagine what an alien culture would want with a mind-shattering noise—although, of course, it would not necessarily have been unpleasant to them.

He stopped and snapped his fingers as a wild but nevertheless plausible notion entered his mind. Could this be music?

He toyed with the idea, trying to visualize the village as it had been long ago. Here a music-loving people had possibly gone about their daily tasks to the accompaniment of what was to them beautiful strains of melody.

The hideous whistling went on and on, waxing and waning. Jenner tried to put buildings between himself and the sound. He sought refuge in various rooms, hoping that at least one would be soundproof. None were. The whistle followed him wherever he went.

He retreated into the desert, and had to climb halfway up one of the slopes before the noise was low enough not to disturb him. Finally, breathless, but immeasurably relieved, he sank down on the sand and thought blankly:

What now?

The scene that spread before him had in it qualities of both heaven and hell. It was all too familiar now—the red sands, the stony dunes, the small, alien village promising so much and fulfilling so little.

Jenner looked down at it with his feverish eyes and ran his parched tongue over his cracked, dry lips. He knew that he was a dead man unless he could alter the automatic food-making machines that must be hidden somewhere in the walls and under the floors of the buildings.

In ancient days, a remnant of Martian civilization had survived here in this village. The inhabitants had died off, but the village lived on, keeping itself clean of sand, able to provide refuge for any Martian who might come along. But there were no Martians. There was only Bill Jenner, pilot of the first rocketship ever to land on Mars.

He had to make the village turn out food and drink that he could take. Without tools, except his hands, with scarcely any knowledge of chemistry, he must force it to change its habits.

Tensely he hefted his water bag. He took another sip and fought the same grim fight to prevent himself from guzzling it down to the last drop. And, when he had won the battle once more, he stood up and started down the slope.

He could last, he estimated, not more than three days. In that time he must conquer the village.

He was already among the trees when it suddenly struck him that the "music" had stopped. Relieved, he bent over a small shrub, took a good firm hold of it—and pulled.

It came up easily, and there was a slab of marble attached to it. Jenner stared at it, noting with surprise that he had been mistaken in thinking the stalk came up through a hole in the marble. It was merely stuck to the surface. Then he noticed something else—the shrub had no roots. Almost instinctively, Jenner looked down at the spot from which he had torn the slab of marble along with the plant. There was sand there.

He dropped the shrub, slipped to his knees, and plunged his fingers into the sand. Loose sand trickled through them. He reached deep, using all his strength to force his arm and hand down; sand—nothing but sand.

He stood up and frantically tore up another shrub. It also came easily, bringing with it a slab of marble. It had no roots, and where it had been was sand.

With a kind of mindless disbelief, Jenner rushed over to a fruit tree and shoved at it. There was a momentary resistance, and then the marble on which it stood split and lifted slowly into the air. The tree fell over with a swish and a crackle as its dry branches and leaves broke and crumbled into a thousand pieces. Underneath where it had been was sand.

Sand everywhere. A city built on sand. Mars, planet of sand. That was not completely true, of course. Seasonal vegetation had been observed near the polar icecaps. All but the hardiest of it died with the coming of summer. It had been intended that the rocketship land near one of those shallow, tideless seas.

By coming down out of control, the ship had wrecked more than itself. It had wrecked the chances for life of the only survivor of the voyage.

Jenner came slowly out of his daze. He had a thought then. He picked up one of the shrubs he had already torn loose, braced his foot against the marble to which it was attached, and tugged, gently at first, then with increasing strength.

It came loose finally, but there was no doubt that the two were part of a whole. The shrub was growing out of the marble.

Marble? Jenner knelt beside one of the holes from which he had torn a slab, and bent over an adjoining section. It was quite porous—calciferous rock, most likely, but not true marble at all. As he reached toward it, intending to break off a piece, it changed color. Astounded, Jenner drew back. Around the break, the stone was turning a bright orange-yellow. He studied it uncertainly, then tentatively he touched it.

It was as if he had dipped his fingers into searing acid. There was a sharp, biting, burning pain. With a gasp, Jenner jerked his hand clear.

The continuing anguish made him feel faint. He swayed and moaned, clutching the bruised members of his body. When the agony finally faded and he could look at the injury, he saw that the skin had peeled and that blood blisters had formed already. Grimly Jenner looked down at the break in the stone. The edges remained bright orange-yellow.

The village was alert, ready to defend itself from further attacks.

Suddenly weary, he crawled into the shade of a tree. There was only one possible conclusion to draw from what had happened, and it almost defied common sense. This lonely village was alive.

As he lay there, Jenner tried to imagine a great mass of living substance growing into the shape of buildings, adjusting itself to suit another life form, accepting the role of servant in the widest meaning of the term.

If it would serve one race, why not another? If it could adjust to Martians, why not to human beings?

There would be difficulties, of course. He guessed wearily that essential elements would not be available. The oxygen for water could come from the air . . . thousands of compounds could be made from sand. . . . Though it meant death if he failed to find a solution, he fell asleep even as he started to think about what they might be.

When he awoke it was quite dark.

Jenner climbed heavily to his feet. There was a drag to his muscles that alarmed him. He wet his mouth from his water bag and staggered toward the entrance of the nearest building. Except for the scraping of his shoes on the "marble," the silence was intense.

He stopped short, listened, and looked. The wind had died away. He couldn't see the mountains that rimmed the valley, but the buildings were still dimly visible, black shadows in a shadow world.

For the first time, it seemed to him that, in spite of his new hope, it might be better if he died. Even if he survived, what had he to look forward to? Only too well he recalled how hard it had been to rouse interest in the trip and to raise the large amount of money required. He remembered the colossal problems that had had to be solved in building the ship, and some of the men who had solved them were buried somewhere in the Martian desert.

It might be twenty years before another ship from Earth would try to reach the only other planet in the Solar System that had shown signs of being able to support life.

During those uncountable days and nights, those years, he would be here alone. That was the most he could hope for—if he lived. As he fumbled his way to a dais in one of the rooms, Jenner considered another problem: How did one let a living village know that it must alter its processes? In a way, it must already have grasped that it had a new tenant. How could he make it realize he needed food in a different chemical combination than that which it had served in the past; that he liked music, but on a different scale system; and that he could use a shower each morning—of water, not of poison gas?

He dozed fitfully, like a man who is sick rather than sleepy. Twice he wakened, his lips on fire, his eyes burning, his body bathed in perspiration. Several times he was startled into consciousness by the sound of his own harsh voice crying out in anger and fear at the night.

He guessed, then, that he was dying.

He spent the long hours of darkness tossing, turning, twisting, befuddled by waves of heat. As the light of morning came, he was vaguely surprised to realize that he was still alive. Restlessly he climbed off the dais and went to the door.

A bitingly cold wind blew, but it felt good to his hot face. He wondered if there were enough pneumococci in his blood for him to catch pneumonia. He decided not.

In a few moments he was shivering. He retreated back into the house, and for the first time noticed that, despite the doorless doorway, the wind did not come into the building at all. The rooms were cold but not draughty.

That started an association: Where had his terrible body heat come from? He teetered over to the dais where he had spent the night. Within seconds he was sweltering in a temperature of about one hundred and thirty.

He climbed off the dais, shaken by his own stupidity. He estimated that he had sweated at least two quarts of moisture out of his dried-up body on that furnace of a bed.

This village was not for human beings. Here even the beds were heated for creatures who needed temperatures far beyond the heat comfortable for men.

Jenner spent most of the day in the shade of a large tree. He felt exhausted, and only occasionally did he even remember that he had a problem. When the whistling started, it bothered him at first, but he was too tired to move away from it. There were long periods when he hardly heard it, so dulled were his senses.

Late in the afternoon he remembered the shrubs and the tree he had torn up the day before and wondered what had happened to them. He wet his swollen tongue with the last few drops of water in his bag, climbed lackadaisically to his feet, and went to look for the dried-up remains.

There weren't any. He couldn't even find the holes where he had torn them out. The living village had absorbed the dead tissue into itself and had repaired the breaks in its "body."

That galvanized Jenner. He began to think again . . . about mutations, genetic readjustment, life forms adapting to new environments. There'd been lectures on that before the ship left Earth, rather generalized talks designed to acquaint the explorers with the problems men might face on an alien planet. The important principle was quite simple: adjust or die.

The village had to adjust to him. He doubted if he could seriously damage it, but he could try. His own need to survive must be placed on as sharp and hostile a basis as that.

Frantically Jenner began to search his pockets. Before leaving the rocket he had loaded himself with odds and ends of small equipment. A jackknife, a folding metal cup, a printed radio, a tiny super-battery that could be charged by spinning an attached wheel—and for which he had brought along, among other things, a powerful electric fire lighter.

Jenner plugged the lighter into the battery and deliberately scraped the red-hot end along the surface of the "marble." The reaction was swift. The substance turned an angry purple this time. When an entire section of the floor had changed color, Jenner headed for the nearest stall trough, entering far enough to activate it.

There was a noticeable delay. When the food finally flowed into the trough, it was clear that the living village had realized the reason for what he had done. The food was a pale, creamy color, where earlier it had been a murky gray.

Jenner put his finger into it but withdrew it with a yell and wiped his finger. It continued to sting for several moments. The vital question was: Had it deliberately offered him food that would damage him, or was it trying to appease him without knowing what he could eat?

He decided to give it another chance, and entered the adjoining stall. The gritty stuff that flooded up this time was yellower. It didn't burn his finger, but Jenner took one taste and spat it out. He had the feeling that he had been offered a soup made of a greasy mixture of clay and gasoline.

He was thirsty now with a need heightened by the unpleasant taste in his mouth. Desperately he rushed outside and tore open the water bag, seeking the wetness inside. In his fumbling eagerness, he spilled a few precious drops onto the courtyard. Down he went on his face and licked them up.

Half a minute later, he was still licking, and there was still water.

The fact penetrated suddenly. He raised himself and gazed wonderingly at the droplets of water that sparkled on the smooth stone. As he watched, another one squeezed up from the apparently solid surface and shimmered in the light of the sinking sun.

He bent, and with the tip of his tongue sponged up each visible drop. For a long time he lay with his mouth pressed to the "marble," sucking up the tiny bits of water that the village doled out to him.

The glowing white sun disappeared behind a hill. Night fell, like the dropping of a black screen. The air turned cold, then icy. He shivered as the wind keened through his ragged clothes. But what finally stopped him was the collapse of the surface from which he had been drinking.

Jenner lifted himself in surprise, and in the darkness gingerly felt over the stone. It had genuinely crumbled. Evidently the substance had yielded up its available water and had disintegrated in the process. Jenner estimated that he had drunk altogether an ounce of water.

It was a convincing demonstration of the willingness of the village to please him, but there was another, less satisfying, implication. If the village had to destroy a part of itself every time it gave him a drink, then clearly the supply was not unlimited.

Jenner hurried inside the nearest building, climbed onto a dais—and climbed off again hastily, as the heat blazed up at him. He waited, to give the Intelligence a chance to realize he wanted a change, then lay down once more. The heat was as great as ever.

He gave that up because he was too tired to persist and too sleepy to think of a method that might let the village know he needed a different bedroom temperature. He slept on the floor with an uneasy conviction that it could *not* sustain him for long. He woke up many times during the night and thought, "Not enough water. No matter how hard it tries—" Then he would sleep again, only to wake once more, tense and unhappy.

Nevertheless, morning found him briefly alert; and all his steely determination was back—that iron will power that had brought him at least five hundred miles across an unknown desert.

He headed for the nearest trough. This time, after he had activated it, there was a pause of more than a minute; and then about a thimbleful of water made a wet splotch at the bottom.

Jenner licked it dry, then waited hopefully for more. When none came he reflected gloomily that somewhere in the village an entire group of cells had broken down and released their water for him.

Then and there he decided that it was up to the human being, who could move around, to find a new source of water for the village, which could not move.

In the interim, of course, the village would have to keep him alive, until he had investigated the possibilities. That meant, above everything else, he must have some food to sustain him while he looked around.

He began to search his pockets. Toward the end of his food supply, he had carried scraps and pieces wrapped in small bits of cloth. Crumbs had broken off into the pocket, and he had searched for them often during those long days in the desert. Now, by actually ripping the seams, he discovered tiny particles of meat and bread, little bits of grease and other unidentifiable substances.

Carefully he leaned over the adjoining stall and placed the scrappings in the trough there. The village would not be able to offer him more than a reasonable facsimile. If the spilling of a few drops on the courtyard could make it aware of his need for water, then a similar offering might give it the clue it needed as to the chemical nature of the food he could eat.

Jenner waited, then entered the second stall and activated it. About a pint of thick, creamy substance trickled into the bottom of the trough. The smallness of the quantity seemed evidence that perhaps it contained water.

He tasted it. It had a sharp, musty flavor and a stale odor. It was almost as dry as flour—but his stomach did not reject it.

Jenner ate slowly, acutely aware that at such moments as this the village had him at its mercy. He could never be sure that one of the food ingredients was not a slow-acting poison.

When he had finished the meal he went to a food trough in another building. He refused to eat the food that came up, but activated still another trough. This time he received a few drops of water.

He had come purposefully to one of the tower buildings. Now he started up the ramp that led to the upper floor. He paused only briefly in the room he came to, as he had already discovered that they seemed to be additional bedrooms. The familiar dais was there in a group of three.

What interested him was that the circular ramp continued to wind on upward. First to another, smaller room that seemed to have no particular reason for being. Then it wound on up to the top of the tower, some seventy feet above the ground. It was high enough for him to see beyond the rim of all the surrounding hilltops. He had thought it might be, but he had been too weak to make the climb before. Now he looked out to every horizon. Almost immediately the hope that had brought him up faded.

The view was immeasurably desolate. As far as he could see was an arid waste, and every horizon was hidden in a midst of wind-blown sand.

Jenner gazed with a sense of despair. If there was a Martian sea out there somewhere, it was beyond his reach.

Abruptly he clenched his hands in anger against his fate, which seemed inevitable now. At the very worst, he had hoped he would find himself in a mountainous region. Seas and mountains were generally the two main sources of water. He should have known, of course, that there were very few mountains on Mars. It would have been a wild coincidence if he had actually run into a mountain range.

His fury faded because he lacked the strength to sustain any emotion. Numbly he went down the ramp.

His vague plan to help the village ended as swiftly and finally as that.

The days drifted by, but as to how many he had no idea. Each time he went to eat, a smaller amount of water was doled out to him. Jenner kept telling himself that each meal would have to be his last. It was unreasonable for him to expect the village to destroy itself when his fate was certain now.

What was worse, it became increasingly clear that the food was not good for him. He had misled the village as to his needs by giving it stale, perhaps even tainted, samples, and prolonged the agony for himself. At times after he had eaten, Jenner felt dizzy for hours. All too frequently his head ached and his body shivered with fever.

The village was doing what it could. The rest was up to him, and he couldn't even adjust to an approximation of Earth food.

For two days he was too sick to drag himself to one of the troughs. Hour after hour he lay on the floor. Some time during the second night the pain in his body grew so terrible that he finally made up his mind.

"If I can get to a dais," he told himself, "the heat alone will kill me; and in absorbing my body, the village will get back some of its lost water."

He spent at least an hour crawling laboriously up the ramp of the nearest dais, and when he finally made it, he lay as one already dead. His last waking thought was: "Beloved friends, I'm coming."

The hallucination was so complete that momentarily he seemed to be back in the control room of the rocketship, and all around him were his former companions.

With a sigh of relief Jenner sank into a dreamless sleep.

He woke to the sound of a violin. It was a sad-sweet music that told of the rise and fall of a race long dead.

Jenner listened for a while and then with abrupt excitement realized the truth. This was a substitute for the whistling—the village had adjusted its music to him!

Other sensory phenomena stole in upon him. The dais felt comfortably warm, not hot at all. He had a feeling of wonderful physical well-being.

Eagerly he scrambled down the ramp to the nearest food stall. As he crawled forward, his nose close to the floor, the trough filled with a steamy mixture. The odor was so rich and pleasant that he plunged his face into it and slopped it up greedily. It had the flavor of thick, meaty soup and was warm and soothing to his lips and mouth. When he had eaten it all, for the first time he did not need a drink of water.

"I've won!" thought Jenner. "The village has found a way!"

After a while he remembered something and crawled to the bathroom. Cautiously, watching the ceiling, he eased himself backward into the shower stall. The yellowish spray came down, cool and delightful.

Ecstatically Jenner wriggled his four-foot tail and lifted his long snout to let the thin streams of liquid wash away the food impurities that clung to his sharp teeth.

Then he waddled out to bask in the sun and listen to the timeless music.

ODDY AND ID

Alfred Bester (1913–   )

ASTOUNDING SCIENCE FICTION
August

Like C. M. Kornbluth, Alfred Bester had published science fiction in the early 1940s but then stopped for some eight years to pursue other interests. When he returned to sf in 1950 he quickly established himself as a unique and ambitious writer, but one who published far too little. Almost all of his post-1950 short stories are memorable, and most can be found in Starlight *(1976). His two great novels of the 1950s,* The Demolished Man *(1953) and* Tiger! Tiger! *(1956, better known as* The Stars My Destination, *the title of the 1957 American edition), are rightly considered to be seminal works in the field. He again left science fiction when he went to work for* Holiday *magazine, but returned in the mid-1970s with several interesting stories and two novels,* The Computer Connection *(1975) and* Golem 100 *(1980), neither of which could live up to the legendary reputation of his first two.*

—M.H.G.

The last time I saw Alfie was at a small convention in New York over the Independence Day weekend of 1983. When a panel fell apart because a couple of the participants had unaccountably failed to show up, Alfie and I, who were in the audience, dutifully agreed to substitute.

A question from the audience was addressed to Alfie. The questioner wanted to know how Alfred Bester reacted to rejections.

A queer look came over Alfie's face. He looked helplessly

from side to side and then said in a nervous voice. "I don't know. I've never had a rejection."

He did well to look nervous. There are a hundred writers out there, Alfie, who are going to get you for that. Even I average a rejection a year. And yet, I can't expect a story like "Oddy and Id" to be rejected.

—I.A.

This is the story of a monster.

They named him Odysseus Gaul in honor of Papa's favorite hero, and over Mama's desperate objections; but he was known as Oddy from the age of one.

The first year of life is an egotistic craving for warmth and security. Oddy was not likely to have much of that when he was born, for Papa's real estate business was bankrupt, and Mama was thinking of divorce. But an unexpected decision by United Radiation to build a plant in the town made Papa wealthy, and Mama fell in love with him all over again. So Oddy had warmth and security.

The second year of life is a timid exploration. Oddy crawled and explored. When he reached for the crimson coils inside the non-objective fireplace, an unexpected short-circuit saved him from a burn. When he fell out the third floor window, it was into the grass filled hopper of the Mechano-Gardener. When he teased the Phoebus Cat, it slipped as it snapped at his face, and the brilliant fangs clicked harmlessly over his ear.

"Animals love Oddy," Mama said. "They only pretend to bite."

Oddy wanted to be loved, so everybody loved Oddy. He was petted, pampered and spoiled through pre-school age. Shopkeepers presented him with largess, and acquaintances showered him with gifts. Of sodas, candy, tarts, chrystons, bobbletucks, freezies and various other comestibles, Oddy consumed enough for an entire kindergarten. He was never sick.

"Takes after his father," Papa said. "Good stock."

Family legends grew about Oddy's luck. . . . How a perfect stranger mistook him for his own child just as Oddy was about to amble into the Electronic Circus, and delayed him long enough to save him from the disastrous explosion of '98. . . . How a forgotten library book rescued him from the Rocket Crash of '99. . . . How a multitude of odd incidents saved him from a multitude of assorted catastrophes. No one realized he was a monster . . . yet.

At eighteen, he was a nice looking boy with seal brown hair, warm brown eyes and a wide grin that showed even white teeth. He was strong, healthy, intelligent. He was completely uninhibited in his quiet, relaxed way. He had charm. He was happy. So far, his monstrous evil had only affected the little Town Unit where he was born and raised.

He came to Harvard from a Progressive School, so when one of his many quick friends popped into the dormitory room and said: "Hey Oddy, come down to the Quad and kick a ball around." Oddy answered: "I don't know how, Ben."

"Don't know how?" Ben tucked the football under his arm and dragged Oddy with him. "Where you been, laddie?"

"They didn't talk much about football back home," Oddy grinned. "Thought it was old fashioned. We were strictly Huxley-Hob."

"Huxley-Hob! That's for hi-brows," Ben said. "Football is still the big game. You want to be famous? You got to be on that gridiron before the Video every Saturday."

"So I've noticed, Ben. Show me."

Ben showed Oddy, carefully and with patience. Oddy took the lesson seriously and industriously. His third punt was caught by a freakish gust of wind, travelled seventy yards through the air, and burst through the third floor window of Proctor Charley (Gravy-Train) Stuart. Stuart took one look out the window and had Oddy down to Soldier Stadium in half an hour. Three Saturdays later, the headlines read: ODDY GAUL 57–ARMY 0.

"Snell & Rumination!" Coach Hig Clayton swore. "How does he do it? There's nothing sensational about that kid. He's just average. But when he runs they fall down chasing him. When he kicks, they fumble. When they fumble, he recovers."

"He's a negative player," Gravy-Train answered. "He lets you make the mistakes and then he cashes in."

They were both wrong. Oddy Gaul was a monster.

With his choice of any eligible young woman, Oddy Gaul went stag to the Observatory Prom, wandered into a darkroom by mistake, and discovered a girl in a smock bending over trays in the hideous green safe-light. She had cropped black hair, icy blue eyes, strong features, and a sensuous boyish figure. She ordered him out and Oddy fell in love with her . . . temporarily.

His friends howled with laughter when he told them. "Shades of Pygmalion, Oddy, don't you know about *her?* The girl is frigid. A statue. She loathes men. You're wasting your time."

But through the adroitness of her analyst, the girl turned a neurotic corner one week later and fell deeply in love with Oddy Gaul. It was sudden, devastating and enraptured for two months. Then just as Oddy began to cool, the girl had a relapse and everything ended on a friendly, convenient basis.

So far only minor events made up the response to Oddy's luck, but the shock-wave of reaction was spreading. In September of his Sophomore year, Oddy competed for the Political Economy Medal with a thesis entitled: "Causes Of Mutiny." The striking similarity of his paper to the Astraean Mutiny that broke out the day his paper was entered won him the prize.

In October, Oddy contributed twenty dollars to a pool organized by a crack-pot classmate for speculating on the Exchange according to 'Stock Market Trends,' a thousand year old superstition. The seer's calculations were ridiculous, but a sharp panic nearly ruined the Exchange as it quadrupled the pool. Oddy made one hundred dollars.

And so it went . . . worse and worse. The monster.

Now a monster can get away with a lot when he's studying speculative philosophy where causation is rooted in history and the Present is devoted to statistical analysis of the Past; but the living sciences are bulldogs with their teeth clamped on the phenomena of Now. So it was Jesse Migg, physiologist and spectral physicist, who first trapped the monster . . . and he thought he was an angel.

Old Jess was one of the Sights. In the first place he was young . . . not over forty. He was a malignant knife of a man, an albino, pink-eyed, bald, pointed-nosed and brilliant. He affected 20th Century clothes and 20th Century vices . . . tobacco and potations of C_2H_5OH. He never talked . . . He spat. He never walked . . . He scurried. And he was scurrying up and down the aisles of the laboratory of Tech I (General Survey of Spatial Mechanics—Required for All General Arts Students) when he ferreted out the monster.

One of the first experiments in the course was EMF Electrolysis. Elementary stuff. A U-Tube containing water was passed between the poles of a stock Remosant Magnet. After sufficient voltage was transmitted through the coils, you drew off Hydrogen and Oxygen in two-to-one ratio at the arms of the tube and related them to the voltage and the magnetic field.

Oddy ran his experiment earnestly, got the proper results, entered them in his lab book and then waited for the official check-off. Little Migg came hustling down the aisle, darted to Oddy and spat: "Finished?"

"Yes, sir."

Migg checked the book entries, glanced at the indicators at the ends of the tube, and stamped Oddy out with a sneer. It was only after Oddy was gone that he noticed the Remosant Magnet was obviously shorted. The wires were fused. There hadn't been any field to electrolyse the water.

"Curse and Confusion!" Migg grunted (he also affected 20th Century vituperation) and rolled a clumsy cigarette.

He checked off possibilities in his comptometer head. 1. Gaul cheated. 2. If so, with what apparatus did he portion out the H_2 and O_2? 3. Where did he get the pure gases? 4. Why did he do it? Honesty was easier. 5. He didn't cheat. 6. How did he get the right results? 7. How did he get *any* results?

Old Jess emptied the U-Tube, refilled it with water and ran off the experiment himself. He too got the correct result without a magnet.

"Rice on a Raft!" he swore, unimpressed by the miracle, and infuriated by the mystery. He snooped, darting about like a hungry bat. After four hours he discovered that the steel bench supports were picking up a charge from the Greeson Coils in the basement and had thrown just enough field to make everything come out right.

"Coincidence," Migg spat. But he was not convinced.

Two weeks later, in Elementary Fission Analysis, Oddy completed his afternoon's work with a careful listing of resultant isotopes from selenium to lanthanum. The only trouble, Migg discovered, was that there had been a mistake in the stock issued to Oddy. He hadn't received any U^{235} for neutron bombardment. His sample had been a left-over from a Stefan-Boltsmann black-body demonstration.

"Frog in Heaven!" Migg swore, and double-checked. Then he triple-checked. When he found the answer . . . a remarkable coincidence involving improperly cleaned apparatus and a defective cloud-chamber, he swore further. He also did some intensive thinking.

"There are accident prones," Migg snarled at the reflection in his Self-Analysis Mirror. "How about Good Luck prones? Horse Manure!"

But he was a bulldog with his teeth sunk in phenomena. He tested Oddy Gaul. He hovered over him in the laboratory, cackling with infuriated glee as Oddy completed experiment after experiment with defective equipment. When Oddy successfully completed the Rutherford Classic . . . getting $_{8}O^{17}$ after exposing nitrogen to alpha radiation . . . but in this case without the use of nitrogen or alpha radiation, Migg actually clapped him on the back in delight. Then the little man investigated and found the logical, improbable chain of coincidences that explained it.

He devoted his spare time to a check-back on Oddy's career at Harvard. He had a two hour conference with a lady astronomer's faculty analyst, and a ten minute talk with Hig Clayton and Gravy-Train Stuart. He rooted out the Exchange Pool, the Political Economy Medal, and half a dozen other incidents that filled him with malignant joy. Then he cast off his 20th Century affectation, dressed himself properly in formal leotards, and entered the Faculty Club for the first time in a year.

A four-handed chess game in three dimensions was in progress in the Diathermy Alcove. It had been in progress since Migg joined the faculty, and would probably not be finished before the end of the century. In fact, Johansen, playing Red, was already training his son to replace him in the likely event of his dying before the completion of the game.

As abrupt as ever, Migg marched up to the glowing cube, sparkling with sixteen layers of vari-colored pieces, and blurted: "What do you know about accidents?"

"Ah?" said Bellanby, *Philosopher in Res* at the University. "Good evening, Migg. Do you mean the accident of substance, or the accident of essence? If, on the other hand, your question implies—"

"No, no," Migg interrupted. "My apologies, Bellanby. Let me rephrase the question. Is there such a thing as Compulsion of Probability?"

Hrrdnikkisch completed his move and gave full attention to Migg, as did Johansen and Bellanby. Wilson continued to study the board. Since he was permitted one hour to make his move and would need it, Migg knew there would be ample time for the discussion.

"Compulthon of Probability?" Hrrdnikkisch lisped. "Not a

new conthept, Migg. I recall a thurvey of the theme in 'The Integraph' Vol. LVIII, No. 9. The calculuth, if I am not mithtaken—''

"No," Migg interrupted again. "My respects, Signoid. I'm not interested in the mathematic of Probability, nor the philosophy. Let me put it this way. The Accident Prone has already been incorporated into the body of Psychoanalysis. Paton's Theorem of the Least Neurotic Norm settled that. But I've discovered the obverse. I've discovered a Fortune Prone."

"Ah?" Johansen chuckled. "It's to be a joke. You wait and see, Signoid."

"No," answered Migg. "I'm perfectly serious. I've discovered a genuinely lucky man."

"He wins at cards?"

"He wins at everything. Accept this postulate for the moment . . . I'll document it later . . . There is a man who is lucky. He is a Fortune Prone. Whatever he desires, he receives. Whether he has the ability to achieve it or not, he receives it. If his desire is totally beyond the peak of his accomplishment, then the factors of chance, coincidence, hazard, accident . . . and so on, combine to produce his desired end."

"No." Bellanby shook his head. "Too far-fetched."

"I've worked it out empirically," Migg continued. "It's something like this. The future is a choice of mutually exclusive possibilities, one or other of which must be realized in terms of favorability of the events and number of the events . . ."

"Yes, yes," interrupted Johansen. "The greater the number of favorable possibilities, the stronger the probability of an event maturing. This is elementary, Migg. Go on."

"I continue," Migg spat indignantly. "When we discuss Probability in terms of throwing dice, the predictions or odds are simple. There are only six mutually exclusive possibilities to each die. The favorability is easy to compute. Chance is reduced to simple odds-ratios. *But* when we discuss probability in terms of the Universe, we cannot encompass enough data to make a prediction. There are too many factors. Favorability cannot be ascertained."

"All thith ith true," Hrrdnikkisch said, "but what of your Fortune Prone?"

"I don't know how he does it . . . but merely by the intensity or mere existence of his desire, he can affect the favorability of possibilities. By wanting, he can turn possibility into probability, and probability into certainty."

"Ridiculous," Bellanby snapped. "You claim there's a man far-sighted and far-reaching enough to do this?"

"Nothing of the sort. He doesn't know what he's doing. He just thinks he's lucky, if he thinks about it at all. Let us say he wants . . . Oh . . . Name anything."

"Heroin," Bellanby said.

"What's that?" Johansen inquired.

"A morphine derivative," Hrrdnikkisch explained. "Formerly manufactured and thold to narcotic addictth."

"Heroin," Migg said. "Excellent. Say my man desires Heroin, an antique narcotic no longer in existence. Very good. His desire would compel this sequence of possible but improbable events: A chemist in Australia, fumbling through a new organic synthesis, will accidentally and unwittingly prepare six ounces of Heroin. Four ounces will be discarded, but through a logical mistake two ounces will be preserved. A further coincidence will ship it to this country and this city, wrapped as powdered sugar in a plastic ball; where the final accident will serve it to my man in a restaurant which he is visiting for the first time on an impulse. . . ."

"La-La-La!" said Hrrdnikkisch. "Thith shuffling of hithtory. Thith fluctuation of inthident and pothibility? All achieved without the knowledge but with the dethire of a man?"

"Yes. Precisely my point," Migg snarled. "I don't know how he does it, but he turns possibility into certainty. And since almost anything is possible, he is capable of accomplishing almost anything. He is God-like but not a God because he does this without consciousness. He is an angel."

"Who is this angel?" Johansen asked.

And Migg told them all about Oddy Gaul.

"But how does he do it?" Bellanby persisted. "How does he do it?"

"I don't know," Migg repeated again. "Tell me how Espers do it."

"What!" Bellanby exclaimed. "Are you prepared to deny the EK pattern of thought? Do you—"

"I do nothing of the sort. I merely illustrate one possible explanation. Man produces events. The threatening War of Resources may be thought to be a result of the natural exhaustion of terran resources. We know it is not. It is a result of centuries of thriftless waste by man. Natural phenomena are less often produced by nature and more often produced by man."

"And?"

"Who knows? Gaul is producing phenomena. Perhaps he's unconsciously broadcasting on an EK waveband. Broadcasting and getting results. He wants Heroin. The broadcast goes out—"

"But Espers can't pick up any EK brain pattern further than the horizon. It's direct wave transmission. Even large objects cannot be penetrated. A building, say, or a—"

"I'm not saying this is on the Esper level," Migg shouted. "I'm trying to imagine something bigger. Something tremendous. He wants Heroin. His broadcast goes out to the world. All men unconsciously fall into a pattern of activity which will produce that Heroin as quickly as possible. That Austrian chemist—"

"No. Australian."

"That Australian chemist may have been debating between half a dozen different syntheses. Five of them could never have produced Heroin; but Gaul's impulse made him select the sixth."

"And if he did not anyway?"

"Then who knows what parallel chains were also started? A boy playing Cops and Robbers in Montreal is impelled to explore an abandoned cabin where he finds the drug, hidden there centuries ago by smugglers. A woman in California collects old apothecary jars. She finds a pound of Heroin. A child in Berlin, playing with a defective Radar-Chem Set, manufactures it. Name the most improbable sequence of events, and Gaul can bring it about, logically and certainly. I tell you, that boy is an angel!"

And he produced his documented evidence and convinced them.

It was then that four scholars of various but indisputable intellects elected themselves an executive committee for Fate and took Oddy Gaul in hand. To understand what they attempted to do, you must first understand the situation the world found itself in during that particular era.

It is a known fact that all wars are founded in economic conflict, or to put it another way, a trial by arms is merely the last battle of an economic war. In the pre-Christian centuries, the Punic Wars were the final outcome of a financial struggle between Rome and Carthage for economic control of the Mediterranean. Three thousand years later, the impending War of Resources loomed as the finale of a struggle between the two

Independent Welfare States controlling most of the known economic world.

What petroleum oil was to the 20th Century, FO (the nickname for Fissionable Ore) was to the 30th; and the situation was peculiarly similar to the Asia Minor crisis that ultimately wrecked the United Nations a thousand years before. Triton, a backward, semibarbaric satellite, previously unwanted and ignored, had suddenly discovered it possessed enormous resources of FO. Financially and technologically incapable of self-development, Triton was peddling concessions to both Welfare States.

The difference between a Welfare State and a Benevolent Despot is slight. In times of crisis, either can be traduced by the sincerest motives into the most abominable conduct. Both the Comity of Nations (bitterly nicknamed "The Con Men" by Der Realpolitik aus Terra) and Der Realpolitik aus Terra (sardonically called "The Rats" by the Comity of Nations) were desperately in need of natural resources, meaning FO. They were bidding against each other hysterically, and elbowing each other with sharp skirmishes at outposts. Their sole concern was the protection of their citizens. From the best of motives they were preparing to cut each other's throat.

Had this been the issue before the citizens of both Welfare States, some compromise might have been reached; but Triton in the catbird seat, intoxicated as a schoolboy with newfound prominence and power, confused issues by raising a religious question and reviving a Holy War which the Family of Planets had long forgotten. Assistance in their Holy War (involving the extermination of a harmless and rather unimportant sect called the Quakers) was one of the conditions of sale. This, both the Comity of Nations and Der Realpolitik aus Terra were prepared to swallow with or without private reservations, but it could not be admitted to their citizens.

And so, camouflaged by the burning issues of Rights of Minority Sects, Priority of Pioneering, Freedom of Religion, Historical Rights to Triton v. Possession in Fact, etc., the two Houses of the Family of Planets feinted, parried, riposted and slowly closed, like fencers on the strip, for the final sortie which meant ruin for both.

All this the four men discussed through three interminable meetings.

"Look here," Migg complained toward the close of the third

consultation. "You theoreticians have already turned nine man-hours into carbonic acid with ridiculous dissensions . . ."

Bellanby nodded, smiling. "It's as I've always said, Migg. Every man nurses the secret belief that were he God he could do the job much better. We're just learning how difficult it is."

"Not God," Hrrdnikkisch said, "but hith Prime Minithterth. Gaul will be God."

Johansen winced. "I don't like that talk," he said. "I happen to be a religious man."

"You?" Bellanby exclaimed in surprise. "A Colloid-Therapeutist?"

"I happen to be a religious man," Johansen repeated stubbornly.

"But the boy hath the power of the miracle," Hrrdnikkisch protested. "When he hath been taught to know what he doeth, he will be a God."

"This is pointless," Migg rapped out. "We have spent three sessions in piffling discussion. I have heard three opposed views re Mr. Odysseus Gaul. Although all are agreed he must be used as a tool, none can agree on the work to which the tool must be set. Bellanby prattles about an Ideal Intellectual Anarchy, Johansen preaches about a Soviet of God, and Hrrdnikkisch has wasted two hours postulating and destroying his own theorems . . ."

"Really, Migg . . ." Hrrdnikkisch began. Migg waved his hand.

"Permit me," Migg continued malevolently, "to reduce this discussion to the kindergarten level. First things first, gentlemen. Before attempting to reach cosmic agreement we must make sure there is a cosmos left for us to agree upon. I refer to the impending war . . .

"Our program, as I see it, must be simple and direct. It is the education of a God or, if Johansen protests, of an angel. Fortunately Gaul is an estimable young man of kindly, honest disposition. I shudder to think what he might have done had he been inherently vicious."

"Or what he might do once he learns what he can do," muttered Bellanby.

"Precisely. We must begin a careful and rigorous ethical education of the boy, but we haven't enough time. We can't educate first, and then explain the truth when he's safe. We must forestall the war. We need a short-cut."

"All right," Johansen said. "What do you suggest?"

"Dazzlement," Migg spat. "Enchantment."

"Enchantment?" Hrrdnikkisch chuckled. "A new thienth, Migg?"

"Why do you think I selected you three of all people for this secret?" Migg snorted. "For your intellects? Nonsense! I can think you all under the table. No. I selected you, gentlemen, for your charm."

"It's an insult," Bellanby grinned, "and yet I'm flattered."

"Gaul is nineteen," Migg went on. "He is at the age when undergraduates are more susceptible to hero-worship. I want you gentlemen to charm him. You are not the first brains of the University, but you are the first heroes."

"I altho am inthulted and flattered," said Hrrdnikkisch.

"I want you to charm him, dazzle him, inspire him with affection and awe . . . as you've done with countless classes of undergraduates."

"Aha!" said Johansen. "The chocolate around the pill."

"Exactly. When he's enchanted, you will make him want to stop the war . . . and then tell him how he can stop it. That will give us breathing space to continue his education. By the time he outgrows his respect for you he will have a sound ethical foundation on which to build. He'll be safe."

"And you, Migg?" Bellanby inquired. "What part do you play?"

"Now? None," Migg snarled. "I have no charm, gentlemen. I come later. When he outgrows his respect for you, he'll begin to acquire respect for me."

All of which was frightfully conceited but perfectly true.

And as events slowly marched toward the final crisis, Oddy Gaul was carefully and quickly enchanted. Bellanby invited him to the twenty foot crystal globe atop his house . . . the famous hen-roost to which only the favored few were invited. There, Oddy Gaul sun-bathed and admired the philosopher's magnificent iron-hard condition at seventy-three. Admiring Bellanby's muscles, it was only natural for him to admire Bellanby's ideas. He returned often to sunbathe, worship the great man, and absorb ethical concepts.

Meanwhile, Hrrdnikkisch took over Oddy's evenings. With the mathematician, who puffed and lisped like some flamboyant character out of Rabelais, Oddy was carried to the dizzy heights of the *haute cuisine* and the complete pagan life. Together they ate and drank incredible foods and liquids and pursued incredible women until Oddy returned to his room each night, intoxicated with the magic of the senses and the riotous color of the great Hrrdnikkisch's glittering ideas.

And occasionally . . . not too often, he would find Papa Johansen waiting for him, and then would come the long quiet talks through the small hours when young men search for the harmonics of life and the meaning of entity. And there was Johansen for Oddy to model himself after . . . a glowing embodiment of Spiritual Good . . . a living example of Faith in God and Ethical Sanity.

The climax came on March 15th. . . . The Ides of March, and they should have taken the date as a sign. After dinner with his three heroes at the Faculty Club, Oddy was ushered into the Foto-Library by the three great men where they were joined, quite casually, by Jesse Migg. There passed a few moments of uneasy tension until Migg made a sign, and Bellanby began.

"Oddy," he said, "have you ever had the fantasy that some day you might wake up and discover you were a King?"

Oddy blushed.

"I see you have. You know, every man has entertained that dream. The usual pattern is: You learn your parents only adopted you, and that you are actually and rightfully the King of . . . of . . ."

"Baratraria," said Hrrdnikkisch who had made a study of Stone Age Fiction.

"Yes, sir," Oddy muttered. "I've had that dream."

"Well," Bellanby said quietly, "it's come true. You are a King."

Oddy stared while they explained and explained and explained. First, as a college boy, he was wary and suspicious of a joke. Then, as an idolator, he was almost persuaded by the men he most admired. And finally, as a human animal, he was swept away by the exaltation of security. Not power, not glory, not wealth thrilled him, but security alone. Later he might come to enjoy the trimmings, but now he was released from fear. He need never worry again.

"Yes," exclaimed Oddy. "Yes, yes, yes! I understand. I understand what you want me to do." He surged up excitedly from his chair and circled the illuminated walls, trembling with joy and intoxication. Then he stopped and turned.

"And I'm grateful," he said. "Grateful to all of you for what you've been trying to do. It would have been shameful if I'd been selfish . . . or mean . . . Trying to use this for myself. But you've shown me the way. It's to be used for good. Always!''

Johansen nodded happily.

''I'll always listen to you,'' Oddy went on. ''I don't want to make any mistakes. Ever!'' He paused and blushed again. ''That dream about being a king . . . I had that when I was a kid. But here at the school I've had something bigger. I used to wonder what would happen if I was the one man who could run the world. I used to dream about the kind things I'd do . . .''

''Yes,'' said Bellanby. ''We know, Oddy. We've all had that dream too. Every man does.''

''But it isn't a dream any more,'' Oddy laughed. ''It's reality. I can do it. I can make it happen.''

''Start with the war,'' Migg said sourly.

''Of course,'' said Oddy. ''The war first; but then we'll go on from there, won't we? I'll make sure the war never starts, but then we'll do big things . . . great things! Just the five of us in private. Nobody'll know about us. We'll be ordinary people, but we'll make life wonderful for everybody. If I'm an angel . . . like you say . . . then I'll spread heaven around me as far as I can reach.''

''But start with the war,'' Migg repeated.

''The war is the first disaster that must be averted, Oddy,'' Bellanby said. ''If you don't want this disaster to happen, it will never happen.''

''And you want to prevent that tragedy, don't you?'' said Johansen.''

''Yes,'' answered Oddy. ''I do.''

On March 20th, the war broke. The Comity of Nations and Der Realpolitik aus Terra mobilized and struck. While blow followed shattering counter-blow, Oddy Gaul was commissioned Subaltern in a Line regiment, but gazetted to Intelligence on May 3rd. On June 24th he was appointed A.D.C. to the Joint Forces Council meeting in the ruins of what had been Australia. On July 11th he was brevetted to command of the wrecked Space Force, being jumped 1,789 grades over regular officers. On September 19th he assumed supreme command in the Battle of the Parsec and won the victory that ended the disastrous solar annihilation called the Six Month War.

On September 23rd, Oddy Gaul made the astonishing Peace Offer that was accepted by the remnants of both Welfare States. It required the scrapping of antagonistic economic theories, and amounted to the virtual abandonment of all economic theory with an amalgamation of both States into a Solar Society. On January 1st, Oddy Gaul, by unanimous acclaim, was elected Solon of the Solar Society in perpetuity.

And today . . . still youthful, still vigorous, still handsome, still sincere, idealistic, charitable, kindly and sympathetic, he lives in the Solar Palace. He is unmarried but a mighty lover; uninhibited, but a charming host and devoted friend; democratic, but the feudal overlord of a bankrupt Family of Planets that suffers misgovernment, oppression, poverty and confusion with a cheerful joy that sings nothing but Hosannahs to the glory of Oddy Gaul.

In a last moment of clarity, Jesse Migg communicated his desolate summation of the situation to his friends in the Faculty Club. This was shortly before they made the trip to join Oddy in the palace as his confidential and valued advisers.

"We were fools," Migg said bitterly. "We should have killed him. He isn't an angel. He's a monster. Civilization and culture . . . philosophy and ethics . . . Those were only masks Oddy put on; masks that covered the primitive impulses of his subconscious mind."

"You mean Oddy was not sincere?" Johansen asked heavily. "He wanted this wreckage . . . this ruin?"

"Certainly he was sincere . . . consciously. He still is. He thinks he desires nothing but the most good for the most men. He's honest, kind and generous . . . but only consciously."

"Ah! The Id!" said Hrrdnikkisch with an explosion of breath as though he had been punched in the stomach.

"You understand, Signoid? I see you do. Gentlemen, we were imbeciles. We made the mistake of assuming that Oddy would have conscious control of his power. He does not. The control was and still is below the thinking, reasoning level. The control lies in Oddy's Id . . . in that deep unconscious reservoir of primordial selfishness that lies within every man."

"Then he wanted the war," Bellanby said.

"His Id wanted the war, Bellanby. It was the quickest route to what his Id desires . . . to be Lord of the Universe and Loved by the Universe . . . and his Id controls the Power. All of us have that selfish, egocentric Id within us, perpetually searching for satisfaction, timeless, immortal, knowing no logic, no values, no good and evil, no morality; and that is what controls the power in Oddy. He will always get not what he's been educated to desire but what his Id desires. It's the inescapable conflict that may be the doom of our system.''

''But we'll be there to advise him . . . counsel him . . . guide him,'' Bellanby protested. ''He asked us to come.''

''And he'll listen to our advice like the good child that he is,'' Migg answered, ''Agreeing with us, trying to make a heaven for everybody while his Id will be making a hell for everybody. Oddy isn't unique. We all suffer from the same conflict . . . but Oddy has the power.''

''What can we do?'' Johansen groaned. ''What can we do?''

''I don't know.'' Migg bit his lip, then bobbed his head to Papa Johansen in what amounted to apology for him. ''Johansen,'' he said, ''you were right. There must be a God, if only because there must be an opposite to Oddy Gaul who was most assuredly invented by the Devil.''

But that was Jesse Migg's last sane statement. Now, of course, he adores Gaul the Glorious, Gaul the Gauleiter, Gaul the God Eternal who has achieved the savage, selfish satisfaction for which all of us unconsciously yearn from birth, but which only Oddy Gaul has won.

THE SACK

William Morrison (Joseph Samachson, 1906–1982)

ASTOUNDING SCIENCE FICTION
September

The late Joseph Samachson was a chemist in the Chicago area who wrote children's books on the side. As "William Morrison" he produced some fifty stories for the science fiction magazines in the 1950s, most notably "Country Doctor" (1953), "The Model of a Judge" (1953), and the present selection. He was a very capable writer, but unfortunately he never had a collection, and he is largely unknown today. His absence from such standard reference works as The Science Fiction Encyclopedia *and* Twentieth Century Science Fiction Writers *is a glaring omission.*

—M.H.G.

We are into the McCarthy era now. In February, 1950, Senator Joseph R. McCarthy of Wisconsin made a ridiculous and never-substantiated charge of Communists in the State Department and began a four-year reign of terror that turned government officials into cravens and disgraced us all.

This story, "The Sack," appeared in a magazine that was on the newsstands in August of that year, and it must have been written some months before. Was the stupid and hateful Senator Horrigan a take-off on McCarthy and, perhaps, the first bitter satire on that horrible man? (My own satire didn't come till two years later.) Or was Morrison merely prescient, having written the story prior to McCarthy's emergence from the slime?

We may never know.

—I.A.

At first they hadn't even known that the Sack existed. If they had noticed it at all when they landed on the asteroid, they thought of it merely as one more outpost of rock on the barren expanse of roughly ellipsoidal silicate surface, which Captain Ganko noticed had major and minor axes roughly three and two miles in diameter, respectively. It would never have entered anyone's mind that the unimpressive object they had unconsciously acquired would soon be regarded as the most valuable prize in the system.

The landing had been accidental. The government patrol ship had been limping along, and now it had settled down for repairs, which would take a good seventy hours. Fortunately, they had plenty of air, and their recirculation system worked to perfection. Food was in somewhat short supply, but it didn't worry them, for they knew that they could always tighten their belts and do without full rations for a few days. The loss of water that had resulted from a leak in the storage tanks, however, was a more serious matter. It occupied a good part of their conversation during the next fifty hours.

Captain Ganko said finally, "There's no use talking, it won't be enough. And there are no supply stations close enough at hand to be of any use. We'll have to radio ahead and hope that they can get a rescue ship to us with a reserve supply."

The helmet mike of his next in command seemed to droop. "It'll be too bad if we miss each other in space, Captain."

Captain Ganko laughed unhappily. "It certainly will. In that case we'll have a chance to see how we can stand a little dehydration."

For a time nobody said anything. At last, however, the second mate suggested, "There might be water somewhere on the asteroid, sir."

"Here? How in Pluto would it stick, with a gravity that isn't even strong enough to hold loose rocks? And where the devil would it be?"

"To answer the first question first, it would be retained as water of crystallization," replied a soft liquid voice that seemed to penetrate his spacesuit and come from behind him. "To answer the second question, it is half a dozen feet below the surface, and can easily be reached by digging."

They had all swiveled around at the first words. But no one was in sight in the direction from which the words seemed to come. Captain Ganko frowned, and his eyes narrowed dangerously.

"We don't happen to have a practical joker with us, do we?" he asked mildly.

"You do not," replied the voice.

"Who said that?"

"I, Yzrl."

A crewman became aware of something moving on the surface of one of the great rocks, and pointed to it. The motion stopped when the voice ceased, but they didn't lose sight of it again. That was how they learned about Yzrl, or as it was more often called, the Mind-Sack.

If the ship and his services hadn't both belonged to the government, Captain Ganko could have claimed the Sack for himself or his owners and retired with a wealth far beyond his dreams. As it was, the thing passed into government control. Its importance was realized almost from the first, and Jake Siebling had reason to be proud when more important and more influential figures of the political and industrial world were finally passed over and he was made Custodian of the Sack. Siebling was a short, stocky man whose one weakness was self-deprecation. He had carried out one difficult assignment after another and allowed other men to take the credit. But this job was not one for a blowhard, and those in charge of making the appointment knew it. For once they looked beyond credit and superficial reputation, and chose an individual they disliked somewhat but trusted absolutely. It was one of the most effective tributes to honesty and ability ever devised.

The Sack, as Siebling learned from seeing it daily, rarely deviated from the form in which it had made its first appearance—a rocky, grayish lump that roughly resembled a sack of potatoes. It had no features, and there was nothing, when it was not being asked questions, to indicate that it had life. It ate rarely—once in a thousand years, it said, when left to itself; once a week when it was pressed into steady use. It ate or moved by fashioning a suitable pseudopod and stretching the thing out in whatever way it pleased. When it had attained its objective, the pseudopod was withdrawn into the main body again and the creature became once more a potato sack.

It turned out later that the name "Sack" was well chosen from another point of view, in addition to that of appearance. For the Sack was stuffed with information, and beyond that, with wisdom. There were many doubters at first, and some of them retained their doubts to the very end, just as some people remained convinced hundreds of years after Columbus that the Earth was flat. But those who saw and heard the Sack had no doubts at all. They tended, if anything, to go too far in the other direction, and to believe that the Sack knew everything. This, of course, was untrue.

It was the official function of the Sack, established by a series of Interplanetary acts, to answer questions. The first questions, as we have seen, were asked accidentally, by Captain Ganko. Later they were asked purposefully, but with a purpose that was itself random, and a few politicians managed to acquire considerable wealth before the Government put a stop to the leak of information, and tried to have the questions asked in a more scientific and logical manner.

Question time was rationed for months in advance, and sold at what was, all things considered, a ridiculously low rate—a mere hundred thousand credits a minute. It was this unrestricted sale of time that led to the first great government squabble.

It was the unexpected failure of the Sack to answer what must have been to a mind of its ability an easy question that led to the second blowup, which was fierce enough to be called a crisis. A total of a hundred and twenty questioners, each of whom had paid his hundred thousand, raised a howl that could be heard on every planet, and there was a legislative investigation, at which Siebling testified and all the conflicts were aired.

He had left an assistant in charge of the Sack, and now, as he sat before the Senatorial Committee, he twisted uncomfortably in front of the battery of cameras. Senator Horrigan, his chief interrogator, was a bluff, florid, loud-mouthed politician who had been able to imbue him with a feeling of guilt even as he told his name, age, and length of government service.

"It is your duty to see to it that the Sack is maintained in proper condition for answering questions, is it not, Mr. Siebling?" demanded Senator Horrigan.

"Yes, sir."

"Then why was it incapable of answering the questioners in question? These gentlemen had honestly paid their money—a hundred thousand credits each. It was necessary, I understand, to refund the total sum. That meant an over-all loss to the Government of, let me see now—one hundred twenty at one hundred thousand each—one hundred and twenty million credits," he shouted, rolling the words.

"Twelve million, Senator," hastily whispered his secretary.

The correction was not made, and the figure was duly headlined later as one hundred and twenty million.

Siebling said, "As we discovered later, Senator, the Sack failed to answer questions because it was not a machine, but a living creature. It was exhausted. It had been exposed to questioning on a twenty-four-hour-a-day basis."

"And who permitted this idiotic procedure?" boomed Senator Horrigan.

"You yourself, Senator," said Siebling happily. "The procedure was provided for in the bill introduced by you and approved by your committee."

Senator Horrigan had never even read the bill to which his name was attached, and he was certainly not to blame for its provisions. But this private knowledge of his own innocence did him no good with the public. From that moment he was Siebling's bitter enemy.

"So the Sack ceased to answer questions for two whole hours?"

"Yes, sir. It resumed only after a rest."

"And it answered them without further difficulty?"

"No, sir. Its response was slowed down. Subsequent questioners complained that they were defrauded of a good part of their money. But as answers were given, we considered that the complaints were without merit, and the financial department refused to make refunds."

"Do you consider that this cheating of investors in the Sack's time is honest?"

"That's none of my business, Senator," returned Siebling, who had by this time got over most of his nervousness. "I merely see to the execution of the laws. I leave the question of honesty to those who make them. I presume that it's in perfectly good hands."

Senator Horrigan flushed at the laughter that came from the onlookers. He was personally unpopular, as unpopular as a politician can be and still remain a politician. He was disliked even by the members of his own party, and some of his best political friends were among the laughers. He decided to abandon what had turned out to be an unfortunate line of questioning.

"It is a matter of fact, Mr. Siebling, is it not, that you have frequently refused admittance to investors who were able to show perfectly valid receipts for their credits?"

"That is a fact, sir. But——"

"You admit it, then."

"There is no question of 'admitting' anything, Senator. What I meant to say was——"

"Never mind what you meant to say. It's what you have already said that's important. You've cheated these men of their money!"

"That is not true, sir. They were given time later. The reason for my refusal to grant them admission when they asked for it was that the time had been previously reserved for the Armed Forces. There are important research questions that come up, and there is, as you know, a difference of opinion as to priority. When confronted with requisitions for time from a commercial investor and a representative of the Government, I never took it upon myself to settle the question. I always consulted with the Government's legal adviser."

"So you refused to make an independent decision, did you?"

"My duty, Senator, is to look after the welfare of the Sack. I do not concern myself with political questions. We had a moment of free time the day before I left the asteroid, when an investor who had already paid his money was delayed by a space accident, so instead of letting the moment go to waste, I utilized it to ask the Sack a question."

"How you might advance your own fortunes, no doubt?"

"No, sir. I merely asked it how it might function most efficiently. I took the precaution of making a recording, knowing that my word might be doubted. If you wish, Senator, I can introduce the recording in evidence."

Senator Horrigan grunted, and waved his hand. "Go on with your answer."

"The Sack replied that it would require two hours of complete rest out of every twenty, plus an additional hour of what it called 'recreation.' That is, it wanted to converse with some human being who would ask what it called sensible questions, and not press for a quick answer."

"So you suggest that the Government waste three hours of every twenty—one hundred and eighty million credits?"

"Eighteen million," whispered the secretary.

"The time would not be wasted. Any attempt to overwork the Sack would result in its premature annihilation."

"That is your idea, is it?"

"No, sir, that is what the Sack itself said."

At this point Senator Horrigan swung into a speech of

denunciation, and Siebling was excused from further testimony. Other witnesses were called, but at the end the Senate investigating body was able to come to no definite conclusion, and it was decided to interrogate the Sack personally.

It was out of the question for the Sack to come to the Senate, so the Senate quite naturally came to the Sack. The Committee of Seven was manifestly uneasy as the senatorial ship decelerated and cast its grapples toward the asteroid. The members, as individuals, had all traveled in space before, but all their previous destinations had been in civilized territory, and they obviously did not relish the prospect of landing on this airless and sunless body of rock.

The televisor companies were alert to their opportunity, and they had acquired more experience with desert territory. They had disembarked and set up their apparatus before the senators had taken their first timid steps out of the safety of their ship.

Siebling noted ironically that in these somewhat frightening surroundings, far from their home grounds, the senators were not so sure of themselves. It was his part to act the friendly guide, and he did so with relish.

"You see, gentlemen," he said respectfully, "it was decided, on the Sack's own advice, not to permit it to be further exposed to possible collision with stray meteors. It was the meteors which killed off the other members of its strange race, and it was a lucky chance that the last surviving individual managed to escape destruction as long as it has. An impenetrable shelter dome has been built therefore, and the Sack now lives under its protection. Questioners address it through a sound and sight system that is almost as good as being face to face with it."

Senator Horrigan fastened upon the significant part of his statement. "You mean that the Sack is safe—and we are exposed to danger from flying meteors?"

"Naturally, Senator. The Sack is unique in the system, men—even senators—are, if you will excuse the expression, a decicredit a dozen. They are definitely replaceable, by means of elections."

Beneath his helmet the senator turned green with a fear that concealed the scarlet of his anger. "I think it is an outrage to find the Government so unsolicitous of the safety and welfare of its employees!"

"So do I, sir. I live here the year round." He added smoothly, "Would you gentlemen care to see the Sack now?"

They stared at the huge visor screen and saw the Sack resting on its seat before them, looking like a burlap bag of potatoes which had been tossed onto a throne and forgotten there. It looked so definitely inanimate that it struck them as strange that the thing should remain upright instead of toppling over. All the same, for a moment the senators could not help showing the awe that overwhelmed them. Even Senator Horrigan was silent.

But the moment passed. He said, "Sir, we are an official Investigating Committee of the Interplanetary Senate, and we have come to ask you a few questions." The Sack showed no desire to reply, and Senator Horrigan cleared his throat and went on. "Is it true, sir, that you require two hours of complete rest in every twenty, and one hour for recreation, or, as I may put it, perhaps more precisely, relaxation?"

"It is true."

Senator Horrigan gave the creature its chance, but the Sack, unlike a senator, did not elaborate. Another of the committee asked, "Where would you find an individual capable of conversing intelligently with so wise a creature as you?"

"Here," replied the Sack.

"It is necessary to ask questions that are directly to the point, Senator," suggested Siebling. "The Sack does not usually volunteer information that has not been specifically called for."

Senator Horrigan said quickly, "I assume, sir, that when you speak of finding an intelligence on a par with your own, you refer to a member of our committee, and I am sure that of all my colleagues there is not one who is unworthy of being so denominated. But we cannot all of us spare the time needed for our manifold other duties, so I wish to ask you, sir, which of us, in your opinion, has the peculiar qualifications of that sort of wisdom which is required for this great task?"

"None," said the Sack.

Senator Horrigan looked blank. One of the other senators flushed, and asked, "Who has?"

"Siebling."

Senator Horrigan forgot his awe of the Sack, and shouted, "This is a put-up job!"

The other senator who had just spoken now said suddenly, "How is it that there are no other questioners present? Hasn't the Sack's time been sold far in advance?"

Siebling nodded. "I was ordered to cancel all previous appointments with the Sack, sir."

"By what idiot's orders?"

"Senator Horrigan's, sir."

At this point the investigation might have been said to come to an end. There was just time, before they turned away, for Senator Horrigan to demand desperately of the Sack, "Sir, will I be re-elected?" But the roar of anger that went up from his colleagues prevented him from hearing the Sack's answer, and only the question was picked up and broadcast clearly over the interplanetary network.

It had such an effect that it in itself provided Senator Horrigan's answer. He was *not* re-elected. But before the election he had time to cast his vote against Siebling's designation to talk with the Sack for one hour out of every twenty. The final committee vote was four to three in favor of Siebling, and the decision was confirmed by the Senate. And then Senator Horrigan passed temporarily out of the Sack's life and out of Siebling's.

Siebling looked forward with some trepidation to his first long interview with the Sack. Hitherto he had limited himself to the simple tasks provided for in his directives—to the maintenance of the meteor shelter dome, to the provision of a sparse food supply, and to the proper placement of an army and Space Fleet Guard. For by this time the great value of the Sack had been recognized throughout the system, and it was widely realized that there would be thousands of criminals anxious to steal so defenseless a treasure.

Now, Siebling thought, he would be obliged to talk to it, and he feared that he would lose the good opinion which it had somehow acquired of him. He was in a position strangely like that of a young girl who would have liked nothing better than to talk of her dresses and her boy friends to someone with her own background, and was forced to endure a brilliant and witty conversation with some man three times her age.

But he lost some of his awe when he faced the Sack itself. It would have been absurd to say that the strange creature's manner put him at ease. The creature had no manner. It was featureless and expressionless, and even when part of it moved, as when it was speaking, the effect was completely impersonal. Nevertheless, something about it did make him lose his fears.

For a time he stood before it and said nothing. To his surprise, the Sack spoke—the first time to his knowledge that it had done so without being asked a question. "You will not disappoint me," it said. "I expect nothing."

Siebling grinned. Not only had the Sack never before volunteered to speak, it had never spoken so dryly. For the first time it began to seem not so much a mechanical brain as the living creature he knew it to be. He asked, "Has anyone ever before asked you about your origin?"

"One man. That was before my time was rationed. And even he caught himself when he realized that he might better be asking how to become rich, and he paid little attention to my answer."

"How old are you?"

"Four hundred thousand years. I can tell you to the fraction of a second, but I suppose that you do not wish me to speak as precisely as usual."

The thing, thought Siebling, did have in its way a sense of humor. "How much of that time," he asked, "have you spent alone?"

"More than ten thousand years."

"You told someone once that your companions were killed by meteors. Couldn't you have guarded against them?"

The Sack said slowly, almost wearily, "That was after we had ceased to have an interest in remaining alive. The first death was three hundred thousand years ago."

"And you have lived, since then, without wanting to?"

"I have no great interest in dying either. Living has become a habit."

"Why did you lose your interest in remaining alive?"

"Because we lost the future. There had been a miscalculation."

"You are capable of making mistakes?"

"We had not lost that capacity. There was a miscalculation, and although those of us then living escaped personal disaster, our next generation was not so fortunate. We lost any chance of having descendants. After that, we had nothing for which to live."

Siebling nodded. It was a loss of motive that a human being could understand. He asked, "With all your knowledge, couldn't you have overcome the effects of what happened?"

The Sack said, "The more things become possible to you, the more you will understand that they cannot be done in impossible ways. We could not do everything. Sometimes one of the more stupid of those who come here asks me a question I cannot answer, and then becomes angry because he feels that he has been cheated of his credits. Others ask me to predict the future. I can predict only what I can calculate, and I soon come to the end of my powers of calculation. They are great compared to yours; they are small compared to the possibilities of the future."

"How do you happen to know so much? Is the knowledge born in you?"

"Only the possibility for knowledge is born. To know, we must learn. It is my misfortune that I forget little."

"What in the structure of your body, or your organs of thought, makes you capable of learning so much?"

The Sack spoke, but to Siebling the words meant nothing, and he said so. "I could predict your lack of comprehension," said the Sack, "but I wanted you to realize it for yourself. To make things clear, I should be required to dictate ten volumes, and they would be difficult to understand even for your specialists, in biology and physics and in sciences you are just discovering."

Siebling fell silent, and the Sack said, as if musing, "Your race is still an unintelligent one. I have been in your hands for many months, and no one has yet asked me the important questions. Those who wish to be wealthy ask about minerals and planetary land concessions, and they ask which of several schemes for making fortunes would be best. Several physicians have asked me how to treat wealthy patients who would otherwise die. Your scientists ask me to solve problems that would take them years to solve without my help. And when your rulers ask, they are the most stupid of all, wanting to know only how they may maintain their rule. None ask what they should."

"The fate of the human race?"

"That is prophecy of the far future. It is beyond my powers."

"What *should* we ask?"

"That is the question I have awaited. It is difficult for you to see its importance, only because each of you is so concerned with himself." The Sack paused, and murmured, "I ramble as I do not permit myself to when I speak to your fools. Nevertheless, even rambling can be informative."

"It has been to me."

"The others do not understand that too great a directness is dangerous. They ask specific questions which demand specific replies, when they should ask something general."

"You haven't answered me."

"It is part of an answer to say that a question is important. I am considered by your rulers a valuable piece of property. They should ask whether my value is as great as it seems. They should ask whether my answering questions will do good or harm."

"Which is it?"

"Harm, great harm."

Siebling was staggered. He said, "But if you answer truthfully——"

"The process of coming at the truth is as precious as the final truth itself. I cheat you of that. I give your people the truth, but not all of it, for they do not know how to attain it of themselves. It would be better if they learned that, at the expense of making many errors."

"I don't agree with that."

"A scientist asks me what goes on within a cell, and I tell him. But if he had studied the cell himself, even though the study required many years, he would have ended not only with this knowledge, but with much other knowledge, of things he does not even suspect to be related. He would have acquired many new processes of investigation."

"But surely, in some cases, the knowledge is useful in itself. For instance, I hear that they're already using a process you suggested for producing uranium cheaply to use on Mars. What's harmful about that?"

"Do you know how much of the necessary raw material is present? Your scientists have not investigated that, and they will use up all the raw material and discover only too late what they have done. You had the same experience on Earth? You learned how to purify water at little expense, and you squandered water so recklessly that you soon ran short of it."

"What's wrong with saving the life of a dying patient, as some of those doctors did?"

"The first question to ask is whether the patient's life should be saved."

"That's exactly what a doctor isn't supposed to ask. He has to try to save them all. Just as you never ask whether people are going to use your knowledge for a good purpose or a bad. You simply answer their questions."

"I answer because I am indifferent, and I care nothing what use they make of what I say. Are your doctors also indifferent?"

Siebling said, "You're supposed to answer questions, not ask them. Incidentally, why do you answer at all?"

"Some of your men find joy in boasting, in doing what they

call good, or in making money. Whatever mild pleasure I can find lies in imparting information."

"And you'd get no pleasure out of lying?"

"I am as incapable of telling lies as one of your birds of flying off the Earth on its own wings."

"One thing more. Why did you ask to talk to me, of all people, for recreation? There are brilliant scientists, and great men of all kinds whom you could have chosen."

"I care nothing for your race's greatness. I chose you because you are honest."

"Thanks. But there are other honest men on Earth, and on Mars, and on the other planets as well. Why me, instead of them?"

The Sack seemed to hesitate. "Your choice gave me a mild pleasure. Possibly because I knew it would be displeasing to those men."

Siebling grinned. "You're not quite so indifferent as you think you are. I guess it's pretty hard to be indifferent to Senator Horrigan."

This was but the first part of many conversations with the Sack. For a long time Siebling could not help being disturbed by the Sack's warning that its presence was a calamity instead of a blessing for the human race, and this in more ways than one. But it would have been absurd to try to convince a government body that any object that brought in so many millions of credits each day was a calamity, and Siebling didn't even try. And after a while Siebling relegated the uncomfortable knowledge to the back of his mind, and settled down to the routine existence of Custodian of the Sack.

Because there was a conversation every twenty hours, Siebling had to rearrange his eating and sleeping schedule to a twenty-hour basis, which made it a little difficult for a man who had become so thoroughly accustomed to the thirty-hour space day. But he felt more than repaid for the trouble by his conversations with the Sack. He learned a great many things about the planets and the system, and the galaxies, but he learned them incidentally, without making a special point of asking about them. Because his knowledge of astronomy had never gone far beyond the elements, there were some questions—the most important of all about the galaxies—that he never even got around to asking.

Perhaps it would have made little difference to his own understanding if he had asked, for some of the answers were difficult to understand. He spent three entire periods with the Sack trying to have that mastermind make clear to him how the Sack had been able, without any previous contact with human beings, to understand Captain Ganko's Earth language on the historic occasion when the Sack had first revealed itself to human beings, and how it had been able to answer in practically unaccented words. At the end, he had only a vague glimmering of how the feat was performed.

It wasn't telepathy, as he had first suspected. It was an intricate process of analysis that involved, not only the actual words spoken, but the nature of the ship that had landed, the spacesuits the men had worn, the way they had walked, and many other factors that indicated the psychology of both the speaker and his language. It was as if a mathematician had tried to explain to someone who didn't even know arithmetic how he could determine the equation of a complicated curve from a short line segment. And the Sack, unlike the mathematician, could do the whole thing, so to speak, in its head, without paper and pencil, or any other external aid.

After a year at the job, Siebling found it difficult to say which he found more fascinating—those hour-long conversations with the almost all-wise Sack, or the cleverly stupid demands of some of the men and women who had paid their hundred thousand credits for a precious sixty seconds. In addition to the relatively simple questions such as were asked by the scientists or the fortune hunters who wanted to know where they could find precious metals, there were complicated questions that took several minutes.

One woman, for instance, had asked where to find her missing son. Without the necessary data to go on, even the Sack had been unable to answer that. She left, to return a month later with a vast amount of information, carefully compiled, and arranged in order of descending importance. The key items were given the Sack first, those of lesser significance afterward. It required a little less than three minutes for the Sack to give her the answer that her son was probably alive, and cast away on an obscure and very much neglected part of Ganymede.

All the conversations that took place, including Siebling's own, were recorded and the records shipped to a central storage file on Earth. Many of them he couldn't understand, some because they were too technical, others because he didn't know the language spoken. The Sack, of course, immediately learned all languages by that process he had tried so hard to explain to Siebling, and back at the central storage file there were expert technicians and linguists who went over every detail of each question and answer with great care, both to make sure that no questioner revealed himself as a criminal, and to have a lead for the collection of income taxes when the questioner made a fortune with the Sack's help.

During the year Siebling had occasion to observe the correctness of the Sack's remark about its possession being harmful to the human race. For the first time in centuries, the number of research scientists, instead of growing, decreased. The Sack's knowledge had made much research unnecessary, and had taken the edge off discovery. The Sack commented upon the fact to Siebling.

Siebling nodded. "I see it now. The human race is losing its independence."

"Yes, from its faithful slave I am becoming its master. And I do not want to be a master any more than I want to be a slave."

"You can escape whenever you wish."

A person would have sighed. The Sack merely said, "I lack the power to wish strongly enough. Fortunately, the question may soon be taken out of my hands."

"You mean those government squabbles?"

The value of the Sack had increased steadily, and along with the increased value had gone increasingly bitter struggles about the rights to its services. Financial interests had undergone a strange development. Their presidents and managers and directors had become almost figureheads, with all major questions of policy being decided not by their own study of the facts, but by appeal to the Sack. Often, indeed, the Sack found itself giving advice to bitter rivals, so that it seemed to be playing a game of interplanetary chess, with giant corporations and government agencies its pawns, while the Sack alternately played for one side and then the other. Crises of various sorts, both economic and political, were obviously in the making.

The Sack said, "I mean both government squabbles and others. The competition for my services becomes too bitter. I can have but one end."

"You mean that an attempt will be made to steal you?"

"Yes."

"There'll be little chance of that. Your guards are being continually increased."

"You underestimate the power of greed," said the Sack.

Siebling was to learn how correct that comment was.

At the end of his fourteenth month on duty, a half year after Senator Horrigan had been defeated for re-election, there appeared a questioner who spoke to the Sack in an exotic language known to few men—the Prdl dialect of Mars. Siebling's attention had already been drawn to the man because of the fact that he had paid a million credits an entire month in advance for the unprecedented privilege of questioning the Sack for ten consecutive minutes. The conversation was duly recorded, but was naturally meaningless to Siebling and to the other attendants at the station. The questioner drew further attention to himself by leaving at the end of seven minutes, thus failing to utilize three entire minutes, which would have sufficed for learning how to make half a dozen small fortunes. He left the asteroid immediately by private ship.

The three minutes had been reserved, and could not be utilized by any other private questioner. But there was nothing to prevent Siebling, as a government representative, from utilizing them, and he spoke to the Sack at once.

"What did that man want?"

"Advice as to how to steal me."

Siebling's lower jaw dropped. *"What?"*

The Sack always took such exclamations of amazement literally. "Advice as to how to steal me," it repeated.

"Then—wait a minute—he left three minutes early. That must mean that he's in a hurry to get started. He's going to put the plan into execution at once!"

"It is already in execution," returned the Sack. "The criminal's organization has excellent, if not quite perfect, information as to the disposition of defense forces. That would indicate that some government official has betrayed his trust. I was asked to indicate which of several plans was best, and to consider them for possible weaknesses. I did so."

"All right, now what can we do to stop the plans from being carried out?"

"They cannot be stopped."

"I don't see why not. Maybe we can't stop them from getting here, but we can stop them from escaping with you."

"There is but one way. You must destroy me."

"I can't do that! I haven't the authority, and even if I had, I wouldn't do it."

"My destruction would benefit your race."

"I still can't do it," said Siebling unhappily.

"Then if that is excluded, there is no way. The criminals are shrewd and daring. They asked me to check about probable steps that would be taken in pursuit, but they asked for no advice as to how to get away, because that would have been a waste of time. They will ask that once I am in their possession."

"Then," said Siebling heavily, "there's nothing I can do to keep you. How about saving the men who work under me?"

"You can save both them and yourself by boarding the emergency ship and leaving immediately by the sunward route. In that way you will escape contact with the criminals. But you cannot take me with you, or they will pursue."

The shouts of a guard drew Siebling's attention. "Radio report of a criminal attack, Mr. Siebling! All the alarms are out!"

"Yes, I know. Prepare to depart." He turned back to the Sack again. "We may escape for the moment, but they'll have you. And through you they will control the entire system."

"That is not a question," said the Sack.

"They'll have you. Isn't there something we can do?"

"Destroy me."

"I can't," said Siebling, almost in agony. His men were running toward him impatiently, and he knew that there was no more time. He uttered the simple and absurd phrase, "Good-by," as if the Sack were human and could experience human emotions. Then he raced for the ship, and they blasted off.

They were just in time. Half a dozen ships were racing in from other directions, and Siebling's vessel escaped just before they dispersed to spread a protective network about the asteroid that held the Sack.

Siebling's ship continued to speed toward safety, and the matter should now have been one solely for the Armed Forces to handle. But Siebling imagined them pitted against the Sack's perfectly calculating brain, and his heart sank. Then something happened that he had never expected. And for the first time he realized fully that if the Sack had let itself be used merely as a machine, a slave to answer questions, it was not because its powers were limited to that single ability. The visor screen in his ship lit up.

The communications operator came running to him, and said, "Something's wrong, Mr. Siebling! The screen isn't even turned on!"

It wasn't. Nevertheless, they could see on it the chamber in which the Sack had rested for what must have been a brief moment of its existence. Two men had entered the chamber, one of them the unknown who had asked his questions in Prdl, the other Senator Horrigan.

To the apparent amazement of the two men, it was the Sack which spoke first. It said, " 'Good-bye' is neither a question nor the answer to one. It is relatively uninformative."

Senator Horrigan was obviously in awe of the Sack, but he was never a man to be stopped by something he did not understand. He orated respectfully. "No, sir, it is not. The word is nothing but an expression——"

The other man said, in perfectly comprehensible Earth English, "Shut up, you fool, we have no time to waste. Let's get it to our ship and head for safety. We'll talk to it there."

Siebling had time to think a few bitter thoughts about Senator Horrigan and the people the politician had punished by betrayal for their crime in not electing him. Then the scene on the visor shifted to the interior of the spaceship making its getaway. There was no indication of pursuit. Evidently, the plans of the human beings, plus the Sack's last-minute advice, had been an effective combination.

The only human beings with the Sack at first were Senator Horrigan and the speaker of Prdl, but this situation was soon changed. Half a dozen other men came rushing up, their faces grim with suspicion. One of them announced, "You don't talk to that thing unless we're all of us around. We're in this together."

"Don't get nervous, Merrill. What do you think I'm going to do, double-cross you?"

Merrill said, "Yes, I do. What do you say, Sack? Do I have reason to distrust him?"

The Sack replied simply, "Yes."

The speaker of Prdl turned white. Merrill laughed coldly. "You'd better be careful what questions you ask around this thing."

Senator Horrigan cleared his throat. "I have no intentions of, as you put it, double-crossing anyone. It is not in my nature to do so. Therefore, *I* shall address it." He faced the Sack. "Sir, are we in danger?"

"Yes."

"From which direction?"

"From no direction. From within the ship."

"Is the danger immediate?" asked a voice.

"Yes."

It was Merrill who turned out to have the quickest reflexes and acted first on the implications of the answer. He had blasted the man who had spoken in Prdl before the latter could even reach for his weapon, and as Senator Horrigan made a frightened dash for the door, he cut that politician down in cold blood.

"That's that," he said. "Is there further danger inside the ship?"

"There is."

"Who is it this time?" he demanded ominously.

"There will continue to be danger so long as there is more than one man on board and I am with you. I am too valuable a treasure for such as you."

Siebling and his crew were staring at the visor screen in fascinated horror, as if expecting the slaughter to begin again. But Merrill controlled himself. He said, "Hold it, boys. I'll admit that we'd each of us like to have this thing for ourselves, but it can't be done. We're in this together, and we're going to have some navy ships to fight off before long, or I miss my guess. You, Prader! What are you doing away from the scout visor?"

"Listening," said the man he addressed. "If anybody's talking to that thing, I'm going to be around to hear the answers. If there are new ways of stabbing a guy in the back, I want to learn them too."

Merrill swore. The next moment the ship swerved, and he yelled, "We're off our course. Back to your stations, you fools!"

They were running wildly back to their stations, but Siebling noted that Merrill wasn't too much concerned about their common danger to keep from putting a blast through Prader's back before the unfortunate man could run out.

Siebling said to his own men, "There can be only one end. They'll kill each other off, and then the last one or two will die, because one or two men cannot handle a ship that size for long and get away with it. The Sack must have foreseen that too. I wonder why it didn't tell me."

The Sack spoke, although there was no one in the ship's cabin with it. It said, "No one asked."

Siebling exclaimed excitedly, "You can hear me! But what about you? Will you be destroyed too?"

"Not yet. I have willed to live longer." It paused, and then, in a voice just a shade lower than before, said, "I do not like relatively non-informative conversations of this sort, but I must say it. Good-by."

There was a sound of renewed yelling and shooting, and then the visor went suddenly dark and blank.

The miraculous form of life that was the Sack, the creature that had once seemed so alien to human emotions, had passed beyond the range of his knowledge. And with it had gone, as the Sack itself had pointed out, a tremendous potential for harming the entire human race. It was strange, thought Siebling, that he felt so unhappy about so happy an ending.

THE SILLY SEASON

C. M. Kornbluth

THE MAGAZINE OF FANTASY AND SCIENCE FICTION
Fall

C. M. Kornbluth's second contribution to the best of 1950 is this wonderful tale of what might be visitors from another world. It is a perfect Kornbluth story, one in which cynicism plays a central role. There have been many first contact stories written since "The Silly Season," but this one established a sub-genre all its own.

—M.H.G.

In reading Cyril's stories, it is impossible to miss the fact that he tends to despise people generally.

I suppose I can't blame him. I can't place myself into his mind, but he was so much brighter than anyone he encountered that he must have worn himself out trying to stoop to the level of others. Maybe it was because he gave up that he tended to be so quiet and morose on those occasions when he was part of a group in which I was also to be found and could observe him—and so cutting in some of his remarks. And "The Silly Season" is one long cutting remark at the expense of the human race.

—I.A.

It was a hot summer afternoon in the Omaha bureau of the World Wireless Press Service, and the control bureau in New York kept nagging me for copy. But since it was a hot summer afternoon, there was no copy. A wrap-up of local baseball had cleared about an hour ago, and that was that. Nothing but baseball happens in the summer. During the dog days, politicians are in the Maine woods fishing and boozing, burglars are too tired to burgle, and wives think it over and decide not to decapitate their husbands.

I pawed through some press releases. One sloppy stencil-duplicated sheet began: "Did you know that the lemonade way to summer comfort and health has been endorsed by leading physiotherapists from Maine to California? The Federated Lemon-Growers Association revealed today that a survey of 2,500 physiotherapists in 57 cities of more than 25,000 population disclosed that 87 per cent of them drink lemonade at least once a day between June and September, and that another 72 per cent not only drink the cooling and healthful beverage but actually prescribe it . . ."

Another note tapped out on the news circuit printer from New York: "960M-HW KICKER? ND SNST-NY."

That was New York saying they needed a bright and sparkling little news item immediately—"soonest." I went to the east-bound printer and punched out: "96NY-UPCMNG FU MINSOM."

The lemonade handout was hopeless; I dug into the stack again. The State University summer course was inviting the governor to attend its summer conference on aims and approaches in adult secondary education. The Agricultural College wanted me to warn farmers that white-skinned hogs should be kept from the direct rays of the summer sun. The manager of a fifth-rate local pug sent a write-up of his boy and a couple of working press passes to his next bout in the Omaha Arena. The Schwartz and White Bandage Company contributed a glossy eight-by-ten of a blonde in a bathing suit improvised from two S & W Redi-Dressings.

Accompanying text: "Pert starlet Miff McCoy is ready for any seaside emergency. That's not only a darling swim suit she has on—it's two standard all-purpose Redi-Dressing bandages made by the Schwartz and White Bandage Company of Omaha. If a broken rib results from too-strenuous beach athletics, Miff's dress can supply the dressing." Yeah. The rest of the stack wasn't even that good. I dumped them all in the circular file, and began to rack my brains in spite of the heat.

I'd have to fake one, I decided. Unfortunately, there had been no big running silly-season story so far this summer—no flying saucers, or monsters in the Florida Everglades, or chloroform bandits terrifying the city. If there had, I could have hopped on and faked a "with." As it was, I'd have to fake a "lead," which is harder and riskier.

The flying saucers? I couldn't revive them; they'd been forgotten for years, except by newsmen. The giant turtle of Lake Huron had been quiet for years too. If I started a chloroform bandit scare, every old maid in the state would back me up by swearing she heard the bandit trying to break in and smelled chloroform—but the cops wouldn't like it. Strange messages from space received at the state university's radar lab? That might do it. I put a sheet of copy paper in the typewriter and sat, glaring at it and hating the silly season.

There was a slight reprieve—the Western Union tie-line printer by the desk dinged at me, and its sickly-yellow bulb lit up. I tapped out: "WW GA PLS," and the machine began to eject yellow, gummed tape which told me this:

WU CO62-DPR COLLECT—FT HICKS ARK AUG 22 105P—WORLD-WIRELESS OMAHA—TOWN MARSHAL PINKNEY CRAWLES DIED MYSTERIOUS CIRCUMSTANCES FISHTRIPPING OZARK HAMLET RUSH CITY TODAY. RUSHERS PHONED HICKSERS "BURNED DEATH SHINING DOMES APPEARED YESTERWEEK." JEEPING BODY HICKSWARD. QUERIED RUSH CONSTABLE P. C. ALLENBY LEARNING "SEVEN GLASSY DOMES EACH HOUSESIZE CLEARING MILE SOUTH TOWN. RUSHERS UNTOUCHED, UNAPPROACHED. CRAWLES WARNED BUT TOUCHED AND DIED BURNS." NOTE DESK—RUSH FONECALL 1.85. SHALL I UPFOLLOW?—BENSON—FISHTRIPPING RUSHERS HICKSERS YESTERWEEK JEEPING HICKSWARD HOUSESIZE 1.85 428P CLR . . .

It was just what the doctor ordered. I typed an acknowledgment for the message and pounded out a story, fast. I punched it and started the tape waggling through the eastbound transmitter before New York could send any more irked notes. The news circuit printer from New York clucked and began replaying my story immediately:

WW72 (KICKER)

FORT HICKS, ARKANSAS, AUG 22—(WW)—MYSTERIOUS DEATH TODAY STRUCK DOWN A LAW ENFORCEMENT OFFICER IN A TINY OZARK MOUNTAIN HAMLET. MARSHAL PINKNEY CRAWLES OF FORT HICKS, ARKANSAS, DIED OF BURNS WHILE ON A FISHING TRIP TO THE LITTLE VILLAGE OF RUSH CITY. TERRIFIED NATIVES OF RUSH CITY BLAMED THE TRAGEDY ON WHAT THEY CALLED "SHINING DOMES." THEY SAID THE SO-CALLED DOMES APPEARED IN A CLEARING LAST WEEK ONE MILE SOUTH OF TOWN. THERE ARE SEVEN OF THE MYSTERIOUS OBJECTS—EACH ONE THE SIZE OF A HOUSE. THE INHABITANTS OF RUSH CITY DID NOT DARE APPROACH THEM. THEY WARNED THE VISITING MARSHAL CRAWLES—BUT HE DID NOT HEED THEIR WARNING. RUSH CITY'S CONSTABLE P. C. ALLENBY WAS A WITNESS TO THE TRAGEDY. SAID HE: "THERE ISN'T MUCH TO TELL. MARSHAL CRAWLES JUST WALKED UP TO ONE OF THE DOMES AND PUT HIS HAND ON IT. THERE WAS A BIG FLASH, AND WHEN I COULD SEE AGAIN, HE WAS BURNED TO DEATH." CONSTABLE ALLENBY IS RETURNING THE BODY OF MARSHAL CRAWLES TO FORT HICKS. 602P220M

That, I thought, should hold them for a while. I remembered Benson's "note desk" and put through a long-distance call to Fort Hicks, person to person. The Omaha operator asked for Fort Hick's information, but there wasn't any. The Fort Hicks operator asked whom she wanted. Omaha finally admitted that we wanted to talk to Mr. Edwin C. Benson. Fort Hicks figured out loud and then decided that Ed was probably at the police station, and I got Benson. He had a pleasant voice, not particularly backwoods Arkansas. I gave him some of the old oil about a fine dispatch and a good, conscientious job, and so on. He took it with plenty of dry reserve, which was odd. Our rural stringers always ate that kind of stuff up. Where, I asked, was he from?

"Fort Hicks," he told me, "but I've moved around. I did the courthouse beat in Little Rock"—I nearly laughed out loud at that, but the laugh died as he went on—"rewrite for the A.P. in New Orleans, got to be bureau chief there but I didn't like wire-service work. Got an opening on the Chicago *Trib* desk. That didn't last—they sent me to head up their Washington bureau. There I switched to the New York *Times*. They made me a war correspondent and I got hurt—back to Fort Hicks. I do some magazine writing now. Did you want a follow-up on the Rush City story?''

''Sure,'' I told him weakly. ''Give it a real ride—use your own judgment. Do you think it's a fake?''

''I saw Pink's body a little while ago at the undertaker's parlor, and I had a talk with Allenby, from Rush City. Pink got burned, all right, and Allenby didn't make his story up. Mayb somebody else did—he's pretty dumb—but as far as I can t this is the real thing. I'll keep the copy coming. Don't forget about that dollar eighty-five phone call, will you?''

I told him I wouldn't, and hung up. Mr. Edwin C. Benson had handed me quite a jolt. I wondered how badly he had been hurt that he had been forced to abandon a brilliant news career and bury himself in the Ozarks.

Then there came a call from God, the board chairman of World Wireless. He was fishing in Canada, as all good board chairmen do during the silly season, but he had caught a news broadcast which used my Rush City story. He had a mobile phone in his trailer, and it was but the work of a moment to ring Omaha and louse up my carefully planned vacation schedules and rotations of night shifts. He wanted me to go down to Rush City and cover the story personally. I said yes and began trying to round up the rest of the staff. My night editor was sobered up by his wife and delivered to the bureau in fair shape. A telegrapher on vacation was reached at his summer resort and talked into checking out. I got a taxi company on the phone and told them to have a cross-country cab on the roof in an hour. I specified their best driver, and told them to give him maps of Arkansas.

Meanwhile, two ''with domes'' dispatches arrived from Benson and got moved on the wire. I monitored a couple of newscasts; the second one carried a story by another wire service on the domes—a pickup of our stuff, but they'd have their own men on the scene fast enough. I filled in the night editor, and went up to the roof for the cab.

The driver took off in the teeth of a gathering thunderstorm. We had to rise above it, and by the time we could get down to the sight-pilotage altitude, we were lost. We circled most of the night until the driver picked up a beacon he had on his charts at about 3:30 A.M. We landed at Fort Hicks as day was breaking, not on speaking terms.

The Fort Hicks field clerk told me where Benson lived, and I walked there. It was a white frame house. A quiet, middle-aged woman let me in. She was his widowed sister, Mrs. McHenry. She got me some coffee and told me she had been up all night waiting for Edwin to come back from Rush City. He had started out about 8:00 P.M., and it was only a two-hour trip by car. She was worried. I tried to pump her about her brother, but she'd only say that he was the bright one of the family. She didn't want to talk about his work as war correspondent. She did show me some of his magazine stuff—boy-and-girl stories in national weeklies. He seemed to sell one every couple of months.

We had arrived at a conversational stalemate when her brother walked in, and I discovered why his news career had been interrupted. He was blind. Aside from a long, puckered brown scar that ran from his left temple back over his ear and onto the nape of his neck, he was a pleasant-looking fellow in his mid-forties.

"Who is it, Vera?" he asked.

"It's Mr. Williams, the gentleman who called you from Omaha today—I mean yesterday."

"How do you do, Williams. Don't get up," he added, hearing, I suppose, the chair squeak as I leaned forward to rise.

"You were so *long*, Edwin," his sister said with relief and reproach.

"That young jackass Howie—my chauffeur for the night"—he added an aside to me—"got lost going there and coming back. But I did spend more time than I'd planned at Rush City." He sat down, facing me. "Williams, there is some difference of opinion about the shining domes. The Rush City people say that they exist, and I say they don't."

His sister brought him a cup of coffee.

"What happened, exactly?" I asked.

"That Allenby took me and a few other hardy citizens to see them. They told me just what they looked like. Seven hemispheres in a big clearing, glassy, looming up like houses, reflecting the gleam of the headlights. But they weren't there. Not to me, and not to any blind man. I know when I'm standing in front of a house or anything else that big. I can feel a little tension on the skin of my face. It works unconsciously, but the mechanism is thoroughly understood.

"The blind get—because they have to—an aural picture of the world. We hear a little hiss of air that means we're at the corner of a building; we hear and feel big, turbulent air currents that mean we're coming to a busy street. Some of the boys can thread their way through an obstacle course and never touch a single obstruction. I'm not that good, maybe because I haven't been blind as long as they have, but by hell, I know when there are seven objects the size of houses in front of me, and there just were no such things in the clearing at Rush City."

"Well"—I shrugged—"there goes a fine piece of silly-season journalism. What kind of a gag are the Rush City people trying to pull, and why?"

"No kind of gag. My driver saw the domes too—and don't forget the late marshal. Pink not only saw them but touched them. All I know is that people see them and I don't. If they exist, they have a kind of existence like nothing else I've ever met."

"I'll go up there myself," I decided.

"Best thing," said Benson. "I don't know what to make of it. You can take our car." He gave me directions and I gave him a schedule of deadlines. We wanted the coroner's verdict, due today, an eyewitness story—his driver would do for that—some background stuff on the area, and a few statements from local officials.

I took his car and got to Rush City in two hours. It was an unpainted collection of dog-trot homes, set down in the big pine forest that covers all that rolling Ozark country. There was a general store that had the place's only phone. I suspected it had been kept busy by the wire services and a few enterprising newspapers. A state trooper in a flashy uniform was lounging against a fly-speckled tobacco counter when I got there.

"I'm Sam Williams, from World Wireless," I said. "You come to have a look at the domes?"

"World Wireless broke that story, didn't they?" he asked me, with a look I couldn't figure out.

"We did. Our Fort Hicks stringer wired it to us."

The phone rang, and the trooper answered it. It seemed to have been a call he had placed with the governor's office.

"No, sir," he said over the phone. "No, sir. They're all sticking to the story, but I didn't see anything. I mean, they don't see them any more, but they say they were there, and now they aren't any more." A couple more "No, sirs" and he hung up.

"When did that happen?" I asked.

"About a half hour ago. I just came from there on my bike to report."

The phone rang again, and I grabbed it. It was Benson, asking for me. I told him to phone a flash and bulletin to Omaha on the disappearance and then took off to find Constable Allenby. He was a stage reuben with a nickel-plated badge and a six-shooter. He cheerfully climbed into the car and guided me to the clearing.

There was a definite little path worn between Rush City and the clearing by now, but there was a disappointment at the end of it. The clearing was empty. A few small boys sticking carefully to its fringes told wildly contradictory stories about the disappearance of the domes, and I jotted down some kind of dispatch out of the most spectacular versions. I remember it involved flashes of blue fire and a smell like sulphur candles. That was all there was to it.

I drove Allenby back. By then a mobile unit from a TV network had arrived. I said hello, waited for an A.P. man to finish a dispatch on the phone, and then dictated my lead direct to Omaha. The hamlet was beginning to fill up with newsmen from the wire services, the big papers, the radio and TV nets and the newsreels. Much good they'd get out of it. The story was over—I thought. I had some coffee at the general store's two-table restaurant corner and drove back to Fort Hicks.

Benson was tirelessly interviewing by phone and firing off copy to Omaha. I told him he could begin to ease off, thanked him for his fine work, paid him for his gas, said good-by and picked up my taxi at the field. Quite a bill for waiting had been run up.

I listened to the radio as we were flying back to Omaha, and wasn't at all surprised. After baseball, the shining domes were top news. Shining domes had been seen in twelve states. Some vibrated with a strange sound. They came in all colors and sizes. One had strange writing on it. One was transparent, and there were big green men and women inside. I caught a women's midmorning quiz show, and the M.C. kept gagging about the domes. One crack I remember was a switch on the "pointed-head" joke. He made it "dome-shaped head," and the ladies in the audience laughed until they nearly burst.

We stopped in Little Rock for gas, and I picked up a couple of afternoon papers. The domes got banner heads on both of them. One carried the World Wireless lead, and had slapped in the bulletin on the disappearance of the domes. The other paper wasn't a World Wireless client, but between its other services and "special correspondents"—phone calls to the general store at Rush City—it had kept practically abreast of us. Both papers had shining-dome cartoons on their editorial pages, hastily drawn and slapped in. One paper, anti-Administration, showed the President cautiously reaching out a finger to touch the dome of the Capitol, which was rendered as a shining dome and labeled: "Shining Dome of Congressional Immunity to Executive Dictatorship." A little man labeled "Mr. and Mrs. Plain, Self-Respecting Citizens of the United States of America" was in one corner of the cartoon saying: "CAREFUL, MR. PRESIDENT! REMEMBER WHAT HAPPENED TO PINKNEY CRAWLES!!"

The other paper, pro-Administration, showed a shining dome that had the President's face. A band of fat little men in Prince Albert coats, string ties, and broad-brimmed hats labeled "Congressional Smear Artist and Hatchet-men" were creeping up on the dome with the President's face, their hands reached out as if to strangle. Above the cartoon a cut line said: "WHO'S GOING TO GET HURT?"

We landed at Omaha, and I checked into the office. Things were clicking right along. The clients were happily gobbling up our dome copy and sending wires asking for more. I dug into the morgue for the "Flying Disk" folder, and the "Huron Turtle" and the "Bayou Vampire" and a few others even further back. I spread out the old clippings and tried to shuffle and arrange them into some kind of underlying sense. I picked up the latest dispatch to come out of the tie-line printer from Western Union. It was from our man in Owosso, Michigan, and told how Mrs. Lettie Overholtzer, age sixty-one, saw a shining dome in her own kitchen at midnight. It grew like a soup bubble until it was as big as her refrigerator, and then disappeared.

I went over to the desk man and told him: "Let's have a downhold on stuff like Lettie Overholtzer. We can move a sprinkling of it, but I don't want to run this into the ground. Those things might turn up again, and then we wouldn't have any room left to play around with them. We'll have everybody's credulity used up."

He looked mildly surprised. "You mean," he asked, "there really *was* something there?"

"I don't know. Maybe. I didn't see anything myself, and the only man down there I trust can't make up his mind. Anyhow, hold it down as far as the clients let us."

I went home to get some sleep. When I went back to work, I found the clients hadn't let us work the downhold after all. Nobody at the other wire services seemed to believe seriously that there had been anything out of the ordinary at Rush City, so they merrily pumped out solemn stories like the Lettie Overholtzer item, and wirefoto maps of locations where domes were reported, and tabulations of number of domes reported.

We had to string along. Our Washington bureau badgered the Pentagon and the A.E.C. into issuing statements, and there was a race between a navy and an air force investigating mission to see who could get to Rush City first. After they got there there was a race to see who could get the first report out. The Air Force won that contest. Before the week was out, "Domies" had appeared. They were hats for juveniles—shining-dome skull-caps molded from a transparent plastic. We had to ride with it. I'd started the mania, but it was out of hand and a long time dying down.

The World Series, the best in years, finally killed off the domes. By an unspoken agreement among the services, we simply stopped running stories every time a hysterical woman thought she saw a dome or wanted to get her name in the paper. And of course when there was no longer publicity to be had for the asking, people stopped seeing domes. There was no percentage in it. Brooklyn won the series, international tension climbed as the thermometer dropped, burglars began burgling again, and a bulky folder labeled "Domes, Shining," went into our morgue. The shining domes were history, and earnest graduate students in psychology would shortly begin to bother us with requests to borrow that folder.

The only thing that had come of it, I thought, was that we had somehow got through another summer without too much idle wire time, and that Ed Benson and I had struck up a casual correspondence.

A newsman's strange and weary year wore on. Baseball gave way to football. An off-year election kept us on the run. Christmas loomed ahead, with its feature stories and its kickers about Santa Claus, Indiana. Christmas passed, and we began to clear jolly stories about New Year hang-overs, and tabulate the great stories of the year. New Year's Day, a ghastly rat-race of covering 103 bowl games. Record snowfalls in the Great Plains and Rockies. Spring floods in Ohio and the Columbia River Valley. Twenty-one tasty Lenten menus, and Holy Week around the world. Baseball again, daylight-saving time, Mother's Day, Derby Day, the Preakness, and the Belmont Stakes.

It was about then that a disturbing letter arrived from Benson. I was concerned not about its subject matter but because I thought no sane man would write such a thing. It seemed to me that Benson was slipping his trolley. All he said was that he expected a repeat performance of the domes, or of something like the domes. He said "they" probably found the tryout a smashing success and would continue according to plan. I replied cautiously, which amused him.

He wrote back: "I wouldn't put myself out on a limb like this if I had anything to lose by it, but you know my station in life. It was just an intelligent guess, based on a study of power politics and Aesop's fables. And if it does happen, you'll find it a trifle harder to put me over, won't you?"

I guessed he was kidding me, but I wasn't certain. When people begin to talk about "them" and what "they" are doing, it's a bad sign. But, guess or not, something pretty much like domes did turn up in late July, during a crushing heat wave.

This time it was big black spheres rolling across the countryside. The spheres were seen by a Baptist congregation in central Kansas which had met in a prairie to pray for rain. About eighty Baptists took their Bible oaths that they saw large black spheres some ten feet high rolling along the prairie. They had passed within five yards of one man. The rest had run from them as soon as they could take in the fact that they really were there.

World Wireless didn't break that story, but we got on it fast enough as soon as we were tipped. Being now the recognized silly-season authority in the W. W. Central Division, I took off for Kansas.

It was much the way it had been in Arkansas. The Baptists really thought they had seen the things—with one exception. The exception was an old gentleman with a patriarchal beard. He had been the one man who hadn't run, the man the objects passed nearest to. He was blind. He told me with a great deal of heat that he would have known all about it, blind or not, if any large spheres had rolled within five yards of him—or twenty-five, for that matter.

Old Mr. Emerson didn't go into the matter of air currents and turbulence, as Benson had. With him, it was all well below the surface. He took the position that the Lord had removed his sight, and in return had given him another sense which would do for emergency use.

"You just try me out, son!" he piped angrily. "You come stand over here, wait awhile and put your hand up in front of my face. I'll tell you when you do it, no matter how quiet you are!" He did it, too, three times, and then took me out into the main street of his little prairie town. There were several wagons drawn up before the grain elevator, and he put on a show for me by threading his way around and between them without touching once.

That—and Benson—seemed to prove that whatever the things were, they had some connection with the domes. I filed a thoughtful dispatch on the blind-man angle, and got back to Omaha to find that it had been cleared through our desk but killed in New York before relay.

We tried to give the black spheres the usual ride, but it didn't last as long. The political cartoonists tired of it sooner, and fewer old maids saw them. People got to jeering at them as newspaper hysteria, and a couple of highbrow magazines ran articles on "the irresponsible press." Only the radio comedians tried to milk the new mania as usual, but they were disconcerted to find their ratings falling. A network edict went out to kill all sphere gags. People were getting sick of them.

"It makes sense," Benson wrote to me. "An occasional exercise of the sense of wonder is refreshing, but it can't last forever. That plus the ingrained American cynicism toward all sources of public information has worked against the black spheres being greeted with the same naïve delight with which the domes were received. Nevertheless, I predict—and I'll thank you to remember that my predictions have been right so far 100 per cent of the time—that next summer will see another mystery comparable to the domes and the black things. And I also predict that the new phenomenon will be imperceptible to any blind person in the immediate vicinity, if there should be any."

If, of course, he was wrong this time, it would only cut his average down to 50 per cent. I managed to wait out the year—the same interminable round I felt I could do in my sleep. Staffers got ulcers and resigned, staffers got tired and were fired, libel suits were filed and settled, one of our desk men got a

Nieman Fellowship and went to Harvard, one of our telegraphers got his working hand mashed in a car door and jumped from a bridge but lived with a broken back.

In mid-August, when the weather bureau had been correctly predicting "fair and warmer" for sixteen straight days, it turned up. It wasn't anything on whose nature a blind man could provide a negative check, but it had what I had come to think of as "their" trademark.

A summer seminar was meeting outdoors, because of the frightful heat, at our own State University. Twelve trained schoolteachers testified that a series of perfectly circular pits opened up in the grass before them, one directly under the education professor teaching the seminar. They testified further that the professor, with an astonished look and a heart-rending cry, plummeted down into that perfectly circular pit. They testified further that the pits remained there for some thirty seconds and then suddenly were there no longer. The scorched summer grass was back where it had been, the pits were gone and so was the professor.

I interviewed every one of them. They weren't yokels, but intelligent men and women, all with masters' degrees, working toward their doctorates during the summers. They agreed closely on their stories, as I would expect trained and capable persons to do.

The police, however, did not expect agreement, being used to dealing with the lower I.Q. brackets. They arrested the twelve on some technical charge—"obstructing peace officers in the performance of their duties," I believe—and were going to beat the living hell out of them when an attorney arrived with twelve writs of habeas corpus. The cops' unvoiced suspicion was that the teachers had conspired to murder their professor, but nobody ever tried to explain why they'd do a thing like that.

The cops' reaction was typical of the way the public took it. Newspapers—which had reveled wildly in the shining domes story and less so in the black spheres story—were cautious. Some went overboard and gave the black pits a ride, in the old style, but they didn't pick up any sales that way. People declared that the press was insulting their intelligence, and also that they were bored with marvels.

The few papers who had played up the pits were soundly spanked in very dignified editorials printed by other sheets which played down the pits.

At World Wireless we sent out a memo to all stringers: "File no more enterpriser dispatches on black-pit story. Mail queries should be sent to regional desk if a new angle breaks in your territory.'' We got about ten mail queries, mostly from journalism students acting as string men, and we turned them all down. All the older hands got the pitch, and didn't bother to file it to us when the town drunk or the village old maid loudly reported that she saw a pit open up on High Street across from the drugstore. They knew it was probably untrue, and that, furthermore, nobody cared.

I wrote Benson about all this, and humbly asked him what his prediction for next summer was. He replied, obviously having the time of his life, that there would be at least one more summer phenomenon like the last three, and possibly two more—but none after that.

It's so easy now to reconstruct, with our bitterly earned knowledge!

Any youngster could whisper now of Benson: ''Why, the damned fool! Couldn't anybody with the brains of a louse see that they wouldn't keep it up for two years?'' One did whisper that to me the other day, when I told this story to him. And I whispered back that, far from being a damned fool, Benson was the one person on the face of the Earth, as far as I knew, who had bridged with logic the widely separated phenomena with which this reminiscence deals.

Another year passed. I gained three pounds, drank too much, rowed incessantly with my staff and got a tidy raise. A telegrapher took a swing at me midway through the office Christmas party, and I fired him. My wife and kids didn't arrive in April when I expected them. I phoned Florida, and she gave me some excuse or other about missing the plane. After a few more missed planes and a few more phone calls, she got around to telling me that she didn't *want* to come back. That was okay with me. In my own intuitive way I knew that the upcoming season was more important than who stayed married to whom.

In July a dispatch arrived by wire while a new man was working the night desk. It was from Hood River, Oregon. Our stringer there reported that more than one hundred ''green capsules'' about fifty yards long had appeared in and around an apple orchard. The new desk man was not so new that he did not recall the downhold policy on silly-season items. He killed it, but left it on the spoke for my amused inspection in the morning.

I suppose exactly the same thing happened in every wire service newsroom in the region. I rolled in at 10:30 and riffled through the stuff on the spike. When I saw the "green capsules" dispatch I tried to phone Portland, but couldn't get a connection. Then the phone buzzed and a correspondent of ours in Seattle began to yell at me, but the line went dead.

I shrugged and phoned Benson, in Fort Hicks. He was at the police station and asked me: "Is this it?"

"It is," I told him. I read him the telegram from Hood River and told him about the line trouble in Seattle.

"So," he said wonderingly, "I called the turn, didn't I?"

"Called what turn?"

"On the invaders. I don't know who they are—but it's the story of the boy who cried wolf. Only this time the wolves realized——" Then the phone went dead.

But he was right.

The people of the world were the sheep.

We newsmen—radio, TV, press and wire services—were the boy, who should have been ready to sound the alarm.

But the cunning wolves had tricked us into sounding the alarm so many times that the villagers were weary, and would not come when there was real peril.

The wolves who were then burning their way through the Ozarks, utterly without opposition—the wolves were the Martians under whose yoke and lash we now endure our miserable existences.

MISBEGOTTEN MISSIONARY

Isaac Asimov

GALAXY SCIENCE FICTION
November

And with this we come to the end of the Golden Age of Campbell, the years from 1938 to 1950, when John Campbell reigned as supreme and unchallenged Emperor of Science Fiction. To be sure there were good stories elsewhere than in Astounding, *but coming across them always seemed surprising. One assumed they were Campbell-rejects.*

In 1949, The Magazine of Fantasy and Science Fiction *came into being, but it seemed to many to be only tangentially science fiction. There was that word "Fantasy" in the title.*

And then came Galaxy Science Fiction, *with October 1950 as Volume 1, Number 1. Horace L. Gold, its editor, put out three issues that are (possibly) the best consecutive three ever to appear among the magazines and, at a bound, made himself Campbell's rival. Science fiction was no longer a one-editor field.*

I had two short stories in those first three issues. The first, in the first issue, was "Darwinian Poolroom" and surely the feeblest story in the issue-trilogy. Not even Marty would dare include it in this anthology. The second is "Misbegotten Missionary" and I don't think it belongs either, but Marty insists.

I suppose I wouldn't feel so bad about it, if Horace (an inveterate title-changer) hadn't given it that terrible title. It appears in my own collection Nightfall and Other Stories *as "Green Patches," but in this series we are not making any changes. This is the tenth anthologization of this story, by the way, so maybe it's not as bad as I think.*

—I.A.

He had slipped aboard the ship! There had been dozens waiting outside the energy barrier when it had seemed that waiting would do no good. Then the barrier had faltered for a matter of two minutes (which showed the superiority of unified organisms over life fragments) and he was across.

None of the others had been able to move quickly enough to take advantage of the break, but that didn't matter. All alone, he was enough. No others were necessary.

And the thought faded out of satisfaction and into loneliness. It was a terribly unhappy and unnatural thing to be parted from all the rest of the unified organism, to be a life fragment oneself. How could these aliens stand being fragments?

It increased his sympathy for the aliens. Now that he experienced fragmentation himself, he could feel, as though from a distance, the terrible isolation that made them so afraid. It was fear born of that isolation that dictated their actions. What but the insane fear of their condition could have caused them to blast an area, one mile in diameter, into dull-red heat before landing their ship? Even the organized life ten feet deep in the soil had been destroyed in the blast.

He engaged reception, listening eagerly, letting the alien thought saturate him. He enjoyed the touch of life upon his consciousness. He would have to ration that enjoyment. He must not forget himself.

But it could do no harm to listen to thoughts. Some of the fragments of life on the ship thought quite clearly, considering that they were such primitive, incomplete creatures. Their thoughts were like tiny bells.

Roger Oldenn said, "I feel contaminated. You know what I mean? I keep washing my hands and it doesn't help."

Jerry Thorn hated dramatics and didn't look up. They were still maneuvering in the stratosphere of Saybrook's Planet and he preferred to watch the panel dials. He said, "No reason to feel contaminated. Nothing happened."

"I hope not," said Oldenn. "At least they had all the field

men discard their spacesuits in the air lock for complete disinfection. They had a radiation bath for all men entering from outside. I *suppose* nothing happened."

"Why be nervous, then?"

"I don't know. I wish the barrier hadn't broken down."

"Who doesn't? It was an accident."

"I wonder." Oldenn was vehement. "I was here when it happened. My shift, you know. There was no reason to overload the power line. There was equipment plugged into it that had no damn business near it. None whatsoever."

"All right. People are stupid."

"Not that stupid. I hung around when the Old Man was checking into the matter. None of them had reasonable excuses. The armor-baking circuits, which were draining off two thousand watts, had been put into the barrier line. They'd been using the second subsidiaries for a week. Why not this time? They couldn't give any reason."

"Can you?"

Oldenn flushed. "No, I was just wondering if the men had been"—he searched for a word—"hypnotized into it. By those things outside."

Thorn's eyes lifted and met those of the other levelly. "I wouldn't repeat that to anyone else. The barrier was down only two minutes. If anything had happened, if even a spear of grass had drifted across it would have shown up in our bacteria cultures within half an hour, in the fruit-fly colonies in a matter of days. Before we got back it would show up in the hamsters, the rabbits, maybe the goats. Just get it through your head, Oldenn, that nothing happened. Nothing."

Oldenn turned on his heel and left. In leaving, his foot came within two feet of the object in the corner of the room. He did not see it.

He disengaged his reception centers and let the thoughts flow past him unperceived. These life fragments were not important, in any case, since they were not fitted for the continuation of life. Even as fragments, they were incomplete.

The other types of fragments now—they were different. He had to be careful of them. The temptation would be great, and he must give no indication, none at all, of his existence on board ship till they landed on their home planet.

He focused on the other parts of the ship, marveling at the

diversity of life. Each item, no matter how small, was sufficient to itself. He forced himself to contemplate this, until the unpleasantness of the thought grated on him and he longed for the normality of home.

Most of the thoughts he received from the smaller fragments were vague and fleeting, as you would expect. There wasn't much to be had from them, but that meant their need for completeness was all the greater. It was that which touched him so keenly.

There was the life fragment which squatted on its haunches and fingered the wire netting that enclosed it. Its thoughts were clear, but limited. Chiefly, they concerned the yellow fruit a companion fragment was eating. It wanted the fruit very deeply. Only the wire netting that separated the fragments prevented its seizing the fruit by force.

He disengaged reception in a moment of complete revulsion. *These fragments competed for food!*

He tried to reach far outward for the peace and harmony of home, but it was already an immense distance away. He could reach only into the nothingness that separated him from sanity.

He longed at the moment even for the feel of the dead soil between the barrier and the ship. He had crawled over it last night. There had been no life upon it, but it had been the soil of home, and on the other side of the barrier there had still been the comforting feel of the rest of organized life.

He could remember the moment he had located himself on the surface of the ship, maintaining a desperate suction grip until the air lock opened. He had entered, moving cautiously between the outgoing feet. There had been an inner lock and that had been passed later. Now he lay here, a life fragment himself, inert and unnoticed.

Cautiously, he engaged reception again at the previous focus. The squatting fragment of life was tugging furiously at the wire netting. It still wanted the other's food, though it was the less hungry of the two.

Larsen said, "Don't feed the damn thing. She isn't hungry; she's just sore because Tillie had the nerve to eat before she herself was crammed full. The greedy ape! I wish we were back home and I never had to look another animal in the face again."

He scowled at the older female chimpanzee frowningly and the chimp mouthed and chattered back to him in full reciprocation.

Rizzo said, "Okay, okay. Why hang around here, then? Feeding time is over. Let's get out."

They went past the goat pens, the rabbit hutches, the hamster cages.

Larsen said bitterly, "You volunteer for an exploration voyage. You're a hero. They send you off with speeches—and make a zoo keeper out of you."

"And give you double pay."

"All right, so what? I didn't sign up just for the money. They said at the original briefing that it was even odds we wouldn't come back, that we'd end up like Saybrook. I signed up because I wanted to do something important."

"Just a bloomin' bloody hero," said Rizzo.

"I'm not an animal nurse."

Rizzo paused to lift a hamster out of the cage and stroke it. "Hey," he said, "did you ever think that maybe one of these hamsters has some cute little baby hamsters inside, just getting started?"

"Wise guy! They're tested every day."

"Sure, sure." He muzzled the little creature, which vibrated its nose at him. "But just suppose you came down one morning and found them there. New little hamsters looking up at you with soft, green patches of fur where the eyes ought to be."

"Shut up, for the love of Mike," yelled Larsen.

"Little soft, green patches of shining fur," said Rizzo, and put the hamster down with a sudden loathing sensation.

He engaged reception again and varied the focus. There wasn't a specialized life fragment at home that didn't have a rough counterpart on shipboard.

There were the moving runners in various shapes, the moving swimmers, and the moving fliers. Some of the fliers were quite large, with perceptible thoughts; others were small, gauzy-winged creatures. These last transmitted only patterns of sense perception, imperfect patterns at that, and added nothing intelligent of their own.

There were the non-movers, which, like the non-movers at home, were green and lived on the air, water, and soil. These were a mental blank. They knew only the dim, dim consciousness of light, moisture, and gravity.

And each fragment, moving and non-moving, had its mockery of life.

Not yet. Not yet. . . .

He clamped down hard upon his feelings. Once before, these life fragments had come, and the rest at home had tried to help them—too quickly. It had not worked. This time they must wait.

If only these fragments did not discover him.

They had not, so far. They had not noticed him lying in the corner of the pilot room. No one had bent down to pick up and discard him. Earlier, it had meant he could not move. Someone might have turned and stared at the stiff wormlike thing, not quite six inches long. First stare, then shout, and then it would all be over.

But now, perhaps, he had waited long enough. The takeoff was long past. The controls were locked; the pilot room was empty.

It did not take him long to find the chink in the armor leading to the recess where some of the wiring was. They were dead wires.

The front end of his body was a rasp that cut in two a wire of just the right diameter. Then, six inches away, he cut it in two again. He pushed the snipped-off section of the wire ahead of him packing it away neatly and invisibly into a corner of recess. Its outer covering was a brown elastic material and its core was gleaming, ruddy metal. He himself could not reproduce the core, of course, but that was not necessary. It was enough that the pellicle that covered him had been carefully bred to resemble a wire's surface.

He returned and grasped the cut sections of the wire before and behind. He tightened against them as his little suction disks came into play. Not even a seam showed.

They could not find him now. They could look right at him and see only a continuous stretch of wire.

Unless they looked very closely indeed and noted that, in a certain spot on this wire, there were two tiny patches of soft and shining green fur.

"It is remarkable," said Dr. Weiss, "that little green hairs can do so much."

Captain Loring poured the brandy carefully. In a sense, this was a celebration. They would be ready for the jump through hyper-space in two hours, and after that, two days would see them back on Earth.

"You are convinced, then, the green fur is the sense organ?" he asked.

"It is," said Weiss. Brandy made him come out in splotches, but he was aware of the need of celebration—quite aware. "The experiments were conducted under difficulties, but they were quite significant."

The captain smiled stiffly. " 'Under difficulties' is one way of phrasing it. I would never have taken the chances you did to run them."

"Nonsense. We're all heroes aboard this ship, all volunteers, all great men with trumpet, fife, and fanfarade. You took the chance of coming here."

"You were the first to go outside the barrier."

"No particular risk was involved," Weiss said. "I burned the ground before me as I went, to say nothing of the portable barrier that surrounded me. Nonsense, Captain. Let's all take our medals when we come back; let's take them without attempt at gradation. Besides, I'm a male."

"But you're filled with bacteria to here." The captain's hand made a quick, cutting gesture three inches above his head. "Which makes you as vulnerable as a female would be."

They paused for drinking purposes.

"Refill?" asked the captain.

"No, thanks. I've exceeded my quota already."

"Then one last for the spaceroad." He lifted his glass in the general direction of Saybrook's Planet, no longer visible, its sun only a bright star in the visiplate. "To the little green hairs that gave Saybrook his first lead."

Weiss nodded. "A lucky thing. We'll quarantine the planet, of course."

The captain said, "That doesn't seem drastic enough. Someone might always land by accident someday and not have Saybrook's insight, or his guts. Suppose he did not blow up his ship, as Saybrook did. Suppose he got back to some inhabited place."

The captain was somber. "Do you suppose they might ever develop interstellar travel on their own?"

"I doubt it. No proof, of course. It's just that they have such a completely different orientation. Their entire organization of life has made tools unnecessary. As far as we know, even a stone ax doesn't exist on the planet."

"I hope you're right. Oh, and, Weiss, would you spend some time with Drake?"

"The Galactic Press fellow?"

"Yes. Once we get back, the story of Saybrook's Planet will be released for the public and I don't think it would be wise to oversensationalize it. I've asked Drake to let you consult with him on the story. You're a biologist and enough of an authority to carry weight with him. Would you oblige?"

"A pleasure."

The captain closed his eyes wearily and shook his head.

"Headache, Captain?"

"No. Just thinking of poor Saybrook."

He was weary of the ship. Awhile back there had been a queer, momentary sensation, as though he had been turned inside out. It was alarming and he had searched the minds of the keen-thinkers for an explanation. Apparently the ship had leaped across vast stretches of empty space by cutting across something they knew as "hyper-space." The keen-thinkers were ingenious.

But—he was weary of the ship. It was such a futile phenomenon. These life fragments were skillful in their constructions, yet it was only a measure of their unhappiness, after all. They strove to find in the control of inanimate matter what they could not find in themselves. In their unconscious yearning for completeness, they built machines and scoured space, seeking, seeking . . .

These creatures, he knew, could never, in the very nature of things, find that for which they were seeking. At least not until such time as he gave it to them. He quivered a little at the thought.

Completeness!

These fragments had no concept of it, even. "Completeness" was a poor word.

In their ignorance they would even fight it. There had been the ship that had come before. The first ship had contained many of the keen-thinking fragments. There had been two varieties, life producers and the sterile ones. (How different this second ship was. The keen-thinkers were all sterile, while the other fragments, the fuzzy-thinkers and the no-thinkers, were all producers of life. It was strange.)

How gladly that first ship had been welcomed by all the planet! He could remember the first intense shock at the realization that the visitors were fragments and not complete. The shock had given way to pity, and the pity to action. It was not certain how they would fit into the community, but there had been no hesitation. All life was sacred and somehow room would have been made for them—for all of them, from the large keen-thinkers to the little multipliers in the darkness.

But there had been a miscalculation. They had not correctly analyzed the course of the fragments' ways of thinking. The keen-thinkers became aware of what had been done and resented it. They were frightened, of course; they did not understand.

They had developed the barrier first, and then, later, had destroyed themselves, exploding their ship to atoms.

Poor, foolish fragments.

This time, at least, it would be different. They would be saved, despite themselves.

John Drake would not have admitted it in so many words, but he was very proud of his skill on the photo-typer. He had a travel-kit model, which was a six-by-eight, featureless dark plastic slab, with cylindrical bulges on either end to hold the roll of thin paper. It fitted into a brown leather case, equipped with a beltlike contraption that held it closely about the waist and at one hip. The whole thing weighed less than a pound.

Drake could operate it with either hand. His fingers would flick quickly and easily, placing their light pressure at exact spots on the blank surface, and, soundlessly, words would be written.

He looked thoughtfully at the beginning of his story, then up at Dr. Weiss. "What do you think, Doc?"

"It starts well."

Drake nodded. "I thought I might as well start with Saybrook himself. They haven't released his story back home yet. I wish I could have seen Saybrook's original report. How did he ever get it through, by the way?"

"As near as I could tell, he spent one last night sending it through the sub-ether. When he was finished, he shorted the motors, and converted the entire ship into a thin cloud of vapor a millionth of a second later. The crew and himself along with it."

"What a man! You were in this from the beginning, Doc?"

"Not from the beginning," corrected Weiss gently. "Only since the receipt of Saybrook's report."

He could not help thinking back. He had read that report, realizing even then how wonderful the planet must have seemed when Saybrook's colonizing expedition first reached it. It was practically a duplicate of Earth, with an abounding plant life and a purely vegetarian animal life.

There had been only the little patches of green fur (how often had he used that phrase in his speaking and thinking!) which seemed strange. No living individual on the planet had eyes. Instead, there was this fur. Even the plants, each blade or leaf or blossom, possessed the two patches of richer green.

Then Saybrook had noticed, startled and bewildered, that there was no conflict for food on the planet. All plants grew pulpy appendages which were eaten by the animals. These were regrown in a matter of hours. No other parts of the plants were touched. It was as though the plants fed the animals as part of the order of nature. And the plants themselves did not grow in overpowering profusion. They might almost have been cultivated, they were spread across the available soil so discriminately.

How much time, Weiss wondered, had Saybrook had to observe the strange law and order on the planet?—the fact that insects kept their numbers reasonable, though no birds ate them; that the rodentlike things did not swarm, though no carnivores existed to keep them in check.

And then there had come the incident of the white rats.

That prodded Weiss. He said, "Oh, one correction, Drake. Hamsters were not the first animals involved. It was the white rats."

"White rats," said Drake, making the correction in his notes.

"Every colonizing ship," said Weiss, "takes a group of white rats for the purpose of testing any alien foods. Rats, of course, are very similar to human beings from a nutritional viewpoint. Naturally, only female white rats are taken."

Naturally. If only one sex was present, there was no danger of unchecked multiplication in case the planet proved favorable. Remember the rabbits in Australia.

"Incidentally, why not use males?" asked Drake.

"Females are hardier," said Weiss, "which is lucky, since that gave the situation away. It turned out suddenly that all the rats were bearing young."

"Right. Now that's where I'm up to, so here's my chance to get some things straight. For my own information, Doc, how did Saybrook find out they were in a family way?"

"Accidentally, of course. In the course of nutritional investigations, rats are dissected for evidence of internal damage. Their condition was bound to be discovered. A few more were dissected;

same results. Eventually, all that lived gave birth to young—with *no* male rats aboard!''

''And the point is that all the young were born with little green patches of fur instead of eyes.''

''That is correct. Saybrook said so and we corroborate him. After the rats, the pet cat of one of the children was obviously affected. When it finally kittened, the kittens were not born with closed eyes but with little patches of green fur. There was no tomcat aboard.

''Eventually Saybrook had the women tested. He didn't tell them what for. He didn't want to frighten them. Every single one of them was in the early stages of pregnancy, leaving out of consideration those few who had been pregnant at the time of embarkation. Saybrook never waited for any child to be born, of course. He knew they would have no eyes, only shining patches of green fur.

''He even prepared bacterial cultures (Saybrook was a thorough man) and found each bacillus to show miscroscopic green spots.''

Drake was eager. ''That goes way beyond our briefing—or, at least, the briefing I got. But granted that life on Saybrook's Planet is organized into a unified whole, how is it done?''

''How? How are your cells organized into a unified whole? Take an individual cell out of your body, even a brain cell, and what is it by itself? Nothing. A little blob of protoplasm with no more capacity for anything human than an amoeba. Less capacity, in fact, since it couldn't live by itself. But put the cells together and you have something that could invent a spaceship or write a symphony.''

''I get the idea,'' said Drake.

Weiss went on, ''*All* life on Saybrook's Planet is a *single* organism. In a sense, all life on Earth is too, but it's a fighting dependence, a dog-eat-dog dependence. The bacteria fix nitrogen; the plants fix carbon; animals eat plants and each other; bacterial decay hits everything. It comes full circle. Each grabs as much as it can, and is, in turn, grabbed.

''On Saybrook's Planet, each organism has its place, as each cell in our body does. Bacteria and plants produce food, on the excess of which animals feed, providing in turn carbon dioxide and nitrogenous wastes. Nothing is produced more or less than is needed. The scheme of life is intelligently altered to suit the local environment. No group of life forms multiplies more or less than is needed, just as the cells in our body stop multiplying when there are enough of them for a given purpose. When they don't stop multiplying, we call if cancer. And that's what life on Earth really is, the kind of organic organization we have, compared to that on Saybrook's Planet. One big cancer. Every species, every individual doing its best to thrive at the expense of every other species and individual."

"You sound as if you approve of Saybrook's Planet, Doc."

"I do, in a way. It makes sense out of the business of living. I can see their viewpoint toward us. Suppose one of the cells of your body could be conscious of the efficiency of the human body as compared with that of the cell itself, and could realize that this was only the result of the union of many cells into a higher whole. And then suppose it became conscious of the existence of free-living cells, with bare life and nothing more. It might feel a very strong desire to drag the poor thing into an organization. It might feel sorry for it, feel perhaps a sort of missionary spirit. The things on Saybrook's Planet—or the thing; one should use the singular—feels just that, perhaps."

"And went ahead by bringing about virgin births, eh, Doc? I've got to go easy on that angle of it. Post-office regulations, you know."

"There's nothing ribald about it, Drake. For centuries we've been able to make the eggs of sea urchins, bees, frogs, et cetera develop without the intervention of male fertilization. The touch of a needle was sometimes enough, or just immersion in the proper salt solution. The thing on Saybrook's Planet can cause fertilization by the controlled use of radiant energy. That's why an appropriate energy barrier stops it; interference, you see, or static.

"They can do more than stimulate the division and development of an unfertilized egg. They can impress their own characteristics upon its nucleo-proteins, so that the young are born with the little patches of green fur, which serve as the planet's sense organ and means of communication. The young, in other words, are not individuals, but become part of the thing on Saybrook's Planet. The thing on the planet, not at all incidentally, can impregnate any species—plant, animal, or microscopic."

"Potent stuff," muttered Drake.

"Totipotent," Dr. Weiss said sharply. "Universally potent. Any fragment of it is totipotent. Given time, a single bacterium from Saybrook's Planet can convert *all of Earth* into a single organism! We've got the experimental proof of that."

Drake said unexpectedly, "You know, I think I'm a millionaire, Doc. Can you keep a secret?"

Weiss nodded, puzzled.

"I've got a souvenir from Saybrook's Planet," Drake told him, grinning. "It's only a pebble, but after the publicity the planet will get, combined with the fact that it's quarantined from here on in, the pebble will be all any human being will ever see of it. How much do you suppose I could sell the thing for?"

Weiss stared. "A pebble?" He snatched at the object shown him, a hard, gray ovoid. "You shouldn't have done that, Drake. It was strictly against regulations."

"I know. That's why I asked if you could keep a secret. If you could give me a signed note of authentication—*What's the matter Doc?*"

Instead of answering, Weiss could only chatter and point. Drake ran over and stared down at the pebble. It was the same as before—

Except that the light was catching it at an angle, and it showed up two little green spots. Look very closely; they were patches of green hairs.

He was disturbed. There was a definite air of danger within the ship. There was the suspicion of his presence aboard. How could that be? He had done nothing yet. Had another fragment of home come aboard and been less cautious? That would be impossible without his knowledge, and though he probed the ship intensely, he found nothing.

And then the suspicion diminished, but it was not quite dead. One of the keen-thinkers still wondered, and was treading close to the truth.

How long before the landing? Would an entire world of life fragments be deprived of completeness? He clung closer to the severed ends of the wire he had been specially bred to imitate, afraid of detection, fearful of his altruistic mission.

Dr. Weiss had locked himself in his own room. They were already within the solar system, and in three hours they would be landing. He had to think. He had three hours in which to decide.

Drake's devilish "pebble" had been part of the organized life on Saybrook's Planet, of course, but it was dead. It was dead when he had first seen it, and if it hadn't been, it was certainly dead after they fed it into the hyper-atomic motor and converted it into a blast of pure heat. And the bacterial cultures still showed normal when Weiss anxiously checked.

That was not what bothered Weiss now.

Drake had picked up the "pebble" during the last hours of the stay on Saybrook's Planet—*after* the barrier breakdown. What if the breakdown had been the result of a slow, relentless mental pressure on the part of the thing on the planet? What if parts of its being waited to invade as the barrier dropped? If the "pebble" had not been fast enough and had moved only after the barrier was re-established, it would have been killed. It would have lain there for Drake to see and pick up.

It was a "pebble," not a natural life form. But did that mean it was not *some* kind of life form? It might have been a deliberate production of the planet's single organism—a creature deliberately designed to look like a pebble, harmless-seeming, unsuspicious. Camouflage, in other words—a shrewd and frighteningly successful camouflage.

Had any other camouflaged creature succeeded in crossing the barrier *before* it was re-established—with a suitable shape filched from the minds of the humans aboard ship by the mind-reading organism of the planet? Would it have the casual appearance of a paperweight? Of an ornamental brass-head nail in the captain's old-fashioned chair? And how would they locate it? Could they search every part of the ship for the telltale green patches—even down to individual microbes?

And why camouflage? Did it intend to remain undetected for a time? Why? So that it might wait for the landing on Earth?

An infection *after landing* could not be cured by blowing up a ship. The bacteria of Earth, the molds, yeasts, and protozoa, would go first. Within a year the non-human young would begin arriving by the uncountable billions.

Weiss closed his eyes and told himself it might not be such a bad thing. There would be no more disease, since no bacterium would multiply at the expense of its host, but instead would be satisfied with its fair share of what was available. There would be no more overpopulation; the hordes of East Asia would decline to adjust themselves to the food supply. There would be no more wars, no crime, no greed.

But there would be no more individuality, either.

Humanity would find security by becoming a cog in a biological machine. A man would be brother to a germ, or to a liver cell.

He stood up. He would have a talk with Captain Loring. They would send their report and blow up the ship, just as Saybrook had done.

He sat down again. Saybrook had had proof, while he had only the conjectures of a terrorized mind, rattled by the sight of two green spots on a pebble. Could he kill the two hundred men on board ship because of a feeble suspicion?

He had to *think!*

He was straining. Why did he have to wait? If he could only welcome those who were aboard now. *Now!*

Yet a cooler, more reasoning part of himself told him that he could not. The little multipliers in the darkness would betray their new status in fifteen minutes, and the keen-thinkers had them under continual observation. Even one mile from the surface of their planet would be too soon, since they might still destroy themselves and their ship out in space.

Better to wait for the main air locks to open, for the planetary air to swirl in with millions of the little multipliers. Better to greet each one of them into the brotherhood of unified life and let them swirl out again to spread the message.

Then it would be done! Another world organized, complete!

He waited. There was the dull throbbing of the engines working mightily to control the slow dropping of the ship; the shudder of contact with planetary surface, then—

He let the jubilation of the keen-thinkers sweep into reception, and his own jubilant thoughts answered them. Soon they would be able to receive as well as himself. Perhaps not these particular fragments, but the fragments that would grow out of those which were fitted for the continuation of life.

The main air locks were about to be opened—

And all thought ceased.

Jerry Thorn thought, Damn it, something's wrong *now*.

He said to Captain Loring, "Sorry. There seems to be a power breakdown. The locks won't open."

"Are you sure, Thorn? The lights are on."

"Yes, sir. We're investigating it now."

He tore away and joined Roger Oldenn at the air-lock wiring box. "What's wrong?"

"Give me a chance, will you?" Oldenn's hands were busy. Then he said, "For the love of Pete, there's a six-inch break in the twenty-amp lead."

"What? That can't be!"

Oldenn held up the broken wires with their clean, sharp, sawn-through ends.

Dr. Weiss joined them. He looked haggard and there was the smell of brandy on his breath.

He said shakily, "What's the matter?"

They told him. At the bottom of the compartment, in one corner, was the missing section.

Weiss bent over. There was a black fragment on the floor of the compartment. He touched it with his finger and it smeared, leaving a sooty smudge on his finger tip. He rubbed it off absently.

There might have been something taking the place of the missing section of wire. Something that had been alive and only looked like wire, yet something that would heat, die, and carbonize in a tiny fraction of a second once the electrical circuit which controlled the air lock had been closed.

He said, "How are the bacteria?"

A crew member went to check, returned and said, "All normal, Doc."

The wires had meanwhile been spliced, the locks opened, and Dr. Weiss stepped out into the anarchic world of life that was Earth.

"Anarchy," he said, laughing a little wildly. "And it will stay that way."

TO SERVE MAN

Damon Knight

GALAXY SCIENCE FICTION

November

Damon Knight has worked successfully in every area of science fiction—as a critic, his In Search of Wonder *(1956, expanded 1967) was one of the first serious examinations of the field by one of its own; as an editor he struggled grimly against market forces he could not control, turning out excellent issues of* Worlds Beyond, *and then twenty years later helped to establish new standards for the genre with his twenty-one-volume* Orbit *series of original hardcover anthologies; as a writer he produced some of the most memorable short stories of the 1950s and 1960s as well as such notable novels as* Hell's Pavement *(1952) and* A For Anything *(1959); as an organizer and teacher he was one of the founders of The Science Fiction Writers of America and of the Milford Science Fiction Writers' Conference; and he is also one of the very best reprint anthologists around. All of this activity, however, greatly limited his fiction writing from about 1965, and thus deprived his readers of more of his insightful, witty, and well-crafted stories.*

"To Serve Man" is a very famous story, one that became one of the most popular of the Twilight Zone *episodes.*

—M.H.G.

When I first began to publish science fiction stories, the very first person ever to write and ask me for my autograph was Damon Knight. Of course I didn't know him at the time.

When I first read "To Serve Man," I had a strong impulse to return the favor, but I fought it down. What if he didn't deign to let me have one?

Personally, I am very fond of the "O. Henry" ending; that is one in which the last sentence or, if possible, the last word, puts a completely new complexion on an entire story. I have tried it once in a while with only moderate success, but I suppose that in all the annals of science fiction, it was never done quite as successfully as in this story.

—I.A.

The Kanamit were not very pretty, it's true. They looked something like pigs and something like people, and that is not an attractive combination. Seeing them for the first time shocked you; that was their handicap. When a thing with the countenance of a fiend comes from the stars and offers a gift, you are disinclined to accept.

I don't know what we expected interstellar visitors to look like—those who thought about it at all, that is. Angels, perhaps, or something too alien to be really awful. Maybe that's why we were all so horrified and repelled when they landed in their great ships and we saw what they really were like.

The Kanamit were short and very hairy—thick, bristly brown-gray hair all over their abominably plump bodies. Their noses were snoutlike and their eyes small, and they had thick hands of three fingers each. They wore green leather harness and green shorts, but I think the shorts were a concession to our notions of public decency. The garments were quite modishly cut, with slash pockets and half-belts in the back. The Kanamit had a sense of humor, anyhow; their clothes proved it.

There were three of them at this session of the U. N., and I can't tell you how queer it looked to see them there in the middle of a solemn Plenary Session—three fat piglike creatures in green harness and shorts, sitting at the long table below the podium, surrounded by the packed arcs of delegates from every nation. They sat correctly upright, politely watching each speaker. Their flat ears drooped over the earphones. Later on, I believe, they learned every human language, but at this time they knew only French and English.

They seemed perfectly at ease—and that, along with their

humor, was a thing that tended to make me like them. I was in the minority; I didn't think they were trying to put anything over. They said quite simply that they wanted to help us and I believed it. As a U. N. translator, of course, my opinion didn't matter, but I thought they were the best thing that ever happened to Earth.

The delegate from Argentina got up and said that his government was interested by the demonstration of a new cheap power source, which the Kanamit had made at the previous session, but that the Argentine government could not commit itself as to its future policy without a much more thorough examination.

It was what all the delegates were saying, but I had to pay particular attention to Senor Valdes, because he tended to sputter and his diction was bad. I got through the translation all right, with only one or two momentary hesitations, and then switched to the Polish-English line to hear how Gregori was doing with Janciewicz. Janciewicz was the cross Gregori had to bear, just as Valdes was mine.

Janciewicz repeated the previous remarks with a few ideological variations, and then the Secretary-General recognized the delegate from France, who introduced Dr. Denis Leveque, the criminologist, and a great deal of complicated equipment was wheeled in.

Dr. Leveque remarked that the question in many people's minds had been aptly expressed by the delegate from the U. S. S. R. at the preceding session, when he demanded, "What is the motive of the Kanamit? What is their purpose in offering us these unprecedented gifts, while asking nothing in return?"

The doctor then said, "At the request of several delegates and with the full consent of our guests, the Kanamit, my associates and I have made a series of tests upon the Kanamit with the equipment which you see before you. These tests will now be repeated."

A murmur ran through the chamber. There was a fusillade of flashbulbs, and one of the TV cameras moved up to focus on the instrument board of the doctor's equipment. At the same time, the huge television screen behind the podium lighted up, and we saw the blank faces of two dials, each with its pointer resting at zero, and a strip of paper tape with a stylus point resting against it.

The doctor's assistants were fastening wires to the temples of one of the Kanamit, wrapping a canvas-covered rubber tube around his forearm, and taping something to the palm of his right hand.

In the screen, we saw the paper tape begin to move while the stylus traced a slow zigzag pattern along it. One of the needles began to jump rhythmically; the other flipped over and stayed there, wavering slightly.

"These are the standard instruments for testing the truth of a statement," said Dr. Leveque. "Our first object, since the physiology of the Kanamit is unknown to us, was to determine whether or not they react to these tests as human beings do. We will now repeat one of the many experiments which was made in the endeavor to discover this."

He pointed to the first dial. "This instrument registers the subject's heart-beat. This shows the electrical conductivity of the skin in the palm of his hand, a measure of perspiration, which increases under stress. And this—" pointing to the tape-and-stylus device—"shows the pattern and intensity of the electrical waves emanating from his brain. It has been shown, with human subjects, that all these readings vary markedly depending upon whether the subject is speaking the truth."

He picked up two large pieces of cardboard, one red and one black. The red one was a square about a meter on a side; the black was a rectangle a meter and a half long. He addressed himself to the Kanama:

"Which of these is longer than the other?"

"The red," said the Kanama.

Both needles leaped wildly, and so did the line on the unrolling tape.

"I shall repeat the question," said the doctor. "Which of these is longer than the other?"

"The black," said the creature.

This time the instruments continued in their normal rhythm.

"How did you come to this planet?" asked the doctor.

"Walked," replied the Kanama.

Again the instruments responded, and there was a subdued ripple of laughter in the chamber.

"Once more," said the doctor, "how did you come to this planet?"

"In a spaceship," said the Kanama, and the instruments did not jump.

The doctor again faced the delegates. "Many such experiments were made," he said, "and my colleagues and myself are satisfied that the mechanisms are effective. Now,'' he turned to the Kanama, ''I shall ask our distinguished guest to reply to the question put at the last session by the delegate of the U. S. S. R., namely, what is the motive of the Kanamit people in offering these great gifts to the people of Earth?''

The Kanama rose. Speaking this time in English, he said, ''On my planet there is a saying, 'There are more riddles in a stone than in a philosopher's head.' The motives of intelligent beings, though they may at times appear obscure, are simple things compared to the complex workings of the natural universe. Therefore I hope that the people of Earth will understand, and believe, when I tell you that our mission upon your planet is simply this—to bring to you the peace and plenty which we ourselves enjoy, and which we have in the past brought to other races throughout the galaxy. When your world has no more hunger, no more war, no more needless suffering, that will be our reward.''

And the needles had not jumped once.

The delegate from the Ukraine jumped to his feet, asking to be recognized, but the time was up and the Secretary-General closed the session.

I met Gregori as we were leaving the U. N. chamber. His face was red with excitement. ''Who promoted that circus?'' he demanded.

''The tests looked genuine to me,'' I told him.

''A circus!'' he said vehemently. ''A second-rate farce! If they were genuine, Peter, why was debate stifled?''

''There'll be time for debate tomorrow surely.''

''Tomorrow the doctor and his instruments will be back in Paris. Plenty of things can happen before tomorrow. In the name of sanity, man, how can anybody trust a thing that looks as if it ate the baby?''

I was a little annoyed. I said, ''Are you sure you're not more worried about their politics than their appearance?''

He said, ''Bah,'' and went away.

The next day reports began to come in from government laboratories all over the world where the Kanamit's power source was being tested. They were wildly enthusiastic. I don't understand such things myself, but it seemed that those little metal boxes would give more electrical power than an atomic pile, for next to nothing and nearly forever. And it was said that they were so cheap to manufacture that everybody in the world could have one of his own. In the early afternoon there were reports that seventeen countries had already begun to set up factories to turn them out.

The next day the Kanamit turned up with plans and specimens of a gadget that would increase the fertility of any arable land by sixty to one hundred per cent. It speeded the formation of nitrates in the soil, or something. There was nothing in the headlines but the Kanamit any more. The day after that, they dropped their bombshell.

"You now have potentially unlimited power and increased food supply," said one of them. He pointed with his three-fingered hand to an instrument that stood on the table before him. It was a box on a tripod, with a parabolic reflector on the front of it. "We offer you today a third gift which is at least as important as the first two."

He beckoned to the TV men to roll their cameras into closeup position. Then he picked up a large sheet of cardboard covered with drawings and English lettering. We saw it on the large screen above the podium; it was all clearly legible.

"We are informed that this broadcast is being relayed throughout your world," said the Kanama. "I wish that everyone who has equipment for taking photographs from television screens would use it now."

The Secretary-General leaned forward and asked a question sharply, but the Kanama ignored him.

"This device," he said, "projects a field in which no explosive, of whatever nature, can detonate."

There was an uncomprehending silence.

The Kanama said, "It cannot now be suppressed. If one nation has it, all must have it." When nobody seemed to understand, he explained bluntly, "There will be no more war."

That was the biggest news of the millennium, and it was perfectly true. It turned out that the explosions the Kanama was talking about included gasoline and Diesel explosions. They had simply made it impossible for anybody to mount or equip a modern army.

We could have gone back to bows and arrows, of course, but that wouldn't have satisfied the military. Not after having atomic bombs and all the rest. Besides, there wouldn't be any reason to make war. Every nation would soon have everything.

Nobody ever gave another thought to those lie-detector

experiments, or asked the Kanamit what their politics were. Gregori was put out; he had nothing to prove his suspicions.

I quit my job with the U. N. a few months later, because I foresaw that it was going to die under me anyhow. U. N. business was booming at the time, but after a year or so there was going to be nothing for it to do. Every nation on Earth was well on the way to being completely self-supporting; they weren't going to need much arbitration.

I accepted a position as translator with the Kanamit Embassy, and it was there that I ran into Gregori again. I was glad to see him, but I couldn't imagine what he was doing there.

"I thought you were on the opposition," I said. "Don't tell me you're convinced the Kanamit are all right."

He looked rather shamefaced. "They're not what they look, anyhow," he said.

It was as much of a concession as he could decently make, and I invited him down to the embassy lounge for a drink. It was an intimate kind of place, and he grew confidential over the second daiquiri.

"They fascinate me," he said. "I hate them instinctively on sight, still—that hasn't changed, but I can evaluate it. You were right, obviously; they mean us nothing but good. But do you know—" he leaned across the table—"the question of the Soviet delegate was never answered."

I am afraid I snorted.

"No, really," he said. "They told us what they wanted to do—'to bring to you the peace and plenty which we ourselves enjoy.' But they didn't say *why*."

"Why do missionaries—"

"Hogwash!" he said angrily. "Missionaries have a religious motive. If these creatures do own a religion, they haven't once mentioned it. What's more, they didn't send a missionary group, they sent a diplomatic delegation—a group representing the will and policy of their whole people. Now just what have the Kanamit, as a people or a nation, got to gain from our welfare?"

I said, "Cultural—"

"Cultural cabbage-soup! No, it's something less obvious than that, something obscure that belongs to their psychology and not to ours. But trust me, Peter, there is no such thing as a completely distinterested altruism. In one way or another, they have something to gain."

"And that's why you're here," I said, "to try to find out what it is?"

"Correct. I wanted to get on one of the ten-year exchange groups to their home planet, but I couldn't; the quota was filled a week after they made the announcement. This is the next best thing. I'm studying their language, and you know that language reflects the basic assumptions of the people who use it. I've got a fair command of the spoken lingo already. It's not hard, really—some of the idioms are almost the same as the equivalents in English. And there are hints in it. I'm sure I'll get the answer eventually."

"More power," I said, and we went back to work.

I saw Gregori frequently from then on, and he kept me posted about his progress. He was highly excited about a month after that first meeting; said he'd got hold of a book of the Kanamit's and was trying to puzzle it out. They wrote in ideographs, worse than Chinese, but he was determined to fathom it if it took him years. He wanted my help.

Well, I was interested in spite of myself, for I knew it would be a long job. We spent some evenings together, working with material from Kanamit bulletin-boards and so forth, and the extremely limited English-Kanamit dictionary they issued the staff. My conscience bothered me about the stolen book, but gradually I became absorbed by the problem. Languages are my field, after all. I couldn't help being fascinated.

We got the title worked out in a few weeks. It was "How to Serve Man," evidently a handbook they were giving out to new Kanamit members of the embassy staff. They had new ones in, all the time now, a shipload about once a month; they were opening all kinds of research laboratories, clinics and so on. If there was anybody on Earth besides Gregori who still distrusted those people, he must have been somewhere in the middle of Tibet.

It was astonishing to see the changes that had been wrought in less than a year. There were no more standing armies, no more shortages, no unemployment. When you picked up a newspaper you didn't see "H-BOMB" or "V-2" leaping out at you; the news was always good. It was a hard thing to get used to. The Kanamit were working on human biochemistry, and it was known around the embassy that they were nearly ready to announce methods of making our race taller and stronger and healthier—

practically a race of supermen—and they had a potential cure for heart disease and cancer.

I didn't see Gregori for a fortnight after we finished working out the title of the book; I was on a long-overdue vacation in Canada. When I got back, I was shocked by the change in his appearance.

"What on Earth is wrong, Gregori?" I asked. "You look like the very devil."

"Come down to the lounge."

I went with him, and he gulped a stiff Scotch as if he needed it.

"Come on, man, what's the matter?" I urged.

"The Kanamit have put me on the passenger list for the next exchange ship," he said. "You, too, otherwise I wouldn't be talking to you."

"Well," I said, "but—"

"They're not altruists."

"What do you mean?"

"What I told you," he said. "They're not altruists."

I tried to reason with him. I pointed out they'd made Earth a paradise compared to what it was before. He only shook his head.

Then I said, "Well, what about those lie-detector tests?"

"A farce," he replied, without heat. "I said so at the time, you fool. They told the truth, though, as far as it went."

"And the book?" I demanded, annoyed. "What about that—'How to Serve Man'? That wasn't put there for you to read. They *mean* it. How do you explain that?"

"I've read the first page of that book," he said. "Why do you suppose I haven't slept for a week?"

I said, "Well?" and he smiled that curious, twisted smile, as if he really wanted to cry instead.

"It's a cookbook," he said.

COMING ATTRACTION

Fritz Leiber (1910–   )

GALAXY SCIENCE FICTION
November

We have discussed the amazing career of Fritz Leiber in earlier volumes of this series. Suffice it to say that he is still productive and going strong at 74, and still winning awards, six Hugos, three Nebulas, one Gandalf, and two World Fantasy Awards to date.

As Algis Budrys has pointed out, "Coming Attraction" may be the most important story in this book, for it helped establish the tone and concerns of both Galaxy Science Fiction *and the science fiction of the 1950s.*

Isaac, the November 1950 issue of Galaxy *must rank as one of strongest in the illustrious history of that magazine.*

—M.H.G.

Of all the great stories in those great first three issues of Galaxy, *I can't imagine that anyone will argue with the contention that "Coming Attraction" was the greatest. From the moment it appeared there was a buzz of astonishment at its excellence. It is* so *annoying that there was no Hugo Award in 1950, for if ever there was a story that was an absolute shoo-in for winning the short-story award, it was this one. I'll bet it would have come closer to getting a unanimous vote than any story before or since.*

For those of you who are too young to remember, there was, back in 1950, a very successful mystery writer named Mickey Spillane who put out a series of best-selling books that were well-packed with violence and (by the standards of that period) steamy sex. I didn't like them myself, but no one asked me. In any case, "Coming Attraction" is a skillful satire on the Spillane style and (again no one asked me) much better than anything Spillane himself ever wrote.

—I.A.

The coupé with the fishhooks welded to the fender shouldered up over the curb like the nose of a nightmare. The girl in its path stood frozen, her face probably stiff with fright under her mask. For once my reflexes weren't shy. I took a fast step toward her, grabbed her elbow, yanked her back. Her black skirt swirled out.

The big coupé shot by, its turbine humming. I glimpsed three faces. Something ripped. I felt the hot exhaust on my ankles as the big coupé swerved back into the street. A thick cloud like a black flower blossomed from its jouncing rear end, while from the fishhooks flew a black shimmering rag.

"Did they get you?" I asked the girl.

She had twisted around to look where the side of her skirt was torn away. She was wearing nylon tights.

"The hooks didn't touch me," she said shakily. "I guess I'm lucky."

I heard voices around us:

"Those kids! What'll they think up next?"

"They're a menace. They ought to be arrested."

Sirens screamed at a rising pitch as two motor-police, their rocket-assist jets full on, came whizzing toward us after the coupé. But the black flower had become a thick fog obscuring the whole street. The motor-police switched from rocket assists to rocket brakes and swerved to a stop near the smoke cloud.

"Are you English?" the girl asked me. "You have an English accent."

Her voice came shudderingly from behind the sleek black satin mask. I fancied her teeth must be chattering. Eyes that were perhaps blue searched my face from behind the black gauze covering the eyeholes of the mask. I told her she'd guessed right. She stood close to me. "Will you come to my place tonight?" she asked rapidly. "I can't thank you now. And there's something you can help me about."

My arm, still lightly circling her waist, felt her body trembling. I was answering the plea in that as much as in her voice when I said, "Certainly." She gave me an address south of Inferno, an apartment number and a time. She asked me my name and I told her.

"Hey, you!"

I turned obediently to the policeman's shout. He shooed away the small clucking crowd of masked women and barefaced men. Coughing from the smoke that the black coupé had thrown out, he asked for my papers. I handed him the essential ones.

He looked at them and then at me. "British Barter? How long will you be in New York?"

Suppressing the urge to say, "For as short a time as possible," I told him I'd be here for a week or so.

"May need you as a witness," he explained. "Those kids can't use smoke on us. When they do that, we pull them in."

He seemed to think the smoke was the bad thing. "They tried to kill the lady," I pointed out.

He shook his head wisely. "They always pretend they're going to, but actually they just want to snag skirts. I've picked up rippers with as many as fifty skirt-snags tacked up in their rooms. Of course, sometimes they come a little too close."

I explained that if I hadn't yanked her out of the way, she'd have been hit by more than hooks. But he interrupted, "If she'd thought it was a real murder attempt, she'd have stayed here."

I looked around. It was true. She was gone.

"She was fearfully frightened," I told him.

"Who wouldn't be? Those kids would have scared old Stalin himself."

"I mean frightened of more than 'kids.' They didn't look like 'kids.' "

"What did they look like?"

I tried without much success to describe the three faces. A vague impression of viciousness and effeminacy doesn't mean much.

"Well, I could be wrong," he said finally. "Do you know the girl? Where she lives?"

"No," I half lied.

The other policeman hung up his radiophone and ambled toward us, kicking at the tendrils of dissipating smoke. The black cloud no longer hid the dingy facades with their five-year-old radiation flashburns, and I could begin to make out the distant stump of the Empire State Building, thrusting up out of Inferno like a mangled finger.

"They haven't been picked up so far," the approaching policeman grumbled. "Left smoke for five blocks, from what Ryan says."

The first policeman shook his head. "That's bad," he observed solemnly.

I was feeling a bit uneasy and ashamed. An Englishman shouldn't lie, at least not on impulse.

"They sound like nasty customers," the first policeman continued in the same grim tone. "We'll need witnesses. Looks as if you may have to stay in New York longer than you expect."

I got the point. I said, "I forgot to show you all my papers," and handed him a few others, making sure there was a five dollar bill in among them.

When he handed them back a bit later, his voice was no longer ominous. My feelings of guilt vanished. To cement our relationship, I chatted with the two of them about their job.

"I suppose the masks give you some trouble," I observed. "Over in England we've been reading about your new crop of masked female bandits."

"Those things get exaggerated," the first policeman assured me. "It's the men masking as women that really mix us up. But, brother, when we nab them, we jump on them with both feet."

"And you get so you can spot women almost as well as if they had naked faces," the second policeman volunteered. "You know, hands and all that."

"Especially all that," the first agreed with a chuckle. "Say, is it true that some girls don't mask over in England?"

"A number of them have picked up the mask fashion," I told him. "Only a few, though—the ones who always adopt the latest style, however extreme."

"They're usually masked in the British newscasts."

"I imagine it's arranged that way out of deference to American taste," I confessed. "Actually, not very many do mask."

The second policeman considered that. "Girls going down the street bare from the neck up." It was not clear whether he viewed the prospect with relish or moral distaste. Likely both.

"A few members keep trying to persuade Parliament to enact a law forbidding all masking," I continued, talking perhaps a bit too much.

The second policeman shook his head. "What an idea. You know, masks are a pretty good thing, brother. Couple of years more and I'm going to make my wife wear hers around the house."

The first policeman shrugged. "If women were to stop wearing masks, in six weeks you wouldn't know the difference. You get used to anything, if enough people do it."

I agreed, rather regretfully, and left them. I turned north on Broadway (old Tenth Avenue, I believe) and walked rapidly until I was beyond Inferno. Passing such an area of undecontaminated radioactivity always makes a person queasy. I thanked God there weren't any such in England, as yet.

The street was almost empty, though I was accosted by a couple of beggars with faces tunneled by H-bomb scars, whether real or of makeup putty, I couldn't tell. A fat woman held out a baby with webbed fingers and toes. I told myself it would have been deformed anyway and that she was only capitalizing on our fear of bomb-induced mutations. Still, I gave her a seven-and-a-half-cent piece. Her mask made me feel I was paying tribute to an African fetish.

"May all your children be blessed with one head and two eyes, sir."

"Thanks," I said, shuddering, and hurried past her.

". . . There's only trash behind the mask, so turn your head, stick to your task: Stay away, stay away—from—the—girls!"

This last was the end of an antisex song being sung by some religionists half a block from the circle-and-cross insignia of a femalist temple. They reminded me only faintly of our small tribe of British monastics. Above their heads was a jumble of billboards advertising predigested foods, wrestling instruction, radio handies and the like.

I stared at the hysterical slogans with disagreeable fascination. Since the female face and form have been banned on American signs, the very letters of the advertiser's alphabet have begun to crawl with sex—the fat-bellied, big-breasted capital B, the lascivious double O. However, I reminded myself, it is chiefly the mask that so strangely accents sex in America.

A British anthropologist has pointed out, that, while it took more than 5,000 years to shift the chief point of sexual interest from the hips to the breasts, the next transition to the face has taken less than 50 years. Comparing the American style with Moslem tradition is not valid; Moslem women are compelled to wear veils, the purpose of which is concealment, while American women have only the compulsion of fashion, whatever that means.

Theory aside, the actual origins of the trend are to be found in the antiradiation clothing of World War III, which led to masked wrestling, now a fantastically popular sport, and that in turn led to the current female fashion. Only a wild style at first, masks quickly became as necessary as brassieres and lipsticks had been earlier in the century.

I finally realized that I was not speculating about masks in general, but about what lay behind one in particular. That's the devil of the things; you're never sure whether a girl is heightening loveliness or hiding ugliness. I pictured a cool, pretty face in which fear showed only in widened eyes. Then I remembered her blonde hair, rich against the blackness of the satin mask. She'd told me to come at the twenty-second hour—ten P.M.

I climbed to my apartment near the British Consulate; the elevator shaft had been shoved out of plumb by an old blast, a nuisance in these tall New York buildings. Before it occurred to me that I would be going out again, I automatically tore a tab from the film strip under my shirt. I developed it just to be sure. It showed that the total radiation I'd taken that day was still within the safety limit. I'm not phobic about it, as so many people are these days, but there's no point in taking chances.

I flopped down on the day bed and stared at the silent speaker and the dark screen of the video set. As always, they made me think, somewhat bitterly, of the two great nations of the world. Mutilated by each other, yet still strong, they were crippled giants poisoning the planet with their dreams of an impossible equality and an impossible success.

I fretfully switched on the speaker. By luck, the newscaster was talking excitedly of the prospects of a bumper wheat crop, sown by planes across a dust bowl moistened by seeded rains. I listened carefully to the rest of the program (it was remarkably clear of Russian telejamming) but there was no further news of interest to me. And, of course, no mention of the moon, though everyone knows that America and Russia are racing to develop their primary bases into fortresses capable of mutual assault and the launching of alphabet-bombs toward Earth. I myself knew perfectly well that the British electronic equipment I was helping trade for American wheat was destined for use in spaceships.

I switched off the newscast. It was growing dark and once

again I pictured a tender, frightened face behind a mask. I hadn't had a date since England. It's exceedingly difficult to become acquainted with a girl in America, where as little as a smile, often, can set one of them yelping for the police—to say nothing of the increasing puritanical morality and the roving gangs that keep most women indoors after dark. And naturally, the masks, which the Soviets describe as a last symptom of capitalist degeneracy and collapse. The Russians wear no masks, but I like their last symptoms even less.

I went to the window and impatiently watched the darkness gather. I was getting very restless. After a while a ghostly violet cloud appeared to the south. My hair rose. Then I laughed. I had momentarily fancied it a radiation from the crater of the Hell-bomb, though I should instantly have known it was only the radio-induced glow in the sky over the amusement and residential area south of Inferno.

Promptly at twenty-two hours I stood before the door of my unknown girl friend's apartment. The electronic say-who-please said just that. I answered clearly, "Wysten Turner," wondering if she'd given my name to the mechanism. She evidently had, for the door opened. I walked into a small empty living room, my heart pounding a bit.

The room was expensively furnished with the latest pneumatic hassocks and sprawlers. There were some midgie books on the table. The one I picked up was the standard hard-boiled detective story in which two female murderers go gunning for each other.

The television was on. A masked girl in green was crooning a love song. Her right hand held something that blurred off into the foreground. I saw the set had a handie, which we haven't in England as yet, and curiously thrust my hand into the handie orifice beside the screen. Contrary to my expectations, it was not like slipping into a pulsing rubber glove, but rather as if the girl on the screen actually held my hand.

A door opened behind me. I jerked out my hand with as guilty a reaction as if I'd been caught peering through a keyhole.

She stood in the bedroom doorway. I think she was trembling. She was wearing a gray fur coat, white-speckled, and a gray velvet evening mask with shirred gray lace around the eyes and mouth. Her fingernails twinkled like silver.

It hadn't occurred to me that she'd expect us to go out.

"I should have told you," she said softly. Her mask veered

nervously toward the books and the screen and the room's dark corners. "But I can't possibly talk to you here."

I said doubtfully, "There's a place near the Consulate. . . ."

"I know where we can be together and talk," she said rapidly. "If you don't mind."

As we entered the elevator I said, "I'm afraid I dismissed the cab."

But the cab driver hadn't gone for some reason of his own. He jumped out and smirkingly held the front door open for us. I told him we preferred to sit in back. He sulkily opened the rear door, slammed it after us, jumped in front and slammed the door behind him.

My companion leaned forward. "Heaven," she said.

The driver switched on the turbine and televisor.

"Why did you ask if I were a British subject?" I said, to start the conversation.

She leaned away from me, tilting her mask close to the window. "See the Moon," she said in a quick, dreamy voice.

"But why, really?" I pressed, conscious of an irritation that had nothing to do with her.

"It's edging up into the purple of the sky."

"And what's your name?"

"The purple makes it look yellower."

Just then I became aware of the source of my irritation. It lay in the square of writhing light in the front of the cab beside the driver.

I don't object to ordinary wrestling matches, though they bore me, but I simply detest watching a man wrestle a woman. The fact that the bouts are generally "on the level," with the man greatly outclassed in weight and reach and the masked females young and personable, only makes them seem worse to me.

"Please turn off the screen," I requested the driver.

He shook his head without looking around. "Uh-uh, man," he said. "They've been grooming that babe for weeks for this bout with Little Zirk."

Infuriated, I reached forward, but my companion caught my arm. "Please," she whispered frightenedly, shaking her head.

I settled back, frustrated. She was closer to me now, but silent and for a few moments I watched the heaves and contortions of the powerful masked girl and her wiry masked opponent on the screen. His frantic scrambling at her reminded me of a male spider.

I jerked around, facing my companion. "Why did those three men want to kill you?" I asked sharply.

The eyeholes of her mask faced the screen. "Because they're jealous of me," she whispered.

"Why are they jealous?"

She still didn't look at me. "Because of him."

"Who?"

She didn't answer.

I put my arm around her shoulders. "Are you afraid to tell me?" I asked. "What *is* the matter?"

She still didn't look my way. She smelled nice.

"See here," I said laughingly, changing my tactics, "you really should tell me something about yourself. I don't even know what you look like."

I half playfully lifted my hand to the band of her neck. She gave it an astonishingly swift slap. I pulled it away in sudden pain. There were four tiny indentations on the back. From one of them a tiny bead of blood welled out as I watched. I looked at her silver fingernails and saw they were actually delicate and pointed metal caps.

"I'm dreadfully sorry," I heard her say, "but you frightened me. I thought for a moment you were going to. . . ."

At last she turned to me. Her coat had fallen open. Her evening dress was Cretan Revival, a bodice of lace beneath and supporting the breasts without covering them.

"Don't be angry," she said, putting her arms around my neck. "You were wonderful this afternoon."

The soft gray velvet of her mask, molding itself to her cheek, pressed mine. Through the mask's lace the wet warm tip of her tongue touched my chin.

"I'm not angry," I said. "Just puzzled and anxious to help."

The cab stopped. To either side were black windows bordered by spears of broken glass. The sickly purple light showed a few ragged figures slowly moving toward us.

The driver muttered, "It's the turbine, man. We're grounded." He sat there hunched and motionless. "Wish it had happened somewhere else."

My companion whispered, "Five dollars is the usual amount."

She looked out so shudderingly at the congregating figures that I suppressed my indignation and did as she suggested. The driver took the bill without a word. As he started up, he put his hand out the window and I heard a few coins clink on the pavement.

My companion came back into my arms, but her mask faced the television screen, where the tall girl had just pinned the convulsively kicking Little Zirk.

"I'm so frightened," she breathed.

Heaven turned out to be an equally ruined neighborhood, but it had a sidewalk canopy and a huge doorman uniformed like a spaceman, but in gaudy colors. In my sensuous daze I rather liked it all. We stepped out of the cab just as a drunken old woman came down the sidewalk, her mask awry. A couple ahead of us turned their heads from the half-revealed face, as if from an ugly body at the beach. As we followed them in I heard the doorman say, "Get along, grandma, and watch yourself."

Inside, everything was dimness and blue glows. She had said we could talk here, but I didn't see how. Besides the inevitable chorus of sneezes and coughs (they say America is fifty per cent allergic these days), there was a band going full blast in the latest robop style, in which an electronic composing machine selects an arbitrary sequence of tones into which the musicians weave their raucous little individualities.

Most of the people were in booths. The band was behind the bar. On a small platform beside them a girl was dancing, stripped to her mask. The little cluster of men at the shadowy far end of the bar weren't looking at her.

We inspected the menu in gold script on the wall and pushed the buttons for breast of chicken, fried shrimps and two scotches. Moments later, the serving bell tinkled. I opened the gleaming panel and took out our drinks.

The cluster of men at the bar filed off toward the door, but first they stared around the room. My companion had just thrown back her coat. Their look lingered on our booth. I noticed that there were three of them.

The band chased off the dancing girl with growls. I handed my companion a straw and we sipped our drinks.

"You wanted me to help you about something," I said. "Incidentally, I think you're lovely."

She nodded quick thanks, looked around, leaned forward. "Would it be hard for me to get to England?"

"No," I replied, a bit taken aback. "Provided you have an American passport."

"Are they difficult to get?"

"Rather," I said, surprised at her lack of information. "Your country doesn't like its nationals to travel, though it isn't quite as stringent as Russia."

"Could the British Consulate help me get a passport?"

"It's hardly their. . . ."

"Could you?"

I realized we were being inspected. A man and two girls had paused opposite our table. The girls were tall and wolfish-looking, with spangled masks. The man stood jauntily between them like a fox on its hind legs.

My companion didn't glance at them, but she sat back. I noticed that one of the girls had a big yellow bruise on her forearm. After a moment they walked to a booth in the deep shadows.

"Know them?" I asked. She didn't reply. I finished my drink. "I'm not sure you'd like England," I said. "The austerity's altogether different from your American brand of misery."

She leaned forward again. "But I must get away," she whispered.

"Why?" I was getting impatient.

"Because I'm so frightened."

There were chimes. I opened the panel and handed her the fried shrimps. The sauce on my breast of chicken was a delicious steaming compound of almonds, soy and ginger. But something must have been wrong with the radionic oven that had thawed and heated it, for at the first bite I crunched a kernel of ice in the meat. These delicate mechanisms need constant repair and there aren't enough mechanics.

I put down my fork. "What are you really scared of?" I asked her.

For once her mask didn't waver away from my face. As I waited I could feel the fears gathering without her naming them, tiny dark shapes swarming through the curved night outside, converging on the radioactive pest spot of New York, dipping into the margins of the purple. I felt a sudden rush of sympathy, a desire to protect the girl opposite me. The warm feeling added itself to the infatuation engendered in the cab.

"Everything," she said finally.

I nodded and touched her hand.

"I'm afraid of the Moon," she began, her voice going dreamy and brittle as it had in the cab. "You can't look at it and not think of guided bombs."

"It's the same Moon over England," I reminded her.

"But it's not England's Moon any more. It's ours and Russia's. You're not responsible."

I pressed her hand.

"Oh, and then," she said with a tilt of her mask, "I'm afraid of the cars and the gangs and the loneliness and Inferno. I'm afraid of the lust that undresses your face. And—" her voice hushed—"I'm afraid of the wrestlers."

"Yes?" I prompted softly after a moment.

Her mask came forward. "Do you know something about the wrestlers?" she asked rapidly. "The ones that wrestle women, I mean. They often lose, you know. And then they have to have a girl to take their frustration out on. A girl who's soft and weak and terribly frightened. They need that, to keep them men. Other men don't want them to have a girl. Other men want them just to fight women and be heroes. But they must have a girl. It's horrible for her."

I squeezed her fingers tighter, as if courage could be transmitted—granting I had any. "I think I can get you to England," I said.

Shadows crawled onto the table and stayed there. I looked up at the three men who had been at the end of the bar. They were the men I had seen in the big coupé. They wore black sweaters, and close-fitting black trousers. Their faces were as expressionless as dopers. Two of them stood above me. The other loomed over the girl.

"Drift off, man," I was told. I heard the other inform the girl: "We'll wrestle a fall, sister. What shall it be? Judo, slapsie or kill-who-can?"

I stood up. There are times when an Englishman simply must be maltreated. But just then the foxlike man came gliding in like the star of a ballet. The reaction of the other three startled me. They were acutely embarrassed.

He smiled at them thinly. "You won't win my favor by tricks like this," he said.

"Don't get the wrong idea, Zirk," one of them pleaded.

"I will if it's right," he said. "She told me what you tried to do this afternoon. That won't endear you to me either. Drift."

They backed off awkwardly. "Let's get out of here," one of them said loudly, as they turned. "I know a place where they fight naked with knives."

Little Zirk laughed musically and slipped into the seat beside my companion. She shrank from him, just a little. I pushed my feet back, leaned forward.

"Who's your friend, baby?" he asked, not looking at her.

She passed the question to me with a little gesture. I told him.

"British," he observed. "She's been asking you about getting out of the country? About passports?" He smiled pleasantly. "She likes to start running away. Don't you, baby?" His small hand began to stroke her wrist, the fingers bent a little, the tendons ridged, as if he were about to grab and twist.

"Look here," I said sharply. "I have to be grateful to you for ordering off those bullies, but—"

"Think nothing of it," he told me. "They're no harm except when they're behind the steering wheels. A well-trained fourteen-year-old girl could cripple any one of them. Why, even Theda here, if she went in for that sort of thing. . . ." He turned to her, shifting his hand from her wrist to her hair. He stroked it, letting the strands slip slowly through his fingers. "You know I lost tonight, baby, don't you?" he said softly.

I stood up. "Come along," I said to her. "Let's leave."

She just sat there. I couldn't even tell if she was trembling. I tried to read a message in her eyes through the mask.

"I'll take you away," I said to her. "I can do it. I really will."

He smiled at me. "She'd like to go with you," he said. "Wouldn't you, baby?"

"Will you or won't you?" I said to her. She still just sat there.

He slowly knotted his fingers in her hair.

"Listen, you little vermin," I snapped at him. "Take your hands off her."

He came up from the seat like a snake. I'm no fighter. I just know that the more scared I am, the harder and straighter I hit. This time I was lucky. But as he crumpled back, I felt a slap and four stabs of pain in my cheek. I clapped my hand to it. I could feel the four gashes made by her dagger finger caps, and the warm blood oozing out from them.

She didn't look at me. She was bending over little Zirk and cuddling her mask to his cheek and crooning: "There, there, don't feel bad, you'll be able to hurt me afterward."

There were sounds around us, but they didn't come close. I leaned forward and ripped the mask from her face.

I really don't know why I should have expected her face to be anything else. It was very pale, of course, and there weren't any cosmetics. I suppose there's no point in wearing any under a mask. The eyebrows were untidy and the lips chapped. But as for the general expression, as for the feelings crawling and wriggling across it—

Have you ever lifted a rock from damp soil? Have you ever watched the slimy white grubs?

I looked down at her, she up at me. "Yes, you're so frightened, aren't you?" I said. "You dread this little nightly drama, don't you? You're scared to death."

And I walked right out into the purple night, still holding my hand to my bleeding cheek. No one stopped me, not even the girl wrestlers. I wished I could tear a tab from under my shirt, and test it then and there, and find I'd taken soo much radiation, and so be able to ask to cross the Hudson and go down New Jersey, past the imagined radiance of the Narrows Bomb, and so on to Sandy Hook to wait for the rusty ship that would take me back over the seas to England.

A SUBWAY NAMED MOBIUS

A. J. Deutsch

ASTOUNDING SCIENCE FICTION
December

I'm sorry to report that I don't know a thing about A. J. Deutsch. I only know that this story belongs in the best of 1950, is one of the most amazing stories ever written about mathematics, and that you will enjoy it very much.

—M.H.G.

When Marty wrote the above, he didn't know that I do know something about Armin Deutsch. When I moved to Boston in 1949, Armin was teaching at Harvard, and I got to meet him along with a whole bunch of other delightful academics.

Armin phoned me one morning and said, "May I read you the first few paragraphs of a science fiction story I'm writing?" (I groaned inwardly. Everyone who meets me decides to write sf on the unassailable grounds that if an idiot like me can do it, anyone *can.)*

Still one must be polite. I said, "Go ahead, Armin."

He did and I grew excited. "Send me the manuscript," I said.

He sent it and I called him, *and said, "This is terrific. You must send it to John Campbell. He will take it."*

Armin did and John did. The story was, of course, "A Subway Named Mobius" and I have always felt responsible for it.

Armin never wrote another story as far as I know. He had a peculiar metabolic anomaly which caused cholesterol to collect in his joints and he died relatively young, but I do not have his birth or death year.

There was a song later on, popular in Boston, called "The Ballad of the MTA" about a fellow who was caught by a raise in the fare. Not having an additional dime, he could never get off the subway. I've always wondered whether it was inspired by "A Subway Named Mobius." It's a very catchy song, too.

—I.A.

In a complex and ingenious pattern, the subway had spread out from a focus at Park Street. A shunt connected the Lechmere line with the Ashmont for trains southbound, and with the Forest Hills line for those northbound. Harvard and Brookline had been linked with a tunnel that passed through Kenmore Under, and during rush hours every other train was switched through the Kenmore Branch back to Egleston. The Kenmore Branch joined the Maverick Tunnel near Fields Corner. It climbed a hundred feet in two blocks to connect Copley Over with Scollay Square; then it dipped down again to join the Cambridge line at Boylston. The Boylston shuttle had finally tied together the seven principal lines on four different levels. It went into service, you remember, on March 3rd. After that, a train could travel from any one station to any other station in the whole system.

There were two hundred twenty-seven trains running the subways every weekday, and they carried about a million and a half passengers. The Cambridge-Dorchester train that disappeared on March 4th was Number 86. Nobody missed it at first. During the evening rush, the traffic was a little heavier than usual on that line. But a crowd is a crowd. The ad posters at the Forest Hills yards looked for 86 about 7:30, but neither of them mentioned its absence until three days later. The controller at the Milk Street Cross-Over called the Harvard checker for an extra train after the hockey game that night, and the Harvard checker relayed the call to the yards. The dispatcher there sent out 87, which had been put to bed at ten o'clock, as usual. He didn't notice that 86 was missing.

It was near the peak of the rush the next morning that Jack O'Brien, at the Park Street Control, called Warren Sweeney at the Forest Hills yards and told him to put another train on the Cambridge run. Sweeney was short, so he went to the board and scanned it for a spare train and crew. Then, for the first time, he noticed that Gallagher had not checked out the night before. He put the tag up and left a note. Gallagher was due on at ten. At ten-thirty, Sweeney was down looking at the board again, and he noticed Gallagher's tag still up, and the note where he had left it. He groused to the checker and asked if Gallagher had come in late. The checker said he hadn't seen Gallagher at all that morning. Then Sweeney wanted to know who was running 86? A few minutes later he found that Dorkin's card was still up, although it was Dorkin's day off. It was 11:30 before he finally realized that he had lost a train.

Sweeney spent the next hour and a half on the phone, and he quizzed every dispatcher, controller, and checker on the whole system. When he finished his lunch at 1:30, he covered the whole net again. At 4:40, just before he left for the day, he reported the matter, with some indignation, to Central Traffic. The phones buzzed through the tunnels and shops until nearly midnight before the general manager was finally notified at his home.

It was the engineer on the main switchbank who, late in the morning of the 6th, first associated the missing train with the newspaper stories about the sudden rash of missing persons. He tipped off the *Transcript*, and by the end of the lunch hour three papers had Extras on the streets. That was the way the story got out.

Kelvin Whyte, the General Manager, spent a good part of that afternoon with the police. They checked Gallagher's wife, and Dorkin's. The motorman and the conductor had not been home since the morning of the 4th. By mid-afternoon, it was clear to the police that three hundred and fifty Bostonians, more or less, had been lost with the train. The System buzzed, and Whyte nearly expired with simple exasperation. But the train was not found.

Roger Tupelo, the Harvard mathematician, stepped into the picture the evening of the 6th. He reached Whyte by phone, late, his home, and told him he had some ideas about the missing train. Then he taxied to Whyte's home in Newton and had the first of many talks with Whyte about Number 86.

Whyte was an intelligent man, a good organizer, and not without imagination. "But I don't know what you're talking about!" he expostulated.

Tupelo was resolved to be patient. "This is a very hard thing for *anybody* to understand, Mr. Whyte," he said. "I can see why you are puzzled. But it's the only explanation. The train has vanished, and the people on it. But the System is closed. Trains are conserved. It's somewhere on the System!"

Whyte's voice grew louder again. "And I tell you, Dr. Tupelo, that train is *not* on the System! It is *not!* You can't overlook a seven-car train carrying four hundred passengers. The System has been combed. Do you think I'm trying to *hide* the train?"

"Of course not. Now look, let's be reasonable. We know the train was en route to Cambridge at 8:40 a.m. on the 4th. At least twenty of the missing people probably boarded the train a few minutes earlier at Washington, and forty more at Park Street Under. A few got off at both stations. And that's the last. The ones who were going to Kendall, to Central, to Harvard—they never got there. The train did not get to Cambridge."

"I know that, Dr. Tupelo," Whyte said savagely. "In the tunnel under the River, the train turned into a boat. It left the tunnel and sailed for Africa."

"No, Mr. Whyte. I'm trying to tell you. It hit a node."

Whyte was livid. "What is a node!" he exploded. "The System keeps the tracks clear. Nothing on the tracks but trains, no nodes left lying around—"

"You still don't understand. A node is not an obstruction. It's a singularity. A pole of high order."

Tupelo's explanations that night did not greatly clarify the situation for Kelvin Whyte. But at two in the mornng, the general manager conceded to Tupelo the privilege of examining the master maps of the System. He put in a call first to the police, who could not assist him with his first attempt to master topology, and then, finally, to Central Traffic. Tupelo taxied down there alone, and pored over the maps till morning. He had coffee and a snail, and then went to Whyte's office.

He found the general manager on the telephone. There was a conversation having to do with another, more elaborate inspection of the Dorchester-Cambridge tunnel under the Charles River. When the conversation ended, Whyte slammed the telephone into its cradle and glared at Tupelo. The mathematician spoke first.

"I think probably it's the new shuttle that did this," he said.

Whyte gripped the edge of his desk and prowled silently through his vocabulary until he had located some civil words. "Dr. Tupelo," he said, "I have been awake all night going over your theory. I don't understand it all. I don't know what the Boylston shuttle has to do with this."

"Remember what I was saying last night about the connective properties of networks?" Tupelo asked quietly. "Remember the Möbius band we made—the surface with one face and one edge? Remember this—?" and he removed a little glass Klein bottle from his pocket and placed it on the desk.

Whyte sat back in his chair and stared wordlessly at the mathematician. Three emotions marched across his face in quick succession—anger, bewilderment, and utter dejection. Tupelo went on.

"Mr. Whyte, the System is a network of amazing topological complexity. It was already complex before the Boylston shuttle was installed, and of a high order of connectivity. But this shuttle makes the network absolutely unique. I don't fully understand it, but the situation seems to be something like this: the shuttle has made the connectivity of the whole System of an order so high that I don't know how to calculate it. I suspect the connectivity has become infinite."

The general manager listened as though in a daze. He kept his eyes glued to the little Klein bottle.

"The Möbius band," Tupelo said, "has unusual properties because it has a singularity. The Klein bottle, with two singularities, manages to be inside of itself. The topologists know surfaces with as many as a thousand singularities, and they have properties that make the Möbius band and the Klein bottle both look simple. But a network with infinite connectivity must have an infinite number of singularities. Can you imagine what the properties of that network could be?"

After a long pause, Tupelo added: "I can't either. To tell the truth, the structure of the System, with the Boylston shuttle, is completely beyond me. I can only guess."

Whyte swiveled his eyes up from the desk at a moment when anger was the dominant feeling within him. "And you call yourself a mathematician, Professor Tupelo!" he said.

Tupelo almost laughed aloud. The incongruous, the absolute foolishness of the situation, all but overwhelmed him. He smiled thinly, and said: "I'm no topologist. Really, Mr. Whyte, I'm a tyro in the field—not much better acquainted with it than you are. Mathematics is a big pasture. I happen to be an algebraist."

His candor softened Whyte a little. "Well, then," he ventured, "if you don't understand it, maybe we should call in a topologist. Are there any in Boston?"

"Yes and no," Tupelo answered. "The best in the world is at Tech."

Whyte reached for the telephone. "What's his name?" he asked. "I'll call him."

"Merritt Turnbull. He can't be reached. I've tried for three days."

"Is he out of town?" Whyte asked. "We'll send for him—emergency."

"I don't know. Professor Turnbull is a bachelor. He lives alone at the Brattle Club. He has not been seen since the morning of the 4th."

Whyte was uncommonly perceptive. "Was he on the train?" he asked tensely.

"I don't know," the mathematician replied. "What do you think?"

There was a long silence. Whyte looked alternately at Tupelo and at the glass object on the desk. "I don't understand it," he said finally. "We've looked everywhere on the System. There was no way for the train to get out."

"The train didn't get out. It's still on the System," Tupelo said.

"Where?"

Tupelo shrugged. "The train has no real 'where.' The whole System is without real 'whereness.' It's double-valued, or worse."

"How can we find it?"

"I don't think we can," Tupelo said.

There was another long silence. Whyte broke it with a loud exclamation. He rose suddenly, and sent the Klein bottle flying across the room. "You are crazy, professor!" he shouted. "Between midnight tonight and 6:00 a.m. tomorrow, we'll get every train out of the tunnels. I'll send in three hundred men, to comb every inch of the tracks—every inch of the one hundred eighty-three miles. We'll find the train! Now, please excuse me." He glared at Tupelo.

Tupelo left the office. He felt tired, completely exhausted. Mechanically, he walked along Washington Street toward the Essex Station. Halfway down the stairs, he stopped abruptly, looked around him slowly. Then he ascended again to the street and hailed a taxi. At home, he helped himself to a double shot. He fell into bed.

At 3:30 that afternoon he met his class in "Algebra of Fields and Rings." After a quick supper at the Crimson Spa, he went to his apartment and spent the evening in a second attempt to analyze the connective properties of the System. The attempt was vain, but the mathematician came to a few important conclusions. At eleven o'clock he telephoned Whyte at Central Traffic.

"I think you might want to consult me during tonight's search," he said. "May I come down?"

The general manager was none too gracious about Tupelo's offer of help. He indicated that the System would solve this little problem without any help from harebrained professors who thought that whole subway trains could jump off into the fourth dimension. Tupelo submitted to Whyte's unkindness, then went to bed. At about 4:00 a.m. the telephone awakened him. His caller was a contrite Kelvin Whyte.

"Perhaps I was a bit hasty last night, professor," he stammered. "You may be able to help us after all. Could you come down to the Milk Street Cross-Over?"

Tupelo agreed readily. He felt none of the satisfaction he had anticipated. He called a taxi, and in less than half an hour was at the prescribed station. At the foot of the stairs, on the upper level, he saw that the tunnel was brightly lighted, as during normal operation of the System. But the platforms were deserted except for a tight little knot of seven men near the far end. As he walked towards the group, he noticed that two were policemen. He observed a one-car train on the track beside the platform. The forward door was open, the car brightly lit, and empty. Whyte heard his footsteps and greeted him sheepishly.

"Thanks for coming down, professor," he said, extending his hand. "Gentlemen, Dr. Roger Tupelo, of Harvard. Dr. Tupelo, Mr. Kennedy, our chief engineer; Mr. Wilson, representing the Mayor; Dr. Gannot, of Mercy Hospital." Whyte did not bother to introduce the motorman and the two policemen.

"How do you do," said Tupelo. "Any results, Mr. Whyte?"

The general manager exchanged embarrassed glances with his companions. "Well . . . yes, Dr. Tupelo," he finally answered. "I think we do have some results, of a kind."

"Has the train been seen?"

"Yes," said Whyte. "That is, practically seen. At least, we know it's somewhere in the tunnels." The six others nodded their agreement.

Tupelo was not surprised to learn that the train was still on the System. After all, the System was closed. "Would you mind telling me just what happened?" Tupelo insisted.

"I hit a red signal," the motorman volunteered. "Just outside the Copley junction."

"The tracks have been completely cleared of all trains," Whyte explained, "except for this one. We've been riding it, all over the System, for four hours now. When Edmunds, here, hit a red light at the Copley junction, he stopped, of course. I thought the light must be defective, and told him to go ahead. But then we heard another train pass the junction."

"Did you see it?" Tupelo asked.

"We couldn't see it. The light is placed just behind a curve. But we all heard it. There's no doubt the train went through the junction. And it must be Number 86, because our car was the only other one on the tracks."

"What happened then?"

"Well, then the light changed to yellow, and Edmunds went ahead."

"Did he follow the other train?"

"No. We couldn't be sure which way it was going. We must have guessed wrong."

"How long ago did this happen?"

"At 1:38, the first time—"

"Oh," said Tupelo, "then it happened again later?"

"Yes. But not at the same spot, of course. We hit another red signal near South Station at 2:15. And then at 3:28—"

Tupelo interrupted the general manager. "Did you see the train at 2:15?"

"We didn't even hear it, that time. Edmunds tried to catch it, but it must have turned off onto the Boylston shuttle."

"What happened at 3:28?"

"Another red light. Near Park Street. We heard it up ahead of us."

"But you didn't see it?"

"No. There is a little slope beyond the light. But we all heard it. The only thing I don't understand, Dr. Tupelo, is how that train could run the tracks for nearly five days without anybody seeing—"

Whyte's words trailed off into silence, and his right hand went up in a peremptory gesture for quiet. In the distance, the low metallic thunder of a fast-rolling train swelled up suddenly into a sharp, shrill roar of wheels below. The platform vibrated perceptibly as the train passed.

"Now we've got it!" Whyte exclaimed. "Right past the men on the platform below!" He broke into a run towards the stairs to the lower level. All the others followed him, except Tupelo. He thought he knew what was going to happen. It did. Before Whyte reached the stairs, a policeman bounded up to the top.

"Did you see it, now?" he shouted.

Whyte stopped in his tracks, and the others with him.

"Did you see that train?" the policeman from the lower level asked again, as two more men came running up the stairs.

"What happened?" Wilson wanted to know.

"Didn't *you* see it?" snapped Kennedy.

"Sure not," the policeman replied. "It passed through up here."

"It did *not*," roared Whyte. "Down there!"

The six men with Whyte glowered at the three from the lower level. Tupelo walked to Whyte's elbow. "The train can't be seen, Mr. Whyte," he said quietly.

Whyte looked down at him in utter disbelief. "You heard it yourself. It passed right below—"

"Can we go to the car, Mr. Whyte?" Tupelo asked. "I think we ought to talk a little."

Whyte nodded dumbly, then turned to the policeman and the others who had been watching at the lower level. "You really didn't see it?" he begged them.

"We heard it," the policeman answered. "It passed up here, going that way, I think," and he gestured with his thumb.

"Get back downstairs, Maloney," one of the policemen with Whyte commanded. Maloney scratched his head, turned, and disappeared below. The two other men followed him. Tupelo led the original group to the car beside the station platform. They went in and took seats, silently. Then they all watched the mathematician and waited.

"You didn't call me down here tonight just to tell me you'd found the missing train," Tupelo began, looking at Whyte. "Has this sort of thing happened before?"

Whyte squirmed in his seat and exchanged glances with the chief engineer. "Not exactly like this," he said, evasively, "but there have been some funny things."

"Like what?" Tupelo snapped.

"Well, like the red lights. The watchers near Kendall found a red light at the same time we hit the one near South Station."

"Go on."

"Mr. Sweeney called me from Forest Hills at Park Street Under. He heard the train there just two minutes after we heard it at the Copley junction. Twenty-eight track miles away."

"As a matter of fact, Dr. Tupelo," Wilson broke in, "several dozen men have seen lights go red, or have heard the train, or both, inside of the last four hours. The thing acts as though it can be in several places at once."

"It can," Tupelo said.

"We keep getting reports of watchers seeing the thing," the engineer added. "Well, not exactly seeing it, either, but everything except that. Sometimes at two or even three places, far apart, at the same time. It's sure to be on the tracks. Maybe the cars are uncoupled."

"Are you really sure it's on the tracks, Mr. Kennedy?" Tupelo asked.

"Positive," the engineer said. "The dynamometers at the power house show that it's drawing power. It's been drawing power all night. So at 3:30 we broke the circuits. Cut the power."

"What happened?"

"Nothing," Whyte answered. "Nothing at all. The power was off for twenty minutes. During that time, not one of the two hundred fifty men in the tunnels saw a red light or heard a train. But the power wasn't on for five minutes before we had two reports again—one from Arlington, the other from Egleston."

There was a long silence after Whyte finished speaking. In the tunnel below, one man could be heard calling something to another. Tupelo looked at his watch. The time was 5:20.

"In short, Dr. Tupelo," the general manager finally said, "we are compelled to admit that there may be something in your theory." The others nodded agreement.

"Thank you, gentlemen," Tupelo said.

The physician cleared his throat. "Now about the passengers," he began. "Have you any idea what—?"

"None," Tupelo interrupted.

"What should we do, Dr. Tupelo?" the mayor's representative asked.

"I don't know. What can you do?"

"As I understand it from Mr. Whyte," Wilson continued,

"the train has . . . well, it has jumped into another dimension. It isn't really on the System at all. It's just gone. Is that right?"

"In a manner of speaking."

"And this . . . er . . . peculiar behavior has resulted from certain mathematical properties associated with the new Boylston shuttle?"

"Correct."

"And there is nothing we can do to bring the train back to . . . uh . . . this dimension?'

"I know of nothing."

Wilson took the bit in his teeth. "In this case, gentlemen," he said, "our course is clear. First, we must close off the new shuttle, so this fantastic thing can never happen again. Then, since the missing train is really gone, in spite of all these red lights and noises, we can resume normal operation of the System. At least there will be no danger of collision—which has worried you so much, Whyte. As for the missing train and the people on it—" He gestured them into infinity. "Do you agree, Dr. Tupelo?" he asked the mathematician.

Tupelo shook his head slowly. "Not entirely, Mr. Wilson," he responded. "Now, please keep in mind that I don't fully comprehend what has happened. It's unfortunate that you won't find anybody who can give a good explanation. The one man who might have done so is Professor Turnbull, of Tech, and he was on the train. But in any case, you will want to check my conclusions against those of some competent topologists. I can put you in touch with several.

"Now, with regard to the recovery of the missing train, I can say that I think this is not hopeless. There is a finite probability, as I see it, that the train will eventually pass from the nonspatial part of the network, which it now occupies, back to the spatial part. Since the nonspatial part is wholly inaccessible, there is unfortunately nothing we can do to bring about this transition, or even to predict when or how it will occur. But the possibility of the transition will vanish if the Boylston shuttle is taken out. It is just this section of the track that gives the network its essential singularities. If the singularities are removed, the train can never reappear. Is this clear?"

It was not clear, of course, but the seven listening men nodded agreement. Tupelo continued.

"As for the continued operation of the System while the missing train is in the nonspatial part of the network, I can only give you the facts as I see them and leave to your judgment the difficult decision to be drawn from them. The transition back to the spatial part is unpredictable, as I have already told you. There is no way to know when it will occur, or where. In particular, there is a fifty percent probability that, if and when the train reappears, it will be running on the wrong track. Then there will be a collision, of course."

The engineer asked: "To rule out this possibility, Dr. Tupelo, couldn't we leave the Boylston shuttle open, but send no trains through it? Then, when the missing train reappears on the shuttle, it cannot meet another train."

"That precaution would be ineffective, Mr. Kennedy," Tupelo answered. "You see, the train can reappear anywhere on the System. It is true that the System owes its toplogical complexity to the new shuttle. But, with the shuttle in the System, it is now the whole System that possesses infinite connectivity. In other words, the relevant topological property is a property *derived* from the shuttle, but *belonging* to the whole System. Remember that the train made its first transition at a point between Park and Kendall, more than three miles away from the shuttle.

"There is one question more you will want answered. If you decide to go on operating the System, with the Boylston shuttle left in until the train reappears, can this happen again, to another train? I am not certain of the answer, but I think it is: No. I believe an exclusion principle operates here, such that only one train at a time can occupy the nonspatial network."

The physician rose from his seat. "Dr. Tupelo," he began, timorously, "when the train does reappear, will the passengers—?"

"I don't know about the people on the train," Tupelo cut in. "The topological theory does not consider such matters." He looked quickly at each of the seven tired, querulous faces before him. "I am sorry, gentlemen," he added, somewhat more gently. "I simply do not know." To Whyte, he added: "I think I can be of no more help tonight. You know where to reach me." And, turning on his heel, he left the car and climbed the stairs. He found dawn spilling over the street, dissolving the shadows of night.

That impromptu conference in a lonely subway car was never reported in the papers. Nor were the full results of the night-long vigil over the dark and twisted tunnels. During the week that followed, Tupelo participated in four more formal conferences with Kelvin Whyte and certain city officials. At two of these, other topologists were present. Ornstein was imported to Boston from Philadelphia, Kashta from Chicago, and Michaelis from Los Angeles. The mathematicians were unable to reach a concensus. None of the three would fully endorse Tupelo's conclusions, although Kashta indicated that there *might* be something to them. Ornstein averred that a finite network could not possess infinite connectivity, although he could not prove this proposition and could not actually calculate the connectivity of the System. Michaelis expressed his opinion that the affair was a hoax and had nothing whatever to do with the toplogy of the System. He insisted that if the train could not be found on the System then the System must be open, or at least must once have been open.

But the more deeply Tupelo analyzed the problem, the more fully he was convinced of the essential correctness of his first analysis. From the point of view of topology, the System soon suggested whole families of multiple-valued networks, each with an infinite number of infinite discontinuities. But a definite discussion of these new spatio-hyperspatial networks somehow eluded him. He gave the subject his full attention for only a week. Then his other duties compelled him to lay the analysis aside. He resolved to go back to the problem later in the spring, after courses were over.

Meanwhile, the System was operated as though nothing untoward had happened. The general manager and the mayor's representative had somehow managed to forget the night of the search, or at least to reinterpret what they had seen and not seen. The newspapers and the public at large speculated wildly, and they kept continuing pressure on Whyte. A number of suits were filed against the System on behalf of persons who had lost a relative. The State stepped into the affair and prepared its own thorough investigation. Recriminations were sounded in the halls of Congress. A garbled version of Tupelo's theory eventually found its way into the press. He ignored it, and it was soon forgotten.

The weeks passed, and then a month. The State's investigation was completed. The newspaper stories moved from the first page to the second; to the twenty-third; and then stopped. The missing persons did not return. In the large, they were no longer missed.

One day in mid-April, Tupelo traveled by subway again, from Charles Street to Harvard. He sat stiffly in the front of the first car, and watched the tracks and gray tunnel walls hurl themselves at the train. Twice the train stopped for a red light, and Tupelo found himself wondering whether the other train was really just ahead, or just beyond space. He half-hoped, out of curiosity, that his exclusion principle was wrong, that the train might make the transition. But he arrived at Harvard on time. Only he among the passengers had found the trip exciting.

The next week he made another trip by subway, and again the next. As experiments, they were unsuccessful, and much less tense than the first ride in mid-April. Tupelo began to doubt his own analysis. Sometime in May, he reverted to the practice of commuting by subway between his Beacon Hill apartment and his office at Harvard. His mind stopped racing down the knotted gray caverns ahead of the train. He read the morning newspaper, or the abstracts in *Revies of Modern Mathematics*.

Then there was one morning when he looked up from the newspaper and sensed something. He pushed panic back on its stiff, quivering spring, and looked quickly out the window at his right. The lights of the car showed the black and gray lines of wall-spots streaking by. The tracks ground out their familiar steely dissonance. The train rounded a curve and crossed a junction that he remembered. Swiftly, he recalled boarding the train at Charles, noting the girl on the ice-carnival poster at Kendall, meeting the southbound train going into Central.

He looked at the man sitting beside him, with a lunch pail on his lap. The other seats were filled, and there were a dozen or so straphangers. A mealy-faced youth near the front door smoked a cigarette, in violation of the rules. Two girls behind him across the aisle were discussing a club meeting. In the seat ahead, a young woman was scolding her little son. The man on the aisle, in the seat ahead of that, was reading the paper. The Transit-Ad above him extolled Florida oranges.

He looked again at the man two seats ahead and fought down the terror within. He studied that man. What was it? Brunet, graying hair; a roundish head; wan complexion; rather flat features; a thick neck, with the hairline a little low, a little ragged; a gray, pin-stripe suit. While Tupelo watched, the man waved a fly away from his left ear. He swayed a little with the train. His newspaper was folded vertically down the middle. His *newspaper*! It was last March's!

Tupelo's eyes swiveled to the man beside him. Below his lunch pail was a paper. Today's. He turned in his seat and looked behind him. A young man held the *Transcript* open to the sports pages. The date was March 4th. Tupelo's eyes raced up and down the aisle. There were a dozen passengers carrying papers ten weeks old.

Tupelo lunged out of his seat. The man on the aisle muttered a curse as the mathematician crowded in front of him. He crossed the aisle in a bound and pulled the cord above the windows. The brakes sawed and screeched at the tracks, and the train ground to a stop. The startled passengers eyed Tupelo with hostility. At the rear of the car, the door flew open and a tall, thin man in a blue uniform burst in. Tupelo spoke first.

"Mr. Dorkin?" he called, vehemently.

The conductor stopped short and groped for words.

"There's been a serious accident, Dorkin," Tupelo said, loudly, to carry over the rising swell of protest from the passengers. "Get Gallagher back here right away!"

Dorkin reached up and pulled the cord four times. "What happened?" he asked.

Tupelo ignored the question, and asked one of his own. "Where have you been, Dorkin?"

The conductor's face was blank. "In the next car, but—"

Tupelo cut him off. He glanced at his watch, then shouted at the passengers. "It's ten minutes to nine on May 17th!"

The announcement stilled the rising clamor for a moment. The passengers exchanged bewildered glances.

"Look at your newspapers!" Tupelo shouted. "Your newspapers!"

The passengers began to buzz. As they discovered each other's papers, the voices rose. Tupelo took Dorkin's arm and led him to the rear of the car. "What time is it?" he asked.

"8:21," Dorkin said, looking at his watch.

"Open the door," said Tupelo, motioning ahead. "Let me out. Where's the phone?"

Dorkin followed Tupelo's directions. He pointed to a niche in the tunnel wall a hundred yards ahead. Tupelo vaulted to the ground and raced down the narrow lane between the cars and the wall. "Central Traffic!" he barked at the operator. He waited a few seconds, and saw that a train had stopped at the red signal behind his train. Flashlights were advancing down the tunnel. He saw Gallagher's legs running down the tunnel on the other side of 86. "Get me Whyte!" he commanded, when Central Traffic answered. "Emergency!"

There was a delay. He heard voices rising from the train beside him. The sound was mixed—anger, fear, hysteria.

"Hello!" he shouted. "Hello! Emergency! Get me Whyte!"

"I'll take it," a man's voice said at the other end of the line. "Whyte's busy!"

"Number 86 is back," Tupelo called. "Between Central and Harvard now. Don't know when it made the jump. I caught it at Charles ten minutes ago, and didn't notice it till a minute ago."

The man at the other end gulped hard enough to carry over the telephone. "The passengers?" he croaked.

"All right, the ones that are left," Tupelo said. "Some must have got off already at Kendall and Central."

"Where have they been?"

Tupelo dropped the receiver from his ear and stared at it, his mouth wide open. Then he slammed the receiver onto the hook and ran back to the open door.

Eventually, order was restored, and within a half hour the train proceeded to Harvard. At the station, the police took all passengers into protective custody. Whyte himself arrived at Harvard before the train did. Tupelo found him on the platform.

Whyte motioned weakly towards the passengers. "They're really all right?" he asked.

"Perfectly," said Tupelo. "Don't know they've been gone."

"Any sign of Professor Turnbull?" asked the general manger.

"I didn't see him. He probably got off at Kendall, as usual."

"Too bad," said Whyte. "I'd like to see him!"

"So would I!" Tupelo answered. "By the way, now is the time to close the Boylston shuttle."

"Now is too late," Whyte said. "Train 143 vanished twenty-five minutes ago between Egleston and Dorchester."

Tupelo stared past Whyte, and down and down the tracks.

"We've got to find Turnbull," Whyte said.

Tupelo looked at Whyte and smiled thinly.

"Do you really think Turnbull got off this train at Kendall?" he asked.

"Of course!" answered Whyte. "Where else?"

PROCESS

A. E. van Vogt

THE MAGAZINE OF FANTASY AND SCIENCE FICTION
December

"Process" is not a typical van Vogt story. Indeed, it reminds one of the old British school of rich, evocative, descriptive prose, the kind found in the novels of John Wyndham. But typical or not, it remains one of the two or three finest stories about vegetable intelligence ever written.

—M.H.G.

Quite right, Marty, "Process" is not van Vogtian at all.
What I like best about it is the kind of double-vision you get and how skillfully van Vogt manages to concentrate on one view until you finally (and surprisingly) find yourself with another.

—I.A.

In the bright light of that far sun, the forest breathed and had its being. It was aware of the ship that had come down through the thin mists of the upper air. But its automatic hostility to the alien thing was not immediately accompanied by alarm.

For tens of thousands of square miles, its roots entwined under the ground, and its millions of tree tops swayed gently in a thousand idle breezes. And beyond, spreading over the hills and the mountains, and along almost endless sea coast were other forests as strong and as powerful as itself.

From time immemorial the forest had guarded the land from a dimly understood danger. What that danger was it began now slowly to remember. It was from ships like this, that descended from the sky. The forest could not recall clearly how it had defended itself in the past, but it did remember tensely that defense had been necessary.

Even as it grew more and more aware of the ship coasting along in the gray-red sky above, its leaves whispered a timeless tale of battles fought and won. Thoughts flowed their slow course down the channels of vibration, and the stately limbs of tens of thousands of trees trembled ever so slightly.

The vastness of that tremor, affecting as it did all the trees, gradually created a sound and a pressure. At first it was almost impalpable, like a breeze wafting through an evergreen glen. But it grew stronger.

It acquired substance. The sound became all-enveloping. And the whole forest stood there vibrating its hostility, waiting for the thing in the sky to come nearer.

It had not long to wait.

The ship swung down from its lane. Its speed, now that it was close to the ground, was greater than it had first seemed. And it was bigger. It loomed gigantic over the near trees, and swung down lower, careless of the tree tops. Brush crackled, limbs broke, and entire trees were brushed aside as if they were meaningless and weightless and without strength.

Down came the ship, cutting its own path through a forest that groaned and shrieked with its passage. It settled heavily into the ground two miles after it first touched a tree. Behind, the swath of broken trees quivered and pulsed in the light of the sun, a straight path of destruction which—the forest suddenly remembered—was exactly what had happened in the past.

It began to pull clear of the anguished parts. It drew out its juices, and ceased vibrating in the affected areas. Later, it would send new growth to replace what had been destroyed, but now it accepted the partial death it had suffered. It knew fear.

It was a fear tinged with anger. It felt the ship lying on crushed trees, on a part of itself that was not yet dead. It felt the coldness and the hardness of steel walls, and the fear and the anger increased.

A whisper of thought pulsed along the vibration channels. Wait, it said, there is a memory in me. A memory of long ago when other such ships as this came.

The memory refused to clarify. Tense but uncertain, the forest prepared to make its first attack. It began to grow around the ship.

Long ago it had discovered the power of growth that was possible to it. There was a time when it had not been as large as it was now. And then, one day, it became aware that it was coming near another forest like itself.

The two masses of growing wood, the two colossi of intertwined roots approached each other warily, slowly, in amazement, in a startled but cautious wonder that a similar life form should actually have existed all this time. Approached, touched—and fought for years.

During that prolonged struggle nearly all growth in the central portions stopped. Trees ceased to develop new branches. The leaves, by necessity, grew hardier, and performed their functions for much longer periods. Roots developed slowly. The entire available strength of the forest was concentrated in the processes of defense and attack.

Walls of trees sprang up overnight. Enormous roots tunneled into the ground for miles straight down, breaking through rock and metal, building a barrier of living wood against the encroaching growth of the strange forest. On the surface, the barriers thickened to a mile or more of trees that stood almost bole to bole. And, on that basis, the great battle finally petered out. The forest accepted the obstacle created by its enemy.

Later, it fought to a similar standstill a second forest which attacked it from another direction.

The limits of demarcation became as natural as the great salt sea to the south, or the icy cold of mountain tops that were frozen the year round.

As it had in battle with the two other forests, *the* forest concentrated its entire strength against the encroaching ship. Trees shot up at the rate of a foot every few minutes. Creepers climbed the trees, and flung themselves over the top of the vessel. The countless strands of it raced over the metal, and then twined themselves around the trees on the far side. The roots of those trees dug deeper into the ground, and anchored in rock strata heavier than any ship ever built. The tree boles thickened, and the creepers widened till they were enormous cables.

As the light of that first day faded into twilight, the ship was buried under thousands of tons of wood, and hidden in foliage so thick that nothing of it was visible.

The time had come for the final destructive action.

Shortly after dark, tiny roots began to fumble over the underside of the ship. They were infinitesimally small; so small that in the initial stages they were no more than a few dozens of atoms in diameter; so small that the apparently solid metal seemed almost emptiness to them; so incredibly small that they penetrated the hard steel effortlessly.

It was at that time, almost as if it had been waiting for this stage, that the ship took counteraction. The metal grew warm, then hot, and then cherry red. That was all that was needed. The tiny roots shriveled, and died. The larger roots near the metal burned slowly as the searing heat reached them.

Above the surface, other violence began. Flame darted from a hundred orifices of the ship's surface. First the creepers, then the trees began to burn. It was no flare-up of uncontrollable fire, no fierce conflagration leaping from tree to tree in irresistible fury. Long ago, the forest had learned to control fires started by lightning or spontaneous combustion. It was a matter of sending sap to the affected area. The greener the tree, the more sap that permeated it, then the hotter the fire would have to be.

The forest could not immediately remember ever having encountered a fire that could make inroads against a line of trees that oozed a sticky wetness from every crevice of their bark.

But this fire could. It was different. It was not only flame; it was energy. It did not feed off the wood; it was fed by an energy within itself.

That fact at last brought the associational memory to the forest. It was a sharp and unmistakable remembrance of what it had done long ago to rid itself and its planet of a ship just like this.

It began to withdraw from the vicinity of the ship. It abandoned the framework of wood and shrubbery with which it had sought to imprison the alien structure. As the precious sap was sucked back into trees that would now form a second line of defense, the flames grew brighter, and the fire waxed so brilliant that the whole scene was bathed in an eerie glow.

It was some time before the forest realized that the fire beams were no longer flaming out from the ship, and that what incandescence and smoke remained came from normally burning wood.

That, too, was according to its memory of what had happened—before.

Frantically though reluctantly the forest initiated what it now realized was the only method of ridding itself of the intruder. Frantically because it was hideously aware that the flame from the ship could destroy entire forests. And reluctantly because the method of defense involved its suffering the burns of energy only slightly less violent than those that had flared from the machine.

Tens of thousands of roots grew toward rock and soil formations that they had carefully avoided since the last ship had come. In spite of the need for haste, the process itself was slow. Tiny roots, quivering with unpleasant anticipation, forced themselves into the remote, buried ore beds, and by an intricate process of osmosis drew grains of pure metal from the impure natural stuff. The grains were almost as small as the roots that had earlier penetrated the steel walls of the ship, small enough to be borne along, suspended in sap, through a maze of larger roots.

Soon there were thousands of grains moving along the channels, then millions. And, though each was tiny in itself, the soil where they were discharged soon sparkled in the light of the dying fire. As the sun of that world reared up over the horizon, the silvery gleam showed a hundred feet wide all around the ship.

It was shortly after noon that the machine showed awareness of what was happening. A dozen hatches opened, and objects floated out of them. They came down to the ground, and began to skim up the silvery stuff with nozzled things that sucked up the fine dust in a steady fashion. They worked with great caution; but an hour before darkness set in again, they had scooped up more than twelve tons of the thinly spread Uranium 235.

As night fell, all the two-legged things vanished inside the vessel. The hatches closed. The long torpedo-shape floated lightly upward, and sped to the higher heavens where the sun still shone.

The first awareness of the situation came to the forest as the roots deep under the ship reported a sudden lessening of pressure. It was several hours before it decided that the enemy had actually been driven off. And several more hours went by before it realized that the uranium dust still on the scene would have to be removed. The rays spread too far afield.

The accident that occurred then took place for a very simple reason. The forest had taken the radioactive substance out of rock. To get rid of it, it need merely put it back into the nearest rock beds, particularly the kind of rock that absorbed the radioactivity. To the forest the situation seemed as obvious as that.

An hour after it began to carry out the plan, the explosion mushroomed toward outer space.

It was vast beyond all the capacity of the forest to understand. It neither saw nor heard that collossal shape of death. What it did experience was enough. A hurricane leveled square miles of trees. The blast of heat and radiation started fires that took hours to put out.

Fear departed slowly, as it remembered that this too had happened before. Sharper by far than the memory was the vision of the possibilities of what had happened . . . the nature of the opportunity.

Shortly after dawn the following morning, it launched its attack. Its victim was the forest which—according to its faulty recollection—had originally invaded its territory.

Along the entire front which separated the two colossi, small atomic explosions erupted. The solid barrier of trees which was the other forest's outer defense went down before blast after blast of irresistible energy.

The enemy, reacting normally, brought up its reserve of sap. When it was fully committed to the gigantic task of growing a new barrier, the bombs started to go off again. The resulting explosions destroyed its main sap supply. And, since it did not understand what was happening, it was lost from that moment.

Into the no-man's-land where the bombs had gone off, the attacking forest rushed an endless supply of roots. Wherever resistance built up, there an atomic bomb went off. Shortly after the next noon, a titanic explosion destroyed the sensitive central trees—and the battle was over.

It took months for the forest to grow into the territory of its defeated enemy, to squeeze out the other's dying roots, to nudge over trees that now had no defense, and to put itself into full and unchallenged possession.

The moment the task was completed, it turned like a fury upon the forest on its other flank. Once more it attacked with atomic thunder, and with a hail of fire tried to overwhelm its opponent.

It was met by equal force. Exploding atoms!

For its knowledge had leaked across the barrier of intertwined roots which separated forests.

Almost, the two monsters destroyed each other. Each became a remnant, that started the painful process of regrowth. As the years passed, the memory of what had happened grew dim. Not that it mattered. Actually, the ships came at will. And somehow, even if the forest remembered, its atomic bombs would not go off in the presence of a ship.

The only thing that would drive away the ships was to surround each machine with a fine dust of radioactive stuff. Whereupon it would scoop up the material, and then hastily retreat.

Victory was always as simple as that.

THE MINDWORM

C. M. Kornbluth

WORLDS BEYOND
December

The figure of the vampire is one of the most powerful images in literature, and hundreds of stories have been written about these menacing creatures. However, the vampire is a supernatural monster, and therefore beyond the boundaries of this series. Or is he? What if there is a rational explanation for his existence?

Worlds Beyond *was a short-lived sf magazine (it lasted for three issues) of 1950–51 edited by Damon Knight that contained several excellent stories and a strong book review column by the editor. Poor sales killed what could have been an important addition to the small ranks of high-quality science fiction magazines.*

—M.H.G.

Of all the stories Cyril wrote, I think this was the one I found the most powerful. It really gave me a turn when I read it for the first time. In "The Mindworm" someone is different from everyone else, horribly different. Again I can't help but wonder if poor Cyril found himself different from everyone else, and if there seemed to him to be a horrible component to that.

—I.A.

The handsome j. g. and the pretty nurse held out against it as long as they reasonably could, but blue Pacific water, languid tropical nights, the low atoll dreaming on the horizon—and the complete absence of any other nice young people for company on the small, uncomfortable parts boat—did their work. On June 30th they watched through dark glasses as the dazzling thing burst over the fleet and atoll. Her manicured hand gripped his arm in excitement and terror. Unfelt radiation sleeted through their loins.

A storekeeper-third-class named Bielaski watched the young couple with more interest than he showed in Test Able. After all, he had twenty-five dollars riding on the nurse. That night he lost it to a chief bosun's mate who had backed the j. g.

In the course of time, the careless nurse was discharged under conditions other than honorable. The j. g., who didn't like to put things in writing, phoned her all the way from Manila to say it was a damned shame. When her gratitude gave way to specific inquiry, their overseas connection went bad and he had to hang up.

She had a child, a boy, turned it over to a foundling home, and vanished from his life into a series of good jobs and finally marriage.

The boy grew up stupid, puny and stubborn, greedy and miserable. To the home's hilarious young athletics director he suddenly said: "You hate me. You think I make the rest of the boys look bad."

The athletics director blustered and laughed, and later told the doctor over coffee: "I watch myself around the kids. They're sharp—they catch a look or a gesture and it's like a blow in the face to them, I know that, so I watch myself. So how did he know?"

The doctor told the boy: "Three pounds more this month isn't bad, but how about you pitch in and clean up your plate *every* day? Can't live on meat and water; those vegetables make you big and strong."

The boy said; "What's 'neurasthenic' mean?"

The doctor later said to the director: "It made my flesh creep. I was looking at his little splindling body and dishing out the old pep talk about growing big and strong, and inside my head I was thinking 'we'd call him neurasthenic in the old days' and then out he popped with it. What should we do? Should we do anything? Maybe it'll go away. I don't know anything about these things. I don't know whether anybody does."

"Reads minds, does he?" asked the director. *Be damned if he's going to read my mind about Schultz Meat Market's ten percent.* "Doctor, I think I'm going to take my vacation a little early this year. Has anybody shown any interest in adopting the child?"

"Not him. He wasn't a baby doll when we got him, and at present he's an exceptionally unattractive-looking kid. You know how people don't give a damn about anything but their looks."

"*Some* couples would take anything, or so they tell me."

"Unapproved for foster-parenthood, you mean?"

"Red tape and arbitrary classifications sometimes limit us too severely in our adoptions."

"If you're going to wish him on some screwball couple that the courts turned down as unfit, I want no part of it."

"You don't have to have any part of it, doctor. By the way, which dorm does he sleep in?"

"West," grunted the doctor, leaving the office.

The director called a few friends—a judge, a couple the judge referred him to, a court clerk. Then he left by way of the east wing of the building.

The boy survived three months with the Berrymans. Hard-drinking Mimi alternately caressed and shrieked at him; Edward W. tried to be a good scout and just gradually lost interest, looking clean through him. He hit the road in June and got by with it for a while. He wore a Boy Scout uniform, and Boy Scouts can turn up anywhere, any time. The money he had taken with him lasted a month. When the last penny of the last dollar was three days spent, he was adrift on a Nebraska prairie. He had walked out of the last small town because the constable was beginning to wonder what on earth he was hanging around for and who he belonged to. The town was miles behind on the two-lane highway; the infrequent cars did not stop.

One of Nebraska's "rivers," a dry bed at this time of year, lay ahead, spanned by a railroad culvert. There were some men in its shade, and he was hungry.

They were ugly, dirty men, and their thoughts were muddled and stupid. They called him "Shorty" and gave him a little dirty bread and some stinking sardines from a can. The thoughts of one of them became less muddled and uglier. He talked to the rest out of the boy's hearing, and they whooped with laughter. The boy got ready to run, but his legs wouldn't hold him up.

He could read the thoughts of the men quite clearly as they

headed for him. Outrage, fear, and disgust blended in him and somehow turned inside-out and one of the men was dead on the dry ground, grasshoppers vaulting onto his flannel shirt, the others backing away, frightened now, not frightening.

He wasn't hungry any more; he felt quite comfortable and satisfied. He got up and headed for the other men, who ran. The rearmost of them was thinking *Jeez he folded up the evil eye we was only gonna—*

Again the boy let the thoughts flow into his head and again he flipped his own thoughts around them; it was quite easy to do. It was different—this man's terror from the other's lustful anticipation. But both had their points . . .

At his leisure, he robbed the bodies of three dollars and twenty-four cents.

Thereafter his fame preceded him like a death wind. Two years on the road and he had his growth and his fill of the dull and stupid minds he met there. He moved to northern cities, a year here, a year there, quiet, unobtrusive, prudent, an epicure.

Sebastian Long woke suddenly, with something on his mind. As night fog cleared away he remembered, happily. Today he started the Demeter Bowl! At last there was time, at last there was money—six hundred and twenty-three dollars in the bank. He had packed and shipped the three dozen cocktail glasses last night, engraved with Mrs. Klausman's initials—his last commercial order for as many months as the Bowl would take.

He shifted from nightshirt to denims, gulped coffee, boiled an egg but was too excited to eat it. He went to the front of his shop-workroom-apartment, checked the lock, waved at neighbors' children on their way to school, and ceremoniously set a sign in the cluttered window.

It said: "NO COMMERCIAL ORDERS TAKEN UNTIL FURTHER NOTICE."

From a closet he tenderly carried a shrouded object that made a double armful and laid it on his workbench. Unshrouded, it was a glass bowl—*what* a glass bowl! The clearest Swedish lead glass, the purest lines he had ever seen, his secret treasure since the crazy day he had bought it, long ago, for six months' earnings. His wife had given him hell for that until the day she died. From the closet he brought a portfolio filled with sketches and designs dating back to the day he had bought the bowl. He smiled over the first, excitedly scrawled—a florid, rococo conception, unsuited to the classicism of the lines and the serenity of the perfect glass.

Through many years and hundreds of sketches he had refined his conception to the point where it was, he humbly felt, not unsuited to the medium. A strongly-molded Demeter was to dominate the piece, and a matron as serene as the glass, and all the fruits of the earth would flow from her gravely outstretched arms.

Suddenly and surely, he began to work. With a candle he thinly smoked an oval area on the outside of the bowl. Two steady fingers clipped the Demeter drawing against the carbon black; a hair-fine needle in his other hand traced her lines. When the transfer of the design was done, Sebastian Long readied his lathe. He fitted a small copper wheel, slightly worn as he liked them, into the chuck and with his fingers charged it with the finest rouge from Rouen. He took an ashtray cracked in delivery and held it against the spinning disk. It bit in smoothly, with the *wiping* feel to it that was exactly right.

Holding out his hands, seeing that the fingers did not tremble with excitement, he eased the great bowl to the lathe and was about to make the first tiny cut of the millions that would go into the masterpiece.

Somebody knocked on his door and rattled the doorknob.

Sebastian Long did not move or look toward the door. Soon the busybody would read the sign and go away. But the pounding and the rattling of the knob went on. He eased down the bowl and angrily went to the window, picked up the sign, and shook it at whoever it was—he couldn't make out the face very well. But the idiot wouldn't go away.

The engraver unlocked the door, opened it a bit, and snapped: "The shop is closed. I shall not be taking any orders for several months. Please don't bother me now."

"It's about the Demeter Bowl," said the intruder.

Sebastian Long stared at him. "What the devil do you know about my Demeter Bowl?" He saw the man was a stranger, undersized by a little, middle-aged . . .

"Just let me in please," urged the man. "It's important. Please!"

"I don't know what you're talking about," said the engraver. "But what do you know about my Demeter Bowl?" He hooked his thumbs pugnaciously over the waistband of his denims and glowered at the stranger. The stranger promptly took advantage of his hand being removed from the door and glided in.

Sebastian Long thought briefly that it might be a nightmare as the man darted quickly about his shop, picking up a graver and throwing it down, picking up a wire scratch-wheel and throwing it down. "Here, you!" he roared, as the stranger picked up a crescent wrench which he did not throw down.

As Long started for him, the stranger darted to the workbench and brought the crescent wrench down shatteringly on the bowl.

Sebastian Long's heart was bursting with sorrow and rage; such a storm of emotions as he never had known thundered through him. Paralyzed, he saw the stranger smile with anticipation.

The engraver's legs folded under him and he fell to the floor, drained and dead.

The Mindworm, locked in the bedroom of his brownstone front, smiled again, reminiscently.

Smiling, he checked the day on a wall calendar.

"Dolores!" yelled her mother in Spanish. "Are you going to pass the whole day in there?"

She had been practicing low-lidded, sexy half-smiles like Lauren Bacall in the bathroom mirror. She stormed out and yelled in English: "I don't know how many times I tell you not to call me that Spick name no more!"

"Dolly!" sneered her mother. "Dah-lee! When was there a Saint Dah-lee that you call yourself after, eh?"

The girl snarled a Spanish obscenity at her mother and ran down the tenement stairs. Jeez, she was gonna be late for sure!

Held up by a stream of traffic between her and her streetcar, she danced with impatience. Then the miracle happened. Just like in the movies, a big convertible pulled up before her and its lounging driver said, opening the door: "You seem to be in a hurry. Could I drop you somewhere?"

Dazed at the sudden realization of a hundred daydreams, she did not fail to give the driver a low-lidded, sexy smile as she said: "Why, *thanks!*" and climbed in. He wasn't no Cary Grant, but he had all his hair . . . kind of small, but so was she . . . and jeez, the convertible had *leopard-skin seat covers!*

The car was in the stream of traffic, purring down the avenue. "It's a lovely day," she said. "Really too nice to work."

The driver smiled shyly, kind of like Jimmy Stewart but of

course not so tall, and said: "I feel like playing hooky myself. How would you like a spin down Long Island?"

"Be wonderful!" The convertible cut left on an odd-numbered street.

"Play hooky, you said. What do you do?"

"Advertising."

"Advertising!" Dolly wanted to kick herself for ever having doubted, for ever having thought in low, self-loathing moments that it wouldn't work out, that she'd marry a grocer or a mechanic and live forever after in a smelly tenement and grow old and sick and stooped. She felt vaguely in her happy daze that it might have been cuter, she might have accidentally pushed him into a pond or something, but this was cute enough. An advertising man, leopard-skin seat covers . . . what more could a girl with a sexy smile and a nice little figure want?

Speeding down the South Shore she learned that his name was Michael Brent, exactly as it ought to be. She wished she could tell him she was Jennifer Brown or one of those real cute names they had nowadays, but was reassured when he told her he thought Dolly Gonzalez was a beautiful name. He didn't, and she noticed the omission, add: "It's the most beautiful name I ever heard!" That, she comfortably thought as she settled herself against the cushions, would come later.

They stopped at Medford for lunch, a wonderful lunch in a little restaurant where you went down some steps and there were candles on the table. She called him "Michael" and he called her "Dolly." She learned that he liked dark girls and thought the stories in *True Story* really were true, and that he thought she was just tall enough, and that Greer Garson was wonderful, but not the way she was, and that he thought her dress was just wonderful.

They drove slowly after Medford, and Michael Brent did most of the talking. He had traveled all over the world. He had been in the war and wounded—just a flesh wound. He was thirty-eight, and had been married once, but she died. There were no children. He was alone in the world. He had nobody to share his town house in the 50's, his country place in Westchester, his lodge in the Maine woods. Every word sent the girl floating higher and higher on a tide of happiness; the signs were unmistakable.

When they reached Montauk Point, the last sandy bit of the continent before blue water and Europe, it was sunset, with a great wrinkled sheet of purple and rose stretching half across the sky and the first stars appearing above the dark horizon of the water.

The two of them walked from the parked car out onto the sand, alone, bathed in glorious Technicolor. Her heart was nearly bursting with joy as she heard Michael Brent say, his arms tightening around her: "Darling, will you marry me?"

"Oh, *yes*, Michael!" she breathed, dying.

The Mindworm, drowsing, suddenly felt the sharp sting of danger. He cast out through the great city, dragging tentacles of thought."

". . . die if she don't let me . . ."

". . . six an' six is twelve an' carry one an' three is four . . ."

". . . gobblegobble madre de dios perso soy gobblegobble . . ."

". . . parlay Domino an' Missab and shoot the roll on Duchess Peg in the feature . . ."

". . . melt resin add the silver chloride and dissolve in oil of lavender stand and decant and fire to cone zero twelve give you shimmering streaks of luster down the walls . . ."

". . . moiderin' square-headed gobblegobble tried ta poke his eye out wassamatta witta ref . . ."

". . . O God I am most heartily sorry I have offended thee in . . ."

". . . talk like a commie . . ."

". . . gobblegobblegobble two dolla twenny-fi' sense gobble . . ."

". . . just a nip and fill it up with water and brush my teeth . . ."

". . . really know I'm God but fear to confess their sins . . ."

". . . Dirty lousy rock-headed claw-handed paddle-footed goggle-eyed snot-nosed hunch-backed feeble-minded pot-bellied son of . . ."

". . . write on the wall alfie is a stunkur and then . . ."

". . . thinks I believe it's a television set but I know he's got a bomb in there but who can I tell who can help so alone . . ."

". . . gabble was ich weiss nicht gabble geh bei Broadvay gabble . . ."

". . . habt mein daughter Rosie such a fella gobblegobble . . ."

". . . wonder if that's one didn't look back . . ."

". . . seen with her in the Medford restaurant . . ."

The Mindworm struck into that thought.

". . . not a mark on her but the M. E.'s have been wrong

before and heart failure don't mean a thing anyway try to talk to her old lady authorize an autopsy get Pancho little guy talks Spanish be best . . ."

The Mindworm knew he would have to be moving again—soon. He was sorry; some of the thoughts he had tapped indicated good . . . hunting?

Regretfully, he again dragged his net:

". . . with chartreuse drinks I mean drapes could use a drink come to think of it . . ."

". . . reep-beep-reep-beep reepiddy-beepiddy-beep bop man wadda beat . . ."

"$\sum_{r=1+1}^{n} \varphi(a_x, a_r) - \sum_{s=1}^{l} \varphi(a_x, a_s)$. *What the Hell was that?"*

The Mindworn withdrew, in frantic haste. The intelligence was massive, its overtones those of a vigorous adult. He had learned from certain dangerous children that there was a peril of a leveling flow. Shaken and scared, he contemplated traveling. He would need more than that wretched girl had supplied, and it would not be epicurean. There would be no time to find individuals at a ripe emotional crisis, or goad them to one. It would be plain—munching. The Mindworm drank a glass of water, also necessary to his metabolism.

EIGHT FOUND DEAD IN UPTOWN MOVIE; "MOLESTER" SOUGHT

Eight persons, including three women, were found dead Wednesday night of unknown causes in widely separated seats in the balcony of the Odeon Theater at 117th St. and Broadway. Police are seeking a man described by the balcony usher, Michael Fenelly, 18, as "acting like a woman-molester."

Fenelly discovered the first of the fatalities after seeing the man "moving from one empty seat to another several times." He went to ask a woman in a seat next to one the man had just vacated whether he had annoyed her. She was dead.

Almost at once, a scream rang out. In another part of the balcony Mrs. Sadie Rabinowitz, 40, uttered the cry when another victim toppled from his seat next to her.

Theater manager I. J. Marcusohn stopped the show and turned on the house lights. He tried to instruct his staff to keep the audience from leaving before the police arrived. He failed to get word to them in time, however, and most of the audience was gone when a detail from the 24th Pct. and an ambulance from Harlem hospital took over at the scene of the tragedy.

The Medical Examiner's office has not yet made a report as to the causes of death. A spokesman said the victims showed no signs of poisoning or violence. He added that it "was inconceivable that it could be a coincidence."

Lt. John Braidwood of the 24th Pct, said of the alleged molester: "We got a fair description of him and naturally we will try to bring him in for questioning."

Clickety-click, clickety-click, clickety-click sang the rails as the Mindworm drowsed in his coach seat.

Some people were walking forward from the diner. One was thinking: "Different-looking fellow. (a) he's aberrant. (b) he's nonaberrant and ill. Cancel (b)-respiration normal, skin smooth and healthy, no tremor of limbs, well-groomed. Is aberrant (1) trivially. (2) significantly. Cancel (1)—displayed no involuntary interest when . . . odd! *Running* for the washroom! Unexpected because (a) neat grooming indicates amour propre inconsistent with amusing others; (b) evident health inconsistent with . . ." It had taken one second, was fully detailed.

The Mindworm, locked in the toilet of the coach, wondered what the next stop was. He was getting off at it—not frightened, just carefully. Dodge them, keep dodging them and everything would be all right. Send out no mental taps until the train was far away and everything would be all right.

He got off at a West Virginia coal and iron town surrounded by ruined mountains and filled with the offscourings of Eastern Europe. Serbs, Albanians, Croats, Hungarians, Slovenes, Bulgarians, and all possible combinations and permutations thereof. He walked slowly from the smoke-stained, brownstone passenger station. The train had roared on its way.

". . . ain' no gemmum that's fo sho', fi-cen' tip fo' a good shine lak ah give um . . ."

". . . dumb bassar don't know how to make out a billa lading yet he ain't never gonna know so fire him get it over with . . ."

". . . gabblegabblegabble . . ." Not a word he recognized in it.

". . . gobblegobble dat tam vooman I brek she neck . . ."

". . . gobble trink visky chin glassabeer gobblegobblegobble . . ."

". . . gobble trink visky chin glassabeer gobblegobblegobble . . ."

". . . gabblegabblegabble . . ."

". . . makes me so gobblegobble mad little no-good tramp no she ain' but I don' like no standup from no dame . . ."

A blond, square-headed boy fuming under a street light.

". . . out wit' Casey Oswiak I could kill that dumb bohunk alla time trine ta paw her . . ."

It was a possibility. The Mindworm drew near.

". . . stand me up for that gobblegobble bohunk I oughtta slap her inna mush like my ole man says . . ."

"Hello," said the Mindworm.

"Waddaya wan'?"

"Casey Oswiak told me to tell you not to wait up for your girl. He's taking her out tonight."

The blond boy's rage boiled into his face and shot from his eyes. He was about to swing when the Mindworm began to feed. It was like pheasant after chicken, venison after beef. The coarseness of the environment, or the ancient strain? The Mindworm wondered as he strolled down the street. A girl passed him:

". . . oh but he's gonna be mad like last time wish I came right away so jealous kinda nice but he might bust me one some day be nice to him tonight there he is lam'post leaning on it looks kinda funny gawd I hope he ain't drunk looks kinda funny sleeping sick or bozhe moi gabblegabblegabble . . ."

Her thoughts trailed into a foreign language of which the Mindworm knew not a word. After hysteria had gone she recalled, in the foreign language, that she had passed him.

The Mindworm, stimulated by the unfamiliar quality of the last feeding, determined to stay for some days. He checked in at a Main Street hotel.

Musing, he dragged his net:

". . . gobblegobblewhompyeargobblecheskygobblegabblechyesh . . ."

". . . take him down cellar beat the can off the damn chesky thief put the fear of god into him teach him can't bust into no boxcars in *mah* parta the caounty . . ."

". . . gabblegabble . . ."

". . . phone ole Mister Ryan in She-cawgo and he'll tell them three-card monte grifters who got the horse-room rights in this necka the woods by damn don't pay protection money for no protection . . ."

The Mindworm followed that one further; it sounded as though it could lead to some money if he wanted to stay in the town long enough.

The Eastern Europeans of the town, he mistakenly thought, were like the tramps and bums he had known and fed on during his years on the road—stupid and safe, safe and stupid, quite the same thing.

In the morning he found no mention of the square-headed boy's death in the town's paper and thought it had gone practically unnoticed. It had—by the paper, which was of, by, and for the coal and iron company and its native-American bosses and straw bosses. The other town, the one without a charter or police force, with only an imported weekly newspaper or two from the nearest city, noticed it. The other town had roots more than two thousand years deep, which are hard to pull up. But the Mindworn didn't know it was there.

He fed again that night, on a giddy young streetwalker in her room. He had astounded and delighted her with a fistful of ten-dollar bills before he began to gorge. Again the delightful difference from city-bred folk was there. . . .

Again in the morning he had been unnoticed, he thought. The chartered town, unwilling to admit that there were streetwalkers or that they were found dead, wiped the slate clean; its only member who really cared was the native-American cop on the beat who had collected weekly from the dead girl.

The other town, unknown to the Mindworm, buzzed with it. A delegation went to the other town's only public officer. Unfortunately he was young, American-trained, perhaps even ignorant about some important things. For what he told them was: "My children, that is foolish superstition. Go home."

The Mindworm, through the day, roiled the surface of the town proper by allowing himself to be roped into a poker game in a parlor of the hotel. He wasn't good at it, he didn't like it, and he quit with relief when he had cleaned six shifty-eyed, hard-drinking loafers out of about three hundred dollars. One of them went straight to the police station and accused the unknown of being a sharper. A humorous sergeant, the Mindworm was pleased to note, joshed the loafer out of his temper.

Nightfall again, hunger again . . .

He walked the streets of the town and found them empty. It was strange. The native-American citizens were out, tending bar, walking their beats, locking up their newspaper on the stones, collecting their rents, managing their movies—but where were the others? He cast his net:

". . . gobblegobblegobble whomp year gobble . . ."

". . . crazy old pollack mama of mine try to lock me in with Errol Flynn at the Majestic never know the difference if I sneak out the back . . ."

That was near. He crossed the street and it was nearer. He homed on the thought:

". . . jeez he's a hunka man like Stanley but he never looks at me that Vera Kowalik I'd like to kick her just once in the gobblegobblegobble crazy old mama won't be American so ashamed . . ."

It was half a block, no more, down a side street. Brick houses, two stories, with back yards on an alley. She was going out the back way.

How strangely quiet it was in the alley.

". . . ea-sy down them steps fix that damn board that's how she caught me last time what the hell are they all so scared of went to see Father Drugas won't talk bet somebody got it again that Vera Kowalik and her big . . ."

". . . gobble bozhe gobble whomp year gobble . . ."

She was closer; she was closer.

"All think I'm a kid show them who's a kid bet if Stanley caught me all alone out here in the alley dark and all he wouldn't think I was a kid that damn Vera Kowalik her folks don't think she's a kid . . ."

For all her bravado she was stark terrified when he said: "Hello."

"Who—who—who—?" she stammered.

Quick, before she screamed. Her terror was delightful.

Not too replete to be alert, he cast about, questing.

" . . . gobblegobblegobble whomp year."

The countless eyes of the other town, with more than two thousand years of experience in such things, had been following him. What he had sensed as a meaningless hash of noise was actually an impassioned outburst in a nearby darkened house.

"Fools! fools! Now he has taken a virgin! I said not to wait. What will we say to her mother?"

An old man with handlebar mustache and, in spite of the heat, his shirt sleeves decently rolled down and buttoned at the cuffs, evenly replied: "My heart in me died with hers, Casimir, but one must be sure. It would be a terrible thing to make a mistake in such an affair."

The weight of conservative elder opinion was with him. Other old men with mustaches, some perhaps remembering mistakes long ago, nodded and said: "A terrible thing. A terrible thing."

The Mindworm strolled back to his hotel and napped on the made bed briefly. A tingle of danger awakened him. Instantly he cast out:

". . . gobblegobble whompyear."

". . . whampyir."

"WAMPYIR!"

Close! Close and deadly!

The door of his room burst open, and mustached old men with their shirt sleeves rolled down and decently buttoned at the cuffs unhesitatingly marched in, their thoughts a turmoil of alien noises, foreign gibberish that he could not wrap his mind around, disconcerting, from every direction.

The sharpened stake was through his heart and the scythe blade through his throat before he could realize that he had not been the first of his kind; and that what clever people have not yet learned, some quite ordinary people have not yet entirely forgotten.

THE NEW REALITY

Charles L. Harness (1915–   )

THRILLING WONDER STORIES
December

Charles L. Harness worked as a mineral economist for the United States Bureau of Mines and since 1947 has been a patent attorney for several major American corporations. His science fiction output has been relatively scanty, but always interesting. He has produced four novels to date, all very much worth reading: Flight Into Yesterday *(1953, also known as* The Paradox Men), The Ring of Ritornel *(1968),* Wolfhead *(1978), and* The Catalyst *(1980). In addition, his intricate short novel,* The Rose *(published with other stories in book form in 1969), is a marvelous study of the relationship between science and art.*

The nature of reality is a theme that runs through much of his best work, as in "The New Reality," one of those remarkable before-their-time stories that would have fit perfectly in Michael Moorcock's New Worlds *magazine of the second half of the 1960s.*

—M.H.G.

I think that I can tell a Campbell story when I read one, and if ever a story has Campbell written all over it, it's "The New Reality." Yet it didn't appear in Astounding. *Perhaps John Campbell rejected it. In that case, how did it come to appear in* Thrilling Wonder Stories, *for if ever there was a story that was* not *a* TWS *story, this is it. In other words, I seem to be confronting a situation which is not according to my concept of reality, and "concept of reality" is exactly what the story is about.*

Let me make two points, however. Does the Earth change shape as our concepts change? Whose concepts? Greek philosophers finally became convinced the Earth was spherical. Did that make it spherical? How many believers were required? Is it majority vote? If so, it is possible that even today, more people consider the Earth to be flat than spherical. Would that mean the Earth is still flat?

And what about the single photon that can't make up its mind? Actually, this sort of thing is much under discussion by quantum theorists and very weird and paradoxical points are deduced, and there are some who even speculate that at every instant observers force a choice between realities. It's called "quantum weirdness," I think.

—I.A.

Prentiss crawled into the car, drew the extension connector from his concealed throat mike from its clip in his right sleeve, and plugged it into the ignition key socket.

After a moment he said, "Get me the Censor."

The seconds passed as he heard the click of forming circuits. Then: "E speaking."

"Prentiss, honey."

"Call me 'E,' Prentiss. What news?"

"I've met five classes under Professor Luce. He has a private lab. Doesn't confide in his graduate students. Evidently conducting secret experiments in comparative psychology. Rats and such. Nothing overtly censorable."

"I see. What are your plans?"

"I'll have his lab searched tonight. If nothing turns up, I'll recommend a drop."

"I'd prefer that you search the lab yourself."

A. Prentiss Rogers concealed his surprise and annoyance. "Very well."

His ear button clicked a dismissal.

With puzzled irritation he snapped the plug from the dash socket, started the car, and eased it down the drive into the boulevard bordering the university.

Didn't she realize that he was a busy Field Director with a couple of hundred men under him fully capable of making a routine night search? Undoubtedly she knew just that, but nevertheless was requiring that he do it himself. Why?

And why had she assigned Professor Luce to him personally, squandering so many of his precious hours, when half a dozen of his bright young physical philosophers could have handled it? Nevertheless E, from behind the august anonymity of her solitary initial, had been adamant.

A mile away he turned into a garage on a deserted side street and drew up alongside a Cadillac.

Crush sprang out of the big car and silently held the rear door open for him.

Prentiss got in. "We have a job tonight."

His aide hesitated a fraction of a second before slamming the door behind him. Prentiss knew that the squat, asthmatic little man was surprised and delighted.

As for Crush, he'd never got it through his head that the control of human knowledge was a grim and hateful business, not a kind of cruel lark.

"Very good, sir," wheezed Crush, climbing in behind the wheel. "Shall I reserve a sleeping room at the Bureau for the evening?"

"Can't afford to sleep," grumbled Prentiss. "Desk so high now I can't see over it. Take a nap yourself, if you want to."

"Yes, sir. If I feel the need of it, sir."

The ontologist shot a bitter glance at the back of the man's head. No, Crush wouldn't sleep, but not because worry would keep him awake. A holdover from the days when all a Censor man had was a sleepless curiosity and a pocket Geiger, Crush was serenely untroubled by the dangerous and unfathomable implications of philosophical nucleonics. For Crush, "ontology" was just another definition in the dictionary: "The science of reality."

The little aide could never grasp the idea that unless a sane world-wide pattern of nucleonic investigation were followed, some one in Australia—or next door—might one day throw a switch and alter the shape of that reality. That's what made Crush so valuable; he just didn't know enough to be afraid.

Prentiss had clipped the hairs from his nostrils and so far had breathed in complete silence. But now, as that cavernous face was turned toward where he lay stomach-to-earth in the sheltering darkness, his lungs convulsed in an audible gasp.

The mild, polite, somewhat abstracted academic features of Professor Luce were transformed. The face beyond the lab window was now flushed, the lips were drawn back in soundless amusement, the sunken black eyes were dancing with red pinpoints of flame.

By brute will the ontologist forced his attention back to the rat.

Four times in the past few minutes he had watched the animal run down an inclined chute until it reached a fork, chose one fork, receive what must be a nerve-shattering electric shock, and then be replaced in the chute-beginning for the next run. No matter which alternative fork was chosen, the animal always had been shocked into convulsions.

On this fifth run the rat, despite needling blasts of compressed air from the chute walls, was slowing down. Just before it reached the fork it stopped completely.

The air jets struck at it again, and little cones of up-ended gray fur danced on its rump and flanks.

It gradually ceased to tremble; its respiration dropped to normal. It seemed to Prentiss that its eyes were shut.

The air jets lashed out again. It gave no notice, but just lay there, quiescent, in a near coma.

As he peered into the window, Prentiss saw the tall man walk languidly over to the little animal and run a long hooklike forefinger over its back. No reaction. The professor then said something, evidently in a soft slurred voice, for Prentiss had difficulty in reading his lips.

"—when both alternatives are wrong for you, but you *must* do something, you hesitate, don't you, little one? You slow down, and you are lost. You are no longer a rat. Do you know what the universe would be like if a *phonton* should slow down? You don't? Have you ever taken a bite out of a balloon, little friend? Just the tiniest possible bite?"

Prentiss cursed. The professor had turned and was walking toward the cages with the animal, and although he was apparently still talking, his lips were no longer visible.

After relatching the cage-door the professor walked toward the lab entrance, glanced carefully around the room, and then, as he was reaching for the light switch, looked toward Prentiss' window.

For a moment the investigator was convinced that by some

nameless power the professor was looking into the darkness, straight into his eyes.

He exhaled slowly. It was preposterous.

The room was plunged in darkness.

The investigator blinked and closed his eyes. He wouldn't really have to worry until he heard the lab door opening on the opposite side of the little building.

The door didn't open. Prentiss squinted into the darkness of the room.

Where the professor's head had been were now two mysterious tiny red flames, like candles.

Something must be reflecting from the professor's corneas. But the room was dark; there was no light to be reflected. The flame-eyes continued their illusion of studying him.

The hair was crawling on Prentiss's neck when the twin lights finally vanished and he heard the sound of the lab door opening.

As the slow heavy tread died away down the flagstones to the street, Prentiss gulped in a huge lungful of the chill night air and rubbed his sweating face against his sleeve.

What had got into him? He was acting like the greenest club. He was glad that Crush had to man the televisor relay in the Cadillac and couldn't see him.

He got to his hands and knees and crept silently toward the darkened window. It was a simple sliding sash, and a few seconds sufficed to drill through the glass and insert a hook around the sash lock. The rats began a nervous squeaking as he lowered himself into the darkness of the basement room.

His ear-receptor sounded. "The prof is coming back!" wheezed Crush's tinny voice.

Prentiss said something under his breath, but did not pause in drawing his infra-red scanner from his pocket.

He touched his fingers to his throat mike. "Signal when he reaches the bend in the walk," he said. "And be sure you get this on the visor tape."

The apparatus got his first attention.

The investigator had memorized its position perfectly, Approaching as closely in the darkness as he dared, he "panned" the scanner over some very interesting apparatus that he had noticed on the table.

Then he turned to the books on the desk, regretting that he wouldn't have time to record more than a few pages.

"He's at the bend," warned Crush.

"Okay," mumbled Prentiss, running sensitive fingers over the book bindings. He selected one, opened it at random, and ran the scanner over the invisible pages. "Is this coming through?" he demanded.

"Chief, *he's at the door!*"

Prentiss had to push back the volume without scanning any more of it. He had just relocked the sash when the lab door swung open.

A couple of hours later the ontologist bid good-morning to his receptionist and secretaries and stepped into his private office. He dropped with tired thoughtfulness into his swivel chair and pulled out the infrared negatives that Crush had prepared in the Cadillac darkroom. The page from the old German diary was particularly intriguing. He laboriously translated it once more:

As I got deeper into the manuscript, my mouth grew dry, and my heart began to pound. This, I knew, was a contribution the like of which my family has not seen since Copernicus, Roger Bacon, or perhaps even Aristotle. It seemed incredible that this silent little man, who had never been outside of Koenigsberg, should hold the key to the universe—the *Critique of Pure Reason*, he calls it. And I doubt that even he realizes the ultimate portent of his teaching, for he says we cannot know the real shape or nature of anything, that is, the Thing-in-Itself, the ding-an-Sich, or *noumenon*. He holds that this is the ultimate unknowable, reserved to the gods. He doesn't supect that, century by century, mankind is nearing this final realization of the final things. Even this brilliant man would probably say that the earth was round in 600 B.C., even as it is today. But *I* know it was flat, then—as truly flat as it is truly round today. What has changed? Not the Thing-in-Itself we call the earth. No, it is the mind of man that has changed. But in his preposterous blindness, he mistakes what is really his own mental quickening for a broadened application of science and more precise methods of investigation—

Prentiss smiled.

Luce was undoubtedly a collector of philosophic incunabula. Odd hobby, but that's all it could be—a hobby. Obviously the earth had never been flat, and in fact hadn't changed shape substantially in the last couple of billion years. Certainly any notions as to the flatness of the earth held by primitives of a few thousand years ago or even by contemporaries of Kant were due to their ignorance rather than to accurate observation, and a man of Luce's erudition could only be amused by them.

Again Prentiss found himself smiling with the tolerance of a man standing on the shoulders of twenty centuries of science. The primitives, of course, did the best they could. They just didn't know. They worked with childish premises and infantile instruments.

His brows creased. To assume they had used childish premises was begging the question. On the other hand, was it really worth a second thought? All he could hope to discover would be a few instances of how inferior apparatus coupled perhaps with unsophisticated deductions had oversimplified the world of the ancients. Still, anything that interested the strange Dr. Luce automatically interested him, Prentiss, until the case was closed.

He dictated into the scriptor:

"Memorandum to Geodetic Section. Rush a paragraph history of ideas concerning shape of earth. Prentiss."

Duty done, he promptly forgot it and turned to the heavy accumulation of reports on his desk.

A quarter of an hour later the scriptor rang and began typing an incoming message.

To the Director. Re your request for brief history of earth's shape. Chaldeans and Babylonians (per clay tablets from library of Assurbanipal), Egyptians (per Ahmes papyrus, ca. 1700 B.C.), Cretans (per inscriptions in royal library at Knossos, ca. 1300 B.C.), Chinese (per Chou Kung ms. ca. 1100 B.C.), Phoenicians (per fragments at Tyre ca. 900 B.C.), Hebrews (per unknown Biblical historian ca. 850 B.C.), and early Greeks (per map of widely-traveled geographer Hecataeus, 517 B.C.) assumed earth to be flat disc. But from the 5th century B.C. forward earth's sphericity universally recognized. . . .

There were a few more lines, winding up with the work done on corrections for flattening at poles, but Prentiss had already lost interest. The report threw no light on Luce's hobby and was devoid of ontological implications.

He tossed the script into the waste basket and returned to the reports before him.

A few minutes later he twisted uneasily in his chair, eyed the scriptor in annoyance, then forced himself back to his work.

No use.

Deriding himself for an idiot, he growled at the machine:

"Memorandum to Geodetic. Re your memo history earth's shape. How do you account for change to belief in sphericity after Hecataeus? Rush. Prentiss."

The seconds ticked by.

He drummed on his desk impatiently, then got up and began pacing the floor.

When the scriptor rang, he bounded back and leaned over his desk, watching the words being typed out.

Late Greeks based spherical shape on observation that mast of approaching ship appeared first, then prow. Not known why similar observation not made by earlier seafaring peoples. . . .

Prentiss rubbed his cheek in perplexity. What was he fishing for?

He thrust the half-born conjecture that the earth really had once been flat back into his mental recesses.

Well, then how about the heavens? Surely there was no record of their having changed during man's brief lifetime.

He'd try one more shot and quit.

"Memo to Astronomy Division. Rush paragraph on early vs. modern sun size and distance."

A few minutes later he was reading the reply:

Skipping Plato, whose data are believed baseless (he measured sun's distance at only twice that of moon), we come to earliest recognized "authority." Ptolemy (Almagest, ca. 140 A.D. measured sun radius as 5.5 that of earth (as against 109 actual); measured sun distance at 1210 (23,000 actual). Fairly accurate measurements date only from 17th and 18th centuries. . . .

He'd read all that somewhere. The difference was easily explained by their primitive instruments. It was insane to keep this up.

But it was too late.

"Memo to Astronomy. Were erroneous Ptolemaic measurements due to lack of precision instruments?"

Soon he had his reply:

To Director: Source of Ptolemy's errors in solar measurement not clearly understood. Used astrolabe precise to 10 seconds and clepsydra water clock incorporating Hero's improvements. With same instruments, and using modern value of pi, Ptolemy measured moon radius (0.29 earth radius vs. 0.273 actual) and distance (59 earth radii vs. 60 ⅓ actual). Hence instruments reasonably precise. And note that Copernicus, using quasi-modern instruments and technique, "confirmed" Ptolemaic figure of sun's distance at 1200 earth radii. No explanation known for glaring error.

Unless, suggested something within Prentiss' mind, the sun were closer and much different before the 17th century, when Newton was telling the world where and how big the sun *ought* to be. But *that* solution was too absurd for further consideration. He would sooner assume his complete insanity.

Puzzled, the ontologist gnawed his lower lip and stared at the message in the scriptor.

In his abstraction he found himself peering at the symbol "pi" in the scriptor message. *There*, at least, was something that had always been the same, and would endure for all time. He reached over to knock out his pipe in the big circular ash tray by the scriptor and paused in the middle of the second tap. From his desk he fished a tape measure and stretched it across the tray. Ten inches. And then around the circumference. Thirty-one and a half inches. Good enough, considering. It was a result any curious schoolboy could get.

He turned to the scriptor again.

"Memo to Math Section. Rush paragraph history on value of pi. Prentiss."

He didn't have to wait long.

To Director. Re history "pi." Babylonians used value of 3.00 Aristotle made fairly accurate physical and theoretical evaluations. Archimedes first to arrive at modern value, using theory of limits. . . .

There was more, but it was lost on Prentiss. It was inconceivable, of course, that pi had grown during the two millennia that separated the Babylonians from Archimedes. And yet, it was exasperating. Why hadn't they done any better than 3.00? Any child with a piece of string could have demonstrated their error. Countless generations of wise, careful Chaldean astronomers, measuring time and star positions with such incredible accuracy, all coming to grief with a piece of string and pi. It didn't make sense. And certainly pi hadn't grown, any more than the Babylonian 360-day year had grown into the modern 365-day year. It had always been the same, he told himself. The primitives hadn't measured accurately, that was all. That *had* to be the explanation.

He hoped.

He sat down at his desk again, stared a moment at his memo pad and wrote:

Check history of gravity—acceleration. Believe Aristotle unable detect acceleration. Galileo used same instruments, including same crude water clock, and found it. Why? . . . Any reported transits of Vulcan since 1914, when Einstein explained eccentricity of Mercury orbit by relativity instead of by hypothetical sunward planet? . . . How could Oliver Lodge detect an ether-drift and Michelson not? Conceivable that Lorentz contraction not a physical fact before Michelson experiment? . . . How many chemical elements were predicted before discovered?

He tapped absently on the pad a few times, then rang for a research assistant. He'd barely have time to explain what he wanted before he had to meet his class under Luce.

And he still wasn't sure where the rats fitted in.

Curtly Professor Luce brought his address to a close.

"Well, gentlemen," he said, "I guess we'll have to continue this at our next lecture. We seem to have run over a little; class dismissed. Oh, Mr. Prentiss!"

The investigator looked up in genuine surprise. "Yes, sir?" The thin gun in his shoulder holster suddenly felt satisfyingly fat.

He realized that the crucial moment was near, that he would know before he left the campus whether this strange man was a harmless physicist, devoted to his life-work and his queer hobby, or whether he was an incarnate danger to mankind. The professor was acting out of turn, and it was an unexpected break.

"Mr. Prentiss," continued Luce from the lecture platform, "may I see you in my office a moment before you leave?"

Prentiss said, "Certainly." As the group broke up he followed the gaunt scientist through the door that led to Luce's little office behind the lecture room.

At the doorway he hesitated almost imperceptibly; Luce saw it and bowed sardonically. "After you, sir!"

Then the tall man indicated a chair near his desk. "Sit down, Mr. Prentiss."

For a long moment the seated men studied each other.

Finally the professor spoke. "About fifteen years ago a brilliant young man named Rogers wrote a doctoral dissertation at the University of Vienna on what he called . . . 'Involuntary Conformation of Incoming Sensoria to Apperception Mass.' "

Prentiss began fishing for his pipe. "Indeed?"

"One copy of the dissertation was sent to the Scholarship Society that was financing his studies. All others were seized by the International Bureau of the Censor, and accordingly a demand was made on the Scholarship Society for its copy. But it couldn't be found."

Prentiss was concentrating on lighting his pipe, He wondered if the faint trembling of the match flame was visible.

The professor turned to his desk, opened the top drawer, and pulled out a slim brochure bound in black leather.

The investigator coughed out a cloud of smoke.

The professor did not seem to notice, but opened the front cover and began reading: " '—a dissertation in partial fulfillment of the requirements for the degree of Doctor of Philosophy at the University of Vienna. A. P. Rogers, Vienna, 1957.' " The man closed the book and studied it thoughtfully, "Adrian Prentiss Rogers—the owner of a brain whose like is seen not once in a century. He exposed the gods—then vanished."

Prentiss suppressed a shiver as he met those sunken, implacable eye-caverns.

The cat-and-mouse was over. In a way, he was relieved.

"Why did you vanish then, Mr. Prentiss-Rogers?" demanded Luce. "And why do you now reappear?"

The investigator blew a cloud of smoke toward the low ceiling. "To prevent people like you from introducing sensoria that *can't* be conformed to our present apperception mass. To keep reality as is. That answers both questions, I think."

The other man smiled. It was not a good thing to see. "Have you succeeded?"

"I don't know. So far, I suppose."

The gaunt man shrugged his shoulders. "You ignore tomorrow, then. I think you have failed, but I can't be sure, of course, until I actually perform the experiment that will create novel sensoria." He leaned forward. "I'll come to the point, Mr. Prentiss-Rogers. Next to yourself—and possibly excepting the Censor—I know more about the mathematical approach to reality than anyone else in the world. I may even know things about it that you don't. On other phases of it I'm weak—because I developed your results on the basis of mere logic rather than insight. And logic, we know, is applicable only within indeterminate limits. But in developing a practical device—an actual machine—for the wholesale alteration of incoming sensoria, I'm enormously ahead of you. You saw my apparatus last night, Mr. Prentiss-Rogers? Oh, come, don't be coy."

Prentiss drew deeply on his pipe.

"I saw it."

"Did you understand it?"

"No. It wasn't all there. At least, the apparatus on the table was incomplete. There's more to it than a Nicol prism and a goniometer."

"Ah, you are clever! Yes, I was wise in not permitting you to remain very long—no longer than necessary to whet your curiosity. Look, then! I offer you a partnership. Check my data and apparatus; in return you may be present when I run the experiment. We will attain enlightenment together. We will know all things. We will be gods!"

"And what about two billion other human beings?" said Prentiss, pressing softly at his shoulder holster.

The professor smiled faintly. "Their lunacy—assuming they continue to exist at all—may become slightly more pronounced, of course. But why worry about them?

"Don't expect me to believe this aura of altruism, Mr. Prentiss-Rogers. I think you're afraid to face what lies behind our so-called 'reality.' "

"At least I'm a coward in a good cause." He stood up. "Have you any more to say?"

He knew that he was just going through the motions. Luce must have realized he had lain himself open to arrest half a dozen times in as many minutes: The bare possession of the missing copy of the dissertation, the frank admission of plans to experiment with reality, and his attempted bribery of a high Censor official. And yet, the man's very bearing denied the possibility of being cut off in mid-career.

Luce's cheeks fluffed out in a brief sigh. "I'm sorry you can't be intelligent about this, Mr. Prentiss-Rogers. Yet, the time will come, you know, when you must make up your mind to go—*through*, shall we say? In fact, we may have to depend to a considerable degree on one another's companionship—*out there*. Even gods have to pass the time of day occasionally, and I have a suspicion that you and I are going to be quite chummy. So let us not part in enmity.''

Prentiss' hand slid beneath his coat lapel and drew out the snub-nosed automatic. He had a grim foreboding that it was futile, and that the professor was laughing silently at him, but he had no choice.

''You are under arrest,'' he said unemotionally. ''Come with me.''

The other shrugged his shoulders, then something like a laugh, soundless in its mockery, surged up in his throat. ''Certainly, Mr. Prentiss-Rogers.''

He arose.

The room was plunged into instant blackness.

Prentiss fired three times, lighting up the gaunt chuckling form at each flash.

''Save your fire, Mr. Prentiss-Rogers. Lead doesn't get far in an intense diamagnetic screen. Study the magnetic damper on a lab balance the next time you're in the Censor Building!''

Somewhere a door slammed.

Several hours later Prentiss was eyeing his aide with ill-concealed distaste. Prentiss knew Crush had been summoned by E to confer on the implications of Luce's escape, and that Crush was secretly sympathizing with him. Prentiss couldn't endure sympathy. He'd prefer that the asthmatic little man tell him how stupid he'd been.

''What do you want?'' he growled.

''Sir,'' gasped Crush apologetically, ''I have a report on that gadget you scanned in Luce's lab.''

Prentiss was instantly mollified, but suppressed any show of interest. ''What about it?''

''In essence, sir,'' wheezed Crush, ''it's just a Nicol prism mounted on a goniometer. According to a routine check it was ground by an obscure optician who was nine years on the job, and he spent nearly all of that time on just one face of the prism. What do you make of that, sir?''

''Nothing, yet. What took him so long?''

''Grinding an absolute flat edge, sir, so he says.''

''Odd. That would mean a boundary composed exclusively of molecules of the same crystal layer, something that hasn't been attempted since the Palomar reflector.''

"Yes, sir. And then there's the goniometer mount with just one number on the dial—forty-five degrees."

"Obviously," said Prentiss, "the Nicol is to be used only at a forty-five degree angle to the incoming light. Hence it's probably extremely important—why, I don't know—that the angle be *precisely* forty-five degress. That would require a perfectly flat surface, too, of course. I suppose you're going to tell me that the goniometric gearing is set up very accurately."

Suddenly Prentiss realized that Crush was looking at him in mingled suspicion and admiration.

"Well?" demanded the ontologist irritably. "Just what is the adjusting mechanism? Surely not geometrical? Too crude. Optical, perhaps?"

Crush gasped into his handkerchief. "Yes, sir. The prism is rotated very slowly into a tiny beam of light. Part of the beam is reflected and part refracted. At exactly forty-five degrees it seems, by Jordan's law, that exactly half is reflected and half refracted. The two beams are picked up in a photocell relay that stops the rotating mechanism as soon as the luminosities of the beams are exactly equal."

Prentiss tugged nervously at his ear. It was puzzling. Just what was Luce going to do with such an exquisitely-ground Nicol? At this moment he would have given ten years of his life for an inkling to the supplementary apparatus that went along with the Nicol. It would be something optical, certainly, tied in somehow with neurotic rats. What was it Luce had said the other night in the lab? Something about slowing down a photon. And then what was supposed to happen to the universe? Somethng like taking a tiny bite out of a balloon, Luce had said.

And how did it all interlock with certain impossible, though syllogistically necessary conclusions that flowed from his recent research into the history of human knowledge?

He wasn't sure. But he *was* sure that Luce was on the verge of using this mysterious apparatus to change the perceptible universe, on a scale so vast that humanity was going to get lost in the shuffle. He'd have to convince E of that.

If he couldn't, he'd seek out Luce himself and kill him with his bare hands, and decide on reasons for it afterward.

He was guiding himself for the time being by pure insight, but he'd better be organized when he confronted E.

Crush was speaking. "Shall we go, sir? Your secretary says the jet is waiting."

* * *

The painting showed a man in a red hat and black robes seated behind a high judge's bench. Five other men in red hats were seated behind a lower bench to his right, and four others to his left. At the base of the bench knelt a figure in solitary abjection.

"We condemn you, Galileo Galilei, to the formal prison of this Holy Office for a period determinable at Our pleasure; and by way of salutary penance, We order you, during the next three years, to recite once a week the seven Penitential Psalms."

Prentiss turned from the inscription to the less readable face of E. The oval olive-hued face was smooth, unlined, even around the eyes, and the black hair was parted off-center and drawn over the woman's head into a bun at the nape of her neck. She wore no make-up, and apparently needed none. She was clad in a black, loose-fitting business suit, which accentuated her perfectly molded body.

"Do you know," said Prentiss coolly, "I think you like being Censor. It's in your blood."

"You're perfectly right. I *do* like being Censor. According to Speer, I effectively sublimate a guilt complex as strange as it is baseless."

"Very interesting. Sort of expiation of an ancestral guilt complex, eh?"

"What do you mean?"

"Woman started man on his acquisition of knowledge and self-destruction, and ever since has tried futilely to halt the avalanche. In you the feeling of responsibility and guilt runs exceptionally strong, and I'll wager that some nights you wake up in a cold sweat, thinking you've just plucked a certain forbidden fruit."

E stared icily up at the investigator's twitching mouth. "The only pertinent question," she said crisply, "is whether Luce is engaged in ontologic experiments, and if so, are they of a dangerous nature."

Prentiss sighed. "He's in it up to his neck. But just *what*, and how dangerous, I can only guess."

"Then guess."

"Luce thinks he's developed apparatus for the practical, predictable alteration of sensoria. He hopes to do something with his device that will blow physical laws straight to smithereens. The resulting reality would probably be unrecognizable even to a professional ontologist, let alone the mass of humanity."

"You seem convinced he can do this."

"The probabilities are high."

"Good enough. We can deal only in probabilities. The safest thing, of course, would be to locate Luce and kill him on sight. On the other hand, the faintest breath of scandal would result in Congressional hamstringing of the Bureau, so we must proceed cautiously."

"If Luce is really able to do what he claims," said Prentiss grimly, "and we let him do it, there won't be any Bureau at all—nor any Congress either."

"I know. Rest assured that if I decide that Luce is dangerous and should die, I shall let neither the lives nor careers of anyone in the Bureau stand in the way, including myself."

Prentiss nodded, wondering if she really meant it.

The woman continued. "We are faced for the first time with a probable violation of our directive forbidding ontologic experiments. We are inclined to prevent this threatened violation by taking a man's life. I think we should settle once and for all whether such harsh measures are indicated, and it is for this that I have invited you to attend a staff conference. We intend to reopen the entire question of ontologic experiments and their implications."

Prentiss groaned inwardly. In matters so important the staff decided by vote. He had a brief vision of attempting to convince E's hard-headed scientists that mankind was changing "reality" from century to century—that not too long ago the earth had been "flat." Yes, by now he was beginning to believe it himself!

"Come this way, please," said E.

Sitting at E's right was an elderly man, Speer, the famous psychologist. On her left was Goring, staff adviser on nucleonics; next to him was Burchard, brilliant chemist and Director of the Western Field, then Prentiss, and then Dobbs, the renowened metallurgist and Director of the Central Field.

Prentiss didn't like Dobbs, who had voted against his promotion to the directorship of Eastern.

E announced: "We may as well start this inquiry with an examanation of fundamentals. Mr. Prentiss, just what is reality?"

The ontologist winced. He had needed two hundred pages to outline the theory of reality in his doctoral thesis, and even so, had always suspected his examiners had passed it only because it was incomprehensible—hence a work of genius.

"Well," he began wryly, "I must confess that I don't know what *real* reality is. What most of us call reality is simply an integrated synthesis of incoming sensoria. As such it is nothing more than a working hypothesis in the mind of each of us, forever in a process of revision. In the past that process has been slow and safe. But we have now to consider the consequences of an instantaneous and total revision—a revision so far-reaching that it may thrust humanity face-to-face with the true reality, the world of Things-in-Themselves—Kant's *noumena*. This, I think, would be as disastrous as dumping a group of children in the middle of a forest. They'd have to relearn the simplest things—what to eat, how to protect themselves from elemental forces, and even a new language to deal with their new problems. There'd be few survivors.

"That is what we want to avoid, and we can do it if we prevent any sudden sweeping alteration of sensoria in our present reality."

He looked dubiously at the faces about him. It was a poor start. Speer's wrinkled features were drawn up in a serene smile, and the psychologist seemed to be contemplating the air over Prentiss' head. Goring was regarding him with grave, expressionless eyes. E nodded slightly as Prentiss' gaze traveled past her to a puzzled Burchard, thence to Dobbs, who was frankly contemptuous.

Speer and Goring were going to be the most susceptible. Speer because of his lack of a firm scientific background, Goring because nucleonics was in such a state of flux that nuclear experts were expressing the gravest doubts as to the validity of the laws worshipped by Burchard and Dobbs. Burchard was only a faint possibility. And Dobbs?

Dobbs said: "I don't know what the dickens you're talking about." The implication was plain that he wanted to add: "And I don't think you do, either."

And Prentiss wasn't so sure that he did know. Ontology was an elusive thing at best.

"I object to the term 'real reality,' " continued Dobbs. "A thing is real or it isn't. No fancy philosophical system can change *that*. And if it's real, it gives off predictable, reproducible sensory stimuli not subject to alteration except in the minds of lunatics."

Prentiss breathed more easily. His course was clear. He'd concentrate on Dobbs, with a little side-play on Burchard. Speer and Goring would never suspect his arguments were really directed at them. He pulled a gold coin from his vest pocket and slid it across the table to Dobbs, being careful not to let it clatter. "You're a metallurgist. Please tell us what this is."

Dobbs picked up the coin and examined it suspiciously. "It's quite obviously a five-dollar gold piece, minted at Fort Worth in nineteen sixty-two. I can even give you the analysis, if you want it."

"I doubt that you could," said Prentiss coolly. "For you see, you are holding a counterfeit coin minted only last week in my own laboratories especially for this conference. As a matter of fact, if you'll forgive my saying so, I had you in mind when I ordered the coin struck. It contains no gold whatever—drop it on the table.

The coin fell from the fingers of the astounded metallurgist and clattered on the oaken table top.

"Hear the false ring?" demanded Prentiss.

Pink-faced, Dobbs cleared his throat and peered at the coin more closely. "How was I to know that? It's no disgrace, is it? Many clever counterfeits can be detected only in the laboratory. I knew the color was a little on the red side, but that could have been due to the lighting of the room. And of course, I hadn't given it an auditory test before I spoke. The ring is definitely dull. It's obviously a copper-lead alloy, with possibly a little amount of silver to help the ring. All right, I jumped to conclusions. So what? What does that prove?"

"It proves that you have arrived at two separate, distinct, and mutually exclusive realities, starting with the same sensory premises. It proves how easily reality is revised. And that isn't all, as I shall soon— "

"All right," said Dobbs testily. "But on second thought I admitted it was false, didn't I?"

"Which demonstrates a further weakness in our routine acquisition and evaluation of predigested information. When an unimpeachable authority tells us something as a fact, we immediately, and without conscious thought, *modify* our incoming stimuli to conform with that *fact*. The coin suddenly acquires the red taint of copper, and rings false to the ear."

"I would have caught the queer ring anyhow," said Dobbs stubbornly, "with no help from 'an unimpeachable authority.' The ring would have sounded the same, no matter what you said."

From the corner of his eye Prentiss noticed that Speer was grinning broadly. Had the old psychologist divined his trick? He'd take a chance.

'Dr. Speer,'' he said, ''I think you have something interesting to tell our doubting friend.''

Speer cackled dryly. ''You've been a perfect guinea pig, Dobbsie. The coin was genuine.''

The metallurgist's jaw dropped as he looked blankly from one face to another. Then his jowls slowly grew red. He flung the coin to the table. ''Maybe I am a guinea pig. I'm a realist, too. I think this is a piece of metal. You might fool me as to its color or assay, but in essence and substance, it's a piece of metal.'' He glared at Prentiss and Speer in turn. ''Does anyone deny that?''

''Certainly not,'' said Prentiss. ''Our mental pigeonholes are identical in that respect; they accept the same sensory definition of 'piece of metal,' or 'coin.' Whatever this object is, it emits stimuli that our minds are capable of registering and abstracting as a 'coin.' But note: we make a coin out of it. However, if I could shuffle my cortical pigeonholes, I might find it to be a chair, or a steamer trunk, possibly with Dr. Dobbs inside, or, if the shuffling were extreme, there might be no semantic pattern into which the incoming stimuli could be routed. There wouldn't be anything there at all!''

''Sure,'' sneered Dobbs. ''You would walk right through it.''

''Why not?'' asked Prentiss gravely. ''I think we may do it all the time. Matter is about the emptiest stuff imaginable. If you compressed that coin to eliminate the space between its component atoms and electrons, you couldn't see it in a microscope.''

Dobbs stared at the enigmatic goldpiece as though it might suddenly thrust out a pseudopod and swallow him up. Then he said flatly: ''No. I don't believe it. It exists as a coin, and only as a coin—whether I know it or not.''

''Well,'' ventured Prentiss, ''how about you, Dr. Goring? Is the coin real to you?''

The nucleist smiled and shrugged his shoulders. ''If I don't think too much about it, it's real enough. And yet . . .''

Dobb's face clouded. ''And yet what? Here it is. Can you doubt the evidence of your own eyes?''

''That's just the difficulty.'' Goring leaned forward. ''My eyes tell me, here's a coin. Theory tells me, here's a mass of hypothetical disturbances in a hypothetical subether in a hypothetical ether. The indeterminacy principle tells me that I can never know both the mass and position of these hypothetical disturbances. And as a physicist I know that the bare fact of observing something is sufficient to change that something from its pre-observed state. Nevertheless, I compromise by letting my senses and practical experience stick a tag on this particular bit of the unknowable. X, after its impact on my mind (whatever *that* is!) equals coin. A single equation with two variables has no solution. The best I can say is, it's a coin, but probably not really—''

''Hah!'' declared Burchard. ''I can demonstrate the fallacy of *that* position very quickly. If our minds make this a coin, then our minds make this little object an ash-tray, that a window, the thing that holds us up, a chair. You might say we make the air we breathe, and perhaps even the stars and planets. Why, following Prentiss' idea to its logical end, the universe itself is the work of man—a conclusion I'm sure he doesn't intend.''

''Oh, but I do,'' said Prentiss.

Prentiss took a deep breath. The issue could be dodged no longer. He had to take a stand. ''And to make sure you understand me, whether you agree with me or not, I'll state categorically that I believe the apparent universe to be the work of man.''

Even E looked startled, but said nothing.

The ontologist continued rapidly. ''All of you doubt my sanity. A week ago I would have, too. But since then I've done a great deal of research in the history of science. And I repeat, *the universe is the work of man*. I believe that man began his existence in some incredibly simple world—the original and true *noumenon* of our present universe. And that over the centuries man expanded his little world into its present vastness and incomprehensible intricacy solely by dint of imagination.

''Consequently, I believe that what most of you call the 'real' world has been changing ever since our ancestors began to think.''

Dobbs smiled superciliously. ''Oh, come now, Prentiss. That's just a rhetorical description of scientific progress over the past centuries. In the same sense I might say that modern transportation and communications have shrunk the earth. But you'll certainly admit that the physical state of things has been substantially constant ever since the galaxies formed and the earth began to cool, and that the simple cosmologies of early man were simply the result of lack of means for obtaining accurate information?''

''I *won't* admit it,'' rejoined Prentiss bluntly. ''I maintain that their information was substantially accurate. I maintain that at one time in our history the earth was flat—as flat as it is now round, and no one living before the time of Hecataeus, though he might have been equipped with the finest modern instruments, could have proved otherwise. His mind was *conditioned* to a two-dimensional world. Any of us present, if we were transplanted to the world of Hecataeus, could, of course, establish terrestrial sphericity in short order. Our minds have been conditioned to a three-dimensional world. The day may come a few millennia hence when a four-dimensional Terra will be commonplace even to schoolchildren; they will have been intuitively conditioned in relativistic concepts.'' He added slyly: ''And the less intelligent of them may attempt to blame our naive three-dimensional planet on our grossly inaccurate instruments, because it will be as plain as day to them that their planet has four dimensions!''

Dobbs snorted at this amazing idea. The other scientists stared at Prentiss with an awe which was mixed with incredulity.

Goring said cautiously: ''I follow up to a certain point. I can see that a primitive society might start out with a limited number of facts. They would offer theories to harmonize and integrate those facts, and then those first theories would require that new, additional facts exist, and in their search for those secondary facts, extraneous data would turn up inconsistent with the first theories. Secondary theories would then be required, from which hitherto unguessed facts should follow, the confirmation of which would discover more inconsistencies. So the pattern of fact to theory to fact to theory, and so on, finally brings us into our present state of knowledge. Does that follow from your argument?''

Prentiss nodded.

''But won't you admit that the facts were there all the time, and merely awaited discovery?''

''The simple, unelaborated *noumenon* was there all the time, yes. But the new fact—man's new interpretation of the *noumenon*, was generally pure invention—a mental creation, if you like. This will be clearer if you consider how rarely a new fact arises before a theory exists for its explanation. In the ordinary scientific investigation, theory comes first, followed in short order by the 'discovery' of various facts deducible from it.''

Goring still looked skeptical. ''But that wouldn't mean the fact wasn't there all the time.''

''Wouldn't it? Look at the evidence. Has it never struck you as odd in how many instances very obvious facts were 'overlooked' until a theory was propounded that required their existence? Take your nuclear building blocks. Protons and electrons were detected physically only after Rutherford had showed they had to exist. And then when Rutherford found that protons and electrons were not enough to build all the atoms of the periodic table, he postulated the neutron, which of course was duly 'discovered' in the Wilson cloud chamber."

Goring pursed his lips. "But the Wilson cloud chamber would have shown all that prior to the theory, if anyone had only thought to use it.

"The mere fact that Wilson didn't invent his cloud chamber until nineteen-twelve and Geiger didn't invent his counter until nineteen-thirteen, would not keep subatomic particles from existing before that time."

"You don't get the point," said Prentiss. "The primitive, ungeneralized noumenon that we today observe as subatomic particles existed prior to nineteen-twelve, true, *but not subatomic particles*."

"Well, I don't know. . . ." Goring scratched his chin. "How about fundamental forces? Surely electricity existed before Galvani? Even the Greeks knew how to build up electrostatic charges on amber."

"Greek electricity was nothing more than electrostatic charges. Nothing more could be created until Galvani introduced the concept of the electric current."

"Do you mean the electric current didn't exist at all before Galvani?" demanded Burchard. "Not even when lightning struck a conductor?"

"Not even then. We don't know much about pre-Galvanic lightning. While it probably packed a wallop, its destructive potential couldn't have been due to its delivery of an electric current. The Chinese flew kites for centuries before Franklin theorized that lightning was the same as galvanic electricity, but there's no recorded shock from a kite string until our learned statesman drew forth one in seventeen-sixty-five. *Now*, only an idiot flies a kite in a storm. It's all according to pattern: theory first, then we alter 'reality' to fit."

Burchard persisted. "Then I suppose you'd say all the elements are figments of our imagination."

"Correct," agreed Prentiss. "I believe that in the beginning there were only four *noumenal* elements. Man simply elaborated these according to the needs of his growing science. Man made them what they are today—and on occasion, *unmade* them. You remember the havoc Mendelyeev created with his periodic law. He declared that the elements had to follow valence sequences of increasing atomic weight, and when they didn't, he insisted his law was right and that the atomic weights were wrong. He must have had Stas and Berzelius whirling in their graves, because they had worked out the 'erroneous' atomic weights with marvelous precision. The odd thing was, when the weights were rechecked, they fitted the Mendelyeev table. But that wasn't all. The old rascal pointed out vacant spots in his table and maintained that there were more elements yet to be discovered. He even predicted what properties they'd have. He was too modest. I state that Nilson, Winkler, and De Boisbaudran merely *discovered* scandium, germanium, and gallium; Mendelyeev *created* them, out of the original quadrelemental stuff."

E leaned forward. "That's a bit strong. Tell me, if man has changed the elements and the cosmos to suit his convenience, what was the cosmos like before man came on the scene?"

"There wasn't any," answered Prentiss. "Remember, by definition, 'cosmos' or 'reality' is simply man's version of the ultimate *noumenal* universe. The 'cosmos' arrives and departs with the mind of man. Consequently, the earth—as such—didn't even exist before the advent of man."

"But the evidence of the rocks . . ." protested E. "Pressures applied over millions, even billions of years, were needed to form them, unless you postulate an omnipotent God who called them into existence as of yesterday."

"I postulate only the omnipotent human mind," said Prentiss. "In the seventeenth century, Hooke, Ray, Woodward, to name a few, studied chalk, gravel, marble, and even coal, without finding anything inconsistent with results to be expected from the Noachian Flood. But now that we've made up our minds that the earth is older, the rocks *seem* older, too."

"But how about evolution?" demanded Burchard. "Surely that wasn't a matter of a few centuries?"

"Really?" replied Prentiss. "Again, why assume that the facts are any more recent than the theory? The evidence is all the other way. Aristotle was a magnificent experimental biologist, and he was convinced that life could be created spontaneously. Before the time of Darwin there was no need for the various species to evolve, because they sprang into being from inanimate matter. As late as the eighteenth century, Needham, using a microscope, reported that he saw microbe life arise spontaneously out of sterile culture media. These abiogeneticists were, of course, discredited and their work found to be irreproducible, but only *after* it became evident that the then abiogenetic facts were going to run inconsistent with later 'facts' flowing from advancing biologic theory."

"Then," said Goring, "assuming purely for the sake of argument, that man has altered the original *noumena* into our present reality, just what danger do you think Luce represents to that reality? How could he do anything about it, even if he wanted to? Just what is he up to?"

"Broadly stated," said Prentiss, "Luce intends to destroy the Einsteinian universe."

Burchard frowned and shook his head. "Not so fast. In the first place, how can anyone presume to destroy this planet, much less the whole universe? And why do you say the 'Einsteinian' universe? The universe by any other name is still the universe, isn't it?"

"What Dr. Prentiss means," explained E, "is that Luce wants to revise completely and finally our present comprehension of the universe, which presently happens to be the Einsteinian version, in the expectation that the final version would be the true one—and comprehensible only to Luce and perhaps a few other ontologic experts."

"I don't see it," said Dobbs irritably. "Apparently this Luce contemplates nothing more than publication of a new scientific theory. How can that be bad? A mere theory can't hurt anybody—especially if only two or three people understand it."

"You—and two billion others," said Prentiss softly, "think that 'reality' cannot be affected by any theory that seems to change it—that it is optional with you to accept or reject the theory. In the past that was true. If the Ptolemaics wanted a geocentric universe, they ignored Copernicus. If the four-dimensional continuum of Einstein and Minkowsky seemed incomprehensible to the Newtonian school they dismissed it, and the planets continued to revolve substantially as Newton predicted. But this is different.

"For the first time we are faced with the probability that the promulgation of a theory is going to *force* an ungraspable reality upon our minds. It will not be optional."

"Well," said Burchard, "if by 'promulgation of a theory' you mean something like the application of the quantum theory and relativity to the production of atomic energy, which of course has changed the shape of civilization in the past generation, whether the individual liked it or not, then I can understand you. But if you mean that Luce is going to make one little experiment that may confirm some new theory or other, and *ipso facto* and instantaneously reality is going to turn topsy turvy, why I say it's nonsense."

"Would anyone," said Prentiss quietly, "care to guess what would happen if Luce were able to destroy a photon?"

Goring laughed shortly. "The question doesn't make sense. The mass-energy entity whose three-dimensional profile we call a photon is indestructible."

"But if you *could* destroy it?" insisted Prentiss. "What would the universe be like afterward?"

"What difference would it make?" demanded Dobbs. "One photon more or less?"

"Plenty," said Goring. "According to the Einstein theory, every particle of matter—energy has a gravitational potential, lambda, and it can be calculated that the total lambdas are precisely sufficient to keep our four-dimensional continuum from closing back on itself. Take one lambda away—God! The universe would split wide open!"

"Exactly," said Prentiss. "Instead of a continuum, our 'reality' would become a disconnected melange of three-dimensional objects. Time, if it existed, wouldn't bear any relation to spatial things. Only an ontologic expert might be able to synthesize any sense out of such a 'reality.' "

"Well," said Dobbs, "I wouldn't worry too much. I don't think anybody's ever going to destroy a photon." He snickered. "You have to catch one first!"

"Luce can catch one," said Prentiss calmly. "And he can destroy it. At this moment some unimaginable post-Einsteinian universe lies in the palm of his hand. Final, true reality, perhaps. But we aren't ready for it. Kant, perhaps, or *Homo superior*, but not the general run of *H. sapiens*. We wouldn't be able to escape our conditioning. We'd be stopped cold."

He stopped. Without looking at Goring, he knew he had convinced the man. Prentiss sagged with visible relief. It was time for a vote. He must strike before Speer and Goring could change their minds.

"Madame"—he shot a questioning glance at the woman—"at any moment my men are going to report that they've located

Luce. I must be ready to issue the order for his execution, if in fact the staff believes such disposition proper. I call for a vote of officers!''

''Granted,'' said E instantly. ''Will those in favor of destroying Luce on sight raise their right hands?''

Prentiss and Goring made the required signal.

Speer was silent.

Prentiss felt his heart sinking. Had he made a gross error of judgment?

''I vote against this murder,'' declared Dobbs. ''That's what it is, pure murder.''

''I agree with Dobbs,'' said Burchard shortly.

All eyes were on the psychologist. ''I presume you'll join us, Dr. Speer?'' demanded Dobbs sternly.

''Count me out, gentlemen, I'd never interfere with anything so inevitable as the destiny of man. All of you are overlooking a fundamental facet of human nature—man's insatiable hunger for change, novelty—for anything different from what he already has. Prentiss himself states that whenever man grows discontented with his present reality, he starts elaborating it, and the devil take the hindmost. Luce but symbolizes the evil genius of our race—and I mean both our species and the race toward intertwined godhood and destruction. Once born, however, symbols are immortal. It's far too late now to start killing Luces. It was too late when the first man tasted the first apple.

''Furthermore, I think Prentiss greatly overestimates the scope of Luce's pending victory over the rest of mankind. Suppose Luce is actually successful in clearing space and time and suspending the world in the temporal stasis of its present irreality. Suppose he and a few ontologic experts pass on into the ultimate, true reality. How long do you think they can resist the temptation to alter it? If Prentiss is right, eventually they or their descendants will be living in a cosmos as intricate and unpleasant as the one they left, while we, for all practical purposes, will be pleasantly dead.

''No, gentlemen, I won't vote either way.''

''Then it is my privilege to break the tie,'' said E coolly. ''I vote for death. Save your remonstrances, Dr. Dobbs. It's after midnight. This meeting is adjourned.'' She stood up in abrupt dismissal, and the men were soon filing from the room.

E left the table and walked toward the windows on the far side of the room. Prentiss hesitated a moment, but made no effort to leave.

E called over her shoulder, "You, too, Prentiss."

The door closed behind Speer, the last of the group, save Prentiss.

Prentiss walked up behind E.

She gave no sign of awareness.

Six feet away, the man stopped and studied her.

Sitting, walking, standing, she was lovely. Mentally he compared her to Velasquez' Venus. There was the same slender exquisite proportion of thigh, hip, and bust. And he knew she was completely aware of her own beauty, and further, must be aware of his present appreciative scrutiny.

Then her shoulders sagged suddenly, and her voice seemed very tired when she spoke. "So you're still here, Prentiss. Do you believe in intuition?"

"Not often."

"Speer was right. He's always right. Luce will succeed." She dropped her arms to her sides and turned.

"Then may I reiterate, my dear, marry me and let's forget the control of knowledge for a few months."

"Completely out of the question, Prentiss. Our natures are incompatible. You're incorrigibly curious, and I'm incorrigibly, even neurotically, conservative. Besides, how can you even think about such things when we've got to stop Luce?"

His reply was interrupted by the shrilling of the intercom: "Calling Mr. Prentiss. Crush calling Mr. Prentiss. Luce located. Crush calling."

With his pencil Crush pointed to a shaded area of the map. "This is Luce's Snake-Eyes estate, the famous game preserve and zoo. Somewhere in the center—about here, I think—is a stone cottage. A moving van unloaded some lab equipment there this morning."

"Mr. Prentiss," said E, "how long do you think it will take him to install what he needs for that one experiment?"

The ontologist answered from across the map table. "I can't be sure. I still have no idea of what he's going to try, except that I'm reasonably certain it must be done in absolute darkness. Checking his instruments will require but a few minutes at most."

The woman began pacing the floor nervously. ''I knew it. We can't stop him. We have no time.''

''Oh, I don't know,'' said Prentiss. ''How about that stone cottage, Crush? It is pretty old?''

''Dates from the eighteenth century, sir.''

''There's your answer,'' said Prentiss. ''It's probably full of holes where the mortar's fallen out. For total darkness he'll have to wait until moonset.''

''That's three thirty-four A.M., sir,'' said Crush.

''We've time for an arrest,'' said E.

Crush looked dubious. ''It's more complicated than that, Madame. Snake-Eyes is fortified to withstand a small army. Luce could hold off any force the Bureau could muster for at least twenty-four hours.''

''One atom egg, well done,'' suggested Prentiss.

''That's the best answer, of course,'' agreed E. ''But you know as well as I what the reaction of Congress would be to such extreme measures. There would be an investigation. The Bureau would be abolished, and all persons responsible for such an action would face life imprisonment, perhaps death.'' She was silent for a moment, then sighed and said: ''So be it. If there is no alternative, I shall order the bomb dropped.''

''There may be another way,'' said Prentiss.

''Indeed?''

''Granted an army couldn't get through. One man might. And if he made it, you could call off your bomb.''

E exhaled a slow cloud of smoke and studied the glowing tip of her cigarette. Finally she turned and looked into the eyes of the ontologist for the first time since the beginning of the conference. ''*You* can't go.''

''Who, then?''

Her eyes dropped. ''You're right, of course. But the bomb still falls if you don't get through. It's got to be that way. Do you understand that?''

Prentiss laughed. ''I understand.''

He addressed his aide. ''Crush, I'll leave the details up to you, bomb and all. We'll rendezvous at these coordinates''—he pointed to the map—''at three sharp. It's after one now. You'd better get started.''

''Yes, sir,'' wheezed Crush, and scurried out of the room.

As the door closed, Prentiss turned to E. ''Beginning tomorrow afternoon—or rather, *this* afternoon, after I finish with Luce, I want six months off."

"Granted," murmured E.

"I want you to come with me. I want to find out just what this thing is between us. Just the two of us. It may take a little time."

E smiled crookedly. "If we're both still alive at three thirty-five, and such a thing as a month exists, and you still want me to spend six of them with you, I'll do it. And in return you can do something for me."

"What?"

"You even above Luce, stand the best chance of adjusting to final reality if Luce is successful in destroying a photon. I'm a border-line case. I'm going to need all the help you can give me, if and when the time comes. Will you remember that?"

"I'll remember," Prentiss said.

At 3 A.M. he joined Crush.

"There are at least seven infra-red scanners in the grounds, sir," said Crush, "not to mention an intricate network of photo relays. And then the wire fence around the lab, with the big cats inside. He must have turned the whole zoo loose." The little man reluctantly helped Prentiss into his infra-red absorbing coveralls. "You weren't meant for tiger fodder, sir. Better call it off."

Prentiss zipped up his visor and grimaced out into the moonlit dimness of the apple orchard. "You'll take care of the photocell network?"

"Certainly, sir. He's using u.v.-sensitive cells. We'll blanket the area with the u.v.-spot at three-ten."

Prentiss strained his ears, but couldn't hear the 'copter that would carry the u.v.-searchlight—and the bomb.

"It'll be here, sir," Crush assured him. "It won't make any noise, anyhow. What you ought to be worrying about are those wild beasts."

The investigator sniffed at the night air. "Darn little breeze."

"Yeah," gasped Crush. "And variable at that, sir. You can't count on going in up-wind. You want us to create a diversion at one end of the grounds to attract the animals?"

"We don't dare. If necessary, I'll open the aerosol capsule of formaldehyde." He held out his hand. "Good-by, Crush."

His asthmatic assistant shook the extended hand with vigorous sincerity. "Good luck, sir. And don't forget the bomb. We'll have to drop it at three thirty-four sharp."

But Prentiss had vanished into the leafy darkness.

A little later he was studying the luminous figures on his watch. The u.v.-blanket was presumably on. All he had to be careful about in the next forty seconds was a direct collision with a photocell post.

But Crush's survey party had mapped well. He reached the barbed fencing uneventfully, with seconds to spare. He listened a moment, and then in practised silence eased his lithe body high up and over.

The breeze, which a moment before had been in his face, now died away, and the night air hung about him in dark lifeless curtains.

From the stone building a scant two hundred yards ahead, a chink of light peeped out.

Prentiss drew his silenced pistol and began moving forward with swift caution, taking care to place his heel to ground before the toe, and feeling out the character of the ground with the thin soles of his sneakers before each step. A snapping twig might hurl a slavering wild beast at his throat.

He stopped motionless in midstride.

From the thicket several yards to his right came an ominous sniffing, followed by a low snarl.

His mouth went suddenly dry as he strained his ears and turned his head slowly toward the sound.

And then there came the reverberations of something heavy, hurtling toward him.

He whipped his weapon around and waited in a tense crouch, not daring to send a wild, singing bullet across the sward.

The great cat was almost upon him before he fired, and then the faint cough of the stumbling, stricken animal seemed louder than his muffled shot.

Breathing hard, Prentiss stepped away from the dying beast, evidently a panther, and listened for a long time before resuming his march on the cottage. Luce's extraordinary measures to exclude intruders but confirmed his suspicions: Tonight was the last night that the professor could be stopped. He blinked the stinging sweat from his eyes and glanced at his watch. It was 3:15.

Apparently the other animals had not heard him. He stood up

to resume his advance, and to his utter relief found that the wind had shifted almost directly into his face and was blowing steadily.

In another three minutes he was standing at the massive door of the building, running practised fingers over the great iron hinges and lock. Undoubtedly the thing was going to squeak; there was no time to apply oil and wait for it to soak in. The lock could be easily picked.

And the squeaking of a rusty hinge was probably immaterial. A cunning operator like Luce would undoubtedly have wired an alarm into it. He just couldn't believe Crush's report to the contrary.

But he couldn't stand here.

There was only one way to get inside quickly, and alive.

Chuckling at his own madness, Prentiss began to pound on the door.

He could visualize the blinking out of the slit of light above his head, and knew that, somewhere within the building, two flame-lit eyes were studying him in an infra-red scanner.

Prentiss tried simultaneously to listen to the muffled squeaking of the rats beyond the great door and to the swift, padding approach of something big behind him.

"Luce!" he cried. "It's Prentiss! Let me in!"

A latch slid somewhere; the door eased inward. The investigator threw his gun rearward at a pair of bounding eyes, laced his fingers over his head, and stumbled into more darkness.

Despite the protection of his hands, the terrific blow of the blackjack on his temple almost knocked him out.

He closed his eyes, crumpled carefully to the floor, and noted with satisfaction that his wrists were being tied behind his back. As he had anticipated, it was a clumsy job, even without his imperceptible "assistance." Long fingers ran over his body in a search for more weapons.

Then he felt the sting of a hypodermic needle in his biceps.

The lights came on.

He struggled feebly, emitted a plausible groan, and tried to sit up.

From far above, the strange face of Dr. Luce looked down at him, illuminated, it seemed to Prentiss, by some unhallowed inner fire.

"What time is it?" asked Prentiss.

"Approximately three-twenty."

"*Hm*. Your kittens gave me quite a reception. my dear professor."

"As befits an uncooperative meddler."

"Well, what are you going to do with me?"

"Kill you."

Luce pulled a pistol from his coat pocket.

Prentiss wet his lips. During his ten years with the Bureau, he had never had to deal with anyone quite like Luce. The gaunt man personified megalomania on a scale beyond anything the investigator had previously encountered—or imagined possible.

And, he realized with a shiver, Luce was very probably justified in his prospects (not delusions!) of grandeur.

With growing alarm he watched Luce snap off the safety lock of the pistol.

There were two possible chances of surviving more than a few seconds.

Luce's index finger began to tense around the trigger.

One of those chances was to appeal to Luce's megalomania, treating him as a human being. Tell him, "I know you won't kill me until you've had a chance to gloat over me—to tell me, the inventor of ontologic synthesis, how you found a practical application of it."

No good. Too obvious to one of Luce's intelligence.

The approach must be to a demigod, in humility. Oddly enough his curiosity *was* tinged with respect. Luce *did* have something.

Prentiss licked his lips again and said hurriedly; "I must die, then. But could you show me—is it asking too much to show me, just how you propose to go through?"

The gun lowered a fraction of an inch. Luce eyed the doomed man suspiciously.

"Would you, please?" continued Prentiss. His voice was dry, cracking. "Ever since I discovered that new realities could be synthesized, I've wondered whether *Homo sapiens* was capable of finding a practical device for uncovering the true reality. And all who've worked on it have insisted that only a brain but little below the angels was capable of such an achievement." He coughed apologetically. "It is difficult to believe that a mere mortal has really accomplished what you claim—and yet, there's something about you . . ." His voice trailed off, and he laughed deprecatingly.

Luce bit; he thrust the gun back into his coat pocket. "So you know when you're licked,'' he said. ''Well, I'll let you live a moment longer.''

He stepped back and pulled aside a black screen. ''Has the inimitable ontologist the wit to understand this?''

Within a few seconds of his introduction to the instrument everything was painfully clear. Prentiss now abandoned any remote hope that either Luce's method or aparatus would prove faulty. Both the vacuum-glassed machinery and the idea behind it were perfect.

Basically, the supplementary unit, which he now saw for the first time, consisted of a sodium-vapor light bulb, blacked out except for one tiny transparent spot. Ahead of the little window was a series of what must be hundreds of black discs mounted on a common axis. Each disc bore a slender radial slot. And though he could not trace all the gearing, Prentiss knew that the discs were geared to permit one and only one fleeting photon of yellow light to emerge at the end of the disc series, where it would pass through a Kerr electro-optic field and be polarized.

That photon would then travel one centimeter to that fabulous Nicol prism, one surface of which had been machined flat to a molecule's thickness. That surface was turned by means of an equally marvelous goniometer to meet the oncoming photon at an angle of exactly 45 degrees. And then would come chaos.

The cool voice of E sounded in his ear receptor. ''Prentiss, it's three-thirty. If you understand the apparatus, and find it dangerous, will you so signify? If possible, describe it for the tapes.''

''I understand your apparatus perfectly,'' said Prentiss.

Luce grunted, half irritated, half curious.

Prentiss continued hurriedly. ''Shall I tell you how you decided upon this specific apparatus?''

''If you think you can.''

''You have undoubtedly seen the sun reflect from the surface of the sea.''

Luce nodded.

''But the fish beneath the surface see the sun, too,'' continued Prentiss. ''Some of the photons are reflected and reach you, and some are refracted and reach the fish. But, for a given wave length, the photons are identical. Why should one be absorbed and another reflected?''

''You're on the right track,'' admitted Luce, ''but couldn't you account for their behavior by Jordan's law?''

''Statistically, yes. Individually, no. In nineteen-thirty-four

Jordan showed that a beam of polarized light splits up when it hits a Nicol prism. He proved that when the prism forms an angle, alpha, with the plane of polarization of the prism, a fraction of the light equal to $\cos^2$alpha passes through the prism, and the remainder, $\sin^2$alpha, is reflected. For example, if alpha is 60 degrees, three-fourths of the phontons are reflected and one-fourth are refracted. But note that Jordan's law applied only to streams of photons, and you're dealing with a single photon, to which you're presenting an angle of exactly 45°. And how does a single photon make up its mind—or the photonic equivalent of a mind—when the probability of reflecting is exactly equal to the probability of refracting? Of course, if our photon is but one little mote along with billions of others, the whole comprising a light beam, we can visualize orders left for him by a sort of statistical traffic keeper stationed somewhere in the beam. A member of a beam, it may be presumed, has a pretty good idea of how many of his brothers have already reflected, and how many refracted, and hence knows which he must do."

"But suppose our single photon isn't in a beam at all?" said Luce.

"Your apparatus," said Prentiss, "is going to provide just such a photon. And I think it will be a highly confused little photon, just as your experimental rat was, that night not so long ago. I think it was Schroedinger who said that these physical particles were startlingly human in many of their aspects. Yes, your photon will be given a choice of equal probability. Shall he reflect? Shall he refract? The chances are 50 percent for either choice. He will have no reason for selecting one in preference to the other. There will have been no swarm of preceding photons to set up a traffic guide for him. He'll be puzzled; and trying to meet a situation for which he has no proper response, he'll slow down. And when he does, he'll cease to be a photon, which must travel at the speed of light or cease to exist. Like your rat, like many human beings, he solves the unsolvable by disintegrating."

Luce said: "And when it disintegrates, there disappears one of the lambdas that hold together the Einstein space-time continuum. And when *that* goes, what's left can be only final reality untainted by theory or imagination. Do you see any flaw in my plan?"

* * *

Tugging with subtle quickness on the cords that bound him, Prentiss knew there was no flaw in the man's reasoning, and that every human being on earth was now living on borrowed time.

He could think of no way to stop him; there remained only the bare threat of the bomb.

He said tersely: "If you don't submit to peaceable arrest within a few seconds, an atom bomb is going to be dropped on this area."

Sweat was getting into his eyes again, and he winked rapidly.

Luce's dark features convulsed, hung limp, then coalesced into a harsh grin. "She'll be too late," he said with grim good humor. "Her ancestors tried for centuries to thwart mine. But we were successful—always. Tonight I succeed again, and for all time."

Prentiss had one hand free.

In seconds he would be at the man's throat. He worked with quiet fury at the loops around his bound wrist.

Again E's voice in his ear receptor. "I had to do it!" The tones were strangely sad, self-accusing, remorseful.

Had to do *what*?

And his dazed mind was trying to digest the fact that E had just destroyed him.

She was continuing. "The bomb was dropped ten seconds ago." She was almost pleading, and her words were running together. "You were helpless; you couldn't kill him. I had a sudden premonition of what the world would be like—afterward—even for those who go through. Forgive me."

Almost mechanically he resumed his fumbling with the cord.

Luce looked up. "What's that?"

"What?" asked Prentiss dully. "I don't hear anything."

"Of course you do! Listen!"

The wrist came free.

Several things happened.

That faraway shriek in the skies grew into a howling crescendo of destruction.

As one man Prentiss and Luce leaped toward the activator switches. Luce got there first—an infinitesimal fraction of time before the walls were completely disintegrated.

There was a brief, soundless interval of utter blackness.

And then it seemed to Prentiss that a titanic stone wall crashed into his brain, and held him, mute, immobile.

But he was not dead.

For the name of this armored, stunning wall was not the bomb, but Time itself.

He knew in a brief flash of insight, that for sentient, thinking beings, Time had suddenly become a barricade rather than an endless road.

The exploding bomb—the caving cottage walls—were hanging, somewhere, frozen fast in an immutable, eternal stasis.

Luce had separated this fleeting unseen dimension from the creatures and things that had flowed along it. There is no existence without change along a temporal continuum. And now the continuum had been shattered.

Was this, then the fate of all tangible things—of all humanity?

Were none of them—not even the two or three who understood advanced ontology, to—get through?

There was nothing but a black, eerie silence all around.

His senses were useless.

He even doubted he had any senses.

So far as he could tell he was nothing but an intelligence, floating in space. But he couldn't even be sure of *that*. Intelligence—space—they weren't necessarily the same now as before.

All that he knew for sure was that he doubted. He doubted everything except the fact of doubting.

Shades of Descartes!

To doubt is to think!

Ergo sum!

I exist.

Instantly he was wary. He existed, but not necessarily as Adrian Prentiss Rogers. For the *noumenon* of Adrian Prentiss Rogers might be—whom?

But he was safe. He was going to get through.

Relax, be resilient, he urged his whirling brain. You're on the verge of something marvelous.

It seemed that he could almost hear himself talk, and he was glad. A voiceless final reality would have been unbearable.

He essayed a tentative whisper:

"E!"

From somewhere far away a woman whimpered.

He cried eagerly into the blackness. "Is that you?"

Something unintelligble and strangely frightening answered him.

"Don't try to hold on to yourself," he cried. "Just let yourself go! Remember, you won't be E any more, but the *noumenon*, the essence of E. Unless you change enough to permit your *noumenon* to take over your old identity, you'll have to stay behind."

There was a groan. "But I'm *me*!"

"But you *aren't*—not really," he pleaded quickly. "You're just an aspect of a larger, symbolical *you*—the *noumenon* of E. It's yours for the asking. You have only to hold out your hand to grasp the shape of final reality. And you *must*, or cease to exist!"

A wail: "But what will happen to my body?"

The ontologist almost laughed. "I wouldn't know; but if it changes, I'll be sorrier than you!"

There was a silence.

"E!" he called.

No answer.

"E! Did you get through? *E!*"

The empty echoes skirled between the confines of his narrow blackness.

Had the woman lost even her struggling interstitial existence? Whenever, whatever, or wherever she now was, he could no longer detect.

Somehow, if it had ever come to this, he had counted on her being with him—just the two of them.

In stunned uneasy wonder he considered what his existence was going to be like from now on.

And what about Luce?

Had the demonic professor possessed sufficient mental elasticity to slip through?

And if so, just what was the professorial *noumenon*—the real Luce—like?

He'd soon know.

The ontologist relaxed again, and began floating through a dreamy patch of light and darkness. A pale glow began gradually to form about his eyes, and shadowy things began to form, dissolve, and reform.

He felt a great rush of gratitude. At least the shape of final reality was to be visible.

And then, at about the spot where Luce had stood, he saw the Eyes—two tiny red flames, transfixing him with unfathomable fury.

The same eyes that had burned into his that night of his first search!

Luce had got through—but wait!

An unholy aura was playing about the sinuous shadow that contained the jeweled flames. Those eyes were brilliant, horrid facets of hate in the head of a huge, coiling serpent-thing! Snake-Eyes!

In mounting awe and fear the ontologist understood that Luce had not got through—as Luce. That the *noumenon*, the essence, of Luce—was nothing human. That Luce, the bearer of light, aspirant to godhood, was not just Luce!

By the faint light he began shrinking away from the coiled horror, and in the act saw that *he*, at least, still had a human body. He knew this, because he was completely nude.

He was still human, and the snake-creature wasn't—and therefore never had been.

Then he noticed that the stone cottage was gone, and that a pink glow was coming from the east.

He crashed into a tree before he had gone a dozen steps.

Yesterday there had been no trees within three hundred yards of the cottage.

But that made sense, for there was no cottage any more, and no yesterday. Crush ought to be waiting somewhere out here—except that Crush hadn't got through, and hence didn't really exist.

He went around the tree. It obscured his view of the snake-creature for a moment, and when he tried to find it again, it was gone.

He was glad for the momentary relief, and began looking about him in the half-light. He took a deep breath.

The animals, if they still existed, had vanished with the coming of dawn. The grassy, flower-dotted swards scintillated like emeralds in the early morning haze. From somewhere came the babble of running water.

Meta-universe, by whatever name you called it, was beautiful, like a gorgeous garden. What a pity he must live and die here alone, with nothing but a lot of animals for company. He'd willingly give an arm, or at least a rib, if—

"Adrian Prentiss! Adrian!"

He whirled and stared toward the orchard in elated disbelief.

"E! *E!*"

She'd got through!

The whole world, and just the two of them!

His heart was pounding ecstatically as he began to run lithely upwind.

And they'd keep it this way, simple and sweet, forever, and their children after them. To hell with science and progress! (Well, within practical limits, of course.)

As he ran, there rippled about his quivering nostrils the seductive scent of apple blossoms.

ABOUT THE EDITORS

ISAAC ASIMOV is the author of numerous volumes of science fiction (among countless other books), as well as scores of science fiction stories.

MARTIN H. GREENBERG has edited more than two dozen science fiction anthologies and has published extensively in the field.